Also by Michael Barnes Selvin

Heaven Walker: The Story of the Master of Cabestany

The Telemachia: A History by Antimenes of Argos

All the Clouds

Mont Valier, France

All Rights Reserved

Copyright © 2018 by Michael Barnes Selvin

First Printing: 2018

ISBN 978-1-387-50427-5

www.michaelbarnesselvin.com

Ordering Information:

Special discounts are available on quantity purchases by corporations, associations, educators, and others. For details, contact the publisher at the above listed address.

U.S. trade bookstores and wholesalers: Please contact above listed address.

Dedicated to:

Fernand and Angèle Jude
Jacqueline Vivès and Paul Nadal

In memory of:

Alain Marco, docteur en médecine

"And all the clouds that lour'd upon our house
In the deep bosom of the ocean buried."
Shakespeare, Richard III

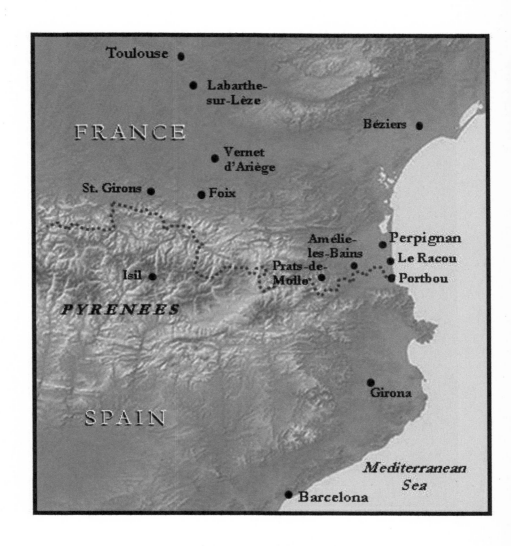

French-Spanish Frontier Region

All the Clouds

Michael Barnes Selvin

Postscript as Prologue

"Do not deny me the opportunity to share with you this final bottle of Champagne. At my age on a winter's night, the date on a bottle has no significance, and a cave full of aged wine is a gentleman's illusion. When will we ever find ourselves together again?"

***

When the Germans first came into Paris, their numbers in strength and their pride ballooned by the surprise of an easy victory to subdue without a fight such a nation of arts and literature. Few cars were on the streets, but the numerous cinemas, theaters, and music halls all functioned as before the occupation. As they marched down the Champs-Élysées, the soldiers wondered how a people whom they felt lacked discipline and commitment could continue their frivolous love of music and divertissement and the café life.

From the day of the beginning of the *drôle de guerre*, the months after France declared war against Germany prior to the invasion and occupation, music fed our need for commonality and conviviality. Popular music helped us keep our grip on indispensable normality. Music has never divided us; rather it has always served to unite us.

"They have a gay air for a vanquished people," the soldiers said to themselves.

Jean Cocteau commented, "Long live our shameful life."

We in the south, in the so-called "free zone," thought, "If Paris can continue, then the rest of France can continue as well."

***

When the hero of the Great War, Maréchal Pétain, signed the armistice with Germany, he felt he understood the problems of the French better than anyone else. He annulled the national motto of the Revolution and government of the Third Republic: liberty, equality, and brotherhood. He found it too inclusive and contrary to what might concern the average person. He substituted his new motto: family, work, and homeland. He felt it captured what the country so desperately needed. He set out to collaborate with the Nazi Occupant, often superseding their expectations.

***

La Résistance. At first, those few actively resisting the Occupant and our own government in Vichy set the table for liberty. Although the place remained vacant, the place setting was always present. The loss of truth dominated our existence. Resistance was no more than the struggle to regain hope for the truth. We risked our lives to instill this hope. So many of us had given up hope and never spoke of serious things.

There were no heroes among us. We did what we could. We did what we felt was right in our own way. Some among us were courageous, risked their lives, and lived a life of sacrifice and fear. But we saved thousands and continued the fight for truth. Many lost their lives doing it.

You may ask why we took such dangerous risks? Why we, like the majority of people, did not sit back hoping for the best, waiting for some solution to this infernal war and occupation, waiting for it to end? Why we did not believe that the old man with his own personal political agenda, ever the hero of the Great War, could somehow protect us and our culture? We knew in our hearts.

***

Music allowed all of us a momentary escape. It allowed us to deceive the Occupant with lyrics he could not understand and double-entendres that gave us a feeling of freedom when we had none. Eat or see a movie was not a difficult decision. The movie theatres were filled to full and the restaurants struggling. Slowly even that changed as the Nazis insinuated their policies, as anti-Semitism laws began limiting the impact of Jewish composers and writers, as American movies and music were prohibited, and as German culture and productions were imported.

Popular singers from the 1930s continued to entertain the troops; only the color of the uniform changed from khaki to verdigris. Music was everywhere. Most everyone had a radio at home, and many had record players. While the Parisian radio stations were controlled by the Occupant, and Vichy controlled the free zone broadcasts, we listened illicitly to Radio-Londres when we could. The popular tunes and movie themes were played everywhere, and the singers were followed closely in periodicals, becoming celebrities and movie stars: Edith Piaf, Léo Marjane, Lucienne Delyle, Suzy Solidor, Tino Rossi, Charles Trenet, and Rina Ketty, to name the most successful during the occupation.

Many of the clubs and music halls remained open all night to allow for the hours of curfew. Music allowed us to get away from the daily insult, the lack of respect, and remember what used to be normal. It took our minds off the news and propaganda, which we knew were all lies.

The rhythm of the music changed. American jazz, at first seen by the Occupant as a threat and a reminder of the American influence, was slowly accepted and transformed into the popular Swing. The Swing, an up tempo beat and irreverent form, allowed people to dance together freely, joyously, and in so doing to put out of their minds the imposed limits on their daily routines. It gave us hope and love during an atmosphere of defeat and hatred.

***

Music sustained the resistance through the sounds and words of truth and hope. Music set us free during a dreadful time to live and love.

> "And maybe what they say is true
> Of war and war's alarms,
> But O that I were young again
> And held her in my arms!"*

*Politics, May 24, 1938, William Butler Yeats.

1

February 1941

> *You pass without seeing me*
> *Without even saying hello*
> *Give me a little hope this evening*
> *I feel such pain.*
> « *Vous qui passez sans me voir,* » *Johnny Hess,*
> *lyrics Paul Misraki/Raoul Breton/Charles Trenet*

I cannot refrain from watching her across the broad expanse of the café/bar. In a light tweed skirt and tight jacket, a loose grey pelerine enveloping her shoulders, dark gloves, and rakish cloche hat covering a chocolate brown schoolgirl bun: overdressed for the occasion, but far from the scabrous black and pink fashion of Parisian couture. She obliterates the light. I would dedicate my life to her for a smile. She feigns not to notice me. In the herd of dancers, the dark watery pools of her antelope eyes remain focused on the portly proprietor of the club.

"We've a month to prepare," the short, swarthy man announces loudly to overcome the hazy hum of diffuse voices. Jordi Pons owns and manages the Club les Tréteaux, a bar turned nightclub in Faubourg Saint-Jean in Perpignan. Many of the people assembled have not seen each other since the successful fall show, *La Belle Epoque.*

"Full rehearsals in three weeks." As Jordi speaks, a Gauloise dribbles ashes onto his filthy apron.

This is her first time at the pre-rehearsal meeting at the small French city on the Mediterranean. Perpignan has a stronger connection to Barcelona than Paris: a "*bourgade espagnole,*" a Spanish barrio, with narrow streets and Majorcan bulwarks. Club les Tréteaux is a rehabilitated nineteenth-century carriage and livery stable. She appears nervous alongside the postured dancers, new among this fine feathered order, younger and less sure of herself.

The hopeful players intend to transform this fore-challenged bar and café into an appealing music hall. Not the Gaieté Parisienne, the ABC, or the Folies Bergère doing so well in Paris, but possibly, in low light and with ample watering, capable of momentarily transporting the despondent imaginations of the inhabitants of Perpignan away from the recent defeat, occupation of our country, and the meager daily diet.

The cavernous, crowded, smoke-filled chamber is weakly lit by industrial pendant lamps, with people positioned all about: seated at tables, packed along the walls, leaning over the railing in the balcony, and those at the zinc counter more interested in their half-filled glasses than listening to the proprietor. Music clubs have mushroomed since the occupation, becoming essential to both Occupant and occupied.

Jordi Pons is a short, near-bald, beer-bellied Catalan, with a tight fist, an eye for the girls, a big heart, and as close to the mayor as to the local strong-arms. Since tourists are few these days, the bar/café serves mostly locals. Jordi initiated the music hall idea several years before, since the large space was sparingly used, and he was barely able to cover his costs. He had been successful in the past with one or two "shows" a year, often earning more in a few evenings than the bar generated in months. In *La Belle Époque*, last fall, Marie Dubas, a mentor of Piaf and a second-tier music-hall singer, *diseuse*, and cinema comedian, captured our hearts. "This evening, I think of my country," began her signature song.

"We're calling it 'The Swing,'" he continues. "Keep that in mind. Jazz: that should bring us forward a few years American style. It's all the rage. We're still auditioning, so no fixed deals. No guarantees. Georges will explain the program."

At his side, Josette, his ample, rosy-cheeked wife, waits. She cooks, manages the bar, and serves as a welcoming host. She prepares short-order sandwiches, sausages, frankfurters, and toasted goat cheese salads, when supplies are available. She also keeps a bubbling cassoulet on the stove at all times. The local white beans are still procurable without a ration card, even as other ingredients have become harder to find. Mostly ignoring her husband, she runs a tight bar: no soliciting, no fighting, no spitting, and no one too drunk to stand. Her two obese sniffers guard the back-bar.

Jordi pauses, drags, and continues. "A bastard of a winter. The floods in October. The influx of foreigners and growing internment camps, not to mention the war. Can't last much longer. So everyone's hoping for an early spring. Paris is hopping, and the Occupant is eating snakes with pleasure; maybe we can prepare a few ourselves. Our hope is to headline Le Grand Charles. He's one of us, and what's the Swing without Trenet? So folks, work hard, ignore everything else, and have a great show, and we'll make a few sou. Let's not become another cinema. Georges, let's break up as soon as possible. Bar service is open." He drops his cigarette, macerates it with his shoe sole, and returns to the bar with his wife.

Georges Doelnitz, the theatrical producer charged with creating this show, is heavyset, large-chested, with unmanageable white hair, and shadowy eyes covered in ashen overgrown brows. He begins naming the participating groups and gesticulating for their attention.

Young Paul Ruiz Broussard ignores him, his eyes fixed on the girl across the way. An old hand after three shows, Paul knows most of the people in the hall and works closely with Georges. Of course, the names that will appear on the marquee and posters are not present. The headliners have no need of these preliminary deliberations. Mistinguett was here in winter of 1939, during the Phony War before the occupation. Chevalier, Fréhel, Piaf, Ketty, and Sablon have remained in Paris at the whim and call of the Occupant. They would not be interested in this jerry-rigged venue in any case. The last show's star, Marie Dubas, recently escaped to Switzerland to avoid arrest. Today, only the supporting cast members are in attendance: hopeful singers, dancers, musicians, comics, stagehands, and other acts. All looking for a chance, all dreaming dreams, indifferent to the possible pittance earned.

Slowly, the chamber begins to empty as Georges announces the group leaders and assignments. Paul watches the neat and trim girl leave with the dance group. He knows he will see her again, but the choppy waters of a dream are tricky to navigate.

After most of the people have departed, Georges Doelnitz comes over to the table where Paul is finishing what used to be called a pâté sandwich, but today who knows really what it contains, and ersatz *café au lait*, made not from coffee beans, but from roasted grains, mixed with a powdered milk substitute. Over the last few years, Georges has been a great help to Paul. They first met on Paul's arrival in Perpignan after graduation from Trinité school in Béziers. Georges helped him settle in the city, giving him part-time work, tiding him over with small loans and food. Since being hired at the Prefecture, Paul has paid him back, and they have remained close friends.

"You can find the time, Paul." Georges says, sitting down heavily.

Paul nods absently, thinking of the girl. Jordi's obtuse announcement of Charles Trenet surprised him. Of course, what motivates Jordi is rarely planned and never announced.

Georges is somewhere in his sixties, a calm, unassuming man having seen and done much in his life, and a safe harbor for many. He first hired Paul as an assistant to do whatever it took to prepare and manage the shows. In the previous show, he had graduated to a backup singer to Mme. Dubas. His previous singing experience had been in the choir of his boarding school, but then Club les Tréteaux wasn't the Paris Opéra.

"You know him, don't you?"

"Who's that?" Paul surfaces from his reverie.

"Charles Trenet...of course."

"I'm the only person who does," he complains. "Jordi knows that."

"You know Jordi," Georges says. "Ruled by his belly. This place has been on the skids for years. He would have been forced out if he didn't own the building. Consider him a victim...like the rest of us."

"Hard to see him in that light," Paul says vaguely. Three years out of school, Paul spent his first two years in Perpignan working for the notary, Lucien Trenet, Charles' father.

"What's the matter with you?"

"Nothing. It gets harder with other demands."

"I know what you mean," Georges says, lighting a Gauloise. "And I'm proud of you, although I must say I worry for your health. You take on too many risks." He pauses and inhales. "Bernadette thinks we should clear out, but we've been here in the south too long. And where to?" That question floats in the air with a series of exhaled smoke rings.

"It could be worse. You could be in Paris." Paul tries to make light, although his days at the Prefecture are filled with people motivated by desperation and anxiety. He's becoming almost accustomed to the despair of the day. Most people have lost their compassion, turning to self-interest. *Je m'en foutism*, they call it. Jean-Paul Sartre called France disgusting, corrupt, inefficient, and racist. Who wants to die for that? Then we discovered the Nazis occupant was far worse. For Paul, as for the country at large, popular music has become a necessary diversion, one of the few remaining. "I need this, Georges."

"We all do. This last winter you impressed Marie Dubas, you know. She said you weren't half-bad as a singer."

"She never mentioned it to me."

"She had her own problems." He suddenly looks at Paul seriously. "You know, my brother is stuck in the occupied zone…"

Paul raises his hand. "You don't have a brother."

"Maybe not, but I may need your help."

"Just say the word," Paul replies honestly.

"We have to survive the bad days to appreciate the good ones. I did it once before. Maybe we can get you a singing role. Let's find out what Charles is up to."

"Okay, let's," Paul agrees sarcastically, knowing that he is the only person who could possibly contact Charles Trenet.

***

After the blitzkrieg defeat in June 1940, the Third Republic fell, and a new government was formed under the leadership of Marshall Pétain. An armistice was quickly signed. Then the new government relocated to Vichy, granted themselves authorization to write a new constitution, and began moving the country in a new direction, vilifying and annulling all aspects of the Third Republic.

The lives of ordinary people in a defeated and occupied France continued, but not as before. More than a million and a half French soldiers remained in prisoner of war camps in the north. People struggled to regain their footing or to simply live their lives. They were frantic for normalcy. So many had died or returned ruined from the Great War of 1914. Every village had seen its youth ripped away, an entire generation. When the Germans occupied the country last summer, they were surprised to discover a nation tired beyond redemption. No fight was left. The Germans divided the country into the occupied zone and the so-called "free zone" in the south. It made little difference. The Vichy government followed the dictates of their German rulers in either zone. Most people attempted to ignore the Nazi occupiers, calling them euphemistically "the Occupant," making them less personal, less real. People fought amongst themselves in support of or against the Vichy government. Only a few resisted silently against the Occupant.

***

Paul walks back to the Prefecture after the meeting. The weather is unfriendly and unkind, frosty and blustery. He's tall, angular, and wiry, not particularly athletic, though a confirmed hiker and climber, having grown up in the nearby Pyrenees. With his badly cropped dark hair falling in his face, you might see him as bookish and serious. His good looks were mostly inherited from his Spanish father. Paul works in the visa section of the Prefecture and has for well over a year. After graduation from La Sainte Trinité in Béziers with a Certificate of Studies, he worked part-time for the notary, Lucien Trenet, providing clerical help and delivering papers. That's where he first met Charles Trenet. He became friendly with the family, seeing Charles when he returned home from Paris. But the work presented no challenges and no future, so after a couple of years, he took a competitive exam and was selected with four others for entry at the Prefecture. The timing was unfortunate. He started under the Third Republic a year before the occupation. After the Vichy regime took power, many faces immediately changed at the Prefecture, including the Prefect. The result was a large shift in direction ministered by Vichy.

The role of the Prefecture was to implement the laws and regulations of the national government. This entailed two functions. An administrative responsibility provided identity cards, driving licenses, passports and visas, residency and work permits, vehicle registration, and registration of associations. The second was a management responsibility of police and firefighters. All functions were sensitive and political.

Those employees supportive of the policies of Pétain were in the ascendency, but still a minority. The great majority were called "*attentistes*," people not yet committed to the armistice and Pétain government, but waiting to see what would happen with the occupation and the war with Britain, cautiously withholding their personal views. A few remaining people immediately resistant to the occupation remained silent, knowing that expressing their views risked arrest. These same factions could be found throughout the country as a whole. "And they that wasted us, required of us mirth."

When Paul arrives at midday, the chief of the visa section, Franco Plana, wants to speak with him. He reluctantly mounts the spiral staircase, not because he dislikes Franco, but because there is never good news in the chief's office. His shoes clack on the circular marble staircase, ringing in the large atrium.

"Where were you when I wanted you, Broussard?" Not even a greeting as he enters the office.

"At lunch." Paul eyes the man, who as a Spanish Republican officer had fled to France during the *Retirada*, the large influx of refugees from the Spanish Civil War. Hundreds of thousands of Spanish refugees had came across the border along the length of the Pyrenees at the end of the Civil War in April 1939. The French army shuttled them into "temporary" refugee camps along the border. Somehow Franco Plana had managed to land on his feet, in two years becoming a force in the Prefecture.

"That music thing again?"

"Yes, sir. Our next show. The Swing it's called."

A slight smile escapes Franco's lips. "Everyone is talking about the Swing, but I have no notion of what it is. We're at war, you know, even if our masters won't admit it. And that's why I wanted to talk. I saw an approved exit visa application this morning, and you know what? It wasn't my signature. I approve all applications. Am I missing something?"

"No, sir." Paul hesitated. Sometimes the best strategy is to fill space with excessive talk, but this one called for tight lips.

"You do this commonly?"

"No, sir."

The chief stares at Paul. "Well?"

"I mean, yes, I signed for you."

"That's a crime. You could be sent away, far away. You want to spend time in Germany?"

"It was important…"

"Broussard, I like you. We understand each other. This is no joke. The Occupant is here in Perpignan. Maybe not in uniform, but believe me he's watching. And our own government is aiding him. The police survey what we do here.

"Yes, sir."

"Have you done this before?"

"A few times, when necessary."

"Now look, you're going to get us both arrested. I don't know who you're working for. I don't want to know, but, at least in this case, let me understand?"

"It was a special request. A German refugee. A famous man of letters and his wife."

"A Jew?"

"Yes."

A large sigh of exasperation comes from the chief. "And did he and his wife leave the country?"

"Yes. You never hear back."

"Listen, Paul, I'm not an ogre. In the future, you come to me to sign these visas. Don't go behind my back. Don't get carried away with what these people tell you, even if you feel it's the right thing to do. This is dangerous…for both of us. Is that clear?"

"Yes, sir."

"Now, out of here. If we have this conversation again, you'll be gone…or arrested."

Paul returns to his desk on the ground floor. He spends much of his time behind the counter facing the public. He fears he has gotten himself in over his head. He feels he must help out, but everyday becomes more complex and more dangerous. Working against the government can be deadly. He has seen this in the mountains and in his work. Though doing nothing seems worse. Seeing so much hatred and anguish without attempting to help is criminal, while helping out is a crime.

***

It was late when Paul approached the entrance to the apartment he shared with his roommate, Robert, on rue de la Gare, with a central tramway running to the train station. The building door was locked. Edith, the concierge, was normally there until ten, listening to the radio and knitting, but always cognizant of comings and goings. Tonight, her small studio window was curtained. Always seemingly annoyed at providing information to strangers, she was also the one source of information on visitors to the building. In her gruff, grandmotherly way, she was smarter than most, exceedingly circumspect in her handling of mail and messages, and trustworthy in her knowledge of the affairs of her clients, the building's inhabitants. She was in love with Robert. Because of his charm and good looks, Robert could do no wrong. Further, his father owned the building and paid her salary and living arrangements.

Paul used his key to open the building door, mounted the three flights to the top, and unlocked the door to the apartment. He crossed the living room, cold and dark, to close the shutters which he had left open to allow sunlight to heat the rooms during the day. Unless they were closed at sunset, any heat gained, rapidly dissipated. The steam heater in the building was erratic and limited, and the small fireplace barely worked. He threw his overcoat on his bed, leaving his jacket on. Paul turned on a small wireless to see if he could hear Radio-Londres, the broadcast of de Gaulle's free French in London. Most of the time, it was barely comprehensible; sometimes, not often, you could hear the news or songs that were never played in France. Tonight, although clear outside, the only sound was hissing static.

There was no food in the apartment. Paul sat at the table in the small and rarely used kitchen, idly chewing bread from the day before and some rapidly aging cheese, sipping a glass of local Grenache, looking forward to bed, where he could warm his chilled body.

"Paul?" Robert arrived, slamming the door and throwing his coat on the couch. "Paul? Oh, there you are."

Robert Bardou was one of the reasons Paul had come to Perpignan after graduation. They had met at school in Béziers. Robert was one of the top students, without even trying, or at least not appearing so. Tall and athletic, he exuded confidence, and the visiting girls loved him. Thanks to Robert's father, their apartment was spacious with two separate bedrooms, nothing they could have afforded on their salaries. Robert was a couple of years older and wildly more experienced. He was raised in Paris and spent summers and vacations in Perpignan and Barcelona. His father owned a commercial real estate development business and was related to the family of Bardou-Job, who had created the famous cigarette paper fortune at the turn of the century.

"How'd it go?" Robert asked, seating himself at the small table and filling a drinking glass with wine. He was large-boned, fair-haired, with a light complexion and masculine good looks. Women found him a touch dangerous, often the most appealing attribute a man can have.

"Not much to report. A few speeches. They want Charles Trenet, but that may be difficult. The Swing show. There was a girl there…"

"Oh?"

"Just an apparition. How about you?"

"An apparition?"

"Nothing happening with you?" Paul asked again, avoiding the subject.

"All we do is talk. Some want to act, but to do what? Most are in a wait-and-see mode. At best, we'll continue with the leaflets and marking the walls with V's, hopelessly reminding people that standing on the sidelines is tantamount to collaboration. It's a hard sell. It's that old saying: *ma pomme, ma pomme, ma pomme* (my apple, my apple, my apple), go along, get along. I'm doing okay, so who cares about you? Can't really blame them. They're exhausted from the wars and the German occupation." He sipped his wine.

"I got caught forging the chief's signature."

Robert startled in surprise. "What?"

"No, it's nothing. You remember that older package I mentioned a few weeks back? A couple from Germany? A writer and philosopher needing false papers. Well, the chief called me in and warned me. Said he would sign in the future. Not to go behind his back."

"It's a confused time. A time of wait and see...no visible future."

***

The next few weeks passed rapidly. The cold and rain carried on like a cranky, spoiled child, with glimpses of drizzly snow. On a sparklingly clear icy day, something that occurred occasionally in winter, Paul made the pilgrimage to rue de la Cloche d'Or, the office of Lucien Trenet, the renowned *Notaire*. Paul greatly admired Lucien, who had been both helpful and sympathetic following his graduation and relocation to Perpignan. Lucien had introduced him to the working life and had acted as a father figure. His real father lived in San Sebastian, Spain. To his surprise, the address no longer held the offices of the Notary; instead a family had moved in, converting the office to living space.

Fearing disaster, Paul walked to the nearby residence of the Trenet family on the rue Bertran de Balanda only a short distance away. He had been welcomed there by Lucien and his wife, Françoise, many times, getting to know the entire family, including Charles on his visits from Paris, playing with the young children, singing, and a few times spending the night. He knocked on the door. The new owners explained that Lucien had moved his family to Arles-sur-Tech, a small town in the mountains a short distance southwest of Perpignan.

That very evening, Robert borrowed his father's car, and they motored to Arles to the new Trenet residence. Lucien graciously welcomed these unexpected visitors at a rather late hour.

"May I offer you something to drink?"

"No. No. Thank you," Paul began, realizing his single-mindedness had resulted in miscalculation. "This is my roommate, Robert Bardou."

"Son of Henri?"

"Yes, Monsieur," Robert said.

"I've worked with your father many times." Lucien looked at the two young men quizzically, but sympathetically. "Now please come in. I'm afraid everyone's settled for the night, but rest a moment. Please."

They entered the spacious living room and sat down.

"Forgive us for barging in," Paul said.

"Paul, you need not excuse yourself. You've earned it. I'm sorry I did not inform you of our move."

"I should have contacted you. Starting at the Prefecture was a shock, and then after adjusting, everything changed."

"I understand."

"We don't want to disturb you. We came to get a contact number for Charles."

"Of course. But first, how is life at the Prefecture?" Lucien questioned.

Paul summarized the remarkable changes he had seen since his hiring. Lucien nodded as he talked.

"And you're working for my friend Franco Plana."

"Yes. He's been a great boss."

"He's very smart, a military man and lawyer. Came here after the Civil War and immediately established himself. And you've found your way into the confused heart of France. You must be careful, but I know you, Paul. Always careful. Politic. Well aware of your surroundings and the risks. You'll be fine."

"I seem to find myself at the center of things. I'm involved in a new music show, Monsieur, and wanted to ask Charles if he might make an appearance. I have no way of contacting him."

"I'm glad to hear you are continuing with music. Although I'm doubtful Charles would return to Perpignan. We haven't seen him since the occupation, but let me give you his contact number. Raoul Breton is Charles' business manager in Paris. Excuse me." He left them sitting uncomfortably, listening to his footsteps ascending the stairs.

He returned shortly. "Here it is," Lucien said, handing a note to Paul. "Let me know what he says. Charles is doing very well in Paris...even with the occupation."

"Thank you. I will." They shook hands and departed.

Over the next few weeks, after a few friendly telegrams, Charles agreed to headline three nights and a matinee on Sunday at the music hall and sent his terms. Jordi Pons was floored by his demands. He agreed, but failed to thank Paul in his shock at the fee request. Charles Trenet was booked.

All the Clouds

***

A few frigid nights later, I boarded a train for Banyuls-sur-Mer, a small fishing and grape-growing village about twenty minutes to the south of Perpignan. The cold but clear sunset splashed crimson across the sky reflected in the chalky Mediterranean waters. I walked into the center of town to meet a young couple at the Café of the Grand Hotel at the end of the harbor. I had been asked to guide them across the local pass into Spain. They were recommended by my contacts. I assumed that they were provided with the appropriate documents. Most of the *passeurs* (guides on mountain trails leading into Spain) had no idea of the official requirements to leave France and to enter Spain, nor cared.

The most critical part of these arrangement was the first glimpse of what we called "the package." My stomach always knotted up and sent shivers along my spine. I hated it. I hated the tension. I hated the stomach-churning knowledge of possible arrest. But I did it anyway, always wondering if it was worth the risk. What did I get out of it? No money. No pat on the back. Just the nebulous knowledge of helping out, helping someone in need, or helping counter the direction of our government and its lack of compassion toward émigrés.

The café was mostly avoided by the locals. It was off from the village center on the coastal route into Spain and frequented by money changers, counterfeiters, passeurs, smugglers, and black market sellers: all seeking to earn a few francs from others' desperation. Occasionally, tourists seeking a view of the sea would stop for a coffee, unaware of its reputation.

As I came upon the café terrace, I immediately spotted a couple in their late twenties looking out of place and nervous. I had no doubt. I watched them for a moment, noting their nervousness and internal focus, never looking at the sea or the roadway. They never met others' eyes and glanced anxiously as people came and went. I moved to their table.

"Bonsoir."

"Bonsoir, Monsieur," the man replied with a heavy eastern European accent, indicating a lack of knowledge of French.

"Marc," I said (aka Paul), offering my hand. They seemed relieved to see me and to hear a name that they had been told would help them. They stared at me, obviously wondering who I was. "Ready to go?"

They both nodded, glancing at one another, understanding the intent of the question. Their contacts had them dressed warmly in local clothing with backpacks, all too new and too clean.

It was rumored that Pétain was about to order all foreigners out of all border areas throughout France. This had already occurred in the occupied zone. So this route had just about served its usefulness. At the beginning of the war, Banyuls had been one of the best routes to exit France by road, train, and overland; it was now overrun by local police, customs, border patrols, and collaborators seeking to interrupt the process.

We began walking through town, crossing a sparkling, silver creek in the full moonlight, coming to Puig del Mas, the original village set away from the Mediterranean in the hills hidden among towering trees. We avoided the well-recognized customs house, where agents usually spied from the front garden on lookout for suspicious people leaving the village. It was cold, and no agents were apparent. Although the couple had been advised to dress as workers, no locals confused them with workers. Everyone in Banyuls knew who the locals were. All others were considered foreigners, whether from outside France, another department within France, or a neighboring village a few kilometers away. The villagers resented the hierarchy of government, but mostly stayed out of politics. Over the last year or so, they ignored much and gave foreigners barely a glance. They knew what was happening, but mostly dismissed it: their husbands, children, relatives all gained from the additional income. The socialist mayor had been helpful to refugees, but recently he had been replaced by a mayor from outside the region chosen by Vichy. This trip would most likely be a final run for me.

We didn't speak as we walked the main vineyard road, beginning the uphill climb into the Alberes, the main easternmost continuation of the Pyrenees. They followed me, obviously nervous about the route and me. We moved off the main trail, to a small footpath below, which paralleled the route, but was obscured from view. Occasionally, we heard voices, but kept out of sight.

I knew the mountain paths well. I had spent warm summers here with a distant cousin of my mother. I had joined the local teenagers in their evening parties and dances in the mountains and vineyards to avoid the prying eyes of our parents and guardians.

We came to the seven pine trees that indicated the direction toward Spain, and here we left the footpath, crossing the main vineyard road, and began climbing directly through vineyards on a steep course. It was a difficult climb, but the couple was in good shape and followed me without trouble. By this time, we were breathing hard, but I felt better, my queasy stomach calming, having passed the most likely places for being stopped.

Higher up we came to another footpath, this one less frequented, and we continued our climb for about an hour before arriving at the summit, which always surprised people. I stopped to show them the direction we had come from. Banyuls with twinkling lights and the French coast spread out along the dark sea. Turning, directly before us, we could see the glimmering Spanish coast and the broad, dark Mediterranean. We were nearly in Spain.

"Wait." I held up my hand, hearing faint rustlings coming from the Spanish side. We moved off the path to hide in a small copse of trees. We watched as three men came into view, obviously relaxed, talking loudly. Smugglers. They knew the trails better than the vineyard workers and cared only to avoid the customs agents. I stepped out to talk.

"Bona tarda senyors," I greeted them in Catalan.

"Bona nit." They looked at me suspiciously, not aggressively. Every centimeter of their bodies was covered in large packs filled to the brim, hanging in nets like pack animals, probably cigarettes and alcohol, maybe some cured legs of ham. I didn't recognize them, but felt that they would be friendly and, possibly, helpful.

"Any problems tonight?"

"You moving people?" The leader asked.

"Yes."

"Border patrol's on the way up. About five, moving fast. You can avoid them."

"Thanks."

"No longer a good path. Too many people. Too easy. And they want to make the passeurs pay. Dangerous. Not worth the money you earn. They killed a passeur a few weeks ago. Wait for them to pass and then ditch the people. Good luck."

They walked on, pleased with themselves.

I returned to the copse.

"We wait here," I signaled, knowing they did not understood much. "Then a small detour. We're in Spain. I can't risk getting caught. Portbou is there." I pointed in the direction of the shore. Where village lights outlined the port like a string of pearls. A small border post can register you."

They nodded their heads as though they understood, and maybe they did. No one is who he pretends to be in this business.

We settled down nervously to wait for the patrol to pass. The trees protected us from the light breeze, and the shivering cold was tolerable. I had work tomorrow, so I couldn't afford to spend the night on the mountain. If we were caught by the French border patrol, they would probably send me to jail, and the couple would be interned in a camp for refugees. Of course, it was nothing like in the occupied zone, where guides were presumed to be in the Resistance and sent to the east for hard labor, no questions asked. Foreigners were returned to their country of origin, often a lethal fate.

The shadow of the occupation has lengthened, becoming a terrible time of compulsory partition by the Occupant, not only of our country, but of families and friends, villages and regions. It's an alienated time of self-interest. A time when contempt rules, and decency is forgotten. A time illuminated by the subdued sights and sounds of an ungodly and silent conflict, often deadly. Our enemy unknown, wintry clouds obscure our vision, our words, our icy thoughts.

Awaiting the passing of the border patrol, my nervousness increased, my heart beating, my mind racing. Should I heed the words of the smuggler: "ditch them?"

2

February 1941

When I leave my house, I can't take a step
Without someone following me, I don't know why
My ears hear enough gallant proposals
The men greeting me and speaking to me of love.
« *On m'suit,* » Mistinguett

Her two best girlfriends challenged her to audition for this new musical show, and on her very first try she had been accepted as a backup dancer over many other girls. She hadn't really thought out what this meant, which was unlike her. Always careful and measured. She took after her father's side of the family: meticulous in all things. "No surprises," her father often warned, but then his paintings, so careful in composition, were filled with jarring colors and unexpected and capricious brushstrokes: all surprises. Perhaps her own life mirrored his art: conscientious and cautious, yet occasionally streaked with startling hues: leaving school, a ruinous love affair, nights of dissolute behavior, nothing to be ashamed of: too much to drink and late nights with friends. Enough to have her parents in a state of alarm. And this success at the audition was certainly a surprise.

After the general meeting at the club, the dancers, mostly young and nervous, met in a dance studio a short distance away. The instructor, Raymond Duras, reminded her of Fred Astaire: middle aged, balding, but slim, light on his feet, and fundamentally enthusiastic. Two dozen girls had made first selection. Now, the auditions continued.

"All right, girls. Just watch what I do." He carefully placed the needle on the record player, and Ginger Rogers' voice sang "Music Makes Me," a popular tune from the film "Flying Down to Rio." "Walk, walk, walk to the right. Walk, walk, walk to the left. Chassé to the right. One, two, three. Chassé to the left. One, two, three. Kick to the right. Kick to the left. Twirl in a free spin, ending with a bravura." He looked at the girls with a smile. "*Bon.* On the downbeat."

The girls behind him, concentrated, attempting to follow his steps. He didn't see it, but he could hear the disaster that followed.

"Now girls, once again."

This time he turned and watched. Only a few girls were able to repeat his moves with any grace. Most failed miserably, some forgetting the steps entirely. Gabrielle tried with all her might to keep up, but knew her counting and mental concentration demolished any flow or elegance of movement. It was as though an unknown foreigner occupied her body, making her awkward and hesitant.

"Again." He reset the needle with a loud scratch and clapped his hands in time and watched.

It continued. Once a simple routine was completed, when enough girls got it, another began. Slowly it became apparent which dancers could follow his moves and which failed wretchedly. She felt somewhere in between, neither among the first dancers to learn the steps, nor the last to fail. She should have taken her dance lessons more seriously, or at least brushed up on the basics. This was not as easy as she and her girlfriends had thought. A lark transforming into an embarrassment.

He began dividing the dancers into groups of twos or threes. After several hours, everyone was exhausted, but at the same time, some were getting it, while others were not. He separated all the girls into two groups, and it was obvious what each group represented. Gabrielle didn't know how, but she seemed in the right group.

"All those in group A are dismissed. Thank you." Monsieur Duras indicated the exit. She remained, drained and unsure, watching half the hopefuls depart despondently.

***

Taking an afternoon off from her job at Les Nouvelles Galeries to attend the audition and being selected felt almost like a defeat to Gabrielle. All her doubts surfaced. In her teen years, this might have ended in tears and days of melancholy. Oaths of: "I didn't really need this," "My friends goaded me on." It wasn't that she was busy or had other things to do, but she realized that time was passing since graduating from an all-girls high school and refusing the two-year study for her baccalaureate, or at least postponing it. She worked in the cosmetics boutique in Nouvelles Galeries and was one of the top salesgirls. She enjoyed it, but she worried what others thought, most importantly her parents. She knew her mother and father were disappointed in her decision to leave school, but their initial panic from her past behavior had dissipated somewhat. They expected her to continue with school, but they recognized that all the young people were deeply affected by the war and occupation.

At school, when she met with her friends, they talked only about boys. She was not ready and doubted she would ever be ready for boys. Although popular at the school, she was never among the most popular "vamp" girls, nor was she among the "whizzes," now at the university. The worst had come during her penultimate year in school: a distressing "love affair" that should never have happened resulted in feelings of hopelessness and self-doubt. As a result, during her final year she suffered a loss of self-confidence and feelings of failure, resulting in below-normal grades, fits of melancholy, and heartfelt fears that she could never fulfill the mostly silent, but clear, expectations of her parents. She made it through, graduated, found a job, and settled down with friends she trusted, ambition in abeyance.

Due to the occupation and new government, time had become meaningless, for young people especially. The future seemed an idea to be avoided, impossible to envisage, everything placed in a state of uncertainty. The breath of the country came haltingly, tentatively, fearfully. People were at war with themselves. They mostly sought an equilibrium of their daily existence.

Gabrielle (which she preferred to Gaby, although quite unsuccessfully) lived in a small house in the Saint-Mathieu district on the rue Maurell. Her father, Auguste Daniel, was a well-known landscape painter and museum curator, and her mother, a housewife. Auguste Daniel had been raised in Paris, a student of Léon Bonnat at the Ecole des Beaux Arts, working with Henri Martin in Toulouse for several years, and finally settling in Perpignan. They lived simply in a three-room townhouse, with her father's small studio on the ground floor. To make ends meet, Auguste Daniel first worked in a framing shop and then found a job as curator at a small art museum operated by the city, always continuing his painting.

Her mother was surprised when she returned from the rehearsals.

"Gabrielle, what's wrong?" Her mother attempted to understand her complicated daughter and allowed her leeway, always defending her from her father, but she was forever anxious. "Oh, my, you didn't get selected?"

"I did. I did, but I can't do it." She began crying.

"What do you mean?" Her mother's voice startled her. "Of course you can."

"I don't know. They're all such good dancers...and beautiful, and they know what to do, and I was lost most of the time. Why did he choose me? It's not a school presentation. It's real, and everyone is older and experienced. They want to be stars. Why did I ever do it? It's all Nuria's fault."

"Her fault?"

"She made me do it. The first audition was easy, but this one was different."

"Go pull yourself together," she dismissed her daughter, exasperated. "Your father will be here shortly. We got a postcard from Fanny."

"She so rarely writes," Gabrielle said, suspending her pout. "What did she say?" Fanny was her grandmother, her mother's mother, a widow living on the outskirts of Paris.

"The community is having problems with foreigners."

"What does that mean?" Her mother, she realized, was concerned.

"I'm not sure, but outsiders causing problems."

"Serious?"

"No. Not yet it seems."

"I hope they're okay."

"We haven't heard from Auguste's parents. I'm sure they're fine."

Gabrielle wandered disconsolately into her room, throwing her coat and jacket in the armoire, kicking her shoes into the closet, and falling onto her bed, staring at her father's paintings on the wall. She loved them. They were full of colors and admiration for the beauty in the region. They filled her heart like a sunny day. He was known as the painter of "*beaux jours*," since he always covered his canvases with the luminous colors of the *Côte Vermeille*, the vermillion coast, and the Roussillon.

Her mom, Julie Daniel, played the peacemaker in the family, but she had a streak of toughness that most people never saw. She insisted that Gabrielle have a career separate from the house, refusing to teach her to cook or allow her to help with housework. "You must be self-sufficient, a woman of purpose, independent," she said frequently from the time Gabrielle entered school, always wanting more for her daughter than she had been allowed herself. While Auguste respected Gabrielle's opinions and was interested in her activities, he was consumed by his painting. Of her parents, Gabrielle suffered the most from her mom's disappointment in her decision not to continue school.

By dinner, her mood had brightened somewhat. She had managed to stifle her reservations and presented a better mien to her father.

"The dancers are experienced, and they're beautiful, with gorgeous bodies, and they know each other. I'm the only outsider."

"Do you want to do this," her father, her most informed and interested critic, asked, "or not?"

"I think I do," Gabrielle said somewhat hesitantly, actually thinking about it for the first time since the afternoon, seeing it as something more than a lark.

"Remember the others are not just thinking about it. They want it." Auguste looked at his daughter strongly. Although quiet, he was always so sure of things, so pointed, so unambiguous. "If you want it, you have to commit to it."

"I know, Papa, but it's hard."

"You can do it, but only if you commit."

"Now Auguste, everyone has doubts. Leave the poor girl alone."

"It's like the baccalaureate. You have to want it."

"Oh, Papa." She began crying.

"Times are hard," her mother said defensively. "You shouldn't make it harder."

Her father softened, and Gabrielle was able to complete the dinner and retire to the safe confines of her bedroom to recover from a traumatic day.

***

At lunchtime the following day, Gabrielle walks along the canal to Le Palmarium, the largest and one of most popular café/restaurants in Perpignan. The anxious rain and wind defer for the second consecutive day, and the air is cool and crisp with weakly warming sunshine. Another sorrowful winter day, waiting for spring with nights of stormy anxiety.

She sits down to wait for her girlfriends, viewing the snow-blanketed Mount Canigou in the distance, the final outcropping of the Pyrenees in their descent into the Mediterranean. Gabrielle's days in the cosmetics boutique are hardly challenging. In fact, in less than a year, she has proven herself, becoming quickly knowledgeable of all the brands and products, aware of the latest fashion trends from Paris, well informed and helpful, and politely forceful. Only when she gets an obnoxious patron, which happens perhaps once a day, does she think about moving elsewhere. She's become an expert on perfumes, able to walk down the street and name each passerby's scent. And lipsticks, blushes, nail polishes are an exercise in colors, something she learned on her father's knees, the complexion is just a canvas. Her salesmanship came from her mother, she supposed: always sensitive to others, warm, and positive, always accommodating, and yet strong.

Nuria and Catie arrive at the café holding hands, animated in their conversation. The clique of three have been best friends from the first day at middle school. After six years of school together, they withhold no secrets. They survived teachers, nights of study, tests, parent problems, sicknesses, thoughtless blunders, and accidents, and, speaking of blunders, boys. They know each other, sometimes better then they know themselves, and they survive together. Only Nuria went on to the baccalaureate, but not to the university. They all did well enough in school, but more study holds no interest to them at the moment.

Catie is petite and adorably blond, the least mature, but also the most traditionally pretty. She is coquettish, repeatedly getting into trouble with boys, but extricating herself well enough with the help of her pals. She works in a baby attire shop as a sales assistant, a job she enjoys, but realizes has no future. Perhaps she is learning sales, but even that is doubtful. Selling baby clothes or strollers to pregnant women presents no challenge.

Nuria, larger and taller, is the conscience of the group. She comes from a Barcelona family and speaks Catalan better than the others, and she's also the most political, the most judgmental, and quick to anger. She's a secretary at la Cimade (*Comité inter mouvements auprès des évacués*). La Cimade was founded in response to the influx of Republicans after the Spanish Civil War to help the émigrés find lodging and work. Today, it is occupied more and more with assisting eastern European refugees. They greet each other with bisous.

"Well…did you?" Nuria asks quickly, sitting down.

"Yes, sort of," Gabrielle replies.

"Sort of?" Her friends pounce on her.

"I mean, I survived the second audition…barely."

Well, congratulations. We knew you could do it," Catie says.

They look at each other and then break out in giggles for no apparent reason.

"You know," Nuria said, "Catie's met a boy."

"Really?" Gabrielle asks dubiously.

"I just met him. He works in the shipping department. As cute as a bug. He asked me to have a drink with him. It was nice."

"His name is Manel," Nuria adds.

"A local boy?" Gabrielle says.

"No. Spanish. Arrived with his parents a couple of years ago. Speaks Catalan and Spanish, but his French is lacking."

"Do we get to meet this Manel?" Nuria asks.

"Not any time soon," Catie says, ending the discussion with a well exercised frown.

They order the day's *prix fixe*, which seems to diminish daily in quantity and quality. Many vegetables are in short supply, and meat is rationed, so restaurants have become imaginative with turnips, sunchokes, and cabbage.

Nuria notices Isabelle Lefèvre walking past and alerts the others. Isabelle was in their class and is currently at the university. She never was very friendly, and not that smart. There is no love lost between them. When she notices the three, she feels obliged to change her direction toward the table.

"Well, the three little kittens," she says. No bisous, no warmth. No one is happy to see her.

"Hi, Isa. How's it going?" Catie asks.

"Excellent." She turns her bland smile on the three. "You ladies busy?"

"Working hard," Nuria says, "for family and country."

"Getting with the order of the day."

"Trouble is," Nuria says, "things aren't improving. In fact…"

"It's all for a purpose," Isabelle interrupts. "You'll see."

"Will we?" Gabrielle asks seriously. "See what? And when?"

"A new order," Isabelle says confidently. "As Celine, my favorite writer, says, 'I'd prefer a dozen Hitlers to an all-powerful Prime Minister Blum.' When the war ends…"

"We'll be speaking German," Nuria adds.

"Mademoiselles," said Isa, "you need to be careful. Lots of *collabos* or informers about: too many Communists, Bolsheviks, unionists, and others. Need I be more specific?"

"You're right, Isa," Gabrielle replies. "We need to clean our closets. Too many old things, offensive colors, not enough of what is proper. Trust our leaders."

Isabelle looks sharply at Gabrielle. "You should know, Gaby."

"What?"

"Jean-Luc asks of you. Why don't you…"

Gabrielle blanches, and her head suddenly turns downward as though slapped.

"You have no idea," Nuria interrupts loudly.

They all know the story. They know the seriousness of the hurt she suffered, though not the extent nor the duration of the pain. They protect Gabrielle.

Isabelle changes the subject. "We must work and sacrifice to make a better path for our country. It depends on each of us: our choices and our compliance. It's a great opportunity, without uninvited guests, freeloaders, and Jews."

"Thanks for the advice," Nuria replies angrily. "We working girls have to get back. See you soon." No one moves.

24

Isabelle looks with distaste. "A bientôt."

They do not reply.

After she leaves, the three look at each other with dismay. It's what they hear everyday. The luncheon is spoiled, and they stand to go their separate ways, giving bisous and planning weekend activities. Catie hugs Gabrielle, who is near tears. Jean-Luc is a name they all abhor and never pronounce.

After Catie leaves, Nuria hugs Gabrielle.

"She's a beast," and then adds seriously: "We're drowning in lies and malice. We have to constantly remind ourselves of the truth. She's right about one thing, we need to watch ourselves."

"Yes," Gabrielle replies absently in a haze, "but a lie is so much more effective and useful than the truth, which is always bathed in complications."

***

Much of my parents' past remains a mystery. Both my parents were raised in Paris, but when they married they immediately departed to work in the south and rarely returned to see their parents. My grandparents on both sides had been strongly set against the union. Although my parents never talked directly to me on the subject, part of their parents' defiance was my father's painting. But I am sure that was not the entire story.

The only time I ever saw my grandparents was on a visit to Paris when I was fifteen years old and my father had an exhibition of his recent paintings at a gallery. The day we visited my father's parents, Paris was unseasonably cold and overcast for a June day, but I was excited to be there. At noon, we rang at the ornate wood and brass door of a large residence in the seventeenth arrondissement. A maid opened the door.

"You must be Auguste...and Gaby. Please come in." No mention of Julie.

We entered an atrium, which was dark, dusty, and cold. Stiff portraits of unknown relatives hung on the walls. As we continued into the house, I spied gloomy rooms crowded with heavy furniture, hidden behind layers of embroidered window curtains, allowing no direct light into the rooms. Potted plants on pedestals and ancient oriental carpets were everywhere. I could barely imagine my father growing up in this soulless house, where a child couldn't find a space to play.

At the end of the hall, we arrived in a sun room, with frosted glass, where I first glimpsed my grandparents. They were old, reminding me of marble statues, without a grain of warmth. They made no effort to welcome us, but remained seated together on a large divan. Both were dressed formally, as though preparing for an elegant evening.

I remained behind my parents as we approached.

"It's good to see you," Auguste said, offering his hand to his seated father. They directed us to sit opposite in oversized chairs, obviously arranged for them. My mother, normally talkative and friendly, remained silent and retreated to a chair.

"This must be Gaby," my grandmother said. "Louise, please find a chair for her."

Louise brought a chair from the nearby table set for lunch, and placed it next to my parents. I sat down, surprised by the reception and my mother's reticence. As the only child of two only children, you would think that I would have been welcomed.

"How have you been, father?" Auguste asked.

"Between bouts of rheumatism and migraines and fatigue I manage. These doctors are worthless. They prescribe the Bayer aspirin for everything, until my ears are ringing. My bad leg from the war continues to bother me, but I can't complain. I still go to the office, and Sarah is holding up." He spoke with a strong eastern European accent, even though they had been in Paris for thirty years.

"You look in good spirits," Auguste added. "And Maman, you look well."

"How is your painting going?" his father asked.

"As I told you, we are here for an exhibition. I was very pleased to be invited to the Voorhies Gallery, along with Dufy, Derain, and Matisse. I'm in good company."

"I don't know them. Are you selling any?"

"Some. It's difficult these days."

"I'm sure. My business is down, but still strong. Good furniture is never out of fashion. You could be of help possibly." He paused, looking at Auguste. "Perhaps you would like a drink before lunch?"

"Yes, please," Julie replied. "I'm thirsty. Water would be fine."

"Louise, please serve them whatever they want. I understand you are working in a museum as well."

"Yes. I'm curator of a small municipal museum."

"I see. And does that pay well."

"We are fine, Papa. We have been there for fifteen years.

My grandmother finally spoke up. "I hope you have found a proper church in the south, Auguste. I am so pleased with our local Sainte-Mairie-des-Batignolles. The priest is wonderful, attentive, and helpful, a true guide in all things." She looked at me. "And you, young lady, you must strive to attain a full understanding of all of God's revelations. I'm afraid Leonard Blum and his government did not appreciate this."

No reply was necessary.

Louise announced lunch, and we moved to the table. During the lunch, they steered clear of any controversy or personal exchange: a meal of strangers. We left shortly afterwards, when polite conversation had run its course and silence dominated. Even Julie did not attempt to enliven the afternoon; she barely spoke.

In the afternoon, we walked around Paris to see some of the sights, the Parc Monceau, the Arc de Triomphe, the Champs-Elysées, but my parents seemed to grow only more cheerless. We soon returned to our hotel room. That evening, we made an appearance at the opening of his exhibition, where, even though well attended, Auguste's parents did not appear. Afterwards, we ate a light supper at a cafeteria.

Early the next morning, we met Fannia, we called her Fanny, my mother's mother. Her welcome was quite different from Auguste's parents. She was happy to see us all and gave everyone kisses and hugs. Her apartment was near Auguste's parents' home, but in an area of downscale apartments. We met her out front of her building.

"My, you're a big girl," Fanny said to me. She was dressed in widow's black, even though her husband had died while I was in primary school, but she was cheery and bright. "Thank you all for coming to visit me. It's been too long since we last met. You all look so tan and healthy. You've lost your Parisian pallor. I guess it's the southern clime."

As planned, she sent my parents off to shop and took me to mass. We walked to the local church.

"Julie looks happy. I'm so pleased." She talked the entire way. "Although she has gained weight. It's the curse of a large woman. She inherited that from her father. She was always headstrong. Never listened to us. Never took her studies seriously. You know, we never knew they were seeing each other until they decided to marry. We wanted so much for her, and his painting seemed to bode poverty. Your grandfather worked hard his entire life, and we never had much, but we never lacked."

I watched her as she talked, never asking about my life or me. She seemed very nice and warm, but somehow sad underneath, or perhaps her life was just very limited.

"Gaby, you need to put your faith in God and work hard in school. Remember, you can learn from books. Always study hard, but you must listen to others smarter than yourself. Your maman never listened to her father."

After mass, we walked back to a small restaurant near her apartment, where we met my parents. She seemed so different from my lively mother, whom I barely recognized in her stories. We said our goodbyes on the street.

"I4'm really sorry," Fanny apologized with tears in her eyes, without further clarification. She embraced me and then her daughter, and shook hands with Auguste. We returned to our hotel to depart the next day.

On the train ride home, my parents barely spoke to each other. They had argued the night before while I pretended to sleep: one of the few quarrels I can remember and certainly the worst. Their low voices and mumbled responses had been incomprehensible, but angry and frustrated. On the train, my mother's mood was morose and sullen, so unlike her, and my father refolded and shook the newspaper as if reading it, while staring out the window.

Back in Perpignan, we never spoke of the ill-fated visit. They never explained their original departure from Paris and the break with their parents. Somewhere, love between the generations had evaporated, and what remained was completely obscured without feelings. I'm sure my parents' argument was about this rupture. My mother was always one to speak her mind, tell the truth, get it out front. My father, though quieter, was often firmer in his beliefs, though he cloistered his true feelings. You never knew what he was thinking. Something had happened in the past that they refused to acknowledge.

While growing up, I always wondered about my grandparents. After this pitiable visit, I had no desire to know them, nor they me, I suppose. As the train made its way south, the weather cleared up, the temperature increased, and our spirits slowly lifted. As far as I know, my parents never visited their parents again. My father on occasion visited Paris for meetings and exhibitions, but never spoke of seeing them.

I have no idea what happened to create this schism. People exhibit from their past only what they want you to know. I'm positive that this kind of dishonesty spoiled several budding relationships I had in school and contributed to the one in particular that damaged me, making me more guarded with all others. At the same time, my visit to my grandparents made me more aware of how important relations with others are and how easily they can be lost.

✳✳✳

Several weekends later, I met Nuria and Catie at the Café de la Poste near the Castillet. The winter weather had become more cordial, and the smell of charcoal-roasted chestnuts had given way to sweet and alluring scents of blooming mimosa and chestnut trees. The flower stalls were filled with fresh-blooming bouquets and potted plants. The auditions were finished, and I was feeling better about dancing. We prepared for two numbers of our own, but also choreographed several smaller dances for backing the band and singers. We provided transitions and impromptu appearances while others were performing.

I became more comfortable with the steps that the instructor, Monsieur Duras, set out for us, and the other girls liked me. General rehearsals with the other acts would not begin for several weeks, and I had no thoughts as to the costumes, whether elegant or skimpy.

Nuria was the first to arrive, dressed to the teeth, looking beautiful in an outfit I did not recognize, smelling of Vol de Nuit by Guerlain, and feeling good about herself.

"*Hola, niña.*" A quick bise.

"If looks could kill," I said to Nuria. "You must have a date."

"With my mother's younger brother from Spain. He's forty, if a day, and looking for work." She lit a cigarette awkwardly. "I have no idea what I will do with him. You interested?

"No, thanks. I have a dance rehearsal this afternoon. I'm feeling much better about the review, although I know very little except the basic choreography. Charles Trenet has agreed to be there."

"That crazy singer? Do you know him?"

"I like some of his songs on the radio."

They turned to see Catie moping along, dressed in baggy pants and an old sweater: her face gaunt and unmade up, her hair disheveled, a colorless scarf circling her shoulders.

"He's gone," she said without greeting.

"Gone?" I said. "He just arrived."

"That's the story of my life," Catie said, flopping down into the waiting chair. "He was so cute. I'm lost…oh so lost."

"The five minute affair," Nuria said.

"He only wanted one thing, and I need a little more reassurance before I give that away. My God, you'd think…"

"So it's all over?"

"Yes." She laughed weakly, "Dead on arrival."

"At least this time you extricated yourself early," Nuria said. "Could have been worse. Just because a guy is cute doesn't mean he's a keeper. You'll survive."

"Thanks. How's the dancer?" Catie asked, perking up.

We were accustomed to Catie recovering rapidly from affairs of the heart. In fact, we had all become fairly resilient. "Great." I said. "I'm slowly remembering my training, and I like the choreographer. He's a superb dancer and knows how to help others improve."

"So, when will we see you perform?" Nuria demanded.

"I'll let you know, but you should come to see Trenet. By the way, we got a new shipment for the spring. Lots of great things. New colors. New products. You have to drop by."

"Your prices are too high," Catie said. "The Bazaar is better."

"You never know what you're getting there," Nuria said. "Since the occupation, all I see are used stuff, worn and worthless."

"Yea, but they're cheap, and we don't get the discount at the Galeries that you do," Catie added.

"You can use my discount. You know that. At least the merchandise is new."

I love them, but sometimes I grow tired. We've been friends too long, know too much, but they're the best. They're the only ones to whom I can tell the truth. My mother gets too worried, and my father is too preoccupied with other things.

Everyone is preoccupied today, though, since the city is filled with people moving through. Tourists are gone, and instead, we have émigrés interested in escaping France. You never know whom you're talking to, whom they represent, or what they be4lieve, but you have to be careful with everyone, just as Isabelle had spitefully said. We are far from the action in Paris, but we feel the spillover in fear and suspicion. Insincerity rules.

We have all been exposed to an insidious sickness and pray that an alchemist can supply us miracle cures. We close our eyes to all that requires vision. The only thing left is to go to movies or bars or nightclubs, where it's warm and you can dream, make believe, and breathe,

3

March 1941

> *Maréchal here we are!*
> *You have given us*
> *Our fatherland reborn*
> *Maréchal, Maréchal here we are!*
> *« Maréchal nous voilà, » André Montagnard and*
> *Charles Courtioux*

On the summit of the frontier with Spain above Banyuls-sur-Mer, the wind had come up, and it was getting colder with a night mist. After the smugglers passed, I waited an hour or so for the border patrol to mount the pass and return to their headquarters in Banyuls. Waiting is the worst: nerve-wracking and stomach-wrenching. The young couple too was becoming increasingly nervous, probably worried that I would desert them or turn them over to the authorities. Finally, I couldn't wait any longer. The border patrol had not passed. A bad sign. They don't spend nights in the mountains. Too lazy for that. They may have returned to the main coastal road, or perhaps were lying in wait if they had been informed of our border crossing.

"We have to go," I said, standing and getting them started again. I knew a secondary path that skirted this route, and eventually ended up in Portbou, a small detour, but less frequented. We began walking silently. Soon we were deep in Spain. The French border patrols had no problem entering Spain in pursuit of foreigners or passeurs. Being caught by them was bad, but the Spanish police were notorious for treating people without papers abusively and taking them to Spanish jails, where the conditions were horrendous. They particularly disliked passeurs.

As we slowly descended the mountain into Spain, I felt more and more ill at ease. Maybe the advice of the smuggler to desert the foreigners was more perceptive than I was willing to admit. I had never done it and was not about to begin now.

We had a clear view of the shining lights of Portbou, with the dark Mediterranean extending to the starry horizon. I stopped.

"I can't go farther." I pointed in the direction of the village. "Portbou."

Suddenly, I clearly heard heavy, stumbling footsteps struggling on the hillside below us. Not the footsteps of people familiar with the hills. We must have been spotted.

"You must go," I gesticulated, hoping they would understand.

They looked at me in shock, but they too heard the approaching footsteps.

"Go now." I pointed in the direction directly toward the village. "Fast. They won't follow you. Go." My voice raised to a pitch that alarmed them. I watched as they moved rapidly along the trail away from the sounds. Then I took off on a path across the hillside, leaving the track. I came to a steep slope running perpendicular to a series of switchbacks. About fifty meters below me I saw a troupe of four or five agents struggling up the hillside, and they saw me.

"Stop," the leader yelled, waving his arms. I knew I was in good shape, and that the border patrol would have a hard time following me. They were older, not familiar with the mountains, and disgracefully out of shape: too much wine and too many cigarettes. They also were deeper into Spain than normal on a steep slope. As I guessed, they had followed me across the mountain side through the loose rocks and desolate winter garrigue, leaving the main track, trying to trap me, but allowing the couple to descend into the village below.

"Stop," one of them yelled again. For an instant, we stared at each other. When he drew his sidearm, I took off on a path I knew led directly up the hillside. I heard a shot fired, but I had lost sight of them, and they could not see me. Two more wild shots were fired in my direction. My heart beating rapidly, I increased my speed. I was able to move rapidly up the mountain, which they couldn't. I came to the summit on the French side and listened for a moment. No sound behind me. I jogged down the hillside, jumping the terraced walls of the vineyards, skirting the rainwater drainage, and coming to the main vineyard road. Without bothering to drop to the trail below, I jogged down the road, arriving late in the night at the train station. Departing trains would begin early in the morning, so I settled down for the rest of the night outside the station. I would arrive just on time at the

Prefecture, tired, clothes unchanged, but ready to pass another day of a different sort of resistance.

***

The occupation and collaboration signal the end of the sun's warmth. The nights are silent; our days are stolen. People talk intimately, but all meaning is lost. Words have no sincerity. Our ears cannot make out the sounds for we hear only lies and half-truths. We hide ourselves, and our false-selves, only acknowledging others' expectations, marking a barren emptiness. A language of proxy and evasion has taken over. The clouds cover us and refuse to lift.

You meet someone and know you will never be friends, either now or in the future. You cannot even know his name. Nor can he know yours. He cannot know where you live or what you do or who you are. Your name is Marc (not Paul). His name is Edmund (not his real name). We meet for the simple reason that we believe, with any luck, that what we are doing has some merit, more merit than doing nothing at all. We are connected by the tenuous confluence of our goals, never expressed, never aligned. The fact is you cannot even be sure that the person you meet is not out to ruin you. So much is in doubt. So much is lost. Yet, in total, so much is important beyond your knowledge or imagination.

You sit on a bench, the third from the entrance on the north side, in the Promenade des Platanes, next to the flower vendors, facing south. A young man about your age arrives and sits down on the other end of the bench. He's nondescript, plain trousers and casual shirt with a canvass jacket and béret. He sits for a moment without looking at you and then turns slightly and says:

"The flowers are blooming along the Têt."

And you say, "Dora is still in Paris."

Then the man says to you, "We need an exit visa." He places an envelope on the bench. "Can you deliver a week from today?"

"I can try."

"Next Tuesday, firm."

"You can look elsewhere."

"All right. All right. Tuesday…if possible."

He stands up and walks away, with the envelope still resting next to you. You sit for a moment and casually glance about you with trepidation, your stomach roiling, and then slip the envelope into your backpack. Your imminent arrest in question, your heart beats rapidly. You leave the bench, anticipating a tap on the back, which this time, thankfully, does not come.

***

Later that afternoon, Paul meets Léon. Léon (not his real name) has worked with him for about six months. Léon had been an art student before the war and now finds that he's better employed, both morally and monetarily, preparing false documents: identity cards, visas, passports, official letters, travel permits, etc. He's quick, accurate, and about ninety percent correct in what he does. That's a lot better than most forgers, and there are many active ones. Some are as fraudulent as their wares. At great risk, Paul has provided him with real letterhead blanks from the Prefecture and has even loaned him rubber stamps, which were duplicated and then returned. As the demand for papers has increased, the letterhead and stamps have taken on greater value at the Prefecture and are now more carefully secured. Once completed, the visa is basically real, except there is no backup paperwork, and, of course, the approval signature is forged.

Café de la Poste is perhaps the most frequented meeting place in Perpignan. It's not a great place for serious meetings, too many people, too many ears, but the morning is clear and cold, and it's a nice walk from the Prefecture. At any time, you can meet just about anyone here on the terrace: the mayor, the Prefect, the chief of police, German agents, businessmen, shop girls, black market sellers, cooks and waiters on breaks, students, housewives, and grandparents with their grandchildren playing in the street alongside. The tables inside the café are occupied only in a downpour.

Léon is a slight fellow, pimpled, appearing malnourished, with long unwashed blond hair falling onto his face, which he ignores.

"Marc."

They shake hands, and Léon sits down. Not exactly happy to see one another, they remain silent until the coffee arrives.

"You busy?" Paul asks. Their voices are low, and they lean toward each other as though in familiar conversation.

Léon nods. "Never busier."

"I have a small job, exit visa," Paul says. He likes the young man, trusts him, and perhaps in another life they might have been friends at the university. Instead, they must avoid each other, or at least limit their contacts, constantly changing the location and timing of their meetings. Paul slides an envelope across the table, which contains the needed data, photo, and francs.

Léon downs his coffee. "Saturday okay?"

"That's fine." They shake hands, and Léon departs.

Paul sits at his place a while longer watching people at the café and passers-by in the street, wondering how many of them are hiding under a pseudonym and false persona. After a deep intake of breath, he returns to the Prefecture.

***

Georges Doelnitz sits at the zinc of the Club les Tréteaux nursing a *jus au citron*, watching Paul eat a sandwich. They have worked together every night for the last two weeks. The review is coming together, although they have yet to initiate a full rehearsal with the entire cast; that will come at the end of next week. After that seven days will remain before the show opens. A simple handbill has been designed by Auguste Daniel, a local artist, from a photograph of Charles Trenet. Above his name in giant type is a splashy red title: "Swing, Swing, Swing at the Club les Tréteaux, 21 rue de la Cloche d'Or, March 24-30, daily at 9 pm, matinee 1 pm on Sunday." It has been pasted all over town for more than a week.

"He's here for only three days, Georges."

"Right. We'll post a bill on top to ensure that the weekend with Charles will be noted. But for the moment, Jordi wants to get word-of-mouth out. We're in pretty good shape. It's coming together."

"Who's doing the Trenet songs the first four days?"

"You feel up to it?"

"Me? I don't know?" His heart skips a beat.

36

"You know the songs?"

"Yeah."

"Just kidding, just kidding. But you know you could do it."

"Wouldn't you be concerned? Trenet has been singing since the review *Allo, Père Pigne* in 1924. He's a major name in Paris and sells plenty of records."

"We'll see. We've got a couple of leads. We've got to start blocking out the scenes."

"Georges," Paul muses, "you know, I've been hearing a lot about the impact of the new laws. There's some resistance to them, foot-dragging, but they're being implemented. Prime Minister Laval is out, but Darlan is no better, and Laval's presence is still there. They're talking about lists of people at the Prefecture. It can only get worse."

"I've been around a long time, Paul. Seen it before."

"I know, but here? I see it daily. One escape route opens, and then it's filled. Slowly they're filling all the holes."

"I understand. This has been going on for ages."

"I'm talking about today, Georges. You don't listen."

"Okay. Okay. But let's get the show completed. Then we talk. Okay?"

"It gets harder. Every day." Paul looks at his mentor, trying to place him with the desperate émigrés he sees in the Visa section. Lucien Trenet, his first boss, and Georges were critical to establishing his life here. Lucien was born in Perpignan and has nothing to worry about. Georges does, but he ignores it.

***

What is fairness or equity? I think most people could agree on what is fair and what it is not. Believing in fairness is pretty simple, but today it's totally absent.

I came to the belief in fairness from my childhood, not directly from my grand-mère or maman or catechism, but from my own struggles. God should, by definition, be fair and must have created a universe intended for fairness. Fairness among humans is based on learned behavior. Children have to be taught to share. Adults must force themselves, or be forced by

37

others or the church, to care for others. Fairness never even crosses the minds of some people, so determined by their own needs (*ma pomme, ma pomme, ma pomme*). Self-interest trumps all.

In principle, our government's role is to ensure fairness with its laws. Yet, fairness is placed at the bottom of a long list of its priorities. In our current situation, people are forced to depart France to survive. The government passes laws excluding certain people from teaching or working in the government or exercising their professional expertise. People escaping the Nazis are returned to their home countries. A million and a half French military are held prisoner in internment camps in Germany and France, even with the armistice signed. The government's agenda is aligned with the goals of the Occupant, and the Occupant allows free rein to the Vichy government's conservative political program as long as it doesn't interfere with the war effort against Britain. And as long as Vichy continues to provide financial, material, and labor support to the Germans.

We often hear these days: "the Occupant is attempting to make a better world." Maréchal Pétain, a hero of the Great War, established a government set up to diametrically change the direction of our country. They said the Third Republic was headed in the wrong direction: led by intellectuals, teachers, workers, freemasons, and Jews. They called it anticlerical, antimilitary, and antifamily. They blamed it for our defeat. They replaced the long-held motto of "*Liberté, Egalité, Fraternité*" (liberty, equality, brotherhood) with "*Travail, Famille, Patrie*" (work, family, fatherland).

The Dreyfus affair at the turn of the century is still relevant today: a young artillery officer, Jewish, was falsely convicted of trading military secrets to the Germans. He was ultimately found to be innocent, thanks in part to Emile Zola's article, "J'accuse!" This scandal created two long-lasting and contentious factions: the progressive, pro-republicans and the conservative, pro-Army, mostly Catholic, "anti-Dreyfusards" The anti-Dreyfusards never forgot. The Dreyfus cultural war continues.

We all want fairness for ourselves. God wants fairness. The effort to disregard fairness requires lying, complicating everything, making everything difficult to understand, and requiring expert interpretation. Unfairness is promulgated by pushing a narrow agenda, never clearly expressed, exclusive and protective of a few, but destructive and anathema to the majority. Above all, it requires lies, propaganda, fear mongering, and restricting free expression.

I lead my life based on fairness. Since the occupation, it has led me in extraordinary directions, entailing significant risks. How much am I willing to give up for fairness? My livelihood, my conscience, my life? I am no hero and do not desire to be one. Yet day by day, I become more deeply involved in the resistance, in my efforts to help people. Day by day, I am more deeply involved in activities that could result in incarceration, here or in Germany, or worse. We read about people in the occupied zone being murdered for far less. Yet, my simple personal equation of fairness that drives me is understandable to children. Perhaps a glimpse of the genesis of this simple philosophy might serve.

***

I remember clearly a wintry afternoon in Amélie-les-Bains, where I was born and raised. I was five years old when one day Grand-mère returned to the house in a distressed, upset state of mind. I was reading a new book I had received for Christmas 1926: an illustrated book called *Les Fables Choisis de Jean de la Fontaine*. My mother had given it to me, and I was not happy with her gift. Even as an early reader, I couldn't understand most of the fables, but with the weather uncooperative, night falling, and nothing else to do, I skimmed through the illustrated stories to find one I liked. I found one and struggled through it: "The Stag who Admired his Reflection," about a vain stag barely escaping from a bloodhound, hindered by his vain antlers.

Grand-mère suddenly arrived home.

"Paul, come with me," she shouted from downstairs. She was in her late fifties, a widow for some time. She rapidly stomped up the wooden stairs, and when she entered I could see she was agonized by some terrible emotion. Immediately, I knew that something unimaginable had happened. I was used to her changes in mood and her quick anger, but this was different. I immediately dropped the book and jumped to my feet.

"Get your overcoat."

39

"Yes, Grand-mère." I was terrified. I went into the small, crammed closet and took out my heavy coat, which was still wet from the afternoon, and I followed her down the staircase. She waited with the door open, truly distressed.

"Come."

"What about Maman and Adèle?"

"Never you mind."

She took my hand forcefully, pulling the door shut behind us. She practically dragged me to the end of the street in the near dusk, in the light rain, past the Mairie, and then along the rue des Thermes. I was convinced that I had committed some terrible offense. She had a temper, and I always steered clear of her when she was in one of her sullen moods. This didn't happen too frequently, but when it did, my mother usually took the brunt of her attacks. If my sister or I happened to be in her sights, my mother would quickly intervene. I feared Grand-mère beyond all others.

We arrived at the church of Saint Quentin and entered the side door. Few people were about, and the chairs in the nave waited vacantly. She genuflected, crossed herself with holy water, and instructed me to do the same. Then I followed her down the central aisle to the first row of chairs before the choir and altar. We sat down. I was still at a loss, fearing the worst.

For a long while, she prayed as seriously as I have ever seen her pray. Finally, she turned to me, no longer in such a rage, but her face distorted with pained tears in her eyes. I had never seen her cry.

"Paul, my child, sometimes things happen. We have no explanation why God in all His goodness allows such things to occur. We cannot begin to fathom his reasons. All we can do is rely on our faith: faith in His grace and truth and love for mankind. He gave His only son into Hell on the cross that we the guilty ones might reconcile with Him and be received into heaven. God sent Him to wash away our sins, so that we may become His adopted children, that we might partake in His divine nature and eternal life. We must never fail to recall the righteousness of God through His son, Jesus Christ."

I had no idea what to reply. I knew it was serious. I remember these words, or words like these, since she repeated this message as I grew up.

"Now you will get down on your knees." She waited, ignoring my look of hopelessness, my lack of understanding, and my appeal for her own grace. As I kneeled, she whispered in my ear: "Now, child, we must pray for your salvation." She paused, waiting, while I prayed silently in my fashion. She began whispering in my ear. "There was an accident. Only God knows what happened, and the good Lord has chosen to take your mother and your sister from us. They now reside in Heaven at His side, and we will miss them. You must say twenty Hail Marys. Hail Mary full of Grace, the Lord is with thee…" She started me off, but then turned silent.

I repeated the words I knew well as she kept count. I must have cried at times, fearing the worst, realizing my mother and sister were gone, wiping away my tears for fear of further enraging her, but not fully convinced. I completed all, twenty times. Questions filled my mind like the first time I saw wild animals in a circus. I remained on my knees pretending to pray, knowing only that something had happened to Maman and Adèle, and they were gone.

After that, she allowed me to rise and sit in my chair. She sat next to me pensively for a long time, obviously within herself somewhere, trying to control her own emotions. The heat from her body comforted me. In one way, I understood what she had said, but in another way, I couldn't believe it. "Taken from us." "Reside in Heaven." I had heard these words before, but never applied to me. It seemed a story told by a stranger. My mind demanded clarification, but she offered none and hushed me as we returned to the house. We walked silently. She no longer held my hand: two separate detached beings. I don't remember anything after that and cannot conceive the night I spent. In all the years I grew up there, played there, attended school there, and during vacations from my secondary school, she never again mentioned a word of the accident or any explanation or solace. I could bring up certain memories of Maman and Adèle. That was permissible. But they were never discussed, and soon these memories too disappeared from our conversations like ghosts at daylight.

Over the years, I often felt treated unfairly by Grand-mère and could not count on her for comfort or understanding. For all her belief in God, the church, and its importance in her life, she never demonstrated any compassion to me. Probably not to anyone.

After some years, I came to understand from others that my mother and sister had died in an automobile accident. My sister was two years younger than I, perhaps four at the time. My mother had been returning from Perpignan driving on the narrow highway leading home. The driving conditions were awful, wet and icy, and the narrow road ran alongside the river with solid rock cliffs on one side and steep precipices on the other side with the river below. Once off the road, the car had broken through bushes and saplings and had landed upside down on the boulders far below alongside the river.

I never have come to terms with the manner of the disappearance of my mother and sister. Too unexpected. Too little information. They were here one day and then disappeared. I kept waiting for them, but they never came back. I'm still waiting.

Years later, I learned that my mother had received news that same afternoon from my father that he was not returning to France. All the time, he had had another family in San Sebastian, Spain. She must have been devastated. We never heard from him again. I'm sure he was absent from the funeral mass and burial, of which I have no memory. I attempted to bury my father along with my beloved mother and sister. The cause of the crash was never known. Was she forced off the road by another car or truck? Was there some mechanical problem? Did she want to die? What about my sister? But these thoughts only led into tangled and ambiguous darkness.

As a result of this, as I grew up I determined to always treat people fairly, as I had not been treated.

After their death, I heard from my father only one more time. He sent money for my schooling. But in the end he finally did aid me, unexpectedly and without his own knowledge. That was years later in Spain.

All the Clouds

***

The following week, Marc (aka Paul) meets Edmund on the opposite bench on the Promenade des Platanes. It's drizzling lightly. He waits nervously, lighting a cigarette, which he does when feeling uneasy. Edmund is late. Paul is tired, working days at the Prefecture and nights at the Club les Tréteaux. He's anxious about this meeting. Léon has prepared the papers, which are up to his normal high standards. So many false documents are hurried, on the wrong type of paper, and badly filled out, often with stamps that would never be used and signatures impossible to decipher. Some fail to pass the simplest measures of the police, to say nothing of the more exigent examinations of the customs and Gestapo in the Occupied Zone. Luckily for the forgers, there are so many different types of passports, visas, identity papers, and forms filled out by so many different countries and agencies and prefectures, that to convince a harried policeman or customs agent, unschooled in the large variety of papers in multiple languages, is not difficult. Gestapo agents, on the other hand, are more informed, have no restrictions with a clear, ultimate aim, and serve as the true test of a forger.

Paul puts out his cigarette prematurely. No one about. Most of the people passing by in raingear and unopened umbrellas hurry without looking around. More and more the world is made up of silent people passing anonymously. Sitting alone on a bench in the drizzle surely must be a sign of something out of the ordinary, and anything out of the ordinary is suspect and open to question by the police or others. Paul is about to leave, when he spies a man making a beeline toward him. His first thought is to get up and run like hell, but the man is dressed as a worker, canvas jacket, blue pants, and work shoes, not police and certainly not Gestapo attire. He manages his fear and waits alertly as the man approaches.

"The flowers are blooming along the Têt," the man says, remaining standing.

And Paul say, "Dora is still in Paris."

"Do you have the papers?"

"Where's Edmund?"

"Do you have them?"

"Yes." He hands them over to the man, who stashes them in his leather reticule without a glance. "We have something else," he says. "Something serious. A package from Britain."

"What can I do?" Paul asks sharply: Britain means military: a death sentence if stopped, His mind reels, as this has been characteristic of his slow descent into strangeness that is engulfing him. Each time he meets with someone, they ask a little more. Each time, it gets a little more serious. And he never knows anyone and just has to go with his gut instinct, totally unsettling his equilibrium and never with explanation, always without information or background. Of course he understands the reasons for this loose, intentionally disconnected series of actions severed one from the other. But it doesn't make it easier. "Go on."

"The common routes along the coast are becoming clogged. Too much traffic. The train to Portbou is teeming with agents and is closely observed at all points. The routes from Banyuls-sur-Mer and nearby villages across the Albère Mountains are also all now closely watched, with customs, police patrols, and agents in the villages…and of course *collabos,* or informers, are everywhere. It's no longer feasible. We have to move farther west into the mountains, and you're familiar with the mountains behind Céret and Amélie-les-Bains. Can you help us out?"

"Maybe. Depends."

"The package is coming from the north. Should be here next week some time. Weekend next."

"I'm busy."

"Nights?"

"Totally filled." That's the final weekend of full rehearsals with the show beginning the following week and wrapping up on Sunday, but that information is withheld. "The next week should be better, April."

"That puts it off possibly a whole week," the young man thinks aloud.

"There are lots of passeurs. "

"I know," he says bitterly. "We'll see." He departs without a word.

"Ingrate," Paul says angrily to himself. They can never get enough, never satisfied, and never a thanks, but then we're all in this together. It's not a world we would create.

4

March 1941

Ah, how sweet and troubling
The moment of the first meeting
When the weary heart beating on its own
Takes off toward a thrilling mystery
You the stranger in a foolish dream
Accept what it brings to you
The joy of love for a lifetime.
« Le premier rendez-vous, » Louis Poterat

Gabrielle's disastrous affair with Jean-Luc was exhumed by Isabelle's mean-spirited ridicule, which brought back the entire affair starkly, so starkly that she cried herself to sleep the next several nights.

She had spent years trying to come to terms with the events of their troubling liaison and move beyond it, but its importance never seemed to diminish. It affected everything about her: her confidence, her pride, her belief in herself. Hearing Isabelle mention it so casually and spitefully, without real knowledge of what had happened, had stunned Gabrielle, sending her back to those awful memories, never attenuated in their import and influence. How can you defend yourself from a lie, when to reveal the truth would be worse than the crime itself?

Whenever Gabrielle is worried or anxious, she walks to quiet her mind. She often walks long distances, across town or in the hills, or on the weekends into the mountains with her father. Walking seems to grant her serenity, for a time.

After a night of insomnia, the day dawned cool and clear in a warmly cerulean blue sky. She left her parents' home on rue Maurell taking a circuitous route to Les Nouvelles Galeries. She left early to allow herself time to transition to work and to think. Her pelerine was tightly wrapped about her. Her sturdy walking shoes will be exchanged for the flats she keeps in her locker at the store. Since the occupation, shoes have been in short supply. Leather and rubber are going to the Occupant's war efforts. Wooden soles have replaced leather, and their caustic clacking is heard more and more frequently along the city sidewalks.

What occupied her mind on this early morning walkabout was a deep, fundamental anguish. Something she wished would diminish with time. Three years before, Gabrielle had had an affair with a boy in her school: Jean-Luc Pineau. He was endlessly praised as the top student in the school, the pride of the faculty, and revered by the other students. Two years ahead of her in school, he intended to sit for the concours examination for the École normale supérieure (ENS) in Paris and was preparing for the baccalaureate examination. Jean-Luc took advantage of his notoriety and their age difference to impress her and to take her under his intellectual wing, as he might have explained it. They met in cafés after school and, on occasion, in the evenings for study or with friends. Soon enough their friends and fellow students assumed that Jean-Luc and Gaby were a "couple." She became the envy of the other girls, who could not believe that shy little Gaby merited such an honor. Her parents knew nothing of all this. Parents are always the last to learn. Jean-Luc lived with his divorced mother and was relatively free to do as he pleased, while Gabrielle was closely monitored and had to account for her time.

Gabrielle was impressed that Jean-Luc might be interested in her. The two-year age difference seemed enormous. To be honest, she was awed by his reputation, and being selected by him abolished her common sense. He was charming and persuasive, backed up by his friends, who were numerous and convinced of his brilliance, based on his remarkable academic achievements. No one spoke negatively of him. Surprised that he had selected Gabrielle, his friends warned her repeatedly to treat him with due respect.

The only person to express doubts was Nuria. She knew Jean-Luc and his friends, but she was concerned that his strong personality and anointed "star" qualities might overwhelm Gabrielle, obscuring her judgment. She also feared that his attraction and pursuit of her might be intended to intimidate and control her. Of course, Catie, like most of Gabrielle's classmates, was impressed with Jean-Luc and amazed that he chose her. Overall, everyone felt this was fortunate for Gabrielle and boded well. She knew all this and also knew that most people assumed it would not last.

One afternoon, after months of seeing each other almost every day during the fall and spring terms, Jean-Luc invited Gabrielle to his mother's apartment. He explained that his mother was anxious to meet her, since he had spoken so frequently of her. Their apartment was near the Castillet along the canal. When they arrived his mother was out. He suggested a glass of wine to await her return, for she would certainly arrive shortly.

She settled into a darkened living room, feeling ill at ease. To her surprise the apartment was modest, poorly furnished, and unappealing, like temporary housing. She accepted a glass of wine, and they talked. However, their conversation, which normally flowed easily and comfortably, soon converged on the importance of sex. Gabrielle explained honestly that she was inexperienced and ill prepared. He seemed surprised and reacted strongly, arguing that one cannot understand oneself without knowledge of one's own sexuality.

"What is sexual desire?" Jean-Luc asked rhetorically. "It's the single most shared experience among humans. It's not complicated or something to fear. It's based on subjective mutual recognition and agreement. A reciprocated look is enough. I am human. I recognize you so that you can realize your own humanity. I caress you so that my flesh can be initiated, as well as your own flesh." He had recently read Anaïs Nin, D. H. Lawrence, and was interested in Jean Paul Sartre, and he spoke on and on in his dialectic manner of the emotional, physical, and spiritual advantages of sexuality.

"How can you know yourself as a modern woman without knowledge of your own sexuality? It frees you. It allows you to understand others and to avoid many of the pitfalls of relationships. It's the sole gateway to love, so important to our psyches." In his fervor and academic approach, he argued to convince her of what she had to gain once she committed to becoming what he called a "modern woman."

What in fact happened was that Gabrielle slowly became terrified. She watched as he seemed to work himself into a frenzy. She never imagined he would attack her, but he became so entrenched in his own words that she worried where they were leading. Seated on a long sofa covered in a sheet, they sat facing each other as he expostulated. The dusty walls, empty save for a few posters, cheap furnishings, and covered windows, all added to her growing alarm. She watched him anxiously, praying his mother would arrive or that he might change the subject. He never paused, never hesitated, continuing to argue the advantages of knowing oneself, its supreme importance. On and on and on.

"Let me show you," he said suddenly, shocking her.

"No," she said, now truly frightened. "Please. I'm not ready. I don't want to." She began crying.

There had been kissing during the months of their friendship, but nothing serious, no groping, no promises, no commitments. They had been alone together in cafés studying, but mostly with friends. Certainly nothing like this had ever happened, nothing hinting of it. He made a move toward her, and she made an attempt to cover herself with a pillow.

"Don't be silly. I'm not going to hurt you," he said stubbornly, verging on anger. "Trust me. This is for you. I would never hurt you, Gaby. I'll not do anything you dislike."

He began pulling at the pillow she clasped like a doll. He jerked it away strongly. She wrapped her arms around her shoulders and breasts to protect herself. She had on a spring cotton dress, tight wasted with ample skirt, buttoned down the front. She attempted to tuck the dress under her legs. He tugged at the skirt, so forcefully that the front buttons popped off the dress. He wrenched it open at her waist.

At first, Gabrielle was too shocked, too embarrassed, and afraid to make a scene. Her reticence soon transformed to horror, realizing that if she resisted his zealous need for her to understand his philosophy, he might hurt her or worse. She was wearing a short slip and wool stockings against the chill. He managed to unhook her garters and pull her stockings and underwear down to her ankles, leaving her totally exposed, covered only by her torn dress and slip. She was mortified, attempting to cover herself but unable to physically resist his strength. Unclear on what he wanted to do and believing he would not harm her, she feared worst of all making a commotion.

He began his forceful demonstration of the superiority of his beliefs, pushing her back and pulling her thighs apart, forcing her knees up and open, ignoring her shoes and underwear around her ankles. He began vehemently to stimulate her, keeping her legs pinned apart and his other arm on her chest and arms. She was petrified, embarrassed to her core, paralyzed by fear and impotence, no longer believing he would not harm her.

"Please, Jean-Luc. Don't."

He ignored her.

"Just relax. It won't work if you're not calm."

He continued more forcefully, disregarding her tears and protestations, believing his knowledge and ideas took precedence to her immature and ill-informed resistance. His strength and vehemence convinced her that struggling was fruitless. She realized he was obsessed, out of his mind. She worried that something far worse might happen. Convinced of the righteousness of his actions, he knew her ambivalent feelings would be resolved if she would only relax and accept the feelings flowing through her body.

Gabrielle's only thoughts were of survival, to get herself out of this sordid, pathetic little apartment. She focused on the dusty ceiling as though it might somehow comfort her like a view of the mountains or the sky.

"Please, Jean-Luc, your mother. I can't."

"Stop," he ordered exasperated. "You will," and he continued aggressively, holding both her arms against her chest.

She froze, feeling only embarrassment and shame. He continued forcefully for some while, finally removing the underwear at her feet. He then moved over her and forced himself on her.

"Jean-Luc. No. Please." She struggled, but could not prevent his overwhelming weight and strength. She felt nothing physically, only her fear and revulsion.

Again he ignored her and continued, no longer satisfied with simply demonstrating, but wanting to take part in his mania to please her. It didn't last long. His demonstration completed.

He stood up, adjusting his clothes, and looked at her smugly as she pulled herself together. He seemed pleased with himself, continuing to ignore her visible embarrassment, humiliation, and horror. She struggled to cover herself.

"Now you're a woman. You know yourself." He paused. "You'll understand tomorrow. I hope I did not scare you, Gaby. I had to be adamant and complete the process. You'll soon comprehend why it was so important to me. You'll thank me. Our relationship has just entered a new era for both of us. We are a union of equals. We can love one another freely. I hope I proved my love for you."

"I need to go," Gabrielle said, her voice hoarse and dry. "Your mother's not going to arrive, and my parents expect me. What will my mother think of my torn dress? Just look at me." It was already later than normal. "I have to go."

She stood up and straightened her torn dress, tugging it together as well as possible, buttoning her jacket to keep it closed. She retreated to the door, praying he would not prevent her leaving. A quick glance in the hallway mirror displayed a stranger, an alarmed young woman she did not recognize. Her long hair disheveled, her makeup a mess, her eyes red, and her washed out complexion reflected the impression of a terrified animal. She closed her eyes to the vision and continued backing out, not looking at him, as if he might change his mind and bar her from leaving. She reached the door, opened it, and walked out. There were no goodbyes.

Gabrielle felt beyond humiliated and guilty. She faulted herself for placing herself in this horrible situation. His fanatical intellectual rationalization had been more frightening than the act itself. He had become possessed, convinced he was giving her a gift. She did not fight him because of his strength, but his obvious crazed state was more frightening than anything else.

She never told anyone of this terrifying and degrading incident, even her best friends. In retrospect, it had changed everything. She became less trusting, more wary, less open. It forced her to become more self-reliant and to listen to her own conscience, her own common sense. She had been too impressed with Jean-Luc, just like all his other friends, and she had believed her good fortune just as everyone told her. She had forgotten her own worth. That was the awful truth.

The events of that evening and her recollection and assimilation of them haunted her and stayed with her. She never told her parents. Her two closest friends knew only that Jean-Luc had attempted to force her and that she had successfully resisted and would no longer see him. They sympathized with her and were friends enough not to push for details. She never spoke to Jean-Luc again, even though he had attempted to talk with her and seemed at first surprised at her reaction and then dismissive. The students assumed he had dropped her, which confirmed their initial belief that she was unworthy. Having excellent results on his Baccalaureate, he was accepted at the ENS and left for Paris at the end of the school year. She never saw him again.

She finished school two years later, without any boyfriends, building close relations with a few trusted girlfriends, but no longer at ease with the academic environment and with no desire to pursue further studies. Although she had disappointed her parents by leaving school, they never suspected the reason behind her decision.

In the early morning haze, she arrived at Les Nouvelles Galeries distraught, exchanging her shoes and entering the first floor cosmetics area prepared to recommend colors and scents, make useful cosmetic suggestions, ring up the purchases, and package them in their fancy new rose bag: "*J'achète tout aux Nouvelles Galeries.*" She turned off one sector of her mind and was able to function. Her coworkers and customers would never have guessed that twenty minutes before she had been, once again, overwhelmed by what had become a recurring nightmare.

***

That evening, I sat at the small dining table with my parents, eating a light, meatless meal. My mother had lit candles, which were in short supply, and my father said a quick grace. Looking at them, I noted that in the last year they had aged. My mother, always bright and cheery, was less so. My father was more preoccupied than normal, even for a man who normally lived very much in his own mind and eyes.

"How are you, Papa?" I asked.

"Okay," he replied, looking up at me, as if this unexpected question had some ulterior reason. "Why do you ask, Gabrielle?"

"Only that everything has changed since the occupation. France is like a ship wrecked on the shoals, being torn apart internally and slowly perishing. Everyone is different, and I sometimes worry about my parents. I love them so."

"Oh, don't worry about us, *ma puce*," my mother said. "We're getting along."

"I know, but Papa seems so distant."

"You're right. It's a terrible time and has been for several years, even before the war." Auguste Daniel looked at his wife and daughter gravely. "It's a dishonest, uncertain time. Everyone is looking after his own interests. There is no love, even in the church. All our lives have been internalized. Most people are waiting for change to come, one way or another. Some few are passionately involved believers, taking advantage of the direction of our country. In the north, people must accept what is happening, since it is in their teeth every day. We are luckier here, but still we are conflicted. Life has focused on hoping for the best, waiting for more people to realize that we cannot continue in this direction. There is only one possible outcome if it continues: the war will be lost, and there will be total domination and loss of our identity and traditions. I have no answers. I'm sorry to be so distracted, but we…" He seemed to drift away into his thoughts, unable or unwilling to explain further.

They were quiet for a moment.

"How's the show coming?" my mother asked in a feeble attempt to lighten the mood.

The evening continued, no one saying what they were thinking. After cleanup, I went to my room feeling uncertain about everything, mostly worried about my father. I know him, and he was under some unusual strain.

I love Papa. He is deeply religious, never raises his voice, and is forever concerned for my welfare. Perhaps his greatest asset is his loyalty, which extends far beyond the family. He believes strongly in the rights of others and the teachings of Jesus Christ, even though he is not a frequent attendee at mass. He lives the doctrine of his faith. He struggled to become an artist and then at my birth had to compromise to continue painting, going to work. Papa fights to preserve Perpignan's artistic and cultural heritage, and he assists artists at all stages of their careers, including teaching school-age students, most of whom worship him. He knows all the leading artists throughout the south.

Many great artists have lived and worked in Perpignan and its environs, and many more have spent time here. Salvador Dali and Joan Miro were born nearby in Spanish Catalonia. Henri Matisse, André Dérain, and Raoul Dufy painted in Collioure, a small fishing village to the south. Pablo Picasso visited Céret in the mountains for several summers. With him came Georges Braque and Juan Gris. Aristide Maillol was born in nearby Banyuls-sur-Mer and sculpted there and in Paris. Gauguin's paintings from Tahiti were first displayed in our Catalan region. The colors of Fauvism and the illusions of Cubism were born here, but to Papa, the god of them all was Cézanne.

As a girl I often went with him on his weekend sketching excursions. He loved the Roussillon, its roots, its people, its landscapes, and the lights and colors of the wind-swept marine and mountainous environments. His paintings were an homage to this enduring love. He never sketched without Gribouille, his dog. Over the years, there had been three Gribouilles, each one more beloved than the former.

While he sketched the landscapes, monuments, churches, and towns for future studio paintings, I would visit them in my own way. I walked through the villages, talked with people, hiked the mountain trails, ambled through the vineyards and orchards, bathed in the sea, rivers, and lakes, talked with the workers, visited the markets and galleries. He gave me an education in the Roussillon that I will always cherish, and he produced a magnificent body of work that will never disappear.

Papa's love of art taught me about the process of art and introduced me to our people, history, and culture. It allowed me to view his deep-seated faith in humanity and built a strong relationship between the two of us. He's a quiet man, but talk about art and you cannot keep him quiet. He measures every scene or person through the practice of painting: the saturation, hue, and intensity of every color, every reflection and depth of every shadow, every tinted nuance of light, the warmth or coolness of shade and highlights. His vision probes beneath the visual perception of people. He sees into their depths and, in so doing, has a more complete understanding of them.

This evening I was worried because I knew something was on his mind, something he was not talking about. Papa is a strong, principled man, unwilling to compromise his ideals. He always allowed my freedom and respected my points of view. Much of my shame at my distressing affair with Jean-Luc was that I failed to recall the lessons of my father: faith, pride, and self-reliance.

***

The participants gather in the Club les Tréteaux. The separate dance rehearsals have concluded. Next week joint rehearsals will be held each night at the hall, combining all the elements of the show, including the music. Gabrielle is no longer anxious about the rehearsals, since she has become comfortable with the other dancers, and the routines have become second nature.

"Quiet please. Quiet. Can we stop for a moment? There will be plenty of time to visit." Georges Doelnitz, the producer of the show, shouts over the assembled people. Everyone is talking, meeting friends, drinking, and generally enjoying themselves. He waits.

At least fifty people gather, casually dressed in rain gear, since an ill-disposed northeastern storm has arrived with strong winds, but the hall is rapidly warming from the crowd. The first general meeting since initiation of rehearsals is noisy and chaotic.

"Sssshush," people begin to shout. "Sssshush." Slowly the sibilant warning works its way through the room, and the noise abates somewhat until Georges can be heard.

"Ladies and gentlemen. Tonight my only goal is to walk through the order of the show. No acting or singing or playing this evening. Just a walkthrough so that everyone can see the chronology of the evening and their contribution. The timing of the show has to be less than three hours. Tomorrow night will be the first rehearsal, and we will continue cropping and adjusting." He pauses as the room becomes quiet. "One announcement: as you know, Charles Trenet has only committed to three nights and a matinee on the weekend. Recently, we received the commitment of Mireille Printemps for the weeknights." Groans from the audience. "I know. I know.

She was popular during the Great War and has not had a hit in ages, but she is a true professional. And best of all, she is available. I'm looking to you to step it up and fill in the vacancy. We'll know soon enough how she will be accepted. We are already getting advance orders for the four shows with Charles." He pauses heavily as though having run a race. "So, good. Here we go. As I call your names, please come forward onto the stage, then retire stage left." A raised platform, has been constructed against the back wall, allowing space for tables, but providing an entrance, a contained surface, and an exit for the acts and performers into a back room out of sight with an exit to the outside back lot of the building.

What should have taken less than an hour takes nearly two hours. Many of the participants appear several times during the program, causing confusion. The musicians stand by idly, taking notes on the order of appearance. The band is made up of locals, five musicians. The pianist leads the group, including a strong drummer, a bright clarinetist, a standup bass player, and a traditional accordionist. Not exactly Duke Ellington or Tommy Dorsey.

Finally, the entire program has been outlined, walked-through, amid confusion, disagreements, suggestions, amendments, and backtracking. Georges is exhausted by the end of the rehearsal.

"Of all the shows I have produced, this one appears to win the award for most disorganized and most unprofessional. I have grave doubts about this show. It could be my last show. Each group must remember how their act fits in and work to make this flow smoothly. Believe me. It's a mess. It's a mess. We gather tomorrow at 7:00 pm. There are more cuts coming." And he turns away angrily.

The dancers are part of the problem, since they are interspersed throughout the show in different numbers and with different routines and different participants. There were several surprises that will require preparing new routines. For instance, the magician wants a few dancers behind him and an assistant, as does the family juggling act.

Raymond Duras groups his dancers together and suggests a meeting prior to the general rehearsal to make assignments and adjust routines. Gabrielle feels confident about her role. She will only be in the two large numbers for the opening and closing and one dance number, which includes all the dancers. The more experienced dancers will be taking on the additional roles. They break for the evening.

***

"How much are they paying you?" Catie asks the next day at lunch. The rain has stopped, and they are seated inside a café along the canal.

"A pittance," Gabrielle replies, "And by the hour, it would be even less. We're slaves, and even the top dancers complain it's not a living, and, of course, no one is planning for that anyway, since most just love the opportunity to dance. Jordi and Georges take every advantage of it, and besides…"

"I've never heard of Mireille Printemps," Nuria interrupts. "Sounds like a stage name."

"I have no idea where they dug her up. Some say she had a career in Paris before the Great War, but she hasn't done much since then. She lives in Bordeaux, and only one of the dancers has had any experience with her, and it was not good. You should attend on the weekend."

"We're going to be there every night," Catie says firmly. "We wouldn't miss it."

"Give me a few days," Gabrielle begs. "I don't want you to see me take a fall."

"It wouldn't be the first time," Nuria jokes.

"Thanks."

"You know, Gabrielle, I was contacted by this man," Nuria says. "He wanted me to distribute flyers, they were anti-Pétain. I told him no, but keep wondering about it."

"I'm not like our friend Isabelle," Catie says, "but two things come to mind. The police are active in routing out the Resistance, so it's dangerous. But also, we need time to see what Pétain can do. He keeps saying that he is shielding us from the harsher realities of the occupation. And certainly, from what I hear, it's much more severe in the occupied zone."

Gabrielle adds: "They just arrested a group from the Musée de l'Homme in Paris for distributing a newspaper called "Résistance." I don't think it's wise right now. I agree with Catie. We should stick with the *attentistes* (people waiting to see what happens) for a while longer. I'm as confused as most people, and the war was so bizarre and then the armistice so quickly signed. Vichy's certainly not doing us any favors. It's not a time to make fast decisions."

"I know," says Nuria, "but so much is changing for the worse, and we all feel the belt tightening. We're lucky here, but it's coming. The soldiers have not returned home. People are losing their jobs. Anti-Semitic laws are being passed. And laws against the newspapers, radio, trade unions, and women. We are all expected to be good housewives now. It's crazy. The forced resignation of Pierre Laval last fall was a good thing. But Vichy is not softening the impact of the occupation. If anything, they are aiding the Nazis.

"You make it sound worse than it is," Catie says. "Suppose we had to deal with the Occupant directly?"

"Vichy is leading the charge," Nuria responds. "They're doing things beyond what the Nazis require or even expect. We need a government that puts the brakes on the occupation and works to regain our independence, not one that uses the armistice as an excuse for dictating their own authoritative ideology. But something's got to give. We are sleepwalking toward a treacherous precipice. I'm not getting involved," Nuria adds. "Not yet, anyway."

5

March 1941

> *The wind propelled the fire*
> *Driving it into the stables*
> *And that's how in one moment*
> *We saw your mare perish*
> *But apart from that, Madame La Marquise*
> *All is well, all is well.*
> > « *Tout va très bien, Madame La Marquise,* » *Paul Misraki*

The brothers at La Sainte Trinité school in Béziers raised me, guided me through adolescence, or so they claimed, and patted me on the back upon my graduation and departure. I never had a favorite brother at Trinité. Instead, the lay professors inspired more in learning and growing. I remember two in particular.

In my fifth year, I encountered a math instructor, who was as regulated in his behavior as in his rules of mathematics. Monsieur Boucher, a tall man with enormous hands and a narrow chin he pointed like a baton to designate a student or an equation of note on the chalkboard. Every morning, he entered the classroom exactly on time. The students shuffled to their feet and watched as he ritualistically turned his back on the class and removed his baseball cap, quickly replacing it with his well-worn béret, which he kept on a hook next to the blackboard. He then rotated to face the class and wished the class a good morning, signaling them to be seated.

Each day he followed this procedure exactly like a cuckoo clock puppet at high noon. At the end of class, after dismissing the students, he repeated the movement in reverse. This became an act that fascinated the students, who came up with many different and creative explanations for his behavior. "Perhaps he is ashamed of his bald head." "No, he must have been a mariner in his day with a naked lady tattooed on the crown of his head." "Absurd, all his thoughts are stored in that béret, he is useless without it." The students could not leave the legend of Boucher alone and discussed him endlessly: his chin, his large hands, and, of course, his béret.

The class itself was extremely rigorous, which furthered the legend, with grading based more on the appropriate formulaic appearance of the proof than the correct answer. Many students failed entirely.

I was normally an excellent student, but I too struggled in his class, although not to the point of failing. One day, I thought of a way to understand Boucher's aberrant behavior. I came to class five minutes early. I had obtained some black carpet thread and proceeded to tie the thread to the blackboard and then attach it to the interior band in the rear of his béret, checking to ensure the béret contained nothing inside as imagined by some students. I left a tether of about two meters of thread. I carefully arranged the thread to the hook and replaced the béret so as not to interfere when Boucher replaced his baseball cap. As the students filed into the classroom they watched me without comment.

Boucher arrived exactly on time, The students expectantly rose to attention: no shuffling, complete silence. Boucher turned to the board, removed his cap, and replaced it quickly with his béret. He turned to the class, greeted them, and motioned them to sit, which they did in unison, without a single smirk. Every eye was fixed on the béret. Boucher moved over to his lectern and leaned over to retrieve the dreaded textbook, and what should happen, but the béret was snatched from his head and fell to the floor. At first, he seemed not to notice what had occurred, then in shock, he realized his béret was adrift and his bald pate liberated. He quickly bent to pick it up off the platform, noting the thread, which he removed with some effort. But too late for him. The secret was revealed.

Without a hint of what had befallen him, Boucher immediately administered the punishment. One hundred times, we neatly printed a phrase in our notebooks that evening after *cenam*, as we called supper. I cannot forget it and worked on it for hours:

> For he that will love life, and see good days, let him refrain his tongue from evil, and his lips that they speak no guile: let him eschew evil, and do good; let him seek peace, and ensue it. For the eyes of the Lord are over the righteous, and his ears are open unto their prayers: but the face of the Lord is against them that do evil. 1 Peter 3: 10-12

From that day on, we had created Boucher's epithet, *Bossu*, for he had an unusually large protuberance on the crown of his head, which was as bald as the day of his birth. This rare natural bulge is commonly referred to as the *bosse des mathématiques*: a marvelous attribute phrenologically speaking. In portraits of no less than Descartes, one can easily observe this bump. The culprit of the unprincipled snare was never identified.

However, I felt guilty about it for weeks. One day, Bossu was absent, which was a rare event. After school, I went on my own to his apartment where many of the instructors outside the order of the brothers resided. I knocked at his door. He came to the door without opening it.

"Who's there?" His voice hoarse and wan.

"Paul Broussard."

"Ah, Monsieur Broussard. What brings you here?' The door cracked open slightly, and I glimpsed him, his *bosse* uncovered. Perhaps we had done him a service, allowing him to publicly and honestly confront a deep-seated dread.

"I wanted to apologize, Monsieur," I said nervously.

"Ah, I might have known it," he said without hesitation, nodding his head and directing his chin directly at me. "The worst of the beans, and yet the most kindhearted. Apology accepted. If only you would apply your ample intelligence to mathematics as you do to your shenanigans." The door closed, not meanly, but firmly. He never ever said another word on this.

I survived Professor Boucher's class as the "worst of the beans." Whatever he meant by that I never knew. I graduated near the top of my class. I never saw Boucher again, but I imagine him loving life and seeing only good days.

The other remarkable instructor appeared a year later, in my final year. I had an engaging third-year English class. The class was small, eight students, all of us top students in the school, all of us facing the unknown: a world in turmoil. Our professor was Malcolm McAllister, an Englishman coming down from Cambridge with a degree in English literature. He had decided to spend a few years in France on a whim, or so we imagined. His epithet, Al, reminded us of a famous American gangster, Al Capone, which seemed appropriate given his informal and impulsive ways. I appreciated him, but he was widely misunderstood among the students.

His classes were casual, and he liked nothing better than bringing in current events for freeform discussion. We hated it, because it resulted in peripatetic verbal excursions demonstrating our ignorance of the language. It also resulted in additional vocabulary words to memorize. As a consequence, the students assessed that he didn't measure up: erratic, disorganized, too loose in his approach, not predictable, and, the worst of all epithets, Anglophilic, which was not surprising, given his nationality, but a blasphemy at that time.

Among his wide interests was horse racing. He always carried the latest track results and racing forms. One day, he attempted to translate his avocation into classroom instruction.

"Gentlemen, let me run down the third-year English handicap at Sainte Trinité. We must whittle down the field to the top three students. Here are my picks." His French was far from perfect, and we always had difficulty following his rapid and vernacular English, but suddenly we followed him with attention and trepidation.

"At 3/1 odds, we have Feinberg: always classy, sometimes a little lazy at the starting gate, but always a dependable finisher." Feinberg, not well liked, was generally considered by all to be one of the top students in the school. He did not go on to university, becoming a goose farmer in the Gers department. A few years later he emigrated to England.

"Next we have Oliver." Oliver was an abnormally stunted boy, who had been sick as a child and never achieved a normal height, but was nevertheless bright and popular and favored by the brothers. Biquet, we called him, "kid goat," for his effective pestering of the brothers and his size.

"Oliver is at 9/2 odds: not that fast in the sprints and a poor mudder, but eager and always a placer, and a pleaser." Everyone laughed, since Biquet was both an easy tease and sensitive. He silently fumed. Whenever we found a soft spot, we manipulated it to our best advantage. Since we all suffered, we all dished it out.

"Ranking a close third, we have Broussard at 5/1 odds: a strong player, somewhat inconsistent, yet an excellent bet playing the conservative long shot.

At this, Biquet guffawed and contradicted the professor. "Broussard most often comes up lame." Biquet thought to capture the spirit of the exercise, but in fact his statement came across as weak and offensive and more revealing of Biquet than of me. Jealousy is the basest of human emotions.

I had known Biquet my entire time at Sainte Trinité; both of us were boarders and on partial scholarships. I always treated him with respect, but obviously he had a low opinion of my intellectual powers and envy of my physical attributes, never before expressed to me. Under the circumstances, he felt he could get away with his comment. I took his remark to heart and thereafter steered clear of Biquet like a bugbear. This was one of the dangers of ranking students, which was a common practice of all the teachers at Trinité, including the brothers.

Once a week, Al brought in an English poem, masking the title and author, making us translate it, analyze it, review the author's intentions, and comment on how it achieved his goals, all without knowing who the poet was. He kept us off balance. Some poets were well known, others were from newspapers or magazines. Then we had to grade the poem on a scale of one to five, with one being a world class work, five being mere dross.

A few weeks after the handicapping, he produced a poem that by chance allowed him to once again link his beloved horses to the classroom.

"Today, we have a short poem from the States," Al began, reading the poem aloud. From our familiarity with his English usage, we guessed he meant the United States. We worked at translating the poem, which he had Biquet copy on the blackboard as he accepted our suggestions. We discussed our translations, definitions, and specific words. This poem was particularly difficult to understand, written in an informal voice based on a bizarre, comic-strip hero named Captain Carpenter, with a mixture of modern, movie-star Western, and archaic language. Once we completed the translation, and its transcription remained on the board in its entirety, we ranked the poem on a scrap of paper with our names on it.

"Oliver, please collect the tickets."

He collected the ratings and handed them to Al, who stood at the lectern before us, the weekly racing form in his back pocket, taking his time, reviewing each ranking.

"Well, we seem to have a horse race here." He looked around, pleased with himself. "There's only one winner. I have seven rankings of five and one ranking of one. Seems clear."

We held our breaths, knowing our own ranking, but wondering about the others and who would be judged correct. I held my breath, wondering if I had failed.

"The long shot has paid off." And he looked at us with an intriguing smile. "High returns on my bet."

I knew exactly what he meant, but the other students had no idea.

He attacked. "Oliver, you rated this a one. Why was that?"

"Sir, I felt it silly and without meaning," he mumbled still standing at the chalkboard.

"Hmm, I see. Silly and meaningless. And if I told you this was a great American poet? Would that help?"

All the students groaned.

"Oliver, I'm waiting."

Oliver shrugged his shoulders, seeing silence as his only alternative to total disgrace.

"The title of the poem, as you might have perceived, had you read it, is Captain Carpenter, the name of the hero, and the poet is John Crowe Ransom. Does that help?"

Everyone shriveled into his exoskeleton, given Al's reaction. Complete silence; no volunteers.

"And the name of the poet helps no one?" He paused for effect. "Okay, last chance. Who is this Captain Carpenter?"

A pin could be heard falling onto the dirty wooden floor. Slowly, I raised my hand.

"Broussard, you have some idea?"

"Yes, sir."

"Enlighten us with your erudition." We barely understood his English.

"Captain Carpenter is a Jesus Christ like figure," I said, not at all certain, but I knew that I had to defend my ranking of number 1, not quite sure why the poem spoke to me.

"Jesus? What a noble idea. How is that Broussard?"

"The bible does not tell us, but Jesus' step-father was a carpenter, or perhaps a builder...an architect. And at that time, the son had to learn his father's trade. If you know who the hero is, you begin to understand the poem, since he suffered his entire life for all of us, but never stopped his efforts."

"Thank you, Broussard. Nicely observed. Anyone else?"

No one knew exactly what was happening, and all were hesitant to dig their graves any deeper, since they had begun to see the handwriting literally on the wall.

"Gentlemen, there is a winner here. Broussard, congratulations. Everyone else had better review in some detail the characteristics and literary devices we have discussed that help identify a world-class poem. I would like to see a written response tomorrow...in English. You are dismissed.

Al kept me after class.

"Good work Broussard. If I can ever be of help, I would be pleased."

"Thank you, sir."

And he did help me when I applied at the Prefecture with a generous letter of support. I'll always remember the last line of that poem:

> The curse of hell upon the sleek upstart
> That got the Captain finally on his back
> And took the red red vitals of his heart
> And made the kites to whet their beaks
> clack clack.

***

"Paul, wake up. Paul."

Paul's roommate, Robert, leaned into the neatly arranged bedroom, where Paul lay fully clothed and exhausted after working all day following a late night spent preparing for the show at the club. The last week had been like that. It was early evening, and Robert knew that Paul was expected at the rehearsal.

"Paul," he called more gently.

The head moved slightly and an elbow pushed the body up to observe the curtained window and last gasps of daylight. "What time?"

"Almost 7:00 pm. You're late. Are you too tired to attend tonight?"

"I can't. I've got to." He muttered to himself, sitting up and turned slowly to look at Robert, who was vaguely smiling at him. "I can't stand your pleasant nature. Leave me be."

"Are you going or not?"

"I am. Now get out."

Paul arrived late for the rehearsal and received a sour look from Georges. Full rehearsals had been going on for four days, and the show was just starting to become more unified. All of the juggling and acrobatic acts had been dismissed. A comedian had been told to tone down his jokes and shorten his act; they didn't want trouble from the police. The bicycle act remained, one of the favorites.

Paul had been standing in for Mireille Printemps, singing in her place at rehearsals until she arrived on Saturday. Most of the songs had been written and performed by Charles Trenet, or the popular duo he sang with, Johnny and Charles (after Johnny Hess, a successful song writer himself and less successful solo singer). Paul knew all the songs, having sung many of them for years, some with Charles. It was important to have the musicians practice with a singer, rehearsing the seven songs allotted to Mlle. Printemps, all recently popular. The musicians and Paul over the last four days had jazzed up the renditions, since dancing would be encouraged. A small, wooden dance floor had been jerry-rigged in front of the stage. Mlle. Printemps' set was midstream, interspersed with the other acts. She returned near the end with a closing love song, which liaised into the finale, combining dancing, singing, and curtain calls (without an actual curtain) for the entire cast.

Luckily, Paul arrived just before Printemps' set and did not delay the rehearsal: as though they would have waited for him in any case. At first, he had been reluctant to stand in for the solo singer, but once he began working with the musicians, he had forgotten any reservations or nervousness. Most of the cast ignored the rehearsal singing, concentrating on their own acts, and the musicians liked to ham it up. Paul followed their lead. Every night he and the band improved until people began to take notice.

Although tired this evening, Paul found himself singing with abandon and infusing the songs with his own emotions. At the end of the set, surprisingly, the cast applauded vigorously. Georges interrupted the rehearsal afterward to announce with Paul standing next to him: "Maybe we should send Printemps a telegram to stay the devil in Bordeaux. We've got our lead singer." The cast reacted spontaneously with great enthusiasm, clapping and whistling, and the rehearsal continued.

The closing number was a Lucienne Boyer song written by Jean Lenoir: *"Parlez-moi d'amour,"* popular in the early 1930's, one that Paul knew well and loved. With the two backup singers behind him, he delivered it with passion, infused with unfeigned honesty. Everyone was moved. The ending of the ballad immediately liaised into the finale, *"Je suis swing,"* written and sung by Johnny Hess, but an up-tempo version made popular by Trenet. All the dancers backed the solo singer on stage, with Paul closing the night. As the song continued, the entire cast appeared on stage and slowly retreated to imagined thundering applause. A spotlight slowly focused on the singers as the night ended, no encores anticipated.

"Lights...curtain," Georges shouted, announcing the end of rehearsal. Spotlights were extinguished, darkening the entire stage area. The band shifted into a slower version to close the evening, but as Jordi had made clear on numerous occasions: "This is a cabaret, not *l'Alhambra* music hall in Paris, not some high-flung concert in the Opera House, not where people get up and file out of the auditorium." The lights in the hall remained illuminated.

"Good work," Georges said to Paul, as the cast slowly departed. They sat at the bar with two Naranjiñas, a nonalcoholic drink imported from Spain, and a few charcuterie meats, thanks to Jordi's wife, Josette. Georges was a recovering alcoholic and hadn't had a drink for five years or so, with a few exceptions, and Paul was exhausted.

"I'm destroying myself," Paul complained. "Too much going on at work and outside, not counting the time I put into this show."

"Take it easy tomorrow. We're almost there. The dress rehearsal should be easy. The costumes have been fitted. Have you heard from Charles?"

"No. I never expected to. When he comes into town, he just shows up. He won't let us down. What about Mlle. Printemps?"

"I have hotel reservations. She should arrive in the afternoon and be available for the dress rehearsal on Sunday.

"What do you think?"

"About what?" Georges asked skeptically.

"About the show."

"Oh. It's okay for an off-circuit venue. It will improve once we have a star. Trenet will do the trick. We are sold out every show with him. Printemps is another matter. I don't expect much. You are more than good enough to carry her role."

"I'll keep my amateur ranking. Stick to backing up." Paul thought of Georges in some ways as a father figure and discounted his compliments.

"You've been crucial to this show. Believe me. Jordi says so, and he rarely compliments anyone. He can barely think beyond his stomach and pocketbook. Even Josette says so. Can't say that any more money will come of it. Printemps and Charles are costing Jordi a mint. For my own part, I am eternally grateful. We'll see what we can do when this is all over."

"I'm going to bed. At least I can sleep in tomorrow. Bonsoir, Georges."

"Goodnight."

***

I knew that I was doing too much. Work at the Prefecture demanded as much as ever, physically and emotionally. People were desperate to leave France, both émigrés and citizens. To obtain a French exit visa required French papers or temporary admittance authorization or citizenship in specific eastern European countries. The rules were constantly in a state of flux, between Vichy and the different Prefectures. Timing and luck played a huge role. The exit visa required a chain of official documents: a travel visa from another country, often Spain, and an entry visa to a third country.

Proof was required of transportation arrangements. The documents were all timed with end dates, so this paper chain had to be executed perfectly among all the countries involved. If one of the interdependent links collapsed, repair was nearly impossible.

As a result of this desperation to find asylum, a great deal of money was involved. Political appointees, wealthy individuals, foreign agencies, interested governments, international rescue organizations, religious foundations, and others contributed financially to the effort. On the receiving end were institutions of good will, including government agencies, transportation companies, the Resistance, and many organizations supporting the departures. A large black market emerged for false papers of all kinds, driven by the demand of desperate people and by the large amounts of money involved, but also attracting fakes, frauds, and outright criminals. With so much money and so much desperation, things often went wrong.

Of course there was also the other side: police, Gestapo, *collabos*, and others attempting to prevent people from leaving, always threatening to denounce them to the authorities. These threats could land you in local internment camps and transit camps, leading to those in Germany, Poland, and other occupied countries in eastern Europe.

At the Prefecture we all played along with the game as best we could. The Prefectures, which at least at the beginning of the war reflected the society, were changing. As Vichy instituted their laws and as the Occupant exercised his authority, the Prefectures began to fall in line with the authoritarianism, helping to identify émigrés and resistants and working with the police to arrest them.

I learned the name of the girl I dreamed about on the first night of planning the show and had only glimpsed after that. Nothing more frustrating on waking from a dream than realizing it was never real, and there's no road back. Her name was Gaby Daniel, and she was twenty years old. I knew where she worked, and I knew her father, the artist, by reputation. When I caught glimpses of her at the rehearsals, I knew that my dream had indeed been real. Too young to be married, she might possibly be seeing someone. I only knew that I had to meet her. Our schedules never

68

coincided enough to talk. I didn't want to ask too much about her as I knew it would get straight back to her. I guess I was also willing to find an excuse for failure.

Only Robert knew of my infatuation. At this point, call it what you will: a glimmer of light or maybe the foolish imaginings of a bleeding heart.

"Does she know who you are?" Robert asked.

"She knows who I am. *Bah*, as she knows Jordi or Georges. Enough to recognize me. I'm quite visible among the cast. All the staff and cast know me. Why shouldn't she?"

"Only a question, Paul."

"Suppose she's engaged."

"You're getting ahead of yourself."

"But a woman as beautiful as she must have plenty of opportunities."

"True, but sometimes beautiful women are the loneliest due to this very thinking. Rarely, mind you. You could walk up to her and introduce yourself," he said with an ironic smile.

"She's constantly off somewhere, leaves early, practicing, surrounded by dancers. I don't know. Maybe she's avoiding me. I must put her off by staring at her like some smitten adolescent. I should know better."

"Next time you see her, introduce yourself. Make a point of it. Force yourself, man."

"You're right, but…"

"Just do it."

"*Bon*. Okay. Okay.

***

The dress rehearsal went very well. After a week of working together, everyone knew their jobs. Everyone knew the order. Everyone contributed. The producer tightened the action. The stage and lighting hands moved quickly to improve the transitions. The players honed their performances, and the orchestra began to get "hot" like Tommy Dorsey or Artie Shaw. The set was a painted backdrop of a Parisian street scene with painted curtains hung on either side, and three real *réverbères* (street lamps) marking the front of the stage. The spotlighting functioned as curtains. Without the spots, the stage was barely lit. The costumes reinforced the excitement of the show, and the music made everyone want to get up and dance.

Georges said that Mireille Printemps had arrived at her hotel and would not be part of the dress rehearsal. She would make her appearance tomorrow evening at the opening. Georges was fuming at her lack of professionalism, treating this show as if it had no importance, but he sent flowers to her room anyway and promised that all would be ready for her. As a result, Paul had to stand in for her with the two other backup singers behind him. By this time, both the band and Paul were accustomed to each other and let go with jazzy renditions of Charles Trenet's well known songs, including *"Je chante"* and ending with the moving solo version of *"Parlez-moi d'amour,"* leading into *"Je suis swing,"* with the entire cast on stage for the finale. After this last song, the entire hall was filled by the sound of the cast shouting and applauding for each other and themselves.

Paul floated off the stage in a state of euphoria, a feeling he had never before experienced. He felt as though he had won an Olympic race, as though he could do anything, as though his father were patting him on the back and his mother and sister hugging and kissing him. He stepped down from the stage, which was only a few centimeters above the bar floor, and everyone was congratulating him, offering him drinks. He was startled and attempted to respond politely.

Even Jordi Pons offered him a free drink, anything he wanted on the house. He looked around the hall, but could only manage to keep walking, advancing toward the bar where he might find Georges. As he reached the bar, she came up to him with a smile. She stood behind him, waiting. There she was, smiling openly: still in her rather skimpy silver satin-like short dress with belled short sleeves and white cummerbund, her face heavily made up. He managed to turn to face her.

"You were great," she said enthusiastically.

"I was," he stopped. Was it a question or a statement?

"Yes. Really," she added needlessly, perhaps to reduce the tension.

He looked into her hazel eyes and her face: bright lipstick, dark eye shadow, and cheeks heavily rouged, her hair in a bun with a small feather headdress. A hint of a perceptive smile remained, and her intelligent eyes darkly focused on him.

"I'm ah...I'd..." By this point, Robert would have kicked him in the pants. "I've been meaning..." but that was not the right direction. He decided to return to basics.

"I'm Paul."

"I'm Gabrielle."

"I know. I know your dad. At least, I know of him. You, and the other dancers, have done a great job." He stared at her. She did not seem to be attempting to escape.

Then twenty-three years of training took over. "A drink?" He caught his breath and held it.

"Oh, no thanks. I have to get back." It was about 10:00 pm and tomorrow was Saturday; there was plenty of time. "Some water?"

Before she could reply, Georges came up to them. "Great job, Paul."

"Thanks. You know Mlle. Daniel."

"Of course."

"You have come quite a ways, Mlle. Daniel. Congratulations. Good job this evening."

"Thank you, Monsieur Doelnitz. You've done a remarkable job yourself. It's finally working."

"I had my doubts," Georges said smiling and slapped Paul on the back, a little more forcefully than necessary. "And this fellow was one of the reasons. We have to pray that Mlle. Printemps does as well."

"I have to head back," Gabrielle said.

"No!" Paul said, way too quickly, a little too harshly. His tempo was totally off. "Please, have a drink with us."

"Thanks. Another time."

"Are you walking?"

"Just a few blocks. It's not far."

"I'll walk with you," Paul said.

"Oh, that's not necessary."

"No. My pleasure." The first bit of sense arrived like a gift from God.

"Okay. Let me change. I'll be back in a jiffy."

"Paul, you okay?" Georges laughed. "Never seen you in such a state. It's the girl."

"I'm a moron."

"True."

"Something about her, Georges. I can't seem to function. I've seen her for the last month and never said a word. This is the first time."

"Well, imagine she's just a normal girl."

"I know. I know. You're right. Exactly. *Bon*. Yes. Yes I will."

***

When they left the bar, it was unusually frigid, but both were dressed warmly. The bracing cold stunned Paul, pulling a watch cap out of his coat pocket and putting on his gloves. The gibbous moon in a clear sky bestowed a yellow glow to the quiet streets.

"I live with my parents on rue Maurell," she said.

"That's not out of my way. I'm on rue de la Gare."

"Not too far out of your way. I appreciate the company. Are you a professional singer?"

"No. Not at all." He swallowed to obtain a breath. "I've always loved singing. School choirs, bathrooms, lullabies for children. I've done my share, but I work at the Prefecture. In the visa section."

"The visa section. That must be busy."

"Right. Too busy and too visible. I have to respond to the needs of distressed people in a set manner. Sort of stressful, depending on your politics."

"And yours?" She looked directly at him, her eyes reflecting the moonlight. He noted a slight nervousness on her part, which gave him a bit of confidence. She seemed willing to listen.

"I'm sympathetic. Probably too sympathetic. Unfortunate in my position. Too much unfairness. I do what I can."

"That's funny. Fairness. We were talking just the other day about fairness where I work, Les Nouvelles Galeries, in the cosmetics section. Many of the girls are older with fixed ideas, and we get into crazy conversations and disagreements. As if anyone would listen to salesgirls,

72

some with husbands in Germany. I'm the youngest. Now where was I going with that?"

"Fairness."

Oh yes." She nodded her head, tucking her hair back under her hood. "Fairness. One of the girls was arrested and lost her job, because she got caught putting up some posters. They said she was lucky. She lost her job and had to leave Perpignan. Talk about fairness."

"I know."

"The only pressure at Nouvelles Galeries is an occasional arrogant and presumptuous client. That's as bad as it gets. 'Hate that perfume.' 'I want something more appealing.' 'That's atrocious.' It's just something you put up with."

"Lot's of changes there?"

"Oh, not much. In Paris a new group took over, and of course some people lost their jobs due to the restrictions on foreigners.

"They weren't foreigners."

"I know.

They walked silently for a moment.

"How did you avoid the army?"

"Timing. I was in school and too young, and then at the Prefecture, and then the war ended."

"I dropped out of school. It really hurt my parents. Nothing to look forward to. How long can this go on?"

"It seems interminable. But you're dancing."

"Oh, that's just a lark. My girlfriends tricked me, and there's no future there. I took lessons in middle school, but that's all."

"But you're good."

"Not as good as some of the others."

They talked easily, without awkward silences, continuing the entire way. They came to rue Maurell and approached the house.

"I'd like to see you again." Paul said honestly.

"I'm sure you will." She glanced shyly at him, her head barely above his chin.

"Outside of this business, I meant."

"We'll talk next week."

"Okay."

"Goodnight and thanks for walking me home."

"Goodnight Gaby."

"Oh, please, Gabrielle."

"Gabrielle."

"See you soon." She ran to the door and disappeared within.

Mme Printemps didn't approve of the set of Trenet songs and wanted to do her own. Georges learned this Saturday afternoon. It would require the band and the three backup singers to learn six or seven new songs before Monday evening. Of course, this also changed the whole theme of "The Swing." Charles Trenet had taken the American sound, the jazz bands and big bands and the singers – Frank Sinatra, Lena Horne, Doris Day, Ella Fitzgerald, Billie Holiday – and had become the Swing master here in France. Mireille Printemps had a few hits in the 1920s, mostly ballads and love songs, down-tempo. Her demand also impacted the dancers, but they could adjust.

Rehearsal on Monday during the day was impossible. Most everyone had a day job. So on Sunday late afternoon, Georges, Mlle. Printemps, the three backup singers, and the band met for the first time. A few people sat drinking at tables, but the bar/café was mostly empty.

"I want the songs I sing," Mlle. Printemps said. "I'm not Charles Trenet. I know who I am."

"You should have mentioned that when we discussed the show," Georges said annoyed, "and your contract. How do you propose to fit your songs into the show?"

"I'm well known and will fill this miserable hall with people interested in hearing my songs. My songs are played on the radio all over. People know me. Who is Trenet anyway? A crazy kid. I've heard enough about him to be disgusted. He's a flash in the pan."

The band sat ready to play, smiling among themselves, enjoying every word, while Paul and the two other backup singers stood to the side, watching.

"Nevertheless," Georges replied, ignoring her statement, "he has made Swing the current fashion. You haven't been to Paris recently, have you? It's everywhere, and it takes peoples' minds off the occupation."

"They need to support the Maréchal. That's all. All these foreigners taking our jobs. Thank God the Jews are out of the business now."

Georges suddenly outraged, looked at her angrily. He knew she needed the pay. Her songs were not currently played. She lived in an apartment in Bordeaux, the most conservative city in France. She was full of hatred for others, thinking she was special, happy that the Occupant had finally ended the Third Republic, hoping it marked a new beginning for her career. The times had passed her by, and her limited talent was not enough to extend her career in a new direction. She was not Mistinguett or Fréhel or Piaf. Georges felt at fault, since he had suggested her to Jordi. But her views turned his stomach.

"That's something we can discuss another time, Mlle. Printemps. You committed to the Swing, and that is what you will do. You can walk away if you choose, but you will sing Trenet. It's what the people want, and, by the way, it's what you contracted to do. You have had the songs for a month, and you refused rehearsals. If you feel you cannot to do them, let's call it a day." He stared at her with true malevolence.

"I don't like the songs."

"You know, and I don't give a damn. We have a good stand-in. You were hired to sing seven songs. We've all worked hard. Do you understand? Your contract was to sing those songs. If not, I'm afraid the contract is voided."

She looked lost for a moment, forgetting her *prima donna* persona, and then drew herself together. "I know the songs, I just don't like the arrangements."

"I do many things I dislike," Georges added. "You have not heard the arrangements. Let's take it from the top. And Mlle. Printemps, let me make this clear, you can consider this an audition. If I'm not satisfied with your performances, you will be asked to leave without any compensation, only a ticket back to Bordeaux."

"Humph."

They spent three hours working on the songs. Mlle. Printemps continued to find everything about them objectionable. The band slowed the tempo, and the jazzy renditions they had worked out were ignored. The backup singers tried to help out, but it was obvious that she had no desire for backup. She had always been a solo singer, mostly in small cabarets and more intimate clubs. She had never appeared in a musical or variety show in a large venue. Several of her songs had been played on the radio after the Great War, but she currently was ignored by Radio Paris, under the control of the Occupant, and by Radio Vichy.

In the final rehearsal, she did a passable job, failing to impart the joy and spirit of the Trenet songs, but a banner with her name had been pasted over the posters throughout Perpignan, along with the actual dates for Charles Trenet.

"She does have a reputation. And we are not in Paris." That's all Georges could say. "It is not even Nice. We can only hope for the best." In the end, Georges accepted the reality of the situation as he always did in his quiet way. He would give Mlle. Printemps a try, not contesting what seemed beyond his control. He had learned this through experience.

6

March 1941

A little rhythm reveals itself
It's the rhythm that makes me that way
Wrapping me up
I am Swing, I am Swing
Zazou, zazou, zazou
It drives me crazy.
« *Je suis swing,* » *Johnny Hess*

On Monday night, the large hall is barely half full. People are here out of curiosity or just happening in for a nightcap. Some have heard of Mireille Printemps. Others have seen the flyers and are hungry for any entertainment. For a few hours, people want to take their minds off the stark reality of a war that has been lost, of being held hostage to the Occupant and Vichy, of paying reparations, supplying food, material, and labor to the war effort, requiring the rationing of their own supplies. A million and a half young soldiers are imprisoned, and there is the constant reminder that foreigners and French alike are frantic to flee the country. For the price of a drink, you can evade the bitter chill and perhaps enjoy a few laughs. Popular music is entertaining all over France and helping the people endure.

Gabrielle views the small crowd cheering and shouting with delight with each act. The dancers are showered with applause. The magician wows the audience and retires to cheers and demands for more, and the timing and skills of the bicycle act amaze everyone, as it always does. The comedian, keeping his act mostly apolitical, draws great guffaws and applause talking about his trials with his wife, their vacation in the Pyrenees, and their farmer neighbor, surprising even himself. The dancers return, again pleasing the audience. All the while, the band keeps the momentum with popular tunes and a strong beat. Several couples take to the dance floor with the Swing backup tunes.

When Mireille Printemps comes out for her set, the lights are lowered, and the band makes its way through relatively slow and doleful renditions of well known Charles Trenet tunes. The set ends with *"Y'a d'la joie"* at half-tempo, lacking any aspect of this wild ode to joy. The three backup singers are side stage, barely audible, invisible, out of the single spot. The audience hardly knows what to do with this performance. No one dances. Polite applause. No catcalling or requests for an encore. Mostly sitting on their hands. After Mireille Printemps exits the stage, the lights on stage come up, and the band reprises a riotous and joyful instrumental of *"Y'a d'la joie,"* which brings the crowd to their feet, shouting, dancing, applauding. This is what they came for.

Paul stands offstage with Georges watching the crowd go crazy.

"I don't understand what she was thinking," Georges says. "This is not a small bistro in Paris with a single spot, glasses of Absinthe, and everyone crying in their cups. I am going to talk to the old lady."

Georges knocks on the door of the only small, private dressing room, probably a tack room at one time, separate from the communal area, and enters. Mireille Printemps is sitting alone on a couch, looking like she has been through the wars, appearing tired and old underneath her bold makeup. When she sees him enter, she straightens up, barely able to hide her exhaustion.

"The band. Rank amateurs." she says instantly. "They ruined me. I should have known better. This isn't France. We might as well be in Spain. And the audience, peasants. They have no appreciation. They don't even speak French. They are only looking to have fun."

"Of course they are," Georges agrees contrarily. "That's exactly why the few that came are here. To have fun."

"And the backup singers…horrible. They need to sing up. I couldn't hear them. What's the use?"

"What about your closing song?" Georges asks.

"What about it?" she ask heatedly.

"It's a love song. You should be able to give it some emotion. No? Then you're off. The backup singers will take over for the finale number: *'Je suis swing.'* If it's not crazy, up tempo, and wild, it could kill the whole thing…the whole week…that's Charles, you know, *Le Fou Chantant* (the singing fool)."

"Humph."

He returns to Paul backstage, scarlet with anger. "You're singing '*Je suis swing*,'" Georges orders Paul. "She's off after her last song. Get that message to the band. Let's see if we can recapture the audience. Word of mouth could destroy us."

The comedian that follows Mireille Printemps finds an audience that is sluggish and uncommunicative like an angry teenager. He struggles through a silent set, not understanding what's going on, expecting the reception of his predecessor. The dancers follow with the entire troupe on the stage, doing their final solo performance. Gabrielle feels the tension among the dancers, affecting their performance and spirit. She attempts to kick higher, to move joyously, to help her sisters, but to no avail. They too receive lukewarm applause. Most people have returned to their drinks and are ignoring much of the proceedings.

She watches from the rear as Mireille Printemps returns for her final song and closing number. The backup singers are placed closer to her, and this time they can be heard. She does an admirable performance of *"Parlez-moi d'amour*," which is much more to her style and gets polite applause.

At the very instant following her bow, as she exits from the stage, the band loudly breaks out into one of the craziest Swing songs of all time: *"Je suis swing,"* playing it as it was written and sung by Trenet and Hess. Paul steps up to the microphone and allows the band to return to the top and then sings the introductory chorus. Then, together, they burn the house down. The crowd rises to their feet. People begin dancing. People join in singing. Gabrielle can feel the change and joins the dancers as they run onto the stage in their final appearance. All the players file onto the stage and join in the melee. Everyone feels the beat of the Swing "that grabs you and never lets you go."

Amazingly, once completed, the band starts all over again, and Paul repeats the song. The audience remain on their feet, refusing to let the song and the feeling go. After the third reprise, the band slows and begins to allow the performers to back off stage. The audience, realizing the end is coming, cheer as the performers depart the stage: the comedians, the magician, the bicyclers, the dancers. Gabrielle is so amazed by Paul's performance and so happy for him. She hugs him spontaneously as he comes offstage with the backup singers, surprising him as others congratulate him. She can see he's flying high like a kite in warm autumn winds.

Finally, the band is alone, and they reprise "*Je suis swing*" to a rollicking instrumental close. It's a great triumph, and, at the end, the audience mostly returns to their tables and continues drinking, and that's the triumph Jordi Pons is looking for.

***

She stands among the dancers backstage, animatedly talking about the evening and their performance, all of them exhilarated, all of them feeling disappointed by Printemps' songs, but happy at their performance on this first night. Having changed to street clothes, she is about to leave by the rear exit. She feels good about the evening and happy for Paul. She has done her part, regardless of Mireille Printemps, regardless of the audience, and Paul turned the evening around. In the end, the final song captured the audience, and that's what's so important.

Paul hurries over to her and receives a bisou. "You saved the show, you know," she tells him.

He waves her comment off and asks, "Can I walk you home?"

She looks up at him surprised, feeling his energy, but doesn't want to be too forward. "You don't need to. I'm fine."

"I would like to," Paul states clearly. After his closing song, he is ecstatic, but he applies the brakes, forcing himself to act calmly and quiet the emotions roiling in his chest, as though his stomach is not knotted, his heart accelerated, and his mind in solid turbulence, as though she is not beautiful, engaging, and all that he desires. He fears alarming her, like a fawn in the forest, with his passionate pursuit; a fawn on the verge of running away and disappearing into the woods.

"That would be nice," she admits comfortably. She too is applying the brakes on her emotions. "Aren't you going to change?"

"Oh, yes. Five minutes. I'll meet you at the bar."

He hurriedly backs away to change into his street trousers, shirt, and jacket. He glances at his image in the makeup mirror, not hating what he sees exactly, but certainly not agreeing to his own attractiveness. He adjusts his long hair, salutes himself sarcastically, then makes a sour face, and leaves rapidly. He's been told he's handsome, but he's never depended on his looks. Always the scholar, light-boned, tall, never particularly athletic, never a girl magnet. Good-looking, but without fanfare. Not a momma's boy, a distracted grandmother's boy perhaps, now perhaps too overly-serious and too consumed by the hazards of his life.

He sees Georges and Jordi talking at the bar with Gabrielle alongside. He joins them. She turns to welcome him with a calmer bisou. The bar is still busy, but Jordi is displeased with sales on the first night. At that moment, Gabrielle sees Isabelle Lefèvre and a friend approaching.

"Well, you two make quite a couple," Isabelle says, viewing Gabrielle and Paul. "This is my friend Françoise." They greet one another with bisous.

"This is the proprietor, Jordi Pons," Gabrielle says without warmth, "and the manager of the show, Georges Doelnitz. I hope you enjoyed the show."

"I'm a real fan of Mireille Printemps," Isabelle responds. "She's a real talent. Too bad the audience was so vulgar and unappreciative."

Paul doesn't know Isabelle, but sees her straightaway: well-dressed, a toasty blond, sure of herself with her own agenda, and no friend of Gabrielle.

"She was not in step with the theme of the show," Gabrielle replies. "The crowd was looking for fun tonight, not a melancholy recital of the current state of affairs. Even you could see the difference when the band took over, and Paul saved the show."

"You're Paul. I'm afraid I don't know Paul."

"Oh, I'm sorry, I thought you had met," she said with conviction. "Paul Broussard."

"Nice to meet you." Paul says offering his hand.

"I enjoyed your rendition, but Mireille has something special."

"Well, maybe we will see you again when Charles arrives," Georges intercedes. "Mlle. Printemps will be here a couple of days more. I have to be off. Nice meeting you. Could we talk a moment, Paul?" He ceremoniously shakes hands with the two girls, excusing himself.

"What was your name?" Isabelle interrupts impertinently.

"Georges."

"No. Your family name."

"Doelnitz."

"Not from around here, or France, for that matter."

"No. Spanish royalty." Georges says irritably. "Who are you?"

"Just a loyal citizen. Bye."

They watch as the two girls leave arm in arm, whispering animatedly. Gabrielle has suffered her theatrics for years, tired of her meddling and her churlish behavior.

"That's what we are up against," Georges comments dismissively. "Though right now we have more pressing issues."

"You're right," Jordi says to Georges. "We need to do something about Printemps, regardless of the young woman's comments. That was a good ending, Paul. We almost lost the crowd. And let me tell you, without word of mouth we're lost. No problem this weekend, but not for the next three days. We need to talk to Printemps. She's set on a disaster course: ours."

"She's convinced she's too good for this venue," Georges replies. "And she disdains the audience. I think we give her one more night, and if she cannot generate some excitement, then adieu. I don't think she can change. Paul will fill in until Charles arrives on Friday night. What do you think?" He turns toward Paul.

"He can do it," Jordi says.

Gabrielle agrees, nodding her head.

"That's not a problem," Paul replies carefully. "The audience may be looking for something different."

"The audience?" Gabrielle says, "loved you. Anyone could see that."

"He's capable," Georges agrees, "more than he's willing to admit."

"If Paul's going to take over for a couple of days," Jordi says, "let's add a second banner to the announcements, reminding people that a local boy is filling in a few nights before Charles arrives. Can't hurt. Should generate some business."

"That's settled." Georges claps Paul on the back. "You kids get going. Work day tomorrow and another show."

***

"Isabelle is something," Gabrielle says as they exit the bar into the cool darkness. A light mist fogs the street lamps.

"Your friend?"

"I've know her since school. Never a real friend."

"Can you trust her?"

"No. Worse than that. She's dangerous. Always was."

"Why?"

"She's aggressive, always wants to be in charge. At school, she was popular and forever stirring the pot, upsetting people, making accusations, or starting rumors, never with any consideration of the impact of her words. You should hear my closest friend, Nuria, on her. And now she seems supportive of Pétain."

They walk in silence for a moment.

"I really meant what I said," she repeats.

"What was that?"

"You saved the show."

"Thanks. Religious choirs at school don't really prepare you."

"I'm no dancer, and there's no future in it, but I enjoy it. Isabelle reminds me how much is uncertain. How can you look to the future, when so much is in doubt in the present? Mlle. Printemps is not going to change. Just like Isabelle, she's convinced she's right. The world is moving back to where she was in the 20s, and she feels vindicated, hoping the past will be our future. That's scary." She shakes her head in doubt.

"What are your friends doing?"

"Not much. People are more worried about where their next meal is coming from than the future. We're all waiting to see what will happen. It can't continue as it is."

"My roommate believes we can change things. He has always been independent and outspoken, but today you don't want to be identified supporting one group. People get revenge in strange ways."

"My father could lose his job, and no one is buying art."

"Why would he lose his job?"

"He works for the commune. What happens when the administration changes? That could change in an instant."

"You're right." Paul has thought just how lucky he is. "If my boss left, I wouldn't last a day. And what then? It's all too depressing."

"My parents have been talking of leaving the region. I guess the one positive is this strange show, and you have a real chance of doing something good."

"You'll see something when Charles arrives."

"You know him?"

"I worked for his father, a notaire, and met Charles several times. He's slightly crazy in a good way. He lives his songs. And he's more poet than songwriter, but he's open and loves people, loves everyone. He lives like he wants to and always has, even as a young man, creating some local scandals. I couldn't live that way, but I really admire him."

When they arrive at her house, the entire street is dark and quiet.

"Thanks, Paul," she says quickly with a smile. "I was very proud of you tonight." She says without thinking. She doesn't know him well enough to say it, but he seems to like her statement. She gives him another bisou on her tiptoes. "Goodnight," and hurries to the door.

***

At lunch with her pals, the day breaks friendly and clear with a transparent blue sky. They are comfortably seated in their normal location outside the Palmarium. Gabrielle goes into great detail on the ups and downs of the prior evening and her meeting with Isabelle Lefèvre.

"I guess we really missed something last night, but we'll be there tonight, for sure." Catie replies.

"Is this Paul real?" Nuria asks seriously.

"He's hard to fathom. He's calm and reserved, but saved the show with his finale performance. Everyone agreed. Something is hidden there like a vein of ore. He seems inexperienced with women. Totally self-sufficient."

"What do you mean?" Catie asks.

"I only know him from our few walks home. You can predict his response to any input. Raised by his grandmother, he developed a pattern of behavior that allowed him to make sense of a senseless world. He is sensitive to others, doesn't want to harm anyone, and is willing to place himself second in most cases. He's committed to do what he believes is right. No surprises. I find that attractive."

"Sounds like he's not ready for a relationship though," Nuria notes.

"I wouldn't disagree."

"He may have a history," Catie says

"Well, I'm sure it's much more layered. I see a young man searching to find stability and acceptance. Like all of us. Not easy to find today."

Nuria nods. "He sounds ideal in some ways. And quite taken with you. Someone willing to be honest with you, faults and all."

"He's gifted at working with others, and his efforts at the show demonstrate an inner strength. He had a tough upbringing, but there's an innocence there. Lost his mother and sister at an early age. Years at boarding school. I've had my ups and downs, my inconsistencies, my emotional reactions, but I have always had my family's support."

"You can be a wilting flower at times," Nuria says.

"Thanks. Paul's a much better person than I am."

"And Charles Trenet is coming tonight?" Catie asks.

"No, Catie. He'll be here on Friday. I think that would be the best day to attend. Let me know and I'll reserve a table."

"What about Wednesday?" Nuria asks. "I shouldn't have to work. I'm not sure about Friday."

"Okay, I'll reserve a table on Wednesday. It's getting late. Tomorrow lunch?"

"Can't," says Nuria.

"Me neither."

"Okay, be that way."

Bisous all around, and they head off in separate directions.

Walking back, Gabrielle wonders about the advisability of telling them her feelings about Paul. She doubts he would like her talking about him and worries that something could happen to change it all. But uncertainty is the basis of all great creations. She laughs at herself and continues on: *zazou, zazou, zazou, he drives me crazy.*

7

March 1941

When you return to Perpignan
You arrive fresh and content
You quickly forget all that you are leaving
Paris and its monuments
Once again you see the Place Arago
The Castillet, the statue of Rigaud
The Loge, the train station
The ducks in le Square
When you return to Perpignan!
  « Quand on vient revoir Perpignan! » Charles
  Trenet, « Le Coq Catalan, » 1933

Arriving at the apartment building after saying goodnight to Gabrielle on Monday evening following the first show, he was surprised to see Edith still in her window.

"Bonsoir, Edith. It's late."

"Bonsoir, Monsieur Paul. I'm finishing a sweater."

"Any messages?"

"No, Monsieur. As quiet as a summer afternoon in the Vaucluse. Monsieur Robert is here."

"Merci. Bonne nuit."

When he entered their apartment, all the lights were on, and Radio-Londres was on their Radiola set.

"Where were you last night?" Paul asked in the small kitchen, while preparing what passed as coffee and a two-day old, soft baguette. "You've not been to bed yet."

"Had a little job."

"Oh? Coffee?"

"Yes. Nothing much. How did the first night go?"

"Horrible. About half full. Mireille Printemps bombed. We'll see if anyone shows up tonight."

"There was someone looking for you yesterday. I don't know how he got this address. I didn't question him, and he didn't leave a message."

"He'll probably catch up with me at the Prefecture."

"You've been busy. This coffee is terrible. The Germans call it *muckefuck*. Have you seen that girl?"

"I've been walking her home after rehearsals. That girl is Gabrielle Daniel. Her father's the painter."

"I know him. He's pretty good. How's she?"

"Beautiful. Funny. Strong personality. Not afraid of speaking her mind, kind of low-key. She holds her own with Georges and Jordi. She works at Les Nouvelles Galeries. Strangely mature. If she's friendly at the end of the show, we'll see. So many people today are nothing but mist and wind."

"Better than nothing."

"I'm hopeful."

"Sounds worth pursuing."

"Unlike any girl I've known before."

"You haven't known that many. Political?"

"I don't think so, but smart. She's on the right side. It's mostly about the show."

"Will you be singing?"

"I have a solo tonight, which I will be doing until Friday when Charles arrives."

"They pasted a notice on the posters. 'Young local talent.' That's you?"

"Georges moves fast. I may have the lead on Wednesday, depending on Printemps."

"What does that mean?"

"She's been told to get on board. The theme is the Swing. That's what people want to hear."

"I'll be there Thursday. My father too."

"Everything will change with Charles. Come on the weekend."

"I will. I'm hitting the sack. I'll be out tomorrow."

***

Tuesday night was a repeat of the first night. Half a crowd. Times of great enthusiasm, followed by the star attraction putting everyone to sleep, which is quite an accomplishment given the popularity of the songs written by Charles Trenet. After the show on Tuesday night, Georges decided a meeting was in order. He knocked on her door.

He barely could make out the weak voice, "I'm not ready."

Ignoring her, he opened the door and pulled a chair into her dressing room, and shut the door. Georges faced Mireille Printemps, almost knee to knee in the small space, the makeup mirror to her back. Her makeup partially removed, her wig off revealing short, solidly grey hair. She looked every year of her age. She retreated as best she could, offering an acidic face of disapproval and arrogance.

"Now Mireille," Georges said gravely and unsympathetically, so unlike him, "it's not working out."

"How could it in this catastrophe of a venue, an empty horse barn, an amateur band, a bunch of no-talent neophytes, a wishy-washy manager, and a rowdy audience that only wants to drink? I quit. No discussion, only I want my full pay."

"We'll pay you the two days you worked. That's it. You can talk to Jordi. You never attracted patrons, even with the publicity. And now another person has to replace you. Take it or leave it."

"My lawyer will talk to you."

"That's fine. In my book you work a day, you get paid a day."

"And that young kid will take my place?"

"Yes. He's shown he can do it. The audience responds to him."

"I've seen them all. He doesn't have it. Trenet has something. And he writes his own material, even though he's a deviant. This boy has nothing."

"Your opinion has no bearing. If you want to get paid, you'll agree to our arrangement. If not you can walk out of here and try to collect your full contract amount."

"That's blackmail. I'll complain to the police."

"Look. It won't work. Everyone knows everyone else. If you follow me, I will get your pay. I am leaving. Goodnight."

Georges dragged the chair into the hall and went to the bar where Jordi and his wife were waiting. The hall was practically empty with a few drinkers hugging their glasses and a couple of employees cleaning up.

"Wait a few minutes," Georges said. "She's coming."

Mireille Printemps soon followed. Jordi handed her a roll of francs, which she accepted.

"We've paid your hotel bill through tonight. Thank you, Mademoiselle."

Jordi and Georges watched as she walked out, feebly attempting a proud exit. They almost felt pity. She never looked back.

"Remind me who recommended her?" Jordi asked knowing the answer.

"Can't win them all."

***

Wednesday night. A better crowd and larger, more lively, and looking for a good time. Even the rain and cold could not reduce the number or their enthusiasm. From the opening act, it was clear that the entire company had breathed a sigh of relief. The hot grogs were selling like sugar crepes. The band played no holds barred, raising the intensity of all the players. Everyone felt it. The audience loved the dancers, who had more energy in their performance, like a race horse after the final turn at Chantilly. The comedian's first set was more political and had the people on their feet. The magician tricked the audience with his slight of hand with ping pong balls. Always the most surprising act, the bicyclers astounded the crowd with their balance, near collisions, and gymnastics. Then Paul's set.

He started out admirably with "*Douce France*," but after that, he and the band exploded. The dance floor overflowed, and the audience couldn't remain seated. Each song fed on the last: "*Je chante*," "*Fleur bleue*," "*Swing troubadour*," "*Un rien me fait chanter*," and "*l'Héritage infernal*," ending in a giant "*Y'a d'la joie*." Paul received his first standing ovation, even from the band, everyone clapping in unison.

At the final song: "*Je suis swing*," which was everyone's favorite, like crème Catalan, he hit his stride. The audience sang along for the three reprises, which had happened every night with this popular song so characteristic of Trenet and his indomitable spirit. The band slowed the beat, and the full company came on stage for final applause and catcalls, slowly withdrawing toward the exit to solidly rhythmic clapping and stamping, until the dancers walked off stage to wild applause, leaving Paul and the two backup singers. Spots off, music slowed and ended, everyone buzzing. The drinks kept coming. The audience never wanted it to end. No thoughts. No worries. No cares. Just dance, dance, dance.

***

As he left the dressing room, everyone surrounded him, clapping him on the back, In the bar, the remaining audience continued to congratulate him, introducing themselves, offering him a drink, just wanting to shake his hand. He accepted the praise gracefully. He moved about the bar area, feeling great, but feeling the need for a safe harbor. The cast and the audience mingled, but he continued to look for Gabrielle, and, then, there she was with two friends.

"Paul, I wanted to introduce you to my two best friends: Nuria and Catie." Paul offered a hand to each, but received joyful bisous instead.

"So you're Paul," Catie said impishly, the others looking on. "You were great."

"Thanks."

"Amazing," she replied, winking at Gabrielle.

"We really enjoyed it," Nuria said more soberly. "We didn't see Printemps, but you were great."

"We've heard all about you," Catie added.

"Gabrielle has spoken of you as well," Paul added politely. "Would you like something to drink?"

"Maybe something not too strong," Nuria said. "White wine."

"Of course," and Paul moved off to get a bottle and glasses. Jordi was behind the bar and pulled the cork and offered the bottle to him.

"You earned it, Paul," Jordi said feeling uncommonly generous. "It's on the house."

Paul laughed to himself at his increase in pay: a bottle of wine. He didn't feel underappreciated or underpaid; this was a separate experience, outside the norm. Nothing about it was authentic. He did it out of respect for Georges and his own sanity surviving the war and occupation: that was enough remuneration.

When he returned, Gabrielle and her friends had procured a table. He found Robert standing there as well. He placed the glasses and wine on the table and turned to Robert.

"Have you introduced yourself? Sit down. Sit down." They scooted over to make a place for him.

"I have indeed," Robert said, "but I must say I was impressed." He gave an unaccustomed bear hug to Paul. "You really did it. I felt very proud, not that I had anything to do with it. Where have you been hiding?"

"Robert is my roommate and friend since college. He's a real local, having been born here. I'm from the mountains."

"Right, fifteen minutes away," Gabrielle added.

"A day's trip in those days," Paul replied.

"In the mountain villages," Robert explained, "people call their neighboring villagers, two kilometers to the north, *gabaches*, foreigners. Here, we're more open, but not too much, mind you."

"And everyone has a Spanish grandmother," Nuria added. "*La Marche Espagnole*, constantly separating battling empires. The Pyrenees basically. It was a large frontier area, where different people traipsed through: the Greeks, Hannibal and his elephants, the Romans, Charlemagne. A great olla, a ragout of peoples…and the mixing continues."

They looked around at each other and then began laughing: a history they all knew well.

"So let's drink," Catie toasts.

"Let's toast to the Club les Tréteaux," Robert said, raising his wine glass. "and Charles Trenet…and Paul Broussard."

"And Georges," Paul added.

They continued until the white wine was finished and Nuria and Catie had departed. Robert then excused himself, telling Paul he would be leaving early tomorrow.

"Well," Paul said. "That was a nice surprise."

"I like Robert, but you know who is taken with him?"

"No."

"Not too difficult to see," Gabrielle said.

"Who?"

"Nuria, silly."

"No. He's not ready to settle down."

"Who is?"

"You're right," Paul said, but he was startled by her quick rejoinder. Was she warning him?

Outside in the fresh air, he felt his heart beating to the tunes reverberating in his head. He looked at Gabrielle, counting her among his intense feelings, wanting to wrap his arms around her. Once again, though, he had to curb his feelings, like driving an Alfa Romeo Spider slowly along the coastal route above Nice.

"God, it was such a difference. It's like we had wings. Everyone felt it." Paul took her hand naturally, hoping it would not be too much. "I can't believe it."

"You made the difference," she said, allowing her hand to remain in his. "The dancers celebrated as if they had won some award, and if that happens often, or even sometimes, I can understand why they are so dedicated. I've never felt exhilaration like this before. I felt like I had accomplished something great, and that's only an inkling how you must feel."

"Everyone contributed tonight."

"I felt I belonged," she said. "It's a good feeling. I've always been on the sidelines, always looking in at other people's enjoyment. Not sure why, though it's probably my parents, who seem so isolated, even though my father works for the city and knows everyone."

"Are they going to come to see you dance?"

"You'd think they would. Papa did the poster, but when I get home, it will be 'How'd it go?' and that will be the end of it. I've always tried to be the dutiful daughter, never cause problems. As a child, no shouting, no running, kind of gloomy, but lots of love and support, just no fuss…or joy for that matter."

"Well, my mother and father never married, and they had two children: me and my sister. My father traveled between Spain and France for the first five years of my life, never staying here more than a few days, never committing to my mother. I remember his short stays, always doting, always the father, always raising my hopes and then leaving. When my mother learned he had another family in Spain, she was devastated. My family was taken from me when I was young. I can remember moments of love coming from my mother, but now I know she was really consumed by her love for a man who never reciprocated. She was nearly as absent as he."

"Do you remember your sister? It's been so long."

"Yes. It was strange for a young boy...losing her. She was my one friend. I blame my father. He paid my private schooling from a distance, but that was all. My grandmother raised me. She had love only for the church and a series of priests who moved through the church up the street. My sister...I always try to feel she's with me, but each year it gets more difficult. I guess I feel guilty. My mother as well. I'm sure she cared, but between her failed love and my grandmother's disapproval of the entire matter, to say nothing of the condemnation of the village, she was left relentlessly unhappy. It's been almost eighteen years since they died."

"Still..."

"Time stood still for them, while it went on for everyone else."

"It must have been devastating."

"What was hard was being raised by my grandmother. You should meet her. Religion was the only pleasure she allowed herself. She lost a daughter and granddaughter, and she never approved of our father. Living with her was like living in a monastery where words were unnecessary. No music. No touch of warmth or love. Only her insistence on the importance of work and her concern for the opinion of the church and village. Boarding school was like a comic opera in comparison, and joining the choir was such an important opening for me. I don't know what I would've done if I had stayed with her as a teenager. I would probably be a tree cutter or a charcoal maker."

They walked on slowly the final few blocks, enjoying the warmth of the experience, hearing the applause in their heads, the music in their hearts. Walking hand in hand, they replayed the show, discussing their fellow performers and the mistakes that the audience never saw. Georges' careful manipulations had made all the difference, allowing the cast to perform at their best. No harsh words. Plenty of encouragement. Understanding each member. He had taken a disparate group of amateurs and carefully arranged and buoyed them, allowing them to work together to create an exciting experience for the audience. He was always available, his advice always sought.

"What will he do when it's all over?" Gabrielle asked.

"Oh, he's retired. He does this because he loves it. He's managed stage shows all over Europe. He and his wife have a small cottage on the coast at le Racou. They may be leaving soon. I guess Jordi's happy. Sold a lot of drinks this evening."

"Friday should be interesting with Charles."

"You'll like him."

They arrived at her parent's house. The street was dark and deserted. No street lamps. For a minute they stood together. She did not retreat or drop his hand. Something pushed him, and he lowered his head for a gentle bisou, but she turned toward him, and their lips met. Just for a moment. Not a bisou, something more meaningful. She smelled of shampoo powder and perfume. She never smelled the" same after a day of work, testing and mixing perfumes for her clients.

She turned and ran to the door, fearing she had been too forward. She didn't understand him, but appreciated his reticence. There was something charming about it: his modesty, his non-aggressiveness, his patience. She found it attractive and exciting, allowing them to find their momentum. Closing the door, she waved at him, deciding that it might be good to see this one through.

Returning to a cold apartment that same evening with Robert asleep, he could still feel the kiss, the press of her soft lips. Her smell. He could feel the warmth suffusing his body: a feeling, an expression, a tenderness so unlike any sensation he had ever experienced before. After a cold snack, he shivered under the sheets and couldn't fall asleep.

***

Thursday morning the Independent summarized the show on page 4 (27 March 1941):

Tired? Hungry? Melancholy? The Swing is happening at the Club les Tréteaux. This neighborhood bar, periodically turned music hall, presents an antidote to glum. Following the dismal performances of Mireille Printemps, substitute singer Paul Broussard, local boy, wowed the audience. The rest of the show entertains. Presented by that sly dog Georges Doelnitz, the show found its feet last night with a makeshift but earnest band and a talented singer. He will headline tonight. Attention: *Le Fou Chantant* stars Friday night. Charles Trenet joins us following his whirlwind success in Paris. Back in his old neighborhood for the first time since 1938, he will be here for four shows through matinee and evening performances on Sunday. Hold on to your hats. Zazou, zazou, zazou.

On Thursday evening the house was full, Paul carried on superbly, and Jordi was satisfied, but on Friday evening, people jammed the club and the street outside, clamoring to enter as if their lives depended on it. Jordi had hired a beefy guard, and once the hall was filled, way beyond what a reasonable person, or a fireman, might find safe, no one else was admitted. Slowly, people left muttering their dissatisfaction after Jordi grumbled in return that Charles Trenet would be there for three more shows, two on Sunday, and first come would be first served.

Inside, the air was thick with cigarette smoke and the smell of booze. Waitresses in skimpy outfits, specially hired for the evening, bustled through the tightly crowded hall, balancing glasses, delivering drinks to tables and standing patrons, collecting money on delivery, and returning with serving trays stacked high. Jordi watched in greedy amazement as the alcohol flooded the room like a spring waterfall. He was beginning to feel good about this show, better than all the others they had done before, far better than the entire month of March. Never before had he seen so much money. August vacation in the Pyrenees was in the cards.

After an opening hour of the variety acts, which were politely accepted by the crowd, but could not gain traction with the hushed anticipation of le Grand Charles, the large and enthusiastic audience finally welcomed the man himself. He could do no wrong.

Charles Trenet came out on stage to a grand ovation, wearing a sky blue, double-breasted suit, somber gray shirt, and yellow tie, with a stingy-brimmed fedora balanced perilously on his head. From the moment of his entrée, he was in charge: in charge of the band, in charge of the evening, in charge of the boisterous crowd at his fingertips. He immediately changed the order of the songs, beginning with "*Y'a d'la joie*" at the very beginning, without the dancers. His voice ranged from strong masculine baritone to moving tenor to the joyous sounds of a countertenor. His charm immediately captured an audience prepared to receive a local hero with adulation. From his first note he proved that he deserved every gram of their reverence. He sang the first song as no other singer could. No one joined in with him. The hall fell silent. His vision and emotive delivery were beyond what anyone anticipated. The crowd glowed in the warmth of his charisma and his message of joy, and returned a standing ovation that wouldn't quit. He finally raised his arms for silence.

"I'm back," he yelled into the microphone to cheers, catcalls, whistles, and thunderous stamping and clapping. "It's good to be back in God's country. The south is my home and welcomes me like a mother welcomes her son." Everyone agreed noisily. "I spent, some say misspent, my youth with the brothers at Trinité in Béziers, but I came of age in Perpignan. I wrote poetry and painted with Fons Godail and was a bit of a hellion. No, probably worse...a lot worse. Albert Bausil and I worked together at the Coq Catalan and on a musical review, '*Allo, Père Pigne!*'" Nineteen twenty-four was long ago, but everyone in the room was at least vaguely aware of the review and had heard of Charles and Albert's reputation. They shouted in approval, forgiving all. "We had a small problem in Vernet-les-Bains at the Hotel Mustapha, but we learn from our mistakes." Again shouts and laughter.

"You know, when I was seventeen I wrote a book. I called it *Les Rois Fainéants* (the lazy kings). A few years ago, I showed it to Max Jacob. He took it and read it carefully, or so he said, and was very impressed. He said it reminded him of his own early work. Great, I thought. I've really arrived. Then he gave me some sound advice: 'Do what I did with my first work. Tear it up and throw it in the garbage and begin again.'" The crowd laughed and booed. "No, he was right. I began again, and by some miracle the next book was published: *Dodo Manières* (the ways of the Dodo bird). It's much better. It's about a failed love affair I had as a teen. It's available, but don't run out and buy it just yet. We've got a great evening planned."

"You might be surprised. The song I just sang, *"Y'a d'la joie..."* The crowd went back into wild applause. "Please...we're all grownups here. Anyway, I gave it to Mistinguett in Paris a few years back. She showed it to her lover, a certain Maurice Chevalier." A few boos from the crowd. "He was lukewarm about it." More boos. "She told him he would be crazy not to sing it and probably threatened to withhold his privileges." The audience cheered. "So he introduced it at the Casino de Paris in his inimitable fashion. The song became a hit, not a big one, mind you, but it introduced me to Paris. Everything changed when I sang that song." Louder cheers. "Chevalier introduced it, but I sang it as it was written to be sung. I sang it like a crazy man, and it became a huge hit." Thunderous applause.

"Let's get this going or we'll be talking all evening." Everyone agreed in one loud voice.

The remainder of his set progressed like a family dinner, everyone hungry for the familiar and satisfying food in the warm atmosphere, with all sibling rivalry and previous insults left in abeyance. When he completed his final song, the room went crazy. He held up his arms and waited. Finally, he said, "Let's give these kids a chance." And he exited the stage. The comedian followed, and to his amazement, everyone loved his stories. The bicycle act brought down the house once again, and the dance number found everyone enthusiastic. The animated audience accepted the closing acts, continually awaiting the return of the master, but enjoying all the acts and ordering fresh drinks.

Charles came back on stage to thunderous applause to begin the finale. He sang *"Parlez-moi d'amour"* as it was intended, with feeling, the entire room silent as he convinced them of the strength of love. When he finished, the audience waited a moment and then broke out in even greater applause, if that were possible. He finally raised his arms to halt the audience, who slowly acquiesced. He signaled for the band to begin the finale, *"Je suis swing,"* but slowly and at a lower volume. The room was hot and buzzing.

People were drinking like there was no tomorrow, and everyone felt amazed to be part of something more important and larger than anything they had ever imagined. They focused on Charles.

Talking over the instrumental, he said, "You know I have a young friend here. I've known him since he graduated from my alma mater and worked for my dad. I understand he did a great job the last two nights as a stand in for Mireille Printemps." Boos. "No, I remember Printemps when I was a kid. She was more mountain climber than singer: she climbed her way to the top, one man at a time." Laughs and hoots. "Got her pretty far, but sooner or later talent is recognized. And this young man has talent. A graduate of La Trinité, and a damned fine singer. Please welcome, Paul Broussard."

Paul listened to the unplanned introduction and came on stage somewhat apprehensively to loud applause. Charles warmly welcomed him and signaled the band to return to the top of "*Je suis swing*."

Following the master's lead, they sang the song, and then Charles began improvising. Paul followed as best he could, never knowing quite where Charles was headed, but the band seemed to be able to follow him, and the audience was singing as well. So Paul caught the tiger by the tail and held on. After several reprises, the band slowed, and once again the audience practically rioted, in good nature, of course.

"Thank you. Thank you." Charles raised his hands for quiet. "Remember, happiness is a game of roulette, sheer chance; joy is discipline and hard work. It's love and joy that create happiness and make life worthwhile, and we need freedom for love and joy to blossom. When you have a song, life cannot treat you meanly." He signaled the band to begin the finale. The cast made their way on to the stage, bowing all together and then departing. All the while, the audience on their feet shouted and yelled, clapping their hands and stamping their feet in unison in thorough appreciation of the evening and of this man, this amazing Charles Trenet.

Later, people filled the backstage. Everyone wanted to meet Charles, or see a friend or family member in the cast. It was impossible to change back into street clothes. People surrounded Paul, congratulating him and wishing him the best. Predicting great things for him.

Gabrielle, still in her show costume, brought her parents, along with Nuria and Catie, backstage to meet Paul and Charles, if possible. They were as thrilled with the evening as the cast members. Gabrielle's parents hesitated, but Gabrielle pulled them forward and introduced them, and Paul shook their hands.

"What a wonderful show," Auguste Daniel said truthfully. Contrary to his name and reputation, he was a small man, short and stocky, with an olive complexion, piercing dark eyes, and a heavy beard, definitely out of his comfort zone in this show and crowded dressing room.

"Thank you, Monsieur Daniel. Tonight was special. I'm glad you could attend."

"We've known Georges for several years. He has one of my paintings."

"I love your voice," Julie added. She was a large woman, husky, with light auburn hair tied up informally on her head. Not at all as Paul had imagined her.

"Thanks. I'm not really a singer."

"We know. Gabrielle told us. She's not really a dancer, you know." They laughed.

"*Bon*," Paul laughed, feeling comfortable with them. "We're seldom what we seem," which no one understood exactly, but laughed at anyway. "Let me introduce you to Charles." Poor Nuria and Catie followed, unable to find space enough to join them. Paul pulled Gabrielle and her parents over to where Charles was attempting to appease a crowd surrounding him, but when he saw Paul and Gabrielle, he freed himself and gave bisous to the girls, noting Gabrielle as he did, and almost shyly, shook hands with Auguste Daniel.

"I have followed your work, Monsieur," Charles said. "I admire you greatly. I was never a great painter, but your paintings and André and Albert helped me discover myself, sometimes in a rather roundabout way." He laughed.

"You're very gracious," was all Auguste replied.

"I'd do anything for this young man," Charles said, patting Paul on the back. "He's got all of us beat by the goodness of his heart. And, you know, he can croon."

Michael Barnes Selvin

***

The Independent review on Saturday morning was unambiguous (29 March 1941):

> This rather antiquated, woebegone venue turned music hall, Club les Tréteaux, managed to pull the coup of the year...decade? With standing room only and people turned away at the door, Charles Trenet, *le Fou Chantant*, demonstrated his deserved success in Paris. This twenty-seven-year-old genius of composition, born in Narbonne of a *Perpignanais* father and a *Narbonnaise* mother, proved that he can deliver his songs better than anyone. Sorry Chevalier. Sorry Sablon. Sorry Fréhel. Sorry Piaf. From *"Douce France"* to *"Y'a d'la joie"* he seduced a willing audience into an evening of rapturous joy. For a moment, for an hour, he turned peoples' hearts inward and made them forget life's difficulties, unifying them and forcing them to remember better times and the importance of joy and love. We will see and hear much more from this writer/performer. Meanwhile, three more shows are planned. The troupe, well coached by impresario Georges Doelnitz, provided a worthy backdrop. A must see.

***

The following shows never strayed from the astounding success of the first show: each one a remarkable achievement with crowds attending every show and people turned away. Each night and matinee, people fought to enter the hall. The booze flowed. The infectious joy spread throughout the starving city like hot pea soup on a snowy and cloudy afternoon. Charles never disappointed. And Jordi went to the bank.

***

On Sunday evening after the final show, Paul and Robert decided to host a cast party at their apartment. Edith was fit to be tied by the lateness of the hour and the number of people asking to be allowed in, waking her and keeping her at her post way beyond her normal time. Warned moments before, she assumed it would be a small party, but a massive crowd

100

continued to arrive, as almost the entire cast made their appearance. However, Charles' arrival repaid her a hundredfold for her pains. All it took was a smile and wave of his hand directed at the concierge melting in her window.

"I have never seen an apartment of men," Gabrielle said on arrival, this her first visit. "How can you expect to have a cast party without any refreshments or hors d'oeuvres?" Robert and Paul stood like two youngsters caught in petty thievery. "What drinks do you have?"

"We have wine and some beer. Not a lot."

"What were you thinking?"

"Gabrielle," Paul complained. "We just thought it would be nice to have the cast over. I didn't hear anyone else suggesting a party. We'll make do."

"Make do?" Gabrielle said, thoroughly frustrated. She looked at Nuria and Catie in horror.

Luckily, others were more prescient. First, Georges and his wife Bernadette arrived with plenty of alcohol and some cold cuts, which were almost impossible to procure since the occupation. Jordi and his wife arrived with enough appetizers to feed an army and, of course, booze. They had shut down the bar, which was unusual, even at this hour, but indicated the level of Jordi's satisfaction with the returns from the show. They knew a *charcutier*, who provided a wealth of prepared meat snacks. Normally, Jordi was as tightfisted as an amateur boxer and would be pushing drinks until late at night, even on a Sunday, to the dismay of the police.

"Paul!" Charles was calling.

Paul looked at Gabrielle and raised his arms despairingly, "I'll take care of setting something up," he said to excuse himself. "Can you help, Robert?" But the women pushed them both out and took charge of the kitchen.

"You've become a singer," Charles enthused. "I remember you a few years ago hanging around my father's office. Sure we sang together a few times, but I never knew you had it in you, kid. Anytime you want to come to Paris, I can get you plenty of work."

"And you," Paul said, "a famous writer and singer in Paris. Friends with all the stars. And now you have a movie coming out."

"Oh, by the way, I invited Django to drop by," Charles said, ignoring Paul. "He saw the end of the show and was quite complementary about your song and our duet. He said he would drop by, but you never know with him."

By this time, the apartment was jammed with people, mostly cast members, but others involved in one way or another or friends or family. People were drinking, so Gabrielle and Robert must have gotten the kitchen together. A table had been set up with snacks, which were disappearing fast. One rarely saw such a display these days.

"You seem to be surviving in Paris," Paul said to Charles.

"Day to day it's okay, not great. The worst is the hatred and distrust on both sides, because there's a great division: the supporters of the Free French and of Vichy. Where you stand on these two ideologies gives an idea of your politics and your confidants: there is rarely contact between the two. The other day *Le Réveil du Peuple* called me a Jew. First of all, what's so bad about that? We know the answer. But secondly, I'm not. Why would the newspaper believe this? It turns out, Trenet is an anagram for Netter. Can you imagine? Netter is a Jewish name, or so they tell me. I've never met anyone named Netter. Trust me, I'm in no position to criticize others, but that was too much. Then, they wanted to do a blood test, as though that might prove something. So many ridiculous theories out there now, not all promulgated by the Occupant, to be sure. They even censored *"Si tu vas à Paris."*

"Anyway," turning to the band with a raised voice. "I have a new song. You all know the words. He hummed a few bars and the band picked up the simple melody. I'm calling it *'Verlaine.'* Johnny Hess thought it pretty good, but since our breakup, he hasn't been too helpful. Still a friend though." Charles began singing.

Everyone recognized Verlaine's great poem, *Chant d'Automne*, now set to music with a simple tune. Every school child learned this poem by heart. Charles introduced the melody, but soon the band was creating their own riffs and breaks. Charles looked on with joy as the entire ensemble sang the song, multiple times. Paul joined in for a solo, and then Charles joined him.

"It's great," Paul said. "Who would think of that? You've done a film, written hits, performed in all the clubs in Paris, and now this song will be sung throughout France. Where do you go from here?"

"Far my friend, and I want you to accompany me." Charles looked at Paul with his playful eyes.

Paul could not reply. This evening, in fact the last three days, had been such a dream. He found it almost impossible to believe. The last week had been an amazing time for him: being part of this successful show, being taken seriously as a singer, but, most of all, his growing attachment to Gabrielle. They were becoming comfortable with each other, enjoying each other's company, seeing each other every day, and, what's more, missing each other when not together. It all combined into a gratifying, sensual pleasure.

This party was the first time they had been together as a couple, or an almost couple, beyond walking home together. Gabrielle was amazing, hosting as if she belonged in the apartment, being gracious with all the invitees, taking charge. She had built up good relations with the dancers and most of the other cast members. Everyone liked her. He watched as she talked with Jordi and Georges in the kitchen.

The party went late into the night. Slowly, people departed, but the band played on. Django Reinhardt never showed, but Charles and the band worked on another new song that he was in the process of writing, which he called "*La mer*." Paul joined Gabrielle, thanking the guests and saying goodnight. Jordi and Josette left early, but Georges and Bernadette were among the last to leave. By the time the band wound up, it was almost dawn. Charles was one of the last to leave, promising to return soon.

"Thanks, Paul. My dad thinks the world of you. Come to Paris. That's where it's happening, and if this war ever ends, Paris will be back on top, believe me. Come for a visit, and bring this beautiful and charming addition." He kissed Gabrielle and then Paul. He left like a warm mistral, surrounding everyone with his infectious joy, and suddenly all was quiet. Robert had gone to bed. Gabrielle and Paul were left alone.

"Wow," Gabrielle said. "He's wonderful and so bright, but I couldn't live with all that energy. It's like an insistent child."

Paul looked at her. "You were wonderful. Everyone loves you, and you took matters into your own hands, creating a great party." He gazed at her, and slowly she came into his arms. He held her like a lifelong lover, comfortably and warmly enveloped by his body. They both were tired, and both had work in a few hours.

"You might as well stay, and we can go to work together. Will your parents mind?

"Maybe, but I'm too tired to care."

He held her around the shoulders and walked her to his bedroom. They lay on the bed fully clothed, their arms around each other. Suddenly she jumped up.

"If I am going to work, I can't sleep in this dress." She unabashedly removed her dress and stockings, folded them neatly on a chair, and returned to the bed in her full length slip.

The thought that he had never truly been with a woman flashed in his mind, but he dismissed it, kissed her, and wrapped her in his arms under a warm duvet like the close friends they had become. Together, they fell contentedly asleep.

8

June 1941

Love, I defy your strong gusts
And the sand that I grasp in my two hands
Slips slowly through my fingers
As the time, as the days, as tomorrow…
« Jeunesse, » poem by Charles Trenet

It's been a slow morning, when we have enough time to go through the stock, rearranging and replacing the various cosmetics. All day long customers come in and switch the lip care and nail colors, move fragrances, mix bath products, eye care, hair care, cleansers and lotions, powders and foundations, blushes, appliances, tools. They move placards and advertising or signs on specials. They move price notations, often without buying anything. I enjoy the mindless ordering and organizing, but I'm interrupted by our manager, our tyrannical, Coco Chanel impersonator.

"Are you busy, Gaby? Can you help out?"

I never thought I would become a cosmetics salesgirl, yet somehow I have become the key salesperson in the department, even though I am the youngest by far. Many of the women have worked here for ages. They come and never leave. Some are good at what they do and are helpful and work hard, while others just show up each day to collect their pay.

"Sure." I walk over to one of our more contentious clients: a wealthy woman dressed to the nines for shopping. I have helped her in the past, and she's difficult in the extreme. The manager makes a hasty retreat.

"Bonjour, Madame. May I help you?"

"My eyes…" She is fondling an eye-liner pencil.

Makeup is like anything; it changes with the times and you have to keep up. Since the war, the style has become more simple and subdued, natural, striking, but understated, perhaps due in large part to the scarcity of replacements and new products. Since movies have become so popular, the stars set the style: Ingrid Bergman, Danielle Darrieux, Ava Gardner, Rita Hayworth. The American look is in, focusing on adorable lips and eyelashes, with eye shadow kept to a minimum. The stars of the makeup industry are

Max Factor, Elizabeth Arden, and Helena Rubinstein. Those are our gods. The deco look is out. Mascara is the keen tool, with nicely plucked, arching eyebrows, not excessively, limited shadow, and long flowing locks.

"Ah, yes. A liner may be too strong, Madame. The shade should be solid from lash to brow and relate to your eye color, but warmer. You have beautiful eyes. Try matte with a little lighter color, closer to your complexion with some gloss. Cherry red is too strong. A hint of brick red."

"I'm not a teenager. I don't want to look like one." She's well into her forties, well-heeled, well-coiffed, and expensively dressed, not from the Galeries, shopping here only because of our lower prices on cosmetics and our larger selection.

"If the brick red is too much, you can reduce it with vaseline and also add a sheen. Here try this, a little red-orange."

"Horrible," she says looking at the colors we have applied to the back of her well manicured hand displaying a large solitaire diamond.

"Well, we can move toward the pink spectrum, warmer, less intense. Try this."

"Hmm..."

"Let's clean up the other colors." I use a cream to wipe away the colors. "Look what gloss can do. It can highlight and reduce the saturation at the same time."

"Hmm...I don't know."

"A little facial powder may help the look. Slightly pinkish cheeks and forehead and the mouth: the triangle."

"I'm not trying to become a street walker."

"Madame, you're a beautiful woman. Vivacious. You only need a hint of color. We could make a complementary appointment with our makeup artist if you like. She's in on Tuesdays and Thursdays." I watch her relax a bit. So many people are tense, and of course money is tight today, even for the wealthy.

"No. That's not necessary. I like the lighter pink with gloss. I'll try it."

"You might want a lighter foundation. We have a special on Elizabeth Arden: Bright and Clear. Very natural."

We try out a few colors to tone down her base with a light blush.

"Often women add color that may be too much in natural light. Before the bathroom mirror it looks okay, but it's too much outdoors. That's why I recommend two sets of makeup: one for natural light and one for evening wear."

"And for evening..."

"You can get away with heavier makeup, and sometimes depending on your dress, even more saturated colors, darker to bring out the eyes and lips. In that case, the brick red may work. Anything more I can help you with Madame?"

"No, that's fine."

"Take this special gift cream. Lightly lavender-scented body lotion for someone special."

She brightens. "Young lady, you seem like a smart young woman. You never know whom you're speaking to these days. Are you native born?"

Gabrielle starts, at first thinking this woman too forward, then softening. "I was born here in Perpignan, and my parents were both born in Paris."

"I see. Well, you can't be too sure these days. So many foreigners. We have to support the Maréchal, you know. He can get us through this muddle, and we can become stronger."

"I hope so," Gabrielle says smiling, exactly as she always replies to these people. "Clotilde, can you please check Madame out. Thank you, Madame. Au revoir, Madame."

***

Later, at lunch with Nuria, Gabrielle complains of the assumption people make that everyone agrees with their own views.

"She just assumed I approved."

"Well," Nuria replies, "it's our official government. The Free French are a long way off, and most people believe Britain will fall. It's just a matter of time before the Free French disappear. It's a pretty good assumption. The Germans keep advancing."

"I guess you're right, but those people who disagree are not vocal, and they can be arrested for simply expressing their views. Newspapers and weeklies are either collaborative or no longer published." Gabrielle looks at Nuria closely, as she appears strained. "How are you getting along?"

"We're struggling. We have no direction. What can we do? What is the best strategy? What's the order of things? So far it's just wait and see. Print up a few sheets and distribute clandestine news that you never hear from government sources. Robert thinks it serves no function."

"Robert?"

"Yes, Paul hasn't told you?"

"No. You're dating Robert?"

"Not exactly. We met at the show and then the cast party, and it turns out we are in the same group."

"That's no good."

"No, I know. It just happened. A friend asked me to help out, and there was Robert...one of the leaders."

"It's dangerous."

"Not so far. I'm just a peanut. It's not Paris, yet. Anyway, you've been busy."

"I have. Work keeps me busy with these crazy customers. People can be so difficult, for no good reason. I've been seeing Paul nearly every evening. He's continued to meet me after work. We talk, and the warmer evenings help out."

"How are you getting along?"

"It's been four months, but it's like a fledgling in its nest, not quite ready to take flight. We seem fixed in the friendship stage. I continue to learn more about him and see how great he is. We hold hands. We kiss goodnight, but he's shy, and that's fine. I'm in no hurry. If you think I'm busy, you should see his schedule."

"I'm sure. He's not very talkative."

"He's reticent with people. Not shy exactly. We have no trouble filling the airspace. We laugh all the time about ourselves or events or silly things. He's had an odd upbringing, so we talk about our families. He never talks about his work. Every week he disappears for a night or two, and he's in the thick of things at the Prefecture, so we talk about normal things, but never about our relationship. Neither one of us is foolish enough to move forward quickly."

"It's bizarre," Nuria says. "Everyone's hiding something, or at least unwilling to commit for fear of retribution. Everyone uses false names. It's impossible to make friends. Honesty and openness don't matter. Is he singing? He was so good the evening I saw him."

"Not really. He and Robert have musical nights with friends, but I don't go. They spend hours working on songs or tunes. It often goes all night. We're having dinner with my parents for the first time."

"Meeting the parents?"

"Yes, no time for romance," I say rather blithely, but also I have my misgivings. "Rule: no quick decisions when it comes to friends or acquaintances. I'm less serious than Paul. He takes everything slowly, approaches everything carefully, never a capricious moment. Sometimes I feel that he doesn't care about me, that we're just friends. It's frustrating at times. I enjoy him as is, and I'm reluctant to do anything that might spoil that. We're both careful." This is an area that she has been thinking about. Whether or not to define the moment. Underneath it all, she feels ready, but she knows she would like to discuss it. She needs clarity.

"No, let it happen naturally. He certainly has passion or he couldn't sing as he does."

"Its late. We've spent all the time talking about me. How about you."

"There are some spring stirrings…but I'm not prepared to have them sprout into the sunshine just yet. Next week perhaps, if the sun is shining, which it most likely will." She stands. "Love you, girl." Bisous.

"Love you, too. Bye, Nuria."

***

They set off for Gabrielle's house. Paul is getting to know all the women in the cosmetics department. They all titter when he arrives, as though she spends all day talking about him, which she definitely does not. Almost always, they offer him a gift: a damaged container or the end of a line. Men's cologne: he never uses it. Or lotion, which he also doesn't use. Fragrance soap, which he appreciates, since it's becoming impossible to find good soap. They've discussed his grooming, but he's never been strong on using scents or deodorants. Just plain unscented Marseilles soap, no shampoo necessary. He says he doesn't shower that often anyway. Maybe once a week and between times a good body wash. That's enough. And he quotes his grandmother, who feels that washing the body is sinful and can cause no end of problems.

Paul sets a rapid pace, and Gabrielle manages to keep up. It's a warm June evening, splendid with a late rosy sunset. After her conversation with Nuria, Gabrielle regards him as though for the first time. He looks good. Tall and slender, his hair always in his face. He doesn't dress well, like a university boy perhaps. He somehow pulls it off, without much variation. He needs help, though, living with Robert with no feminine involvement.

"You've done something to your hair," Paul says in defense of her obviously observing him.

"Just a trim."

"It's nice…a little shorter."

"Yes. You noticed."

"Haven't I been improving?"

"Hardly. You're such a male."

"Well, I'm preoccupied."

"As if you're the only one."

"I know, but I see more than most. I see first hand the people trying to get out of France any way they can. I see the government trying constantly to make it harder and harder and always threatening the foreign-born with expulsion to their country of origin. You know, they're making lists. And I have no idea where the lists go. At least to Vichy. Anyway, I don't have to tell you."

"I don't see what you see. But I am aware."

"Sorry. I'm a little nervous?"

"No need. It's too lovely this evening, and my parents are not difficult. You are not under examination."

"Well, you know, I'm anxious that they like me, or at least don't find me objectionable."

"Don't worry about that."

"Am I the first?"

"The first?" She pauses, her mind suddenly escaping her. "The first boy I have introduced to my parents? Why does that matter?"

"Well, I don't know. I guess I'll be compared to the others."

"What? The others? There have been no others. You're the first…to meet my parents. What can I call you? Boyfriend? You've met my parents before." After her discussion with Nuria, she can't contain herself. "What are we anyway, Paul? We've known each other for months, and we're pretty close friends, but is that all?"

"I'm at fault. I enjoy being with you, and I don't want to lose that. It's all I have. No family, boarding school, and work, that's been my entire life. Not exactly circumstances for forging friendships. And with my life as it is now, it's impossible to make attachments. We're all waiting to see what happens with the country, to say nothing of our lives. That makes it difficult, and I'm not exactly experienced in these things."

"These things?"

"You know. Dating. Having a girlfriend."

"Let's postpone this," she says quickly. She has been thinking more seriously about him. She loves much about him, but also she will never love him without his commitment. One day at a time. That's plenty. That's all she asks. They can't continue to skate on the edge of the pond.

They arrive at the house on rue Maurell. Gabrielle uses her key, and Paul follows her up the stairs. Gabrielle watches him react to the strange mixture of odors from fresh cooking and painting solvents. They enter the living room.

"Maman, we're here."

Julie Daniel comes from the kitchen in an apron, with a cooking cloth in her hand. She's a tall woman.

"Bonjour, Paul," Julie says warmly, offering a handshake.

"Bonjour Madame. How are you?" Paul returns her strong handshake, and she laughs.

"Very well," and she kisses her daughter. "Your father's running late. Come in. Come in."

They follow her into the small open kitchen off the salon and dining area, where she offers them a local white wine.

"Show Paul around. Auguste should be here any time now."

"Not much to show," Gabrielle says, leading Paul down the hall. "My parents' room. Bath. Toilet. My room." She cracks the door to her orderly room, not highly decorated. Her father's unframed paintings fill every wall, surrounding a desk and mirror, a single bed, and a large oriental carpet, with a single window to the rear. "My domain."

He leans in to better view her room. "Very nice." He approves the sparse furnishings, minimum of feminine details, and collection of her father's art. He never had a room of his own. As a child he slept with his mother and sister in a small bedroom on the top floor. After they were gone, the small bedroom on the third floor was converted to a maid's quarters, and a small utility room was converted to a sleeping area with a desk and ship's bunk, without a window or air, which was particularly uncomfortable in the summer months.

They return to the salon and sit down with their drinks. All the walls are covered with paintings. She watches as Paul observes the many works. He begins on one wall and moves around the small room, perhaps a little nervously, as in a museum.

"These are my dad's most recent paintings. His studio's on the ground floor, and whenever he completes a painting, he stores it here in the living room temporarily, and that's why we live with the constant smell of linseed oil. And then the paintings slowly leave for a gallery or an exhibition and are replaced. The walls constantly change, except the ones in my room, which I love and are not part of the rotation."

The paintings are brightly colored, highly saturated hues right out of the tube, mostly impasto with under-colors showing through. She loves what may appear at first to be frustration in applying the colors, quick dashes over a completely different hue or last daubs over contrasting colors, without mixing or blending on the canvas. The effect is one of multiple layers, followed by corrections, all in primary colors, but also hints of spontaneity and capriciousness. Her father is called by the critics a "post-Cezannian fauve."

Of the paintings of Auguste Daniel on the walls of the salon, Paul admires the landscapes, and less so, the portraits, still lifes, and family portraits. Most are oils, but also ink, charcoal sketches, and watercolors. All are in a recognizable style with a common palette, particularly a strong use of a variety of blues.

They hear the door open downstairs. From the rear comes the scampering feet of Gribouille, a small dog, at high speed to welcome him. Auguste appears to be in a dour frame of mind, but greets Paul kindly and kisses his daughter. He is shorter than his wife and certainly less hefty.

A small table for four has been set up just off the salon. Auguste disappears and then quickly returns to take his place at the table. Julie and Gabrielle bring in the serving dishes: a white bean stew with greens on the side. Auguste opens a bottle of red wine and serves the plates, setting a dish on the floor next to him where Gribouille waits impatiently.

"So, young man, we certainly enjoyed your performance. Gabrielle tells me you work at the Prefecture. You enjoy your work?"

"I find it a challenge, Monsieur. It's stressful. I work directly with people desperate to secure what they believe are life or death papers, but which most likely will not be authorized."

"Gabrielle told me you are in the document section." Auguste Daniel looks closely at Paul. "What I'm saying is it must be difficult working in the new environment. What with the Pétain government and the National Revolution. I have a similar challenge. I met the new Prefect. He seems cut from that same mold."

"I have a sympathetic boss. We try to help people, but you're right, of course, we are limited in what we can do. I have met the Prefect once only."

"Auguste, let Paul eat," Julie says.

Gabrielle watches Paul realize he hasn't touched the food before him. He rarely discusses his job. It's impossible and perhaps dangerous to describe what he does. He does what he can, often pushing the constraints applied by Vichy. It's a risky tightrope that only a few others in his section even attempt to walk. Most are content to respond strictly according to regulations and provide little or no help.

"A singer in the Prefecture," Auguste Daniel says sardonically.

Ignoring the comment, Paul replies: "I've always been interested in music. I sang in the school choir, and I worked with several successful singers here."

"It's not a great time for singing," Auguste Daniel says. "Not with the problems we have. I know everyone wants to forget what is happening. There are people who cannot, their lives depend on it."

"Actually, as Charles Trenet says, it's the best time for singing. Popular music is becoming so popular because it helps us get through the days." Gabrielle sees him regret his comment the moment he says it.

"You know, Paul," Auguste replies, and to her surprise his countenance changes, relaxing, "I take it back. Excuse me. You're probably right."

He has shocked Paul and pleased his daughter.

"It's been a hard day."

"I really like your paintings," Paul says. "I've seen some in galleries, but never like this."

"Are you interested in art?"

"Yes," Paul hesitates. "I am." But then backtracks. "I've never had any talent."

"Well," Auguste says, again startling Gabrielle, who has not heard this before. "What you see here is dross. One in ten is good. The rest can be burned. Unfortunately, most people do not understand good painting and like whatever their eye finds pleasing. Ask a six year old to pick his favorite picture and sure enough he will find one of the good ones. But older people see in art what they want in themselves. There is much more to art than people admit, much in the eye of the beholder, but I love an instinctive, unformed reaction. That's why I love teaching children."

The remainder of the dinner goes on in a similar fashion. Julie tries to temper her husband's statements. Gabrielle feels that Paul is constantly under scrutiny: exactly what she told him would not happen. He is not used to family dinners and the play of honesty. At his grandmother's house, he ate mostly in the kitchen with the cook, and at the school refectory he ate with his mates, talking of classes or vacations. Lately, Robert and he rarely eat at home, preferring a quick meal at a cheap cafeteria or brasserie.

After dinner, Auguste takes Paul down to his studio at the insistence of his daughter, while she and her mother clear up. Gribouille follows. The walls of the small studio are covered. Canvasses are stacked against the walls. The room has three easels with paintings in progress and several tables covered in paint tubes, jars, cans, charcoal, solvents, brushes, and knives and other implements and tools. The floor is a work of art in itself, never cleaned, spotted with paint of all hues and covered with pieces of canvas, discarded brushes, old paint tubes and jars. Everything is in a state of disorder except the three paintings in progress: the same image in different hues. It's amazing that Auguste can find anything while working. Paul loves order in his rooms, his workspace, his life, to the extent that Robert constantly complains of his meddling to create order.

"Few people are permitted entry," Auguste states matter-of-factly. "It's an image of my mind. I'm a very visual person. I see only skin deep. Sometimes people find me obtuse and insensitive, and rightly so, because I'm always viewing the surface, the play of light and shadow, the reflections, the interplay of hues. I'll admit it. If I offended you this evening, please excuse me. I care desperately for people. Comes with my old-world heritage. First generation French, and still listening to the whispers of the elders in my head. Unlike our current masters, who are so set on avenging old wrongs and transforming conditions. I could go on. I assume you are not one of them, since you seem to be successfully friendly with my daughter."

"I'm half Spanish and half Catalan and all French. I have been on my own most of my life. My mother's gone. My father has never been in evidence. I was raised by a strict Catholic grandmother. Not a recipe for humanitarianism. And yet my lack of guidance somehow allowed me to believe in the goodness of people. That's what guides me. Not politics. Not religion. But a belief in people. Their basic decency. Hard to maintain under the current circumstances."

"And in your position. I think I like you, Paul. I like your honesty, and I understand. I expect we will see more of you around here. Come on, Gribouille. Let's go upstairs."

***

Outside the house, after coffee and sweets and pear eau de vie, after a warming of the ambiance, after talk of the state of the war, and after the parents decide it's late, Gabrielle and Paul say good night alone outside. The night is warm and balmy. The narrow street is deserted and dark, only a few reflected lights from the neighbors' first floor windows. Gabrielle feels tense and shy. Their faces barely visible in the darkness, they stand facing each other on the sidewalk.

"I hope my parents didn't put you off," she breaks the silence.

"Not at all. They're both great. Your father's amazing: his art, his sincerity, and his candor, and Julie is calm and accepting. No surprise they've raised a wonderful daughter."

"I wanted you to see them first hand without attempting to edit them. You survived well." She waits. She allows him time and space to respond, but respond he must. She watches him building up his courage or, more likely, just not knowing how to begin.

"I really like your parents." He pauses. "I've thought about what you said earlier." She looks at him strongly. "About our friendship, you know, earlier this evening. I don't want to be friends. Your parents can't change that, even though your father was a bit of a grouch."

"He likes you," she interrupts quickly, frightened by his literal words.

"Yes. And I like him. We came to an understanding, I think." He pauses. "But I like you especially. And that's why I want to be more than friends. You have to forgive my inexperience and reserve. This is all new territory for me."

She looks at him closely and moves toward him. A delicate kiss on the lips not too different from the kisses they have exchanged before, but unmistakable as an admission of her desire for more than friendship. They look at each other, followed by a grateful and confirming embrace. Then a longer, more searching kiss, more sensual and with abandon. She clings to him for a moment, attempting to reclaim her equilibrium. She backs away with her hands in his.

"Does that make my intentions clear?" he asks.

"I think so."

116

"Totally honorable. Bear with me."

"I'm not exactly an old hand," she laughs. An inopportune memory of a shabby apartment in Perpignan and Jean-Luc flashes in her mind. "We'll get along *poc a poc*" (little by little).

"Thank you." She can see his relief.

"Good night," she says with a quick kiss and then runs like a little girl to the door and waves before she closes it.

9

July 1941

Walled town and port
Death's tranquil sanctuary
Breezes caress the grey seas
All sleep.
« Les Djinns, » poem by Victor Hugo

We seem to be in a dark, endless night, well below the level of the sea, so deep that no shelter is possible, swamped by the currents, unable to surface, no further breath exists. Germany seems to be winning on all fronts. They are taking over North Africa. Yugoslavia and Greece have surrendered. At the end of June, Adolf Hitler launched Operation Barbarossa, Germany's invasion of the Soviet Union. Finland joined the Axis in this invasion, after helping the Nazis overrun the Baltic states. Jacques Doriot, an ex-communist turned fascist collaborator, is leading one thousand Frenchmen in a unit of the Wehrmacht actually fighting alongside the Germans in this invasion. Britain is under heavy bombing, and Leningrad is now under siege. Certainly, the end is near.

In the unoccupied south, we are better off than the north, especially Paris, where daily life is a struggle. Yet even here, commodities are rationed, and foodstuffs are in short supply. You can buy most anything in the black market, which is thriving, but at a much higher price. There are rumors of the farmers withholding produce or hoarding to get better prices; people call this the peasants' revenge. Everyone looks to their relatives in the countryside to lend a hand.

The French military captured in the German blitzkrieg still languish in prison camps despite the more and more apparently dubious efforts of Maréchal Pétain. No one is content with Prime Minister Flandin, the tall anglophile who replaced Pierre Laval in December last year. With the support of the Occupant, Laval remains on the sidelines, disagreeing with *le bon Vieux* (the old man) on all accounts, and rumors are rife of Germany forcing Laval's return.

The Resistance is stymied with a waking dream. The disparate groups cannot decide on a strategy or unified plan. They are uncoordinated, without communications or even knowledge of their comrades. They make extravagant plans in isolation, but they cannot act. Mostly, they focus on escape routes and avoid any espionage or outright sabotage. Either they are afraid of retribution or just don't know what is effective. Weapons are sparse. In the south, the Communists and Spanish Republicans lead the charge, but they too have agendas that are not necessarily aligned with the common people. In London, de Gaulle and the Free French Forces fight the allies for recognition and representation and fight among themselves about the role of the Resistance in France. Communications with London remain stymied, nearly impossible at this point. There is too much distrust, differing aims, and intense political competitiveness.

It's been two years since the humiliating defeat and armistice. We are learning that Vichy is not the answer. We cannot depend on Vichy to negotiate any kind of settlement or demonstrate any pushback. Vichy is too focused on their National Revolution and the denigration of the Third Republic, ridding France permanently of what they call its Bolshevik policies. What is the answer? Do we become a part of the greater Germany, of the New Europe? Everyone keeps his opinion to himself. It's not a topic discussed publicly or in the newspapers.

And yet life goes on with happiness just another form of anxiety.

***

There is no reduction in the demands on the Prefecture, especially the Visa Section. On a sunny day just before the August recess, Franco Plana, chief of the visa section, calls a meeting of the agents in his section. A very busy man, he has to balance the demands of the Prefect and the long lines of people queuing up for assistance: pressure from the top and from the bottom. About twenty people attend, mostly the frontline people interfacing with the public.

"Good morning, everyone." No smile or warmth. "To be blunt, it has come to the notice of the Prefect that this section leads all Prefectures in the free zone in the issuance of exit visas. We are on the scale of Bordeaux,

119

although that Prefecture is many times larger. Obviously, being the closest to Spain has much to do with it, but nevertheless we are under microscopic scrutiny. There is pressure to issue exit visas to citizens only. If Vichy has its way, all foreign individuals within France will be returned to their country of origin. This is only being discussed, but stand ready, it could come to pass."

Paul has heard this speech before. It's the talk of the extreme collaborationists, the ones who actively support the Occupant and his demands. Those demands are rarely explicitly stated and certainly not publicly. The Occupant ensures compliance privately at the top levels, depending on Vichy's own collaborative measures and governance on implementation and enforcement.

He looks out the window into the clear blue sky, wishing to be elsewhere. Since the show, he has felt disheartened. His work at the Prefecture is ineffective, and his extracurricular activities are highly risky and constantly being ratcheted upwards into more dangerous trips. Each time he successfully helps someone across the border, he is asked for more. Each day the border becomes more difficult to cross, and passeurs are caught and arrested or worse. Robert too now spends many nights away. They never discuss their activities, and Paul senses that Robert is getting involved in something much deeper, more dangerous. Arrests are made daily, and people are frequently sent to spend time in the many growing internment camps in the region.

His one inspiration is Gabrielle. She gives him hope. He loves having someone to care about. They spend many enjoyable hours together, both in the evenings and on the weekends, when they are free. They have come to depend emotionally on each other, yet there still seems to be some barrier that prevents a closer friendship. Perhaps this is natural. It just takes time. Neither is experienced, and both have some hesitation about committing. In a world that cannot be trusted and which is veering in an unknown direction, it is difficult to think beyond tomorrow. So they just enjoy each other and love spending time together, and avoid talking about a future. And this is acceptable to both. Without a future, time has become meaningless.

"As we all know," Franco continues, "our Prefect is not an extreme individual. His career depends on doing what the government tells him to do and staying within the laws of the country. We may feel that our goal is to help people, but we cannot make policy decisions. We are governed by the laws and policies of Vichy. I know this is not news, but since the 1940 Census, we need to update our statistics. Every person who comes to seek our services must fill out the background forms without exception. We need to know who these people are, where they come from, and their intentions. That is the message that the Prefect has made perfectly clear."

Paul notes this statement. It's not a change exactly, but in the past it was ignored in many cases. There are plenty of émigrés living in the department without papers of any sort. This is a matter for the police when it comes to their attention, usually on an individual basis. A census was taken early in the occupation at the insistence of the Occupant, but many people escaped it, and the continuing influx of émigrés in the south has greatly increased their numbers during the last year.

"Our section is under scrutiny. We are in a region at the forefront of this activity. We cannot be party to illegal emigration, and if it continues we will all be in trouble, and not just with Vichy. Are there any questions?"

"What about naturalized French citizens?" someone asks.

"French citizens? We are here to support our country and that includes everyone: naturalized and native-born. The government is concerned that foreign elements here may cause problems. Bolsheviks, Communists, foreign agents, escaping military or foreign government personnel, and others are intent on upsetting the apple cart. I'm afraid it is not clear-cut, but let me make this clear, we are not the police. We are not here to arrest people, foreign or not. We cannot forget our mission of responding to people's legitimate needs." He looked around the room.

"Well, then," Paul thinks to himself, "what exactly is the message?"

Everyone in the room remains quiet, not looking around, not feeling confident that expressing an opinion or questioning the bureau chief would serve any purpose. They stare at their feet. The politics and opinions of the individual agents are not subjects of conversation. They want to keep their jobs and to progress in their careers. As a result, the atmosphere is non-collegial and uncooperative.

"Very good," Franco says, "Thank you, gentlemen."

Paul returns to his desk, but he wonders about the mention of data collection, something that made him take notice. Later in the morning, he meets a secretary from the Prefect's office in the hallway.

"Bonjour, Agnes." At one point he thought he might like to get to know her outside the Prefecture, but never pursued it. She is attractive and somewhat older and party to many of the rumors, real or imagined, throughout the organization.

"Bonjour, Paul. Haven't seen you in a while."

"Busy. The visa section met this morning. There was talk of a list of foreigners. Have you seen such a thing?"

"You haven't been attentive after your show business success. New girl friend?" Agnes smiles seductively at him.

"Hardly success. Thanks. I've been busy, Agnes. You know…"

"Not really," she says, looking curiously at him. "To answer your question. There's a compilation of the foreigners living in the Pyrenees-Orientales department, including those naturalized. It's a joint effort with the Gendarmerie. I've a copy in preparation."

"Is there some way I could see it?"

"It's pretty hush-hush."

"Just a glance."

"Well, drop by this evening after five pm. I'm working late. You'll sing me a song?"

"Thanks, Agnes. You're a doll."

"Yes, porcelain."

***

After work, he headed up to the administrative floor. Agnes was waiting, looking like she had been working too hard, her hair a mess, not the spry ingénue of the morning.

"The Prefect left a while ago. Most others are gone. Take a quick look. You'll owe me. You spend too much time in the Visa section. You never get out." But you could tell her heart was not into banter. She took out four thick files containing thousands of cards. "This is being updated, but it's nearly complete." She motioned for Paul to sit down. "Looking for someone special? Your girl friend?"

"No, just want to check on a friend and his wife."

The cards were not in perfect alphabetical order, but segregated by letter. He opened the "D" section and began skimming through.

"It's an updated version of the 1939 census ordered by the Occupant in 1940," she said. "They're experts at data collection. And it includes the summer census collected by Vichy. Besides foreigners, it includes naturalized citizens in the department. Lots of people have been on the move, particularly out of the occupied zone, and many have evaded the local census, or so they say. And then there're the others." She talked vaguely as though it had no real significance, just a task to be accomplished.

"The others?"

"Yes, you know."

"I don't, Agnes."

"Well, the undesirables…the Bolsheviks and the others."

Paul ignored her, knowing exactly what she meant, and continued skimming the "D's," not seeing what he was looking for. Then he stumbled on a name "Daniel," and stopped. He could not believe what he saw: Daniel, Auguste and Julie, and their parents' names. How? Why? He had not been looking for them. Each line contained, name, address, country of origin, date of entry, date of naturalization, household data, and a code, indicating further information elsewhere. In their case, the address on rue Maurell was correct and the names of the family members, but as native citizens their names shouldn't have been there. After a startled moment, he continued on.

"You see someone?" she asked.

"No, I thought I had, but was wrong."

His finger traced down the cards, moving quickly until the last few. Then it stopped on Doelnitz, Georges and Bernadette, le Racou, correct address, no family members, date of naturalization, 1920, and a similar code to the Daniels'. There it was: his worst fears confirmed, and now complicated with the unexpected and shocking name of "Daniel," which had to be in error. He pulled back in a state of complete stupefaction.

"What is it?" Agnes asked, aware of his alarm.

"I'm not sure. It could be…could be wrong. Right? Maybe an error. I'm sorry. Thanks, Agnes. I've got to go. I owe you for sure." He walked out immediately without a further word. Suddenly, an unanticipated complication made everything else even more convoluted.

***

Georges looked at him with doleful, tired eyes, shaking his head in disbelief. Not that he didn't believe, only that it was something he felt would happen sometime in the future, not today. Why today? They looked at each other.

"Don't tell Bernadette. It would kill her."

They sat on the porch of Georges' small bungalow in Le Racou, a small community off the beaten path near Argelès Plage on the coast 40 kilometers south of Perpignan. Between neighboring homes, one could glimpse the blue sky and sea, a short stroll to the beach. The day had dawned warm and would be hot in the afternoon: excellent swimming weather with the water temperature rising every day. Paul had no thoughts of swimming. He had too much on his mind and had not seen Gabrielle the night before. He knew the importance of the information he had recovered at the Prefecture. Even if it were based on misinformation, it was dangerous. And he knew just how dangerous. Luckily the census was still going on, and no one was prepared to act on the information. He knew that it would likely be used at some future date, months off. There was time.

Paul looked at the only man who even approached a father-figure in his life. A man in his sixties, mostly retired. A man with great talents, who had done much in his life and seen much. A man often sought for his opinion or advice on delicate matters. A trusted man with a humanitarian touch. Paul had never pursued Georges' history before his arrival in France. He didn't know exactly the date of their arrival. Naturalized in 1920. That should have made him immune to deportation, unlike most of the recent naturalizations and newly arrived émigrés, He talked with his clients daily and his clandestine clients at night, so he was sensitive to the discussion of dates of naturalization. Vichy continued to argue on a date certain for exempting naturalized citizens from deportation, but xenophobia and intolerance were on the ascendency.

"Nothing will happen soon," Paul said, "but you need to be aware."

"I know. I know." Georges unconsciously tapped the table. "I know. It is a tune I have heard before. We have been naturalized for more than twenty years. I did everything right. No problems. I worked hard, made a few sou. You can only run a few times in your life. The human is like a tree. Although the fruit is blind, the tree has vision. You might uproot him a few times, but one time too many and he withers and dies. My roots were in Poland, and we were transplanted here. Now they are here. You just get tired."

"I can help you, Georges."

He ignored Paul. "This is an old refrain, excuse the metaphor. Heard it before. Ageless. It'll never stop, and, you understand, it is crazy. The worst of it is that people stupidly believe this kind of hatred."

"Georges, this is real. They don't forget these lists. I can get you out of France today, with false papers. These people are not playing."

"Paul, you're a youngster. You have your life spread out before you like some tropical beach with coconut palms and gently lapping water. You're flexible, but these old and brittle bones are about finished. When I was your age, I was a prize fighter. Middleweight. I sparred with Jan Gerbich in the Warsaw Boxing Club. Never was any good, and I got out before I was too beat up, but I learned one thing. You can survive in the ring if you keep your wits about you. No anger, no rage. You can pretend for the press, but in the ring you must be in full control. Emotions have their place…in the bedroom or with your kids. But don't let them rule you. Anyway, how's that girl friend? You seeing her?"

"Yes. Gabrielle." Paul knew that he could not convince him of anything. Georges was set in his ways, not fearful, perhaps too tolerant. Too forgiving and understanding. Most of the people Paul saw were so desperate that they exposed themselves to great risks, trusting no one. And this attitude, to him, made better sense.

"You don't sound convinced."

"What?" He was taken aback, but adjusted. "Gabrielle is the best thing that has ever happened. Not that I'm some great Lothario. Something seems to hold us back. I remember my mother, and I was young at the time, saying, 'with people or friends, never make snap decisions. Always give them time.' I guess she was excusing herself for never pressing my father, never marrying him, and losing him. Probably not great advice."

"Gabrielle seems like a wonderful girl."

Paul hesitated. "I think she is, only…"

"What?"

"I'm not sure. We both are hesitant. I suppose, having been on my own for so long. I'm kind of cautious to commit, afraid it won't work out."

"Listen, Paul. It's not something you can plan or prepare for. Don't over-think it. You have to allow it to happen. It doesn't have to be rapid, just be open to it. I've been married some thirty years. Hate to add it all up, but in the end it warrants the effort. And believe me, it takes effort. There's more to life than just work and play."

"I'm open to it, but I'm not sure she is."

"It's not up to her. You both have to make a go of it. You talk to her?"

"Yes."

"Than just be honest. If it fails, so be it. Tell her what you're thinking, or what you're afraid of. In other words, put your cards on the table face up. She'll appreciate it. Give her credit."

"Yes, but…"

"Anything on the music front?" Georges said, changing the subject. "I don't think Jordi will have another show until next year, possibly during the holidays."

"Some of the band members and others have been meeting occasionally. Just jamming-out. Nothing serious. Charles will be staying in Paris for the duration. Lots of work, and he feels comfortable there. He recorded that great song he played at the cast party, '*La Mer*,' his memories of the Catalan coast."

They talked a while longer, as the day warmed and the sun rose in the sky. Before Paul departed, he made one last attempt.

"I'll let you know if something changes. It won't be too soon."

"Thanks, Paul. I'll keep in touch. Oh, by the way, our name on your list may have nothing to do with our citizenship." He smiled distantly.

Paul realized exactly what Georges was referring to, but said nothing. They had never discussed it. After a strong hug and a bristly bisou, he left to catch the train returning to Perpignan.

***

That evening, I met Gabrielle at a small brasserie for a light supper. I was really puzzled on how to handle the information on her family. We have become closer friends. Kissing, sometimes passionately, but not taking it beyond that. Never before have I had someone I could confide in, someone I could trust. She was always open, interested, and gave in kind. Now I feel a familial trust in her, something that never existed in my own family: an opening to an area I had never entered previously like a garden gate finally unlocked.

"You look beautiful tonight," I said honestly. And she did, her dark eyes and dark chocolate hair reflecting the multicolored lights above the patio of the restaurant. She wore a short-sleeved light-grey dress, belted, with shoulder pads.

"Why, thank you."

We ordered a snack and coffee.

"I missed you yesterday. I was looking for some information, and I found it, but I also found something else." I paused, wondering how to present this gently, without discounting its importance. It was the kind of information that could not be ignored.

"Is it something you can talk about?"

"Yes." What will this mean to her? I had thought about it, knowing what it might mean. There was probably a good explanation.

"Well?" She could see my thoughts and responded with a mixture of fright and irritation.

"The Pyrénées-Orientales is conducting another census, working with Vichy and, ultimately with the Germans. This census focuses on foreigners in the department, but it goes beyond that. It's combined with the 1940 census with naturalized citizens. I was looking for Georges Doelnitz, as I worry about him with the recent bias laws. And I found him and his wife listed."

"What does that mean?" she asked, feeling relieved.

"As naturalized citizens prior to 1935, he and his wife shouldn't be on the list. But they are. At the same time, I noted that your mother and father were listed."

"What? My mother and father! How's that possible?"

"I don't know. Both your parents were born in Paris, right?"

"Yes." She looked at me as though I were the problem. Doubts rose as I reconsidered what I might be revealing.

"I don't know why they would be on the list, but they were. The list is secret. I was allowed to look up Georges' name, but there were perhaps tens of thousands of names. Vichy is pushing the census, but the Germans are behind it. They are set on returning the foreigners in France to their countries of origin. Vichy has an element that wants France for the French: their code for outlawing foreigners in France. They blame the foreigners for the Third Republic, for the loss of the war, and for any other problem they can think of.

"But my parents are French." She looked concerned, pale and alarmed. I took her hand. The waiter came to our table, but we asked for more time.

"Yes. And your grandparents as well?" She nodded. "Then there is only one other conclusion I can see, assuming it's not an error."

"What's that?"

"In March," I said, lowering my voice. "Vichy created the *Commissariat Général aux Questions juives*, under Xavier Vallat, to manage Jewish assets and to organize anti-Jewish propaganda. Vichy passed the second *Statut des Juifs* in June and began the process of registration in both occupied and non-occupied zones. This was coupled with the prior census and registrations. If there is one thing the Germans are good at, it's compiling and maintaining data.

"I'm pretty sure the current census is being used to count Jews, Free Masons, Gypsies, and others: the so-called undesirables as well as émigrés. No one will say that. We've all seen the flyers and papers published in Paris by Charles Maurras, most notably, and others. We know the steps Vichy took to remove Jews from government, teaching, law, medicine, the armed forces, entertainment, and other professions. There is a large and single-minded group that wants to rid France of these so-called undesirables, whether foreign, naturalized, or citizens, and Vichy and the Germans approve.

"Paul. Paul. What does all that have to do with me? I was born here, baptized here, and confirmed. I'm Catholic, as are my parents, and their parents as well. I don't understand." I saw a moment of doubt in her face, a cloud of uncertainty.

"I'm sorry. I'm just worried. You need to tell your parents, and I will do all I can to help. The census in the Pyrenees-Orientales will not be completed until the end of the year. Nothing will happen immediately."

"Oh, my God. I thought it couldn't get any worse," Gabrielle said dejectedly. "I can't believe it." She stood and exited the restaurant. I left a bill on the table and followed her out.

People were in the streets. I stopped her as she began walking precipitously home. I grabbed her close and held her.

"You'll be fine. I'll make sure of that."

"I need to go," she said, backing off. Practically in tears, she looked at me with fear in her eyes. Maybe I shouldn't have said anything, or maybe I had presented too much. Never in my life have I wanted to protect anyone as I did now.

"I have to go," she repeated.

"I know. But I never wanted to hurt you or your family. I was just worried. I love you." The first time I had ever used those words. I hadn't planned it. "I wanted to warn you. To do the right thing."

"You did. Thank you, Paul." She rested a moment in my arms.

"I'll walk you home."

"No, don't. I need to think. I'll talk to you tomorrow. A bientôt." She kissed me and hurried down the street.

***

You take a late afternoon train to the small mountain village of Amélie-les-Bains. The train is crowded with shoppers returning from Perpignan, where supplies are more plentiful. Small shopping bags, unlike before the war when goods were plentiful, contain mostly hard goods and some prepared foodstuffs from the town market. People are friendly, as this is a common trip. Marc (aka Paul) quietly reads a novel, Malraux's *L'espoir*, on the Spanish Civil War, ignoring the chatter. If you knew him well, you might notice a strained forehead and nervous movements of his hands, swiping aside the dark hair falling over his forehead. He is dressed in colorless, but warm, worker's clothes, with a heavy jacket on his lap, boots, and a small rucksack. These days people are reticent to ask questions or converse with strangers.

Since the snows have dissipated, the mountain cols (passes) are open. Though the cols are patrolled by customs agents, Gendarmes, and occasional police details, more strangers are appearing: people seeking escape and the ever-present smugglers. Desperation drives people to gamble with their lives, for to be caught leaving the country without papers is a crime. From the window of the train, you note the first views of Mount Canigou, the highest peak standing alone in view of the entire region, snow-covered, partially masked by transparent clouds in the reddish sunlight of the afternoon.

You probably don't have a grandmother in Amélie, few people do. Paul's grandmother lives in a stone building close to the station in the center of the village on rue Paul Pujade. It consists of three stories with an entrance on the street and looks pretty much like the other houses in the center of town. She was born in the house, married in the house, and raised Paul's mother in the house. Paul as an infant and young boy spent many years there. His mother never recovered from the affair with Paul's father and never married, and her mother never forgave her. Paul and his sister, Adèle, were the only positive results, although the most severe neighbors considered them illegitimate without redemption.

Even when his mother was alive, his grandmother was the primary caregiver, if you can call it that. His mother was too far gone with her unrequited love and the enmity of the neighbors to care for her two children. His grandmother ruled over both her daughter and grandchildren with an autocratic and demonizing stance. She was never poor. The town's people suspected but were never sure of a substantial nest egg, as she had inherited the house and an ample estate from her father, once mayor of the village. Her own marriage had been short-lived to an older man who had died after a decade or so of marriage, having contributed his seed and probably recognized soon enough his mistake.

Grand-mère always said she lived by the eleventh commandment: thou shalt not suffer sloth. She frequently reminded anyone who would listen that any problem could be solved by hard work and diligence. She never quite expressed it in those words, nor had she ever worked a minute in her life. The new national motto pleased her: "*travail, famille, patrie.*" It reinforced her belief, placing work at the forefront. Paul agreed with her to a limited extent, having imbibed this concept from birth. Growing up, he heard whispers that his maman had suffered the consequences of a slothful life. As a result, he became a hard worker: before school, during school, and once he graduated. He took work seriously, whether cleaning his room, an essay, a delivery, or a service of some sort. He did not believe in the religious significance of work.

Grand-mère's tightfistedness was relaxed only to allow her generous giving to the Eglise Saint Quentin, an easy walk from her house. She was one of the church's key benefactors. At twelve, Paul happily departed Amélie les Bains to attend a boarding school well over a hundred kilometers from his home and childhood friends, realizing, even at that young age, living with Grand-mère would ultimately drive him mad. After he left for school, he returned to visit only during the longer school breaks.

Upon arrival at the Amélie train station, Paul, without visiting his grandmother, walks a short distance to the Grand Café de Paris. He orders a coffee and sits facing the entrance. The café is empty save for a couple of workers in blues at the bar laughing and drinking red wine from tumblers. Pernod, which they normally would be drinking, had been banned by Vichy. He waits, not knowing what to expect, a little tense and anxious: his stomach upset, eyes noting every movement, every person passing on the street.

Amélie-les Bains is a typical mountain village built on two sides of the rapidly flowing Tech River on a secondary highway to Spain. In the past, the hot baths and casino supported the village. However, in October last year after a torrential rainfall lasting days, the Tech overran its embankments and flooded the town and several other towns along its descent into the Vallespir plain. The great inundation of 1940 destroyed the roads, bridges, homes, and lives of many inhabitants. Amélie spent months separated from the region, without rail or roads, without electricity, without telephones, and without even the ability to cross the river. Today, the two bridges have been restored, the road and rail to the coast are operating, and the casino and health spas are open, but the village is still in the process of rebuilding. Grand-mère survived admirably before, during, and after the flood, just as St. Quentin, the patron saint of her church, had during his lifetime until finally being beheaded.

A middle-aged couple enters the café together with a younger man. They are clearly not locals, although dressed in ill-fitting casual clothes. They are too old, too well-coiffed, and their faces are sophisticated beyond their dress. The younger man greets the locals perfunctorily and orders. The couple seats themselves at a table near the entrance. Once he has delivered the coffee, or what serves as coffee, the man approaches Paul.

"The cherry trees of Céret are ripening rapidly," he says in a lowered voice.

Paul has to think a bit. "This summer should be a hot one."

The stranger sits down, leaving the couple at their table with their coffees.

"I'm René. And you are?"

"Marc." In this exotic ritual, the two shake hands while his companions remain at their table. An observer might think them long absent friends or distant family members. Probably not notable.

"Are you prepared?"

"Yes, but I'm not sure of your friends. Are they capable? This is not an easy route." He acts somewhat annoyed.

"Of course. Prepared and advised. I did not choose the route."

"We can't delay. Tonight or not at all. We'll meet in front of the town hall."

"Agreed." He returns to his table and finishes his coffee in one gulp. They stand up and walk out. The men at the bar never give them a second glance.

A few minutes later, Paul leaves, watching if anyone follows. He strolls toward the town hall, unhurried, watching the three people, and window shops, all the time aware of his surroundings, anything out of the ordinary. The initial meeting is always the most stressful. His stomach and heartbeat respond to the danger, which could come from any direction and any person. He crosses the street and joins them, shaking hands with the couple. At this hour, very few people are about. Most are on some errand or returning home.

Paul and the couple begin walking up the street in the direction of Arles-sur-Tech about fifteen kilometers to the west, Paul leading, attempting to maintain a peripheral view of his surroundings without appearing obviously edgy. Before long, he turns off to a secondary road in the direction of Montalbà, a tiny village in the mountains. The couple follows with some difficulty. They begin walking on a rough, unpaved road, barely negotiable by car, though not too steep, leading toward the looming mountains. After about an hour, and no signs of being followed, they leave the road and turn off onto an unmarked mountain track. The older couple is now struggling.

Paul waits for them, not saying a word. Some of the "packages" have difficulties, and some are injured in one way or another or handicapped or sick. He's doubtful this older couple can make the hike.

"Do you speak French?"

The couple look at each other with mistrust. They don't know him and probably have been moved from person to person over the last few days or weeks. They haven't eaten well, and, most importantly, they are older, in their fifties. They've been warned not to talk to the passeur.

"Yes. We have been in France since before the Great War," the man says fluently in a heavy German accent. They regard Paul intently.

"We have a mountain to climb. If we go too far and you fail to make it, I will have to leave you, and tomorrow you will be picked up by the customs or police. If you turn back now, you can return to Perpignan; otherwise you will be arrested. Understood?"

"Yes, Monsieur."

The man looks at him carefully. "Young man, you don't seem to understand. We have no choice."

"Okay," he softens. "We'll take it easy. No talking."

"Thank you."

They continue walking as the light fades, more slowly this time, and then begin a steeper and rougher climb. The darkness has now closed about them, but the clear skies and full moon allow them to continue without danger. The path is rutted from the summer rains, but passable and not muddy. Paul knows the way, comfortable with the routes of his childhood. He keeps his eyes and ears open on the trail ahead and behind. So far they have seen no one and heard only an occasional bird or owl. The mountainside is dry, sparsely covered with low-growing dry shrubs and rocks, with occasional stands of juniper, beech, and larger copses of chestnuts.

They stop to rest. The fresh air has become redolent of herbs and the small brush of the rocky and dry garrigue.

"Do you do this often?" the man asks in a low voice, breathing hard. His wife sits nearby, holding her head in her hands, all reserve absent, too tired to maintain an acceptable facade.

"As little as possible." Paul is getting comfortable that tonight will not be a problem and relaxes. One advantage of this trail, though more difficult, is that it is not yet patrolled as the closer-in routes are in the coastal mountains, the Albères.

"German?" he asks.

"No, French. Naturalized."

"Ah."

"My name is Emile Liebmann, and my wife, Magda.

"No names please. Five more hours or so. The worst is yet to come."

"Why do you do this? Help people escape?"

"It seems the right thing to do. No?"

134

"Of course, young man. But today, so many people avoid doing the right thing."

"It's a difficult time."

"I have lost everything. I had a successful jewelry business in Paris. My business was taken without compensation. My home in St. Cloud as well." He looks at his exhausted wife. "Our two boys made it out, and we are joining them in America, God willing. We leave with only our lives and passage to join them. Why did this happen? I cannot tell you. And it is not the first time. We have only love in our hearts for this country. No malice for anyone."

Paul watches the man tear up and reach for his wife's hand. "Are you okay?"

She nods.

They begin walking again. After a switchback, they follow the crest of a hillside, steep but passable. The weather is not cold, and the track is visible. They walk along the crest a few kilometers and then rest at a switchback until they catch their breath. They continue on the main trail at a junction. Every so often, Paul stops to listen for sounds, voices, footsteps, rocks falling. This evening nothing but night sounds. His legs are feeling the incline, but it's a good feeling. He has hiked these mountains for years, knows all the trails, and has built up his muscles and power, which he has to recall relative to the people he is helping. The couple is struggling to keep up, but not complaining.

On the next turn, he hears voices. He quickly pulls the couple off the path behind some rocks and low brush. They wait and listen. There is no noise, only night sounds. They wait. Then they hear footsteps descending and voices talking normally in Catalan from the cadence. Finally, three men pass below on the path, not worrying about being heard, joking and laughing, not expecting to see anyone. A good sign. They all support heavy backpacks. Paul waits until their voices pass and the night sounds return.

"Smugglers. Cigarettes and alcohol probably. We can go."

Two more hours of climbing and resting. The couple is exhausted and must rest every quarter hour. When they finally reach the crest, near the Col de Doña Morta, it's early in the morning, and the couple can barely move.

They camp for half an hour to give them time to recover. Paul offers them water from a canteen and pieces of sausage. They slowly come round.

"That's the worst," he tells them, hoping to ease their burden.

They proceed west along the crest for a kilometer or so, and then, thankfully for the couple, begin the descent into Spain on a better trail, although it crosses several streams. Most passeurs would leave them here, but the trail is not an easy one to follow.

"Thank you for helping us," the man says, feeling better on the down grade. "We loved our life. So many people like you, willing to help. We were given a second chance in Paris, long before the Great War. We thought we had found paradise. People who believed in freedom, equality, and brotherhood. We raised two children. Educated them. Gave them everything. Now all is changed. All because of that man, Hitler. He woke the beast from its deep slumber. In every generation, the ravenous beast stirs from his forgetfulness and must be confronted and sent back to hibernate.

"Once a man gave up his afterlife in heaven to help a family in trouble. 'Aren't you miserable knowing you will never see heaven?' people asked him. He answered forthrightly. 'I found my service to God was for all the wrong reasons. Now I serve Him solely out of love and devotion to others.' That man was Shimon. You call him Peter. And you, young man, have led us to freedom, and we thank you."

He looks at this earnest man so driven to arrive at the truth. "Thank you, Monsieur. I must leave you soon."

"Are you married?"

"No. I have a girl friend, but we haven't talked about marriage."

"Is she the right one?"

"The right one?" He hesitates. "I don't know. We get along together. Well."

"Passion? You need passion."

You look at this well-meaning stranger. "Yes, of course." But in his mind he questions this.

"Passion is not rational. You must give it reign and be prepared for heartbreak or euphoria. But without it you are only existing.

"Yes." This thought startles him.

136

"Is she intelligent?"

"Very."

"With intelligence and mutual passion, don't let her get away."

"I'm only twenty-three. Too much in doubt."

"You have a job, beyond passeur?"

"Yes."

"Then marry her. You're a hard worker. Don't worry about the world. It can take care of itself. Commitment is not a practical consideration. It's in your heart. You can't go wrong if you follow the dictates of your heart."

Paul questions the simplicity, not because he disbelieves, but because of its implied wisdom.

"Life is not complicated," the older man continues. "It's people who make it so. Making things complicated secures your position, your work, your life. Don't believe them. Don't listen to them. Listen to your heart."

"That's easy to say," Paul replies, attempting to conceal his thinking.

"I know you. You have the right instincts, young man. You're smart and generous. It's all there. Just listen to yourself. Trust yourself."

"If only I were trustworthy," he jokes, but it offends the seriousness of what this stranger is trying to say.

The stranger looks at him with intensity. "Perhaps you need to be a little more trusting." He pauses. "How far from here?"

He waits for his emotions to calm. "Less than two kilometers to a better track. Are your papers in order?"

"Yes. That is not a problem for us."

He looks at them. He probably paid a mint for the papers. "Just conserve your strength."

The path begins to descend steeply. The dawn light is coloring the dark sky. Spots of illumination can be seen in the distance. They continue downhill. At a switchback descent they keep to the east toward the sea. As a boy, Paul walked this path with his more adventurous friends. The border is not marked, but he knows they've been in Spain for some time. They come to a larger path, one he recognizes. It leads to Maçanet de Cabrenys, a Spanish village much smaller than Amélie. He stops.

"I have to leave you now. This path leads to a Spanish village with a police presence. Just ask anyone. As long as your papers are in order, they will help. Always keep to the east, toward the sea." He points in the direction.

He sees mistrust in their eyes. Being deserted? Left to the wolves? They are afraid for good reason: lots of horror stories of banditry and fraud by passeurs.

"Keep to this main path. It will grow in size as you descend. You will arrive at the village. I can't go farther. I'll be arrested, and Spanish jails are the worst."

In the dawn light, he makes out their facial expressions and sees a hesitancy. They are in pretty good shape for old people, just nervous.

"*Bon*. Believe me, you'll be okay. This is the final step. You've made it." He attempts to reassure them. "The Catalan have a different attitude, you'll see. Wait for the village to awaken. Maybe find a spot to rest. Good luck." They shake hands.

"Thank you. You are a very brave young man."

"Perhaps a little foolish." Paul smiles, the self-deprecation falling on deaf ears.

"No. You're doing the right thing." He takes an envelope from his pack and hands it to him.

"No. No." He waves his hand. "I can't."

"For your girlfriend. It could cause me troubles. I do not intend to return. Believe me, we are fortunate. Of all the people who have helped us, you have been the kindest. I see goodness in your heart."

He forces the small envelope into Paul's rucksack and shakes his hand again. "Emile Liebmann and Magda. You have helped us. I understand why you don't want to disclose names, but names are always important. We are our names." At last he must feel the ordeal over. "Many have aided us. There are many good people. We know that. Thank you." They shake hands again, as does his wife, who has not said a word the entire trek.

"Good luck. My name is Paul Broussard." He will never see them again. Never know if they arrive at their final destination, if they will survive to find a sanctuary. And they will never know if he followed their advice. Sad

138

when humans cannot connect. They walk hesitantly down the path, disappearing into the haze. He hears their footsteps, and then there is silence.

Paul turns and reverses the hike. It takes about four hours to arrive in Amélie, much faster than the outbound trip, but the anxiety and stress have departed. He arrives in time to catch the mid-morning train and dozes on his way back to Perpignan, tired but content, as though he has made a small difference.

10

Speak to me of love, whispering tender caresses
Yet my heart cannot hear your gentle utterances
Unless you repeat endlessly these incomparable words
I love you.
   « Parlez-moi d'amour, » Jean Lenoir

Gabrielle arrived home after dinner in time to join her parents before her father descended into his studio to work. Her parents were in the kitchen, still at the table.

"Bonsoir," she said and quickly ducked into the bathroom to touch up her makeup and check her eyes.

"*Ma puce*," Julie called in a concerned voice, "I thought you were dining with Paul this evening."

"I was. I did," she called from the bathroom, wiping all her makeup off with cream and quickly cleaning her face.

"Why are you home early?" Again in her best motherly pitch, but with an undertone of solicitude.

She entered the kitchen and sat down quickly, not looking at her parents.

"Okay," Auguste said, perhaps a little too harshly. "Out with it."

"Nothing." She looked at her hands as she attempted to relate her confusion. "Paul told me he saw your names on a list at the Prefecture."

"What sort of list?" Auguste asked sharply.

"A census of all foreigners in France."

"And our names were on this list?"

"Yes, but it's more than foreigners. It includes French Jews and others. They call them the 'undesirables.'" She looked up at her parents.

"French Jews?" Julie enunciated warily.

"Yes, he said the list is being updated here for the department, based on the 1940 census, which the Germans first required of the government."

She watched as her parents regarded each other, as only a long married couple can.

"It must be a mistake," Auguste said, although she could hear anxiety in his voice. "They certainly make mistakes." He paused. "Once you're on a list, you remain there. Mistake or not, it becomes their truth." He scratched his balding head. "Did he say anything else?"

"Yes. He said the new census will not be completed before year-end.

"We knew this would happen," Julie said unexpectedly to Auguste, looking at him fiercely.

"No," he replied firmly. "I refuse to argue. We are not our parents. We are not hiding. We are who we are."

"Papa. I don't understand."

"Let me see if I can explain. Our parents, your grandparents, left Lithuania and came to France in the early 1880's. They were escaping from all the hatred in northern Europe. In France, they hoped for a new life. They worked hard, joined the Catholic church, became naturalized citizens, and raised their children as French children. Growing up, they rarely heard a word of Yiddish or Russian.

"We were born and raised French, both of us. Our parents wanted to retain nothing of their past. We were French by birth. Both our parents made sure we were raised in the church. We may not be practicing Catholics today, but like millions of people in France, we are *croyant:* we are believers.

"As young French adults, we became dissatisfied with the restrictions and limits imposed by the strict community we had been raised in. We revolted in every way we could. Finally, against our parents' wishes, we fell in love, married, and left the community...as did most of our friends.

"Yes, our parents were Jews. They lived in fear of the pogroms they had experienced in Lithuania. And once in a new country, this fear never departed. It colored every aspect of their lives, even after conversion to Catholicism. They attempted to protect us by not talking of the past.

"We raised you in the church. We believed all that we had heard during our early lives. So are we, who have known no other religion save Catholicism, now suddenly Jews? Some would probably say we are, but the laws of the country and church protect us.

"We know, despite all the propaganda, that the Occupant is in charge. Vichy knows this well and acts without having to be ordered. Further, we know that the Nazis will not stop until they rule all of Europe: Britain and Russia included. What we do not know is how far the Germans will go with their successful game of blaming Jews. It got them into office, and they will never forget their hatred of Jews. The "Free Zone" means nothing. And your news today confirms that we may still be seen as Jews. Hard to believe. In Spain the Sephardic Jews converted en mass in the fifteenth century, however, the ostracism continued for generations and eventually most left to save their lives.

"I will talk to some people to see what they think. We have time. And if we continue to resist, we may be able to turn the direction of the war or shorten its duration. Tonight, I suggest we be thankful for what we have and for our belief in the goodness of others and the French ideals we have all been raised with. Most people do not agree with Vichy, but day by day the sickness of this regime is pushed to extremes by the Occupant without ethics and principles, without civilized bounds.

"I'm ashamed to have this information come to you in this way, Gabrielle. We thought it was in the past and was irrelevant. And by God, it is the past. But I suddenly see how foolish we were. Were we fools to believe in this country? I cannot answer that with certainty. I can only say we have done nothing wrong, even according to Vichy. Let's wait for things to become clearer. I hope you will forgive us, Gabrielle. None of us is prepared for this." He looked at her as only a father can look at his daughter, one who has always been such a gift in his life.

Gabrielle didn't know what to reply. She rose and hugged her father, whom she loved beyond reason, and then her mother. But she was confused and needed time. She retired to her room for a sleepless night, reconsidering who she was and who her parents were. The facts of her life suddenly crashed and collided like pins from a bowling strike.

***

The next day, Saturday, she takes off from work early and hurriedly walks to the Prefecture. It's a bright and clear afternoon, another sultry day, a day for bathing in the sea, with only a whisper of a breeze. At the reception, she asks for Paul, who immediately comes down to the lobby.

"Gabrielle, what's wrong?"

She looks at him intensely as if meeting him for the first time, but somehow knows all about him. He is tall, muscularly thin, with small, darkly piercing eyes, a narrow nose, and ears slightly obtruding through his long hair. Handsome, but not traditionally so. Not a footballer. An academic or a professional, perhaps. Who is he anyway? A boy she met in a music hall, who could carry a tune, knew many people, and was courteous and well-liked. Someone who confidently knew himself and was smart and hardworking. A boy who thought for himself, didn't need religion for a moral foundation, and stood on his own two feet. Someone whom you would grow to like and depend on for his consistency. Someone willing to stand up for what he felt was right and willing to fight for what he believed, well aware of the tremendous risks involved.

She hugs him closely for a moment, aware they are being observed.

"I need to talk."

"Okay. Let me run upstairs. It's almost quitting time anyway. I'll be back in an instant."

She walks outside into the warm afternoon to wait on the portico. He soon joins her and takes her hand.

"Where to?"

"Your apartment, where we can talk privately."

"Fine. Robert is rarely there these days. We have nothing to eat. Stop for something?" He looks at her with concern, knowing she is in a state, but not able to discern her mood specifically. Knowing that this must have something to do with the information he revealed the evening before, he hesitates to initiate the dialogue.

"I'm not hungry."

"*Bon.* Okay."

They begin walking along the canal, not talking. The apartment is about two kilometers from the Prefecture. She seems agitated. Determined. Resolved. As if she has come to some decision and will not be deterred.

At the entrance to the apartment, Gabrielle and Paul see Edith in her window.

"Bonjour, Edith," Gabrielle says, having been accepted by the concierge over the last few months.

"Bonsoir, Mademoiselle Gabrielle and Monsieur Paul." Her eyes take in the scene.

"Edith, you haven't come to the Galeries yet. I'm ready to serve your cosmetic needs." She smiles.

"Thank you. I'm quite beautiful without all the folderol."

"It's true, Edith," Gabrielle says. "You have the natural complexion that all women would die for."

Edith responds with a full-toothed smile, watching them pass, knowing all, just as the old village gossips do in the Vaucluse.

When they arrive, the apartment is warm from the morning's heat. It's going to be another hot day. He opens a window onto the street to allow some air into the room. She sits on the couch.

"Something to drink? Wine? Robert was able to find some good white wine."

"No, thanks."

He joins her on the couch. For a moment, they sit is silence, Paul waiting. She seems calm, slightly nervous. A long pause ensues, unusual, a little uncomfortably. She prepares her thoughts, deciding on the best way to proceed.

"Paul, I told my parents," she glances at him. "About the list..."

He waits openly.

"They did not know what to make of it. But it initiated a discussion that should have been broached years ago. It answered many questions. As an only child, I was the most important thing in their lives. Nothing was too good. My father took me everywhere and protected me, and yet I suspected there was something withheld about their past. Last night was a revelation.

"When I was fifteen, we visited my grandparents in Paris. It was a strange visit, and I discovered that no love existed between the generations. My grandparents were cold and proper, while my parents made no effort to change that, accepting it as though it were natural. I now have a better idea of what was happening at that visit.

"My grandparents, both sides, emigrated from Lithuania in the 1880s. They came to Paris because of the hatred against Jews in their town and the pogroms occurring in the country. They had known each other in Vilnius, and they settled in a community of Lithuanian émigrés in Paris. My parents were born and raised within the community. The community remains to this day somewhat isolated, finding some comfort in a shared past. My parents went to the same schools, had the same friends, and grew up together. Not surprisingly, they fell in love. What was surprising was their parents' reaction of disapproval. Their parents blamed each other, starting a disagreement that continues to this day. It forced my parents to move as far away as possible. This was not unusual. The older generation remained ensconced in their Paris community, while the first French-born generation moved out. To my parents, the community was like a prison; once out, they never wanted to return.

"I was raised without knowledge of this struggle. I can't really relate to it, but the secret I discovered was that my grandparents were Jewish émigrés.

"Once in Paris, my grandparents quickly converted to Catholicism and set a course of assimilation, dropping their language, culture, and traditions. They attempted to eradicate their past. But they remained within this colony of émigrés and never really became French in their hearts. They all became naturalized citizens, and they raised their children as assimilated French, and, as a result, almost all these children rebelled and departed.

"When I visited, I did not know this story. Now I think I have a better comprehension of these people seeking a better, more secure future for themselves, but mostly for their children. In fact, it created a gulf with the French-born, and the second generation grew up without knowledge of the traditions of their grandparents. The one commonality was Catholicism, and since my parents raised me freely within the church, that did not work out very well for me.

"Their names on that list delivered the past to their doorstep and now to me. Someone never quit thinking of them as anything but Jewish. So there you have it. Your girlfriend is a Jew."

Paul looked at her in disbelief, shaking his head in incredulity, not knowing whether to laugh or cry. "I see you. You're beautiful, delightful, intelligent. That's all." He looked at her strongly. "Is this meant to scare me off?" He paused. "I felt I had to tell you about the list. I also feared that it might affect us."

"You were right to have told me, and now you know why our name is on the list. You guessed anyway, but I thought you needed to know from me." She looked at him closely, examining his reaction.

"I figured it might be that." Paul pulled her over to him and held her. She joined him willingly. "We just need to use this information so no one gets hurt: you or your parents."

"A day ago," she said, "you told me you loved me. It feels like ancient history. I was a different person, and I never replied. I'm sorry for that because I love you as much as anyone I have ever known. More. I want to be with you: Jewish, Catholic, Free Mason, Communist, or agnostic. I believe in you." His mouth met hers, and their bodies entwined.

She broke away.

"And that's not all. I want to be with you entirely and do all that it takes to make us happy. I'm yours today and forever."

"I accept," he said laughing. "And I love it."

"And no stopping."

Slowly they began making love. His hands slid up and down her graceful body, feeling her thighs and hips and waist and back, until she could scream. Their mouths never disengaged. She felt his desire and her own. She pulled back.

"Wait. Not here. Let's go to the bedroom."

"It's a mess."

"You should have thought of that."

"Not for this."

"I know. Let's go."

Jumping up, she ran into the bedroom, removing her clothes as she went. She had never felt so free and full of life. He followed her, in awe. She quickly disrobed to her underwear and turned toward him."

"Well?"

"I want to watch."

She smiled and sat down on the side of the bed and slowly removed one stocking and then the next. She unclasped her bra and allowed it to fall on the floor, exposing her full breasts. Then she stood to remove her slip and panties and faced him in her nakedness, hands on her hips, posing. He was overwhelmed at her beauty. Never before had he seen such beauty.

"I love you, and I want you. I'm not exactly…"

"Shut up and get to work."

For an instant, and only an instant, she remembered a cold apartment, a crazed boy, a desperate appeal to rationality, a violent exploitation. Then as rapidly as it flashed in her mind, the image disappeared.

"Your turn," she laughed, indicating his clothes.

He looked at her in surprise and then quickly removed his pants and underwear, drawing his pullover over his head.

"You're beautiful, you know," she said.

"Not really."

"Well, it's the truth. Come here," and she fell backwards onto the unmade bed, quickly covering herself with the duvet. He was not far behind her.

"You know," he said, "I don't ever want to hurt you. We don't have to do anything."

"Are we going to do this, or are we going to talk about it?"

He joined her under the duvet. She felt his body against her own, a sensation she had never experienced before. She moved against him slowly, her mouth seeking his, and they melted into one another. The daylight in the room made no difference, and the light underneath the covers created a yellowish world of their own. They were together as a single body. She helped him and welcomed him with her own desire. Nothing could stop them. They loved as only lovers can, without shame, without foreknowledge, joyously exploring, knowing their only desire was to please each other: joining together in a timeless universe without modesty or fear, conscious only of their union. When she flinched momentarily he stopped, but she held him even tighter with her body, insistent that he continue. Together, their joint passion led them, directed them, allowed them to move together, to fuse together as though they could never be parted, as though they were born to be together, beyond all time and space.

***

She awoke the next morning to see him staring at her. Her first thought was that she must be a fright, that her makeup must be all over her face, but his face indicated otherwise, or at least that it made no difference. Images and feelings of the day and night flooded her consciousness. She had made love to him and had enjoyed it. He had been gentle with her and had helped her, just as she had helped him, and together they had pursued their love and passion for one another as friends and lovers. They parted only to eat scraps of what remained in the kitchen, to drink a little wine, but mostly water, and to quickly return to their lovers' bower. She felt grown up and confident, relaxed and beautiful. She peacefully closed her eyes and slept again.

The rising sun finally intruded into their universe with a long line of light across the floor and on the edge of the bed. Paul watched her with her eyes still closed and her hands sheltering her head. She breathed slowly. Her hair in disarray, falling over the bolster and covers and hiding one eye. He gently brushed it aside.

She smiled shyly at him. She had slept naked for the first time in her life, and she loved it. She pulled the covers tightly around her neck and watched him. He seemed changed. Often she found him distant in his moods, away somewhere in his mind. Today, he observed her closely, watched her every move, waiting patiently for her to wake.

"I'm famished. Are you going to make some coffee? You promised."

"Of course."

He jumped from bed and walked rapidly to the kitchen. She watched his narrow hips and long, muscular legs move away. She wondered what this meant, this rapid decision. She had not planned it. The news of her family's background had jolted her, but that was not the main factor. She sought some stability in her life, and Paul seemed such a determined soul, so clear on the right and wrong of things, probably to his detriment, but it was a beacon for him. He did what he felt was right, and people could feel it and trusted him. They were lovers now, and she knew she could trust him in all aspects of this: keeping it a secret if needed, supporting her needs, committing to her, and always being faithful to her in all ways. She felt relaxed and comfortable.

"Tea is all we have," he called, carrying a platter of tea, cups, and some packaged biscuits he had discovered at the rear of a cupboard." He set it on the bed and jumped in. "At your service, Madame," he joked."

She thought about it. "Madame." It felt true, and she felt no loss. She was a woman now, not quite a Madame perhaps, but pleased with herself all the same. Not at all concerned with the implied departure of her youth. She wanted it, and she had always wanted it, but it had to be given to the right man, and in her heart she was content with her decision. Like so many of her choices, it was made at an emotional nexus. She was too much her father's daughter.

***

She met Nuria and Catie at the Café du Square in the afternoon. They noticed immediately that something had changed.

"What have you gone and done?" Nuria said. "No make up. Natural hair. A bounce to your step. The cat has eaten the mouse."

Gabrielle laughed, still dressed in her skirt and blouse from the day before. Something she never approved of, but didn't care this day.

Catie examined her. "Rosy cheeks, bright eyes, no makeup…must either be a day at the beach yesterday or you won a prize."

"The latter," Gabrielle said with a sly smile that revealed all.

"You didn't," Nuria roared.

"Really?" Catie asked, not sure what Nuria knew.

"Yes, I did." Gabrielle said completely self-satisfied.

"You're kidding," Nuria said. "You must have won the Paulist medal, normally only earned after 50 years of hard labor."

"It only took six months."

149

"Unbelievable," Catie said. "Now what are we going to do? We have to get busy, and it's such a dreary outlook for any kind of success. I'm so jealous. You always surprise us, Gaby. What is it about you? But I'm so happy for you. Of course we saw it coming."

They ordered coffee and waited in the warm shade under an umbrella. The square was crowded with people going on their Sunday business after mass or visiting friends or just out walking after the mid-day meal. It could have been an ordinary day, if things were different. If the world was not in such turmoil, if bombs were not falling on London and Paris, and lately on German targets. If émigrés, airmen, and French citizens were not urgently roving all over the south looking for a refuge.

Nuria wisely examined Gabrielle more closely. "But that is not your only news of the day. I can see it written clearly on you like a billboard poster."

"You're right," Gabrielle said, turning serious. "I'm afraid it's a bit convoluted and all interrelated in a way I can barely begin to understand, and it's a rather long story."

"But my dears, what else have we to do today?" Catie said happily.

Gabrielle told them the story of the discovery of her parents' names on the Vichy list, much as she had told Paul. They listened, occasionally asking her to clarify, absorbed in her heartfelt openness. In the end, they were more concerned than shocked.

"What are you going to do?" Nuria asked.

"Nothing, for a while. It's too far-fetched to believe, and Paul says the census data search and compiling will continue until the end of the year."

"It must be a mistake," Catie said.

"It's no mistake, because it's based on something real. Ordinarily, it would be a travesty of justice and a betrayal of all this country stands for."

"You're right," Nuria said. "Last week, a German soldier was assassinated in the Paris subway, and they shot fifty hostages in retaliation. Now that's insane. And you know what? Vichy carefully selected the victims based on their own criteria. Communists mostly, but other undesirables."

"My God, when will it end?" Catie asked

"I hate that word," Gabrielle said, "undesirables."

"It's pure hatred. It could go on for a long time. This could be our future."

"You're always so cheerful, Nuria."

"It's the truth."

"Yes, but somehow…"

They continued talking into the afternoon and then split up to return to their homes. The warmth of the day belied their exchange which had irremediably led them into the shadowy darkness of night.

***

Have you ever returned to your parents' house feeling grown up and mature, only to have them look on you as a child? Parents always see their children as infants.

"We missed you last night," Julie said, before Gabrielle could escape to her bedroom to change and fix herself up.

She considered the many explanations she could provide her mother and decided on the limited truth.

"I stayed over at Paul's apartment. It got late, and I just didn't feel like walking home."

"I suppose that's your right, but, *Cherie*, we were worried. You must let us know."

"Maman, I did not plan it. I'm sorry."

"It's just that we worried that our discussion of our past might have upset you."

"It did. For sure. But I decided it makes no difference to me. I am who I am, and nothing has changed. I feel no different. I can't change the past. If it hadn't been for this idiotic war, we would never have known. Somehow, for some reason, it would have come out anyway."

"Now, Gabrielle, this was not our fault."

"It doesn't matter. But it shouldn't have been a secret. That was a mistake. I need to clean up."

"You're coming to dinner?"

"Of course."

After dinner, Auguste suggested a walk, and Gabrielle accompanied him.

"Come on, Gribouille." The small dog jumped up and ran around, anxious to come with them. They took the common evening stroll around the Palace of the Kings of Majorca.

"I don't want this disclosure to be hard on you."

"No, Papa. It's not really. Just a shock."

"Yes, indeed. It was a story we first learned at a somewhat younger age than you and was also not exactly a surprise. Our parents never talked about it, nor did the neighborhood. Yet many people in the community continued speaking Yiddish and hid nothing. People around us always knew, especially neighbors, and that's probably why our names are listed. People have long memories."

As they walked in the pleasant evening air, Gribouille ran here and there, smelling everything, enjoying.

"You and Paul getting along?"

"Yes, Papa. I think I'm in love."

"Well, he seems a very mature young man. Don't jump into the water without testing the temperature." He paused. "Sounds like my father talking. Always the aphorisms rather than the simple truth. I'm happy for you. I have full confidence in your ability in these matters. I just wish the times augured better."

"Do we need to be worried?"

"Frankly, yes we do. The Occupant is on a path of exclusion of the Jews. We've seen that Vichy does all that is demanded, and more, to force Jews from their lives in France. That's why I help out as much as I can. No one looks on us as Jews, publicly or privately. The secret remains for the moment. But one day it could turn on us."

On the rear side of the palace, they watched a police car approach swiftly. An officer in the first car jumped out and warned them back as it crossed in front of them. Auguste called Gribouille. The car entered a long apron leading up to the Citadelle. Following closely behind was a van. As it passed, they viewed two soldiers with carbines sitting on either side of the van. Behind the soldiers they glimpsed people looking out the back, wide eyed, staring out into the weakening evening light. Recently, the police had been using the Citadelle as a temporary holding area for émigrés and undesirables arrested without papers. The two vehicles disappeared up the road. They continued their walk without comment.

"Paul said he will watch for any changes that may affect us and will warn us."

"He sees both sides. It's good to have him with us."

As they completed their walk, Auguste stopped before the house.

"Gabrielle, it's hard on a father to see his only daughter growing up, but I'm proud of the woman you have become."

They embraced for a moment and then entered the house, Gribouille scooting right behind them.

***

I'm not beautiful. I have always known that. I'm attractive, and people find me so, but I've never taken my appearance seriously. My father and mother raised me to see well beyond a person's looks and to discover a person's heart. My best friend Nuria is also plain, perhaps a little manly due to her size, not to demean her. She's smart and lively, and I love her, and she is very feminine and sexy, but in a large girl way, not slim and light-boned. Catie is more traditionally pretty: short, good figure, with long blond locks, and she takes care of herself. At school we were a threesome, and the boys left us pretty much alone. We did well in school, but we followed politics more closely than many of our classmates and were more to the left than most. We survived on our smarts and our lack of interest in boys. Only Catie was interested in boys, but we were able to help guide her on the right path.

Papa always doted on me, but what he enjoyed most was my brightness, my insights, my own opinions. When I spotted a red fox on one of our walks, which he had missed, he continually spoke of my sharp eyes. My father knew the importance of eyes. A painter looks at nature differently than most people. The painter's eye understands light in all its variations and learns how to simplify these observations and to reproduce them, but it's all a trick, as he says. You can fool the eye on canvas by controlling the use of paint. In nature, color exists in infinite variations, but on canvas paints have only limited variations. The trick is to fool the eye of the viewer into believing that he is viewing nature. Look to the masters. A simple brushstroke, a right color choice, a mixture of hues, a highlight: all can create a unity that even a child testifies is true to nature, but actually is far from nature and quite artificial: a trick.

I always was able to see clearly where others could not, and by see I mean both the visual surface and the underlying attributes. I only failed on one occasion: Jean-Luc. He tricked me into believing in him, along with his friends and most of my classmates. He fooled me by playing on my own feelings of insecurity. I made sure that Paul was the one and only person who knew the details of this incident. At first he was angry, although he had never set eyes on Jean-Luc, but after much discussion of my point of view he came to accept it as I have. He never would agree with me on one count: that it was my fault, even to the least degree. It was a crime, he said simply. He should have gone to jail for it. I didn't disagree.

11

Fall 1941

I know you are lovely
The sweetness filling your eyes has charmed my heart
And that's for life
I know it's foolish
Tomorrow, for pleasure, you will make me suffer
I know, I know you are lovely
>   « *Je sais que tu es belle,* » Antoine Le Grand/Pierre
>   Bayle

It took months, and perhaps a spell of biting northwest tramontane winds and the cascade of the large reddish leaves from the plane trees onto the streets, for me to remember the contents of the drawer next to my side of the bed. Gabrielle slept peacefully.

Fall was remarkable. Up to that point there had been one piece of bad news after another. Paris was full of bright lights for the Occupant, but the Parisians were starving and tortured by the constant strain of being surrounded by arrogant German troops. They flooded the streets, the metro, the best restaurants, and night clubs. Maxims and La Tour d'Argent were fully booked by *les Boches*. Marching bands played in the morning and at rallies; Nazi uniforms were ubiquitous. The worst were the plain soldiers in groups posing as innocent tourists, enjoying themselves a jot self-consciously, asking for directions, smiling at the girls, being gallant, while the Parisians sought to ignore them or pled incomprehension of their abominable French.

The souvenir of the defeat and subservience to another nation, one bent on ruling all of Europe and withdrawing their liberty, was indelibly etched in every vision every single day. The curfew, always a consideration, hampered the night life of all but those with money and influence: the powerful collaborators and the senior German military looking for fun. If you were wealthy, you could do most anything for a price. The ordinary Parisians were forced to hurry for sanctuary to avoid being accosted by a Gendarme, or worse, a German soldier.

Everyone said it: the voice of Paris is a growling stomach. Not the propaganda on the radio. Not the collaborationist newspapers and magazines. Any news that could partially shade the glorious advances of the Occupant or tarnish the successes of Vichy disappeared into the nether world. There was only one truth: whitewashed, nearly baseless, and untrustworthy. Increasingly, people scrambled to survive. Foreigners or people who looked different were stopped and if they could not produce proper identification were sent to the numerous camps around the Ile de France. This activity was not mentioned in the news, but everyone knew it was occurring, as friends, colleagues, and neighbors disappeared without a word.

The south of France waited its turn.

Gabrielle stirred and turned when she realized Paul was sitting up in bed.

"It's early," she said.

"Not so early. It's our anniversary."

"Our anniversary?"

"Yes, three months to the day. Your parents have been great. And my grandmother is blissfully ignorant."

"Hmm."

"You know," he said, allowing her time to come to full consciousness. "I guided an older couple, a Jewish couple, into Spain about four months ago, and the man gave me an envelope. At first I refused it, worried it could be used against me. But he was adamant. So I brought it back. Threw it in a drawer. Forgot about it. Stupid, don't you think?"

"If it's important or incriminating, how could you ignore it? You're normally so careful."

"I know, but somehow it was different. He was different."

"Really?" she plumped the bolster and pulled herself up a bit, looking at me with interest. "What was it?"

"I don't know."

"You don't know?"

"Never looked at it."

"Oh, God, Paul. Now on our anniversary, you suddenly want to find out what it is."

156

"I was thinking of Robert. He's due back, and something reminded me of it. I'm sure it's nothing. Maybe some cash."

"Good. Where is it?"

"Right here." He reached over and took a plain envelope, postcard size, from the bedside table.

She sat up expectantly and watched him.

He tore open the envelope and discovered a small sealed packet in heavy card paper. Opening it, a key dropped out onto the duvet. It was a small key, smaller than a door key, and had a number etched on it. He pulled out a carefully folded sheet of paper and opened it. There were two pages: one handwritten on airmail paper and the other some sort of official document, signed and sealed by a notary in Paris. With Gabrielle hanging over his shoulder, he unfolded the thin paper, revealing an old-fashioned elegant script:

20 March 1941

To Whom it May Concern:

My name is Emile Liebmann. My wife Magda and I are leaving France with documentation and passage for the United States. We are naturalized citizens of France as of 12 December 1914. I was a jeweler in Paris for twenty-two years, following French service in the Great War. Under Germany's second decree on the so-called "aryanization" process, Vichy initiated procedures to sell our wholly-owned store, Jeanne de Lille, 152 rue Saint-Honoré, owned by Société Anonyme LIEBMANN & FROIDE, trading in gold, custom jewelry, gems, watches, and other fine jewelry. Vichy's Commissariat-General for Jewish Affairs (CGQJ) initiated the process. On April 21, Jean-Marie Dessous of the CGQJ was appointed provisional administrator of the Paris store. The value and inventory were worth conservatively 4.5 million francs. Our home in Saint Cloud, 42 rue Royale, is also in process of being sold, but will not be completed for several years due to ownership disputes. Approximate value is 1.2 million francs. The proceeds from these sales are to be paid into government accounts and held in escrow for us or our benefactors, less the fees charged by the administrator and a ten percent share to cover the costs of the CGQJ. I have left on deposit in the Banque Générale de Perpignan, 1.5 million francs. Due to events and the tenor of the times, I am convinced I will receive nothing or a pittance of the value on any of my assets. The system is rife with greed and corruption. However, with the assistance of my legal advisor and notary, I have moved minor assets into a safe deposit box, No. 601, at this same bank, legally free from administration by the CGQJ. The bearer of the attached document will be given free access, without contention, and any and all contents will become property of the bearer under French law to do with as he pleases.

I pray for you and my adopted country,

Signed: Emile Liebmann/Magda Liebmann

He checked the key, which indeed was stamped 601.

The next document was official-looking with a large red notary stamp, a waxed seal, and a black stamp of the Banque Générale de Perpignan, initialed: FBM:

Bearer Note

The bearer of this document is entitled to access to Lockbox 601 at the Banque Générale de Perpignan, 28 rue de la Main de Fer, Perpignan, France. Unrestricted access is guaranteed under former and current laws of France until 25 May 1946 and by the authority of the undersigned officer of the bank. Within this time, all rights and obligations remain in force with the bank, its assigns, and successors, regardless of any future changes in the charter or ownership of the bank. All fees and maintenance costs are waived in return for the prepayment of one franc. The bearer of this note and key will be given unhindered access to the box without disputation. Any and all contents will become the property of the bearer without inventory and in total confidentiality.

Signed: Paul-Marie Béguy
Notaire, Paris and his seal

Signed: François B. Mota, President
BGP and its seal

Signed: Xavier Vallat, Commissioner
Commissariat-General for
Jewish Affairs

Date: 15 February 1941

"Well, what do you think?"

"We're rich." she laughed.

"Probably not. It looks real, but who knows? The bank may not honor it. Or there may be nothing in the box. We'll have to think of a way to view the contents without getting into trouble ourselves."

"What would they do?"

"I don't know, but Jewish property is being seized all over the country: businesses, homes, personal property, art and antiques, all properly and legally, according to the laws of Vichy. No one is going to welcome us to take the contents of this box. But this document has been carefully prepared and must have cost thousands in payoffs to make it legal, including the deposit of a large sum in the bank. I'll show this to a lawyer at the Prefecture and see what he says."

"It's still early," she said, falling back into the duvet, smiling at him. "I may be unwashed, but I'm ready and willing, my wealthy lover."

Paul cautiously returned the papers and key to the envelope, slipped it into the drawer next to the bed, and happily joined Gabrielle under the warmth and darkness of the duvet.

***

On Monday, I walked to the Prefecture, thinking about the changes occurring in my life. Everything was moving fast. A month earlier, Gabrielle had decided to move in with me. We had discussed it for several months and come to a rational conclusion: that we wanted to be together. Not just on the weekends and dates during the week, but together as much as possible. It was not a difficult decision on my part. Gabrielle had a more challenging concern, although fully committed. She had her parents to think of, but surprisingly they were supportive. By this time, I knew them well, and I think they liked and trusted me.

We did not move in together innocently without thought. We discussed marriage, which seemed right, but felt that we would prefer to wait for the war to end before the actual ceremony. In fact, though, we both felt in our hearts and freely expressed to each other that we were committed as strongly as we could possibly be regardless of actual civil documentation and church blessing. Too much doubt surrounded us in our personal and private lives. It was a time of doubt. People were being forced to make important decisions that ordinarily could have been delayed or even ignored.

We celebrated moving in at the Daniels' house with a roast chicken purchased from a friend in the countryside. Auguste contributed a wine he had saved for just such an occasion. My grandmother in Amélie would not have approved of any of this and was, therefore, left uninformed.

On my part, this was a decision fraught with disturbing thoughts on the casual evanescence of life: the loss of my mother, my sister. My years of protecting myself, of building a mechanism of survival, of working hard to shield myself from loss. I had no one to turn to for advice or direction, but I was in love, deeply, desperately, beyond recall. I committed myself without allowing my history or inclination to interfere.

Part of this decision was made easier since Robert had been away from the apartment for many weeks. He was now working in Lyon, but he never talked about his work or his comings and goings. Anyone with an ounce of sense knew that Lyon was the center of the Resistance and that he was deeply involved. However, he kept this entirely to himself. He was due back before the holidays, but even that was not certain. In his absence, I had taken over management of the apartment building.

In the south, the resistance was attempting to expand its operations, still with almost no coordination or communication between groups. Everyday, life became more complicated. More was asked of participants and supporters, however loosely affiliated. I was pushed to increase my activities, both in the Prefecture and in my actions as a passeur. My slow entry into the resistance was like water building up above a tiny leak. More and more I had less control of my activities and less say in what I did, and, as a consequence, the risk mounted to a dangerous level. Once committed, I could not withdraw.

I had continued to provide help to people seeking papers to allow them to leave the country or, in fact, to help them stay here legally. Franco Plana, my boss, helped me in this, and when he differed I sought false papers. Also, I had been actively guiding people over the Pyrénées from Amélie and Céret. I hated acting as a passeur and tried to avoid it, but the demands of the Resistance and their needs were too insistent to avoid entirely. I did it carefully, only over the ranges I knew well from my youth. As the routes along the coast had became more controlled and, thus, riskier, other routes opened up to the west, farther from Spain and more difficult to cross, but less regulated and patrolled. In our region, the escape routes from the Vallespir, a valley contiguous with the frontier carved out by the Tech river, were becoming more common. Amélie-les-Bains and Ceret were centered here.

I continuously worried about being caught assisting others or as a passeur. I had had a few close calls, but not like others had. It was rumored that some guides were captured and shot on site. It was risky, perilous work, but, unless you knew the individual involved, you never heard back when they were stopped or arrested. They just disappeared.

Recently, with the increased bombing flights over France, downed English flyers had become more numerous. The British military supported them, knowing their return was much more cost-effective than training new flyers. In return for assistance, London helped the Resistance with money and, reluctantly, with arms. Providing aid to the flyers involved many people, entire networks were built up. For the British airmen it was like being put on a tram without exits: it just kept moving rapidly, changing faces and locations, advancing toward a final destination, never with explanation, constantly adjusting and recalibrating, but always pressing forward. They were transported from the north to the south, then to North Africa or Spain and Portugal, and eventually to London. Most were transported successfully.

When I arrived at the Prefecture, I went directly to see Franco Plana.

"Bonjour, Franco. Thank you for seeing me."

"It's always a pleasure, Paul. You're doing a good job, but I worry about you, and, of course, your outside activities."

"That's why I wanted a word."

"Yes," he said hesitantly.

"I received a document and didn't quite know how to handle it. It has nothing to do with the Prefecture."

"Do I need to see this?"

"I can trust no one. There is no liability for you to view it. I need some legal advice."

I handed the bearer note to Franco and waited as the chief perused it.

"Ah, it seems straightforward. It should not have any consequences to you as bearer. You have the right to open the box in confidentiality and do with the contents as you see fit. The bank cannot view the contents of the box and cannot prevent you from taking them. Now, that is all fine and good, but today banks are acting rather unpredictably. One possibility is that the safe deposit box has been looted. With the new laws, Jewish safe deposits and lockboxes have become the property of the government. Assuming this is not a Jewish denoted box, which I believe is the attempt here, you may be in luck. You will be required to show identification and sign for being admitted to the safe. I guess the police could follow up after you see the contents.

"Here's my advice. Visit the bank as soon as possible. Get in and out rapidly. Take whatever there is. Find a secure place to hide the contents. If someone questions you, you can say there was nothing in the box. Difficult to prove otherwise.

"One thing going for you is the witness, Xavier Vallat, Commissioner of the CGJA. He's a top official of Vichy. My guess is that he was paid off to sign this and would not like to see it made public.

"Now, I never saw this and do not want to know anything further. Is that clear? Get back to work and keep your head down. You know the census is almost complete, and one can only speculate on what the Occupant plans to do with it. I don't have to remind you that we are seeing just the beginning."

Franco paused. In another life, he might have been a friend. As a boss, he was great, but, as he constantly reminded his staff, things change. A friend one day may become an enemy the next.

"Thank you, Franco."

"Stay safe, and maybe we'll both survive."

***

The Banque Générale de Perpignan is a small, nondescript local bank, located in the commercial center, neighboring the Casa Xanxo, the sixteenth century Gothic residence of Bernat Xanxo, a wealthy cloth merchant. Like many local banks, the BGP is barely surviving, but reflects a time during the 1920's when business was buzzing. Paul opens the door and enters with trepidation. He's wearing an overcoat, scarf, and béret. With Franco's advice in his ear, he's still feeling vulnerable. The wood-grained atrium is empty of customers, with a single teller, a middle aged woman smoking behind the counter, totally bored. Three other teller windows are closed. A stairwell on one side of the room leads up to the first floor, and an iron grill on the other side is obviously an entry into the vault.

"Good morning, Monsieur. How may we serve you today?"

"Good morning. I would like access to the locked boxes."

"Do you have a box?"

"Yes."

"And identification?"

"Is Monsieur Mota here?"

"Monsieur Mota?" she asks herself, looking slightly put out, as though she has never heard of him or this is some inconvenience. "Yes. Yes he is."

"May I see him."

"You have an appointment? He's a busy man." She smashes her cigarette in a large ashtray already overflowing with ashes and butts.

"May I talk with him, please?"

"He's upstairs."

"Could you inform him?" he replies, not impatiently, but firmly. He just wants to get this over as quickly as possible, and he prefers to leave as little evidence of his visit as he can.

"One moment, Monsieur." She turns to the wall behind her and pulls a chain. He hears a bell ringing on the floor above. After a few moments of silent discomfort, a short, obese man appears in rolled shirtsleeves and suspenders. He looks down at his teller, ignoring Paul.

"Yes, Madame Soler?"

"A young man to see you, Monsieur."

He turns his gaze on Paul, not pleased with what he sees, and with a great sigh of nuisance, makes his way down the stairs with difficulty.

"Yes, what can I do for you," with an emphasis on the "you." No greeting or salutation.

Paul takes the notarized document from his sack and hands it to Monsieur Mota, who holds it far from his eyes to be able to read it without his glasses. He scrutinizes the page, nodding his head irritably. He has seen it before.

"I see. I see. Is this some kind of deception?"

"No, Monsieur. Paul Béguy, my notary, gave me this document."

"So," he says distractedly. "I assume you have the key?"

"Of course."

"May I see it?"

Paul shows him the numbered key without releasing it.

"Follow me." Paul trails him as he opens the grill. He unlocks a large iron vault door and turns to the right, where a small station is set up before a closed wooden door. "Please sign the register." Paul signs his name quickly, illegibly, and writes down the number of the box. Monsieur Mota opens the door with his own key, turns on a light, and holds it open.

"May I have the document back, please?"

The rotund man hands him the document, which he stores in his backpack. Entering the small chamber, he says, "Please shut the door." The door closes behind him.

With less than fifty boxes in total, he quickly finds box 601, inserts the key, and easily opens the metal door. Inside is a wooden drawer just barely smaller than the space. A copper drawer pull allows him to take the drawer entirely out of the box. He places the drawer on a counter on the side of the tiny room. He opens the top of the container and sees a small round leather sac, nothing else. He quickly places it in his rucksack. It weighs almost nothing. Closing the empty drawer, he returns it to the box, secures the door, and removes the key, putting it in his trouser pocket. Monsieur Mota is awaiting his exit. He passes without a word.

"Did you find what you were looking for?"

Paul continues without turning. "Merci, Monsieur."

As he exits, he hears the man say in *sotto voce*, clearly meant for Paul: "*Sales Youpins.*"

***

After work, I pick up Gabrielle at Les Nouvelles Galeries. It has turned cold. The wind has died down for the moment, but it's the tramontane season: a cooling breeze off the Pyrenees in the summer that can turn into a viciously freezing maelstrom in the winter, blowing objects and people off the roads. We hustle out of the store into the fading light.

"Good to see you," I tell her, always moved by her beauty. We kiss for a moment on the stoop, without abusing her makeup, which is not easy. She tends to add makeup and perfume as her day progresses, and by the end of the day looks and smells like a model for the *3 Suisses* catalog. I don't appreciate kissing her with heavy makeup and lipstick, and she, in turn, protects her makeup like a best friend. Fortunately, it's the first thing she removes once at the apartment. We bundle up for the walk.

"How did it go?" Gabrielle asks innocently, tugging down a red-knitted, wool skull cap and wrapping her gray woolen scarf about her neck.

"No problem. Not a pleasant experience, but I emptied the box without raising too much interest. I'm sure the bank president knew what the box contained, and he called me a "dirty Yid" on the way out. He knew the box was associated with Jews. Probably lucky that the contents weren't appropriated by the state."

"Well?"

"What?"

She looks at me as if I were the family dog who had just ingested the dinner capon.

"I saved that for you."

"Really? You weren't curious?"

"Of course, but I wanted to open it at our apartment. By the way, Jordi sent a postcard with a note to drop by the Club tonight. Is that okay?"

"Sure. But curiosity is my catnip."

The Club les Tréteaux is deserted. Josette is behind the bar cleaning up, and her two bulldogs come yipping out from behind the bar. We have managed to become friends, the dogs and I, since they normally are standoffish to all save the steadfast regulars. Probably because food scraps from my plate often find a way to their tiny mouths.

"Bonjour, Josette. How are you?"

"Fine. Fine. These windy, cold nights are terrible for business." She comes out from behind the zinc and hugs both of us. It's like being hugged by your grandmother, all warmth and abundance. "*Dites donc*, I found a pig's head this morning, and the cassoulet is great at the moment. Sit down. Sit down. Jordi's cooking. I know he wanted to talk, and Georges is expected as well." She walks back to the kitchen.

We drape our coats on a spare chair and sit down at the table, keeping our jackets on. The barn-like structure is costly to heat, and without patrons it tends to become chilly. Josette bustles back from the kitchen with two steaming bowls and place settings and sets them before us. Her cassoulet has suffered with the times as the white beans became dominant to the meat and sausage, but is great anyway.

"What are you drinking?" she asks.

"Two drafts. The soup smells delicious."

"You children need your protein. Eat. Eat." And she rushes over to the counter and leans over from the customer side to pull two draft beers.

"Thank you," Gabrielle says, smiling at the soup. "We are all starved."

We silently examine the thick soup, which gives off a strong meaty aroma, though still mostly white beans. No sausage visible. She returns with two full glasses and carefully arranges herself on a chair at the table. The bulldogs settle down at our feet, waiting impatiently.

"This is incredible," I say. "How do you manage, Josette?"

"Oh, you know, the "Système D." *On se débrouille…on se démerde.* Make do with what you've got. Think, adapt, and improvise. I trade a hard-to-find illegal bottle of Pastis for a pig's head and some garlic sausage. Works every time. Jordi's family supplies us with duck fat."

We are unable to talk while the rich soup suffuses our mouths with pleasure.

"That cassoulet has been on the stove for twenty years. God knows, it changes with the times, but you can always find beans and something to add, if nothing more than rutabagas, God forbid. If a scientist could save a spoonful every day, he could observe the history of our region: from fat to thin, from duck to pig, from Spain to Germany, from rotgut to Banyuls."

Jordi comes in from the kitchen, still wearing his apron and chef's toque.

"You make a great soup," Gabrielle tells him, standing to give a bisou.

"*Hé*, I was doing the dishes. The soup's Josette's. How's it going?"

"Good. And you, Jordi." I received an unexpected bisou from him. Something is up for sure.

"Paul. Paul. Paul. We think of you. Another show. Another extravaganza."

"You'll never get Charles here. He's too busy in Paris."

"Georges has some ideas. Where is he anyway? Never here when you need him, and always snooping about when you have no use for him."

Jordi joins us at the table. The older couple watches the young couple eat like two starving school kids. We talk about getting along: advice on shops that have certain foodstuffs, village markets that are better than others, farmers with special offers, black market providers, movies, and the current news of the war. Finally, Georges comes in from the cold. Jordi is first up to welcome him. Georges looks suspiciously at Jordi as he receives another unusual bisou. He looks ruddy and well, perhaps a little above his fighting weight.

"What's new, Jordi?" Georges says, winking at the table. "You're a cat who's found a new mouse hole?"

"Come on, Georges. What would you have? Anything you like. Drink? Soup? Josette?"

We laugh at Jordi's bald performance and offensive joke. Josette looks at him as if looks could kill. I get up to give Georges a hug, really happy to see him.

"How've you been?"

"Staying away from evil influences and booze. Haven't been in Perpignan for ages." He goes to Josette and Gabrielle for bisous and sits down in Jordi's seat.

"I'm hiding out at Le Racou with my wife and Argut, our Spaniel. Excuse me," he apologizes to the two bulldogs waiting for their treats. "I love it. We go to Argelès for shopping and Collioure for an occasional aperitif. When the wind dies down, we have the white light off the sea, the high billowing clouds passing rapidly, and the noisy, riotous seagulls flying circles in the airstreams. Can't beat it.

"What's on your mind, Jordi. By the way, I'll have a tea, whatever herbal you have. I'm off the stuff for a while."

Jordi has pulled another chair up to the table and sits listening to Georges. "I'm thinking of another show this spring. We need it. People barely come to the bar these days. No one ventures out after dark. We need some gaiety. We need some beauties to rest our eyes on like Gabrielle; some music to calm our souls; some wine to change the color of the earth."

"Jordi, you've become a poet," Georges says. "I'm retired. I'm happy. Relaxed for the first time. If it weren't for this *sacré* war and all the rotten news, I'd be in heaven...on earth, that is."

"Don't let them get us down," Jordi says. "I've always been a non-political kind of guy. You know me, go along, get along. Keep my head to the grindstone. Don't worry about the other guy. *Je m'en fou.* I don't care. But even I have my limits, and of course business sense. Let's do a show. We talked about it after the last one, which was such a success, really because of the people in this room."

Josette notices several people enter. "Jordi, take care of the customers." She is not going to take care of them and is still fuming from Jordi's supposed joke.

"Think about it, Georges." He leaves to attend the bar.

"Let me translate for you," Josette responds quickly in his absence. "Jordi's at his wits' end. He needs to tide us over or lose everything we have worked for. The show last spring kept us going, but now we barely make enough to pay the electric company. Everyone goes to the movies today: sits

168

in the dark, hisses at the newsreels, and escapes with the films. Then they return to hide out at home. We had a moment last spring. Can we do it again? Maybe share the proceeds more equitably." She stands up and addresses Gabrielle. "Come along, I have something to show you," and they both leave to the kitchen.

Georges looks at me with concern. I have been as busy as ever and have not thought of singing or music for the last six months. An occasional jam-out with friends at the apartment, but nothing serious. The last session was in the summer, when Georges Ulmer and Pierre Fouad, the Hot Club drummer, got together. That worked well. But nothing since.

"What are you thinking?" Georges asks me.

"Well, Django Reinhardt might be interested. He's here when his Gypsy caravan comes to Argelès-sur-Mer in April or possibly before, on their way to the annual meetup at Saintes-Maries-de-la-Mer in late May. He's busy in Paris, performing and selling records, mostly made before Stéphane Grappelli left for London. They've added a clarinetist to the quintet to replace him, which of course is impossible."

"You think you could get them?" Georges asks.

"I don't know. He's capricious like the Gypsy he is. Difficult to tie him down."

"If you could get Django," Georges says, "I might consider one last fight. Once a pugilist, always ready to fight...until your brains are mush. Bernadette will think me crazy, but she has always known that."

Jordi returns with tea for Georges and sits down. "Well, you figured it all out?"

They ignore him. "I could send a note to Pierre," I say.

"We might be able to produce something, provided we could get Django to commit."

"That's the problem. You have to know Django. If he needs money, he may be interested. We'd have to pay him up front. Jordi's not going to like it."

"You're right about that," Jordi interjects.

"Let's give it some thought," Georges adds. "We'll get back to you, Jordi. Give us some time."

Before we leave, I find a moment alone with Georges.

"Have you thought of getting out?"

"Frankly," Georges says, "I haven't."

"Well the census is nearly complete, but it will be some time before they act on it, but they will. If not Vichy, then the Occupant. I can get you papers."

"No, Paul. We're good here. I've been uprooted too many times in my life. I'm getting too old for this. We'll tough it out."

"I'll keep you posted."

"You don't have to worry about us. We're fine. But thanks."

"I do, Georges," I nod in resignation. "I do worry." How I respect this man, even his obstinacy.

***

Gabrielle and Paul return to the apartment late that evening, Josette having given Gabrielle more cassoulet and some other things she carries in a paper bag. It's been a day of anticipation, and they're tired. At the front door of the building a man comes out from Edith's studio. Paul has never seen anyone exit the studio of the concierge, even the concierge herself. He is not sure when she leaves her spot to shop or takes care of personal needs. Never a visitor, never a guest. The man is well dressed in a tailored coat, tie, and dark fedora, probably in his fifties.

"Nice to see you again, Paul?"

Paul does a double-take and then recognizes him, having met him once before.

"You're Robert's father."

"Yes." They shake hands. "Henri Bardou."

"This is my fiancée, Gabrielle Daniel."

"Happy to meet you." He shakes her hand. "You must be Auguste Daniel's daughter. He has spoken of you many times when I've seen him at town meetings. We always compare notes on our children." He turns to face Paul. "I wanted to talk with you."

"Please come up. It's cold here." Paul sees Edith's face behind the thin curtains in her window, observing. He waves.

"No. I don't want to bother you. I'm worried about Robert. Haven't heard from him since last summer. Have you seen him?"

"No. He's been away nearly six months."

"Not a call. Not a postcard. Nothing. Do you know where he is?"

"No. My guess, though, is he's in Lyon. That's the center of, of…"

"The center?"

"Yes, of the, you know…" Paul glances at Edith's visage.

"Of the Resistance?" Henri notes Paul's reticence.

"Yes."

"Ah. I might have known. I see. It seems to run in the family. You can trust Edith. She has been in my employ for almost thirty years, ever since her husband, a distant relative, was killed in the Great War. We need to talk to him, Paul. His sister was arrested in Chartres last week. She's being held at the camp at Gurs, but that's all they will say. Can't see her. Can't help her. They say we can send a package once a month, but who knows if she would ever see it, or how long she will be there. The Swiss Red Cross visits, but they're no more helpful."

"Again, I'm just guessing, but I'm sure they work for the same man. Robert most likely knows about his sister."

"Who do they work for?"

Paul is uncomfortable. "I don't know his name, but he's one of the top men. There are so many competing groups that barely communicate."

"Can you contact him?"

"I can try. It's not like they want to be found. If we could find him, so could the police. But I'll try. Actually, I was expecting Robert over the holidays."

"Please keep me informed."

"Yes, of course."

The man turns to leave. "Oh, by the way. Robert thinks the world of you, and thanks for taking care of managing the building."

"That's the least I can do. Sorry I'm not more help."

They mount the stairs and enter a freezing apartment.

"Maybe I said too much," Paul mused.

"Do you know more?"

"Not really."

They enter the bedroom and shut the door to try to reduce the draft. The day has been an emotional roller coaster: getting into the lockbox, meeting with Jordi and Georges, and now Robert's father. His life seems to get more complicated each day, and he continues his own battles. His one anchor has been Gabrielle. He wonders vaguely how he existed before her. She snuggles next to him, warming him.

"Let's get into bed and warm up. It's freezing," she says.

"Good idea."

They undress quickly and hide under the covers. The heavy winter duvet seems more cold than the room itself. Coming together, they are able to warm each other. They remain embraced, rubbing their bodies and entwining their legs, with only the reading lamp on.

"God, it's cold. How come you are not more curious?" Gabrielle whispers.

"I guess I don't feel that whatever's in the sac belongs to us."

"But he gave it to you."

"He had no choice. I was the last in the line. It belongs to him. They have children. And who knows, it may be nothing."

"It might be something."

"True." He extends an arm from under the covers and opens his rucksack on his side of the bed and takes out a small leather sac with a leather drawstring. He hadn't given it a good look at the bank. He opens the sac to produce a small leather container.

"What's that?" she asks.

"That's what was in the safe deposit box."

"That's extraordinary. It's a Hermès tambour bag. Probably cost a mint. I've seen some similar, but it must be a custom order, since it's smaller than the commercial sizes."

They both sit up. It's barrel-shaped, about twenty centimeters high and ten in diameter, a hard leather top tied with leather laces interlaced from top to bottom entirely around the barrel like a drum. Finally, after unlacing all the way around, Paul pries the top off. Inside is a large maroon felt cloth rolled carefully and sized to fit exactly into the container. They come out from under the cover ignoring the ambient temperature, and he places the cloth between them. Slowly, he unrolls the cloth. The first stone appears, followed at each turn by another stone, never touching one another. When the cloth is fully unrolled, he counts fifteen cut diamonds, or at least what appear to be diamonds, each glittering as though a source of light.

Gabrielle is breathing heavily. "They're matched, the same size and color. Remarkable, as though for a necklace. And they're probably three carets each or more. They're beautiful."

"Are they real?"

"Of course they are," she says smugly. "I see them every day on the wealthy ladies who come into the shop, except they never have more than one and rarely as large as these, but I can have one tested by the expert at the store. They're easy to lose. We'll have to be careful."

Paul laughed. "We never had this problem before." He kissed her, "Careful."

He rewraps the jewels in the cloth and places them into the container and laces it up.

"What will we do with this?" She asks. "We'll just worry."

He looks at her. "Insurance."

"What do you mean."

"These may be useful."

"For what?"

"For us, my little cabbage." He places the bag in a drawer in the side table and takes her in his arms. "You didn't know you were sleeping with a wealthy man."

"No more noble thoughts?"

"I guess my greed got the best of me. He gave them to me."

"Yes, dear...to us."

The bed is warm , and they make love with ease and familiarity. The war ceases. The occupation is terminated. Robert is forgotten. The Prefecture and Les Nouvelles Galeries disappear. The cold is made warm, and the world unifies in a timeless embrace. An embrace for yesterday, today, and tomorrow. An embrace whispering to each other their happiness, pledging their lives free of all limits and borders.

12

December 1941

In a tiny village of long ago
I saw the last of the shepherdesses
At eighteen years, a princess of virtue
The wisest girl in the village
Spinning her wool and guarding her sheep
Wearing cotton stockings and mocking the village boys.
« La dernière bergère, » Alexandre Siniavine, L.
Sauvat; Django Reinhardt

Café des Arts is a small bar/restaurant, very popular, centrally located, but without much of a menu. It's one of their haunts when a light lunch is in order. For the last three days, it has been cloudy and drizzly, and today is the first day in some time to bring out tables and chairs into the cool sunshine, even if temporarily. Gabrielle secures a table under the entrance awning, just in case. She waves as the girls arrive.

They hurry over, each bending to give her a *bise*.

"We never see you any more," Nuria says, chastising.

"I've been busy at the store. Lots of changes. We're losing some brands, and cosmetic choices are becoming limited. Everything is going to the war effort, and of course the management doesn't know what they're doing. Our sales are way down, and our faithful clients not as faithful. Why spend on lipstick, if you haven't any meat to eat?"

"Our store is way down," Catie says. "I may be out of a job soon if sales don't pick up. People aren't having babies. The baby makers are in POW camps or hiding. But that's not the reason you've been busy. You're practically married."

"Not really. You'll be the first to know when we consider marriage, and it's not a great time, even if you've found the right man."

"You have," Nuria says.

"We get along." She orders a tea and a pâté sandwich.

"The special salad. Thanks"

"I'll take a *croque-monsieur*. Thanks.

"Anything to drink?" the *garçon* asks.

174

"Tea all around."

"Who would have believed it?" Catie says. "Six months ago, we were looking for any man. And now you've found one, and we are still looking. You're lucky. What's it like?"

"My God, Catie. Leave her be," Nuria says. "At la Cimade, we're swamped by the number of émigrés arriving. And our center started working with the internment camps in the south: Argelès, St. Cyprien, Rivesaltes, Rivel, Bram, Le Vernet...even Gurs. The internees used to be mostly Spanish, but now they're all eastern Europeans, more every day. I've been visiting the camps. My desk job is turning into a liaison with the internees in the camps. We provide food, clothing, medical supplies, and books to the camps, and keep statistics, watching what they're doing, working with the Quakers and the OSE (*Oeuvre de Secours aux Enfants*), helping the incarcerated children, evacuating as many as possible."

"Are you still involved in other things?" Gabrielle asks her.

"No. Just la Cimade. But it's getting interesting and more involved."

"Not as risky?"

"Well, I wouldn't say that exactly. We're getting more outside funding now. And, well, you know."

"What do you mean?" Catie asks.

"She just means, helping people is more difficult," Gabrielle says quickly. "The world war has begun now with the Americans joining after the Japanese bombing of Pearl Harbor. They declared war on Japan and then on Germany a few days later. The US just confiscated SS Normandie this morning. The fastest trans-Atlantic ship in operation, and that didn't sit well with Vichy."

"Maybe she'll become a troop ship, Nuria adds. "It's only been a few days, and the ship has been in New York for months. Couldn't have been a surprise to Vichy."

"What's it like," Catie asks Gabrielle quite seriously.

"What?"

"Living with your boyfriend?"

"It's nice, Catie." Gabrielle answers pensively, considering the question. "It's comfortable, but exciting at the same time, knowing someone cares and allows you to be yourself. Paul is very considerate, but I'm the one who should be worrying. He's always off doing something, always helping people." Her thoughts flash on the diamonds, which they hid in a floorboard under the bed along with some cash.

"That's great," Catie replies, honestly impressed. "You deserve it, Gabrielle."

"What's your problem, Catie?" Nuria says, slightly annoyed. "You'll find someone. You're always so negative. Men won't make you happy."

"I know. But it's hard. So few men about."

"Well, they'll return. Relax. Quit looking, and one will show up. Believe me." Nuria's tone is perhaps a little harsh, but then they all have their own lives and directions and pressures. It's not like school days.

Nuria and Catie return to their respective jobs, leaving Gabrielle to finish her tea, now cold. She knows that Nuria is becoming involved with the Resistance through la Cimade. It started out as a Protestant assistance agency for displaced persons, Spanish refugees primarily, but recently has become more active in the growing internment camps. Their funding originally came from Protestant ministries, but has become much more diverse with the war and the changing priorities.

Gabrielle ponders Catie's innocent question. She has never felt so free to be herself, as though she had been suddenly allowed to grow up, but then living with your parents is kind of stultifying: always the child, living in the same room that you were raised in, from your bed with your favorite covering to your much loved paintings by your Papa. She has left one world and entered another, one of her own choosing.

Paul has been considerate, worried that she might not be happy with her choice, but at the same time preoccupied with his own affairs, which seemed to be occupying his thoughts more than ever. Now with a possible spring show at Club les Tréteaux, although it's not clear if there will be any dancers, this show being focused on jazz, he would be busier than ever. But she never felt that she was not pivotal to his life, just that he had too many demands on his time. She never complained when he returned after a two-day trip, never asked for additional information, never pushed him, always allowed him his life. She knew that when he returned, he was hers alone, and she basked in this knowledge, comfortable with the role she played, and her new-found freedom. One nagging thought tugs at her occasionally: it all happened so quickly in response to her discovery of her family's secret. She never had time to focus on herself: what this meant to her. Did it have no meaning at all? Was it irrelevant to her life? Did she merely substitute Paul for another family that she didn't understand?

Even with the world upside down, she leaves the café to return to work, feeling comfortable for the first time in her life.

***

That evening they have dinner at the Daniels. Paul is late from the Prefecture, and they arrive at the house about an hour late in the darkness and cold.

"Maman, it smells so good," Gabrielle calls from the hall downstairs.

"Come in. Come up." Julie's voice reverberates in the stairwell as they mount to the first floor.

"We're late."

"Don't worry, your father hasn't arrived yet." Julie welcomes them with hugs and kisses. "You both look beautiful. In good shape, I'd say. I just get older and fatter regardless of my diet."

"You're not fat, Maman."

"Paul, will you open a wine. At least we can have a drink. It's another vegetable stew. That's all we eat these days. I managed to find some lard. That's what you smell. I also managed to get a fresh baguette. So life is beautiful."

They settle in the salon with wine, everyone exhausted. No one talking.

"So what have you been up to?" Julie looks at them.

"We've been fine. Working hard. Paul was away last weekend in Amélie visiting his grandmother, and Jordi is thinking of another show this spring."

"How is your grandmother?" Julie asks politely.

"The same. Never changes." Paul sips from his glass. "She loves Pétain and the Catholic church. So we don't have much to talk about."

"It must be nice to see her. Gabrielle's grandparents are so distant. We barely hear from them, especially since the occupation."

"Oh, Maman. We rarely heard from them before the occupation."

"I got a postcard from my mother last week."

"What?" Gabrielle looked at her sharply. "What did she say?"

"It seems they're having a hard time. She wasn't more specific. But you know that Paris is getting the worst of the occupation. We can't really do anything, even if she would accept our help."

The door opens below, Gribouille scampers from the bedroom, and Auguste's footsteps can be heard as he mounts the stairs. Gabrielle rises to greet him at the top of the stairs.

"Oh, Papa, I miss you so much." She hugs him strongly.

"I'm always here, my daughter." He looks up at Paul. "How are you, Paul? Working hard, I'm sure." He enters the salon and kisses his wife and Paul, his daughter still hanging on his arm. "Sorry to be late."

"Dinner is ready," Julie says, moving toward the kitchen.

"Everything's a battle these days. You must know that, Paul. Every discussion turns into a contest of whose voice is the loudest. Every issue is seen as a test to prove your point, and show the failure of others' views. One day we may sort it out, God help us, but for now it's a constant muddle. Where's the wine?"

Paul rises to get another glass.

At the table, they eat their stew in silence. Auguste is obviously in a dark mood, eating rapidly, not looking up, concentrating on his thoughts. Julie smiles occasionally, uncomfortably. Gabrielle seems upset and not willing to break the silence. Paul, not being attuned to the family dynamics, hesitates, but feels the need to fill the space.

"I sent a card to Django in care of Jane Stick in Paris. They have been there this fall, playing to large audiences."

"What's Jane Stick," Auguste demands. "And who's Django."

"Sorry," Paul says. "Jordi Pons wants a new spring show, and Georges suggested Django Reinhardt, who is well known and has been very successful in Paris this year. He's a jazz guitarist with a small quintet called the Hot Club. I met him a few times with Charles Trenet, when they got together for a jam-out. Django's a free spirit and moves around constantly.

He's a Gypsy and joins the caravans of his friends and refuses to be held to a schedule."

"Never heard of him."

"Oh, Papa. He's well known and sells plenty of records and is on the radio in Paris, or used to be."

"Anyway, Ninine replied that they were coming to Lyon and Nice, and a week in Perpignan might align with an annual caravan in Argelès in the spring."

"Ninine?"

"That's his Gypsy name. Eugène Vées, a relative of Django. He's also a guitarist with the band."

"You know these people?"

"I've met a few of them. Django has been here, but I don't believe the quintet has played here. He's friendly with Georges Ulmer, a popular singer from the region and friend of Charles."

"Well," Auguste looks up for the first time, "I hope you can pull it together. Jordi owes you. Don't let him take advantage." He paused. "You know, Paul, I've thought a lot about what you told us of the new census. You can't discount anything in this environment. We know the Germans blame the Jews for all their problems. But France is different. Even if we have some well-known anti-Semites, and Vichy is kowtowing to the Occupant, the people will not stand for it, particularly for the deportation of French Jews. I don't see that happening…ever."

"No one is objecting to the 'Jewish laws,'" Gabrielle says disputing her father. "Even as professionals lose their jobs."

"You're right, my daughter," Auguste muses. "This is our country, and it is a nation of laws and tradition. How far Vichy will go to support the Occupant and its own National Revolution is the question. Today, we close our eyes. Given Vichy's orientation and past legislation, we can't assume anything, particularly that they will honor the rights of their citizens."

No one replies.

Paul looks around at his adopted family. A family that has welcomed and accepted him. He hears the scuttlebutt at the Prefecture. He hears the hateful views expressed at some of their meetings; what some believe the government should do. It's a time when people feel free to express their intolerable views and are not discouraged, not even tempered, by their colleagues. He has few illusions of the lengths Vichy might go to in order to forward their cause, even beyond the cause of the Occupant.

"I will hear when the policies of the Pyrénées-Orientales change," Paul offers.

Everyone around the table is silent.

***

When Gabrielle and Paul return to their apartment, it's late. Edith's window is curtained. Paul uses his key. They mount the stairs slowly, not speaking, thinking about the evening, not a happy gathering. It's gotten that way with dinners with the Daniels: too much left unsaid, too much hidden.

Paul opens the door and sees the lights on. They must have left them on since early morning. They enter slowly, hesitantly. The salon is empty. They enter the hallway. All the doors are closed. Their room is dark, and Paul turns on the lamp. Nothing is out of order. He returns to the hallway and knocks on Robert's door. Nothing. He opens it to a dark room. He turns on the overhead, and sees the bed occupied by a fully dressed, bearded individual, who turns groggily to see who turned on the light.

"Robert?"

"Turn off the light. We'll talk tomorrow." He turns back into the bolster. Paul pulls the bedcover over him and recedes from the room.

In their room, Gabrielle is nervously waiting.

"Well?"

"He's here."

She relaxes visibly and sits down on the side of the bed. He sits down next to her and puts his arm around her shoulders.

"What were you thinking?"

"I don't know," she says. "After tonight, I don't know what to think. My father is so disheartened. Even that speech in support of the country he loves. It's not like him."

"He's strong. We'll get through this."

"I don't know what else to do." She feels a pain in her side. Everything seems to be moving in the wrong direction. She can't hear her own heart beating; her eyes cloud over. When will it end?

***

The next morning, Robert is waiting for them at the small kitchen table.

"Bonjour, my friend," Robert rises, giving Paul a bisou.

"Your father was here," Paul says irritably. "He hadn't heard from you in months...and with the holidays on us..."

"I called him last night. I'll try to do better, but it's difficult. There's lots going on. London is finally taking some interest. You'll see. Everything will change in the next few months, or we'll all be arrested or dead."

"That's a positive view," Paul says sarcastically. "I wish there was some way we could stay in contact."

"I'll send a postcard now and then. I'm headed back at the first of the year. I'm on vacation for the while."

"You look terrible. You need a vacation. You can use my razor."

"How are you guys anyway?" he whispers.

"We're fine," Paul says firmly."

"I might have known it. You were always the type, quiet, studious, never rocking the boat. Nothing for years, and then the one and only appears. I've been in the market for an eternity, and what have I got to show for it? Nothing. Not even a date if I wanted one."

"Maybe we can do something about that."

"It's terminal, my friend. Terminal."

Gabrielle comes into the kitchen and kisses Paul and then stops at Robert, looking at him, and finally gives him a bisou on his bearded cheeks. "You're not going to get a woman with that growth."

"Bonjour, Gabrielle."

"Bonjour, Robert." She smiles.

She begins making tea and toasting some of the last pieces of a baguette from several days ago.

"How are you, Robert?" Paul asks.

"Exhausted. Living on the road, never changing, never bathing. Once I washed in the frigid Rhone. Drinking too much, smoking too much. But other than that…"

"What about your sister?"

Robert looks hard at Paul and replies. "She was arrested. They took her to Gurs near Pau in the western Pyrenees. That's all we know."

'We've got a contact now," Gabrielle says. "Nuria. She's working for la Cimade."

"I've heard of them, helping immigrants. Not an ideal job in this climate."

"They have developed contacts in the Vichy-run internment camps. She mentioned Gurs the other day. We might be able to find out more. Will you be available for lunch at noon, Les Nouvelles Galeries?"

"Sure, after a bath and shave, I should be fairly presentable."

"I can't make it," Paul says. "I have a meeting today, and this weekend I'm away for two days."

"When were you going to tell me?" Gabrielle asks.

"I didn't have time last night."

"So…" Gabrielle says, accusing him.

"I just did tell you."

"Thanks."

***

To the delight of the other clerks in the cosmetics department, Robert presented himself, newly shaved and clean, looking like an eligible young man in clean clothing. Even the bags under his eyes were less apparent.

Gabrielle was waiting on a customer, so Robert walked around like the perennial bull in a china shop, eyeing the exotic assembly of different items used for making up women's faces and bodies. The perfumes alone lined an entire wall: myriad products, brands, presentations, and specials, all in different sizes and options. Open jars for testing. Spray bottles. Sets of perfumes, eau de cologne, bath salts, scented creams, and washes. Robert stared at the objects, realizing at that moment what he did not know, would never know, and would never understand: women.

Gabrielle finished with her client and welcomed Robert with a kiss. She then took Robert around, introducing him as the best friend of Paul, making it perfectly clear that she was not cheating. They walked out together to the Palmarium up the street along the canal. The day was one of the gifts of December that frequently occur in Perpignan: a crisp, blue, temperate day with strong sunshine. The girls were waiting at an outdoor table.

Robert had met them briefly at the spring show at the Club les Tréteaux. Gabrielle reintroduced them. In this setting, in the sunlight, they appeared more sophisticated, more attractive, particularly Nuria. Catie was not his type.

"Robert is back from a long business trip in central France," Gabrielle told them. "You may remember him from the show last spring. He's Paul's roommate, and mine I suppose." She laughed. "He's an ideal roommate: never there."

"Not at my own choosing," Robert replied. "And I'm returning soon to Lyon." He waved down a *garçon*, and they all ordered light lunches. When he saw a local red wine on the menu he quickly ordered a bottle. Wines were becoming scarce due to the Occupant's appetite for French wines.

"What do you do?" Nuria said, breaking the current convention of not asking specific questions, only because she knew approximately what he was involved in and wondered what his answer would be.

"I'm a petty administrator of a currently small, but growing service company. My job is boring, and I'm on holiday until the end of the year. Things may get more interesting. Right now, I really prefer hearing what you beautiful ladies are up to."

Nuria told him about la Cimade, and Catie timidly admitted that she clerked in a children's clothing boutique. Gabrielle subtly filled in the missing information that both were available without complications. When the wine and food arrived, the conversation became more animated.

"Gabrielle told me a little about your duties, Nuria," he said. "She thought you might be able to help. My family is going crazy. My sister, Véronique Bardou, was arrested last month, and we have heard nothing from her. We did learn that she was taken to Gurs."

"Where was she arrested?" Nuria asked.

"In Chartres."

"Well, it's surprising, and lucky she wasn't taken to Drancy outside of Paris. It may just be coincidental. One thing is certain, there are no rules. It depends on who makes the arrest, whether German or French and, in either case, the official making the arrest matters: Gestapo, SS, military, Gendarmerie, or local police. I'm guessing, but it sounds like she was not suspected of serious misbehavior or at least a lesser level. Gurs is not fun, but it's better than others, and it's in the unoccupied zone, run by Vichy. Some camps are controlled by the Germans as way-stations for deportees in transit. At Gurs she should be able to write and receive letters. Have you written to her?"

"We only discovered her arrest by word of mouth a few weeks ago and only recently that she was at Gurs. She knows very little, I'm sure," Robert said. "I worry about interrogation and coercion for information."

"Gurs is large, about fifteen thousand internees," Nuria explained. I visited it a few months ago. The largest percentage are Jews, but there are many Spanish republicans still there as well. The Germans doubled its population a year ago by relocating about seven thousand Jews from the Baden region. Mostly women, children, and the elderly. It's overcrowded. Food is meager. There is little plumbing, sanitation, or running water. And there is poor drainage in an area with heavy rainfall. Conditions are terrible, but the inmates are working to improve the camp. Escapes are frequent due to the large number of inmates and few guards. That's just the physical description; the politics and behavior of the inmates is one of the largest dangers."

"Sounds horrible," Robert said.

"There are worse."

"God."

"Robert, I'll see if we can get a report on your sister. Véronique Bardou? She will be suffering, but not in danger, and there are lots of comings and goings."

"Yes. Thanks for anything. I'm shocked. It's one thing to read about it cursorily in the papers. And we know the papers leave out anything that sounds negative. It's entirely different to hear you talk of it. I've got to leave at the end of December, but my father may be able to help things. He would be a good contact for you in any case."

"Let's see what our Intern Reps find out. You'd be surprised at the internal communications at the camps and their ability to know who's there. They have plenty of time on their hands, and they believe in the importance of information on the internees."

"Nuria, I would love to find out more about your job. Maybe we can meet one evening at the apartment with Paul."

"Of course," Nuria said smiling.

"And you too, Catie. I'm sorry we didn't get more time to talk."

"I understand," Catie replied sympathetically, but looking a little shocked by the conversation and her lack of knowledge.

"I'll let you know," Gabrielle said.

"*Garçon*, the bill please. This is my treat," Robert said. "And thanks again."

***

I went to visit my parents a few days before Christmas. In just a few short weeks, the winter temperatures in Perpignan have fallen to historic lows, icing and freezing the streets and jeopardizing the subtropical plants planted throughout the city: palms, bougainvillea, jacaranda, mimosa, and citrus. I bundled up as best I could and walked to my parents' house. Everyone was feeling the effects of the freezing temperature: oil in short supply, coal and charcoal expensive and difficult to obtain, and wood impossible to purchase in town. The winter of 1941-42 was turning out to be one of the coldest on record in normally balmy Perpignan.

The news distributed underground gave a ray of hope. The controlled press made light of the United States' declaration of war on Germany, just as they had done when Japan attacked Pearl Harbor. It seemed to presage that any help from the US would be slow in coming and not significant enough to turn the German tide. Vichy discussed declaring war on the Allies, but failed to come to a decision. Nevertheless, however it was officially portrayed and propagandized, people recognized the US declaration as a positive in a sea of bad news.

The freeze on the Russian plain was worse. The gossip was that the Wehrmacht were bogged down, being unprepared for a long winter fight to take over the country of its former non-aggression partner. "General Winter" once again put a hold on the German advance outside of Moscow. We heard only glowing reports from Vichy, but the BBC and common sense told us that the German army was halted in the east, at least temporarily.

When I arrived, the house was colder inside than outside and deathly silent, and Papa was in his studio painting, dressed as if he were climbing in snow covered mountains. Maman sat in the kitchen, wrapped in an old blanket, looking terrible. She was embarrassed at my unexpected visit and fought to make light of the stressful situation.

"Gabrielle, how good to see you." She smiled vaguely. "It's so cold, the only place I can warm up is in my bed under a ton of blankets. I'm just making some tea. You must be freezing. Where's Paul?"

I nodded yes to the tea. "Paul is off on one of his errands in Amélie. Robert went with him. They'll be back tomorrow."

"Did Robert hear about his sister?"

"Yes, Nuria found her, and she's okay, in good spirits, but the camp is awful. She is expected to be released in the spring, and the family is in communication by post."

"What's happening to our country?" Julie lamented, pouring hot water over what they called "tea."

"The world's gone crazy. Nuria said there are thousands of prisoners in Gurs, and there are many other similar camps in France, and everyone's talking about the German and Polish camps, which the BBC described as widespread butchery, worse than the Mongols. We never hear about the French camps."

"I don't know. I guess we're lucky here, although you really wouldn't know it." She set three cups on the table.

"Auguste," she yelled down the stairs. "Come for tea. Your daughter's here."

They waited hearing the footsteps trudge up the stairs.

"I know she's here," he replied bitterly. He sat down at the table.

All the Clouds

I had never seen my parents in such a state of misery. My mother, always upbeat, only allowing her resources to run down on rare occasions. I can remember a few breakdowns during my childhood, tears, anger, harsh accusations, and recriminations against Papa. They always evaporated by the next morning and only a handful of times, but I do recall them.

"Where's Paul?" he asked.

"He and Robert went to Amélie and will return tomorrow. I can see that you two are struggling and need a vacation or a getaway."

"It's a harsh winter," Auguste said. "The city is shut down. People are hibernating in their homes. There is no fuel. As though God is punishing us. We can only pray for an early spring."

"We're all waiting," Julie said. "Waiting for change. Waiting for something good to happen. Something different. It can't continue like this."

"We thought we would celebrate *Réveillon* at the apartment next Wednesday night," Gabrielle announced. "At least we have a little heat. Would you be interested? Robert will be leaving the next day, and his father will be there and Nuria and Catie. This will be a sad Christmas, but perhaps one of faith, which I guess it's supposed to be."

"Oh, I don't know," Julie said. "Maybe we're not up to it."

"What do you mean. You're not sick."

"No. It's just not a festive year."

"Julie, we would love to come." Auguste corrected her. "It's been hard on us, *ma puce*. There's so much for us to consider."

"Our roots?"

"Yes that, but really our only heritage is French. We had a card from your grandmother Sarah. She said the entire community is in a state of shock. Only the older people understand the depths of anti-Semitism. Paris is under the thumb of the Occupant, and we know they are rabid. But so are many of the French as well. They are led by Charles Maurras' *Action Française* and the Vichy collaborators, such as Rebatet, Brasillach, Laval, and Déat. And just people in the street. It's retribution for the Dreyfus affair and the Third Republic. We just don't know what is going to happen. The beauty and grandeur and legacy of this country are menaced by lying, common squabbles, and demonizing." He shakes his head in disbelief.

***

I left that evening to return to our apartment. I undressed quickly and jumped under the covers. There I spent the night in turmoil never quite falling asleep. I grew up in a welcoming and loving atmosphere, a warm region and a warm people. I learned Catalan from my playmates and never felt different. I felt like I belonged here in Perpignan. My parents were accepted and even revered for contributing to the region: my father, well known, created iconic images of the charm and colors of the Roussillon.

So much has changed in the last year and a half: the defeat, the war, the new government, and now the continuing battle against foreigners, and, what they call, the undesirables: aliens, Communists, Freemasons, and Bolsheviks, even naturalized citizens. And, of course, the Jews were included, inaudibly in most situations, but understood as the worst of the demons. Many saw this as an opening to a better world: a new Europe, united and strong. Still under the thumb of the Germans and their violent racism and disrespect for human rights. Others saw this as the end of much of what France had stood for since the revolution. France the champion of *Liberté, Egalité, et Fraternité.*

I never felt I belonged to any of these groups, but suddenly I have to begin to rethink what I am. How much of me comes from who I believed myself to be and was raised to be. And how much of me is due to my genes and biology, my ancestors, or "my liver, my spleen, and my ovaries," as Louis Darquier de Pellepoix has recently written, a fictitious name of an opportunistic leader of the anti-Semites.

Paul is wonderful and supportive, listening to my family and me, never questioning, never showing the least reservation, but does he know who I am? He seems accommodating, understanding. It's not even been a topic of conversation for us. I think I would die if there were a hint of doubt in him. We've known each other for nearly a year. We allow each other total freedom, and at the same time know we can trust each other. It's not anything we consciously talk about. It's just there.

Is it fair to link his fate with mine? I have never doubted him, and now I include him in my dark and dismal thoughts. We live so much on a day-to-

188

day basis. The future seems remote and hazy. The entire world dares not think of the future.

What's it like to have children? We have talked of that, and he is more open than I am. I'm not ready for children or to give birth to a child. It's something both lovely and terrifying to envision. To me, Paul's attitude is the strongest indication of our love. His willingness to have a child with me. How can you doubt someone who professes to want your children?

People believe I'm Christian, but what would be their reaction if they knew I was Jewish? Even Nuria and Catie were shocked when I told them. Nothing has changed, just a history lesson. Genes and ovaries. Does that change who I am? Does that place Paul even further at risk?

Maybe growing up means coming to terms with the true nature of evil, with people who only care for themselves, willing to sacrifice others and their own values to get ahead. A world of deathly competition and ruthless struggle, sanitized so that nothing is apparent, nothing spoken, only codes that they understand.

No. It's not like that. It must be better. Why have children and grandchildren? Why live? Why struggle? Why dream? Why? For paradise? No, it has to be better. Better. Some end. Joy. Love. Procreation. Humanity. It must be better...

***

On Wednesday afternoon and evening, Christmas Eve 1941, everyone gathers at the apartment on rue de la Gare. Some arrive for a short visit, having to return to their own family celebrations. Others come for hours. Some come for dinner, while others seek the music and party. It's unusual for a celebration that is traditionally reserved for family to be expanded to a large gathering, but then nothing is usual these days.

The freezing weather continues with sleety rain. Outer garments fill the entrance hall in a disorderly heap, leaving a narrow path for the guests. Everyone's there: Robert, Gabrielle and Paul, Robert's father, Gabrielle's parents, Jordi Pons and Josette, Georges Doelnitz and Bernadette, Catie and Nuria, some cast members from the last show at Club les Tréteaux, including the musicians and dancers, and a few uninvited guests.

Gabrielle has been working all day, attempting to assemble a festive dinner party given the lack of available produce and supplies. Fortunately, the guests understandingly bring whatever they have saved beyond their normal sparse diets: lots of alcohol and wine, some quite good, even a few bottles of champagne from the Bardou family, fresh baguettes, cakes and pastries, vegetable casseroles, appetizers, including some fresh oysters, homemade foie gras and pâtés, cooked sausages, dates and chestnuts, and more alcohol. Everyone has saved or worked to make the occasion special.

The windows of the apartment, almost immediately fog up and are carefully cracked opened, but everyone is comfortably warm from the crush of bodies filling the hallway, salon, and kitchen.

"Where can we set up?" one of the band members asks Paul.

"Behind the sofa, against the windows."

They crowd into the small space, the drummer on the outside, a clarinet, a bass, and an accordion. Enough to replay some of the Trenet songs from the last show. To everyone's surprise, Georges Ulmer and Django Reinhardt arrive together, Django with his guitar. Paul knows Georges Ulmer from several functions with Charles, and he rushes to welcome them.

"Georges, thanks for coming."

"I ran into Django last night and invited him when he said that you had been inquiring about a gig here in Perpignan. You've met him before, haven't you?"

"Yes, but it's been a while."

"Django, this is Paul Broussard."

"Happy to meet you, my young friend. I remember you with Charles in '38, no? And I saw you jam last March with Charles. Pretty good." With a tailored suit and tie, a wide brim hat, and a pencil thin mustache, Django's almond eyes sparkle in delight with an aura of sincerity.

"Thanks. I'm out of practice." Paul quickly waves at Jordi and Georges Doelnitz, who had been watching the interaction with interest, recognizing both men.

"Maybe we get you going tonight. You sing like Armstrong. 'Come on down, you do de do da la re pa pa, papa gotta do the Heebie Jeebies.'" By this time, all the guests are listening.

"I want you to meet Jordi Pons," Paul says. "He's the owner of the music hall and would like to have the Hot Club come for a week in the spring. And Georges Doelnitz, the musical producer." Both push through the guests to greet the newcomers. "This is Django Reinhardt. And you know Georges Ulmer."

"Nice to see you both," Georges Doelnitz says, shaking both their hands. "We worked together in Nice."

"You're right," Django says smiling and pointing at Georges. "I remember you. One tough cookie."

"Musicians need some discipline," Georges replies.

"You telling me? Turned out well though, as I recall. Nin-Nin, normally the calm and reserved one, will never forget you, and your rules."

"How is your brother?" Georges asks honestly.

"Wasting his money on broads, gambling, and drink, not in that order, but then that's what we all do."

Georges laughs and introduces both men to Jordi, who has been standing there, not understanding exactly what's going on, and then the four of them move aside for a private conversation.

Gabrielle comes up to Paul.

"So that's Django?"

"Yes, He's amazing. At least his records. And Georges Ulmer is a great singer. He's got a lot of records out as well. I think they're both ahead of us in the drink department though. Are you surviving?"

"I've got help, otherwise I'd be sunk. We're going to have a buffet. It's not proper, but I didn't expect all these people. Have you noticed Robert and Nuria? They seem to be getting along. Catie has been a big help, along with Maman, and Josette and Georges' wife, Bernadette. I love her. Robert's father brought ten bottles of champagne. It's going fast. I've got to move. My dad looks lost. Can you check in?"

"I love you."

"You should," she says, hurrying off toward the kitchen.

The band begins warming up and sounding pretty good for not practicing together for almost a year. The drummer calls for Paul."

"Hey, Paul. Let's go."

"Give me a moment," he waves. "I'm coming."

Paul moves over to Auguste Daniel standing against the wall like a Corinthian column. By the time he reaches him, the band is playing, and conversation is becoming difficult.

"Are you okay?" Paul almost shouts. He leans close to Auguste's ear. "You know people here, don't you?"

"It's not that, Paul. It seems that the area where my parents live in Paris was surrounded a few days ago by German military police and the SS, assisted by Gendarmes, and they began questioning everyone. Looking for foreigners. And they arrested some."

Paul looks at Auguste, who seems in a state of shock.

"Auguste," he says closer to his ear. "Is there some risk to your parents?"

"That's not the issue, Paul. The Germans have made the first move, aided by Vichy. We've seen this before. Our parents are old, to say nothing of their naturalized citizenship and conversion to Catholicism. They're okay. I can't believe what is happening, and yet it's real. I don't mean to be a wet blanket, and we've said nothing to Gabrielle. It's a terrible omen."

"I agree." Paul hears his name called again.

"You go on," Auguste says. "Julie and I will be leaving early, but we'll see you both tomorrow."

"Of course. I'm truly sorry, Auguste." He rushes to the band and joins them in a Trenet song from the show. Without an amplifier his voice joins the music and noise of conversation in the small room. Django and Georges join him after his first song.

Django draws up a chair and begins directing the musicians, all of whom know who he is and are awed by his reputation and obvious talent. This rag-tag group of part-time players realizes they are in the presence of one of the greats, two, counting Georges Ulmer. They begin to straighten up and take their music more seriously. No longer a pickup gig; they're playing for real.

"I have a special song," Django says loudly. "One I'm working on. I call it 'Nuages.'" And he begins playing the straight melody. It's a soft, gentle tune. The guests quiet as they are taken by the sounds coming from the lone guitar. One by one the musicians pick up the tune and begin playing together, giving Django the ability to improvise and play off the main melody. Paul and Georges Ulmer stand aside.

"No lyrics yet," Django mouths, winking.

As though in a rehearsal, they play *"Nuages"* countless times, each time a little better. Then they begin playing standards. Django takes control, just as he does with the Hot Club. There seems to be no song he doesn't know. He begins each with a guitar entry, forcing the players to follow his lead. His upfront improvisations are often difficult to understand: where he expects the band to join him and even what song he's playing, but then he returns to the melody, and the musicians join in. It takes a while for them to catch on to his energy and direction, but Django is supportive and generous, allowing everyone to add to each song in a solo or improvisation, with Georges and Paul singing at times together and alone. Georges sings his hit comic song, *"Quand allons-nous nous marier?"* When are we going to get married? The lyrics ending with "We'll do it another year, my adorable cowboy."

The guests now are casually eating on borrowed plates and utensils, listening to the music, and joining in when they know the lyrics. A few couples are dancing carefully for lack of space. In the small kitchen, Gabrielle, Julie, Josette, Bernadette, and Catie find a moment to relax, pleased to watch the guests enjoying themselves.

"It's getting late, dear," Julie says.

"I couldn't have done it without your help, Maman." Gabrielle hugs her, then Catie, then Josette.

"What a celebration," Catie says. "It figures for a year of goodness."

"I hope so," Julie says. "You stay. I'm going to grab Auguste off the wall and take him home. We'll see you tomorrow." She leaves. Others are beginning to leave as well.

"Where did Nuria go?" Catie asks.

"I haven't seen her."

"And Robert."

"Hmm, you're right. Well…"

"Now I'm jealous of both of you."

Together, they look at the nearly empty table and the mountains of bottles, plates, and utensils, wrapping paper, and empty containers. The kitchen is in total disarray. The entire apartment is filled with the detritus of a joyous celebration, and it continues. Catie looks seriously at the dirty dishes.'

"Don't you dare. That's for tomorrow. Don't even think about it. Let's join the party." Gabrielle takes Catie by the hand, and they join the dancers, repeating some of the dance routines to the delight of the band and other guests. People are sitting on the floor against the walls, smoking their last cigarettes. Others are leaving, struggling to find their coats and politely thanking everyone. Paul is occupied saying goodnight, wanting a chance to work with Django. Everyone is cheerful, slowed down, and there is a feeling of camaraderie and hope. Christmas will be happy this year, regardless. It can't be otherwise.

The celebration continues late into the night. While many celebrants depart, a strong group remains, talking and enjoying the band. The room is clearer, and people are able to dance. The elders have departed: Jordi and Josette, Monsieur Bardou, Georges and Bernadette. The band remains together, grateful to be able to play with Django, who appears to be just beginning the evening, a cigarette in his mouth and a full drinking glass of Cognac next to him. Paul and Georges Ulmer stand on the side, singing when they can.

"Quite a night Monsieur Broussard," Gabrielle joins them. She snuggles up to Paul, and he welcomes her, while focusing on the music. Then she sees Robert and Nuria in the hallway, cozying up. She elbows Paul, and he smiles at her in acknowledgement, without losing the beat.

"Georges and Django have agreed to join our show in April," Paul whispers in her ear. "Jordi declared that it cost him the skin off his butt, but it will be worth it. I'm not sure how much. He was very pleased. And Georges is elated to work with Django."

"I'm going to bed."

"I'll join you, but I can't leave them right now." He kisses her, but his attention is on the band.

In the bedroom, Gabrielle disrobes and settles under the duvet. She has become accustomed to sleeping in the nude, even in the coldest weather. It's a feeling of freedom, and once the sheets warm up it's more comfortable, no more pulling of nightdresses. The buffered sound of the music from the salon echoes, but she is exhausted, feeling good about the evening. The music somehow calms her. The soft refrains of *"Nuages"* continue to be interspersed with standards. She listens. Each instrument interprets the melody and then they play together. She listens as Paul sings a solo and then Georges Ulmer, and then they sing together. The warmth of the evening and the love in her heart shelter her. She cannot bear thoughts of the future, and she dreams one day at a time, one day with Paul, with Robert and Nuria, with Catie. Her parents so disturbed this evening. The guests all welcoming a chance to enjoy a brief moment of happiness among friends. Christmas tomorrow. It's already tomorrow. Mass and then dinner with her parents. When will the weather turn? When will the warming spring winds and the white blooming almond blossoms return? When will the nightmare end?

***

The next morning, I wake early for some reason. I barely heard Paul enter the bedroom at dawn. I managed to fall back asleep. Paul is now fast asleep next to me, and I watch him for a moment. How wonderful to be sleeping next to him, hearing his gentle breathing, touching him in his sleep. A gift.

There is much to clean up, so I put on a nightgown and my heavy robe and make my way into the salon. Amazingly, someone has cleaned up. In the kitchen I surprise Nuria and Robert, sitting at the cleared table talking intimately, drinking our imitation coffee. They are both dressed and appear ready to depart.

"Good morning," Nuria says, smiling slyly.

"Good morning." I know Nuria as well as anyone, and she does not make decisions lightly; at the same time, she never shies at taking what she wants.

"Robert has to leave this morning to get back," she says. "I'm going to walk him to the station. We didn't sleep at all. It was a wonderful party."

I couldn't help myself. "I'm sorry you missed it."

She doesn't miss a beat. "I'm not." And she looks directly at Robert, who acknowledges her expression, agreeing. He seems to be quite smitten.

"Gabrielle, dear roommate, don't be so judgmental," he says lovingly. "Sometimes you have to seize the moment. Nuria is like a warm summer vacation. I love her, and I love you, and I really needed to be here. It's been a balm for my heart." He turns and kisses Nuria on the cheek.

All I can think is, my God, they're in love. What a wonderful thing.

"You needn't have cleaned up."

"We seemed to have a surfeit of energy." She smiles.

"We're heading out to catch the train to Marseille. I am, at least. And Nuria is coming with me to the station. Give Paul a big kiss for me. We heard him singing. We were here, you know."

"I know," I reassure him. "You'll have to get used to female humor."

"That would be my fondest desire." Again his eyes are on Nuria.

They stand, and I give each a bisou and a large hug, especially since both Paul and I know the risks he's taking.

"When will we see you again?" I demand, hearing my mother's voice.

"Probably around Easter. Can't promise anything, but now I have a huge incentive to return to Perpignan for the show." He put his arm around Nuria, and they walk out of the kitchen At the door, Robert turns to blow me a kiss, and then the door closes. I feel the warmth of their meeting, but somehow it's unable to assuage my wakeful doubts about my family and my future.

13

January-February 1942

Darling, I want to hold you
Tighter in our embrace
To feel you against me
And the heat of your body
Enough promises, enough vows
We are in the folly of the moment
We know our oaths of love
Will never last forever.
« *La Java Bleue,* » *Vincent Scotto*

In late January, Paul was summoned to the Prefect's office. He didn't know the Prefect, who had arrived about a year before. They had met briefly, had shaken hands, and had passed in the halls and foyer without greeting. The coldest winter on record continued into the spring, but the day was clear and sunny. The Prefect's office was on the second floor with a wide view on the Têt canal, the commercial zone, and the frosted mountains in the distance. Before he could sit down to wait, Agnes, the secretary signaled him to enter the office without regarding him. He knocked and then entered the large, naturally illuminated room.

"Monsieur *le Préfet,* bonjour," he greeted the Prefect. Then he noticed Franco Plana sitting comfortably on a couch to the side in a small conversation area.

"Monsieur Broussard, welcome. We've met on several occasions, and Franco has spoken highly of you. Please sit down." He indicated the conversation area on the side of the room. Paul shook hands with Franco and sat down on the other end of the couch. The Prefect, a tall man, thin and nervous, light-complexioned, was definitely not a local. He came over and sat opposite them in an overstuffed chair, sitting bolt upright. "Would you like something to drink?"

"No thank you, Monsieur. I just had breakfast."

Paul looked at these two men, both in their fifties, graying hair and easy assurance. One he knew well and trusted. The other was an appointee of Vichy, and Paul had no idea of the man. The previous Prefect had been

197

appointed by the Third Republic administration of the Ministry of the Interior prior to the fall of the government. Monsieur Bonville, the new Prefect, a native of the Savoie and a career administrator, had served in several other Prefectures in increasingly responsible posts. Paul knew that he was a "company man" and a politician of the first order.

There was a pause for a moment. Both Paul and Franco waited for the Prefect to commence.

"How long have you worked here, Paul? Since before the war?"

"I was hired in a competition just before the war. I worked for a notary after graduation from school."

"I see. Our function, as you know, is to implement the desires of the state. We do not set policy. We do not create regulations. We implement them. Obviously, just as in everything, there are gray areas where we must make judgments, or areas of informed decision-making, but always with the view of our nation as interpreted by the Minister of the Interior. We are not free to interpret the law based on what we think is right or wrong." He stopped for a moment, rubbing his hands.

Paul knew where this was going. It had a thoroughly familiar cadence. He was fairly sure it was not about his extra-curricular activities. It was only about his work here. He knew he had pushed the boundaries in providing help to some people. Franco knew it as well and had warned him, although continuing to aid him at times. Since his conversation with Franco, he had tried to be more circumspect, and Franco had helped him by signing the papers. The one thought in his head was that he didn't want to implicate Franco.

"It's come to our attention, and the attention of others, that you have been, shall we say, overzealous in your assistance in certain cases. Now, I am the last person not to realize that we are a bastion for needy people. But our job, again, is to defend the state. When Marshal Pétain says that foreign nationals must be returned to their country of origin, then I work in that direction. As an administrator, I cannot take into account what the actions of other countries will be.

"I will give you one example. An older couple is seeking a French exit visa when they have ignored the rules of their own country and entered our country illegally. They are sought by their own country. Do we disregard the laws of their national origin? Do I ignore both their national laws and the laws of our country to some higher power or morality?

"You are a young man with a fine future ahead of you. As I understand it, you were number one of the new interns the year you were hired. And you have done well. This meeting is simply to inform you that others have become aware of your more liberal activities. Perhaps you can maintain a lower profile, but we all must function appropriately in an environment within my direct control. If this were left entirely to me, I might give you a warning. It is not, I'm sorry to say. You would not be the first agent arrested from a Prefecture. I hope you will take this very seriously. How do you feel, Franco?"

"I agree with you, Monsieur." Franco looked down at his hands uncomfortably.

Paul replied quickly. "I take this very seriously, Monsieur." He was somewhat at a loss to understand the unspoken part of the message, or at least the reason behind the message. Where was it coming from? Who knew anything about his activities? No one. That was certain. He thought perhaps it might have to do more with his extra-curricular activities than he at first suspected. Someone must have informed, a disgruntled former colleague or a current employee. Possibly someone he didn't even know.

The Prefect stood, as did Franco and Paul.

"Thank you, gentlemen."

They left the office together and slowly walked down the stairs. At the first floor, Franco kept walking down the stairs instead of going to his office.

"Let's take a little walk," he suggested.

They exited the Prefecture and crossed the street. It was cold and neither one had an overcoat, but the sun was shining. They walked along the canal without talking for a while, then Franco turned to him.

"I think you know exactly where I am coming from," he said. "I'm proud of you, but his message was clear. Monsieur Bonville is a politician, and his job depends on Vichy. We are a little more free, but still we have to remember who we work for. There are plenty of people using Vichy as a way to enhance their careers, as a way of getting back at people they dislike or are in competition with, and as a tool to push their own beliefs. It's a time of reprisals. Political power can be a terrible weapon. The French excel at that."

They stopped and sat down on a bench with a view of the mountains. Franco lit a cigarette, and offered one to Paul. He took it and lit up. For a moment they watched people passing, going or coming from appointments, taking early lunch, shopping, or just out for a promenade after several rainy days.

"In his example of an older couple," Paul said, "what if their country of origin intends to incarcerate them for no reason other than who they are? What if their laws are racist or immoral?"

"You know the answer."

"I guess I'm in the wrong business."

"No. It's just the wrong time." He looked at Paul seriously. "You're not married, are you?"

"No."

"You've got a girlfriend?"

"Yes."

"You planning?"

"No."

"But you're serious."

"Yes. We've been together for some time. Gabrielle Daniel, daughter of Auguste."

"I see. Who's Auguste?"

"The painter."

"Sorry. I don't get out much. I just wanted to understand your living situation."

"You think I should resign?" Paul spoke somewhere between a question and a statement of fact.

"I warned you six months ago, but now the Prefect is warning you as well. Someone has identified you. Who exactly I don't know, but it really doesn't matter." He paused. "Paul, you're as smart as anyone in the Prefecture, but it's a place where politics trump performance. I will help your career anyway I can. But right now, it's time to make a tactical retreat without retribution or ruin to your reputation."

"I understand," Paul said thoughtfully. "It's something I had not really contemplated. Of course it's always at the back of your head. You have always treated me with respect. Thank you."

"You won't get rid of me that easily. I think we share many of the same values. I tried to support you and protect you, but others believe the lies we hear and see daily from Vichy…believe it or not. It's time, before something more serious happens. And then you wouldn't have any recourse. Besides, you can be more useful elsewhere. I have a contact, and I recommended you to him. He's someone you can trust, and I say that knowing you can't trust many people today. At least you can trust him at this moment in time, if you want to continue working for what you believe in." He handed Paul a name and address handwritten on a scrap of paper: Louis, 85 rue Jeanne d'Arc. "Tell him 'all the clouds have lowered upon our house.' And believe me, this will not continue indefinitely." It was not entirely clear what he was referring to: the Prefect, the war, Vichy, Europe, the world.

They stood up and walked back to the Prefecture together. As they entered the building, Franco said: "Let me know what you decide in the next few days. If you want, we could move you out of harm's way, but it would be a backward career move. You can leave now, and when things change…"

"Merci, Monsieur."

***

After work, I walk across the river to Les Nouvelles Galeries, wondering how to approach this topic with Gabrielle. She tends to worry. I worry, but not in the same way. All my life I have lived among raging mountains and cold tramontane winds. I have always survived. I'm not one to ruminate or to have periods of great darkness. I have learned to regulate my life: like sailing, keeping an even keel, trimming to the changing winds, always ready to furl the mainsail. I have difficulty trusting others. This was one of the reasons I was so slow in becoming involved with Gabrielle. You can lose with impunity what you don't commit to. That's all changed. I'm now in deep emotional debt to her, exposed, you might say, with all my heart.

Leaving my job at the Prefecture will not have an immediate impact on our finances. I have saved a large part of my salary for the last two years. The apartment shared with Robert in his father's building has been a boon to my savings, since neither of us pays rent. Although Gabrielle's earnings are meager, it would be enough to survive on a daily basis. And right now that's all you need. I guess one question is what would I do with my time. The contact Franco gave me is certainly a Resistance member, possibly a serious one, not just a publisher of anti-Vichy tracts, but an active participant in aiding the Free French, possibly a military wing.

During the holidays, Robert confessed what we all knew: he is active in a small Resistance group in Lyons. His chief is named Joseph Mercier, *nom de guerre*, who recently returned from London with the assignment from de Gaulle of unifying the diverse Resistance groups throughout France. His assignment would be in the cross-hairs of the Occupant. Am I ready for this kind of commitment and risk?

I arrive at the Galeries early. Gabrielle is helping a well-dressed woman, so I stand around waiting, surveying the amazing array of cosmetics.

"Paul?"

I turn around and see a young woman I recognize vaguely but cannot place.

"Bonjour," I reply.

"I'm Isabelle Lefèvre," she says. She's attractive, small, blond hair, well made up, and a fresh open smile as though I should know who she is. "I'm a friend of Gabrielle."

"Oh, well I'm waiting for her." I still have no idea who this person is.

"I know. I see you here often."

"Do you work here?"

"Silly. You really don't remember me. I went to school with Gabrielle, and we met at the show with Mireille Printemps."

"I'm sorry. Of course," but I only vaguely recognize her.

"It's okay. You're still at the Prefecture?" she asks smiling.

"Yes." It's curious she knows this.

"I'm friends with Julien."

"Julien?"

"Oh. You know, Julien Bonville."

"*Ah Oui*. The Prefect."

"Yes. He's a family friend."

"I see," wanting to terminate this unsettling dialogue. Gabrielle arrives.

"Bonjour, Isa. How are you?"

"I'm good. Just browsing. It's pretty expensive. You look good, Gaby."

"Thanks, Isa, but we have to be going. Nice to see you." She grabs my arm firmly. We turn to leave.

"Gabrielle. You don't fool me."

"What?" Gabrielle turns and assaults her with her eyes.

"You know," Isabelle says with assurance.

"I have no idea."

"You may have a pretty boyfriend, but that doesn't change anything."

"Go to hell."

"I will, but not before you."

"God, Isabelle. Get a life."

We quickly leave into the fresh cold air, bundling up.

"What was that?"

"I'm not sure. She was a friend in school. Never a close one. One of the popular girls who never cared for us. Now she's taken a personal dislike of me. Her politics have veered to the right. Her father's at the Prefecture: Monsieur Lefèvre?"

"I don't know him. What section?"

"Something to do with the police."

"Ah. I rarely deal with that side. A close friend of the Prefect. No wonder. Not surprising her politics are to the right. By the way, let's stop for dinner. I have some ration tickets about to expire."

"What's the occasion?"

"We need to talk."

She glances at him nervously.

We stop at one of our regular restaurants, frequented mostly by retirees from the surrounding apartment buildings and pensions. The best thing about it is the price and fresh fries. If you're a good customer, Madame Porras will give you a second helping. The rest of the food is ordinary.

The atmosphere is subdued, limited lighting, heating to a minimum, no music, and low voices. Madame Porras welcomes us and gives us a good table in the back near the kitchen where it's warmer. The menu of the day: choice of vegetable pâté, deep fried cauliflower, cut blood sausage, or vegetable soup, followed by a ragout of pork, very lightly influenced by meat or meat stock, and choice of dessert, petit-suisse or eggless caramel custard, and a quarter carafe of red or white wine. We take off our coats and relax for a moment. It's always amazing how good Gabrielle looks at the end of a work day. She looks at me, knowing that something is up. I wait until the first course is served.

"I had a discussion with the Prefect today. First time I've ever spoken to him." I lowered my voice to ensure we were not overheard. "He indicated that someone identified me as too free with visas. Probably someone from inside the Prefecture. He didn't discharge me, but he wants me gone. Franco was more to the point. He said it was time." I looked at the surprise on her face.

"You're going to leave?" she said, looking upset.

"I don't have a choice. It's either that or eventually be arrested." I watch her closely, as the news sinks in and questions come to her mind.

"But...what will you do?"

"I'm not sure. We'll have to see. We have the show coming up, so that will occupy my time for a while. Georges is giving me more responsibility, and I will be paid. I have no idea how much? Most likely, it won't be much. It gives me time to think about the future. I've been working for more than three years since graduation. I may want to think about returning to working for a notary or even eventually becoming a lawyer. "What do you think?"

"What about singing?"

"Charles offered to sponsor me in Paris. But that's crazy."

"It's not. I think you could do it. It's not the best time, of course. You could also talk to Robert's father."

"Robert's father? He's a commercial property owner." I think about it for a moment. "That's an idea. Let's give it time to sink in. I'll submit my resignation at the Prefecture. Franco will continue to support me and remains a friend I can trust."

"Paul, you can do anything you set your mind to. My father may have some ideas."

"He's got his own problems."

"You mean the names on the list?"

"No, more than that." I have been thinking about this, but never expressed it.

"What, then?"

"I think your father may be involved in the Resistance."

"Really? I don't know..." She pauses considering it. "He's been so different lately. And he goes off to these meetings almost every evening and never says anything about them. God, it's so impossible. Let's go home."

"What about dessert?"

"I just want to be with you," she says firmly.

My heart is overflowing. I have never felt such love and respect for anyone as I feel for this uncompromisingly strong woman. We leave the restaurant and walk in the cold air to the apartment, our coats tightly wrapped and our arms around each other. With her love and support I can do anything. It feels like our bond is too strong for anyone ever to hurt us; I can suffer anything as long as I have her.

***

Louis at 85 rue Jeanne d'Arc turned out to be quite different from any other figure Paul had met in the Resistance. He was open and friendly. Short and heavy-set, gruff, with calves as thick as giant sausages, probably rugby, and a strong, intelligent face, with unruly eyebrows. He immediately impressed Paul with his strength of character, his honesty, and his no-nonsense attitude, but above all his warmth. Somewhere in his fifties, he had the movement and vitality of a younger man. After a bone-cracking handshake, he pulled Paul into a dark apartment, sparsely furnished, unkempt, with packing boxes lining the walls. In the kitchen, which was more a bar than a kitchen and certainly never functioned for cooking, he rinsed two water glasses and topped them with red wine.

"Sit," he ordered, pulling two chairs up to the round table, overflowing with papers, surrounded with opened cases of wine, booze, tins of food, cartons of foodstuffs, and many unopened crates.

His first reaction was that he could trust this man, although he realized that working for him could expose him to the armed side of the Resistance. A further ratcheting of the danger involved.

"I know you, Paul." He spoke fluent French with a heavy Spanish accent: another refugee from the Spanish Civil War.

"How's that?"

"It's my job. I know most of the things going on in this town. I know you are one of the top passeurs in the region through contacts in the network. I know Franco Plana well. I fought with him in the Civil War. He worked for Vicente Rojo Lluch, and at the end was promoted to colonel. About as bright as they come. And also I know the Prefecture. Franco said you were the right person. Already involved helping others. I checked on it. When he recommends someone, I know I have found a valuable asset."

Paul was shocked. "What kind of job?"

"You leave that to me," he laughed. "I know who you are. A singer. An administrator. A person who knows right from wrong. Self-contained. Confident, yet not arrogant. I'm not talking about sabotage and executions. I'm talking about handling an assignment needing confidence and people skills. Doing your job, and keeping your mouth shut."

Paul swallowed deeply, his mind reeling. What had he gotten himself into?

"We need someone with a familiarity of the border crossings. We want to set up a secure system to move aviators out of France, to return them to England by truck. Not by hiking. We'll supply the truck and set you up in business. Know anything about charcoal?"

Paul shrugged shoulders. "We have a steam heater...when it functions."

"Well, you'll learn. It's the best source we have these days for heating, cooking, and vehicles. It's in strong demand, and supplies are limited. How's your Spanish?

"Conversational."

"Okay. That's great. You know Céret and Amélie-les-Bains, the Vallespir, and the mountain passes. Are you interested?"

"I haven't the faintest idea."

He laughed. "Good answer."

"Is it dangerous?"

"Probably…somewhat more that your passeur activities. If caught, you could be in a host of problems. I don't want to underestimate the risks, but today, if we believe in what we are doing, we all accept these risks. If you do it right, I think the risks are reasonable. Here's the deal…"

And he began to explain in detail the operation. Paul listened until his mind felt like a sieve. Louis noticed and postponed further discussion. Paul left in a haze. It would take a few days to digest all the information: working for the Resistance, the risks involved, and the assignment itself.

After a light supper that evening, he sat with Gabrielle and described the conversation.

"Is it dangerous?" she asked.

"I don't know."

***

In February, Paul left the Prefecture. He said his adieux to the few people who meant something to him and left without fanfare: no celebration, no announcement, no severance compensation. He had been one of the bright young men selected prior to the fall of the Third Republic. After his departure, of the four selected by examination, only one remained. He remained in the police section and his politics were in line with the Vichy government. Paul left feeling good about his experience there, and somehow he felt his dismissal did not detract from what he had gained. As his first working experience in a collegial environment, he had not been prepared for the politics, the infighting, the vague performance measurements, and the competitive atmosphere. He had survived, but had not excelled. He had learned that whom he knew was more important than his contribution or commitment, that his ability to please his superiors at all levels was more important than getting on with his colleagues. He had entered as an innocent without any experience, and he left with a knowledge of the system and how to get ahead. He doubted he would ever seek such a work environment again. A singing career seemed easy by comparison.

His one disappointment was that his activities in supporting the resistance via the prefecture were immediately curtailed.

***

He took no time off. He spent a week talking with Louis at the apartment in Perpignan. He arrived each morning to discuss the job, but also everything else that came up. He related his entire life to Louis: his boyhood, his family, his schooling, his work, his singing, and his love for Gabrielle. In return, Louis, against all protocol of the Resistance, introduced himself as Francisco Giner Macias, nicknamed Paco, from a Catalan family. He had earned a post as an instructor of Spanish literature at the University of Barcelona, specializing in Baroque literature of the seventeenth century. He had been active in the Second Spanish Republic before the coup and had supported the Republicans against the Nationalists before joining the *Retirada* and fleeing for his life into France. Through academic contacts in France, he had been offered a teaching position at the University of Perpignan. He believed strongly, like many of the Spanish refugees in France, that if he supported the Free French in ridding the country of the Occupant and establishing a government based on the true ideals of France, then France would in turn support the ouster of Franco from Spain. Married twice, he freely admitted his failure with women and was currently, adamantly unattached.

***

The day dawns dark and cold. They drive the short distance to Ceret where the charcoal operation is centered. Over the last week, Paul has gotten to know Paco Macias. He trusts him and feels he will support him if any difficulties arise. He has no idea of the connections in the organization above Paco or how he fits into the order, whether high or low. He assumes high. The job is clearly defined and limited to the practical aspects, exactly the way Paco described.

They drive a few kilometers outside of Ceret on the road to Amélie. These are the roads of his childhood, on foot and on bicycle. He thought he knew every street and byway, but he's surprised when they turn off into a large parking area filled with vehicles of all kinds. A warehouse is in the rear. On one side of the warehouse, trucks, wagons, and carts are being filled from a massive charcoal pile. On the other side, large trucks are being emptied of their charcoal loads, building another mound. Every centimeter of the ground is layered with a thick coating of black dust. Everyone working around the charcoal is covered with dust. The drivers stand back talking or watching the men shovel the charcoal into the truck beds. The workers shoveling are totally black. Even in the cool weather, the sweat lines on their faces give them the look of other worldly beings. The yard is surrounded by high trees, but the clean, snow-covered heights of Canigou can be seen above this dark, shadowy underworld.

"Here we are," Paco says pulling up to an office at the side of the warehouse. He parks but remains in the car a moment.

"Remember, the operators here know nothing of our business. They may suspect, but they don't ask. We do our job of delivering coal. With the occupation and the increasing demand for charcoal, they need all the haulers they can get. You are an independent driver. You follow our orders, and they pay you by the load. Come on, let's meet the boss."

They enter the office.

"Good morning, Lucien," Paco leads the way, shaking hands with a short, square man, who quickly rises from his desk behind a counter. "Let me introduce you to Marco. He's the young man I told you about. He's from the region and is comfortable in Spanish." They shake hands.

"Where you from?" Lucien asks.

"I was raised in Amélie and lived there until I was twelve and left for school. I used to ride my bike past here on my way to Ceret, but I never saw this warehouse."

"It's new. When the Occupant cut the supply of oil and gas, we had to do something. Now charcoal runs our cars, heats our homes, cooks our food. The French are lazy bastards. It's the Spanish who produce the charcoal. We can sell all we get our hands on. We pay by the load. Simple as that. If you bring a good load, we pay. You got contacts in Spain?"

Paul looks to Paco to answer.

209

"We've got three mills and more coming on line," Paco replied. "I'm just giving Marco a tour of the operation. He'll work with one of our drivers for a while and then haul on his own."

"Well, as I said, you're welcome. We're open all day, every day. Just bring it in. How many haulers you got now, Paco?"

"Hard to say, Lucien. They come and go."

"Whatever you say. Good luck to you, kid. I'll look for you."

"Thanks."

Back out in the yard, Paco's car is turning dark like all the others. "You got time to visit Spain?"

"Sure."

"Okay, let's see the other side of the operation." They begin driving up the highway toward the border.

"Once you get to know the people, the business is easy. It's at that point that we complicate your life."

Paul knows exactly what he means.

They drive up the highway into the Pyrenees toward Spain and arrive at the border crossing about thirty minutes later after passing through Prats-de-Mollo, the last French town on the highway. It's cold, the hills and roadside are scattered with snow, but snow on the road has melted off. Very few cars are passing in either direction. Paco stops the car at the Col d'Ares, the French border crossing, where two soldiers and a policeman are stationed.

"Bonjour, Messieurs," the policeman says. "Your papers, *s'il vous plaît*."

They offer their French identification papers and passports.

He looks at the papers and then bends down to look at each of them and inside the car.

"The purpose of your visit?"

"We have business near Beget."

The policeman returns the papers. "How long today, Monsieur Macias?"

"Not long just showing a new driver the ropes. A few hours. You'll be seeing him often."

"*Très bien*." He signals for them to continue.

A little farther into Spain along the road is the Spanish crossing, with two Spanish border guards out front of a small station. They recognize Paco and allow him to continue without question, waving him through. They turn off after a few kilometers onto a rural path into a forested area. They come to a cleared level area and stop. Before them are three high completed mounds and a fourth under construction. They get out, and a workman comes over to the car.

"*Benvingut, Senyor* Macias. Welcome. I heard you coming." He's an older man, balding with a growth of beard and narrow eyes, dressed in filthy clothes and sandals.

"*Hola, com estàs*, Alberto? This is a new driver, who will be helping out. Paul." They shake hands. "He'll be working with Eric for a while and then driving on his own."

"Welcome."

"How are things coming?" Paco asks.

"We have four kilns close to finished. One we lit this evening." He looks over at Paul. "You ever seen charcoal fabricated before?"

"Never."

"Well, it's a delicate process. If you're not careful, you get ashes. Let's walk over to the mound we are currently building." They pass three completed mounds, which look like large burial out-croppings from the earth. Farther along the plateau, they come to a mound in process. Two men are placing cut logs vertically in a circle. The ground has been totally cleared.

"We build what you call *meules*, high mounds of wood." Alberto explains. "We construct a chimney in the center and surround it with dry logs. Sometimes the logs are green, but that's not so good for combustion. Then a log floor. Then the process of slabbing. The large logs are arranged vertically in the center, with smaller ones around the edge. It's about twenty meters in diameter and ten meters high. Once all the logs are slabbed, we cover the entire structure with a thick layer of grassy soil and moss to seal the pile from air and keep the cover from falling in. The cover is earth with plenty of sand...not flammable. We have good soil here that serves us well.

"Once completed, we leave the *meule* to dry a few days and then light it from the bottom. The whole idea is a controlled burn so that it turns the wood into charcoal without burning it altogether. About fifty percent of the wood remains as charcoal, if we do it right. Once lit, the kiln must be watched day and night, about five days in total. The amount and color of the smoke from the chimney tells everything: how the combustion is proceeding, if the temperature is too hot, or if it's burning, or if there are cold spots. You adjust by plugging holes or making holes as the wood is slowly consumed inwardly and upwardly, until it is completely combusted. It takes about two days to cool. Then we can load your truck.

"It's not a job for the French, though. The Spanish have been doing it for centuries, and we are hard workers. We move from forest to forest. It's hard work, but we know how to do it."

"Marco will be assisting Eric, and then he'll have his own truck, so you can plan on more production."

"Okay, boss. You can depend on us."

"I know, Alberto."

They walk back to the car and begin the trip back to Perpignan.

"We plan on two or three trips per week," Paco explains. "That way you get to know the border guards and the workers. This has to be as normal as possible, so everyone knows you, sees you a couple times a week, and assumes what you're up to. Gets so used to you that they don't want to see your face. Then you can begin to earn your keep."

***

"I'm frightened," Gabrielle says quietly with an immense sigh. "I'm so tired of all this. All these changes."

Paul takes her hand from across the table and doesn't reply. He can't. Gabrielle has changed since he started his new job. She feels trapped in a succession of events they cannot control. Paul is more sanguine and relaxed, more adaptable, but nervous.

January and February have been the coldest on record, and only recently have hints of spring appeared: sunny days interspersed with cold rains and snow flurries. They are in the Café Deixonne huddled side by side at a back table.

"You are always away and return exhausted late in the evenings. I hate my job. It's beyond boring, and it's difficult dealing with all the people.

212

Lately, Nuria is away traveling, and Catie is so tedious, we practically never see each other any more. My mother tries to be cheerful, but she's terrified for my father, whom I rarely see. He's out during the day and doesn't return until late at night, and he's not painting, so Gribouille just mopes about the house."

"Gabrielle, I cannot..."

"I know. I know. I'm not complaining. It's not your fault. I just wonder what is becoming of us."

"I'm earning more than before, and I'm learning skills I never knew I possessed."

"What about us? We're like an old married couple. Never doing anything interesting or different. Never going anywhere, and our diet is terrible. My mom gives us vegetables and fruits, but we never have time to shop." She pauses. "I guess I'm just tired. I know it's nothing you can change. I can't seem to warm up. The war. The demands of Vichy. The hopelessness. Even the news from the BBC is horrible and depressing and much of it unbelievable.

"Let's go home," he says.

"That's not going to make anything better."

"I've got lots of charcoal now. We can light up the brazier and have some prune eau de vie your mother gave us. Tomorrow's a free day. I don't have to be anywhere. We could go for a drive."

"I hate that truck. It's so noisy and uncomfortable and big. And talk about cold. You're always fiddling with this or that to keep it going or to get it going."

"I can't help that."

"I know. It's just the clouds never seems to lighten." She stands up quickly.

Outside the cold air shocks them. They button up their heavy coats and pull their scarves about their necks and their hats down over their heads. He takes her arm, and they walk closely together.

"We could stop by my parents house. It's on the way, and it's not too late."

"If you want. Should we just drop in?"

"Please."

"Okay."

The Daniels are in and are surprised and pleased to see their daughter and her fiancé. Upstairs the brazier is going slowly, and they settle on the couch with Auguste in his chair.

"How's the new job?" Auguste asks, after producing four glasses of wine.

"I'm getting used to it. It's much more physical than the Prefecture, but it's also more interesting. Nothing is routine. Getting to know lots of people, out in the fresh air, and I love driving my truck."

"What is it exactly you're doing," Julie asks innocently. Auguste looks at her skeptically.

"Oh, just delivering charcoal from Spain to a warehouse in Ceret, where people buy it for resale. It's a big business. The warehouse manager says he could sell twice as much charcoal, but supplies are limited. They're cutting thousands of cords of wood in Spain, maybe millions, all aimed at the charcoal market in France. It's being used more and more."

"And who's your boss?" Julie continues.

"A Spanish Republican, who was a professor at the university here. I believe he knows you, Auguste."

"I know him. He's a good man, without doubt. Now Julie, leave the poor boy alone to enjoy his wine."

For a while they sit in silence, enjoying the warm fire.

"Maybe you should start burning charcoal," Paul suggests. "It's a great heat producer. I'll bring you a sack. I'm already an enthusiast."

"I have my source of dried oak and vine clippings. It's fine. My problem is the studio: no fireplace or way to heat the room. It's colder there than outdoors. I can't work, even if I had the time."

"Oh, Gabrielle," Julie says. "We got a note from my mother. The Occupant has arrested many of the foreigners in the area and continues to make life miserable for the residents. Everyone is a suspect. Many have left the community, moved to the countryside, and more have sent their children away. Auguste's parents haven't written in ages. We're lucky living apart from all that."

Gabrielle says nothing.

"I'm having an exhibition in June," Auguste adds.

"That's great," Paul says. "We're having another show sometime in April/May with Django Reinhardt. He'll be here for a gathering in Argelès, but to get him to set an exact date is nearly impossible."

"Georges Doelnitz asked me to come up with an advertising poster. I've been thinking about it. Since I've never seen the man, I'm sort of stumped."

"Robert has a couple of his albums I could loan to you."

"Thanks. Georges loaned me a few. Most people know who he is, but have never seen him."

Gabrielle and Paul return to their cold apartment. Gabrielle barely talked at her parents' house, even when her mother described her grandparents' trials in Paris, and she continues to be uncommunicative. It's just the winter blues and the common despondency over the war. Paul feels a little better from the familial atmosphere and the wine, and the warmth.

***

I'm delighted with the light Renault flatbed truck, enclosed with a canvas cover and surrounding rails. It's relatively new, having been built in 1936 and converted to the latest gasogene system burning charcoal in 1941. The spare tire in the rear was removed, and a gasogene unit built into the tire well. A tool compartment has been retrofitted on the right side above the unused gas tank. I park the truck behind the apartment building. Normally, it takes about fifteen minutes to get the combustion chamber heated enough to throw off gas at the proper temperature for the engine to ignite. This morning for some reason it takes longer. One load of charcoal in the burner lasts about 100 kilometers before refill. That's more than enough for a trip to the charcoal production site, where the fire box can cool and then be refilled for the return trip.

The weather changed in late February. The freezing temperatures have been fewer, alternating with days of warming sunlight. I'm dressed in my worker's costume, as I call it, supplied by Paco, well-used, but my size for the most part. Dark heavy dungarees with suspenders over a heavy shirt, a vest, wool scarf, heavy indigo chore coat, an eight-sided soft cap, and black leather boots. I was lucky to find real boots in my size. Both leather and rubber supplies are entirely taken by the Occupant.

I love the drive into the mountains through the Vallespir. The roads are dry and the sky blue; winter's warriors are being defeated. I pass my grandmother's house in Amélie-les-Bains. I remind myself to visit her, since it's been several months since I last saw her, not that she notices, or complains.

I arrive at the border mid-morning with snow dotting the passage. The French border police now recognize me and wave me through without stopping, having become accustomed to my double passage two or three times a week. The Spanish guards stop me, but after a cursory view of my papers and empty bed, they signal me through. I arrive at the mountain clearing a few minutes later. It takes a few hours to fill the bed. Alberto comes forward to welcome me and climbs into the truck with me.

"*Hola, amigo.* A good day, no?" We shake hands.

"Bonjour, Alberto. How's it going?" Always dressed in filthy clothes and smelling of wood smoke, due to the shepherding of the fires day and night; he is remarkably nimble for his years. We've become friends when he learned that my father's Spanish and my grandmother Catalan and I speak Catalan.

"Everything is great." They are slowly moving new mounds along the ridge line, keeping as close as possible to the wood supply, while allowing access to the trucks. "The completed kiln is up the road, a little rough for this truck, but you can make it. We're doing a lot of cutting and stacking. We're nearly out of dry wood, so pickups will slow over the next two months. With a good sun, we should be back in business soon."

We drive slowly through the woods past old sites returned to the earth. The workers are careful to replace the soil, and the ashes from the kilns are a good additive and soon disappear with the rain and snow. I see a mound ahead opened to reveal the carbonized wood, ready to be loaded.

"Back up there," Alberto points to a step-down, making loading easier for the workers, three of whom are standing about waiting with their wide shovels.

I maneuver the truck as closely as possible into the space and turn off the motor. Jumping down, I switch the gas exhaust valve to the exterior and close down the fire box.

"Come, Marco. Let's get something to eat."

We walk down the hillside to a tented area, where a table and benches have been set up. On the side, two enormous work horses are loosely harnessed to a giant wagon piled high with chopped wood. Beautiful, giant beasts with heavy manes and uncut fetlocks, they look up at our approach and then return to grazing peacefully. Alberto pours two large glasses of wine, and I sit down opposite him.

"How are you doing?" he asks.

"With the cold weather, everything is more difficult. It must be hard living here in the mountains during the winter."

"What can you do? The war can't last forever. I'll soon be back at work in the valley."

"What do you do in normal times?"

"Like everyone else, I have a small vineyard, not enough to live on, though I should be able to get a larger one when this ends. I teach school. You know, small kids. My wife too is a teacher. The Civil War changed everything. It's harder now for the small guy. You know what I mean. What about yourself? You married? I got three kids and a fat wife. Loves to eat, but warm at night. You know what I mean." He talks while cutting sausage and bread.

"I worked for the government, but now I only have this job. My girl friend works in Perpignan in a large department store."

"You work for *Senyor* Macias?"

"He manages the business. I'm just a driver."

"He's a big man." Alberto pushes the cut sausages and bread to the center of the table, along with a large unwrapped cheese. "Drink and eat." He leans over to me and whispers confidentially. "You know he was an officer in the Republican army."

"He was a teacher before that."

"Yes, but a big man, you know. He's going to save all of us." He winks with his knife in the air, a piece of sausage on the end.

217

"I hope you're right, Alberto."

"I know I'm right. What else you do?"

"I sing a little."

"Sing? Everyone sings. How you mean?"

"I sing with a band in concerts."

"You mean like Raquel Meller? La Violetera." He begins singing a popular Spanish song, which we never hear in France.

"I don't know her."

"Never mind. What do you sing?"

"Popular songs. French songs.

"Oh. Maybe you sing for us."

"There will be a concert in May in Perpignan."

"They put me in jail. And if I sing in Catalan, Franco put me in jail."

Two workers join them for lunch. They are totally black, except for slightly washed faces and hands.

"All finished?" Alberto asks the men.

"No problem."

"Thanks for lunch."

"It's okay. We have another load for you next week. Okay?"

"Yes, thanks," and then to the workers, "*Bon profit*. See you, Alberto."

"*Adéu*."

I have no idea of the payment to Alberto and his men. Paco takes care of all that. I assume Alberto's making more here than he could in any other occupation, given the current economy in Catalonia. He must make arrangements to pay the property owners for the wood. Probably more complicated than I imagine.

Back at the mound, now reduced to a pile of ash and dirt, I check the load, which is about half full, throw a tarpaulin over the charcoal, and start the fire in the fire box.

The return through the borders goes without incident. The Spanish guards wave me through, and the French do a cursory examination of the contents. I make my contribution to their comfort, a bag of charcoal, and head for Ceret. At the warehouse I back the truck to the offloading area, leaving the motor idling. The truck is quickly unloaded, and I receive an envelope with cash. I'm back in Perpignan before long and park the truck, clean up the gasifier, and discard the waste. It's early, so I walk over to Paco's apartment and knock on the door. He cracks open the door.

"Oh, Paul. One moment." He closes the door behind him.

I wait for several minutes. When the door finally opens, a man leaves rapidly. I've never seen him before, and Paco makes no effort to introduce us.

"Sorry, Paul. Come on in." He opens a window. The rooms reeks of sweat, as though there has been some heavy work or a heated argument of some sort. "Something to drink?"

"No, thanks. I had a large glass of wine with Alberto."

"How did it go?"

"Great." I hand him the envelope.

"Not a large load?" he asks, counting the notes.

"About half full. He'll have another load next week, but after that things will slow down."

"Too bad. We've got a backlog. And you've gotten to the point of being comfortable, no?"

"Yes."

"Test run next week. Prepared?"

"I guess."

"You've done it before."

"This is different."

"It'll be fine."

"I hope so," I said, not entirely convinced.

"Me too," he added.

I wasn't sure if he was half serious or pulling my leg. Here's this intelligent man with all sorts of experience. Even if I trust him, do I trust the system we're setting up. There's always an element of doubt. I know the consequences of being caught. Is it worth it? One thing I have learned of Paco, he's got a hard side, and I'm not sure how deep that vein runs in his nature. He knows people, can read people, but how much sympathy goes along with this understanding?

"You're worried?" he asks.

"Yes."

"Don't be. Think about your contribution. It's not inconsequential, you know. If this works, it could be enormous. This is a big war, and we are in it for the duration. A lot depends on what we do today, believe me. I've seen it in Spain, and we failed sadly, and now the country is mired in a personal autocracy. And how many died? How many are permanent exiles? How many were reduced to penury and disgrace?"

"I understand what's right, and I know it rationally. It's just my guts that are the problem. Aiding military to escape? That's a death sentence..."

"We're all in this together. And you know what...it's dangerous. We are all under death sentences."

14

March 1942

> *But alas at Saint-Jean as everywhere*
> *A promise is nothing more than a trap*
> *I was crazy to believe in happiness*
> *And to want to keep his love*
> *How can you not lose your mind*
> *When embraced in his bold arms*
> *Since you believed his tender words.*
> « *Mon amant de Saint-Jean,* » *Emile Carrara and Léon Agel*

I tried. I blinded myself for a moment that I had escaped the sea storm of my life unscathed. I've been miserable lately, and I'm not sure exactly when or why it suddenly began. I sleep only in the early morning hours. Maybe because of the lack of sunshine and the retarding of hopeful spring weather, but everything makes me miserable.

I tried talking to Paul about it the other night, but he has his own problems, and I hate to burden him. He's on the cusp of a gigantic change in his business. I know that, but he's only been half-aware of me, and I seem to be always complaining, the harpy, and I'm sure he feels it. It's affecting everything I do, our relationship, and even my performance at work.

We don't eat well. No meat to speak of, no butter, no milk, and vegetables, vegetables, vegetables, far from the best, mostly tubers and rutabagas, cabbage, Brussels sprouts, broccoli, and some greens, if we're lucky. No one is friendly. Everyone is veiled and fearful. My parents are struggling. We cannot even expect the help of God in this godless land. Billowing waves drown all reality in their senseless commotion. We're all lost, like wilting flowers.

A few days before, my mother allowed me to read a letter from my grandmother Fanny. In the past, this would never have happened, but with the occupation my parents' relations with their families are changing, so she told me not to mention the note to Papa. He's too busy and disheartened on his own, she said. Papa's parents barely communicate, an occasional postcard without content. My grandmother's recent handwritten note was more telling, in a cursive, old world script:

9 February 1942

My dear Julie,

I hope this letter finds you in good health. I have been a poor correspondent over the years. Recently, the errors of the past seem to have lost significance in comparison to those of the present. So much has been lost. I pray that you will understand your parents one day. The occupation has changed everything here in Paris and in our community. Each day life has become more and more difficult. I think of my parents when they first came to France. The whispered stories I heard from their generation of the old country. Today, our life has returned to that. We are never sure of what is happening. Police patrol our community day and night. People, foreigners are taken away. Even their relatives never hear back. The authorities say they are being returned to the east to relocation camps. We are all afraid to leave our houses. Children are falling sick, and in many cases their parents are sending them to rural areas to hide them. All because of this pursuit of undesirables. We mark our transoms with lamb's blood to remind God and the Egyptians to pass over our homes. We just received a letter from an army friend of your father who served with him in Bulgaria. He says life in the Vilnius ghetto is intolerable today. People with yellow permits were moved to the small ghetto. Mostly poor and uneducated. People in the big ghetto without work papers or hiding out were rounded up and taken away. He said murders are being carried out near the village of Paneriai. You may remember summer vacations there. In October the small ghetto was shut down, but they continue bringing people there. It seems to be some sort of center of incarceration. There are rumors far worse is happening. My life is small and dark. Thank God for my priest. Auguste's parents also find themselves more and more restricted. They send their regards. God protect you and keep you and Auguste and Gabrielle,

Fanny

My grandmother's note shocked me: perhaps an augury of the future and, at the same time, a replaying of a past believed beyond recall. Her note seemed to bring the horror of occupation into perspective. I read it again and again. I realized my understanding of my history was changing. It was not as I had been led to believe.

We all pore over the one-sided newspapers and listen to the news from both sides, and always the rumors, the lies and the half-truths. We are in the hands of a government with its own agenda, milking our resources without respect or empathy. All in support of the Nazis.

The note raised the most basic questions. Am I part of my grandmother's history? Can I stand by and watch the human disaster occurring? Isn't this my disaster? And if so, does my birthright expose Paul? I try to contain my doubts, but at times I cannot. I need to find something for myself. He is so self-contained. I know it's not easy on him, but he never complains or expresses doubts. He never hesitated when the truth of my Jewish heritage was admitted. I'm sure my unhappiness discourages him from opening up to me. I need to be strong, independent, and only then can our love have a chance.

How can I think of marriage or children? How can people plan for good weather when the stormy clouds keep advancing, where the seas rage and the winds dominate? All seems useless.

***

After Paul left to go to the mountains, I wake late, too late for work, and I decide to take the day off. I sneak out to catch a train to Argelès-sur-Mer, debarking at Le Racou, a small resort village on the sea nearby. I don't want to see my parents today. I'm going to visit Georges Doelnitz and his wife, Bernadette. I had met her only once before and immediately liked her. I developed a good relationship with Georges during the show, and Paul thinks the world of him. Why the Doelnitz? Maybe they can better understand.

I arrive just before noon. I knock on the door of their small cottage off the rue Principale. I hope I'm not being too presumptuous.

The door opens wide, and the warmth of the house and smell of dying embers rush out to welcome me.

"Gabrielle," Georges says in candid surprise, his small dog at his feet. "Come in. Come in." Bernadette enters into the salon, certainly not dressed to greet anyone, in a bulky wool sweater and loose men's pants. They both look at me and realize something is amiss. Bernadette comes up to me and takes me in her arms as a mother would a child. She holds me without saying anything, reading my face and posture. I never thought it was so apparent and cannot contain my tears, but also I feel a flood of relief, just to be with someone who might understand.

"I'm so sorry."

"Hush. Come sit down. Georges, get us a strong drink and snacks and stoke the fire, please." She sits down next to me on the soft couch. She touches her finger to my lips to stop me from attempting to explain.

Georges hurries about, while I sink into the pillowy coziness and warmth of the sofa. I don't know where to begin. They must fear the worst, that I'm leaving Paul or that he's been arrested or hurt or worse.

Bernadette begins soothing me with her words. "Quiet. Relax and take off your jacket. You are absolutely at home here. We've been meaning to see you and Paul, but you know how things are. We get into our comfy cottage. We walk along the seashore in the mornings when it's clear. We build fires. We open a good book. We eat, not so well anymore, and we just allow time to dissolve without notice. Argut, get down. You and Paul are so important to us." The small black and white spaniel reluctantly gets off the couch to lie at my feet, as though I were a long-lost friend.

Georges brings in a freshly opened bottle of Calvados and pours three small snifters: one full and the others one finger. Somehow he produces a plate of sliced ham, soft cheese, and a fresh baguette and places them next to the drinks on the coffee table. Sitting down in an easy chair opposite us, he watches calmly with cagey eyes.

"Now, Gabrielle," he says, "how's Paul? We've not seen him since the beginning of the year."

I take a deep breath and taste the concentrated liquor with a jolt. "He's fine. He left the Prefecture…"

"What?" they say simultaneously.

"Yes…he was forced out by the new Prefect."

"I never would have suspected that," Georges said, "but, then again, nothing is too strange any more. I assume that's not the reason for your visit."

"No. He's got a new job. He drives a truck and delivers charcoal from Spain to France."

"Paul?" he laughs. "Leave it to Paul. He drives a truck?"

"He works for a Spanish Republican who taught at the university."

"And he delivers charcoal?"

"Yes. He's away almost every day, but now he's finished training and will be home more often, at least that's what he says. He never goes into detail."

"And you?" Georges asks gently.

"I'm still at Les Nouvelles Galeries." Turning to Bernadette, "You should come and visit. Lots of spring specials and remainders."

"Oh, honey. I've all I need." She laughs. "It's not that I have given up. It's just that I just don't need much anymore."

"I'm not sure why I'm here. But I don't want to be an inconvenience."

"Listen, Gabrielle," Georges interrupts. "You will never be an inconvenience. We are the only parents Paul has." He pauses and asks cautiously, "Is it okay between you two?"

"Yes. We're great. It's me…" I begin crying, the tears flowing, not really knowing exactly why, embarrassed and exasperated with myself. I didn't come here to collapse in tears.

Bernadette leans over and puts her arm around my back. Georges looks uncomfortable but concerned. Argut, the spaniel, manages to sneak back up onto the couch and burrows in next to me.

"I'm sorry. I didn't mean to break down."

"My dear," Bernadette says, "have something to eat. We are all automobiles without gasoline these days, parked for the duration. We need to fill up now and them."

I drink and eat a little, and I begin to talk, first about my parents, and then the community of Lithuanians my grandparents belong to in Paris, and then about the note from my grandmother. Slowly, the entire story emerges of my revealed Jewish heritage, its forced unveiling due to the lists, the history of the Lithuanian community in Paris, the difficulties my grandparents are having, my parents' reactions, and their own struggles. They listen to me sympathetically, nodding and understanding, and by the time I complete this account, my cup is empty, and I have eaten half the ham and cheese.

"You know, Gabrielle, our names are on that same list," Georges says softly. "I can't believe your father and mother have anything to worry about. They are native-born. And you certainly are not liable. Anyone naturalized is different. Vichy argues about the exact date. Any time before the thirties, though, is considered exempt from deportation. Your grandparents were naturalized before the turn of the century. We were naturalized in 1920, so I don't think any of us should have a problem.

"What is happening in Lithuania is more disturbing. We've certainly seen enough here and in the old country to know the Occupant's depth of hatred. We've seen it firsthand in Poland. We've seen the orders and directives and discrimination here, and we're in France. Believe me, whatever is happening here, eastern Europe is far worse. To go there today with the Nazis in charge is probably a death sentence, as your grandmother hints. People have no respect, no appreciation of history, laws, or human rights. It comes and goes. Historical events and movements repeat themselves: pride and suspicion, avarice and poverty, lies and truth. We never learn.

"You're a beautiful and intelligent young woman. You love and are loved. You have nothing but clear sailing ahead of you. There may be rough patches, but it will recede into vague memories. People eventually come to their senses. There are enough good people to overcome the narrow-minded and ignorant dogmatists, excuse my language, Argut. Things improve." He paused, seeming to consider.

"Maybe this is not about the occupation and war. Has this revelation been upsetting?"

"No," but than I changed my mind, finally recognizing the fact. "Yes. It was so far outside anything I would have imagined. At first, I thought

226

nothing had changed. I am the same person. But something has changed. I ignored my feelings, but the more I thought about it, the more I didn't know who I was. It forced me to question my current life and how I wanted to live in the future. I realized I had been raised with something missing."

"You are not alone," Georges said. "This is happening throughout Europe. Jews who never thought twice about their heritage, religion, or culture are being forced to confront this imposed reality. It's not easy, and everyone has a unique approach to handling it."

"I can't continue like this. I can't be a shop girl. I can't watch while others suffer. That's where I am right now. Dissatisfied with myself. Some spoiled child, exempt from all, disconnected, lunching with friends, worried about the rain or cold. Waiting for spring to feed our roots and warm our souls...while others are in desperate pain."

"We all fight in our own ways," Bernadette added. "No matter who we are. Plenty of Jews are happy to hide out and hope time will solve all. Others run. Some fight. You have to do what is right for you...regardless of your past. We are old and tired, finished with struggling, just wanting to enjoy a few more years together. Probably wrong...pig-headed...but that's where we are."

"I have not been to a synagogue in years," Georges says, "but I am Jewish. I am proud of my heritage. We have been dispersed, scattered, yet we maintain an inner strength that unites us...and that is within you as well. You can accept all of it or part or none at all, but it is there to provide a moral strength in adversity. Believe me. Never be ashamed. One day it may be your saving grace...God's unconditional love for mankind."

"I worry that it could hurt Paul. If something happened to me..."

"That's not impossible, I suppose. It's true that being Jewish today is a definite liability. We must live with that, but leave that up to Paul."

"You don't worry?"

"Yes, we do, but we are so fortunate...like a bird that never needs to land."

I look at Georges and then Bernadette, so open, so loving, in spite of what they have suffered, so full of hope. I listen to his words, and they enter my consciousness like a memory. For a while, we remain quiet, pensive, and then Georges speaks up.

"Now, the next show is going to be a good one. Jordi wants both Paul and you to return. Maybe we can bring a little warmth into peoples' lives. That's something. I'll tell you what. We've been meaning to see Jordi for some time. Why don't we all drive into Perpignan and have dinner with Jordi and Josette. I think I have enough gas. Let's see. It's almost five o'clock now. What's Paul up to?"

"He should be back by now. Probably getting ready to pick me up after work. He has no idea I took the day off."

"We can be there before he arrives. He'll never know. Give us a few moments to get dressed. You might want to walk Argut to the beach. He's been cooped up all day with the old folks, and he seems to have taken to you."

"That would be lovely."

I walk the dog across the street to the beach. He's happy to come with me, happy to be out. The sun has turned the day into spring. The low clouds have lifted, and the beach is welcoming. A long white sandy stretch with the descent of a hillside blocking the beach in one direction and a break-water far in the opposite heading. Few people are out. We walk along the shoreline toward the rocky hillside. I'm mesmerized by the sound of the waves. I let Argut off his leash, and he skips along the breaking waves, barking, but always carefully jumping away to avoid the foamy water.

I see my life in this endless cycle, caught up and released time after time. I do not have an exact idea of why I came here to see Georges and Bernadette. I surprised myself with what I told them. I'm sure the fact they're Jewish has much to do with my visit, that they might better understand. I hadn't planned on telling them the whole story, although I think they knew some of it from Paul. Somehow, I knew they would understand better than most people. I thought I could skip past it like a little girl with a jump rope, but I cannot.

I thought I could just continue on, but that is not going to happen. I am not who I was a few months ago.

***

When Paul arrived at Les Nouvelles Galeries, he was pleased to see Georges and Bernadette. He was nicely dressed, out of his worker's outfit and clean-shaven. Rather than visit the Club les Tréteaux, Georges suggested a restaurant on Place de la République, one that usually managed to find enough scrap fish for a fisherman's soup with vegetables. They settled into a booth with Argut on Bernadette's lap. Georges ordered a carafe of local grenache, and they awaited a decent dinner.

"I hear you are a working man these days," Georges said to Paul.

"Gabrielle told you. I'm delivering charcoal produced in Spain to a depot in Ceret. It keeps me busy."

"What about the Prefecture? I hadn't heard." Georges eyed Paul seriously.

"They decided that I didn't fit in with their goals, which was quite correct." Paul took a drink, wondering how much to say. "Franco thought I could be more helpful elsewhere."

"I know your new boss," Georges said suspiciously.

"He's a good man."

"Yes. He's that. But he runs in a rough crowd."

"A rough crowd?" Paul reacted negatively. "We cannot ignore what's going on. You have to understand. I might want to marry and have children and a home of my own one day. I might want a career of some sort, and not in entertainment. I might want a normal life, free to choose whatever direction I want. At some point, nice doesn't work."

"Paul, stop," Georges said firmly. "We too want all that for you. I am only concerned for your health."

Paul shook his head. "So am I."

Gabrielle and Bernadette were clearly becoming uneasy with the conversation. "Maybe we can talk about this elsewhere," Gabrielle finally said, watching the two men facing each other.

"Of course we can," Georges agreed.

A waiter arrived with the soups, interrupting the conversation. He set the dishes down, topped the wine glasses, and departed. "*Bon appétit.*"

Georges looked at Paul, addressing him more gently. "We could have talked before you became involved."

"I don't want to talk about it," Paul said strongly. "It's not something open to your opinion versus mine."

"No. At your age…"

"Too many people want comfort…to be left alone. That's a losing strategy."

"You are right." Georges stares at Paul a moment, nodding his head. Perhaps remembering himself at that age.

"What's going on with the show?" Paul asks.

"We have some pretty good ideas, and Jordi wants to involve you and Gabrielle."

"Has anyone contacted Django or his brother?"

"No. Weren't you going to do that?"

"I've been busy. Besides, I may not understand the financial aspects, but it seems to me that last show made a ton of money and nothing ever filtered down to the participants. Everyone's appreciative, but it has to be handled more honestly. Jordi paid Django something as a retainer. I have no idea how much, but you would think there would be some arrangement involved with us: some promise on his part. I love being involved, but I think you and Jordi have to play fair."

"Don't misunderstand. I'm not getting rich from these shows, and you make a good point. Let's talk with Jordi."

"Fine. I'm a little on edge. I seem to be getting cranky with my new job, and it hasn't even really begun. Am I cranky, Gabrielle?"

"Yes. Yes you are, but first of all, we need to eat." They began to eat. Cut pieces of yesterday's bread were shared around. Georges ordered another carafe of wine. Bernadette dunked some bread into her bowl and fed Argut. For a moment they all felt separated and alone. Two couples, as close as anyone can be, at odds.

"I'm sorry," Paul finally apologized. "I've been working too hard. Forgive me."

"We're all under stress," Bernadette said. "We hadn't seen you in such a long time, and Gabrielle came for a lovely visit. We just thought it would be a good idea to get together. We love you both and only want the best for you." Gabrielle reached over warmly and cupped Bernadette's hand.

The remainder of dinner, which was not really very satisfying, was spent on the mundane, ignoring the war, the occupation, and local politics. After dinner, Georges insisted on paying. Outside they walked a few blocks to the car, which was along the river. At the car, they said goodnight, exchanged bisous, and promised to meet again soon. Gabrielle and Paul declined a ride to their apartment, insisting on walking. It was cool but clear. Georges and Bernadette drove off, and Gabrielle and Paul walked the several blocks back to rue de la Gare.

***

Back in their apartment, the first words out of Paul's mouth: "You didn't work today?"

"I took the day off. I wasn't feeling well, and the idea of visiting them seemed a good way to pass the day pleasurably and peacefully.

"Why?" Paul demanded. "If you were sick..."

"I wasn't sick. It just seemed the right thing."

"You could have talked to me."

She didn't feel like talking about it, just as he didn't want to talk about his work. She went to the bathroom in the hallway feeling misunderstood and changed into her old nightgown. When she returned, Paul was sitting up in bed. She quickly slipped into the cold bed on her side.

"What did you talk about?" he asked coldly.

"Nothing special. We walked on the beach. Had a drink and some aperitifs. They had a fire going, and it felt nice. I got to know Bernadette, and Georges is great."

"I wish you had told me."

"I decided after you left. I don't report to you," she retorted.

"You told them about the letter from your grandmother?"

"Yes."

"And the situation in the Lithuanian community in Paris?"

"Yes..."

"You told them about your Jewish connection."

"Connection? Yes, about my heritage. I thought they might understand."

"You mean because they're Jewish?"

"Probably. Yes."

"And did they?"

"They were sympathetic. They understood far more than I expressed. They were more sympathetic simply because they are Jewish…and because they love you."

"I don't know. We haven't really discussed it. You gave me the impression that it was just a blemish. That it was a fact and really didn't influence who you are." Paul watched her. He knew something had been bothering her, and after the revelation he had anticipated a reaction, but it had never come. It probably would have been better if it had happened sooner than later, but now it had arrived.

"I trusted them."

"We never discussed it. You've been upset for weeks. Do you think I don't see these things?"

"I don't know what you see. We never talk about anything. Your mind is always elsewhere."

"It's my fault?"

"No. I'm not blaming you. We're both strained."

"Maybe, but I have a job to do."

"And I don't?" She felt hurt to the core. "I have my little meaningless job. I'm ashamed of my little friends and my useless life." She began to cry softly. It was all coming out so badly, so mixed up, so defensively.

"I didn't mean that," Paul said, changing his tone. His mind was reeling. He didn't mean to have the evening end this way. No one understood. He had too much on his plate and nowhere to go with it, no one to tell, no one to help him. And it was only beginning. He turned away and pretended sleep.

Gabrielle felt his movement, felt his coldness, but she could never reach for him. He would not allow it, would think her weak. She pulled the covers over her head, hid her face in the bolster to muffle her sobs, and waited for sleep.

***

The next morning, Gabrielle went to work, hoping that returning to her daily routine might lighten the burden weighting her heart. Paul had a meeting with Paco Macias later that morning, and he didn't stir as she left the apartment. She waved to Edith as she passed the concierge's window. The window opened with a clack.

"You look lovely," Edith called out.

"Thanks, Edith. *Bonne journée.*"

"You too."

She wondered what this meant. Edith was normally silent and uncommunicative. As far as Gabrielle knew, Edith sat in her booth ten hours a day, eating, drinking, knitting, controlling the door, suspicious of every unfamiliar face seeking entrance, and turning away hawkers and salespeople. She reviewed her dress and dark wool pelerine. Felt her hair. She wondered if last night remained evident on her face, barely made up. She would see to that. She hurried along the street.

At half-past noon, she walked rapidly to the Palmarium to meet her chums, whom she had not seen since the holidays. She spied Nuria and Catie sitting at an outside table. The sun was shining, but it was a little cool to eat outside.

"Only tables left were on the terrace," Catie said, jumping up and giving Gabrielle a big hug and bisou. Nuria remained in her seat. Gabrielle bent over to give her a bisou, noting a sour look on her face.

"We can find another restaurant." Nuria said.

"Yes. Let's," Catie responded. "I've been freezing all morning. How about Ubu's? It's not so popular, and the food's fair, and it won't be crowded." They all stood up, hooked arms, like the girls they had once been. At the restaurant, they settled at a small table well inside the doorway and ordered salads. It wasn't much warmer than outside.

"Gosh, Nuria, it's been a long time," Catie said.

"A few months since the holidays." She spoke without enthusiasm.

"Where have you been?"

"Oh, moving around mostly. I've been working for la Cimade, but also with an export company in Lyon. I might as well be out with it. I've become involved with Robert.

"Involved?" Catie asked.

"Well, more than that. We've been living together in Lyon."

"And you're working with his company?" Gabrielle demanded, knowing the answer. She was examining Nuria closely. Something was wrong. She had lost weight. She no longer applied any makeup at all, and her hair was dry and unkempt. Her face was hard and lacked animation as she took out a cigarette and began smoking.

"Yes, but with la Cimade as well. They work well together. I've seen enough for a lifetime, I'll tell you that. I've seen camps in the free zone and a few in the occupied area. We work with the Swiss Red Cross, the Quakers, the YMCA, the OSE (*Oeuvre de Secours aux Enfants*), and others. We're trying to make sense of what is happening: who is being arrested, where they are being taken, and what is the process for individuals caught up in the system. It's a well-thought-out system, believe me: it's sick, and, as we delve deeper, it's getting sicker. Robert's been working with a group of people in Lyon. It's dangerous for him, and his hair is turning gray. But I've found my man. No doubt. I wish we could flee from all the extraneous noise."

The salads arrived. They just looked at the woeful lettuce and nameless vegetables: without a tomato or radish or anchovy in sight, and the dressing was a wan hodge-podge.

"I'm so jealous," Catie said to Nuria. Catie seemed the only one to be happy to be back with her friends.

"If you need some help, let me know," Gabrielle added. "I'm feeling out of things here in Perpignan."

"What do you mean? You and Paul are still together?"

"Yes," Gabrielle admitted.

"It's always a bumpy road," Nuria replied, noting Gabrielle's unease.

"Well, we had a big bump last night. I'm not contributing anything. I'm just marking time. He's always away if not in body, then in mind."

"I heard he left the Prefecture?" Nuria said.

"Yes. He's got a new job, even more precarious."

"Are you serious about wanting to work?" Nuria asked.

"Yes. I don't enjoy the Galeries anymore. Not that I ever did. My parents are having problems, and my father is no longer painting and away all the time.

"I know what you mean," Catie said vaguely. "But what can we girls do?"

"We can make a difference, Catie," Nuria said forcefully. "They need us. It's not a man's world out there. You would be surprised at the number of women arrested, and not for lack of documentation." She turned to Gabrielle. "What are you going to do?"

Gabrielle shook her head.

"I'll tell you," Nuria continued. "It's hard being with Robert. He drinks and smokes too much. He disappears frequently and can never say when he's going or where he's been. It's like living with a ghost. And he has that same vacancy when at rest, as though his mind is a thousand kilometers away. But don't misunderstand, when we focus on each other, everything else dissolves into nothingness. It never lasts long, but it's enough."

"Does he respect what you do?" Gabrielle asked desperately.

"Yes. He's all about organization, working with others, convincing others, wheedling and cajoling and threatening. His boss is even worse, keeping everything to himself, trusting no one, and driving everyone crazy. But they both understand the importance of uncovering what the Occupant is up to beyond the headlines and public statements. It's what unifies us and hopefully will convince other groups to join."

Gabrielle watched her while she talked. Maybe she's grown up over the last few months. She was always the smartest in the class, but she managed to have a lightness about her, an ability to laugh, to enjoy. Some of the innocence and femininity have been submerged. Her joy seemed gone.

"I can't deal with his double life," Gabrielle replied, "especially when I get so little time allotted to me. If I had more going on in my own life it might be different, but as a salesgirl I'm marginal. It still leaves me without a life of my own."

"Sounds serious," Catie said without thought.

"You may be right." Gabrielle snapped. "We're all being forced to change. And it's only going to get worse. No one's making any progress."

Nuria glared at Gabrielle. "Yes, but we can't give up. We have to do what is right."

Gabrielle returned to work feeling no better, but determined to stem this constant ebb and flow of emotions.

***

Paul walked to Paco Macia's apartment on rue Jeanne d'Arc, the day cool and the skies blue. The door opened immediately, as though Paco were expecting him.

"*Hola, amic meu.* How are you? Come in. Come in. I only hear good things about you. Come and have a drink."

Paul sat down at the old wooden table, while Paco opened a bottle of red wine.

"It's the best of the Alt Empordà. It can compete with any wine in France, though not easy to come by these days. How have you been?"

"Good, or I should say okay."

"Why okay."

"Well, it's Gabrielle. She's having a hard time."

"Ah, *mujeres hermosas.* They always have special problems. They're happiest when they're pregnant. It must be the hormones. Any ideas."

Paul frowned. "That's not about to happen."

"I know. You need a night out. You've earned it. You've got Alberto pushing his crew harder than ever. But you know, we're not in the charcoal business. We're in the business of saving people. And that's why I wanted to chat. Tomorrow we have our first package. That's what you passeurs call it, no?"

Paul looked at this man, this educated man, not finding him amusing. He took a drink of wine, not smiling at his antics.

"Listen, Paul. I'm only going to tell you this once. You have to learn to live two lives. One while working and the other when at home with Gabrielle. I'm a perfectly serious fellow, despite what you may think. I am forced to do very grave things and to take decisive actions. But that is not

236

who I am. You might not like that other person. You might even be a bit scared of him. I like this other one better myself. I hope to be able to return to this one full-time. Here's a bonus. Go home. Treat Gabrielle. Find that person who entertains others, who sings love songs, and become that person. Tomorrow pick me up here at 7:00 am, and you can become the serious man you are right now.

***

That evening, Gabrielle and Paul have a night out. Paul chooses to go to one of the most talked about restaurants in Perpignan. The owner welcomes them warmly, but they feel immediately out of place with the other diners, well-dressed, older, obviously well-off. The waiters are solicitous, but in a way that suggests they are not the normal caliber welcomed here. Paul realizes instantly that this is the wrong restaurant. He has made a large mistake.

They order from a menu that looks as though it was printed before the war. The bill of fare actually offers meat dishes, salads, real desserts, and wines.

"How can we pay for this?" Gabrielle whispers, feeling uncomfortable as well. She notes the effort Paul is making. She wants nothing more than to make it all work, tonight and for all their life together. He can't just dress up, comb his hair, and take her to an expensive restaurant and expect all to change like a magician's slight of hand.

"Paco gave me a bonus. He said I had earned it."

"That's wonderful," she says doubtfully. "Maybe we should have saved it, rather than spending it on a dinner like this."

Paul looks at her, hurt.

Each course of their dinner comes with grandeur. First a salad of fois gras with toast and fig confit. Then roasted rack of lamb on a bed of white beans with tiny cepe mushrooms in a butter sauce and house baked bread. A salad follows with choice from a large cheese platter. Dessert is profiteroles with real cream and grated chocolate. Where these ingredients come from they will never know. The people in the restaurant are obviously not suffering from the occupation. The waiters act as though this is normal fare, but for Gabrielle and Paul it's fantasy, so far from reality that it's embarrassing and distressing. They are both so uncomfortable, conversation is impossible.

"I think we both deserve it," Paul says, hoping to rationalize the extravagance and discomfort. "I know it's hard on you. I'm sorry I can't seem to shake off my day job. You mean the world to me. I want your happiness more than anything."

Suddenly, Gabrielle loses herself. She stands to leave, wanting to scream hatred at these privileged peacocks without a bit of concern for what is happening to their country. The diners watch closely. The restaurant becomes hushed. Before she can make a move, she notices a face that she has not seen for years. A tall, thin young man exits the kitchen. With long, uncropped hair, a Roman chinstrap beard encircles his thin face. He approaches them. She can't speak. She can't move.

"Gaby?"

She looks at him completely at a loss, her mind unable to retain all her thoughts like a overflowing cistern.

"It's Jean-Luc Pineau. How are you?" He looks at her closely. Seeing her dazed eyes and lack of response, he turns to Paul.

"I'm a friend from school." He offers his hand, which Paul accepts hesitantly, not knowing exactly who he is, but also aware of Gabrielle's reaction.

"What are you doing here?" Jean-Luc asks Gabrielle.

Gabrielle shakes her head, unable to confront this image from the past.

"You must be doing well. You're not…one of them…are you?" he asks in an undertone.

"No." She finally says, shaking her head.

The restaurant is now totally quiet. Everyone focuses on the three young people, wondering where this will lead, without an inkling of the undercurrent.

"I have to go," Gabrielle says quickly, feeling sick to her stomach from the rich food, but also from the years of storing away her feelings, hoping for them to pass. Once again, she is flooded with shame. It's as if three years have dissolved into a single night, as strongly as the day it occurred: a streak of Venetian red over blue cobalt, a bloody slash, bringing her instantly back. Nothing has changed.

"Listen, Gaby," he replies hurriedly, becoming wound up. "I'm sorry. I meant to talk with you, but everything was crazy that last semester. I believed what everyone told me. I'm doing well at the École Normale Supérieure. I'm surrounded by the smartest people at the best institution in France. It's simply amazing. I haven't been back to Perpignan since I left for Paris. My mother works here. Would you like to meet her?"

"No." Then Gabrielle remembers. "You haven't seen Isabelle Lefèvre since you graduated?" Gabrielle demands.

"No, I barely knew her anyway."

"I need to go," she repeats, feeling even sicker, wanting this horrifying scene to end.

He begins talking earnestly, wanting her to understand. "I'm so sorry. I'm doing better now, but it's dangerous. They follow me sometimes. In the back of the bus I see them…they don't know it. And I have to change buses. My instructors. The head of Social Sciences and Economics sometimes follows me in a car. I think they believe I have secrets…

Ignoring him, Gabrielle turns to the room. "What's wrong with you people?" she yells. "Leave us alone," The diners drop their heads. The restaurant is totally silent. "You can all go to hell," she shouts.

Paul, mortified, pays the bill, and extricates himself. "I'm sorry," he apologizes to the owner.

"No," he says sympathetically. "I understand, Monsieur. Merci."

As he leaves, the diners return to their meals with whispered explanations.

Outside, Gabrielle is waiting, shivering, having vomited in the street. He approaches her, wanting to comfort her or to understand. He's never seen her is such a state. She warns him back.

"You know who that was?" she asks.

"Yes. At first I had no idea, but it became clear."

"And what did that mean to you?" Gabrielle asks in anger, striking out at him, but then quickly corrects herself. This is not his fault. She needs to take responsibility for her life at this very moment. She can't expect him to repair her deep despondency. Jean-Luc made clear her worthlessness: today as years before.

"He seemed lost."

"Nothing has changed. It's gone on too long," she sighs, "too far. And it won't stop. I'm eternally tired. I can't pull myself from this abyss. It's not helping either of us."

"What do you mean?"

"We can't continue as though nothing has changed. You've become more and more involved. You lost your job, and now you've started another one, even more dangerous. You might as well be fighting in the front lines. A passeur was caught in the Albère Mountains a few days ago. He was killed outright by the border patrol. No questions."

"I've become a person without a country. My entire life is a lie. I have no idea what to do. Everything has been thrown into disorder, and my father hasn't the time to take notice. My mother's suffering. My friends have become strangers."

"It's the war," Paul says. "You're not alone. It's a plague on all our houses."

"Jean-Luc brought it all back. So clearly. I can't live with it. I have nothing. I only have you, and you don't need me. I'm just a liability. I will only bring you pain…or worse. Right now I need to help myself."

"I try, Gabrielle."

"You're the sweetest man on the planet. And I love you, and this is not your fault. But I can't go on living with you. Tonight pointed it out so clearly."

"What?" He envisages what she is saying, how much he would be losing. "It was all a mistake. And who thought we would meet that crazy man?"

"Did you see them looking at me?" she asks, exasperated, wheeling around gesticulating. "They all knew."

"That's not true."

"Maybe something will change, but right now I need time. I can think only of myself and my family, not the country, not Jean-Luc, not even you. I need to save myself before it's too late."

Paul feels a sickening pain of defeat and loss in his stomach. For the first time, he has found someone to share his life, someone he loves, a family, a place of his own, and now it is dissolving as abruptly as the lives in his past. And now he is losing what he committed to, contradicting everything he had justified in his lonely existence. He has failed.

"I trusted you, Gabrielle…with everything."

"I will only hurt you."

Gabrielle sees the pain in his face and eyes, the pain she is imposing. She wants to take it all back, fearing she will never find love again. This is her last opportunity, and she is throwing it out like a petulant child. She can't see any other way to escape her feelings. Just like the people crossing the mountains into Spain, she is hazarding all to free herself: she has no alternative.

They return to the apartment. The dinner and its aftermath have been a disaster. Gabrielle says nothing on the way back. Once in the apartment, neither speaks, both too deflated and too hurt. They retire to their bed as uncomfortably as two strangers. They have no resources to draw on for reconciliation. The distance separating them is fixed, firm, and final.

***

The next morning, Paul wakes early for the meeting with Paco. After another night of tossing and turning, I lie inert, listening to him make his way through the apartment until the door finally shuts. I get up, wash myself, and pack my belongings. There really is not that much of me in the apartment after nearly a year of living together. One bag and a valise of memories. I leave the keys on the hall table and close the door. I will be late for work. Hailing a taxi, I return to my parents' house, feeling the very same defeat I assume Paul feels. There is nothing good about this separation. It will not help either one of us. The past and present have conjoined to beat us. Jean-Luc has won. Truth is defeated. The present has only contempt for us. We have only an illusion of a future. These once innocent wild flowers have become a bouquet of weeds.

Michael Barnes Selvin

Maréchal Philippe Pétain, Chef de l'Etat français:
July 1940-August 1944

Paul, his father, and his twin aunts,
San Sebastian, Spain, 1925

Paul with his mother and sister, 1927

Paul with his grandmother and 9neighbor, Amélie-les-Bains, 1936

Portrait of Gabrielle (Girl with Rabbit),
Auguste Daniel, 1930)

Gabrielle, Perpignan, 1932

Robert in his graduating class (first row, second on right), 1936

Hot charcoal mound in the Spanish Pyrenees

Renault AGR-2, retrofitted with Gasogene and tool box

Paul, Paco Macias, and Gabrielle

An de Trasse

Dans ma petite ville de chef-lieu de Canton
(Chine), j'ai toujours, lorsque je prenais le train,
été fasciné par une image réclamé, qui dans
la petite gare en fleurs, incitait à visiter
l'Allemagne. Par un moyen secret que je ne
puis divulguer ici, j'ai été "amené," à voir
ce pays gratuitement. Ce pays c'est un
immense espace entouré de fils de fer barbelés
dans lequel les habitants sont enfermés, seuls
nous sommes libres, malheureusement il y a
trop de monde dans le susdit pays, aussi
"jouissons" nous d'un espace plutôt restreint,
c'est dommage. Ce fameux lieu où nous
sommes libres s'appelle un "concentrionslager"
et notre hôte ne reculant devant aucun
sacrifice, nous loge, nous nourrit "sans qualificatif"
avec une "courtoisie" qui ne peut avoir d'égal.
Lorsque je suis arrivé à Buchenwald, vous ne vous
douteriez pas ce qui m'a frappé le plus, se sont
"les ceusses" qui nous attendaient à la gare avec leurs
chiens. Je ne t'oublierai jamais ce petit coin de
Thuringe, le temps que je passe dans la forêt est à
jamais imprimé dans mon cœur. Malheureusement
dans ce coin de paradis terrestre, on rencontre de
mauvais camarades auxquels on s'habitue. Je t'ai
rencontré mon vieux Roger, et je me suis habitué
à toi et malgré toutes tes défauts lorsque l'on nous
obligera à rentrer, c'est avec une certaine joie que
je te retrouverai afin de te rappeler notre grand
voyage dans l'inconnu. Amicalement,

Ton vieux ami

Anonymous letter from Buchenwald, Germany, 1941

Gabrielle and Paul, December 1942

Camp du Vernet in the Ariège

15

April 1942

> *If you were gone*
> *How could I live*
> *I would never know*
> *The happiness that intoxicates me*
> *When I am in your arms*
> *And my joyous heart surrenders*
> *How could I live*
> *If you were gone.*
> « *Si tu n'étais pas là,* » *Gaston Claret and Pierre Bayle"*

I leave the apartment early with Gabrielle feigning sleep. I knew it, but couldn't bring myself to say something to her or to kiss her goodbye. I feel a stranger. Anything I could say or do would be taken negatively, whether expressing my love for her or censuring her for her selfishness. In either case, I would be wrong. I'm exhausted by last night: our uncompromising argument, our inability to change the direction of the tide. The patrons understood what we were saying. They clearly interpreted our emotions and discomfort. We were the entertainment. The restaurant, le Saint Jean, was the wrong choice. This restaurant serves as the domain of collaborators and black market people, wealthy people with money to burn. We were the youngest diners by far. We were not dressed appropriately. The obsequious waiters made no effort to hide their disdain. It was clear on everyone's face that we were aliens.

Gabrielle has been feeling morose since she discovered her family's heritage. At first she seemed to accept it with equanimity. She admitted to being shocked by it, but not seriously, not at any depth. However, it wore on her, made her reconsider long-held assumptions. I thought she was assimilating it well enough, but I guess it had dominated her inner thoughts. The fact that she went to Georges and Bernadette to express her feelings was a strong indication of her inability to manage the questions herself, and of my failure to help her. Her parents didn't see it.

I have been so consumed by my new job for the past two months that I missed the significance of her internal turmoil. I failed wretchedly. Gabrielle means more to me than anything in my life. For the first time in my life, I was comfortable with the strength of our devotion. I made no concession to time or limits or pressures to our attachment. I assumed its continuity. And yet we were not strong enough to survive. We were divided by the need to understand and the despair that we were not able.

I'm feeling sick at heart for Gabrielle, and at the same time I'm setting out on the most difficult challenge I have ever faced in my life: transporting British airmen across the border. This is not like a passeur, where there is control of the process: timing, route, awareness of the surroundings, and knowledge of the habits of the patrols, and always the choice to turn back. There is no retreat. If the border police stop and examine the truck carefully, they may find the secret compartment. If they discover a downed British airman, there will be no questions asked. The military police will come, and we will both be arrested, taken to transport camps, probably aimed eventually at German or Polish camps. We will be lucky not to be executed on the spot, which could happen in the occupied zone.

At the parking area behind the apartment, I fill the fuel box with charcoal and light the fire. I stoke it until it heats sufficiently, providing the hot gas essential for combustion, and then switch the gas valve emitting the gas into the engine. I turn the ignition. The engine sputters, catches, and starts, roughly at first, but then begins idling comfortably. I back up and leave the parking lot. Arriving a little late to pick up Paco, he is waiting out front of his apartment building.

"Bonjour, Paco. How's it going?"

"Okay, you're late."

"I know. Rough start. Rough night."

"So, let's go." He climbs into the cab, and we take off.

"Where to?" He has told me nothing of the day, except that this is a trial run.

"It's on the way to Ceret. I'll show you when we get there. You can leave me at Ceret. I have some business, and then you can pick me up at the depot when you return with your load. Alberto said that he has moved the operation and has hired more tree cutters and stackers, so production should double by summer. Why a rough night?"

We continue on the highway to Ceret. I think about his question a moment. "Had an argument with Gabrielle."

"*Zut*. Serious?"

"Yes. I took her out for a nice dinner at le Saint Jean, but it fell apart almost immediately."

"After three wives, I can't be trusted handing out advice on relations with women. They're impossible anyway. I've been single since coming to France. Oh, I've had my *petites affaires*. French women expect too much, and they offer nothing unique from Spanish women. Probably the wrong choice of restaurant."

"She's leaving me, returning to her parents' house. Said I was not the reason. But I feel responsible."

Paco does not respond immediately, thinking about it. "Sounds like she wants a stronger commitment. They always want to be reassured. Marriage?"

"No. You're wrong. We've talked about it, and I'm open to it. My commitment was not a factor. She needs time away from me. Perhaps the idea of marriage frightened her. It does me."

"It's one of the most serious things in life that you can do rather casually. It would terrify me at your age. How was the food?"

"What?"

"The food at the restaurant?"

"Not the right choice." That's all I could say.

We come to the bridge over the Tech River and begin the climb up the river valley. The day is a little overcast. It's building toward rain. We are paralleling a large vineyard running alongside the highway with a view of Mount Canigou hiding in the misty clouds.

"Turn off on the next dirt road."

I see the entrance to a vineyard and make a sharp turn onto a farm road. We drive along the rough path about five hundred meters and come to a stone farmhouse hidden from the main road. I slow to a stop before a fence and gate.

"Wait here. I'll be back in a moment." He jumps out of the truck, opens the gate, and disappears to one side of the house.

I take out a cigarette and settle back with the engine idling, feeling the tension departing with each breath. I listen, but all is silent. I'm feeling queasy. Whether it's my stomach from last night or my nerves due to the upcoming frontier crossing. I see Paco and another man coming around the house. He's young, a head taller than Paco, and walking with a limp.

"This is my friend," Paco introduces me. We shake hands."

"Good to meet you," I say.

The stranger doesn't reply, but smiles awkwardly. He's dressed in work clothes with a heavy jacket, but his hair is long and his hands are not those of a worker.

"He's going over the hill with you," Paco says. "He doesn't speak any French or Spanish." I look at him, probably my age, but I understand this is my package.

Paco goes over to the tool box on the side of the truck and reaches into the compartment and removes the shovels, brooms, and other tools. For a moment his upper torso is lost in the interior as he struggles. Finally, he emerges with a long board.

"It's not that easy to get out," he turns to me. "Here, let me show you. I stand behind him and watch him reinsert the board. The board fits snuggly into the back of the tool box. There are two tiny, almost imperceptible, levers that raise and lower to catch the board. The stranger stands away from us watching intently, nervously.

"Now you take it out," Paco orders.

I reach into the box, manage to push the levers down, and coax the barrier board out. I can see the space for a single person with breathing holes on the far side.

"Well done." He signals to the stranger, who climbs into the box with difficulty and scoots to the back. "Okay?" He lifts his thumb. I see the man return the sign.

"Are you okay?" I ask in my best English from McAllister's class at Trinité.

"Right-oh."

I don't remember that word from class, but get the meaning.

Paco nods to me, and I replace the board carefully, not wanting to crush the man, but it fits nicely, and there is room remaining for the man to position himself, but not much. I lift the levers, and the board is fixed in place.

"Throw some dirt into the box to hide the levers."

I toss several handfuls of dirt into the box, just enough to look natural and replace the tools, closing the compartment.

"There you have your package," Paco says. "There's plenty of air for him, and these flyers are not claustrophobic. They know the drill. When you get across the border drive past the charcoal facility toward Rocabruna. You'll be stopped on the road before you get to the village. They'll ask you, 'do you know the way to Barcelona,' and you reply, 'You're a long way from Madrid.' Okay?"

"Yes," but now my stomach is churning and my heart beating rapidly. There's no turning back.

"Let's go."

We return to the highway toward Ceret, which we reach in a few minutes. I drop Paco at the entrance to town.

"See you back at the depot in about four hours."

"Good luck," he says and waves.

I continue up the valley, aware of the clear blue skies and fresh air, arriving at Prats-de-Mollo, in about thirty minutes. As we approach the French crossing, my heart is racing. I'm comfortable that my truck looks no different, but you never know. There have been no sounds from under the truck. I see the border guards standing alongside the road and two soldiers behind them with their rifles on their shoulders. I recognize one of the guards. I slow to stop, but the guard signals me through. I wave and pass slowly through the gates.

At the Spanish side, the soldiers look more serious, and there's an automobile stopped with an inspection going on. A well dressed man stands with a soldier on the side. The border guards look up from their search and recognize me, and once again I'm waved through. One soldier standing back from the inspection with his automatic rifle cradled in his arms eyes me as I pass. I slowly drive through the final border gate, my heart speeding and my stomach roiling. I move off, glad to be across. That was too easy.

Taking my normal route, I continue past the forested entrance to the charcoal facility. My heart slows, but I'm still tense, not knowing what to expect. I drive carefully toward Rocabruna. The truck is wider than normal traffic, and the road is narrow, barely able to support a single lane with constant curves on the downgrade. In order to pass, vehicles must drive along the soft shoulder. Luckily, there is little traffic. I come to a fork, and a man dressed in peasant clothes is standing beside the road. Seeing the truck, he waves. I stop alongside and roll down the window.

"*Hola, Senyor.*"

He approaches the cab. "Do you know the way to Barcelona?" he asks in broken French.

"You're a long way from Madrid."

He raises his hand to shake mine and switches to Catalan. "Follow me. There's a farm road down the way." He turns and walks down the road for about fifty meters and then signals the turnoff. The truck barely makes the turn onto a rough dirt path. I stop just off the road afraid of getting stuck and jump out, the engine idling. I'm worried about the fuel supply, nearing the end of the fire.

"We'll take it from here," he says brightly. "No problem at the crossing?"

"None."

I walk around the truck to the tool box, open it, and throw out the tools. I reach in to pull the board out. Almost immediately, the man slithers out and comes to his feet. He stretches his arms and legs, but looks no worse for the experience. He's probably been through much tighter spaces. He comes over to me and takes my hand in both of his.

"You are now in Spain," I say in English.

"Much thanks," he replies, brushing back his blond locks. "Much thanks, indeed." He looks practically cheery, rosy cheeks, a little tired perhaps: a good-looking young man, his innocent face staring into mine.

"Thank you for your service to our country," I say in careful English.

What he replies I will never know, but he has a lot to say, rapidly. We shake hands again, and I close the tool box. I go round and mount the cab. Waving, I back out onto the road and return the way I came.

Arriving at the new charcoal area, I back up to a cold mound with Alberto and two workers signaling me. I turn off the engine. For a moment I sit in the cab, allowing my fears to subside and my body to readjust. I've never been happier to see anyone. I shake all the workers' hands, smiling, happy to be outside, glad to be free of the anxiety. They look at me somewhat surprised, since they know nothing of my delivery. I feel twenty pounds lighter, ready to fly. I'm thirsty and hungry.

"*Hola*, Alberto. It's good to see you." I pat him on the back.

This pattern repeats itself, two sometimes four times a week, and I grow to accept the risks, never feeling comfortable, but the routine nature, the ease of passing the border, and the appreciation of the packages, mainly British airmen, allow me to come to an accord with my job. I know that this is a mirage. The terrible risk is constantly there and cannot be ignored. It could change in an instant, depending on the indolence of the guards. For the next month or so it continues without incident, and then I hit a large bump in the road, literally.

***

In the late afternoon at Club les Tréteaux, Jordi lit a cigar, sitting across from Georges and Paul. He stared at them harshly, unwilling to negotiate, but Georges had presented his case well, and the old man sat back, drew a long breath, and allowed the cigar smoke to slowly escape his nose like an industrial chimney. The club looked as seedy as ever, the only warmth coming from the kitchen where the cassoulet bubbled like hot tar, the smell great. Two bowls of the historic white bean stew rested before the two interlocutors. Jordi nursed a glass of beer. Josette had welcomed Georges and Paul with bosomy bisous and then retreated to continue her dinner preparations, perhaps aware of the potential negotiations.

"You guys know how tough times are for proprietors of public houses? Look around." There were less than a handful of drinkers. "I paid that man a month's salary; he may be a Gypsy, but he's no fool. He's got to come through, and you started this, both of you. Now I'm out a bundle."

"And who stands to gain?" Georges demanded, ignoring the jarring clichés." Paul tasted his cassoulet, mostly staying out of the discussion.

"I hear you, Georges. But you got to consider my side. I take all the risks, pay all the salaries, fund all the improvements."

"These shows remind people you're still in business. They come to the show, and they come back for a drink or two. We're not asking for residuals, just a fair share of the show's profits: a 40:60 split is fair, since we arrange the show, bring the talent, and attract the audience. We're only here because we're old friends and want to help the club. We could walk away. Paul is busy, and I'm retired to the seashore. Think about it."

"Well, I appreciate your friendship, but still I'm in business. Twenty percent seems fair to me."

"With your bookkeeping, we'd be out money. Thirty-five is the bottom. We can't go below that. And we're taking risks as well. Your accounting for one. We're not asking for guarantees."

"Georges, we've been together a long time. I can go to twenty-five, and that's final. Josette will kill me."

"This stew is tasty, but it's our last supper." Georges pushed back from the table, leaving a half-empty bowl.

"Hold on, Georges. I'm dying. Thirty." He coughed and dropped ash all over the table.

"You'll survive. Come on Paul."

Paul looked at these men, both elder citizens, without a worry, acting like they were on stage in some seamy drama. "Split the difference, thirty-two five, and we'll share equally anything above twenty thousand francs net. You've never had profits exceeding that in any of the shows, excluding Trenet. I know you did well on that one, and this one will be for five days." Paul had no idea of where this came from, it just seemed right, and the twenty thousand an informed guess.

Both of the men looked at Paul.

"I guess you've been doing your homework," Jordi said, patting Paul on the shoulder in a not entirely negative fashion. It's my funeral, but you give me no choice. Let's do it. You guys are on. Partners. Now get what's-his-name down here, and let's get this show on the road.

Georges fixed Jordi, still standing. "That's thirty-two five and anything above twenty is split two ways. You okay with that?"

"Yea, yea. Eh, what do you think? I wouldn't do it for my brother, if I had one. But for you guys...I love you...in a funny sort of way. Now, sit down, Georges."

They shook hands all around, and Josette came out of the kitchen, obviously having listened to the entire proceedings.

"Finish your stew. I've got a special dessert. Jordi, put out that cigar, you'll run off the few customers we have." She stood behind Paul with both hands massaging his shoulders. "How's Gabrielle? You haven't been in for a while."

"She's fine," Paul said hesitantly.

"Fine? What's that mean? Your dog is fine. Your maman's fine. Not your lover."

"Lay off the boy, Josette," Jordi interjected.

"I mean," Paul added, "she's going through some stuff. You know, with the occupation and work."

"I wasn't asking about the state of the union. Just about her. Send her down here, and you can come if she decides you're worth it." Josette turned and returned to her domain.

"How you been keeping, Paul?" Jordi asked. "Really?"

"I've been working too much, worrying too much, and Gabrielle resents it. She doesn't want to be dependent on me, and I'm sort of independent."

"You guys still together?" Georges asked, concerned.

"I'm not sure at this point," Paul replied uncomfortably, honestly.

"When we talked," Georges said, "I realized she was really upset. She experienced a big shock. Don't underestimate it. Something that most of us will never have to face. Her world upset. It'll take time to adjust. It could be years, a lifetime. But it also meant she needs to make changes in her life."

"What are you talking about?" Jordi said, not anticipating a full explanation.

"Gabrielle discovered some relatives in Paris she never knew she had," Paul explained.

"So? That's a good thing. Just the other day, my cousin from Toulouse introduced me to his daughter. I never knew he had a daughter, and she's a looker."

"You're right," Paul said. "It's a good thing in most cases, but not in all."

"Listen, Paul," Georges changed the conversation. "When are you going to talk with Django?"

"I'll send a telegram to Pierre Fouad or Ninine, his brother. Not sure where they're playing or even if they're in Paris."

"Okay. I have to get going," Georges said. "We'll start rehearsals in three weeks or so, Jordi. It's not going to be as big a cast. We'll not require the full room until the end." He stood and shook hands with Jordi. "Paul, walk with me? I left the car down the street."

"Sure. Thanks, Jordi. Let me say goodbye to the sniffers. We'll drop by to let you know the progress in the next week or so." They embraced. Paul put on his coat and walked back into the kitchen. "Josette?"

"Oh, Paul," Josette turned from her cutting board. "I'm sorry if I was a little harsh. I overheard your conversation, but don't let her get away. She's worth it. Sometimes, you have to give a woman time, breathing space, but not too much. You guys belong together." She came over to him and gave him a full bear hug, meaning he had work to do as far as she was concerned.

"Thanks, Josette."

He walked over to the basket next to the stove containing the two bulldogs. They had been suspiciously watching him with their bulging eyes, but not wanting to leave the warmth of their container. He rubbed their ears and small bodies, which they allowed and seemed to like.

"We'll drop by. See you soon."

Outside, Georges was waiting for him. They began walking toward the car.

"Paul, you have to understand the magnitude of this on Gabrielle's life. It puts into question everything that has happened to her. Her life has been a lie. She will have to reexamine everything in a new context, particularly given the current environment. What she might have disliked before has now become personal, but I know how strong she is. Being a Jew today is dangerous. Give her some time and support her. She may want to make some pretty drastic changes."

"I know you're right, Georges. Right now, I'm not sure what to do. We'll talk in a few days."

"Let us know, if we can help in any way."

It was late, too late to meet Gabrielle at the Galeries. He walked slowly back to the apartment. When he arrived, he looked for Edith as though she were Cerberus. The door opened, but she remained out of view. He walked up the three flights and opened the door into a dark and cold apartment.

"Gabrielle," he called needlessly.

He went straight back to the bedroom. Everything was picked up. He went to the closet. Her clothes were gone. All her toiletries were removed from the bathroom. She was gone. He ate some crackers and cheese and then sat down in the salon in the dark, his mind empty, his life frozen. A few hours later, he went to bed. The apartment was cold, and the bed no warmer. He lay in the cold sheets, smelling of Gabrielle. She could not take that away. Sleep took a long time coming.

***

The next day, Paul has no appointments. He wakes late to a cold and deserted apartment, smelling of dust and ringing in silence. He makes his way through his daily ablutions and then leaves the now empty apartment and finds his way to his normal café on the rue de la Gare. He orders an imitation coffee and non-butter croissant and sits out on the sidewalk, mindlessly watching the trains full of people pass on the tramway and travelers with their valises hurrying on their way to the train station. The weather has warmed, but he leaves his coat buttoned. He sits there until he can no longer and then gets up to walk.

He has no new arguments. He could apologize and promise to be more attuned to her needs. She seems to have run the course with Les Nouvelles Galeries. She wants more meaningful work, but that is only a part of what is bothering her. The occupation certainly, and her discovery of being Jewish. Most of what is driving her is out of his control.

At the normal time for meeting her, after several coffees and cigarettes, after walking throughout the town, he makes his way to the Galeries. In the cosmetics boutique, he does not see her, but one of the girls approaches.

"Did Gabrielle leave early?" he asked.

"Nope. She didn't come in today. Called in sick."

"She didn't tell me," Paul replied, hoping it wasn't clear that they were having problems.

"She is taking the remainder of the week off."

"Oh. Thanks. I better be getting back."

"I hope she's feeling better."

"Thanks."

He leaves, and without really thinking, walks to her parents' house on rue Maurell. It's about dinner time, so he meanders, all the while his mind preparing ways to approach her, to talk to her, to explain. By the time he nears the house, it's totally dark and almost too late. Knocking on the door, he hears some voices from the second floor. Finally, the knob turns and Julie opens the door.

"Paul," she says, not surprised, but awkwardly. "Gabrielle is here, but…" She changes her mind. "Come on up."

Paul follows her up the stairs. Auguste is sitting in his easy chair with the paper in his lap and Gribouille at his feet.

"Good evening, Monsieur."

"Paul. Nice to see you."

From behind him, Julie whispers, "she's in her room. You go on down there. She's in a state."

Paul walks down the hallway and knocks on her door. No answer. He knocks again.

"Go away, Paul."

He opens the door, and she is sitting on the bed facing the door.

"I don't want to talk with you right now. You've got to give me time."

"I want to help," Paul says. "It's no good this way."

"You can't."

"Why's that?"

"Because you don't understand. Even if you did, it's got nothing to do with you."

"Gabrielle…"

"I have to do this, Paul."

"So you don't want to see me?"

"I want some time, that's all."

"Should I call?"

"No."

He watches her. She looks terrible: her hair a mess, no makeup, her eyes red. He wants to hold her, to soothe her, wanting to feel the comfort of her body against him, wanting to save her from herself, and, by doing so, save himself.

"There's nothing I can do?"

"No."

"It's not fair."

"I'm sorry, Paul. It's not about you. There's nothing you can do. Please go."

"Okay. I don't want to lose you. Talking might help."

"Not now. Please leave."

"Okay, but when can I see you?"

"I don't know."

"Okay. Sorry. You can count on me, Gabrielle. I know you don't want to hear this, but I love you."

"Goodnight, Paul."

"Goodnight."

Back in the salon, her parents are standing as though waiting for him. He sighs and walks awkwardly to the stairs. "Goodnight."

"Paul," Julie says, "she'll call. Don't fret."

"Thanks."

16

April-May 1942

> *I'm alone this evening with my dreams*
> *I'm alone this evening without my love*
> *The day falls, my joy ends*
> *All is broken in my heavy heart*
> *I'm alone this evening with my pain*
> *I've lost all hope of your return*
> *Yet still I love you and always will.*
> *« Je suis seule ce soir, » Charles Trenet*

"Gabrielle."

The voice breaks onto the beach, advancing up the damp shore, and then announces its raucous withdrawal.

"Gabrielle."

Waking with a start, Gabrielle realizes the voice is not a dream, but her mother calling. Struggling to come to consciousness, she looks about. She can see the glimmer of the morning sun on the shutters on her window. It's later than normal, and she needs to go to work. Another day has dawned.

She pulls herself awake and marches to the toilet. When she returns to her room, she dresses much as she dressed yesterday. They have no meaning, clothes. Less so, makeup. But she needs to get out of her room. Too much time spent alone in her cell, contemplating what was, what is, and what could be. She realizes the strange despondency she has fallen into. It's warmth is comforting, even though you know in your heart and mind that you must disentangle yourself from its false embrace. Nothing has any value.

She exits the house with her mother talking gibberish to her. She can't hear; she can't see. She walks quickly to Les Nouvelles Galeries. The comforting thought of Paul is too painful. She hasn't seen him for a month, since he came to her house. He's probably beginning to work on the show at the Club les Tréteaux. She really doesn't want to know. She doesn't want to see her friends. She can no longer tolerate Catie and her inanities, and Nuria continues to work and live in Lyon, as far as she knows. She doesn't really care. She works. She eats meagerly. She lives. She doesn't read the papers, so full of lies. She avoids the BBC broadcasts that are so important to her father. She ignores the gossip and advice of her colleagues at work. She is hermetically secluded, incapable of focusing on the bizarre buzz of other people. After being warned several times by her manager, she attempted weakly to improve her attitude and demeanor. Still her dress is unacceptable, and she needs to take better care of herself. How can you sell beauty products if you yourself are without makeup, without conditioning, without scent? Strangely, though, she continues to be one of the best girls, selling more than any of the others. If this were not true, she would have been fired weeks ago.

"Madame," she tells one client, "today the trend is less: less blush, lighter colors, flesh colors. Try the spring collection, a light foundation, and add powder. Light browns for the eyes and mascara applied with a brush, not too much. With lips use a lighter color, an amber perhaps, or orange, leave the hot colors to Hollywood, and dilute with vaseline, which is becoming harder to find, but we keep a supply. We have a great new gloss, which gives a soft glow in the evenings, but who goes out anymore? Eyebrows simply groomed. We have special tweezers. And nail colors to match, leaving the cuticle and tip uncolored. Let me show you. And remember we no longer carry stockings, so if you can't find any, we have beautiful liquid stockings in colors that work well and last.

At home at mealtime, she endures her parents.

"Cherie, you seem so unhappy. You need to get out more."

"I know, Maman."

"Have you heard from Paul? He saw Papa yesterday about a poster for the next show. It's a man called Jean, or something like that. I've never heard of him."

"His name is Django."

"Have they talked to you about dancing?"

"I told you. It's just music. Jazz. No magicians. No jugglers or acrobats. No dancers."

"Julie," Auguste says. "Leave her alone. Can't you see, she wants to be allowed to eat in peace."

"Yes, but she has no friends and never goes out."

"She's a grownup."

"I'm not so sure," Julie adds.

"The weather has improved. I can begin looking for scenes to paint. And Gribouille needs to run. I'm going this weekend. Would you like to come? With snow still on Canigou and late almond trees still in bloom, you can always find a new and interesting vantage point."

No response.

After dinner Gabrielle retreats to her room. She has some novels to read, but she cannot focus, reading a sentence and then forgetting it or getting carried away by her chattering mind. She usually puts on a housecoat and lies on her bed, reading sporadically, often falling asleep, until she finally turns out the light and attempts to sleep the night. Where once she fell asleep at peace with the coming dawn, now she falls asleep to exist a few more hours.

She knows she is sick at heart, but is unable to halt the slide into her deepest fears. Nothing is rational about her state. Nothing is controllable. What seems easy to correct to an outsider is a tangled mass of thoughts of uncertain depth that is impossible to disentangle and that traps her. She is barely able to lift a finger without contrary thoughts. Lost without possibility of rescue.

"What will become of me? In the end, we will become the food of foolish insects."

***

On a weekend in late April, her father asks her to join him on one of his sketching treks, and she accepts. They take a train to Prades and walk up the road to St. Michel de Cuxa, an ancient abbey in a state of disrepair, but remarkable even in its current condition. They have not been there for years, and the site is splendid, with the walls of the abbey and high bell tower intact. The roof has given way, some of the supporting pillars have fallen, and many of the outbuildings are in a similar state of disrepair. As a consequence, the structures, including the church itself, are closed to visitors and worshippers. The abbey is in the foothills of Canigou, surrounded by the mountains, still with snow on the heights, and private vineyards and blooming orchards. Auguste goes sketching on the grounds with Gribouille, while Gabrielle visits the ancient abbey. The sun is out, but the steady, moderate breeze keeps the temperature fresh.

Much of the cloister was sold to an American at the turn of the century, when the abbey was in its worst state, and many masterpieces of sculpture were shipped to the United States. Since then, the Cistercians, aided by the local commune and inhabitants, have attempted to restore the church to its original elegance. However, the Great War and the Spanish Civil War interrupted much of the progress, and the current war continues to hold everything in abeyance. The high bell tower is magnificent, and the church walls and footprint are elegant and suggest its ancient splendor. Gabrielle walks around the edifice and through the grounds, feeling the sunlight and listening to the birds and an occasional cock crowing in the distance. After a while, she joins her father, who is sketching the abbey from the direction of Prades to the north.

After several hours, they walk back to Prades. Today, the town is peaceful like many of the mountain villages. Since the occupation, the town has lost some of its population with the departure of tourists and young people. Recently, though, the influx of immigrants from the Spanish Civil War, including Pablo Casals, the famous Spanish cellist, and émigrés from the current war have more than restored the population. They find a café serving lunch and sit down inside; the terrace is unoccupied even though the sun is shining. They are late, but the server allows them to lunch among the patrons, most of whom are locals and know each other.

They are served a fresh green salad with a few cooked vegetables and fresh browned goat's cheese, and a pleasant local white wine. Auguste pours the wine and toasts his daughter.

"To you, *ma Cherie*, a true gift to your parents."

She drinks. "I'm afraid I feel a failure. I haven't done anything right."

"Oh, it's not about what you have done; it's about who you are. You understand?"

"Yes, Papa," but she stops and is silent.

"Is this about Paul?" he asks carefully.

"No. It's really not, no more than it's about you and Maman."

"What is it then? You've not been very talkative the last weeks and obviously out of sorts. It's unlike you."

"I have difficulty defining it myself. I feel at a loss, and nothing is quite right. It's as though I have awakened from a nightmare and no longer know who I am. Whether I'm dreaming or the dream is merely reality." She looks at him, her father, her solid, dependable enthusiast, the one person she has always been able to count on.

"He looks sharply at her. "Is this about being Jewish?"

"Yes, some. It started there anyway."

"You know, I have expressed the shame I feel that we handled this so very badly, just as my parents handled it badly. Worse perhaps. I don't want this to resolve itself in the same way we did with our parents, through silence and frigidity." He paused to think. "As a boy growing up, I always suspected something, and many of the people in the community never attempted to hide their past. Some who were not particularly religious continued with their traditions, even though they claimed to be Christian. Others were outright Jewish, speaking Yiddish, attending the temple, dressing the part. We, the next generation, knew they were all different, and, thus, we were different. By the time my parents and Julie's decided to explain, it was not much of a surprise. I think it was no surprise to my school chums, but it was never a subject of discussion. We made fun of those who continued the old ways. We hated our parents and attended the church without sincerity. When I learned the truth, I felt a little duped, but it answered a lot of questions. The difference with you was that we had decamped the community and raised you in a totally free environment. You never felt different. We should have told you from the start, and then it wouldn't have been such a shock, more natural, acceptable." He paused to sip his wine.

"I have thought about this my entire life. I know I'm Christian. I was raised Christian. I was baptized and attended church, and I believe in Jesus and in what he symbolizes. But I also know I'm Jewish. If I talked to a Jew, he would tell you that I am Jewish, but he would only be partially correct. I'm both. I'm both a Christian and a Jew, and I'm proud of it. When Pétain first introduced all the anti-Semitic legislation, it insulted me directly, although it did not affect me materially. When I hear of the treatment of the Jews in Eastern Europe by the Nazis, I feel I am one of them and feel more than sympathy: outrage and anger. When I meet a Jew, something special happens. There is a connection for me, even though he may have no knowledge of any relation and considers me, rightly, a Christian.

"It's strange. These two distinct parts of my being have always existed with me. Today, people want to believe, even the most liberal, that Jews are different…aliens from some other world. They want to blame Jews for all that ails them. They use this as a device to aid their ambitions, to steal, to kill. They lie to themselves that we are rich, that we are members of a cult to control the world, that we are in constant communication with one another, that we commit ritual murder, that our traditions are somehow dangerous and contrary to their beliefs. And they benefit from disseminating these myths.

"How can I help you, my daughter? Here is all I can say. Be proud of your forebears. They were people of conscience. They had an unquenchable belief in humanity…regardless of how they were treated. They believed in right and wrong, and were always respectful of others. These are our Christian values as well. Jewish ideals are not foreign or subversive. They are shared by intelligent, clear-thinking individuals throughout the world, whatever their religion.

"You are Christian. You are Jewish. These are not contradictory or inconsistent. They are you, just like they were Jesus. You can continue being Catholic with the knowledge of who you are. There is no conflict. You are a wonderful, caring person. That's who you are. No one can change that. And anyone who tries based on a religious label is ignorant.

"Unfortunately, we are confronted today with ignorance. Many people are only interested in self-promotion and obtaining money and power, all at the expense of others. And they are doing great harm. They will eventually fail, but in the meantime, they are accusing the Jews and, at the same time, attempting to bring down a nation of great humanitarian traditions. And we have to do what we can to ensure these traditions are not lost.

"You can help," he adds enigmatically, "and it may in turn help you."

It's getting late, and they are the only remaining patrons. They pay and leave for the train station. Gabrielle feels she knows her father a little better, and she's proud to be his daughter. She always was, but he has opened up to her. She is unsure how this affects her. She wants to let it settle in so she can better understand his message. Somehow, though, like an unidentified puzzle of a thousand pieces dropped on the floor, through the identification of patterns, colors, shapes, and the recognition of an order, the pieces eventually fit back together.

***

I returned to work the next week with an improved spirit. I realized I could never return to who I was, and I wasn't sure yet who I would become. I felt that first I had to apologize to Paul. This was not his fault. There was nothing he had done to cause it, either through his actions or inactions.

I think there is a lesson here for me. I'm very emotional like my mother. More susceptible to being knocked off my track or to make assumptions that affect me negatively. Quick to judgment, slow to forgive. Paul's ability to stay in tune affected the entire orchestra, made it better. He may pay a price emotionally, closing himself off to an extent, leaving off the high notes perhaps, but he earned the gift of consistency and longevity.

It was not time to contact him. I just wanted to be more focused on myself before I allowed him entrance. I still had to decide what this meant to my life. It could be a gamble. If I lost, I would lose him. I know I will never find another like him, and each night I fall asleep in a pool of tears.

I could quit my job and do something else. Join the Resistance, as I now realized my father had suggested. Go back to school. Unfortunately, at this time there weren't many options. I wish Nuria were here. She knows herself and what she wants, and she goes after it. I have always impressed people, but somehow that is not enough. I got my job at Les Nouvelles Galeries by being forceful, by convincing my manager that I knew more about makeup and sales than any of the other employees. So she hired me. I think I was right, and my experience at the store has shown that I have a talent, but I'm not sure where that talent leads me. Could I find a place as a business person at a house of couture in Paris? I think I could, but it would require resettling, something that would be nearly impossible today.

When I returned to work, I was a different person. I was my old self as far as anyone could see, but underneath I was recast, a transfiguration in progress. I closely observed every person I worked with and every person I met. I was looking for something better, something that fit me, allowing me to be myself and to develop a meaningful life. And one day, I found it.

17

May-June 1942

> *The train departs...*
> *A cloud stretches out above its blue canopy*
> *And in passing seems to pronounce*
> *A sorrowful farewell*
> *To all that I loved*
> *The train rounds the curve*
> *In a billow of vapid smoke*
> *Disappearing forever.*
> *« Nuages, » Django Reinhardt, Jacques Larue*

The posters designed by Auguste Daniel were a great success, posted throughout the city with a remarkably detailed image in pen and ink of Django and the Hot Club, lettering in three colors. Just like the Trenet concert, the first evening attracted a large crowd with standing room only, and people were turned away at the door. The few scantily-costumed servers couldn't serve the crowd fast enough. With the whole warehouse heated up by the crowd, people began drinking even faster.

Django Reinhardt and the Hot Club arrived an hour late. Obviously, everyone knew his reputation: Gypsy time. They allowed him latitude, continuing to drink peacefully. There were no cast, no dancers, or others to fill in. Georges had decided to limit the show to the Hot Club. Finally the small band reduced to a piano and accordion, having planned only to back up the Hot Club, opened with Paul singing some of the Trenet songs from the prior show. The audience was in an accepting mood, and welcomed the local singer enthusiastically. They got into the swing of things immediately, as if they had only come to see him. They sang along, danced, caroused, and drank.

By the time Django finally arrived, the hall was jumping, and the crowd was amiably soused. Dancing had been condemned by Vichy, but this off-circuit venue was able to get away with it, at least for short periods. Paul finished his tenth Trenet song, singing with passion *"Je suis seule ce soir,"* which was exactly what the crowd craved. Everyone could relate to the permissible, but clearly anti-war, lyrics. The slow-tempo romantic song allowed the audience to rest and to dance slowly and intimately. During the previous up-tempo songs, the crowd had danced wildly, with some talented couples leading with lifts and throws. With this romantic ballad, the married couples and lovers were able to return to the dance floor.

The first sign of Django was a spattering of applause in the middle of Paul's rendition of "*Si tu va à Paris,*" a Trenet classic from the 1930s, which had been censored in Paris. The Hot Club entered with panache. They obviously were well along on a joyous and well-watered evening. They mounted the stage and, without interrupting the song, set up and slowly joined in.

This evening the Hot Club consisted of Django and his brother, Joseph, on guitars, Pierre Fouad at drums, and Eugène Vées (Ninine), a rustic relative of Django, playing guitar. Since the departure of the violinist Stéphane Grappelli. key to the Hot Club sound, Hubert Rostaing had joined on clarinet. The ever-changing group was still capable of keeping up with the ingenious and irrepressible Django.

When Paul completed the song with the entire Hot Club supporting him, Django walked up to the microphone and hugged him.

"This young man has quite a voice, quite a future. You can be proud, and you'll be hearing more of him this evening." He turned to the audience and shouted, "Paul Broussard." Paul departed the stage, to cheers and whistles. "Now let's do some shin-cracking."

Django took over the evening, starting with an up-tempo version of "*Si j'aime Suzy.*"

By the time Paul had finished his song, he had had a taste of Django's jazz. Not only did Django join the Trenet song, but he made it his own, improvising, repeating, extending, twisting, and turning phrases. Paul managed to keep up, singing during the returns to the melody, but often found himself listening to the band extemporize with its own version. The piano and accordion also followed, but with difficulty.

"Wow," was all Paul could say when he joined Georges at the bar.

"He's a whirlwind, all right," Georges said.

"It's like singing with a force of nature. You never know where he's going; it's constantly surprising. But they love him."

"They do," Georges said. "Who else could have kept this crowd happy? Trenet?"

"Singing with a real musician makes me humble. I've got a lot to learn."

Django entertained the house for three hours straight, drinking as they played his hits from the 1930s up to his current songs and some that he was still working on *"Djangology,"* "Ain't misbehavin," *"J'attendrai,"* *"Georgia on my mind,"* *"Hungaria,"* *"Belleville,"* "I'll see you in my dreams," "I can't give you anything but love," *"Daphné,"* *"Minor Swing,"* "All of me," among others. He called Paul back onto the stage at times to sing, *"Nuages"* and several Trenet hits that Paul knew well and that Django had played with Josette Daydé, his last vocalist, and recorded with Jean Sablon.

At midnight Django and the Hot Club took a break to smoke. A half-hour later they were back at it for another full set. No one left.

Georges and Paul went outside during the break. As a late spring had broken the icy hold of winter, and the evening was gentle and humid. Paul offered Georges a cigarette, and they smoked together in silence for a few moments. Finally, Georges broke the spell.

"How's she getting along?"

"Frankly, I don't know. She refuses to talk, but recently she's gotten into something. I'm not quite sure what. She's been away. The only reason I know is that her parents at first thought it had to do with me, and questioned me, but I haven't seen her for nearly two months."

"What do you think?"

"I'm afraid to guess. She still works at Les Nouvelles Galeries, but on a part-time basis. They let her get away with it because she's one of the most productive girls in her department."

"You miss her?"

"I do nothing but work. I exist. But I'm only half there. I've trained myself not to miss anyone, but, yes, I miss her."

"Can't you break into her life?"

"I've tried. Now her parents won't speak to me. I think they blame me. All I can do is pray she comes to her senses."

Jordi came out to where they were sitting.

"I can't believe it," he said, wiping the sweat from his forehead. "They've been going for hours. And we've got them for five more nights. Is that right, Paul?"

"That's what Ninine said. No guarantees."

"*Bah*, I'm almost out of stock. I'll have to make a run tomorrow. It's incredible."

"Good?" Georges asks Jordi.

"*Hé*, better than that."

Paul returned several times for tunes he knew, and the musicians supported him enthusiastically. He felt more comfortable, and they were used to working with vocalists and stuck to the melody, allowing the singer to lead. Then they would play a jazz tune, improvising, playing solo credenzas, deconstructing the melody, and finally returning to put it all back together. The crowd loved it. During the evening, the dancing never stopped whether up-tempo or slow-romantic. As a finale they took up "Nuages" again, and Paul joined to cheers. Jacques Larue had recently added lyrics for this instrumental song written by Django, which was becoming one of his standards. The solo song had become an instant hit for Lucienne Delyle. Paul knew it well, having worked with Django at the holiday party and had followed its success on the radio.

People began slowly to leave the club at 1:00 am. By 2:00 pm more people were leaving, but the Hot Club played on. The band slowly finished the last encore and retired, and the club emptied at half-past, everyone exhausted but buoyant, realizing that they had shared an extraordinary moment together. One they would never forget. The war was forgotten, politics were put to bed, and good spirits and joy were shared by all. Walking out of the club was like leaving a wondrous dream.

***

The next day in the Bits and Pieces column in the morning Independent (26 May 1942):

> Unbridled talent presented itself last night in our sleepy southern abode at the Club les Tréteaux. Together, Jordi Pons and Georges Doelnitz seem to have a knack for

attracting top Parisian talent. Last night was no
exception: King Django Reinhardt and the Hot Club held
court. They journeyed into the farthest reaches of
modern music: pure jazz with an American flavor. Our
own local talent, Paul Broussard, anchored the vocals,
but it was the Hot Club that filled the club, passionately
playing Django standards and new additions, such as his
latest Parisian hit *"Nuages"* and the romantic ballads. It
was his jazz renditions that got people off their seats.
Certainly, Django's genius is to never stand pat, always
testing the limits, knowing what people want to hear and
expanding on it. Hubert Rostaing on the clarinet filled in
admirably for the violin of Stephane Grappelli. The
gendarmes worried about the late hour and wild dancing,
but they allowed the show to go on. Runs five more
nights through Sunday. An opportunity not to be missed.

***

For the rest of the week, the show continued in the same vein. A constant
flow of people filled the hall each night, increasing on the weekend,
drinking, dancing, and enjoying the riotous and spirited Hot Club until late.
People came in droves, many more than one night, grooving with the band
and the songs. Paul sang every night. He had worked on several of Django's
compositions and joined the band on the next nights: *"Un amour comme le
nôtre," "Je sais que vous êtes jolie,"* and *"La derniere bergère."* Paul found
it easy to perform with them. By the last night, he was completely
comfortable with the band, and they with him. Together, they were able to
satisfy the crowd beyond their expectations.

Paul was surprised by Django's work ethic. Once in his chair with his
guitar on his right thigh and his glass of cognac and water on his left, he
gave his all, more than the audience expected, drawing out songs that
captivated, playing requested songs, favorites, and always encores. His
public reputation, though mythologized rather than actually earned, was as
an erratic and irascible entertainer, often angering his audiences by his
foibles and self-absorption, but that spring in Perpignan he was on his best
behavior, fulfilling everyone's wishes. Every night they played late. In the
late afternoons before each performance, the band assembled in the hall for

short rehearsals, leaving for dinner at various restaurants and then returning for the show.

On the last night, Django joined the club late, having returned from a small casino in Argelès, a short distance from Perpignan. He had won ninety thousand francs. He loved gambling and often was a big loser, but this evening was a lucky one for him, and he played his last evening with the spirit of his good fortune. The band and Paul had started without him. They were in top form when he finally joined them. And the Hot Club without Django was like a professional fighter throwing a fight; with him they were a world champion.

After the club closed the final night, after the cheers and rhythmic applause, after the drinks had run out, the band and a few others gathered at Georges' home in le Racou for a small celebration. The evening was temperate. The entire week hinted of an early and hot summer. The attendees at le Racou relaxed together. Bernadette and Josette had prepared a table overflowing with food and drink, including a large roast turkey that Josette had amazingly obtained from a source in the countryside: no one had seen a turkey in years.

The Hot Club made a short appearance, but Django soon left to gamble with his winnings from prior nights. He wanted one last go at cards, but the others gathered in the small house, spilling out onto the porch and front yard. The local musicians showed up for a brief appearance, but the evening turned out to be mostly close friends and associates. No music was played, and the low-key evening reflected more the times than the success of the show. Jordi and Josette soon left, as did most of the others. Much of the food remained.

Paul settled on the couch, nursing a large glass of pressed lemon juice and sugar. Paul rarely drank more than a beer, and although he was feeling high from his performance and the show in general, a lingering absence filled him, preventing him from fully enjoying his success. He had delayed several deliveries to and from Spain for the show and had not spoken to Paco in almost a week.

"You look like the weight of the world is on your shoulders," Bernadette said, cozying up to him on the couch. He was sleepy after the late night, barely keeping his eyes open. He felt her warmth and desire to assuage his feelings.

"Georges said you did very well, and that you were among the top musicians in the country."

"Thanks, Bernadette. Just tired, and next week will be a heavy one. And Gabrielle..." he paused. "I know she's doing better. She has a lot on her mind and is in charge."

"You know, Paul, she's a wonderful and sensitive girl. She's a little lost right now. She's trying to find an explanation, a way forward."

"She never came this week..."

"I'm sure she wanted to. She's just not ready. I'm sure it's not about you. She loves you, believe me."

"I'm part of the problem, I know, because she measured everything in her life by what I was doing. It sounds sort of strange, but she looks at herself from what she thinks is my perspective. She assesses that she doesn't measure up in my eyes. And that's ridiculous. She thinks I believe her job isn't professional. She wants to be special and appreciated like her father. She is skilled at her work, but it's not enough. And then when she learned about her roots, that seemed to tip the scales. I don't know. I could have been more understanding, more loving." He paused. "It's hard."

"It's not that hard, Paul, and you were very good with her and for her. As I said, you're not the problem. Other issues fill her mind. You're right about her wanting more. She wants to be your partner. She's smart and wants to be independent. But she has to come to terms with who she is right now. That's a big order. You know what? She'll be back."

"How long do I wait?"

"As long as it takes. If a woman is astounding, she will be difficult. You have to accept her ways. Don't give up, and you will be rewarded by her soaring nature."

"Mon Dieu. That's too much."

"There you are," she said simply and squeezed his hand.

"Oh," Paul looked at Bernadette. "How are you doing?"

"Okay," she smiled, putting her arm around his shoulders. "I'm glad it's over. Georges is so proud of you."

Georges came into the salon and joined them, sitting on the other side of Paul.

"Bernadette. Give the boy some breathing space."

"He's so attractive. What can I do?"

"It's been a good run," he said to Paul, ignoring his wife. "Now we have to think sensibly. Things are changing at Vichy. What are your thoughts, Paul? We haven't had time to talk."

"I haven't visited the Prefecture recently. I could get you both out with papers. It's up to you."

"I think we're okay for the while. They're not deporting sixty year olds yet, at least from what I hear. I guess we're too comfortable here. You know what they say, 'Whenever a Jew gets too comfortable, it's time to move on.'"

"Let me do some investigating. How do you think we did as partners with Jordi?"

"He'll rob us blind, but I think he did so well that he might be feeling generous. I'll do a little investigating on my own. I think he owes us some money. You especially. You made the whole thing work from start to finish. My role was minimal."

***

Each year of the occupation seemed to have a new title, and this one seemed to be dawning with less hope and more stories of atrocities. The year of the phony war, 1939. The implausible defeat and armistice of 1940. The casual year of wait and see, 1941. And now that had changed into the year of hopelessness, 1942. The audience at the club and the cast reflected this. Everyone was thrilled with the performance, but everyone was exhausted by the bad news, the shocking politics, the lack of nutrition, and Vichy. And Vichy was changing. Pierre Laval had returned to power as Prime Minister in April. He was far more accommodating to the Nazis, and he undermined any authority that remained with Pétain. The Occupant was putting more pressure on Vichy to increase the sacrifice for the war effort, taking all the country could produce. They demanded workers, materiel, and industrial and manufacturing support. And, and never uttered, they wanted the undesirables gone.

***

Paul visits the Prefecture the next day and is shepherded into his ex-boss' office immediately. Franco Plana looks older, drawn and thinner. Paul sits down before his large wooden desk. The filtered light gives the office a warm glow.

"Bonjour, Paul."

"Bonjour, Franco. How are you?"

"Nice to see you. To answer your question, I've been better. You look pretty good. You've been working?"

"Of course. I stay busy."

"That's good. I've had a few setbacks. Every day gets tougher here. You were lucky to get out when you did. Life here is crazy, between the zealots and the obstructionists, although few enough of these remain, and they're very careful. Can I help you with something?"

"I wonder if you could counsel me a bit."

"Sure, Paul."

"I have some friends whose names appeared on the list last fall. I'm worried about them."

"Well, how can I say this. I'm worried for most of the foreigners here in the department. Are they foreigners?"

"Naturalized just after the Great War. Over sixty and Jewish."

"They seem to be keying on 1935 as the final date. After that all naturalizations will be nullified. They should be okay. But they're talking of mounting a major effort this summer in the north. How much of this will come south, I can't say. Or let me put it another way. I'm not aware of any preparations here. But I do know there is great pressure to round up people and ship them east without questions: lock, stock, and barrel. No one's talking about where they're going or why or even if they have facilities to receive them. Millions of people are being rounded up throughout Europe. Where are the camps of sufficient size to house them? Reports vary, but none are helpful. Requests for visas here have fallen off greatly. People are frankly afraid to register. I don't blame them." He pauses. "Jewish you said?"

"Yes."

"Well, no one's talking. All bets are off, even French Jews."

"Today, it seems that what goes unsaid is more important than what is said."

"You're referring to what I just said?"

"Yes."

"You're right. If talking too much can cause trouble, people stop talking. And Vichy does more silently than vocally for sure. Lies can be vocalized, while truth must progress mutely. I'll tell you what, Paul, you're working with Paco, no?"

Paul nods.

"Good. Just making sure. Here's what I'm willing to do. If I hear of any imminent preparations here, I'll let you know. In any other time, you'd have my job by now. That's how much I think of you."

"Thank you. It means a great deal to me."

"How's Gabrielle?"

"You remember her name?"

"It's my job."

"We split up."

"Sorry. I thought you had found the right one. You need a wife, that's important. A good one." He starts coughing, pulling out a handkerchief and stopping with difficulty.

"I'd better be going," Paul says, looking closely at him. "You okay?"

"Take care of yourself, Paul."

"Thanks."

***

After a brief discussion with Paco Macias, Paul reinitiates his hauling duties postponed by the show. He begins in earnest hauling three to four packages a week. The scheme that went so well over the last two months continues unabated, but one day in late June it takes an unexpected turn.

The day dawns bright and sparkling, forcing a light mist to dissipate. He has to pick up a package from the safe-house outside Ceret. This time it's a short man with grey hair, dressed in workers' clothing, but his nails are neatly trimmed and groomed. He looks more like a French man than the typical passenger and is certainly not a worker. Something strikes Paul: he's not an émigré, nor military, nor Jewish. They shake hands, but not a word is spoken, which is normal with military and European émigrés. But this time, something bothers him. He helps the man into the truck. He has been briefed and understands the specifics of the transport. The man seems unconcerned with the dirt and debris in the tool box and scoots into the compartment. Paul cautiously closes the barrier and then replaces the camouflage dirt and tools.

The drive up the hill is relaxed in good weather, with wild flowers blooming along the roadside and trees filling out with emerald leaves. Everything is green and fresh and healthy smelling. He feels good, although as always there is still the nagging anxiety in the back of his head. The truck motors smoothly on the highway by Amélie-les-Bains and his grandmother's house. It's been too many months since he has seen her. His grandmother never complains, but he feels guilty. She never met Gabrielle.

He passes through Prats-de-Mollo, but just outside the town the truck is stopped at an impromptu roadblock by a detachment of gendarmes checking papers of all vehicles entering and leaving France. This has happened before without problem. He slows to a stop, waits in a line of a few vehicles, and removes his business and personal papers.

When his turn comes, a gendarme approaches, about Paul's age, tall, with hard eyes "Good morning, Monsieur. Your papers, *s'il vous plait*."

"Bonjour, Monsieur." He hands several papers to the officer.

The officer scrutinizes each document, carefully, and hands them back. "Can you step out of your cab?"

Paul lays the papers on the seat next to him and steps out, his head buzzing.

"Your name?"

"Paul Ruiz Broussard."

"How long have you been delivering charcoal?"

"About six months."

"Have you any contraband?"

"No. You are welcome to inspect the truck, Monsieur." By this time, Paul is worried, his heart beating just like his first crossing, but outwardly he attempts calm.

"That won't be necessary. One moment please."

The policeman walks over to where two other gendarmes are standing. There is no traffic in either direction, and no other vehicles are behind his truck. They confer for a moment, and the officer returns.

"Thank you, Monsieur. You may proceed. *Bonne route.*"

"Thank you." Paul mounts the cab and puts the truck into gear, slowly moving through the roadblock. He continues up the road for about a kilometer, wondering what is going on, his heart continues to race and his breath comes in spurts. He turns off onto a farm road to rest and breathe, proceeding until he finds a turnaround out of sight of the highway. He turns the truck around, realizing that by changing his routine he may be exposing himself, but he's concerned by the traffic stop and the doubts about his package. He gets out of the truck to smoke a cigarette, leaving the engine idling, and to calm his tense nerves. Suddenly, he hears struggling and banging on the side of the box and muffled yelling. Surprised, he opens the tool chest and removes the tools. He pulls the retaining door open and helps the man out.

"What's happening," the man asks in perfect French, looking around apprehensively at the surrounding high trees, brush, and narrow road. The man is clearly taken aback at the location.

"We were stopped," Paul says, realizing that this is too much to be ordinary. The packages are told to remain absolutely silent during the entire trip, regardless.

"Where are we?" the man demands. He seems nervous, trying to get his bearings.

"Near the frontier." Paul eyes the man, knowing he is hiding something.

"Still in France?"

"Yes."

"Oh, *mon Dieu!*" Suddenly, he is unreasonably angry, stomping about and swearing, loosening his muscles, flexing his arms.

"Why did you make a racket?" Paul asks, further troubled by the man's odd behavior, his looks, and his language.

"I'm claustrophobic, you *petit con*." Mixed with the anger, he sees frustration on the man's face, as though he missed a train or lost a sports match.

Paul is taken aback by the epithet. He looks at the man to try to identify him, and his behavior, but cannot. He knows something is deathly wrong.

"Who are you?" he demands.

"Just trying to get out," he says, exasperated.

"No," Paul says, doubting what he's seeing. Doubting the act. Doubting the man. "You're lying."

"You're in trouble now."

"Me? What? Who are you?"

"Listen, you're a driver. Just do your job."

"Simple question."

"Yeah, and none of your business."

Paul realizes he cannot continue with the man. He angrily replaces the barrier in the tool box, throws in the tools, and shuts the door. Ignoring the man, he quickly mounts the cab, slams the door, and shifts the idling engine into gear.

"Where are you going?" the man demands indignantly, coming around the truck to the driver's door.

"I'm leaving."

"You can't do that."

"You want to get across the border, walk."

"You're under arrest," the man says, holding a pistol up to the window. "Get out of the truck." From his voice, the man is used to getting his way, but it doesn't add up.

"Arrest?" Paul opens the door quickly with his foot, catching the man full on, knocking his off his feet onto his back.

He quickly accelerates up the rough road, but the man rights himself and runs alongside, grabs the locked door handle, and steps onto the small running board below the door. His face is at the open window, the pistol in the frame of the window.

"Stop. Stop or you're in big trouble," he yells, banging on the window and barely hanging on as the truck accelerates, bouncing on the uneven surface.

Paul ignores him, as the truck picks up speed. Seeing a thick grove of high rushes on his left, he veers toward the plants, and drives as close as he can, while he steps on the accelerator pedal. He doesn't want to kill the man, but he wants to get rid of him. The high plants, reaching above the cab, whip along the side. With increasing speed, he turns into the heavier branches, forcing the man to lose his footing and finally his handhold. The truck continues on without him.

In the mirror, Paul sees the man thrown against the body of the truck bed, falling onto the trail, but he quickly loses sight of him. At the highway, he turns in the direction of Spain.

He cannot understand what the man was attempting to do, but he must continue the trip to pick up charcoal or raise suspicion on his return. His mind racing, he slows at the French border, but he is waved through normally. The Spanish border guards are even more friendly. He crosses the border without a problem or inspection at either outpost. By the time he arrives at the charcoal production area, his shirt is wet with sweat, and he is breathing as though having completed a marathon race. He sees a few workers who signal him to an exposed charcoal mound, where he backs up, turns off the engine, and jumps out of the truck.

He's exhausted. He greets the workers and utters, "Where's Alberto?" He feels totally rung out, not understanding what happened, not knowing who the man was, who's side he's on, or what he's likely to do.

"He's not here right now. You can go down to the camp. Get something to eat. Wait for him."

Paul nervously lights another cigarette. He's been exceeding his normal two or three per day. In fact, his smoking has been increasing ever since Gabrielle left. He sits at the table rehashing in his mind the events of the two stops. What would have happened if he had not stopped in the forest? He wondered if the man knew where he was and was planning to make noise at the second stop. He couldn't have anticipated the unexpected traffic stop, and must have thought the second stop was the Spanish border crossing. But why the Spanish border? He knows that the man was up to no good, which could have cost the entire operation. It still can. He wonders about the risk of the return trip.

"*Hola, amic meu.*" Alberto sits down across from him.

"Alberto, good to see you." Alberto probably would have been politically sympathetic, but he is ignorant of Paul's activities. He is a business acquaintance and a friend. "How's it going?"

"We have another site down the road and have been cutting there. Where have you been?"

"The last two weeks were taken by a musical show with Django Reinhardt." His metabolism begins to slow down. The cigarettes helped.

"Who is this?"

"A guitarist."

"Ah, flamenco. I love it. We all love it."

"No, jazz."

"Jazz? No, I don't understand it. Let me get you something to eat. You look hungry...and tired. Eh, are you okay?" He looks more carefully at Paul. "I have a small bottle of my mother-in-law's *aiguardent*. Try it." He pours a small amount into a glass and hands it to Paul, then disappears into the tent. Paul sips the strong local liquor. It's intense, and the flavor suffuses his mouth. It cools his mouth and throat, and it relaxes him. Slowly, he forces himself to slow down.

Alberto returns. "Not much today." He puts some cheese on the table with cut bread and some cooked peppers and wild asparagus served cold."

"Perfect lunch, my friend," Paul says, finally returning to near-normal, postponing his fears.

"No problem. With the new property, we will have charcoal through the summer. Tell your boss. The price is going up throughout the mountains. Can't help it, even for good friends. You like my wife's vegetables. That's not all she can cook. You need one."

"A vegetable?" he jokes.

"No, *Senyor*. A wife," he replies seriously.

"I'm not ready and have no prospects."

"I thought you had a girlfriend."

"Yes, but she left."

"Ah, they do that. Let her go. She doesn't know what she has."

By this time the truck is fully loaded and the workers have joined them for a late lunch. Paul is feeling better. His stomach is quenched with the strong liquor and tasty vegetables and cheese. He leaves after sharing his Gauloise cigarettes all around and saying he will return in two days.

***

Although he was as apprehensive as he has ever been, the return from the mountains is without incident. He's waved through both border stations, dropping off a sac with the French border guards, and delivers his load at the Ceret depot. He arrives back in Perpignan late afternoon, parks the truck, and immediately walks to Paco's apartment without returning to his own. He knocks on the door, and Paco cracks it cautiously.

"Paul. Something wrong?"

"I'm not sure. I need to talk."

"One moment."

He listens as Paco converses with someone. Then the door opens.

"Sorry, Paul. Come in."

Paul enters. The daylight is just departing, and the room is dimly lit. He looks around and sees her sitting casually on the couch with papers on her lap. She's the last person he would expect to see here.

"Gabrielle!" He doesn't mean to say it with such force, but he's dazed, and the day has been so full of unexpected shocks. He doesn't know what to say.

Paco interprets the surprise on his face. "I think you know each other. Gabrielle has been helping out with administration. I know this is awkward, but it's time. You're not kids. No?"

They look at each other.

"Why didn't you tell me?" Paul says emotionally without thought.

"I wasn't ready. I'm just not ready…"

"Ready?" He can't assimilate the idea with her sitting in this office where he spent weeks learning his assignment.

Paul looks at Paco, who is standing awkwardly between them, hearing the emotions flowing through them, though not their depth.

"But, why?" Paul asks. "You never gave me a chance."

"I don't want to talk about it," Gabrielle replies firmly. She's fixed on him, but holding herself back. She's not backtracking, not giving in, not a centimeter, protecting her independence.

No moment in his life has ever been so hurtful. Not since his grandmother dragged him to the church to announce the death of his mother and sister. He feels a similar loss. He sees it clearly in her darkly fixed eyes, and it cuts to the quick of his heart. He's lost her. She sits there resolutely, maintaining her independence. He's crushed.

"Okay, you two," Paco announces. "Sorry, Paul, it shouldn't have happened this way. I should have told you earlier, but you were not expected here. Was there a problem?"

"*Ben, oui.*" His mind has been derailed. He pushes his feelings aside for a moment. "May I speak with you outside?"

"Of course. I'm afraid she is one of us now. Let's take a walk."

As they stroll around the city block, Paul recounts the troubling events of the delivery. Paco listens with interest, nodding, and signaling his comprehension. When Paul ends his story, he questions Paco.

"Who was that man? You knew him?"

"No," Paco says. "I'm not sure what gives. Though outside our normal network, he was recommended. I've got to talk to the safe-house. I never met the man.

"He was French."

"Yes? I don't know, Paul. This is serious, and you are grounded until we get to the bottom of this. He knows too much. It could be that we have been exposed. I don't know, but let's keep this to ourselves. Take a week off, Paul. We'll talk."

Paul looks at Paco; suddenly he questions if he can trust this man. Without realizing it, the interview is terminated. He starts, glances quickly about, and then says, "Thanks." He doesn't know what else to say.

"How did the show go?"

"Well. It has no significance." He looks at this man he barely knows. "By the way, I hope you are not exposing Gabrielle to any information that could be deadly."

"I take my role seriously. I protect my people with my life. Believe me. I'll contact you soon, Paul," Paco says loudly. "You need to cool off."

As he walks away, all he can think is how beautiful she appeared and that she never looked at him. How much he misses her. How much he wants her. The deep hurt tugs at his heart and stomach, so hurtful that it makes him weak with resentment. A Romanesque cathedral reduced to rubble and carried away. The last lingering embers, kept warm by ignorance, are now dashed with finality. How can he continue to work with Paco? How can he go on at all?

"What a disaster, today."

Paul walks on into the night alone with aching thoughts and a mélange of feelings of hurt, fear, and anger. The terrible cruelty we suffer: without a future, without remedy to our sickness, accelerating into the unknown. All that remains is a stark black and white image of her stern, unfeeling eyes, those of a stranger.

Loneliness is a motherless child.

18

> *The evening wind slaps against my door*
> *Reminding me of long lost loves*
> *In front of a long extinguished fire*
> *It's an autumn song...*
> *What remains of our loves?*
> *What remains of those beautiful days?*
> *An old photo of my youth*
> *What remains of our love letters?*
> *The months of April, our rendezvous*
> *Memories that haunt me ceaselessly.*
> « *Que reste-t-il de nos amours?* » *C. Trenet and L.*
> *Chauliac/lyrics C. Trenet*

I believe after months of cloudy storms that I'm moving in a worthwhile direction. The last weeks have opened my eyes and allowed me to see myself and the world in a newly focused light. My healing began a month ago.

After moving out of the apartment, my despair worsened, but I discovered later that it was an essential first step. It took a month, with my mother and father deeply worried. I went to work each day, feeling that I was doing nothing of value and that my customers were ignoring the authentic dangers, wasting their time in self-satisfying emollients and cleansers. I recalled discussions with Paul about adjusting to his new job. Normally, he never mentioned names, but for some reason he mentioned that he had been working with Paco Macias. I had no idea who he was. I was fairly certain he was a member of the Resistance, but even that title, which hardly ever passed peoples' lips, was an abstract, confused concept.

As I thought more about my background, and the struggles of these people, and what was happening around me, and, yes, Paul's quiet determination, how could I continue with my unguents and scents and colors? How could I walk down the street knowing that last year, last year mind you, Churchill announced on the BBC that whole districts in Eastern Europe were being exterminated and that "we are in the presence of a crime without a name." And no one talks about it, but it's only getting worse. How can I continue guided in ignorance.

My return to Les Nouvelles Galeries was the first step. The next step occurred two months later. I pulled myself out of my self-imposed gloom, and I went to visit Paco Macias. Some time before our breakup, I had surreptitiously followed Paul, not that I didn't trust him, but out of curiosity and, perhaps, some envy. He said he had a meeting and left early, and I followed him at a distance and watched as he entered a building and hurried to see him knocking on the door of a ground-floor apartment.

I walked to this same location and same door during lunch one day, not having planned it in any concrete terms. I knocked on the door. An older, distinguished man with bushy eyebrows and a trimmed beard opened the door and looked at me. He was almost as tall as Paul, but heavier set. He opened the door wider, removing a cigarette from his mouth. "You're Gabrielle. No?"

"Yes," I replied surprised. "How did you know?"

"It wasn't too difficult. Few if any pretty girls knock at my door, and Paul can't contain himself from talking about you. I'm sure my advice to him had nothing to do with the dissolution. I'm sorry if it did, but I would never actually recommend separation as a course of action. It solves nothing. You just continue on with the exact same issues that caused the problem in the first place. Come in. Come in." His face glowed with warmth and intelligence.

I had to smile at his explanation. I entered the living area of a small apartment in a complete state of disorder. Boxes and cartons piled against the walls. Bottles, cans, glasses, plates and utensils, and shopping sacs covered every surface. The round central table obviously served as an office desk and as a meeting center. Two gigantic ashtrays were filled to overflowing with cigarette butts. A settee was buried under papers, clothes, and books. The daylight was obscured by shuttered windows and drawn curtains. It smelled of smoke, mold, and old clothes. A man cave, so unlike Paul.

"Sit down. I would have arranged things if I had been notified of your visit."

"Sorry to surprise you, but I wanted to talk."

"I'm all ears. Obviously, I'm already familiar with your activities and background."

"I want a job." This came to me automatically without forethought.

"Now, that's direct, and not the subject I had anticipated." He looked at me quizzically. "What do you want to do?"

"I want to help stop the madness in our country."

"That's an admirable goal, but it's not a good start. Right now, what you call madness, I would refer to as a sickness of feeble morality and amnesia. We have been infected by the Occupant. I believe this malady is a temporary illness, but like saddleback fever it can come roaring back at any time." He sighed. "We need to be more specific. What can you do to assist in this goal?"

"I'm smart and well-organized. I know marketing and sales, which I believe are valuable in any circumstances. I don't mind hard work, and I'm not afraid of getting my hands dirty. I write well and work well with disagreeable people."

"Hmm."

"I can handle all sorts of people..."

"But not your lover..."

I started and looked up at this older man in surprise, wondering how much he knew? Was he joking?

"Sorry, a low blow. As I said, I am past-president of this common hazard."

"No. You're right. I needed a break. Everything was moving too fast. I love Paul. But he doesn't need me. At least, he gets along very well by himself."

"Well, that's the first thing you've said with which I disagree. Let's leave that for another day. I'm quite the fan of Paul, you know. The first rule here is to separate your private life from what goes on here. The second rule is to keep your mouth shut. Do you think you can do that?"

I liked that. "Yes. I can. My mother would find this an impossibility, but my father would have no trouble."

"Your father is Auguste Daniel?"

I nodded. "Everyone in Perpignan knows him."

"Yes they do."

"He's having a show."

"I know. I see him at Town Hall meetings. When this war is concluded, assuming we have extinguished the evil and have survived, what do you want to do?"

"That's a hard question. Since the occupation, I have postponed thinking about the future. I would like to continue with school, perhaps learn more about business. I would like to have a marriage like my parents. Children one day."

"Yes, but you have to plan the future today, even if it seems bleak and nebulous and without hope." He paused a moment as though in thought. I guessed this was a test: whether I could keep my mouth shut or not.

He continued, "I'm tempted to try you out and see how helpful you can be. I'm currently in a state of continual disorder to my own detriment, as you can see. I need an assistant. Someone to keep track of my appointments and rendezvous. In other words, someone to organize my life a touch. I'm good at some things, but I have never been good at systematizing, bookkeeping, or organizing. And it continues to get harder, more complex, and busier every day." He paused, looking for my reaction.

I remained attentive, not replying.

"As the war changes, so does the nature of our activities. The number of our associations, and, I might add, our financial situation, ebbs and flows. As a movement, we need to be more unified and more powerful. This is slowly coming about and today is our current focus. When we do manage to defeat our adversary, which is absolutely mandatory, we will become a major political movement. I know this. A force against tyranny in all countries." He pulled his beard.

"Perhaps we could start out by working mornings. I want you to continue with your current job, if possible. The pay here is not good. We barter for much of our recompense, and even that is mostly cigarettes and wine and liquor. Certain of our activities are highly compensated. You could also help organize this apartment.

"Don't mistake me. This is dangerous, risky work. As dangerous as it gets. I want to keep you immune as much as possible, but even showing up here could get you arrested. We will not be friends. We will not see each other anywhere but in this room. What you learn here must be kept secret. I insist on a Chinese wall between you and any of my associates or my activities. I don't want you here for any meetings. I don't want you to meet anyone here, ever. Is that clear? You can keep my schedule, but at the same time have no direct knowledge of what it means and the identity of people involved. Your work for me will be between the two of us. *Fini*. You will never know what it is I do, how I do it, or where. Is that clear."

I nodded my head in agreement, slightly scared of what I was volunteering for, remembering my conversations with Nuria.

"I want you, as much as possible, to be in the dark. Is that clear? And you will have to handle your affairs with Paul like an adult. It will not be a topic here. Let me make that entirely clear. Right now, believe me, he is the most important asset we have. He earns all our keep. I refuse to allow your relations to upset that apple cart. You understand?"

"Yes."

"I'll see you early next Monday. By the way, I am not that disagreeable, regardless of what Paul has told you."

***

That was a month ago. Since then I have quickly gotten my arms around his calendar of appointments, which we coded, and the physical aspects of the office, for that is what I call the combined kitchen/dining area and common area. Paco has a bedroom, but it's his private domain with his private files. I never go near it, and the door is always locked as it should be. Normally, I'm in the office only in the mornings. The day of Paul's unexpected visit, we were going over the books and ran late into the evening. I had just managed to bring some order to the flow of money through Paco's hands, mostly cash income and expenses, but sometimes large amounts. We had to code everything and agree on the coding so we both could understand without exposing ourselves. From time to time, his safe contained more than fifty thousand francs. I also was learning by association about this small operation. Nothing that placed me in jeopardy, but an understanding of the concrete goals and objectives.

Paul's visit was a shock. My first impulse was to go to him and hold him in my arms. I could see his consternation, but I wanted him to see that I was surviving without him. It was the most difficult performance of my life. My heart grieved at his appearance. I could see his surprise and dismay and growing anger at me. I'm not sure how long he will tolerate my behavior. I want to store him like grape shoots from old growth vines for future harvests. It's cruel and selfish. He's my family, but he will have to endure my obsessive character in this case. I'm aware of the risk of losing him, something I accept. I cannot be with him as an appendage. I have to be his equal: two strong and independent hearts beating as one.

***

Auguste Daniel's exhibition took place at the ancient Town Hall in early July, in the center of the city. It was held in a large hall in the ancient rundown building. The walls were covered with his paintings from floor to ceiling: landscapes, portraits, and images of life in Perpignan and the surrounding region. Gabrielle had no idea where all these paintings came from, many she barely remembered, all brightly colored, all real locations and people, and all in his signature style. She had refused to allow him to take her favorite paintings from her room, but he still managed to fill the hall to overflowing.

When she arrived, the room was crowded with people: dignitaries, city workers, fellow artists, students, friends, and acquaintances. Few enough celebrations were held during this time, so people flocked to this type of event. Everyone was in a celebratory mood, and Auguste modestly accepted the congratulations and comments of the many friends surrounding him. He was uncomfortable, she could tell, but was gracious and friendly. Gribouille remained at home.

She greeted her mother with a kiss.

"How are you and Papa?" She had been busy the last month, leaving early to work at the office and returning from working late at the Galeries, usually eating at cheap restaurants. She had almost returned to feeling normal about her life, compulsively occupying herself and keeping her roving mind in check.

"We're fine. He's been dreading this for ages, but he seems to be surviving. How's work? We almost never talk anymore. You're working so hard."

"I'm busy and becoming involved in all sorts of things. I have lots on my plate. So much so that I can barely think of anything else." She saw Catie enter the hall and waved.

Catie immediately came over, greeting Gabrielle and her mother with bisous.

"How are you?" she asked Gabrielle. "Haven't seen you in ages."

"I'm great. Working at a new job and spending less time at the Galeries."

"What's that?"

"Oh, working as a personal secretary for a business man. I'm learning about bookkeeping, managing an office, arranging affairs, and controlling an agenda. How about you?"

"The same. Still selling clothes to new mothers. My hours have been cut back though. We're just not doing that well. We have to have lunch. You do eat?"

"Yes, for sure next week. I got a postcard from Nuria. She's still in Lyon, but totally dedicated to her work. She's planning a visit this summer."

They watched her father from a distance. Auguste was short, and the crowd surrounding him almost obscured him from view. He was more comfortable sketching in the foothills of Canigou than greeting admirers.

Ferdinand Coudray, the mayor, called a momentary halt to the loud commotion and celebration. He waited for the hall to quiet down.

"Ladies and gentlemen, I would like to welcome you to this amazing exhibition. We all know Auguste, but we are not familiar with his newest work. We have over two hundred paintings exhibited here and all of them wonderful. Salvador Dali, eat your heart out. No, actually Dali is one of Auguste's friends, as are many famous artists: Dufy, Picasso, Miro, Derain, Matisse, and others. And of course our local artists, many of whom have been his confidants, worked with him, or have been his students: Descossy, Schmidt, Susplugas, Manolo, Vivès, Giner, Desnoyer, Maillol, Fons-Godail,

Poncelet, and many, many others. I'm proud to present his recent work, so that we can all see our Roussillon through his astonishing eyes. No artist presents a more encyclopedic view of our region of French Catalonia: infused with the intense colors of our days and nights, of our sunlight, of our waters and shores, and of course ourselves. No other artist both sees our home with such bright, loving, respectful, eloquent eyes and is capable of reproducing this extraordinary vision.

"Auguste, please join me for a few words."

There was a motion in the crowd, allowing Auguste to approach the mayor. They shake hands and embrace.

"Thank all of you for coming," Auguste said, looking around at the sea of faces of the expectant well-wishers. He paused. "I paint what I see, what I love. I paint the colors of our country. I paint all of our habitats: the mountains, rivers, and seashores, the vineyards, the fishing boats, the people who labor here to make our soil fertile and to feed us. I paint the amazing gifts God has given us, and I paint freedom and liberty for..." He stopped in mid-sentence. The mayor quickly embraced him and continued.

"We thank Auguste for his contributions. He has been instrumental in helping the Spanish émigrés and continues his work helping others. He is deeply involved with my administration in preserving and enhancing the cultural gifts that bless us. Please join me in applauding his accomplishments, and I'm looking forward to many more years of his vision."

The room applauded loudly and then returned to viewing the paintings, greeting old friends, and meeting new ones. People once again surrounded Auguste, and those who knew the family came to Julie and Gabrielle to congratulate them.

Out of the corner of her eye, Gabrielle saw Paul enter the hall hesitantly, looking around uncomfortably. He saw her and came across the room. It had been almost a month since their meeting at Paco's apartment.

"Bonsoir," he said, giving Gabrielle, Julie, and Catie bisous. "How are you?" he asked, looking at Gabrielle.

"Fine. Thanks. Working hard." Julie remained nervously silent.

"Congratulations, Julie," Paul said. "This is really a great celebration for Auguste. I think I'll see if I can get close enough to wish him well. Excuse me." He began working his way over to where people were surrounding Auguste.

"That was a surprise," Julie said irritably.

"Maman, it's not like that at all. Paul is not to blame. Please." She sighed heavily, her heart beating rapidly.

At that moment, she caught sight of Isabelle Lefèvre. Her heart sank. Isabelle came directly toward them to greet them, as though she were someone special. A man accompanying her stood back, watched, not eager to be introduced.

"Bonsoir Gaby, Madame, Catie. Quite a gathering here, no? Very impressive." Isabelle stood back haughtily. No bisous offered or received. She was formally-dressed, as though attending an opera or concert. Most of the people attending were casually dressed.

"You still seeing your boyfriend?"

"Yes, of course, thank you," Gabrielle said with mild rancor.

"I heard you had broken up."

"Well, you can't trust rumors."

"Not rumors. I know what's going on."

"Good. We don't have to chat."

"You're prickly this evening, Gaby. Working too hard? Nuria is working in Lyon, I understand."

"I wouldn't know. Listen, Isa, we're not friends and never were. We don't have to pretend." She meant to finish the conversation. This had happened too many times in the past, and she could not stomach Isabelle's egotistical support of Vichy and its politics.

"Well, well." She looked slightly irritated. "You have become quite the ingrate. Times are changing, and we all need to move on. You needn't be so impolite. You never know who you're talking to."

"I owe you nothing," Gabrielle replied firmly. "Now please, this is an important celebration for our family, and there are few enough celebrations amid the restrictions. Please respect us."

"I see," Isabelle replied, speaking rapid fire staccato. "You're wrong. You owe me. You need to realize it. I know you, Gaby. I know your friends and Paul. Watch yourselves." She turned and stormed away with her companion.

"What was that about?" Julie questioned. "She used to be one of your best friends at school."

"Never. She's never been my friend. And for some reason she seems to loath Catie, Nuria, and me. It's always been about Isabelle. We never did anything to harm her. She was always popular, but somehow she had a problem with us. Isn't that right, Catie."

"I have no idea what her problem is." Catie said. "She's successful and runs with a fast bunch. I see her in clubs and restaurants. She's always with that same guy."

"Who's that?" Gabrielle asked.

"He was in my brother's class, four years ahead of us. His name is…I'm thinking…Joseph Tena. After graduation, he continued to hang around the lycee, even when we were there."

Paul returned from a few words with Auguste, having missed the quarrel with Isabelle.

"I'm heading home," Paul announced. "Nice to see you all. Glad to hear your job is working out, Gabrielle. I hope it goes well."

"Thanks. It's been good for me, reducing my time at the Galeries. How is your work?"

"It's grueling in a strange way, but rewarding." He looked at her as one would an old friend imbued with memories, mingling good and bad. "Goodnight, all." He turned and moved off toward the exit.

"He seems in good shape," Julie said. "Last time we saw him, he was in such an agitated state. Distraught. He made your father so angry, until we had to ask him to leave. Sad, we liked him so."

Gabrielle listened to her mother, watching Paul depart. She knew him too well. She could see the effort it took him to maintain his composure and to keep his true feelings to himself. She realized that he was like an iceberg, not in the sense of cold, but with many times more subsurface commotion stirring fiercely than appeared above surface. She knew he had honestly come to wish her father well, whom he truly liked and admired. But she was also aware that his feelings for her were only contained with the greatest of efforts. These feelings were no longer all positive.

***

Sometimes a name dwells with you. You hear it repeated in your head. You try to place it, and usually after thinking about it, you realize who it is. Someone from your past, a distant friend, or just someone you have heard talk of. But in this case, Gabrielle had no memory. She could not place the name. In the office a few days later, she recalled the name and asked Paco.

"Do you know a man by the name of Joseph Tena? He was mentioned to me as though I should know him, but I couldn't place him."

"Joseph Tena? What was the context?" Paco wrinkled his heavy brows, looking at her seriously.

"He's a friend of a school chum: Isabelle Lefèvre. She was in my class, but never a true friend. They were at Papa's exhibition, where I saw him."

"*Zut*. Joseph Tena? What did they say?"

"Oh, nothing much. Isabelle was there, being her normal bloodhound self, believing she was the smartest in the room, but she didn't introduce her companion, Joseph Tena. Another friend recognized him afterwards."

"I see," Paco said. "I don't know Joseph Tena, but I'm aware that he is an active collaborator. Quite vocal, he has caused some problems for us. He is one of the leaders here of *Action Française*, the right-wing party supporting Vichy, and works with the police. I would avoid both of them."

"I'd love to, but she seems to always show up at the wrong time, professing to know all about me and my affairs."

"What did she say...specifically?"

"Nothing specific. That she knows what's going on. That she knows all about Paul and me."

"Anything else?" Paco asked very seriously, looking concerned.

"That's all. She knew Nuria was in Lyon. She said to watch myself."

"I would take her seriously. We will do a little research. If you hear more from her, let me know. They may suspect something, and they are dead set against our goals, dangerously so."

"I'm sorry I said anything."

"No. You need to be aware of your movements and patterns. The fact is, as long as this war continues, we're enemies. Our aim is to convert these enemies into responsible adversaries or else..."

***

Thinking is often used as the cause and excuse for inaction, and I'm no different. My thoughts were confused, but they are becoming more focused. I keep Paul from my thoughts until late at night, and even then I'm parsimonious in allowing myself to consider him, or to think about us, if there is such a relation. During the day, I occupy my mind with my immediate duties in the office and at the store, but at night my thoughts run ragged. I can't read, and I'm a poor conversationalist with my parents. I see no one else, and they've grown used to my behavior and accept it as long as I'm no longer as unhappy as I was. My mother worries, but she has worried my entire life, and as long as I'm eating and cheerful, she keeps her worries to herself.

At night I dream, and I startle awake and tell myself it was just a dream, a meaningless dream, but I wish it would never end. It always does, leaving me cheerless and without hope. Dawn never brings solace.

Working with Paco is like an education in understanding other people and, as a consequence, managing my behavior. They seem to go hand in glove. I'm skilled at handling strangers with cheer and charm and always keeping them at arm's length. My work has improved at the store as well, and I have become much more cautious in my movements.

I am now able to come to terms easily with the mundane aspects of Paco's business: the flows of people, money, and supplies. He never explains any of his affairs, and I'm never party to his meetings. People visit his apartment, only in the afternoon when I am not there and are never identified.

I'm beginning to understand the Resistance. Actually, there is no "Resistance," only people and small groups that disagree in a wide variety of ways with the direction of our country, with the facts of the occupation, and the motivations of the Occupant. It is made up of people from all different backgrounds: French, Spanish, Catalan, Communists, and Republicans, Gypsies, workers and professionals, *attentistes,* and even supporters of Vichy, émigrés and Catholics, Jews and Free Masons. Some people join small groups. Some resist individually in their own ways, marking V's on walls, delivering tracts, or just complaining to their friends. This miscellaneous set of individuals, mostly unguided and without knowledge of each other or any coordination, is growing. Information slowly filters down, because all media is watchfully controlled to ensure the point of view of Vichy. As the occupation continues, as we hear of actual atrocities by word of mouth and attempt to digest unthinkable rumors, more people resist. At this point, the sundry resistants are uncounted, totally disorganized, and share only one thing in common: they are against the occupation of their country. The one saving grace, the Resistance is hope. We all need hope.

Paco travels frequently for a day here or two days there. I never make arrangements; never know where he's going nor with whom he meets. When he returns, he organizes meeting after meeting with people I never see and only know from code names. We talk, but never of his business. Sometimes the apartment is filled up with crates and boxes, but these slowly disappear as they are distributed. The money, in similar fashion, grows, filling the safe, and then is rapidly distributed. I never know the specifics of where things come from nor where they go. Strange job, but I respect Paco and know exactly why he doesn't involve me more. Not that he doesn't trust me; it's insurance that protects me from implicating myself in his business. Since I cannot provide specifics, I should be held harmless on being questioned. Of course there is risk to this job. I am fully aware.

"Here," he says, "take these bottles home to your parents. Take a few cans from that box. Might be better than the normal fare. Here's some extra cash. Go shopping."

We don't eat together, other than a morning croissant or brioche and coffee. We are never seen in public together. He apologized for not attending my father's opening, but said that he had talked with him afterwards and congratulated him.

One morning I was in the office, and he was out. Someone knocked strongly on the door. When I didn't respond, whoever it was began banging on the door as though to break it down and yelling in Spanish. Finally, when I felt the neighbors were being aroused and someone might call the police, I cracked the door to explain that Paco was out. Instead, the door flew open and a large man dressed in worker's clothes burst in. I was propelled backwards and barely kept my balance.

"Where is he?" the man shouted in Spanish.

"He's not here. He doesn't allow anyone here when he's out."

"I need help," he shouted. I realized the man's stomach was covered in blood.

"Quiet, or the police will come," I said firmly, which seemed to work, as he lowered his voice.

"Help me." He began slumping to the floor. I grabbed him, allowing him to fall gently on his back. He was breathing hard and held his stomach with his right hand. His head was lolling back and forth.

I grabbed a towel and knelt next to him. I pulled his hand to the side and lifted his shirt. I saw a nasty wound on his side, but it didn't appear to be mortal. I went to the sink and wetted the towel. I cleaned the wound, which continued to discharge blood, but slowly and didn't appear to be too deep. We didn't have any emergency supplies, so I pulled his belt loose and tightly folded the cloth over the wound and tightened the belt around the cloth to put pressure on the wound. The man did not complain.

I ran to the phone. There was a special number for emergencies, which he had told me once that I would likely never use. I told the operator the number and waited.

"Yes," an abrupt male voice answered, no more.

"85 rue Jeanne d'Arc. Emergency. It's heavy."

There was a pause on the line. "Okay. We're coming."

Two men showed up almost immediately and knocked gently. One was a huge, hulking man in working blues and a béret, and the other fair and slight with long blond hair, dressed in a sweater and slacks with a light red scarf. I had never seen either one of them before. I allowed them in.

"What's this?" the slight man asked, without introduction.

"He just showed up. He's hurt."

"I can see that. We'll take care of it."

The men lifted the wounded man and supported him between them as if he were merely drunk and needed help home. They walked him out the door, without a word of thanks or goodbye, nothing.

I cleaned up, remaining in the apartment until noontime and then locked up. Strange episode. I never learned anything about it. When I told Paco the next day, he said not to worry. "It will be taken care of." He never mentioned it again.

That's my life with Paco. Always busy, always learning, always intriguing, always on the edge of something I know exists but that remains mysterious. Questions unanswered. Events scheduled without knowing what they mean. I realize the purpose of its structure and accept it for what it is. In any other time, I think I might have enjoyed knowing him, like a favorite teacher, but I realize this will never happen or at least not under the current circumstances. We might have been friends. It's not to be. Sad, but it's a sad time, and the saddest is yet to come.

19

July-August 1942

I will wait day and night
I will wait forever for your return
I will wait because the bird who flies away
Returns to find forgetfulness in its nest
Time passes and flows by
Sadly beating in my heavy heart
Yet, I will await your return
Yet, I will await your return.
« J'attendrai, » D. Olivieri; Poterat/Rastelli

Of all the prior months of the war, the summer months of 1942 were the worst, the best, and the busiest. Laval negotiated with the Occupant. He offered a plan to return one French prisoner of war being held in Germany in exchange for each volunteer worker from France committed to work in Germany. Germany finally negotiated: one French soldier returned for every three French workers in Germany. Laval called this the Service du Travail Obligatoire, the *relève.* He declared at the same time: "I wish for a German victory" as insurance against the triumph of Bolshevism in Europe. Not the words you would expect from a French Prime Minister. Negotiation or collusion?

During the first week of July, I had a meeting with Paco. He decided to accompany me on a pickup. I drove unhurriedly toward Ceret on a bright azure day, clear and pristine, with a refreshing tramontane whistling a tune of renewal. We talked about general things, but I was still concerned about my altercation with the package I'd left on the roadside.

"I wonder about that man," I said, having never closed the episode. It weighed on me. I had made many deliveries since then at his assurance of no change in risk, but I thought these were rather reckless. No changes were made at the border, no more police barricades, no modifications that might have raised my suspicions of any intelligence or movement against us.

"I meant to tell you, but I thought you understood."

"Understood what?" I demanded slightly miffed.

"You were right about him, Paul. He was a collaborator and planted to expose us. I'm not sure exactly how he found his way into our network and safe-house, but he did. The people there did not know. They accepted the word of the contact that delivered him. Both men have been removed. The fact that he was a Frenchman raised some issues, but he was convincing and answered our questions. The system failed, and we repaired the leak."

"But he's still out there, no?"

"He's gone."

"Gone?"

"Yes. He was taken care of. We were not exposed."

"You mean…"

"No, of course not. He was forced to the conclusion that any word from him would result in deadly consequences. He was not working alone, and he identified his co-conspirators. They have all been silenced." He paused to gather his thoughts.

"The collaborators of Vichy and the Occupant are becoming a serious threat. They are organizing. Benefactors are willing to provide such groups financial support, primarily the Occupant through a network. They are becoming more active in Perpignan, but in the north they are a force to be reckoned with. Joseph Tena is leading the effort here, but the only reason for their existence is the largesse of their benefactors; it's not necessarily politics.

"Once occupation began, there were locals providing information to the police, stealing vegetables in the market or fish from the fishermen, and forcing people to their petty wills. Now they can earn a little money as well. The man you discovered happened to get himself in too deeply, underestimating our network, and, once in the system, was unable to extract himself."

"Are you sure he will not inform on us? It's my skin."

"Absolutely. He's out of action. You have to understand the importance of your activities to our network. You have delivered how many packages?"

"Not sure. Maybe twenty or so. I haven't kept count."

"Well, I have. I would say you underestimate the number by more than half. London is very happy with the return of their airmen. We are just one stop, a critical stop, in a long network that operates between Belgium, France, Spain, and London. It saves the Allies millions by returning trained, experienced airmen. Hundreds of them. One at a time. Helped by perhaps hundreds of people willing to accept the risks."

"I guided many people on foot over the mountains, and I always wondered what became of them."

"And we won't know in our case as well. That reminds me. There is a demonstration on Independence Day in Perpignan. I want you to go very discretely to report for me. It's the first such demonstration, and we can get away with it because the Occupant is distant."

We arrived at the vineyard and turned into the safe-house. I parked around the back of the house, where the vigneron and his wife were waiting for us with two young men standing awkwardly alongside.

"Bonjour."

"Bonjour." We recognized each other well enough by now, but never said more than a greeting. Paco exited the truck and began arguing with the grower privately, while I opened the tool carrier and emptied the compartment. I waited until Paco returned.

"They screwed up. There are two," he said.

"We can only take one," I said. "Two would mean that even a cursory search would easily discover them both, and then the whole thing would be a bust."

"How many times have you been stopped?" he asked.

"Once."

"Did they search the tool compartment?"

"No."

"Well? It's up to you."

"I think it's dim-witted."

"I agree," Paco said, smiling.

"Sort of like betting a heap on the black or red in Roulette, the odds are good, but the bet is dumb. The house eventually wins. Can they keep one of the men for a few days?"

"That would be dangerous for the vigneron and his wife."

I nodded. I guess I was the expendable link in the chain, I laughed to myself. It didn't matter. "Okay," I replied straight-faced. I signaled for the two men to come. They gathered next to me peering into the tool case. "It is very small," I said in English; I had no idea of their French facility.

"We are very grateful," one said, an Englishman. "I understood you. If you can do it, we can." And he shook my hand.

I nodded my head for them to enter. They scooted next to each other.

"You can't move, and if the board falls you will not be able to pull it back in place, leaving you exposed." I pushed the divider in, unhinged, next to the second man. It would remain upright unless someone tested it, and then it would probably fall open. I picked up a dead branch, breaking off a piece to use as a shim. I also tossed in more dirt than normal, and then the tools to help maintain the loose divider. I carefully closed the door to the box and secured it.

"Bon. Au revoir."

We got into the cab and took off. I dropped Paco at the entrance to Ceret and continued up the highway into the mountains. It was a little more nerve-racking than usual, my heart in my mouth and my sweaty hands gripping the steering wheel. I slowed at the French frontier, but they were not interested and waved me through. At the Spanish border I slowed again, receiving a warmer welcome from the two guards, both helpfully waving me through. No problem as it turned out. I just didn't want this to become standard procedure. Once in Spain, we were met on the road by a contact who took the two airmen on the next stage of their journey. Everyone was happy. I returned to Perpignan with a full load of charcoal, not as happy, not even satisfied, feeling uneasy that my fate was controlled by others for their own gain. They made the decisions, and I took the risks. Anything goes wrong, and it's my neck. Now I know how soldiers feel. This was the first time I doubted Paco, but not the last.

***

On his days off, Paul occupied himself by reading, walking, relaxing in cafés, working on the truck, generally not doing anything special. He felt downhearted and lonely, upset with himself for his indolence. He listened to

306

the BBC and read the local papers and Resistance tracts, an armchair resister. He saw few people. Robert remained absent, and Georges and Jordi, although they talked about a new variety show, did so half-heartedly. Paul dined at the club once a week, where Josette welcomed him with bosomy hugs and remarkable soups. He had received his pay from the Django Reinhardt concert, some 3,000 francs, which he squirreled away in his savings under the floorboards, along with most of his earnings from the past four years, since he spent little on his living expenses. He wondered how long Monsieur Bardou would continue to allow him to occupy the apartment with Robert absent most of the last year, although he did manage the building, maintaining common areas, collecting rents, fixing repairs himself or having a workman do it when he could not, and of course maintaining good relations with Edith.

He recently read a popular novel, though clandestine: *The Silence of the Sea*, by Vercors. It told the story of a cultured German officer, a musician and composer in private life, who was billeted with a French man and his attractive daughter. The officer spoke French fluently and had studied the great writers and musicians of both countries, and he proposed a Beauty and the Beast analogy to his hosts. Beauty was France (and the host's daughter he was falling madly in love with); and the Beast was his own country, who was misunderstood and needed love to discover what truly was in its heart. He suggested a marriage of the two countries. The daughter and her father remained silent throughout his entire stay, never allowing him an opening. Never acknowledging his humanity. Never a word. They literally resisted. Something France had not done. Before the officer left, he quoted Shakespeare's Macbeth, expressing disillusionment: "Those he commands move only in command, nothing in love." He departed, disillusioned by his country, his hosts, his hopeless love, and his naïve idealism, volunteering for the Eastern front.

One night, Paul mindlessly read the back page classified ads in the local paper, his insight into public life. Mme. Feckler was having difficulty finding a maid. Workers were being sought for a furniture factory in Bordeaux and couldn't be found. Many women were selling their furs. From the volume of ads, patent medicines seemed to be selling off the shelf, and movies were popular, with German films replacing the American ones. Notaries were working on forced sales of properties. Soccer was becoming more popular, while rugby continued in popularity in the south. Few people were marrying. Announcements of deaths swamped births. A farmer in Rennes was hiring and finding it impossible to get copper sulfate for his vines and fertilizer for his wheat fields, and he worried about getting sufficient hands for the harvest. Mme. Dietsch purchased two pigs in the country, one for herself and one for a friend. She was arrested, but claimed she had an authorization from the president of the Food Supplies Committee. She was quoted, "I did nothing wrong. They took my pigs illegally, which I wanted to send to my husband who is a prisoner in Germany. Now I have nothing to send him."

The phone rang. It never rang. Robert's father had installed a phone a year before. Most homes were without phones, and people made local calls from the telephone exchange at the post office. International calls were not allowed on home phones. Monsieur Bardou believed in this new device, but Robert and Paul had little need of it. Since Robert's absence, it had rested quietly in the entryway, gaining dust with disuse. It rang again. He thought it must be Paco calling with some emergency, although he had never called before. He tossed the paper aside and walked slowly into the living room in his stocking feet. The phone continued to ring. Finally, he picked it up, fearing the worst.

"*Allo?*'

"Hello Paul."

A pause.

"Gabrielle?" he asked incredulously.

Then a longer pause. He waited an eternity. His eyes instantly clouded over. His heart halted his breathing. All he could hear were the sounds of its beating: poum-poum, poum-poum, poum-poum.

"Is something wrong?" he asked.

"I miss you." Her voice rose from some depths on the verge of tears, and he could hear the effort in her breathing. How much effort it must have taken her to make this call, and then she was silent.

His mind parsed through all his internal conversations, arguments, imagined reactions in his fantasies to what he had desired for so long, but really had given up anticipating.

"Why now?" he asked awkwardly, as a placeholder, screaming in his mind, not meanly, but gently. He prayed.

Of course he had dreamed of a meeting. In his unprepared state, he became instantly at odds with himself: should he act as if the last three months had not existed, or should he be distant, angry? Or must she take ownership and give him some justification, an apology? Did he bear some responsibility? Yes, certainly. He had come to this conclusion soon after the breakup. He wanted her back, he knew that, to be with her, to have her and the sunny brilliance of her love. He needed her. But at what price?

"I think I haven't been honest with you."

"Honest with me?" he repeated. "You haven't even talked to me." He hadn't focused on honesty as being one of the issues.

"What I mean is that I hurt you. I know that. Because of something that had nothing to do with you. It was all about me, and I was selfish. My father always warned me as a child not to get caught in setting my own trap, but I did not do this out of anger or spite, and it began and ended with me. Burning down the house we had constructed meant that I burned down my own home...our home. It seemed necessary at the time. And I'm so sorry."

Paul swallowed hard, hearing her, instantly modifying his reaction, without giving way to feelings of anger or revenge. "It wasn't all your fault. I was so consumed with my own life that I ignored yours. I knew you were suffering, and I was no help." Again doubt. What did she want?

"No. We need to be able to lead separate lives. I knew you were entering a new phase in your work, one with some danger, and I was not supportive. You continued along and did not blame me. I thought by separating I might be able to address my problems better, as though you were an obstruction, and it was never true. I have to fight my own battles. We can be sympathetic and understanding and supportive and loving, but we must take primary responsibility for ourselves."

He gave up any pretence of distance. "No, I'm a failure at opening myself to others."

"No. You were understanding, and I knew you loved me. I needed to do battle with my own demons; something you could not help me with. I know that now, Paul. I love you. I never stopped loving you. I don't ever want to lose you. I'm so sorry for the pain I caused you. I was wrong."

Paul just heard his imagined hopes expressed in a few words. They both paused and listened to the noise on the line. The faraway sound of a man could be heard talking in the background. But Paul heard the joy and wonder of his heartbeat like air to a drowning soul.

"Sometimes you have to allow yourself happiness," he said. "Protecting yourself from being hurt means you will never find happiness. I sound like a Charles Trenet song: 'Happiness is like a roulette wheel, but joy is a discipline in action.'"

"I miss you. I would like to see you."

"I would like to see you as well."

"When?"

"Whenever you like." Paul held his breath.

"Now."

"Now?"

"Yes."

"I'm coming over."

"I'm not at home. I'm at the post office."

"Oh, yes."

"I'll meet you at Aux Dames de France."

"Okay. I'm coming."

Without thinking, he ran to the bedroom, dressed, pulled a light jersey over his head and headed out to the hallway. He halted and turned around to view the mess of months of not caring. It was past midnight, but the temperature remained balmy. He began kicking clothes into a pile, taking away old packages and wrappings, picking up glasses and plates, moving dust of months around. He finally gave up. It was what it was and walked out.

He walked rapidly: one of the longest walks in his life along rue de la Gare to the main crossroad and the building Aux Dames de France across the street. The buildings and few blocks seemed interminable. Hardly any cars. Streets deserted. Blinds drawn. There was no curfew in the free zone, but at night people remained in their homes and apartments, and it was late. He finally came around the corner and saw her across the main byway, coming toward him on the large public square. He could see her, hugging herself, not waiting, but crossing the empty intersection toward him, impatiently. He began hurrying, afraid of a dream of endless pursuit, until he came to her, and she to him, in the middle of the intersection. They fell into each others' open arms, their bodies joined, their mouths searched each other, their minds drained. It was all so familiar, all so comfortable, as if nothing had changed. As if time did not exist. Something so valuable had been allowed to slip away so easily. And now, nothing separated them.

They began hurrying back to the apartment, holding on to each other, their hips joined, their arms around their backs, their steps in unison. They stopped to embrace and kiss and reassure each other of their resolution. But did not speak.

Once in the apartment, they ran to the bedroom laughing, falling onto the bed, stripping off their clothes joyously. In the dark, they forgave each other. They recommitted. They laughed. They struggled together, like two starved animals. They feasted until they could feast no more. And then they lay exhausted, separated, yet together. How could they have allowed this to happen? Never again. Listen to your heart.

Finally, Paul rose to get glasses for an orange liqueur, and they lay together sipping the sharp pleasure of the alcohol. Neither talked, and when Gabrielle felt obligated to continue her explanation, Paul covered her lips with his own. It all began again: a dream of reality. They were together.

***

On Independence Day, July 14, 1942, I walked to the demonstration being held in the Place Arago. For weeks, posters throughout the city had announced the celebration. The local government allowed it to happen. The weather was windy and a little cool but clear. The plaza was warmer and rapidly filling with the street blocked. There were hundreds of people. All around I noticed friends meeting who had not seen each other since the end of the phony war. The conversations were excited and intense. For the first time in two years, people gathered in support of an idea, never before seeing those who felt as they did.

Although not a Resistance event per se, celebrating independence resonated among people disappointed with the armistice, the direction of our government, and the loss of freedom in a country synonymous with the idea. The participants were mostly unaffiliated individuals wanting to celebrate an important ideal, as they had done since birth. Resistance groups were among them, but not identifiable.

Tracts were being freely handed out: *Combat, Libération, Franc-Tireur, et l'Humanité.* I noted a few city policemen standing on the outskirts, watching intently, trying to remain nonthreatening. Most likely, there were out-of-uniform police and agents of the Occupant sprinkled throughout like red peppers in a spicy paella. Of course even more anonymously, collaborators acted the role of supporters. They all discreetly monitored rather than attempting to upset the event. The gendarmes were powerless to prevent the gathering. There were just too many people in good cheer, desiring to celebrate our national day of independence. Every year since July 14, 1789 people celebrated with laughter and gaiety and dancing in the streets.

Since the occupation, Maréchal Pétain stated that this day should be a day of mourning. He laid a wreath on the Vichy memorial for the war dead in the morning and attended mass in the afternoon. This approach, purposely ignoring the revolutionary past, greatly pleased the Occupant. In Paris, instead of the traditional military parade on the Champs Elysees, Germans troops marched with few spectators.

The people of Perpignan fearlessly gathered in the traditional spirit of the day. No speeches were made, no bands played, no military marched. The crowd spontaneously broke into la Marseillaise, singing all three familiar verses and then repeating the prohibited song. After singing, the demonstration broke up into smaller groupings, watching and meeting each other with wonder. These people with different goals and agendas and plans of action looked about, realizing that others shared their distaste for the occupation. I was amazed. It was clear that the people assembled shared common interests. It was also clear that there was little or no communication between the groups and no coordination. People continued to meet old friends unexpectedly. I realized what Paco had said on many occasions that the Resistance would be of little consequence without joining together with shared goals or at the very least with coordination of their activities.

I continued walking through the crowd, which was beginning to thin out. Within one of the groupings, I saw a familiar face: Nuria, Gabrielle's best friend, whom we had not seen for six months. As far as I knew, she had been living and working in Lyon with Robert. I walked over to where she was talking, surrounded by many people, and I waited patiently until I caught her eye. She smiled, excusing herself, breaking out of the group, and came over.

"Paul. How wonderful to see you." She gave me a bisou and a warm hug.

"I thought you were in Lyon."

"I was. I mean I am. My father died unexpectedly, Paul. That's why I couldn't contact Gabrielle. And I came to help my mother. I'm here with my family until next week. I'm so proud of my birthplace and pray that this can move things along. We will talk. I haven't had time to contact Gabrielle, but wouldn't miss her for the world. Have you seen her?"

"I'm sorry to hear about your father. It's true, we split up for a time, but we're back together. I'm sure she would love to see you."

"Can we get together this weekend. I have lots on my plate for the next few days."

"What about Robert? We never hear from him."

"He's totally committed to Joseph Mercier, our leader. Robert is indispensible it would seem. They are constantly on the move throughout the country. Headquarters remain in Lyon, and it would take an act of parliament, if we had one, to get him away. But we, like you, are stronger than ever."

"That's wonderful to hear. Can you come to the apartment this Sunday?"

"Of course. I'm worn out and would love to pass a peaceful day. I leave on Monday."

"Great. I'll tell Gabrielle. She may want to contact you earlier."

"I'll be in and out of my parents' house. We can catch up on Sunday. I'm so glad we met. Give Gabrielle a big kiss." She bussed me lightly and returned to her group, obviously an important person.

I didn't know Nuria that well, but of Gabrielle's friends, she seemed the most intelligent and driven. She certainly was Gabrielle's best friend and confidant. Her absence may have made Gabrielle's temporary retreat more difficult. I knew it would be a boon to Gabrielle to see her. Although being together had alleviated our loneliness, we had few friends and rarely socialized. Our jobs were primary in our lives and occupied our minds day and night.

On the way out of the plaza, I saw Auguste Daniel walking determinedly. I caught up with him to greet him. We had dined with Gabrielle's parents a few times since getting back together, and they seemed pleased and were warm and welcoming to me as before.

"Auguste," I called from behind him. He turned quickly and saw me.

"Well, Paul. What brings you here?"

"Probably the same thing that brought you here," I said, tired of his quiet assumptions. I knew why he was here, but he had always kept it a secret from his wife and daughter. And he knew why I was here. Gabrielle had suffered too many secrets, and it frustrated me. Among loved ones, secrets only serve to sabotage.

"What would that be?" he asked, looking harshly at me.

"Love for our country."

"We all love our country," he said banally.

"Yes, some more than others, and some rather foolishly. And some without respect for others."

"It's too bad we can't be more open these days," he said.

"We can. We just have to be careful."

"I was referring in general."

"So was I."

"It depends on many factors, young man," Auguste said, showing some irritation. "You are not a member of the family...not yet."

"I've never had a family. Perhaps I'm naïve. And I'm in no place to comment, but I love your daughter with all the best intentions."

"I'm not sure where this is leading, but I think we should postpone this discussion. We were both here to celebrate our independence, I agree. And I may have been a little dismissive, but there are appropriate occasions and venues. Is that clear?"

"Yes, Monsieur."

"Nice seeing you, Paul."

We separated, and I returned to the apartment. Auguste was part of the problem. Julie was sweetly concerned with her family, but it was Auguste who ruled. Gabrielle worshipped him. She saw herself only through his eyes, and she felt she had never measured up. Much of this was inferred from his silences, and much was due to her own feelings. He was much more sympathetic to her than she was to herself. But no one knows what others are thinking without talking, and little enough talking occurred within her family, and there were always the secrets.

***

Sunday dawned warm and inviting, another hot day. We opened the windows wide and aired out the apartment. Gabrielle somehow managed to purchase a small lamb shinbone and slowly stewed it with white beans and available vegetables: onions, greens, turnips, and parsley. You can add anything to lamb and have it come out like a Michelin three-star restaurant. The redolence filled the rooms. Normally, we are not active housekeepers, but I had forced myself to become neater, and we kept things picked up and in their places. We had spent Saturday cleaning everything, and for the first time since she departed we enjoyed the fresh aroma of a clean apartment. Gabrielle had invited Catie, but she was the only other guest. We envisaged a day of relaxation and catching up. She wore a loose blouse and shorts.

Just before noon, Nuria arrived with a bag full of provisions. We could see immediately that she was exhausted. She was dressed in a loose blue blouse and white pantaloons. She and Gabrielle hugged for a long time, not joyously, but like two close friends who had been separated and anticipated further separation. I took the supplies into the kitchen, while they rested next to each other on the couch like two puppies happy to see each other, but a little reserved.

I delivered large glasses of iced white wine, which they accepted gladly. I sat down in the easy chair across from them.

"It's been a rough year," Gabrielle admitted honestly. "I started a new job and am now working part-time at Les Nouvelles Galeries in the afternoons until closing. Paul and I are back together, and I think I've grown immensely since the last time we saw you and Robert."

Nuria discarded her sandals and rested lethargically, with her feet on the coffee table and her head on a pillow, forcing herself to occasionally sit up to sip her wine, but feeling comfortably at ease. "What's your new job?"

"I'm a personal secretary to a man involved in a host of activities, including the charcoal business where Paul is working. I do everything for him, from coordinating his calendar to keeping his books. It's a cash business with lots of barter, so I manage the ins and outs. I keep clear of his business activities, though. How about you? What are you up to?"

"I work for a very determined man, Joseph Mercier, who is a unifying force, traveling throughout the occupied and free zones, determined to convince people of the importance of working together. My understanding of the refugee camps was very helpful, and we continue to help émigrés." She seemed to wilt for a moment, taking a fast sip of her wine.

"You may not have heard," she continued, "but two day ago the police and the Nazis arrested thousands of Jews in and around Paris. They were supposed to arrest only foreign Jews, but they arrested every Jew they could get their hands on, including children and seniors, two classes supposedly exempt from deportation. Truly a roundup. They moved through the suburbs based on lists of people, but they arrested everyone they could find: the French police led but with the active participation of the Germans. They transported these people to the Velodrome d'Hiver, which once served for indoor bicycle racing, but now is used as a sports arena. It's outside Paris and not configured in any way to be an internment camp, even for short periods. A blanket and a change of clothes was all that the arrestees were allowed to bring. They filled several other internment camps as well. Literally, thousands of people crammed together without facilities, knowing nothing of their fates, women, children, the infirm, and the elderly. No one is being allowed in, including international rights groups and the Red Cross.

316

I'm sure from my past experience that the conditions are horrendous. It's rumored that this is just a temporary move and that they are preparing to transport everyone to the north. This is not the first time for mass arrests of Jews, but it is the clearest evidence of our Occupant's intentions, and they seem to be ramping up. From talking with internees of the camps, I learned that they believe Auschwitz to be an extermination camp. Massive killing of innocents has been going on in the east, but now they're taking people from our own country. It's inconceivable."

"That's awful," Gabrielle said, her eyes watering. "My dad's parents and my grandmother live in a community of Jews in Paris. They became citizens before the Great War, and they're all Catholics, and they're all old. I can't believe they would be caught up in all this. What's happening to us?" She began crying gently to herself.

"That's okay, Gabrielle," Nuria said, moving closer to her. "We're all working to end this nightmare."

"I know. I know. But it's too much to comprehend."

I was astonished by the news. I watched Gabrielle as Nuria described the roundup. I saw the terrible impact it was making on her. "Maybe you want to call your parents," I suggested, "and tell them about it. They may have word from your grandparents."

"I doubt it," but she wandered off to the phone.

"What are you doing now," Nuria asked me.

"I'm doing what you're doing," I said, tired of candy-coating my job. Tired of all the lies. "Trying to help people. I've been doing this since the war started and before. Now I'm helping airmen escape from this country. The demonstration on Independence Day was a remarkable insight, so many people of good will wanting to change the direction, and indeed, some working to change it, but unknown to each other and without any communication between them."

"That's exactly what my boss is doing. He's trying to pull people together, but it's nearly impossible. He's been charged by de Gaulle to unify the various groups. No one wants to work together. Everyone has his own reasons, has his own turf, has his own ambitions and fears. It's easy for the Nazis; they do what they're told with little question and no thought. Here, the few who give a damn are all so bigheaded that everything becomes a battle of egos. How can a country that doesn't work together compete with a totalitarian state? There are just too many cheeses in France, too many differences. How can freedom compete with fascism?"

Gabrielle returned in a state. "My mother knew about it. She received a postcard from her mother, and my father talked with people in Paris. It's horrible, and to think my grandmother may be a victim of this hatred and my father's parents. There has been no word since the roundup occurred. She does not know whether they were taken or not."

There was a knock on the door, and I went to answer it.

"Bonjour, Catie."

"Bonjour, Paul." She gave me a bisou. She was dressed in a flowered shirtwaist dress and pumps.

When we entered the salon, everyone welcomed her, but the air had been released from the balloon. Kisses all around, but she found herself in a room of zombies. I rushed to get her some wine.

"What's wrong?"

Nuria remained standing and summarized the conversation while pacing.

"I can't believe it, and your grandparents were arrested?"

"We don't know," Gabrielle said stiffly.

"Maybe I shouldn't have said anything," Nuria said.

"No. I'm glad you did," Gabrielle said. "And it's not like it's a surprise. It's just another step in the evil slowly enveloping us like a low cloud of darkness. What I don't understand is why more people don't stand up."

"I think you're exactly right," Paul said, looking at the bereft women standing before him. "How about a walk to a café before we have something to eat. We need some fresh air. Nuria returns to Lyon tomorrow. It's so important to keep our spirits up, all of us."

The day never recovered. The walk and fresh air helped little. The dinner was eaten without enthusiasm, although it was probably the best meal we've had in months. The three best friends tried to brighten the gloom, but it was not to be. Catie left early, and Gabrielle and Nuria returned to the couch gossiping about friends. We snacked for dinner.

Later in the evening when we said farewell, Nuria confessed another bit of her insight.

"You know, Robert is in very deep. There are four or five of them, and they carry guns. They have to be aware of everything and everyone. Robert is basically consumed when he returns for a few days, not from the trip or the meetings, but from pure, unadulterated fear: fear of being denounced, fear of the collaborators, fear of the agents of the Occupant. They know they are targets, and they cannot rest their vigilance a single moment. It's awful."

Gabrielle and Nuria hugged as if they would never see each other again. She left in tears, and Gabrielle collapsed on the bed. I left her there and cleaned up a bit, finally turning out the lights and joining her on the bed. We lay there without talking, staring at the ceiling, not touching, waiting, waiting for sleep to wrap her warm arms about us like Lethe, the river of forgetfulness.

***

Gabrielle and Paul visited Auguste and Julie the next day at noon, before Paul left for a delivery. They were both at home and were happy to see the young couple. Auguste especially seemed to be making more of an effort to be outgoing. It could have been his discussion with Paul or perhaps it was his response to reading the recent note from Julie's mother in Paris, or both. Julie handed the postcard to Gabrielle, who read it carefully and fell into a chair, saying nothing, the tears flowing from her eyes silently.

10 July 1942

My dears Julie and Auguste,

It's been very difficult here. I remember when we were kids in Vilnius, and our parents told us to run and hide under the beds. We lay shivering and hoping the angry people would pass over our house. Each time, they spared ours, but others were not so lucky. I am not convinced we will be spared here. Daily something awful takes place. People are hurt or taken away. Others just disappear. You never hear anything. Everyone is afraid and hides in their houses. So much is unsaid.

I wanted to let you know I am thinking of you and your family. That I love you all. I feel so sorry for our past. What is most important in life is often ignored until too late, and the past has no significance.

"Do not compete with the evildoers; do not envy those who commit injustice. For they will be speedily cut off like grass and wither like dry vegetation. Trust in the Lord and do good; dwell in the land and be nourished by faith."

Your loving mother,

Fanny

She handed it to Paul, who read it more slowly, going over it several times. He realized that Gabrielle's grandmother had painted a monumental portrait. He could taste the bitterroot of fear, the smell of hatred and injustice, and hear the terrible agony of regret. He walked around to the back of the chair and placed his hands on her shoulders.

"I'm sorry," was all he could manage.

***

Sometimes, you have to make a stony commitment even with the odds stacked against you, or so you may think at the time. The future winds of change are so obscure and unsettled as to frighten any progress. You are anchored in the bay of your desire for assurance and certainty. How can you move forward, with so many childish hopes and desires, so many opinions of your friends, so many stories of achievements and conquests? How can you ever grow up?

Early the next week, Paul drives the truck into the mountains. The warmth of the coastal plain diminishes as the road begins ascending. No wind, but the clouds huddle around the peaks of Canigou. This time Paul has a passenger sitting next to him, and their destination is his grandmother's house in Amélie-les-Bains.

"It's been years since I've been to the mountains." Gabrielle says, her eyes searching the landscape. "It's so beautiful: the steep green hillsides of the mountains beside the narrow road, covered with trees and lush growth. Even my father now mostly stays in Perpignan for his painting."

"It's time to get out."

"People are afraid. Traveling is so difficult and scary these days."

"Yes. I probably wouldn't do it if I could avoid it. We are all home-bound."

They arrive at the entrance to the village of Amélie-les-Bains. The streets are relatively empty. It's nearing lunch time. They pass the buildings housing the briny baths so effective against the diseases of the liver and spleen. They continue into town and find a large parking area off the street. Well into the mountains, the heat diminishes somewhat, still not a breath of wind. Paul leads them down a side street to a view of the Tech River, low during the summer months, but still cascading over the rocks through the center of the village. They watch the river and feel the coolness rising from the rocky bed. The Tech is an untrustworthy river, like a friend who plans and talks behind your back, periodically flooding. The village is still recovering from the massively destructive inundation two years before. They walk through the commercial center of town to the rue de Thermes near the church of Saint-Quentin, so dear to his grandmother. Paul stops before the home of his grandmother, rue de Paul Pujade, remembering so much.

It's after the morning service, so she should be at home. He knocks on the familiar door and waits. They listen to someone slowly descending the creaky wooden staircase. A lace curtain is pulled back for an instant on a side window, and finally, the door is opened.

"Bonjour, Grand-mère."

"Paul. How nice to see you." There is no bisou or contact between the grandson and his grandmother. "And who is this?"

"This is Gabrielle Daniel."

Gabrielle hesitates a moment before deciding to give the diminutive woman a bise, realizing immediately that she has committed her first faux pas. She backs off.

"Bonjour, Madame."

"Bonjour Mademoiselle. How are you doing?" she asks using the formal pronoun, *vous*. She uses the familiar pronoun, *tu*, only with her direct family, of whom only Paul remains, and never ever used it with her husband.

"Thank you, I'm well."

His grandmother is dressed entirely in black, with a black scarf tied around her head. She is round and remarkably short, but her eyes shine brightly. She must be somewhere in her eighties, but she moves spryly and appears very well.

"Come in, Paul."

She shows them into a dark salon, furnished with furniture from the Belle Epoque, not truly antique, but well-made and aging in that direction. The room is full of diffused daylight through the lace curtains, smelling dusty and unaired. Paul and Gabrielle sit down on a hard davenport, and his grandmother sits down in her armchair, not making an effort to serve them.

"I've been very busy," Paul begins, "working and travelling…"

"Too busy to visit your ancient grandmaman?" she smiles.

Paul hesitates and then sighs. It's like he's never left. He's still the quiet boy, always trying to please his guardian. "I suppose you're correct. But now I'm visiting you and finding you in good form."

"The good lord will provide, you know. I taught you well as a child."

"And I'm thankful, Grand-mère. I wanted to stop by to introduce you to my fiancée. We have been together for almost a year and will be marrying soon."

She looks over at Gabrielle, who returns her gaze.

"Marrying?"

"Yes, Grand-mère."

"I married your grandfather when I was sixteen. The war in China took him from us, God protect him, leaving me with a single child, your mother. A great disappointment to me. God protect her. A great disappointment. I won't speak ill of your father, but I have never believed in marriage. There is only one true marriage, and that is the marriage to Jesus Christ. Are you married to Jesus, Gabrielle?"

Gabrielle is shocked to be directly addressed and that Madame has remembered her name. She has a moment, trying to prepare a response to the question.

"It shouldn't require so much thought," his grandmother says calmly.

"I'm a good Catholic," Gabrielle finally responds. "I was raised in the church."

"As believers in Jesus Christ, we anticipate the day when we will be united with our Bridegroom. Until then, we remain faithful to Him. That is the text."

No one spoke for a moment, wondering where the conversation was leading. Paul was used to his grandmother and finally ended the silence.

"Grand-mère, we have come a long way and are thirsty. Do you have some tea?"

"Why don't you make some, Paul. You know where it is. I'd like to talk with your fiancée."

Paul glanced at Gabrielle and rose to go to the kitchen.

"What do you do, child?"

"I work at Les Nouvelles Galeries and also as a private secretary."

"Two jobs?"

"Yes, Madame."

"And your parents?"

"My father is a curator in a museum in Perpignan and an artist. My mother is a housewife."

"And are they supporters of our leader, Maréchal Pétain?"

"We make every effort to be good citizens. We hope for an end to the war."

"I see. My pastor says we must support our government to prevent the ungodly Bolsheviks from gaining power as they did a few years ago. Do you cook?"

"I do. I'm a very good cook." Gabrielle decides to go with the tenor of the conversation, even if it means outright lies.

"That's important in any marriage. Are you a clean girl?"

Gabrielle hesitates, "clean?"

"Yes, are you a virgin with a clean uterus?"

Gabrielle looks at her, "Why, yes," leaving it at that.

"That also is important. I had a clean uterus. Only one man my entire life. And only one child, a disappointment. I have a good grandchild, though

323

I don't see him as much as I would like, but I know these children today. You know," she leans toward Gabrielle and whispers, "his father was not married to my daughter, and he was born out of wedlock. But he is a good boy. Smart. Takes after my father, God bless him, the spitting image. He was mayor, you know, and a respected notary."

Paul hurries from the kitchen with tea and cups and saucers. He sets it down on the table to let it steep.

"Paul, I like your fiancée. Children today don't understand the value of work. She's a hard worker."

He pours the tea, serves his grandmother, and then Gabrielle.

"We have biscuits. How can you serve tea without biscuits?"

"I couldn't find any."

"In the top cupboard. Go and look."

"You know, Gabrielle, men are helpless," she says conspiratorially laughing.

"I know what you mean," Gabrielle agrees.

Paul returns with a box of biscuits and offers them around. His grandmother takes two. They all drink their tea.

They are able to extricate themselves before the clock strikes one hour along with the church bells, thanking her effusively and promising to return and to keep her appraised of their wedding plans.

"She's amazing," Gabrielle says on the way back. "Solid as a rock. No doubts there. I wish my mother were a little more like her. Of course her views are a little dated, and she could be a spokesperson for the church."

"She was not a loving guardian, but at least a consistent one. I'm glad you met her."

"Me too. I thought she would be much worse based on your descriptions of her. She's quite nice.

"On her best behavior or maybe mellowing a touch."

"I thought she would object to you getting married."

"If she only knew the truth."

20

September 1942

> *Each gentle evening*
> *I hear him singing under my window*
> *Each evening my lover*
> *Returns to rouse me from my sleep*
> *Si, si, si, it's only a serenade*
> *Si, si, si, a serenade without hope.*
> « *Sérénade sans espoir,* » *Melle Weersma/H.*
> *Halifax/André Hornez*

One balmy evening, the gift after a summer of variable weather, we were returning to the apartment from the Galeries after a snack at our favorite café. We had been working hard, from early morning to late. I had spent the afternoon stocking the shelves at the store, but lately the replenishments of the products had become less frequent and fewer. Many of the products were discontinued. Coco Chanel had closed all her retail outlets, some said in retaliation for the labor problems in Paris, which she blamed on the Bolsheviks. She even shut down her couture house. Chanel No. 5, her most popular brand, continued to sell better than ever, even after a squabble with the Jewish directors of *Parfums Chanel*. The cosmetics industry was suffering, the war effort stealing too many of the raw materials and the dearth of workers, with people being pressured to go to Germany to work under Laval's relève program. Not surprisingly, the quid pro quo of the relève program with the Occupant to release French soldiers from incarceration never materialized. The program like all others our government had proposed for our benefit was a lie in support of the war effort.

Edith knocked on her window as we were about to enter the apartment building. We waved. Paul went over, and the window opened.

"*Bonsoir*, Edith."

"*Bonsoir*, Monsieur Paul. A telegram for you." Her hand exited the window, and Paul took a grey envelope.

"Thank you, Edith."

"*Pas de quoi*, Monsieur. *Bonne soirée.*"

"Bonne soirée à vous."

When we entered the apartment, I went to open the windows and shutters, and Paul sat in the salon, opening the envelope. I watched him peruse the telegram carefully and then slap it down on the couch angrily.

"What is it?"

He never talked when he was angry. He pointed to the letter, indicating that I should look for myself. I picked up the telegram and read it:

Télégramme
Perpignan 22216 33/30 20 3/9/42 7ᴴ35

HOPE YOUR FRIENDS ENJOYED STAY
SORRY THEY HAVE TO LEAVE = CESC

"What in the world does it mean?"

"It means that roundups are about to commence in the Pyrénées Orientales.

"Really? Who is Cesc?"

"My ex-boss at the Prefecture. It's his Catalan name."

"Franco?"

"Yes, he promised to send me advance warning of roundups in the department. It means that the police have been ordered to arrest known foreigners in the area."

"You mean Jews."

"Yes and no. Mostly, of course. You remember that list I saw over a year ago? Georges and Bernadette were on it."

"So were my parents."

"Yes, but they are native-born. They don't have to worry. Vichy and the Occupant are not focused on native-born citizens, particularly in the PO. Not yet anyway. It means I must warn Georges and Bernadette."

"I want to go with you."

"Of course."

***

The next morning, while Paul was in the rear preparing the truck, I packed some items. One of my co-workers had shared a piece of home-made fois gras. had saved it for a special occasion. I added some sausage and a bottle of champagne and threw in our bathing suits, just in case. On the way, we stopped at our favorite baker for two fresh baguettes. It was early and the line had not yet formed. I scooted in and out while Paul waited. The day dawned clear and crisp, but the sun had not heated the beach, maybe not swimming weather.

When we arrived at Le Racou, the mist still hovered over the sea, and the clouds obscured the sea. The village was packed with vacationers, even though the swimming weather had been below par, and it was just outside the season. Like all seaside resorts, the inhabitants were older and mostly late starters, and Georges and Bernadette were no exception. When we knocked on the door, it took some time before Georges appeared in the living room in his dressing gown and opened the door with his dog Argut at his slippered feet.

"What are you two doing here?"

"We wanted to have breakfast with you," Paul said. "We miss you."

"That's very nice, but Bernadette is still asleep," he groused, and then thought better, "but come in, come in."

The house smelled of sleep, with late night cinders still smoldering in the fireplace.

"We have some things for you," I said, entering the kitchen, which was open to the living area, and proceeded to prepare some snacks.

"Let me get dressed and see if I can rouse my spouse. We had rather too much to drink last night. I'm afraid I fell off the wagon celebrating our fortieth. The gift of alcohol is that it temporarily silences the demons. Can you believe it? Married 1902. This rotten weather spoiled the summer. Only the tourists swim with the cool water and constant breezes. All the merchants are complaining about the lack of commerce this year. But they always complain, every year. Just a minute." He disappeared into the back of the house.

A few minutes later he appeared in shorts and t-shirt with a loose, open yellow cardigan sweater.

"Did you hear the news?"

Paul looked up. "What news?" he asked cautiously. There had been too much grim news lately.

"The allies raided Dieppe. Canadian and British commandos led the battle for a beachhead. It was a disaster from the start. They never penetrated the seawall. The Germans were prepared, and they were well-ensconced along the cliffs. The invaders were pinned down on the beach the moment they landed. They did manage to land some tanks, but the tanks were contained along the beach by the seawall and large concrete obstacles. Luckily, as it turned out, the tanks facilitated the withdrawal. Without them, it would have been a killing field. There was a tremendous air battle above the ships, and the Royal Air Force managed to protect the ships, but at a heavy toll. The Allies are not ready to invade, and the Germans continue to improve their defenses. Doesn't look good. Of course, it made all the papers...a great victory."

"Maybe it's time to leave," Paul said.

"What?"

Bernadette entered the room, looking sleepy in a loose blouse, green sweater, floppy shorts, and pink mules. "What are you kids up to?"

"We came for a visit," I said, giving her a warm hug and kisses. "And you too, Georges." I gave him a big hug and began setting out the fois gras, cut sausage, bread. I gave him the champagne. "Can you open this?"

"He looked at me skeptically. "What's the occasion?"

"Well, if you pour the champagne we will tell you."

Paul looked at me doubtfully. I knew his mind was only on one thing, but I wanted this meeting to have more than a negative tone. The separate announcements could be made jointly without conflict if the timing was right.

Georges poured four champagne flutes and offered them around. Paul stood to make a toast.

"You know we love you both. You have been such a help to me and to us. We want you to be part of our lives forever." Again, Georges pulled a

328

distrustful countenance. Before Paul could charge forward, I interrupted him.

"First order of business is to toast your anniversary. Congratulations, and you should have told us. Next year, we will know. Secondly, salute to our friendship and to our health." I raised my glass, and everyone tasted the champagne. "Now, Paul has two announcements. The first about us, and the second about you."

Paul was slightly startled, but acquiesced to my manipulation of the order of the announcements. "Gabrielle and I have decided to get married. We felt we couldn't postpone it any longer, even though this is a lousy time to do anything." He put his arms around me. "Anyway, we're in love…more than ever."

"Well, this is exciting," Georges said looking pleased. "We are so happy for you. We certainly wish you the very best and will do anything to aid you. It's a big adventure, but, believe me, it's worthwhile." He glanced at his wife. After all the hugs and kisses, he said, "can an old man sit down for the next announcement?"

"Please," Paul replied. And we all sat closely together on the couch, glasses in hand, Argut at our feet, facing Georges. Bernadette was hugging Gabrielle with tears in her eyes, and Georges was facing Paul, still wondering what was going on.

"The next announcement, in its way, is also positive," Paul said. "I received a telegram from the Prefecture last evening. It appears that the Occupant was not satisfied with the number of arrestees in the recent roundups in the occupied zone and is forcing Vichy to come up with departmental quotas. Well, my ex-boss informs me that a roundup in the PO is imminent. Hard to say how soon and how thorough, but I would guess, knowing the machinations of the police, in a matter of days, not weeks. It's time to get out."

"What about our naturalization date?" Georges said pugnaciously. It was way before the deadline announced by Laval."

"That's true. But I wouldn't bet on it. Your names were on that list, and once on a list you never get removed. The police will not quibble. They're not mathematicians. They follow orders without much thought and no discussion."

"I know what you mean," Georges said, suddenly seriously. "But there are so many issues. How? Where would we go? What happens to our house? What about our savings? What of my pension? We are not wealthy. Not only were we naturalized long before the critical date, we also are above the age limit."

"Do you trust Vichy?" Paul demanded.

"No," Georges admitted taken aback by Paul's strong tone.

"Then why trust them with your lives? We know they are being pushed by the Occupant, who has no respect. They don't care about dates or age. They don't care if you are naturalized or born here. The recent Vel d'Hiv roundup included a large percentage of children and seniors, and, let's be clear, French Jews. There was no discussion of the Vichy guidelines. They took everyone they could get their hands on. This is not some legitimate judicial action."

"I know, Paul. I know. We have been thinking about it. We have no relatives. We are the end of the line, and we are comfortable here. Give us a few days."

"We just want to help you. You are very important to us."

"Yes, and you to us. God knows, we want to be around for our grandchildren." For the first time, Georges was moved and had to wipe his eyes.

"I can arrange papers for you. We can drive you across the border with very little risk. But you have to decide, and you will need identity papers and travel documents."

"I know. I know." He drank a large gulp of champagne. "What do you think, Bernie?"

"I don't know. You kids have so much to look forward to. We've had a good long life together. Eh, Georges? We've seen some horrible things, but we've lived well and loved every minute of it. We never could have kids, never thought too much about it, but it just never happened. You're all we have. I think we may need to leave. We've been together forty years. I'm afraid that today happiness is just another form of anxiety. Let's have some snacks and relax. Allow us time to think about it and talk about it."

We spent the entire day with them, talking, eating, drinking, and taking two short walks with Argut. I have never felt closer to anyone. Bernadette and Georges are so warm and open, so forgiving, so understanding. Since they never had children, everyone is their child. Paul attempted a few times to discuss the warning and the possible alternatives, but they were not open. We planned an evening early the following week at the apartment. It was sad when we left. The disparity of our two announcements, but also the importance of both. I love them so. I couldn't help from crying on the way home, not for them but for all of us. Too many tears, too little time, too much uncertainty.

***

Sunday evening we spend with my parents. I have never seen Papa in such a state, He's nervous, not focusing on the conversation, obviously occupied with something else. Even Gribouille notes his preoccupation, whimpering tiny sighs at his feet. We settle in the salon with tasteless tea, but relaxed after a nice dinner of bean soup.

"Papa, come and sit down."

"Auguste, what is wrong with you this evening," Julie asks. "Gabrielle and Paul have an announcement. It's important. Can't you suspend your thoughts for a few moments. You can attend to your affairs afterwards."

Papa huffs, but sits down in his easy chair across from us, and Gribouille settles at his feet.

"Maman, Papa, Paul and I have decided to marry. We have been thinking about this and avoiding it for months. We know that it's not a good time to marry, but we decided that to wait will serve nothing. We are committed. We told Paul's grandmother, and she gave us her blessings. We don't want this to be a big affair. A simple civil wedding. Nothing fancy. Just family. Maybe a dinner at our apartment."

My father looks concerned. "I know it seems the right thing to do, but the timing is not good." He pauses. "So much is happening. You're young and there will be time if we can ever rid our country of this pestilence. Why rush into this?"

"Auguste," Julie says, sharply for her, "do you remember our wedding?"

"Of course," he replies annoyed.

"Well, then, you will remember that all of our parents were dead set against it. What did we do? Ran away and married on our own, without any family or friends. You had served your time before the conscription law changed to three years, but you were required to serve again in the Great War. It finally ended, but times were tough. We had no money, no prospects. You had a job in a framing shop earning next to nothing. We left Paris in 1920. You were twenty-seven and I was twenty-three. We went as far away as possible, and we married. Gabrielle was born two years later. There was nothing sensible about our elopement and marriage. We were running away, simple as that. Gabrielle and Paul are both level-headed, hard-working. We can help them if they run into trouble, which seems doubtful. If they feel they want to marry, we should support them with all our means and love. Simple as that."

My mother hadn't made such a speech in her entire life.

"Thank you, Maman. I love you both."

"And we love you, my little one. Auguste is grumpy tonight. We can ignore this for the time being."

"Julie," Papa replies sourly. "Life is just not that simple. Paul knows that. Every day is a test, and it's only getting worse. There's talk that the Occupant is disgusted with Vichy. With the Allies making headway in North Africa, it won't be long before the Germans decide to come south. That will change everything. Forgive me, I have a lot on my mind. Both of you are adults, about as responsible as it gets. I will support you with all my might. Gabrielle, your mother is not alone in loving you and respecting you. I will enthusiastically give you away in marriage to Paul. I only wish times were different."

"So do I, Monsieur. Thank you for your confidence," Paul says formally.

"Paul, let's be friends. Now that you're in the family. About our little discussion. I will try to be more open. It's for the best. Agreed?"

"Yes, agreed."

***

Paul arranged it all. The banns were posted for ten days. On 10 September 1942 just before noon, Gabrielle and Paul were married by the mayor in a simple ceremony in his office at the Mairie. Gabrielle's parents were there, but Paul's grandmother could not make the trip. Catie and two surprise witnesses, Nuria and Robert, joined them. Everyone was pleased that they felt this occasion was special enough to make the trip for a single night's stay.

Gabrielle's parents drove them to the town hall. Paul looked very dapper in a dark-blue suit. Gabrielle didn't even know he owned one, and she wore a practical white sheath and chapeau with a partial veil. Her friends at Les Nouvelles Galeries sent a beautiful bouquet, which she carried. Auguste knew the mayor well, who welcomed them. He wore his blue, white, and red official sash and was especially jovial and thoughtful. The wedding party was invited into his office, leaving the door open during the entire time for this public ceremony. After reading the requisite portions of the civil code related to marriage, he requested two witnesses sign the wedding register. First Nuria and then Robert signed. Robert was running on fumes, and he looked thin and gaunt. He had rested on the night train from Lyon, but he smoked constantly and, unlike him, he looked nervous. After the signatures, the newlyweds exchanged simple gold bands and kissed.

Then the mayor spoke: "It pleases me greatly to marry this young couple, whom I know very well. This is evidence in the future of our country. Marriage is an institution honored by all. Some of our friends might try to use marriage as a way of instituting their ideas on genetics through the prenuptial certificate, but as long as I'm mayor, which may not be long, I will marry all young couples who want to join hands in love and respect. Please, Paul and Gabrielle, accept my congratulations and best wishes for a long and fruitful life. Congratulations."

The mayor went around the room shaking hands and bussing the women. It took maybe fifteen minutes to complete the ceremony. The party exited his office and went to a café to have quick drinks before returning to the apartment. Auguste remained in the office a moment talking with the mayor in serious, hushed tones.

When everyone returned to the apartment, Edith came out of her room for the first time ever. She was surprisingly thin and nicely dressed. Gabrielle gave her the bouquet and a big kiss on each cheek. She was so pleased to see Robert that she could barely contain herself.

"Monsieur Robert. It's you. What a miracle. One moment please." She ran back into her room and returned with a jar. "This is my home-made tisane, which contains a mixture of restorative herbs."

"Why thank you, Edith. I will take it faithfully. I definitely need it." He gave her a kiss on each blushing cheek, and she retired like a young girl to her window seat and knitting, her flowers dancing.

Once in the apartment, everyone relaxed and began to catch up with each other. The guests arrived with sacks of provisions, and Gabrielle had slow-baked a black-market pork shoulder, which remained in the oven, warm and redolent, meat falling off the bone. Julie went into the kitchen to prepare the ceremonial lunch. Jordi and Josette arrived with a large kettle of a real coq au vin, some fresh green beans, and a large plate of hors d'oeuvres; Julie had prepared a wedding dessert: *croquembouche*, a small tower of cream puffs and late season strawberries, drizzled with caramel and, amazingly, real chocolate. There was even some real coffee, cream, and butter: such luxury. Georges and Bernadette were late.

In his bedroom, Robert and Paul had a long, meaningful hug like two prize fighters after a grueling match, exhausted and leaning on each other for balance. Paul was surprised to feel a pistol in the rear of Robert's pants and looked at him in surprise.

"Oh that. My boss is a wanted man by Vichy, and we all carry some protection. It doesn't mean anything."

"That's not true, Robert."

"Well, it's dangerous out there."

"In addition, you look terrible."

"And you as well, sonny. We must be doing something right." Neither laughed.

Nuria, Catie, and Gabrielle hurried to Paul's bedroom, where they could talk a moment without concern.

They hugged like schoolgirls and giggled innocently as they had years before.

"Thank you for bringing Robert," Gabrielle said to Nuria. "But he looks so tired and older. He needs a vacation."

"Believe me, we all do. You girls look good, both of you. What are you doing, Catie? Is there a man in the picture?" She squinted at Catie.

"I'm not ready to admit it. I've been dating a man, but right now I just want to enjoy him without planning some romantic future. If it turns real, you'll meet him." She laughed. "And you and Robert?"

"We're all growing up," Nuria said. "Robert and I are not thinking marriage, if that's what you're suggesting. We're taking it day to day, not on account of our connection, but the uncertainty of the times and our jobs. We can't take it any other way. It's draining. But with Robert I have never had such emotions, such a commitment, as though tomorrow has no significance. It's like bright fireworks that scintillate brilliant colors and you never know how many, how intense, or how long they will last, and you don't ask."

"We're like an old married couple," Gabrielle added, not despairingly, but with pride. "A drop of stability, or what passes as stability, in a sea of doubt."

There was a knock on the door, and Jordi announced the opening of the champagne. The girls joined everyone in the main room, where he filled a variety of glasses.

"This is a 1934 Veuve Clicquot" Jordi announced, "so enjoy. Let me propose a toast to the newlyweds, Gabrielle and Paul. May you enjoy great wealth, a graceful life, and grateful children." He must have read this somewhere.

"Here, here," Robert said. "To Paul, my school chum, the conscience of Trinité, and that's saying a lot. To the couple of the year." He raised his glass in salute. "We have much to learn from them."

Nuria raised her glass. "We pray that this atrocious war comes to an early end, and we can all be free to lead normal lives."

"Ah, normality," Auguste began. "Today, we celebrate Gabrielle and Paul. Tomorrow will be a new day, and one day all the clouds will dissipate and be buried in the sea, and the sun will return to warmth and cheer. But first we must find our way out of this evil, ungodly nightmare. Put away childish notions, for we are no longer children." Then he paused uncomfortably and in a muted, pitchy, wavering voice began to sing: "*Allons enfants de la Patrie; le jour de gloire est arrivé…*"

And everyone joined him in singing La Marseillaise, the forbidden national anthem. This act, so uncharacteristic of Auguste, filled their hearts with love for him and our country. Thank goodness that Paul's strong voice joined in to lead the small amateur and unrehearsed choir.

When the song finished, the hors d'oeuvre plate was passed around, and the dining table was loaded with servings. Everyone was relaxed and talking. At the table, they crowded around with barely enough space, but managed. Soused, Jordi opened another of his wines, a red Pomerol and passed the bottle around casually for a wine fit for royalty.

"Where is Georges?" Jordi asked. "He hasn't dropped into the bar recently, and I wanted to talk about a variety show this spring."

"I don't know," Paul said, expressing the full weight of his concern. "We visited them ten days ago. They promised to see us this week, but we didn't hear from them. They knew all about the wedding, and I sent a telegram to remind them. I don't know what to think." But all his fears surfaced.

Everyone remained silent for a moment, considering Paul's words, but eating and enjoying the excellent food.

"How was your exhibition, Monsieur Daniel?" Nuria asked.

"It has been going very well, attracting many people. It's still up until next month. Only a few sales, though. Who would buy a painting today?"

The dinner was a mixture of warmth and sadness. The room was warmed by love, yet it was tragic that among the best of friends, what was left unspoken took on greater import than what was said. Like a large family reunion so much had transpired, so many changes, so many lives moving on different trajectories, so many unresolved memories of the past. Everyone shared partial stories of each other, but no one knew the full details, and it was the details that meant the difference between life and death.

The dinner continued with mostly small talk. Jordi, Julie, and Catie told their anecdotes. Gabrielle tried to make everyone comfortable. The wine flowed, and by the end of dinner, everyone relaxed with the evening and the conversation. What a strange affair, where honesty was limited and the truth parsed out like delicious macarons.

A loud knock on the door woke everyone. Paul went to answer. The sound of the door opening and a loud voice broke the silence: "I wouldn't have missed it for the world. Where is she?"

Gabrielle recognized the stentorian voice. He came into the salon like a force of nature and, to her surprise, picked her up, hugging her tightly, swinging her about. "I'm so happy, *la meva filla.* So happy for you and Paul. But who cares about the groom." He finally put her down. She loved Paco, but there had always been an understood restraint on their friendship. This was an unexpected surprise. Today, he felt free to be the other person he had described. Gabrielle introduced him breathlessly.

"This is our boss, Paco. He's a professor of Spanish at the university."

He circled the table shaking hands and introducing himself. He knew Auguste, although nothing was stated, and kissed Julie. When he came to Nuria, they spoke in Catalan. "Why you're the spitting image of my brother's daughter. What is your family name?"

"Danon."

"Danon…from Barcelona?"

"My family…yes, my grandparents"

"We are related: Sephardic Jews."

"What? Really?" The surprise was apparent in Nuria's composure.

"Of course. Could be three hundred years ago, but close enough. Danon was a common Sephardic name. Nice to meet you. Gabrielle talks of you." Nuria looked perplexed and confounded, totally taken aback.

Julie carried in an extra setting and forced Paco to sit in her place, which she cleaned up a bit. Soon Josette joined her in the kitchen.

"Well, this is an extraordinary gathering," Paco said. "And Jordi. It was your café where Paul got his start, no?"

"He's good boy," Jordi replied, well along the path of inebriation.

"Yes he is," Paco admitted. "Excellent choice of words. You know, today is the celebration of a wondrous event. I wish I had been better at marriage. I attempted twice, and failed twice. One never learns. But these two are strong individuals and are perfectly matched to grow together like two trees in the wind, moving joyously in concert, but fully respectful of their separateness. Omar Khayyam. I see a bright future.

"Today, I am told, the Occupant tore up the armistice and is heading south. Vichy is no more. Vichy has lost everything: their zone of supposed independence, their Army and Navy, and their empire in North Africa: a bunch of embittered old men fantasizing, lying, dreaming of recovering their disgraceful past, powerless marionettes, to be discarded on the rubbish heap of history like a burlap bag full of rotting potatoes. But from now on, we will have the Occupant here in the south to further complicate our lives."

"In the Free Zone?" Catie asked.

"If you could ever call it that, yes, my dear. We will see them in our daily comings and goings. They will be constructing their fortifications along the Mediterranean coast and enforcing their profane ideology in our cities, towns, and villages and pursuing their ruthless ambitions."

"That changes everything," Robert said, suddenly animated and consumed. "It's a sign of their weakness. Also, a sign that Vichy really never had any power or purpose. It's a sign that the Germans are now on the defensive. The reality of the occupation won't change, but it may become darker. In fact, this summer has been the darkest yet, but it's also the end of the beginning, and the beginning of the end." He glanced up at Paul. He had been mostly silent the entire afternoon, responding to people, but holding back. "It means that now more than ever we must unify. We can't just wait with petty arguments and fiefdoms." No one pressed him on what he meant exactly; no one had to; everyone knew.

"The bright side of our work," Nuria added, "is we know more than most people about what's going on, and believe me it's not good. We…"

"Georges and his wife are naturalized, right?" Robert suddenly interrupted.

"That's why we're worried," Paul replied, frustrated.

"Well, the police are arresting Jews throughout the south. Thousands, according to our estimates. They started in August after the Paris roundups. There seems to be a new strategy in the south. The north has already been purged."

"Laval cannot do enough to appease the Occupant," Nuria added. "Vichy is rounding up more than their quota."

"In June alone, we counted four new train convoys leaving France full of arrestees," Robert said. "And we know that July and August were the heaviest roundups ever, and they continue to arrest and fill the trains heading to the east. They are sending prisoners from internment camps in the south, Gurs, Récébédou, Noé, Milles, le Vernet, Rivesaltes. As we talk, roundups are occurring in Limoges, Toulouse, Lyon, Marseille, and Montpellier. These are the ones we hear about, although never in the newspapers, and there are many more."

"The waiting is over," Paco said. "It's over. We cannot wait to see what will happen, and I'm not talking about my friends in this room. I'm talking about the great majority who refuse to admit what is happening. The shopkeepers. The *attentistes*. The *je m'en fous*. The *ma pommes*. The anti-Dreyfusards. The Catholic church."

In the end, Gabrielle wasn't pleased with the tenor of the evening, but what do you expect getting married at such a time. The dinner ended well enough. Everyone enjoyed the food and each other. The wine never ran out. First Jordi and Josette left happily. Then the Daniels departed along with Paco. It seems they are closer than anyone realized. Robert and Nuria excused themselves to his bedroom. Gabrielle walked Catie to her house nearby and returned. She turned out the lights and joined Paul in their bedroom. He was in bed feeling down.

"You're thinking of Georges and Bernadette?"

"Yes. I'm scared. Papers take time. I haven't done anything."

"We need to visit them tomorrow. I'm sure Paco will not miss me."

"Do you think the conversation got out of hand?"

"Yes, but that's where we live today: our wedding in the middle of a thunder and lightning storm. It's impossible not to discuss it. Maybe one day we can look back on it with good thoughts. It's our marriage after all."

"Now it's our honeymoon, you know."

"I do."

"Come to bed."

"I was hoping you would invite me."

339

Gabrielle discarded her clothes, turned out the light, and slid under the covers next to him. She felt his warmth against her body. He wrapped his arms about her. She felt protected, desired. He enhanced her life in so many ways. She liked Paco's analogy of twin trees in the breeze and was glad they had married despite all: the uncertainty, the occupation, the future. It felt right.

She held him and refused to him let go. She held him for tonight, tomorrow, for all time. Eternity measured in lifetimes.

21

Fall 1942

If you visit Paris
Tell all my friends hello
And that my heart will always be faithful
If you see my neighborhood
More beautiful than the entire world
If you see my house, sing my favorite song...
If you see rue Lepic, my concierge Sylvie
Tell her that one day I will come
Perhaps tomorrow, one never knows
When I will return home
When I will meet all of that again
Forever
« Si tu vas à Paris, » Charles Trenet

Love and war are intricately linked. They are the mysterious mountain peaks of human emotion: good and evil, beauty and ugliness. Love is not countable or measurable, while war may be counted and estimated, its direction and duration cannot be known. Neither one can be foreseen. They are the two inexplicable and puzzling faces of God.

The next day, as they drive to le Racou, they note the German troops, troop carriers, and armaments moving about, having arrived during the night in Perpignan. It hadn't taken them long. It's quiet, and people go about their business, but it's a sea change for the worse in already troubled waters.

At le Racou, the summer influx of vacationers and people with vacation homes have departed. The sky is clear, but autumn is in the air with a cool breeze along the seashore. The street is nearly vacant, and parking is no problem. Paul knocks on the door. No answer. He knocks again. Nothing. He has a key that Georges gave him a year ago or so. It turns the lock and opens the door. The interior is cold and still, no people, no dog. They look around. Nothing out of order. Paul goes into the rear bedrooms, while Gabrielle looks in the kitchen.

"Gabrielle."

She turns, startled, and goes to the back. Paul is standing in the bedroom. Everything is in disorder. Clothes strewn about. Shoes flung in all

341

directions. Drawers open. The dressing area is a mess. Yet, on the closet door hangs a cream silk party dress, ready for a celebration.

"I wonder what happened?" Gabrielle says. "They definitely left precipitously."

They search all the rooms for clues of their departure. They sit on the couch, wondering what to do, their minds running wildly. Then they hear footsteps approach on the porch.

"Hello?"

Paul goes to the door.

"Yes?"

"Bonjour. I'm the next door neighbor."

Hearing this, Gabrielle joins them at the door. "Bonjour. I'm Gabrielle and this is Paul. We are the closest friends the Doelnitz have here. They have no relatives."

"The gendarmes were here," the short, bald man, still in summer dress, blurts out. "Early morning this Thursday, before daybreak, two cars and a wagon and lots of talking. We're not used to that. Woke us up. We heard them hammering on the front door until Monsieur Doelnitz opened it. I couldn't see well, but I could hear. They went into the house, while others waited on the front walk. I could see them smoking. Must have been six policemen or so. Took awhile, but finally I see them leading Georges and his wife out and putting them into their wagon with a couple of officers. Drove away."

"Did they have baggage?" Paul asks.

"I think they did. Maybe a single piece between them. They were dressed warmly, like in winter clothes, heavy overcoats, but disheveled. Strange. It all happened so fast."

"Well, thanks for letting us know."

"We're new to the neighborhood. We didn't know them well, but they seemed like ordinary people. You know, nice people."

"Yes, thanks."

They return to the living room in a haze.

"I'll have to look into this. Where were they taken? They should know at the Prefecture. Whether they'll tell me or not, I can't say. Franco asked me not to return."

"Nothing we can do right now." Gabrielle says devastated. "Let me pee, and we can go."

Paul waits, upset and anxious. He knows what happened. It happened exactly as he had heard many times. A quick pickup early in the morning, a trip to the Citadelle, where they would be interviewed, and then transport out. He doubted the local police would concern themselves with innocent people, wrongly accused.

Gabrielle returns. "I found a scribbled note in an envelope addressed to us. It was hidden in the medicine cabinet." She handed it to Paul.

Dear Paul and Gabrielle,

We expect you to find this as a married couple. We wish you so much happiness and regret not being with you. You both deserve it. I can't thank you enough. What you warned has happened. They listen to nothing Georges says. Others will correct any problem. Just following orders. No information on where they are taking us. Only one bag. This is my fault. You would think I would know better. Not the first time. Nothing you can do, and do not worry, I believe we can straighten this out. Hope to see you soon, and if later, then know that we love you both,

Bernadette

They close up the cottage, and Gabrielle gets into the truck. Paul starts the fire in the combustion chamber.

Once he gets the engine started he remembers. "Oh, I almost forget," he says. "Give me a second."

He runs back into the house, walks straight through, and exits the back door onto a stone patio surrounded by a small, neatly tended garden. He walks into the garden and sees what he's looking for. A small brown and white corpse: a Cocker Spaniel named Argut, his neck distended in an unnatural position. He bends over to feel for a sign of life where there is none. Kicking a small grave in the loose sod, he picks up the lifeless body, lays him in the small grave, and covers him with the fresh earth. He stands there for several minutes, wiping his eyes filling with tears, staring at the newly turned ground, He isn't crying just for the unfortunate dog, but for everyone, and himself.

"RIP Argut." He decides not to mention it to Gabrielle.

***

Franco Plana, chief of the visa section, looked sincerely at Paul. It was Monday, three days after the Germans arrived in Perpignan.

"Sorry about that. He was correct. He and his wife should never have been taken. I can't speak for the efficiency of our police or the Gendarmerie. They, like the society at large, are by no means unified, but they follow orders. Without question. Anyway, give me a moment." He left the room, Paul wondering what he was up to.

It took a long time, long enough to smoke a cigarette and to view the canal and strolling shoppers from his windows. He watched a German guard detachment march along the canal and then turn to enter the commercial sector and Hotel de Ville. Finally, Franco returned with a grey folder, which he was rifling through, quickly reading portions. He stood before his desk.

"'Arrested at five o'clock on the morning of September 9. Taken to the Citadelle. Transferred to the *Centre national de rassemblement des Israélites*.' That's the new center in Rivesaltes set up to receive foreign émigrés. 'Scheduled to be transported to Drancy internment camp on Convoy No. 7, September 10 at 19:13 with estimated one hundred and seventy-five internees, to arrive at Drancy on 11 September at 14:25.'"

Paul interrupted: "They were on the way as we were marrying."

"Here, this is interesting. An added note. 'Representatives of Vichy and the SNCF determined a schedule of one train per day beginning August 31 until all foreign internees in the south are transferred to Drancy. The convoys will consist of open freight carriages with sliding doors for approximately seventy-five people per car, covered cars for approximately forty people per car, four or five covered cars for baggage, and one car for approximately twenty to thirty guards. Itinerary: Sète, Nîmes, Sorgues-Châteauneuf-du-Pape, where it connects with a train from Milles internment camp, to the demarcation line at Chalon-sur-Saône, terminating at Drancy in a northeastern suburb of Paris, supposed to be a modernist urban habitat, *La Cité de La Muette* (City of the Silent Woman). The entire complex was confiscated by the Occupant to be used as a major housing area in the Ile de France. The detention camp itself is run by French police, but it's a transit camp totally surrounded and under the control of the Occupant."

He paused to sit down at his desk, considering the disturbing and enervating information. They didn't speak. Paul was astounded at the information, so organized, so close at hand, and most likely highly confidential.

"What can I do?" he asked despairingly.

"Nothing. Drancy is locked up tight. No visitors. Even the Red Cross has trouble visiting. There is nothing you can do. I checked and Convoy 7 left on schedule."

"They arrived at Drancy on our wedding day," Paul repeated rancorously. "What about his arguments of his arrest being contrary to French guidelines?"

"All I can say is that you know as well as I that Vichy guidelines are ignored by the Occupant. And now, Vichy has been superseded. I'm not sure what will become of us here at the Prefecture. My guess is we will be mostly ignored. The gendarmes and the local police are caught in an impossible trap. What can they do? And I don't know how much longer I can hold out here. The Prefect hasn't made an appearance since the takeover of the free zone. No one knows or is talking about what's happening."

"I'm sorry, Franco. If you hear anything, let me know."

"You can pray. Maybe by some miracle they may be interned in France. I'm really sorry. I know what they meant to you. We tried."

"Yes. We tried." But Paul was sick at heart, disconsolate, like in the midst of a rapid cascade of freezing water barely holding on for life. Georges had been his stalwart supporter for all his years in Perpignan. He had no closer friend, except Gabrielle, of course. Georges and Bernadette disappeared like others in his life. He prayed it would not be as final.

***

That next week, another postcard arrived from Paris. This time, surprisingly, it came from Auguste's mother, written two months before.

Vel d'Hiv   18 July 1942

To my son and daughter-in-law,

A note. Picked up Thursday at 15:30. Taken to the Velodrome d'Hiver near Eiffel Tower. We are unhappy. Isadore sick with heart problems, cannot endure a train trip. New people arrive. There are pregnant women, blind people, handicapped people, crazy people, small children. We sleep on the ground. Not a German in sight.

They give milk to children less than ten. Adults get a piece of toast, chocolate, a Madeleine, and cold pasta.

We cannot survive here for any time. Fanny is with us, in bad shape, and can't take much more. At our age. It is even more hurtful when the women say awful things and can no longer stand up and fall down and those with a little courage lose patience little by little.

I cannot any longer. I am giving this note to a person who promises to mail it, but I have given up. I am praying for you. If you receive this, pray for us.

Sarah

***

I picked up an English airman for delivery into the Pyrenees. He was wounded, but maintained a bright and heartening demeanor. I helped him into the concealed compartment behind the tool box. The days had been getting much colder, and rain was frequent. In the mountains, the temperature was near freezing, and the first snow remained alongside the road and on the brambles and branches of trees. The cab was very cold, and I was dressed in a heavy coat, cold weather underwear, gloves, and a heavy ski toque. Still, I shivered uncontrollably.

For a few months after the arrival of the Occupant, everything at the borders remained the same, and I continued with my deliveries. But this day all that changed. No problem driving to Prats-de-Mollo, but when I arrived at the French post, the border patrol officers I knew over the many months had disappeared. Instead, I found gendarmes and customs agents and a small contingent of Weimar soldiers. I slowed, and they signaled me over near the small enclosure. For the first time, I saw the Pétain police as well, in blue uniforms and caps.

A policeman in blue came up to the window. "Bonjour. Your papers please." He was not from the region by his accent. The Wehrmacht soldiers wore heavy slate-grey coats over their grey tunics and dark trousers. They remained stoical like manikins with their machine guns cradled in their arms, watching everything, but understanding nothing. The easy run was finished.

I handed him my papers, which included my personal identification papers, the certificates of transportation, and the identification of the charcoal company. He read through the papers without expression.

"Please step out of the truck."

I did so, leaving the motor idling.

"Step aside, please."

I moved over toward the enclosure. Two border patrol agents came over to search the truck. One of them gave me a sheepish look, as though he empathized with me. The other examined the truck from top to bottom, even inspecting the undercarriage.

"What are you carrying?" one asked.

"I transport charcoal two or three times per week from our production area in Spain to the depot in Ceret. I'm empty going over and carry a full load on return." I stopped myself, remembering the warning never to offer information.

"Okay," the blue-dressed officer said. "What's in the side compartment?"

"Tools." I was beginning to become concerned. I felt my body shivering, from the cold, but more likely the tension. I took a deep breath and stepped forward to open the door. For a moment, I wondered if he knew what he was looking for. Had they been tipped off?

"Step back," the policeman commanded sharply.

He signaled for one of the guards to open the chamber. He pulled out the dirty tools, finding it distasteful, getting his uniform dirty and his hands filthy, spilling charcoal debris and dirt onto the ground, getting his gloves and boots covered in black dust. All that remained was the dirt and powdered charcoal dust, which I always carefully refilled to hide the tiny levers holding the barrier in place. He flashed a torch into the obscurity to observe the interior and straightened up.

"Okay." He backed off, not making any effort to return the shovels and tools.

"You need to obtain an authority to transport charcoal," the Vichy officer said malevolently.

"I've been doing this for almost a year. I have the transportation certificate."

He looked at me sharply, the border guards standing behind watching curiously. The Germans were totally disinterested. "See your local Gendarmerie. I can't do your business for you. Without it next time, you won't be allowed through." The guard handed my papers back and signaled for me to leave.

"Okay. Thanks."

He churlishly nodded at me. I went over to get my work gloves from the cab. I picked up the tools and tossed them carelessly into the compartment, dropping my gloves on top, and shut the exterior door. I slapped my trousers to remove some of the dust, but it was hopeless. Hopping into the cab, I put the motor in gear and moved slowly forward. When I rounded the curve out of sight, my pulse was racing. I slowed, breathing deeply. I progressed slowly along the empty route and gradually approached the Spanish border. By the time I neared the Spanish frontier post, I was partially recovered. The Spanish guards had not changed. I was comforted to see a face I recognized and to be waved through.

I arrived a few minutes later at the meeting point with the contact standing along the side of the road. I helped the airman out of the compartment. He seemed to have survived, perhaps not even knowing how close he had come to being discovered.

"Okay?" I asked him.

He nodded his head and raised his thumb. I shook his hand and watched as the two departed. I guardedly replaced the barrier and hid it more diligently than usual with mud, dirt, and charcoal debris. I replaced the tools and closed the compartment. I wasn't sure I could continue this charade. Slowly the risks increased, particularly with the mute German soldiers. After my conversation with Paco, I had kept count. The number of packages totaled maybe ninety after about seven months. I had no idea how important this effort was, but I questioned its tenure given the arrival of the Occupant. That would entail a conversation with Paco.

Of course, the frontier was not the only place changing because of the Occupant. All the coastal villages were being disrupted: people forced to move out of their homes, homes taken over by Germans, the Mediterranean coast cleared of all but necessary inhabitants, creating a prohibited zone, reserved for the military and essential locals. Construction of the southern seawall took on a new urgency, building concrete walls, bunkers and emplacements for troops and armaments, tank barriers, and other defensive structures. The German military architects hired thousands of locals to help with the construction. Financing for the works came straight from Vichy payments under the armistice. With the fall of North Africa to the allies, the Germans were feeling vulnerable: however, that did not slow their pressure on Vichy to remove the undesirables from the south; in fact, it accelerated: quotas from Berlin had to be filled.

***

Gabrielle is working late, restocking and repairing the damages of a busy Friday afternoon. The store is mostly empty, about to close. They both continue to be disturbed by the arrest of Georges and Bernadette. No information of any kind has filtered back to them. The disappearance without a word haunts them like the loss of an heirloom pocket watch you felt was merely misplaced, but never reappeared. The situation with Gabrielle's grandparents is even more concerning, since receiving the note from Sarah, particularly due to the rumors circulating around the Val d'Hiv roundup and its outcome. It's a time of disappearances without notification, as if the value of life has degraded to simple rubbish, silently carted away to some undisclosed disposal site. The French soldiers remain in prison in Germany, émigrés disappear, people in villages leave without word, friends vanish, relatives are lost, and enemies are dealt with mutely. The French police are occupied with more important issues: keeping the borders closed, controlling the complicated rationing system, thus ensuring the flourishing black market, responding to the needs of the Occupant, and hanging on desperately to their jobs with a confusing hierarchy of command and personal morality. The presence of the Occupant is like a picador at a bullfight, enraging the virile bull, while at the same time emasculating him for the final battle.

Gabrielle finds the mindless restocking calming, redressing and ameliorating the errors of the past. She is busy in the cosmetics area, when once again she shockingly views her old school chum, Isabelle Lefèvre. After their last encounter, you would think that she could find someone else to bother. Isabelle walks in as though she owns the store, followed by her paramour, Joseph Tena. She advances quickly, without any pretense of shopping, obviously having come to see Gabrielle.

"Bonjour, Gaby," she says with her habitual smirk on her hard, not-quite-pretty face and long blond hair.

Gabrielle doesn't reply, irately staring at her, which does not prevent Isabelle from addressing her.

"You and your friends are in big trouble…as you probably know. I warned you. You're all on the wrong side, and we know everything about you, your hubby, and your father. You're stirring a pot that is boiling over and will scald you. Remember who your friends are. It's finished."

Gabrielle watches her bitter mouth and the pleased countenance of the man with her.

"Isa, leave me be," Gabrielle replies, having no idea what she knows, and, indeed, doubts she knows much of anything. She knew Gabrielle's parents during school informally, but has had no other real knowledge or contact since then.

"Things are changing here in Perpignan. If you choose not to participate, you will be left behind. It's a new world order."

She stops her work. Angry and irritated, she confronts Isabelle: "What are you talking about? Why are you doing this?"

At the tone, Isabelle backs off a bit, but her companion comes closer. "We know what's going on with your husband and your parents," he says, his face pocked-marked from an adolescent battle with acne. "With the new changes, we are becoming recognized for our activities. It will be made official in a few days. Groups that continue their resistance to the order will be arrested or worse. If you can't imagine the future, then you are doomed to remain in the past."

Again, Gabrielle can't think of anything to reply. "Please leave," is all she says. "You know nothing about me or my family."

At the same time, Isabelle is examining a display of Helena Rubinstein special lipsticks, thirty francs each. She picks up one and puts it in her purse. She smiles, pleased with herself, and walks out of the store.

Gabrielle feels exposed and exhausted, and at the same time she realizes that there must be some truth to what they say. She is scared. She stops her work and abruptly leaves the store.

When she arrives back at the apartment, Paul has a small dinner waiting and a glass of wine. She flops down on the couch and describes the encounter. Paul sympathizes with her and takes it very seriously.

"I've heard of this group," he replies. "It's a fascist movement in support of the government, but it's becoming a quasi-military organization in support of the Occupant and paid by the Occupant, or at least that is the rumor. They are being armed by the Occupant: another policing force among many active ones. But, Gabrielle, why would they need to tell you anything, if they really knew so much?"

"Why focus on me at all? I'm not doing anything of value. And I'm sure they have no idea of your activities. And my parents, how are they implicated?"

"It's probably a lot of conjecture and bluster, but I think it's important for us not to ignore the warning. We'll talk with Paco."

"Oh, I forgot to tell you. He plans to move his office. He hasn't said where, but we're packing up."

"Make a date for us to meet with him at a different location. I haven't seen him since the reinforcements at the frontier. And you need to be more conscious of being followed. We need to take this seriously."

***

At noon a few days later, Paul waited to meet Paco and Gabrielle at a restaurant outside the city center, nursing an ersatz espresso. He had an appointment that afternoon with Henri Bardou, who had called and asked to speak with him. He had not said why, but Paul assumed it was about Robert or the apartment or both.

They arrived shortly. This was the only time they met in public since working together. Paco sat down and lit a cigarette. Gabrielle came around the table, kissed Paul, and sat down next to him, taking his hand.

"Sorry to miss you, Paul. We haven't spoken since last week. I have been traveling, and Gabrielle has been trying to get everything arranged for our move. From what Gabrielle told me, the border crossing has changed completely. What exactly is happening?"

"The border has been reorganized, most likely by the Occupant. The normal customs agents are gone, replaced by uniformed Vichy policemen, backed by Wehrmacht soldiers with automatic weapons. I didn't recognize anyone. They are not friendly and did the first serious search of the truck, but luckily found nothing. I don't think they have any knowledge of us at this point. One policeman, the most aggressive, seemingly in charge, said that I needed to have authority to transport charcoal. Whatever that authority may be. They let me carry a load back that day, but reminded me to get the approval from the local Gendarmerie. It was nerve-racking."

"Well, the entire network is readjusting," Paco said. "Like everyone, we were caught with our pants down with the Occupant coming south. It means that our work will change. We have to be more careful. The gendarmes and local police, and even the Vichy police, are more forgiving, willing to overlook things if it serves them or their pocketbook. That has changed. The Wehrmacht soldiers understand almost nothing, but they are not willing to look aside. The Gestapo probably were here before, but now they can work openly with the military administration, which includes the

Sicherheitsdienst, the intelligence service of the SS, and the Sicherheitspolizei, its security police. The Gestapo is much smarter and absolutely dedicated to destroying us. The SS is not as smart. They're the ruthless hoodlums. They're all dedicated to the Fuehrer. So our enemies have increased in number, are more committed, and are better trained. The game's changed." He lit another cigarette with the butt. He seemed more nervous than usual.

"In addition, a new party has joined the hunt. Gabrielle met them the other day. What used to be rag-tag groups of collaborators, Vichy supporters are now becoming more professional. They are calling themselves the Milice, and they are more unified and outfitted by the Occupant throughout France. They are paid, plus they steal on the side. Mostly, it is composed of disaffected, thug fascists, who have always been with us, but now under the new occupying forces will feel empowered. They understand what is happening locally, like your nominal friends, Gabrielle. They can be a source of information and names to the Gestapo, and now they can be dangerous in their own right. It depends on how many French citizens want to work for the enemy. It cannot be underestimated.

"After thinking about it, I realize I knew Joseph Tena at the university a few years ago," he continued. "A middling student, without passion. No one to remember. He seems now to be leader of the Milice here in Perpignan. He will be used by the Occupant, so we need to be concerned about him and his girlfriend, what was her name?"

"Isabelle Lefèvre."

"Yes. I don't want to scare you, but we are all in more danger now. They know something. Perhaps not enough to make a move, and it may be based on suspicions, but we need to make changes, including your parents, Gabrielle. I am postponing the office move. I'll contact you both in a week or so. You can help us move with the truck, Paul, but no more deliveries until we better understand the situation. You're on leave until next year. I really want to keep the two of you out of harm's way. Gabrielle will help out for a few days with the move, but you're both out of work until you hear from me in a few weeks. By that time, we should have a better idea of how much is known, and we'll be better organized at all levels. Okay?"

Paul nodded his head. He recognized that the changes at the border meant that the risks had multiplied greatly. Particularly when the Milice seemed to smell something. He certainly didn't want to be arrested with a military package. Today, that could mean immediate execution on the spot by the occupying army, no questions asked.

They departed concerned and uncertain, each in a different direction: Paco back to the office, Gabrielle to Les Nouvelles Galeries, Paul to meet Robert's father.

***

Henri Bardou stood at the window of his office in a *hôtel particulier*, a large free-standing private residence with courtyard and private entrance, like you see in Paris. The room was appointed in classical style with high arched windows, a large desk, wainscoting, darkly wooded bookshelves, a large chandelier, and a fireplace, mostly useless in the south. The elegant building and décor forced Paul to reconsider his opinion of the man, and his son. Henri welcomed him, shaking his hand in a friendly fashion, pointing to a settee and chairs.

"I'm really sorry I was away and missed your marriage ceremony. Congratulations. I understand Robert made it."

"Yes, Monsieur. He was here for only a few hours. He came expressly for the wedding."

"He could have left a note," he commented to himself out loud. "How did he look?"

"He looked tired and anxious. He's totally committed."

"Doesn't sounds like him, but I'm not certain to what."

Paul watched this father, greatly concerned for the welfare of his son, but he remained silent.

"He's always been talented in everything he touches, but never willing to put in the effort to succeed. Raised with everything he ever wanted, he found school unchallenging, as you probably know better than I. Never concerned with his own interests. Always looking for loyalty from his friends, but always disappointed in the end. You have been the one consistent friend. He always had me to fall back on. Great charm, but constantly making bad choices."

"I don't think you have to worry about that, Monsieur."

"How's that?"

"Well, he's consumed by his job. And my guess is he's fighting for this country as few people are these days. His talents are recognized at the highest levels. He's being tested to the limit of his resources."

"Interesting. Still with that girl?"

"Nuria? Yes. They're quite devoted to one another."

"I only met her once, but found her too pushy, too strong-willed."

"She knows herself and is aggressive. I like her, but outwardly she's not warmth and charm. Once you're her friend, though, she'll do anything for you. She's fighting for the soul of her country…just as Robert is."

"Paul. Are you involved in this movement?"

"What are you referring to?"

"You know exactly what I am referring to."

Paul had no idea why Monsieur Bardou had invited him here, and it was becoming less clear. He looked at this wealthy man, sure of himself, independent, obviously well-connected. He knew Robert's politics veered to the left, and he wondered where his father's loyalties lay.

"I do what I can."

Henri chose to allow Paul's evasion to stand. "What are you doing now. You're no longer at the Prefecture."

"I'm working for a company that imports charcoal from Spain." He began feeling warm, sweating, wondering where this was headed.

"I know. You're driving a truck. Do you find this rewarding?"

"I don't plan this as a career, Monsieur, if that's your meaning. It keeps me busy and out of the relève."

"I'm sure it does. What about your singing career?"

"Singing? I never saw it as a career. It's been an interest, a hobby, nothing more." He watched the tall man, sitting comfortably, his legs crossed. Here was a successful businessman, never exposing himself, never giving you an idea of what was on his mind, used to negotiating and dealing with others. Charming, effective, easy to work with, but fixed in his ways.

Strong-willed and capable of obtaining whatever he desired. His failure was that he took for granted his success and privileged position, and he judged others less successful harshly, without empathy or understanding. Paul knew that Robert's mother had died of cancer while they were at school together. He was unclear on how to relate to this man, having had little exposure to men like Henri Bardou. It was a world apart from his experience. He thought of Paco Macias, of Paco's ease and warmth with others, of his idealism and belief in others. Paco had a hard side, Paul knew that, but Paco also appreciated others with differing backgrounds.

"Anyway, I don't want our conversation to be disconcerting to you. Here is why I asked you to join me today. I have long been impressed with your combination of intelligence and practical skills. I know how Robert feels about you, and you have been managing the apartment building on rue de la Gare as well as it's ever been managed. I'm looking for an assistant to learn the commercial real estate business. I own a large number of buildings in the region, mostly office and retail business locations, and I am rapidly expanding. Due to the war, there are many opportunities available today. I am fortunate to be in a position to purchase additional sites, but this has always been a one-person firm. When the war ends, I'm thinking of purchasing raw land and becoming involved in development, again remaining in my niche of commercial activities. It's become too much for one person. I need a smart young man, someone I can trust, who can work with all kinds of people.

"I never do business with people with whom I do not have a personal relationship. I get along with the powers that be, but I am very flexible. I'm not political. I don't allow politics to determine my activities. You may find that reprehensible, and it verges on this today, since we have to deal with a corrupt government and an enemy in our midst. I definitely disagree with the goals of this government and their tactics. That's between us," he smiled. "But I need to work with everyone. I'm not a predator, and I believe in offering fair prices for properties. Not a bottom-feeder. There are plenty of those today working with the *Commissariat Général aux Questions Juives* (CGQJ), picking up properties for a sou at the cost to other people. Vultures all, and they will get their comeuppance. I expect after this period is over, and the dues have been paid, there will be a time of growth, and I want to be situated to join and aid that growth. I do not want any suits or judicial entanglements.

"What I am offering is a chance for you to join a real estate firm at an introductory level and to grow with this firm. Does this have any appeal to you? It's nothing Robert ever considered, although he would be welcome. There's plenty of room."

Paul wasn't sure he liked this man. He didn't dislike him either. He saw a realistic honesty, a man of affairs. Not a humanitarian by any means, at least in outward appearance. If he hadn't known Robert so well, his answer would certainly have been negative. He just wasn't in a position to decide.

"You don't have to say anything," Henri Bardou said smiling at him. "Think about it. Let's have dinner with Gabrielle in a few weeks, before the holidays. Is that fair?"

"Yes. Thank you for the opportunity, Monsieur. I am flattered. There are many things right now..."

"Think about it," he interrupted. "Any questions or doubts, just ask. That's all. And I apologize about putting you on the spot in regards to Robert, just a father trying to understand an uncommunicative son, but your information was therapeutic. Thank you.

"I understand, and I thank you."

***

In June, Vichy had passed a law requiring all young men and single women to be subject to work requirements of the government: the so-called relève, the same name given to this new law, the *Service du Travail Obligatoire*, aimed primarily at men in their twenties, the class of 1942. It was fully functional by the fall. The law made it clear that all workers were subject to the Occupant's work needs, working here or in Germany. Although it never facilitated the release of many French prisoners of war, it was a constant pressure, forcing people to work for the war cause. No one liked the law, most resisted, and it never fulfilled Vichy's goals: an irritant in all ways.

In mid-September, there was an explosion and fire in the office of the STO in the City Hall of Perpignan intending to delay local implementation of the law. To most people, it was a well-chosen action, complicating the departmental actions and postponing its implementation for several more months until the records could be reestablished.

Strangely, the local newspaper reported it. Most negative news was never published. Stories focused on Vichy, the locations and deaths from the bombardments of the Allies, the hopeful changes in Italy, Hitler's speeches, and opinion pieces on the future role of France in the New Europe. Never anything on resistance or deportation or Allied gains. Paul noticed a tiny article in the Independent on page 2:

> Bolsheviks at it again
> Hoping to devastate the relève, Perpignan STO office
> bombed with little impact on its operations
>
> Perpignan 16. – Yesterday a small fire broke out and was quickly contained in the Office of the STO at City Hall. In this poorly instigated raid, little damage was incurred, and no other parts of the City Hall were affected. It is believed that this was an inside conspiracy, since no other offices were damaged, and there was no sign of forced entry into the building itself. The police are investigating and say they are on the trail of the perpetrators. The attempted destruction failed in an effort to eliminate the office, its contents and records, and its functioning. The police promise to bring the criminals involved to justice in the next few days and to punish them to the full extent of the law.

***

Two nights later, Gabrielle returns from the Galeries, and they walk over to her parents' house. Julie had insisted that they come for dinner. Something is up. The house is cold and inhospitable. The salon is in a state of disorder, unkempt, with piles of clothes, files, paintings, and other things lining the walls.

Julie welcomes them affectionately. "Come in. Come in."

"Maman, the house is freezing. What's happening?"

"I know. I should have warned you. We'll light the stove, but it doesn't do much. We have to wait for your father to arrive to explain. How have you been?"

"Working," Gabrielle replies. "Paco is moving to a new location. He wants to be in place by the new year. Paul has been furloughed for the time being. No more trips to Spain. He's learning to cook, and he's always there to pick me up after work."

"Hmm, nice." Julie smiles at Paul. "How are you?"

"I'm okay," Paul says, eyeing the disorder of the room. First time in years I'm not fully occupied, with time to relax. It won't last long."

"He's been offered a job," Gabrielle adds. "Henri Bardou. You know him?"

"Kind of. I met him, I guess. Your father knows him. What sort of job?"

"Commercial real estate development," Paul replies."

"How nice. Can you get the fire going, Paul? You're an angel to provide all that charcoal. Your father's running late as usual." She pours some wine, and the dog scampers from the back of the house, through the salon, down the stairs, to the door. "That's him."

We hear Gribouille whining happily and the door opening. The two come slowly up the stairs and into the salon.

"*Bonsoir, tous*," Auguste says, kissing his wife. Gabrielle gives him a bisou. He throws his coat over a chair in the kitchen and pours himself a large glass of Banyuls sweet wine. You can tell something is up. He's avoiding eyes and clearly occupied and edgy. Unlike him.

"Well, how are my kids?"

"We're fine, Papa. How are you?"

"That depends. We will postpone serious talk until after dinner. What is it, Julie?"

"Beef stew, without any beef, just a few bones the butcher saved for me. And a little marrow. But plenty of good red wine, a bit of smoked bacon, carrots, fresh cepes, rutabaga, and turnips, of course, shallots, garlic, and zest. I can't believe I found them in the market this morning."

Auguste produces a fine Burgundy wine. "Special occasion."

After a quiet, tense dinner, they retire to the salon with a liqueur, leaving the dishes piled in the sink. Gribouille curls up at Auguste's feet. The house has heated up a bit from the hot coals.

"Well?" Gabrielle says, looking at her father.

Auguste clears his throat nervously. Always the hint of impending bad news. "We have decided to leave Perpignan."

"What?"

"It's not what you may think. And it's only temporary. We are going into hiding. Can't be helped. With the Occupant at our doorstep, it was decided that we needed some fresh country air."

Paul thrusts himself backwards sharply. "You promised, Auguste. We're big people now. You can tell us the truth."

"Life was so simple before you joined the family, Paul, but we're glad you did. Yes, let me explain. I have been involved in an effort to establish a unified Resistance movement in France. It's being called *Mouvements Unis de la Resistance* (MUR). I won't go into it any further. Anyway, we were denounced and then, thanks to some friends, warned in advance. We are off to a small village in the Fenouillèdes, a wine-growing region on the French border of Catalonia. We have use of a small house and should be quite comfortable"

"How long, Papa? And can we visit? How will we communicate? What about this house? When are you going?"

"The less you know the safer you are...and we are. I don't know who denounced me, but Julie and I are leaving tomorrow before dawn. We will be there for the duration. That's better than an internment camp in the north. We will communicate, but you will not be able to visit, nor even know our location. It can't be long. Things seem to be turning. The Soviets appear to have stopped the advance at Stalingrad, and Rommel is trapped in Tunisia. North Africa belongs to the Allies. Two critical defeats for the Axis powers. And the Allies are gaining with their bombing."

"You know, Auguste," Paul says. "We too will be out of the fray by year end. The relocation of the Occupant has heated everything up, bringing the war to our doorstep."

"We've made progress," Auguste says. "Things are going to change. I'm glad that I can breathe easier with both of you out."

"Any word from the north?" Gabrielle asked, knowing the answer.

"Nothing," Julie says, tearing up.

The evening ends emotionally. We clean up the dishes, empty their cupboards, and help get the house in some order. We leave with large sacs full of dry goods and produce and several paintings. Intense feelings of love pass between the family members, with strong and meaningful hugs and kisses, not knowing when they will see each other again, but feeling relief that they will be removed from the crosshairs.

***

Later in bed, Gabrielle and Paul curl up, keeping each other warm. She has stopped crying and lies comfortably in the curve of his body.

"What does it mean…their leaving?"

"I think I know, but I'm not sure. I think your father might surprise you."

"He always has. But why do they have to leave?"

"He fears being arrested. He's more involved than we thought."

"In what?"

"In saving a country he loves…"

The more that transpires, the more the vice closes, Paul thinks. The world seems to be growing smaller. It's now everyone for himself. No one ever says it outright, but fear is everywhere. If someone doesn't share your ideas, then you're enemies. A *couvre-feu* (curfew) is instituted from eight in the evening to seven in the morning. At night, the advent of nightly German patrols constantly remind people of the occupation; a knock of a gun butt on the window or door means to cover or extinguish any visible interior lights. Everyone has double curtains, so no one can see into your house. You have to be careful of what you say and whom you say it to. Horse-pulled wagons and gazogène camionettas carry household goods as people move off the coast into the mountains. It's affecting all of us.

The Daniels' leaving. The Doelnitz arrested. Gabrielle's grandparents caught up in a roundup. The borders being tightened up by the Occupant.

When will it end? The noose is tightening. We must not become entrapped, for there may be no escape, and both of us are deeply exposed.

"I'm glad they're leaving, for at least they will be safe."

22

December 1942-January 1943
> *Look across the salty ponds*
> *Those elegant sodden reeds*
> *Look at those white gulls*
> *And those rusty colored houses*
> *The sea has gently embraced us*
> *Along the shores of clear lagoons*
> *And like a tender love song*
> *The sea has cradled my heart for life.*
> « *La Mer,* » *C. Trenet*

I awake groggy again, late, feeling nauseous, and I run to the bathroom and vomit into the bidet, knowing after several weeks what is happening to my body. Paul left early this morning, but he has no idea of the changes that are occurring, and I refuse to tell him for a month or so, just to be sure. He cannot see the phenomenon before his eyes, the farthest thing from his mind. Well, so be it. I'm glad. I made every attempt to prevent this pregnancy: too much unbridled passion and not enough forethought. It's not the right time, but is there ever a good time, as Georges asked?

Tomorrow will be Christmas, my first Christmas without my parents, and the first as a married woman. It's strange to think of this, but that's the proper category, and it's not a bad one. The New Year 1943 is coming rapidly upon us. Almost three years of war, death, misery, shame, and the loss of our freedom.

My parents have sent one cryptic note, passed through friends, telling us that they have settled into a comfortable farmhouse with a view of the Agly River, running through a cultivated river valley, with plenty of woodlands in the foothills for firewood. Papa is sketching and painting the hills, valleys, people, and animals, particularly the horses, of the Fenouillèdes. Probably for the first time in his life, he finds himself free to paint without restraint, although I'm sure he maintains a low profile. The locale is remote and has become home to many new inhabitants: few questions are asked of newcomers. New occupants are widespread in rural villages throughout the country.

I dress and head down to the store. I've been working near full-time since the postponement of the office move, but may help Paco for a few days at the new office in the new year. Unusual for the day before a holiday, few customers wander the aisles, but there is no usual today? It's been cold and rainy, and with the occupation and the curfew, people have been staying closer to home. The shelves look like one of those impoverished stores you see in the outskirts. Diminishing items to choose from and limited stock. We make an attempt to fill the shelves and to make the cosmetics area attractive, but our hearts aren't in it, and the result is meager, unexciting offerings. As stocks are depleted, it's difficult to find replacements, and the major brands are providing less in the way of promotional material. Several girls have been furloughed. Our makeup artist has been reduced to one day a week, but even then she isn't busy. We'll probably close early today.

I meet Catie for lunch at the Grand Café in the center of town. Normally busy midday, it's practically empty, and the surly waiters are friendly for a change and glad to be of service.

"How have you been?" Catie asks innocently. She's aware of the major events in my life, as we usually meet once a week.

"We both are free this week, until the new year. Paul is finished with hauling, and I may work a few days early next year, but that's it. We are unemployed after that."

"What will you do?" Catie asks anxiously.

"I haven't a ghost of an idea."

"I broke up with my latest. You didn't even meet him, thank God. I just have no luck. I guess I should just become a nun."

"I wouldn't give up quite yet."

"I think I need to focus on myself. Maybe a new job. Something different. My parents keep questioning what I'm doing, but it's hard with all the changes. I don't blame them."

"Oh, come on. You can't depend on some prince charming to change everything and make you happy. You have to do that yourself, even married. Look at Nuria."

"I know, but she's so smart, and she's always been inspired by things. Remember when she wanted to be a doctor and volunteered at the hospital, only to find she hated cleaning up after people and all the blood? Then it was politics, working for local candidates. Then la Cimade, helping immigrants and internees. And now, God knows what she's doing, probably something worthwhile, while I'm selling strollers and diapers."

"Quit worrying about it. Once this is over, it will all change." But that phrase is heard too often to be believable, I think to myself. The Occupant seems only to be strengthening, and the war is continuing at its own sluggish pace. Any good news is never printed and difficult to find.

"No one's having babies. I'll probably be out of a job next year."

"Well, I'm sure you'll find something, maybe something you really want to do."

"Nice to think, no? But what would it be?"

"If you don't know…"

I feel sorry for Catie, she seems so lost. Perhaps a man would make a big difference in her life, but it would be like the lottery: high payoff, but terrible odds.

***

There had been no sign or word from Robert and Nuria during the holidays. We assumed they were unable to disentangle themselves from this critical period of change.

On Christmas Eve, Gabrielle and Paul went to midnight Mass at the cathedral of Saint Jean Baptiste. It had been a tradition for Gabrielle growing up. Only in the last few years had her parents reduced their attendance at services. She always enjoyed the music and the ritual, the nativity choir and the organ music. They sat in the rear of the church, trying to participate in the ceremony, to be moved by the Latin mass and the singing, to become part of the service, to feel the miraculous birth of Jesus, but slowly they found it unbelievable, irrelevant to their daily life and the events surrounding them. They noticed some Germans in uniform taking part. It seemed totally incongruous.

Gabrielle watched the people begin to line up to take Holy Communion. It reminded her of the daily lines you see for bread, meat, and vegetables.

Suddenly she recognized a face. She turned away quickly, but not before she was recognized, their eyes meeting for an instant.

"I just saw Isabelle," Gabrielle said, horrified. "And she smiled at me."

"Let's go," Paul suggested. "I'm feeling that this Christmas season is missing the point."

"Me too."

They departed rapidly into the cold evening and walked slowly back to the apartment. People were in the streets, even with the curfew.

"What are we going to do?"

"Tonight? It's late."

"I know. I mean next week, we're both off, and, in fact, we both may be out of jobs next year. What will we do?"

"Well, I'll talk to Monsieur Bardou for one. It all depends on Paco. I think he's changing his strategy. Vichy's helping, with the STO, even with the problems here in Perpignan, throwing a wrench into the complicated works, a wrench in our favor across the whole country."

"I would be required to aid the war effort if I registered, which I will not. Particularly since the department's records have been destroyed…at least temporarily. It's perfectly clear whose side our government is on."

"What would you do?"

"I'm not going. It's forcing men my age to flee the country and attempt to get to London to fight for the *Forces françaises libres* (FFL), the free French forces. The mountains are filled with locals attempting escape. But it's also filling the ranks of the Resistance, particularly the Maquis. I think Paco's in a recruiting mode for the various Maquis groups. That's why he doesn't need us, and he doesn't see us in this role."

"He's been meeting constantly with many more people than usual, I know that."

"I think it's becoming more serious, more military in nature."

"The relève is a great recruiting tool for the Resistance and the FFL."

When they arrived at the apartment, Paul poured two snifters of Grand Marnier, which he brought into the bedroom.

"*Joyeux Noel, mon amour,*" he said, handing her a glass.

"Come to bed. It's too late for wine."

"He stripped and got under the cold covers, finding her body warmed up. They lay together for a minute, when her mouth sought his. They kissed passionately, and all was forgotten, except the importance of each other. She welcomed him with mind and soul, and they melted together without a thought. Two people on an isolated island in the warm sun and sand, enlivened by their one certainty: their love for one another.

Afterwards, they both lay back and laughed like paired finches.

"What was that?" he demanded.

"I don't know, I'm just feeling a little crazy, and I think it was the mass and the people and our discussion."

"But, what about...birth control?"

"It's about that time of the month."

"Oh?" He looked at her: hair disheveled, no makeup, lying candidly on her back, sipping from the liqueur, oblivious to all.

"Don't worry," she said, gently outlining his face with her fingers. "I'll take care of you," and she began laughing hysterically, until tears came to her eyes and she began coughing. "I needed that."

"I guess you did. I love you.

"And my dear, I hope you know how much I love you."

***

The new year began with contentious and despondent weather. It was as if the elements mirrored the moods of the people and had set out to display their psyches: potent, disturbing winds, biting temperatures, and dark clouds of ceaseless rain and drizzle. Most people celebrated Noël in private, staying inside and feasting on whatever they could obtain, which was very little. They prayed that signs of a turn in the war were real and lasting. The Germans had failed at Moscow, and now they were surrounded by the Soviets outside of Stalingrad and were unable to extricate themselves. The Allies had secured control of North Africa, opening a backdoor to Europe. François Darlan, Admiral of the Fleet and commander in chief of the French Navy, had made a deal with the Allies, committing all French troops in North Africa to the Allies. He was assassinated a few days later, just before Christmas. The Resistance had also made progress, quietly infiltrating the

National Gendarmerie and the post office. In response, the Occupant continued feverish construction of the Südwall, using thousands of local STO's. But, incredibly, the Germans became even more aggressive in rounding up and deporting those they termed *"Untermenschen,"* or undesirables: Jews, Communists, Bolsheviks, Gypsies, eastern European émigrés, Africans and persons of color, anti-Nazis, gays, and anyone else they found objectionable. You would think they would focus on the war.

The Occupant was joined in this effort by the Milice Française, a new paramilitary force created by Joseph Darnand of Vichy and funded by the Occupant. The Milice was made up of French fascists particularly determined to defeat the Resistance, but also to aid in discovering and exposing *Untermenschen*. Dressed in blue jackets and trousers, with brown shirts and blue bérets, they suddenly became visible, more daring.

In response, the Resistance moved more toward military tactics, still struggling with sub-rosa efforts to coordinate and unify their goals and to control the various groupings. The Maquis were greatly boosted in membership by the *réfractaires,* those young men and women refusing and running from the STO. The Maquis received little pay and operated under rigorous discipline and commitment. Their uniform, less visible than the Milice, was high-waisted trousers, jaunty bérets, and knotted kerchiefs. And they were prepared to fight, though still not well-equipped.

Needless to say, the two groups, the Milice and the Maquis, had been raised together, knew each other, and reviled each other with a terrible loathing: siblings at war.

***

A few weeks into the new year, Gabrielle walked to the new office on rue de Jean Payra with her umbrella shielding her from the worst of the rain. The office move had occurred in early January. Paco, Paul, Gabrielle, and several strong-backed helpers had moved everything into the new building. It had taken only two days, and Paco had requested help from Gabrielle for a few more days to start up the office.

After a weekend of cold but clear weather, the rain began falling steadily, never halting, filling the gutters and streams. The storm clouds coming from the northeast, which normally with the marine winds would have passed quickly, lay heavily over Perpignan, funneling water and hail on the city. Luckily, the new office was closer to their apartment. Paco was waiting for her. He had placed a towel to keep water from coming in under the door, the price tag of having a ground floor office with a side entrance in an older building.

"Bonjour, Paco," she said, leaving the umbrella at the entrance. "It's really coming down."

"Bonjour, *Petite*. Take off your coat and come in and dry off. There is some hot water for tea." A steam-heater under the window barely functioned. The office consisted of a great room, looking as disordered as the old office before she had arranged and ordered everything. Several other rooms were closed off.

"I need your help to reorganize everything once again. It's all mixed up. I'm out for two days, but I'll be back on Thursday, and we can get it together in a few days. Don't worry about the heavy boxes. I'll move them if you get the rest set up. Two more desks will be delivered in the next day or so."

"We have too many files," she said. "It's not smart. Let me get rid of some."

"You know, you're right. I haven't had time to think about it. I don't think there's anything incriminating, but there may be some interesting things there. We discarded much of our stuff before moving, but take a second look." He seemed occupied, his mind elsewhere, not his normal self, but she began working.

She spent three days organizing: moving files, filling boxes, finding cash and securing it in one location, and selecting old files for disposal. Only Paco knew the combination for the safe, so she kept all cash separate in a large envelope. She arranged the desks after their delivery. Filling many cartons with old and useless files at the front of the room, she decided to have them removed for disposal without awaiting his return, knowing he would just vacillate as usual over discarding them. She had accomplished the impossible: organizing and assembling a usable office space. In the back of the room were the heavier boxes filled with foodstuffs and alcohol and other miscellaneous contributions.

On Thursday, the rain finally let up, and she arrived early. Paco had arrived earlier and had moved all the heavy boxes to a back room. For once the office was spacious, with room for several people and three desks, a meeting table, and a conversation area near the entrance. Gabrielle had arranged the files, but there was still more to do.

"Bonjour, Gabrielle. I have no idea how you did it. Amazing. It's much improved."

"Welcome back," she said, placing her coat on a rack and sitting down at the meeting table.

"Where are the older files? I thought we decided to wait."

"Never. You would just be unable to decide. I dumped all I thought should be."

"I don't know," Paco said shaking his head. "I may need some of them. But you're probably right." She could see his dissatisfaction.

"This depressing weather tires me out, and Paul gets nervous being cooped up and needs to get out."

"Maybe we can get him busy again, but things are getting rough. Last night a small group in Thuir was arrested, but today we celebrate. I have a bottle of Champagne," he added.

"Your last day, at least for a while. You have been wonderfully helpful and hopefully have learned a thing or two. I don't want to expose you further."

"We're still in a state of disarray."

"That may be true, but that seems to be life itself, doesn't it?" He popped the cork and filled two glasses, and set one on the table before Gabrielle.

"To you and Paul," and he raised his glass.

They clinked glasses and tasted the sparkling freshness. He sat down at the table.

"So what are your plans? I heard Paul might have a job offer, a good one."

"Yes. He said he was going to talk with Monsieur Bardou. Do you know him?"

"Yes. We don't run in the same circles mind you. He's…"

Three light knocks sounded on the entrance door. Annoyed, Paco rose and went to open it. He cracked the door, but the instant the door opened slightly, it was pushed forcefully from the exterior, thumping Paco solidly on the forehead, throwing him back into the room. He lost his footing and fell backwards onto the wood flooring. Three large gendarmes burst into the room. Gabrielle was so surprised that she dropped the glass of Champagne on the floor, splashing her shoes and stockings. The police warned her to remain where she stood, and they leaned over Paco, roughly turning him over and handcuffing him. They left him lying on his stomach, unable to utter a sound, perhaps hurt.

Two German officers entered the room in clean, grey uniforms with police shoulder boards and green underlay. They looked around haughtily and signaled for the police to remove Paco. The police hefted the heavy man by his arms and dragged him out. He was either unconscious or in a state of shock, muting him.

One of the German officers came over to Gabrielle, who was visibly shaking. "And who are you, Mademoiselle?" His French was flawless, with barely an accent.

"My name is Gabrielle Daniel."

"I see. And what is your role here?"

"My role? I'm his secretary." This was serious, but she had no idea of how serious it might be. She had never envisaged such a scene, even in her wildest imaginings, and was unable to plan her responses. All their discussions of lowering their profile and being more careful had come to naught. Not surprisingly, they came at the exact time of day Paco returned to work from a trip. They knew his schedule. At least Paul was not here. She hoped he would not be caught up.

"Are there any illegal armaments here?"

"No," she said, shaking her head, surprised by the question.

"You will come with us for a few questions. I'm sure this will amount to nothing, Mademoiselle. Your boss has more to answer to."

23

January 1943

> *She listens to the java*
> *She hears the java*
> *She closes her eyes*
> *Her fingers dry and nervous*
> *The music flows through her skin*
> *From below, from above*
> *She wants to cry out bodily*
> *And so to forget.*
> « *L'accordéoniste,* » *Michel Emer*

Due to the persistent torrential rain, he drove the truck to Les Nouvelles Galeries to meet Gabrielle after her work. When he entered the cosmetic department, one of the more senior women looked up at him with surprise and slight annoyance

"Well?" she said ambiguously.

"Has she left already?"

"We never saw her today. No word. Her clients have been asking for her. We thought her sick."

"No. She left the house this morning, and I was expecting to pick her up."

"Sorry. She never showed."

Paul felt a deep unsettling pain in his stomach. She was as regular as the bells of St. Jean. He was the one who had to be reminded or was occasionally late. Never Gabrielle. The only place she might be would be at Paco's office. He drove the few blocks to rue de Jean Payra and double-parked. The door was wide open, and Paul could see at approaching that several people were cleaning up, that the office had been ransacked. Binders and papers and stripped open boxes lay all over the floor: the room reeked of spilled wine and alcohol.

"What happened?" he asked, not recognizing any of the men working inside or out.

"Who are you?" an older man dressed in a suit asked him rudely.

"I'm a friend. Who are you?"

"The police raided this morning, or that's what the neighbors tell us."

"Oh, my God. What about his secretary?"

"Don't know. Never saw a secretary. Why the questions?"

"My wife worked here."

"The police tore this place apart, taking what they wanted. We warned him. We urged him to leave, but he wouldn't listen. God damned academic. Now we're all in trouble. You as well, probably."

Paul nodded his head. "Thanks."

At the Prefecture, Franco Plana was not happy to see Paul, although he did allow him into his office, seeing the strain in his face.

"I don't want you coming here. It's way too dangerous for both of us. Is that clear?"

"I know. I know. It's Gabrielle, Franco," he said dejectedly. "I'm not sure, but she's disappeared. I can only presume she's been arrested."

"When?" Franco asked curtly.

"This morning between nine o'clock and noon."

"You sure?"

"No."

"Well, I suggest you investigate other possibilities. In any case, if she was arrested, we won't know about it for several days. Everything is changing around here. We're not calling the shots." He paused for a moment. "Listen, Paul. I understand. But you can't come here, for both our well-being. I'll look into this, but it'll be several days, and we'll have to meet elsewhere. I know how important this is to you. It may be a false alarm. I'll contact you, but no more visits. Agreed?"

"Yes." Paul understood, but he couldn't help himself from looking at Franco differently. He was running scared. He had never seen Franco, the hero of the Spanish Civil War, in such a state of disorientation and fear. There must be more at stake than his job.

He left and passed by the Daniels' house, but it was locked up tight with no evidence of life. He finally returned to his apartment, half hoping to see her. No. Her absence was palpable: like after a terrible storm when the wind and rain and thunder finally die down: the emptiness, the silence, the humid absence. He couldn't sit, he couldn't sleep, he couldn't listen to the BBC

373

news, his mind reeling. There could be no other explanation for her disappearance. She left the apartment normally, going to work. He searched her closet. Nothing out of the normal. The bathroom, the toothbrushes, the dental paste, the water cup all in order. In the kitchen, a teacup and knife in the sink, a cut baguette, and her mother's jam on the counter.

He finally perched on the edge of the bed, still unmade from the morning, and like a wary bird held his head in his hands. He saw his entire life dissolving, slipping away. His mind hurtled from one improbable notion to the next. He thought of her parents. He had no idea where they were and no way to contact them. He thought of Catie, but dismissed that idea. There was no other explanation. If Paco was arrested, she would be as well. She was there, and they had both disappeared. The police ask no questions, they follow orders. They pick people up and take them to the Citadelle to be interviewed. And that was usually the end of it. Information rarely filtered back. Very few returned. Going to the Citadelle would serve no purpose. It was locked up tight, and visitors were not allowed. The mere fact of asking questions about someone would definitely pique their interest in him and expose him. And that would help no one.

The next few days passed interminable. He had nothing to do except ponder the possibilities, assuming she was arrested. He pretty much gave up on any other explanation. In desperation, he thought of returning to the Prefecture, but decided to heed Franco's advice. He would be contacted if there was any information available. That would be the only possibility remaining to give him some sliver of hope, of direction. How long could this uncertainty last?

For almost a week, he existed in misery, not eating, not going out, not taking care of himself. He saw no one. He remained in a state of suspended animation. Unhappy. Grieving. Angry. Upset with himself. Hating others. By far the worst week of his life. And behind it all was the knowledge that Paco might expose him if he were forced to, and that would end his freedom, or worse.

Finally he received a telegram from Franco to meet at the Palmarium. The weather had stabilized to clear and cold. He arrived early, waiting nervously for Franco at an exterior table, nursing a coffee. He felt like a small boy waiting for Christmas to begin after returning from mass, waiting for his mother and grandmother to descend the staircase to begin the celebration, full of anticipation, yet knowing he would be disappointed.

"*Hola*, Paul?

"Bonjour," he replied at the end of his wits.

Franco sat down and waved off a *garçon*. "I found some information. She was arrested by the Gestapo on the morning of January 12th."

"Oh, God. I knew it."

"She was arrested as a member of the Resistance, but had no information of value. That's what the report says. She was arrested with Francisco Macias, who was sent to Gurs. She was sent to Camp du Vernet d'Ariège."

"I've heard of it, but I know nothing about it. Why was he sent to Gurs and she to Vernet?"

"Well," Franco hesitated uncomfortably, "it's not a good sign. Le Vernet has become a transit camp for undesirables, including women and children. Mostly Jews, in other words."

"That's why she went to le Vernet, and Paco to Gurs?"

"Yes, perhaps. I didn't think she was Jewish."

"She's not. The Germans might think so. So she's being treated like an undesirable?"

"I'm not sure. Much information is left off the Prefecture reports."

"What will they do with her?"

"I have a Republican friend in the village of le Vernet, Miguel Serrano, who has first-hand information and may be able to help. He spent a few years in the camp himself after the Retirada, and when he was released, he took up residence in the region to help the Spanish internees." He handed me a piece of note paper with a name and address scratched on it. "That's all I know, and all we will ever know at the Prefecture. No reports back. Control and coordination of deportation is handled by the Occupant with the cooperation of Vichy and the SNCF."

"Deportation?"

"I'm afraid that's what le Vernet has become. There are deportation convoys leaving once a month or so to the north. I'm sorry."

"No. I really appreciate it, and I'm sorry that I involved you. At least I know her location at the moment. I'll talk with your friend."

"Paul, a word of advice. Take this a step at a time. You will need all your resources. Get some rest and be careful. You look terrible."

"I'm not concerned with my own health. I'll do anything. Without her, I'm lost."

"First, get yourself together. This may be the fight of your life."

Thanks, Franco."

"I wish you success. I hope one day we can meet as friends. *Bon courage*."

Internally, he felt a slight lift of liberation. He could start working toward a solution, the one grace his grandmother had successfully instilled. He began working immediately.

***

You are Paul Broussard. What can you do except commit to freeing her? You have no idea how to go about this, but your mind is consumed with nothing else. Any connection you may have had with the Resistance is gone. Even your contacts with the evasion networks over the mountains have been lost. The routes in the eastern Pyrenees have mostly been busted, except for locals escaping on isolated trails they know personally. Further, with the Occupant now improving defenses in the south, the frontiers have been beefed up, and the consequences of being caught are much more severe, if not fatal. You have savings. Not a lot, but enough to survive?

Your daily existence is nothing. An empty apartment. A worthless life. You are worried about the STO, refusing to register. Many people your age are refusing as well, escaping France or joining the Maquis or other Resistance groups. You are not considering joining a group yet. The entire direction of your life is determined by Gabrielle's circumstances, and nothing will detract you from that until you find some resolution or a stone wall.

Gabrielle and her family gave you something you hadn't even realized was missing from your life: love, compassion, and respect. It's like your first taste of fois gras and the realization that this rich flavor exists. You never knew of its existence. You never missed it. And suddenly you are awarded a flavor so intense and satisfying that you never want to lose it. And then, appallingly, it's removed. The value of all that you have lost is clear. Others who were raised with some aspects of a family take them for granted, rebel against them, hate them, think them too controlling, or ignore their importance. You, on the other hand, will do anything to reclaim your love: regardless of the chances of success.

***

Paul's mind is deluged with unanswered questions. He paces the apartment constantly. Food is of no consequence. It rains. The evenings are often filled with lightning and thunder. The sunny days are ignored. He walks from one room to the next. He sits on his side of the bed. He cannot read. The radio offers little. He waits. He thinks. He plans.

Then one day he remembers and rushes over to the side of the room and lifts a floorboard near the wall. He pokes his hand into the cavity and pulls out some francs in a roll, but also the small paper sac. Inside, he takes out the leather reticule. What did she call it. A tambour bag by one of the Parisian designers. He can't remember: Hermès maybe. He takes his time opening the small drum, until the heavy fabric can be pulled out. He opens it carefully on the bed. Fifteen diamonds slowly appear as he unrolls the cloth. Even in the low light, fifteen beautiful cut stones sparkle and shine like miniature fireworks. How much are they worth?

The next day he walks to a jeweler on rue Louis Blanc across the bridge from Les Nouvelles Galeries, la Maison Pallarès. He enters the small store. A man wearing a jeweler's eyepiece greets him. He's wearing a white shirt and trousers.

"Bonjour."

"Bonjour, Monsieur."

"May I help you."

"I want an appraisal of some cut stones."

"Of course. My brother's in the back. He's an expert on gems. Let me get him." He crosses the room, leaving Paul alone in the shop, a good sign. He walks around looking at the watches, mostly, but jewelry as well.

"*Oui,* Monsieur." An older man, white-haired, with a lab coat enters the room. "You have some cut stones to appraise?"

"Yes"

"Come to the back, please."

He follows the man to a workroom at the rear, mostly filled with hundreds of timepieces and clocks in various states of repair. The man sits down at a high desk and turns on a heavy desk lamp. He motions for Paul to sit next to him on a stool. Paul takes the tambour bag out of his rucksack, while the jeweler watches him with interest. He opens the leather case and pulls out the cloth, carefully placing it on the desk before the man, and unrolling it. He notes the jeweler's surprise, who puts on his loupe with increased interest, like a birder observing a rare migratory water fowl never before seen in the area.

"This is quite amazing," the jeweler says to himself. "Twelve. Sized to perfection. All fine stones. Very, very fine." He puts each on a small scale. "Amazingly matched. All three point three carats." He adjusts his loupe and scours the diamonds. Very fine indeed. Very clear. No inclusions. All well cut. I would have to study them carefully, but I think you have valuable stones here. The market for diamonds has recently doubled due to the demand by the Occupant. In Paris, these would be purchased immediately for a high price Here it may be a little more difficult, but that should not be reflected in the price. I'm getting ahead of myself, excuse me. I'm unsure of what you want to do with them. These days of misfortune, we get many people wanting to sell cut stones and family jewelry." He sighs, lifts his eyepiece, and observes Paul.

"I want to sell them."

"I understand. I would hazard they would be priced between two thousand and three thousand francs. That's a guess."

"All of them?"

"No. Each one. And they are much more valuable in a set like this. We charge five percent of the total sales price, but you can be assured that you would be getting the best price possible here in Perpignan. And you would have all the paperwork to guarantee the sales price and their authenticity and the price paid by the buyer. But I will have to study them. This is a transaction that demands honesty, trust, and confidentiality. Our family has been in business here in Perpignan since eighteen sixty-five. You can count on our family. We will be here for some time to come.

Paul was shocked by their value. A year's wages for an office worker were maybe fifteen hundred francs. A flat could cost twelve thousand francs and a beautiful mansion could be purchased for less than fifty thousand francs.

"One question, you might consider. In this environment, the likely buyer will be German. Does that bother you?"

"Yes, some. But other things bother me more."

He left the stones at the store with a receipt. Somehow he trusted this man, and he was convinced that they would obtain the best price and that other appraisals would not be necessary. He had no idea of the value of the diamonds. To him, the value was zero. He had kept three stones out of the transaction for Gabrielle. He walked back to the apartment attempting to recall the name of the couple that had given him the stones. He couldn't recollect. There had been too many packages in the interim, but he could picture them. He remembered the man's earnestly voiced insistence on following your own heart and the importance of names. Two concepts that had been new to him at the time, that he had never really considered before. Perhaps this man and his wife had had a larger impact on him than he realized. He hoped they had found a way out.

***

Paul had met several people with Paco Macias. One in particular had impressed him. He knew when he first met him that he was involved in quasi-military operations. Paco called him Bouloc, *nom de guerre*. Paul guessed from casual comments and bits of intelligence that he was involved in organizing groups throughout the region to undertake sabotage and the execution of judgments of the military tribunal of the local Maquis. His achievement, which Paco recounted, was unifying three regional Resistance movements. These groups had graduated from publishing tracts, with real news from London, to actual operations against the Occupant and local Milice groups. Bouloc, he believed, was important in this secret army of the

Languedoc-Roussillon. After several failed attempts and tons of convincing through his own résumé and experience, Paul managed to set up a meeting with him.

Surprisingly, Bouloc came alone to a small café off the beaten path. They had not seen each other for over a year, but they easily recognized one another.

"Bonjour, nice to see you," Paul greeted him with a firm handshake. He was in his forties, bearded, with a tweed jacket and black béret. His face radiated intelligence and firm strength, but had a tightness around the eyes, hinting at intensity and, perhaps, ruthlessness. They ordered coffee and sat alone outside in the cool air where no one could overhear them.

"Bouloc...and you're Paul." Real names.

"Yes."

"I was very sorry to hear about Paco," he said immediately, after a brief introduction by Paul. "The Gestapo have no idea of who he is. Someone informed, and they picked him up, but according to my informants, he survived some pretty rough interrogation and was sent off to Gurs, giving them nothing, and he's okay. I assume that means you're okay...for the moment."

"My wife was picked up with him, and she knew absolutely nothing of his business."

"Sorry, *hombre*. I saw her on a few occasions at the office. I don't think she knew who I was. Hey, you were one of Paco's true success stories. Good work. Lots of danger and exposure, but you got away with it. Anyway, we're here to discuss your wife. She's the daughter of Auguste Daniel, no?

"Yes."

"He's quite the man."

"He's a great painter."

"No, I mean his recent operation. Caught them by surprise and destroyed everything."

"Operation?" Paul asked, not understanding.

"Oh," Bouloc said taken sharply aback. He paused, knowing he had violated one of the key provisions of the Resistance, and began again. "She's at le Vernet, not a great place."

Paul looked at him quizzically, but didn't want to be sidetracked. It was, in any case, something he had suspected.

"No. I'm trying to set up a way to communicate with her. I've written a few letters, but no response. I have a contact in the village of le Vernet, and I'm hopeful he can help. What I want to discuss with you is a way to get her out, to free her."

"Eh, that's no easy feat, *hombre*. I pretty much know the circumstances. She's in the women's section, and in danger of being transported any day. Let's think about this. The camps are well secured, and with the Occupant taking over management, they are becoming fortresses. The men we've heard about who have escaped le Vernet did it on their own. Mostly lucky, right circumstances. The failed attempts are not known, but I've heard they're treated badly or just disappear. I don't see that for your wife." He paused and thought for a moment.

"One idea. I've heard a few stories of people escaping transport trains, no easy matter and dangerous, jumping from moving trains. Northern France, Holland, Belgium. You have to slow them down. In Belgium, I heard there have been a few examples of blocked transport trains, with wholesale escapes, but never in France. And information is scarce, since the Occupant controls any negative information that makes them look bad. The trains here aren't guarded that well, although that's changing, but they move rapidly in open country, making it difficult for any disruption to occur. I don't know. It's not easy, *hombre*."

Paul hesitated, but finally added. "I have money to make this happen, enough to get arms and explosives or whatever it takes."

"Sounds good, but we would need the help of the Brits to pull off something like this, at least in getting supplies, and I'm not sure stopping a transport train would be in their best interests at this point. Today, the trains are full of undesirables. I hate that term. You know, people the Occupant wants out of the way. They're mostly not part of the war, but its innocent victims just the same, victims of hatred and ignorance, combined. Sorry. Getting off the point.

"I'll tell you what. Get in touch with your wife. Let's understand her situation. It may not be as grave as you think. One last point. We've been told by London to cool it on the military assaults. They want us to hold back. They have their own plans, and the big boys in Lyon are attempting to pull everyone onto the same boat. If that happens and the Allies manage to get a foothold here, things will change."

"Meanwhile, my wife is in danger of being transported to the north."

"I get it, Paul. I get it. Let's take this step by step. I'm willing to do what I can. Let me see what I can do on my end, and you work on gaining insight on the camp. Okay? One thing to remember. Everything changes on a daily basis. Rules of yesterday will no longer be in effect today."

"Yes," he said, but he was disappointed. He realized he couldn't expect others to jump to his aid. This was his problem, and he needed to make it work. They set up another rendezvous in two weeks. He had no idea what tomorrow would bring, so time seemed to stretch out into an eternity.

24

February 1943

> *The lingering sobs of autumn's violins*
> *Wound my heart with their long, languorous tone*
> *All around me suffocating and ghostly*
> *When the hour sounds*
> *I recall times past, and I cry*
> *And I leave to an evil wind*
> *That carries me here, there, as if I were a dry leaf.*
> « *Chanson d'automne,* » *poem by Paul Verlaine, set*
> *to music by Charles Trenet*

A gendarme accompanied her to the police car and helped her get in the back. In addition, a police wagon and a black Citroen were doubled parked. The police wagon took off, followed by the car with Gabrielle. They crossed the canal, passed Les Nouvelles Galeries, and headed toward the Palais des Rois de Majorque, near her parents' home. The thirteenth century structure once served as the capital of the Majorcan king, but was now a failing structure; a portion in the rear, called the Citadelle, was used as a holding area by the Gendarmerie and now the Occupant.

They pulled up at the entry gate and entered a courtyard. Gabrielle was escorted into an atrium of the foreboding ancient stone structure, where the policeman handed her off to a man in plainclothes. He led her through a series of doors, ending finally in an area with a cold and dreary row of steel doors. He opened one with his set of keys, indicating she should enter, and he closed the door behind her, with a final clash of the door and the keys turning in the antique lock. The cell was empty save for a chamber pot and some straw piled in one corner on the stone floor, which she assumed served as a mattress. Recently occupied, the cell was filthy. A small barred window was far above her head, and allowed only a hint of light to enter the cell. A horrible stench filled the air of sewage and stale humidity. There was no noise; it was unnaturally quiet. She sat down on the floor, mentally and physically exhausted, not knowing what to think.

She couldn't believe it. It had all passed so rapidly, without any explanation and with only a few questions. She wondered where Paco was and if he were hurt. She thought of Nuria, who had spent some time with la Cimade visiting camps and prisons, whose descriptions seemed so far beyond anything she could conceive of. She remembered, but hadn't really internalized these descriptions, so beyond her experience. Yet here she was in similar circumstances, alone with nothing, knowing nothing, without any recourse. Thank God she had grabbed her heavy coat before leaving the office.

She wondered how long she would be here and what the process would be. She waited expectantly, but time seemed of no significance. After a few hours without a word or a visit, she lost track of time. The light in the cell varied little with the passage of the sun, which was mostly clouded over anyway. The one thing she knew and was grateful for was that Paco had kept her from any knowledge of his activities, and she hoped this might save her from any serious consequences. She wasn't naïve and knew the stories, however filtered, but she also knew that her participation in his affairs was minor, and she could not provide any information of value to the Occupant, but she also had to admit that she suspected his work was extensive, beyond what she had ever conceived. She finally wrapped her coat about her and lay down on the filthy straw in a fetal position, waiting.

Later, the noise of someone in the hallway woke her. The steps on the stone floor passed by. She wouldn't allow herself to daydream about Paul. How would he find out about her disappearance? What would he think of her absence? Instead, she waited obliviously, tracing the mortar between the flat flooring stones with her fingers, examining the lines and abrasions on the ancient stones, trying to keep warm, which was impossible, and praying to stop the chatter of her anxious mind.

She thought of Isabelle and her boyfriend. The warning repeated in her head. Was this their doing? No. She was working for one of the top figures in the Resistance in the Pyrenees Orientales. That was the problem. It wasn't a question of being careful. She was trapped. Now she had no idea what would happen. How could she contact Paul? It all seemed unreal, and yet very real in the extreme. She dozed.

The noise of the lock turning in her door forced her to open her eyes in the obscurity. She must have fallen asleep. The door opened noisily, and a metal dish clanked on the floor. The door closed. She had no idea of the time. A vapid cloud of steam rose from the liquid in the dish. Hoping for warmth, she turned over and pulled the dish closer. It was a clear broth, without vegetables. Lacking a spoon, she sipped from the bowl its lukewarm contents. It tasted of ashes and decay, but there was something in its savor that attracted her physically, perhaps some hint of vitamins or oil. Besides, she was thirsty. She finished it. And then returned to waiting. For what? Her mind stirred about quixotically, fabricating the worst and the best and the unimaginable. The possibility of Paul's arrest darted through her chattering mind.

Slowly, the dim light departed the chamber, leaving her in total blackness, and she settled into a wakeful slumber, never actually sleeping, always shivering from the cold and humidity. It was impossible to prevent scenes and thoughts of her life from intruding. As she slipped in and out of sleep, her thoughts veered back to tender memories until the reality of her shivering and discomfort prevented her from sleeping. The tug and pull of her recollections left her in a somnolent state without ever giving her reprieve from her real circumstances nor allowing mental escape.

The longest night she ever spent, like waiting endlessly for an examination in a hospital, came to an end with key sounds and the door opening.

"Come with me," a uniformed guard said.

She stood awkwardly, almost losing her balance, her limbs sorely aching from the hard, cold floor. She forced her chilled extremities to function. Following him, door after door, she attempted to brush her hair, arrange her dress, and keep her coat wrapped about her. Finally, they came to an occupied area somewhat warmer before a desk.

"What is your name?" an older man in civilian attire asked her.

She had to think. "Gabrielle Daniel."

"Your cell number?"

"I don't know."

"One forty-two, C-block." He wrote in a book without looking at her.

She felt faint and reached out to the desk to steady herself.

"Have a seat," the man said.

She looked about and saw a bench against the wall. She carefully walked over and sat down. How could this continue, she thought to herself. One day and I'm a wreck. I have to be stronger. The thought alone made her feel somewhat better. She sat and waited.

Some time later, the man stood and entered the door behind his desk. He was gone for some time, but then returned and sat down. After a while, another man, a tall policeman, entered and signaled for her to follow him. More doors, each door a new room, progressively warmer and more lifelike. Finally, the policeman knocked on a door, opened it, and forced her ahead of him. In a bare room with sparse furnishings and a single desk, she saw the same German officer who had talked to her at the office. The policeman pulled a chair up to the desk and gestured for her to sit. The German was dressed impeccably, not a note missed, his hat sat before him on a clear desk, except for a single file folder in the center. His salt-and-pepper hair was neatly razor-cut short on the sides, long on top, parted high on the head, and slicked down with Royal Crown pomade. The room reeked of Cologne aftershave.

"Gabrielle Daniel Broussard?"

"Yes." This miniscule admission of her name comforted her.

"Where is your father?"

"My father?" she asked. "I don't know."

"You don't know where your own father is?" he asked in a mockingly surprising tone.

"No, Monsieur. Both my parents left without telling me, intentionally of course." Keep your mouth shut, her mind yelled.

"*Ach so*. How long have you been in the Resistance?"

"I'm not, Monsieur. I work at Les Nouvelles Galeries."

"Mademoiselle Daniel, let me warn you, your answers will determine your fate. We know who you are and who you work for. So may we proceed truthfully. I would hate to see it get more serious."

"In the mornings, I work for the man you arrested. In the afternoons, I work at the Galeries."

"I see. And you are not in the Resistance?"

"No, Monsieur."

"You work for one of the leaders of the Resistance. Are you aware of that?"

"I was an assistant and knew nothing of his affairs."

"You expect me to believe that?"

"Yes. I just balanced his books and kept his calendar. I never met a single contact or attended a single meeting, of which he had many." Shut up, Gabrielle.

"You admit you knew he worked in the Resistance?"

"No. He's a businessman."

The officer sneered in disbelief. "Don't toy with me. You don't know a man named Jean Robert?"

"No."

"And Henri Fontaine?"

"No."

"What about Louis Torcatis?"

"Never."

"Tell me about the flow of money."

"I accounted for the money."

"How did it come in?

"Paco, Monsieur Macias, always gave it to me, and I entered it in a ledger and put it into the safe."

"And you have the combination"

Thank you, Paco, she thought. "He was the only one who knew the combination."

"I see. What about his meetings?"

"I kept a calendar without names, only dates and times."

"Really. And travel?"

"He arranged his own travel."

"You expect me to believe this."

"It's the truth."

"*Ach so.*" He looked at her, seemingly sympathetic. Then surprisingly, "are you Jewish, Mademoiselle?"

"Madame. I'm Catholic."

"That's not what I asked."

"My parents are Catholic, born in Paris. I was born here in Perpignan."

"I see. You are not Jewish?"

"I'm not, nor my parents…"

"But their parents were Jewish."

"I beg your pardon? All my grandparents are Catholic. My maternal grandmother took me to mass when we last visited Paris. My father's parents both attend church."

"You continue to play games. I warned you. Your grandparents were born in Lithuania of Jewish parentage. We know that. They are…" but he stopped himself. "They were Jewish, and they still are."

"I was baptized and raised in the church, as were my parents."

"You miss my point," he said shaking his head, as though she were a slow child and his mission was to teach her, or make certain she agreed. "Your own government has defined Jews as anyone with at least three Jewish grandparents. 'Baptism cannot change your liver, your spleen, your ovaries,' to quote your own countryman, Louis Darquier."

Gabrielle's spirit and energy drained, and she could not focus. She had lost all fight in her after only twenty-four hours in captivity. She had no reserves. Even her hatred. She could only see this man in his spiffy outfit pretending to be sympathetic.

"*So.* We seem to be at an impasse. You are very uncooperative, Madame Daniel. And your husband, what does he do?"

"He left the Prefecture six months ago or so, and he drove a truck delivering charcoal, but that job ended."

"From the Prefecture to driving a truck. Where is he now?"

"I don't know. I presume at our apartment."

"And where is that?" She thought miserably that they surely must know that, if they knew all the rest.

"27 rue de la Gare."

"And this man, Francisco Macias?"

"You arrested him."

"Your husband works for him as well?"

She glanced at him, asking herself how much he knew. "He worked for a charcoal company."

"*Ach so.*" He nodded his head as though truthfully considering her answer. He observed her closely, tapping his finger on the file before him. "I'm inclined to give you the benefit of the doubt. Perhaps another night might aid your memory."

"I'm telling you what I know."

"*So.*"

He stood, and she helped herself to her feet, her head down. The door to his office opened, and a soldier came in and escorted her back to the cell. Thank God for Paco, for keeping me out of his affairs. And for Paul as well. I think my innocence of the details saved me from the harsher questioning that Nuria described. I think the German officer realized I had little or nothing of interest to him. Only time will tell, and time weighed heavily. Once in the cell, she lay down and fell into a troubled slumber.

***

Early the next morning, I was aroused by a rough hand on my shoulder. For an instant, I did not know where I was, but all too soon it came flooding back to me with a terrible realization. I was frozen from a sleepless night. I pulled my coat about me, adjusted my dress, and struggled to my feet. The guard watched me without emotion.

"Hurry up."

I stood, my head bleary, and followed him into the hallway. Other men and women waited. I joined them. We slowly advanced, until the entire block was cleared, everyone in line. There was no word of what was happening, where we were going, and I assumed no one knew. When we whispered, we were warned to keep quiet. I followed another woman, older, with a sophisticated air, who a few days before might have been considered nicely dressed. She had long blond hair, but she walked with a pronounced limp, and wore only a light coat. We walked through the building, again one door after the next, until finally a door opened to the outside and fresh air welcomed us. It was cold and drizzly, no sun, and low clouds misted the distance. Several municipal buses waited, and we were forced into a bus until no one else could enter, with people standing in the aisle. Then the remaining people were forced into the next one. I was lucky to get a seat.

I watched the city of Perpignan disappear. We passed directly in front of our apartment on the rue de la Gare and stopped before the train station. Waiting police guards, forced us into a group and directed us into the station to the departure area, harshly warning observers away from our group and opening a passageway. People swiftly moved aside, allowing us to pass, watching us curiously, understanding that we were the undesirables that everyone spoke of, but also surprised that we looked like the normal citizens we were. We slowly entered the waiting train. I saw a sign noting the Toulouse Special, which I knew well and had taken numerous times to visit Toulouse, about two hundred kilometers from Perpignan. I managed to get a wooden seat in the ordinary third-class section.

We arrived at Toulouse four hours later without making any stops. I was able to watch the landscape pass swiftly as we left behind the city of my birth. We moved rapidly along a spit of land between seawater lagoons and the seashore. "*La mer qui on voit danser le long des golfes clairs.*" The line from Charles Trenet's song, sung by Paul Broussard so many times, repeated itself. The train then turned west before Narbonne into the Corbière foothills, past vineyards now dormant, reaching the large medieval fortified city of Carcassonne. We had visited it numerous times. It all seemed so unreal. The familiar sounds of the train and the familiar countryside creating a Hollywood motion picture. In the Toulouse station, our train sat on a side track for several hours until we began moving again, more slowly, through flat farming lands with the Pyrenees painted in lead white with hints of Prussian blue outstanding in the far distance.

We were a small group that descended from the train at a tiny station with a sign saying Le Vernet d'Ariège. Our train had not stopped at any station to allow passengers on or off. Guards had circulated along the crowded aisles the entire trip. We had not eaten since the night before, and it was well into the afternoon when we arrived. All our minds were elsewhere, imagining what we had lost and where we were going. We debarked onto an empty platform, with additional guards waiting. They began yelling and commanding us into a rag-tag formation. We followed orders to march in parade fashion on a path that paralleled the tracks. The weather had cooperated; it was overcast and cold, but the rain had abated. I could see the white-crested mountains stretching into the distance. We were all strangers and speaking was forbidden by the guards. We all walked in our separate worlds, trailing the minutiae of our lives, separately, not wanting to confront the reality of what was happening to us.

We had no baggage. Most of us had been given no time to prepare, so we moved along. There were a few tears expressed, some oaths sworn. Hunger affected all of us, and fear of the absolute unknown lingered. Our first foretaste of the camp was a group of men marching rapidly with guards alongside. They were dressed in rags and carried work implements, looking destitute of mind and spirit. They all marched roughly together to a caustic *un-deux, un-deux, un-deux,* ignoring us, marching in time to the gruffly shouted count.

It was bizarre that our group of people, normal people, barely introduced to the environment everyone knew was coming, could accept being herded like animals and coerced without complaint into passive acceptance. Much of the control was exercised by withholding any information, keeping the herd without any knowledge or influence, but it also was a time, and had been for years, when so much was in doubt that people went along without question. It was not a time for revolutionaries. No one spoke as we approached the barbed wire enclosure, not one enclosure, but actually three different rows of fences of barbed wire high above our heads. We marched to the formidable entryway. We waited as the guards conferred and were finally allowed entrance. We looked at the barbed wire fences welcoming us, all of us noting the large wooden sign hanging above us from the gateposts like the entry to Dante's Inferno:

CAMP DU VERNET

We marched into a holding area, where the few women in our group were separated and led off to a building.

"All clothes off," a female guard ordered.

We stripped and waited shamefully in the unfurnished cold hut. I could see that the entire camp was made up of similar wooden structures, hutments with waterproofed paper outside, much of it torn by the winds and rains, revealing the wooden walls constructed haphazardly, without concern for insulation. It was as cold and almost as windy as the exterior. Spaced around the grounds were high guardposts with strategic views of the entire camp. A woman prisoner searched us for valuables, bundled up our clothes and tossed them aside. I had nothing of value, but I noticed several women try to retrieve an earring or gold ring. They allowed us to keep our underwear, but gave us loose colorless tunics of rough woven linen, appearing dirty and used. A piece of cardboard with a number was handed out to each of us, which we were told to drape around our necks.

We were then marched to another barrack, where we were processed, answering a few questions: name, date of birth, place of residence, and other questions filled out by the interviewer. Then we moved to a new barrack in Section C for women, where we were processed again and assigned a bunk, randomly as it turned out. Inside the temporary housing, two rows of contiguous bunks on two levels ran the length of the building. About thirty women were housed in each side. A prisoner handed the new arrivals a single blanket. "Keep this securely," an unsmiling and unsympathetic prisoner warned us. "There will be no replacements."

All this took hours, waiting in line for something as simple and uncomplicated as registering at a hotel, though this was far different from that.

Finished, we waited in the barrack for the occupants to return, again afraid to talk or inquire. There were perhaps a dozen of us. The prisoners began arriving at twilight, tired, not happy to see new additions to their building. There were no greetings, no welcomes, and no initiation of the new arrivals. The evening meal consisted of an insipid liquid, which might have been heated at one time, containing a dearth of fat globules, a few chickpeas, and, perhaps, some unidentifiable morsels of vegetable matter. I was given a spoon and tin cup, which I was warned to keep secure as it would not be replaced. I drank the soup in one gulp and placed the implements under my blanket on my assigned bunk. I watched the other women talking to each other. I noted many Spanish prisoners and eastern European, but few French women.

We were allowed to move around freely after the soup. The yard of our enclosure was rocky and devoid of any vegetation. Rainwater pooled in spots and drained down to the toilet facilities of the next enclosure in a vile unnatural drainage trough. Our enclosure was small in comparison to the men's barracks. We could see through the barbed wire fences, but there was no ability to communicate and, as I soon learned, to attempt was harshly punished. To pass from one enclosure to another was impossible. The toilet was on the side of our barrack, somewhat obscured from the neighboring barrack. It consisted of an open area with rocks. There was nothing to clean yourself with, and it was impossible to find a location clear of detritus. Horrified, I finished quickly and escaped.

Returned to the barrack, I found two women fighting physically, rolling around pulling each other's hair, while others stood about leaving them to their fight. After a while, the two women quit, both crying and complaining about something in a language I could not understand. I went to my bunk to lie down, when a woman came up.

"Why are you here, darling?"

I looked at her: middle aged, heavyset. She could have been a farmer's wife, and she might have once been attractive in a healthy way. Tonight, she was gaunt and emotionless.

"I'm not sure. I was arrested, and somehow I arrived here."

"You didn't win the *Loterie Nationale*?"

"No." Somehow this attempt at humor made me feel worse.

"This is a new section, not that it's any better than the others. It was built to house women, who are new to this camp. There appears to be a current overflow. So here we are. It's a transit camp, so don't expect to be here for any while. Although some of the Spanish women have been here since the *Retirada*. You're a local?"

"Perpignan."

"Before that?"

"Before that?"

"You know, your nationality. How long have you been in France?'

"I was born here."

"Ah, you're not foreign born?"

"No." I was beginning to understand her direction. "And you."

"Oh, I married a Frenchman after the Great War, and we moved to Marseille. I was born in Germany. He was native born, and a butcher, but he got involved in the black market and was arrested and sent to Rivesaltes. Gone about a year. They caught me recently during a roundup, and my boys, mostly grown up, and my parents were taken as well. God knows where they are. We all were sent in separate directions."

"Why?"

"Me? Just like most of the women here." She shrugged her shoulders assuming I understood. "Just be glad you weren't sent to Dachau or Auschwitz, although, God knows, we may get there yet. They murder people there, you know. Here they just starve you to death. You need friends here, otherwise you'll be bulldozed by the toughs. I've got my friends, and you seem a good sort. Stick with us."

"Sure. I don't know anyone. I'm Gabrielle."

"Rachel. You'll meet plenty of women here, but hold on to your panties, *ma petite cherie*. They'll steal you blind. I'm across the way," she said pointing to the opposite row of bunks. Upper is better. Dryer, better air, less filth. You should move."

"Thanks."

"Say. You're Jewish aren't you?"

"No."

"Really?"

"I mean I'm Catholic, but Jewish grandparents. So I guess I am too."

"With the recent roundups, they've had to find a spot to house us, if you can call it that. So they just opened up a new section here at Le Vernet. You don't have to worry until we fill up, and then they clean house. I made it past the last roll call. God knows why. This section was set up mostly for Jewish women and children here temporarily after the roundups. Our barrack has no children, thank God. They're next door.

***

It took several weeks for Gabrielle to come to terms with the camp procedures and the desperate culture of the women prisoners. The tedious days without sufficient nourishment, a mindless disciplinary schedule, lack of warmth and clothing, sleepless nights, and the constant awareness of the dangers from other prisoners, rapidly changed everyone into wan-faced, empty-eyed, listless, shattered women. Almost all the women spent time in the infirmary now and then, returning to the barrack in most cases with antiseptic or nothing at all. Some never returned.

The outline and routine of the camp were quickly learned. The camp at large consisted of sixty hectares or so with three large sections, separated by barbed wire enclosures and trenches. One for non-Jewish political prisoners or extremists, as they called them. One for aliens with criminal records. And one for political suspects without definite charges on record. All men, thousands of them. The women's barracks were added later to temporarily contain the overflow from other camps of Jews: women and their children.

Food consisted of about a baguette per day made from the dregs of adulterated flour. A cup of unsugared black coffee, or what passed as coffee, in the morning with a cup of watery soup at midday, and in the evening usually a cup with a few chickpeas, lentils, or vermicelli in some variety of weak and tepid infusion of fat. The roll call, sometimes three per day, required all residents to stand motionless during the naming. Any name missing a response, required another roll call from the beginning, until all were accounted for. Offenses were announced and punished at these roll calls with fists, leather crops, or imprisonment without food or drink for short durations and only bread and water for longer incarcerations. If the accommodations were bleak in the barracks, the so-called "prison" facilities were far worse.

For the men, this was a work camp: senseless demeaning work. Work consisted of maintaining the camp, digging, cleaning the filth and waste from the yards, removing the detritus, working on roads and drainage ditches inside and outside, clearing and cutting, chopping and transporting wood for the camp administration and guard quarters, and other duties around the facility. From word of mouth, Le Vernet was notoriously considered the worst concentration camp in France, worse than German and Polish camps. And this opinion was based on the prisoners' views, well informed by their matriculation at many different holding facilities and other camps.

Gabrielle, relatively innocent, coming from a loving, stable family, morally firm and upright, and supportive, was lost at Le Vernet. For weeks, she could only process her ruin: loss of husband, family, job, friends, and liberty. Loss of all she held dear: believing that by acting for the good of others and working hard she could control her life. All was removed from her footing, and there was nothing remaining. She was an empty umbrella blown across the land by the winds.

Slowly she met other women, mainly women who understood she was in a territory where she had never treaded before, where her resources failed her, and where she would not survive alone. She felt different from the others. She was like an exotic greenhouse plant that had been uprooted, torn from all the tethered roots supporting her existence, and placed outside in ill weather either to survive or wither away. But maybe everyone felt that way.

***

"How long have you been married?" Rachel asks one day.

Our days are mostly made up of roll calls and long periods of inactivity. We are not required to work. A few help out in the so-called infirmary. Others may aid the administration, but for the most part we are left to our own devices, wandering around in the yard when the weather permits and when the mud has dried sufficiently, gossiping and telling tales. I've been reticent to join these free-form and ill-informed discussions: everyone speaking at the same time, gesticulating and quoting their husbands, Lenin, and the Bible. The guards view us from afar with frosty disdain like the comical beasts we have become.

"Four months," I tell her.

We have become friends in a strange way. She is one of the few sympathetic women here. I don't think we would be friends outside, but here she mentors me, and I am thankful for it. Left to my own resources, I think I would be destroyed. She and her friends insulate me from the guards and other prisoners and from our barrack head (*chef de groupe*): a tough Spanish Republican named Maria. She looks and acts more like a man. Our barrack has been slowly filling; each week new arrivals join us. So I'm no longer the new pigeon. No one is happy to see these additions, since the rations do not seem to increase proportionately. Everyone watches the bunks fill, knowing that a full barrack means overcrowding and sharing bunks, and finally the reality of selective deportation to the German and Polish camps.

"You're just a pup. Is he the one?" Rachel asks.

"He's the only one."

"No kidding. He's a good Jewish boy?" She still doesn't believe I'm not Jewish.

"He's Catalan and Spanish."

These questions keep coming up from the Jewish women. I have discovered that there are few others among us, and the only acceptable relation is with another Jew. They know it, but they totally disregard that I was raised a Christian and never had any other thoughts. No Jewish traditions in my family. They just assume.

"I've had Christian lovers," Rachel says, "long before my husband, God protect him. Jewish men are too quick. You know what I mean and not thankful. My husband always said better a butcher than a calf, and then he would laugh, but he tried at least. He smelled of rotten meat, but I loved him and bore his children. I'm considered an alien. They ignore my marriage to a French Christian."

When I first met the head of our barrack, Maria, I was totally frightened. She was heavyset, and bullish, with plenty of control over the barrack. She divvies the food, chooses the cleanup details, sends women to the infirmary or not, bullies, and generally gets her way. She has a group of sycophants, who are at her beck and call. With nothing to do, the women gossip endlessly about each other. She heard I was married to a Spaniard and that seemed to make a big difference to her. She has not been exactly friendly, but she leaves me alone, which is a gift, while she picks on the others.

Maria is decidedly not Jewish, and I think fundamentally she agrees with the common idea that Jews are at the very foundation of the problems facing Europe and their elimination will certainly make everything better. I think she feels she is being punished by being placed in charge of a Jewish barrack. She accepts me as non-Jewish and with all the benefits that affords: none, save a slightly improved attitude.

"You need to beef up," Maria says to me, laughing. There is no beef in our diet. Even she is well below her fighting weight, I'm sure.

I have lost weight. No mirrors and, certainly no scales, but I feel it on my thighs and my arms. I'm often weak and lackadaisical, physically and mentally. I feel and see the slow transformation of my body due to my pregnancy, which is now confirmed by a second or third month. I'm not sure which. My waist, my sore breasts and back, my moods, and my wild hair all signal the advent. At the same time, the camp has begun to leave its marks. I fear I will lose the baby if this incarceration continues much longer, but I tell no one.

It's strange, but my life here has regularized. Somehow I see this as proof of man's ability to adapt to anything, any environment, with the limitless will to survive. Even those condemned to Purgatory, for that is where we are, on our way to the Inferno, must come to terms with their surroundings. They are able to create a temporarily and deliberately false sheltered existence. Cheerfulness is perhaps possible for moments, even though the stark reality of despondent misery keeps intruding.

Parcels come, some from family connections and some from the Red Cross. They are supposed to be distributed to all prisoners, although my experience is that little or nothing finds its way to the inmates. Initially picked over and distributed from the top, almost nothing is left for those of us at the bottom. Letters do arrive, but there is nothing to write with or on, and I have yet to receive a single word. Does anyone know where I am? There is a canteen, but only if you have access to money from relatives. Who knows how much cash is actually given to the rightful recipient. Some women are able to buy cigarettes at the canteen and use the cigarettes to obtain additional food and privileges.

News of the outside is mainly brought in with new women. Its effect is like vitamins, passing though the camp as a necessary ingredient to life, but with each dose of vitamins comes a taste of poison. The population is frequently the victim of bouts of dysentery, infecting everyone, requiring frequent trips to the exterior horrific facilities in daylight and nighttime, in good weather or downpours, that is, those who are capable of making the journey. Others remain in their bunks. A further reason for Rachel's upper bunk rule, which I followed as soon as I could secure one. They say there's a hospital for the sick outside the camp, but I only hear of the infirmary.

I miss Paul so much. I cannot focus on him and maintain my sanity. My only hope is that he knows where I am and is actively trying to make some type of contact. I have full confidence in his capacity to solve any problem, although this one may be beyond even him. I love him, and I refuse to allow myself to wallow in self-pity and despair, while my mind is taken over with dreams of what could and should have been. Two trees standing firm against the blustery winds. One tree now uprooted and replanted without thought or care. My greatest hope is that he remains rooted as before.

Paul, my love, my cherished, darling husband, I love you more than you will ever know. I fear I will never find you again?

Michael Barnes Selvin

25

February 1943

> *Laura, sweet face barely glimpsed*
> *Laura, fragile image of evening*
> *Echo of a laugh scarcely heard*
> *Memory of a failed hope*
> *Along the shoreline*
> *Your dress seemed to whirl*
> *Laura, her gentle movement left*
> *Only a name in the summer wind*
> *And the dream of always singing of you.*
> « *Laura,* » *David Raksin; (French lyrics: Jean Sablon)*

Paul sat on the train watching the scenery pass, wondering what Gabrielle had seen on this very same trip. The sunshine shimmered outside in the cold, transparent indigo morning, captured so often by Auguste Daniel with his favorite blue hues. He had heard from Miguel Serrano. Miguel owned a small farm near Camp du Vernet and was active in working for the rights of Spanish prisoners, some there for years, although now a minority due to the new influx of European arrestees and transferees. Miguel worked with human rights groups to ensure fair treatment of the internees and to obtain their release. The Occupant had other goals, he explained.

Paul anxiously regarded the landscape swiftly passing as the train left Perpignan and raced along the sea, through the swampy lagoons that Trenet had remembered. The Corbière hills passed on either side with dormant vineyard after vineyard fleeing the train. He watched as the train skirted the large medieval city of Carcassonne dominating the town and countryside. They continued on to Toulouse, where he changed trains, waiting in the station until the local took off. After countless stops, the commuter train finally arrived at the station at Le Vernet, a small rural village in the Ariège River valley, dwarfed by the population of the concentration camp, which was totally isolated from the village. In the distance, the Pyrenees stood out like a massive protective wall. The clouds and the mountains competed for preeminence, with the mountain peaks firmly establishing their dominance in a never-ending procession.

Paul immediately spotted an older man smoking nervously, pacing back and forth on the rail platform, surveying the few people disembarking the train. He assumed the short, solidly built man, dressed in well-used farm clothes with curly locks barely contained under his watch cap, was Miguel.

"*Hola*," Paul called out, and Miguel broke into a wide grin, dropped and stamped his cigarette butt, and gave Paul a firm bear hug.

"You're late."

"I just missed a connection in Toulouse, and there are not many coming in this direction."

"Besides the daily local, the only others are closed trains. Are you hungry?"

"Well…"

"I know. I know. But we'll get to that. First a little nourishment. We do pretty well here with all the farms and a weekly market. People come from Toulouse to shop here. Anyway, let's go."

They ate fresh bread and coffee with homemade prune jam in a small restaurant, Le Moulin, where everyone seemed to know everyone else. Miguel questioned Paul in detail about his background and experience, avoiding talk of the camp. Miguel was born in Barcelona about fifty years ago and had fought with the Republicans during the Civil War. He was arrested crossing into France and spent a year incarcerated at le Vernet, but was released thanks to a job offer. He never forgot his time there and on departing vowed to remain close to help others. He never anticipated the change in demographics, which had exploded the camp with immigrants from northern Europe and then the flood of so-called undesirables.

"Let's take a walk," he suggested.

When Paul attempted to pay for the meal, Miguel wouldn't hear of it, and the waitress sided with her friend. They walked out of town along the river.

"Your ex-boss, Franco Plana, was my commanding officer during the war," he said, initiating the conversation when they were alone. "He saved my life and the lives of many through his wise and careful leadership. I am indebted to him forever. He said you were a great person, so I'm prepared to assist you. I understand your wife was arrested. Her name?"

"Gabrielle Daniel Broussard. We've been married only a few months."

"She's foreign born?"

"No. French, as are her parents."

"And her parents were arrested as well."

"No. They went into hiding a few weeks before. She was arrested with a member of the Resistance. They sent him to Gurs, but I tracked Gabrielle down to Le Vernet."

"I see. Typically, they send political prisoners to other camps. Le Vernet has become a transit camp for undesirables. She's Jewish?"

"Her grandparents converted. Her parents were baptized and raised Catholic, as she was."

"Oh, looks like she was in the wrong place at the wrong time. Six months ago, she would have had her wrist slapped. Today, with the Occupant in command, things have changed. What do you want to do, as if I couldn't guess?"

"One, I want to be able to communicate with her. Two, I will take care of the rest."

"The rest? Communications, we can set up. The rest, as you call it, is nearly impossible. There are occasional escapes, usually men from the work details. Some few make it out with their lives. The only visitors are the Red Cross and a few other agencies, carefully controlled. No relatives. No lawyers. No spouses or children. Most of the new arrivals are temporary. They leave on closed trains for the north. I would guess that the average stay at the camp is a month or two. With the continued inflow, her stay may be reduced. You'll have to work fast. Let me see if I can help you establish a communication link."

"Thank you. I have money and will pay."

"Just *pourboires*. It's not a business. Many people don't like what they see today. Guards, maintenance, delivery services, and others that work in the camp. That's our main inroad. It's enough to pass word of mouth in both directions. Written communication is possible, but not desirable: too risky. Also we can provide information: changes being made that might affect your wife, sicknesses, and other day-to-day news, such as moves, punishments, or deaths, to be frank. It's not a healthy place. Planning for transit is more secure, but we have ins at the SNCF. The international agencies have little impact, and now with women and children in the camp…"

"Any information you can provide would be great. The main thing today is that I want her to know I'm committed to helping her. How? I am not sure. But I won't rest until we are together again. I will do all that it takes to free her. Can she get that message?"

"Let me see what I can do. It's too early to say. You have a telephone?"

"Yes, but we have to be careful. It's easy to eavesdrop."

"I understand. I will contact you. You used to be a truck driver, no?"

Paul smiled. "Yes, for a while."

"Well I'm a small farmer and grape grower, trying to find a variety that can survive the climate here. For hundreds of years, this area produced remarkable wines, but with the Phylloxera almost all production ceased. Now it's slowly coming back. We'll have to move fast though to find her and learn what's going on. Agreed?"

"Yes. I don't know how to thank you."

"Then don't for the time being."

They continued talking, gaining confidence in one another, establishing a rapport, and initiating a friendship.

***

A few days later, two notes arrived in the mail in a single envelope. The first one was a postcard from Miguel Serrano with a picture of Mount Valier in the high Pyrenees, the highest peak visible from Le Vernet:

5 February 1943

Paul,

Thank you for meeting with me on delivery transport. We were successful in getting several other growers to participate. We look forward to working with you. Please meet me on Monday next week at the same time and location. Yours,

Miguel

The next was a letter on scrap paper in a separate envelope. He tore open an envelope and discovered a note from Gabrielle. It was written in pencil on a torn piece of paper in a hand he never would have recognized.

25 January 1943

My Darling Husband,

I'm okay. I received word that you had visited the village and were concerned. My health is good. It's not easy here, but please don't worry too much about me. I am with some good women, and we work together to help one another. Some few letters come through via the Red Cross. Please write soon. My stay here is nothing compared to missing you. I love you, my dearest, and this love will never be extinguished. Your devoted wife,

Gabrielle

The tears poured from his eyes as he read and reread the short note, trying to pry open the simple words to see her inner thoughts. It could have been written from a summer camp, with no indication of what he had been told about the life in Camp du Vernet. Regardless, he slept that night for the first time in weeks, just knowing that she was alive and that she knew he was making efforts to contact her.

***

On his next trip to the village of Le Vernet, Miguel was waiting for him at the restaurant. It seemed like meeting a close friend. They quickly ate and left the restaurant.

"We're going to my house," he said, walking toward the outskirts of the village to a small farmhouse, with a large attached garage and a tractor parked in front. Inside was a warm home, obviously decorated by a woman, without evidence of small children.

"This is it," Miguel said. "Please sit down. Would you like something to drink?"

"To drink?"

"Coffee, water, a beer?"

"I'm fine."

He went to the back, and someone knocked on the door.

"I'll get it."

Paul heard him talking with a woman in Spanish. A large woman entered, probably in her thirties, dressed in workers' clothes, heavy jacket, pants, and boots. She shook Paul's hand and sat down across from him, appearing at ease in this house.

"So, you're Paul," she said in Spanish, assessing him carefully.

"Marta is a neighbor and a guard in the women's section of the camp," Miguel explained. "She's a good contact, but we have to be careful. People talk."

Paul didn't know what to say. "How is she?"

"Oh, she's adjusting well. She's fine...for the moment."

"Can I give you a note to take to her?"

"I can't. I'm sorry. I'm happy to let you know what's going on, and anything in the camp that might be important. Or relay a verbal message from you. I'll keep in touch with Miguel."

"What about deportation?" Paul asked.

"We usually feel the rumblings, but little is known beforehand. It's announced at roll call, and everyone whose name is called is expected to go immediately. Right now her section is half full, so the next transport shouldn't be announced until next month or the month after. It's really a function of filling the train for the camp administrators. Some weird kind of efficiency. They are nothing if not efficient."

Paul felt light-headed, his heart beating rapidly. "Can you tell her I love her, and I'm trying to get her out. You know she's native-born and Catholic. She should not have been arrested."

"You'd be surprised who's there," Marta replied. "By the time they get to le Vernet, they're in the system. It's too late. I don't mean to be harsh, but the camp is a transit station, and questions of legality or false imprisonment or mistakes are not pertinent, unless you know someone high up in Vichy. I don't ever recall an internee being released. There are only two directions:

transit or the cemetery. Most of the Republicans have been released to work, but that was a different war."

Paul watched her hardened features and acceptance of her job. He didn't want in any way to antagonize or make her uncomfortable. "I appreciate your helping out." He reached into his pocket to retrieve his wallet.

"No," Miguel ordered. "We'll see how this goes."

"Can I give you money for supplies for Gabrielle, paper and writing implements perhaps or food?"Paul asked.

The woman stood up. "I like Gabrielle. I'll help her as much as I can. Anything else you want me to tell her?" She accepted fifty francs.

"Just tell her I miss her, and I'm okay. I'm working for her. Thank you."

After the woman left, Miguel held Paul back.

"You have to understand her position."

"I do. I do. I guess. I'm just worried."

"I know. I'll keep in touch. We usually get some advance notice on transport, and as Marta said, you have some time."

***

He visited the Bijouterie Pallarès the next week. The jeweler had studied the diamonds and had offered them for sale. Several offers had been received. He felt the best one came from a broker, a wholesale jewelry dealer. His offer was for two thousand six hundred and fifty francs each, or thirty thousand two hundred and ten francs in his pocket.

Paul accepted. He would pick up the cash in three days. He had only one fleeting chance, like the light from a rapidly dissolving sun. All the dangerous risks he had taken in the last two years paled in comparison to what he would risk to free Gabrielle.

26

When you see your village again
When you see the clock tower again
Your house, your parents, your school friends
You will say that nothing has changed at home.
Your lover has been faithful and smart
She will come to look for you
When you see your village again.
    « Quand tu reverras ton village, » C. Trenet

The roll call is announced early one morning.

"Up and out, you lazy bitches. Out or else the penalty box. Don't play sick with me you worthless *connes*." The screaming and yelling continues until even the bedridden are roused and pulled from their bunks. "Bring all your rubbish. You're not coming back." Some have to be aided out and others carried out of the barrack.

This is the call to our fate by Lucifer, like death anticipated, never arriving at an auspicious time. I have no idea of the date, nor how long I have been here: more than a month? I'm as well aware of the crowded barrack as others are. We stumble out expecting the worst, grumbling, holding our cup and plate, our blanket, and anything else we might prize. Most people have nothing. In our filthy, hand-woven linen nightdresses, in our unwashed state, our fetid redolence and freakish hairdos, in our sicknesses, we form a loose assembly of ghouls and zombies.

The head of our barrack, Maria, yells at us as if we were school children. Many of us are barely able physically to join this godless congregation. What has become of us, squatters and pee-ers, without modesty, too far gone to care? Our nails bitten to the quick, our hair falling out in shards, our breasts wizened like bunches of sour grapes, our scent of sewage and decay, our bodies festering with lice and fleas. We live in a frozen oubliette, where all is ancient history; we, the embroidered society of the lost, are shielded from our God in some far off corner. We have become so accustomed to death that many of us no longer fear it, almost welcome it. We never talk about it, except with our closest friends. It visits us, just as the slow

407

degradation of our comrades' bodies breaks out, just like some canker or gangrene or cancer. It greets us in the morning and occupies our minds at night.

At the first roll call of every day, the internees search the barrack for those who can no longer rise to the assembly, test their respiration, and, if we detect no movement, remove their bodies as quickly as possible. They may just be the lucky ones. Mud, dirt, filth, scum, refuse, detritus lead us all to pray to the god that no one truly believes exists.

The weakling sun is barely risen, obscured by low-lying fog, and the cold chills our exposed bones to the quick. Our barrack of some sixty bunks now contains almost one hundred women of all ages, forced to accept their unknown destination. We are quickly shaped by days of misery; we barely sleep, remaining drowsy, until the anticipated, but never truly expected, call arrives. We refuse to talk of it. Then suddenly it's here like a foolish prophet of doom. We know it; we've heard the stories from other people from other internment camps, and those who cannot stand lean on others or sink into the oozy filth in our yard.

The *Chef du Camp*, not normally present for daily roll calls, surrounded by guards, joins our assembly carrying our fates on a typed piece of paper, a profane document of horror. I can only imagine that some execrable law or statute must require his presence, some carefully considered legal justification, absolving all within the administration of this abominable crime. We all know the outcome, but can't call it by its proper name.

"Quiet," the head of our barrack yells once again. "When your name is called march to the entry gate and wait."

The head is an older prisoner tough but fair. That's why she's lasted. And even in her role of kowtowing to the hierarchy of powers, she is able to maintain her eternal hatred for all of them.

The camp chief begins reading: "Pauline Dahan, Michèle Attia, Alice Carré, Monique Ibrahim, Kirsten Bergdoll, Mélina Dessin, Marie-Estelle Sebban, Muriel Cohen, Sylvie Madar, Sophie Mongès, Karine Moreau, Céline Morel..."

There appears to be no order, just random names without faces, daughters of their parents, unknown, a name disappearing into the ether.

"Anne-Mairie Pomel, Caroline Abensur, Sophia Begin, Margo Warshauer, Veronique Chafetz, Selma Kusminsky, Doris Principale, Janna Minski, Katerina Chompsky, Rhonda Charon, et cetera, et cetera, et cetera, for the time it takes for a hundred breaths, or a dozen prayers, or twenty Hail Mary's, or eight hundred heartbeats of an over-active heart. Fifty-three names, half of our barracks. And how many other barracks are there with names called? Not that many, maybe four or five, not counting the barracks with mothers and children, or the male barracks for that matter, but they will be on the transport as well.

There is little discrimination between the sexes and the ages with transport judgment. This careful God is not biased among the chosen. Many of the chosen were the newest arrivals, again randomly selected we assume, given barely enough time to make friends or adjust to the hideous daily routine. Each name is called to a gasp, sigh, sniffle, puff, or pant. Tears. Sobs. Silence. Names are our only connection to our past and now the hint of our future, selected with so much thought and love, suddenly turned into curses.

The rhythm of the names terrorizes and hypnotizes me. I remember a strange letter Nuria gave me from one of the German camps describing the transit. It hadn't meant much to me at the time, but I couldn't throw it away, even though I didn't understand it. With the catalogue of names ringing in my head, gasping for breath, I see the image of the letter clearly in my mind. Why did it stay with me? Please don't read my name, I demand of God, as I listen for my godforsaken fate. I remember the letter and its locale: Weimar, Thuringia, land of Luther and Goethe and Schiller:

Year of Filth, 1941

In my village near Canton (China), I always take the train. A poster shows a small train station decked with red and violet geraniums for a visit to Germany. I visited this country for free. This space is surrounded by barbed wire. Unfortunately, there are too many in this small space. Too bad. This famous place is called a "*Konzentrationslager*," and our host never shies from any sacrifice. When I arrived at Buchenwald, I never questioned our welcome at this train station. I will never forget Thuringia, the time I spent here engraved on my arm. Not at all like the poster. Unfortunately, we met many unfriendly comrades. I met you, my old friend, and despite all your faults, I will meet you again one day to remind you of our wonderful voyage into the unknown. Sincerely,

Your old friend

I think of secondary school. I remember waiting with the entire class for the professor to return papers and exams with snide remarks, carefully ordered, always in descending order, leaving the worst for the last. I half-feared, half-listened as the papers were returned, often flung across the room in mock anger. Daniel, good job. Or Daniel, sorry you weren't here, as I waited before him. Never the first. Always midstream. Nuria, frequently first, received bouquets of enthusiastic comments. Her papers returned by a polite hand. Danon, Bravo. Danon, felicitations. Danon, charming. Catie had to endure the longest wait to receive her comments. Ferrer, banal. Ferrer, obvious. Ferrer, abysmal.

The names finally come to an end. Fifty-three and not mine. The camp chief departs to his next roll call, while the women named are still struggling toward the gate, some trudging, some crying, some moving robotically, their minds in some other locale. I watch them. I pray for them. And why them? What criteria is used to judge us? Why am I not included? Did I do something that saved me from the gallows this time, or is it pure dumb chance, or did some wise judge adjudicate my past for guilt or innocence? I don't know. I don't care. I have more time. Thank you God, wherever you are.

***

I distractedly wander back to the barrack to return my blanket and dining utensils, now feeling relief and guilt. I'm sure the rations will be adjusted accordingly, but life is just a bit easier for a moment with fewer sharing our accommodations. I feel a twinge of remorse at that thought, but the camp is run with such a mixture of corruption and ignominy and in such a laissez-faire manner that it becomes almost self-governing, self-perpetuating. I'm still learning my way here.

The guards do as little as possible. Some guards come from the Garde Mobile, or gendarmerie, the rotten ones, whose goal is to have nothing bother them and take exceptional measures only when things go against them. These are the guards that rampage in their drunken stupor at night, beating, raping, and terrorizing. Other guards come from the village and are more humane, if such a word can be used. Somehow, one of them took an interest in me and even met Paul and related his words to me. He loves me and will do everything to aid me. God, what can he do? The guard, her name is Marta, is a tough cookie like all of them, but underneath beats a concealed heart. Few enough people have hearts here, even among the prisoners, and those that do are soon relieved of any benevolent feelings. I'm lucky to be friends with Rachel and her group. She and the others in the group all survived the roll call this morning. Why?

I'm not sure how many women sections there are. I know there is one with mothers and children, rumored to have been decimated in this recent call. All the sections are isolated, but rumors move rapidly. This roll call occurred without any notice, so obviously the rumor mill is not to be trusted entirely. Within our section, we have free movement. The latrines are frequently used at night. Perhaps there is some modesty here, though you wouldn't know it, and it is a trait that falls low on the list of behaviors. During the day, we walk about conversing, gossiping. On Sundays we are free to do what we like. Catholic services are held by some prisoners, but not appreciated, particularly by the Jews, who are by far the majority in our barrack. I have mixed emotions and have attended both Catholic and Jewish meetings. Of course, there are no priests or rabbis here, only women with deeply felt convictions.

Also on Sundays, there are performances. People put on plays about the camp, the guards, or the inmates. No one is exempt. They sing popular songs. Only the *Marseillaise* is forbidden. Instruments appear. A violin. An accordion. A tub drum. There are dances. Writers read their stories from notepapers, and a number of camp poets love nothing more than reciting

411

their recent poems. I picture Paul and our show in the Club les Tréteaux, a lifetime ago.

There is no equality here and no morality. Some women get weekly packages or letters or money sent to them. They are the wealthy (relatively) matrons, and everyone looks up to them. Others are destitute and become the servers of the wealthy. There are items or favors that can be bought or traded from inmates or guards, and there is a very limited commissary where supplies can be purchased. Cigarettes are a common currency for whatever anyone wants. Paper and pens are available. Books are traded or passed around with some type of payment. Favors are frequent: work details, cleaning up, help in any manner of things, and personal services. Intimate services. Guards are not above accepting bribes and doing favors. It's a "free" market without bounds, regulations, or morality.

***

After the roll call, we fell back into what has become normal life. A political discussion began on what the roll call means: laboring in some far off location for the war or working in some industrial factory in Germany or certain death in a gas chamber. Everyone seems to have a fixed idea on where these trains and prisoners are headed. Past experience in other camps, rumors, prohibited newspaper accounts, BBC reports, letters, disappearance of relatives all feed these differing views of the future. Some few internees have seen things with their own eyes, but they are no more believable than others reporting gossip and hearsay, or irrational wishes.

A fight broke out over midday rations, with two women rolling around in the mud, pulling out the little hair that remains on their skulls. Fights have to be stopped on occasion before someone is killed. If a fight continues too long, the guards will take over. They enjoy beating women with their truncheons. They also will take the worst offenders to a punishment box in the open, where food is not given for several days, or bread and water only if the punishment lasts longer. This fight today was stopped early by the witnesses. People had had enough for one day.

A week or so later, the guards raided our barrack. They came in late one night and forced us outside into the rain. They ransacked the bunks and searched everywhere. They walked out with extra blankets, hidden drugs, jewelry, knives, and other items considered contraband. We were finally allowed back in, but rain-soaked with little ability to dry ourselves. The next day I was sick, my body aching, especially my back, which had never bothered me before. Except for roll calls, I remained in my bunk the entire day, fearing the worst: the loss of my still undisclosed baby. By the evening I noted spotting. I called Rachel, and she thought I should go to the infirmary. I hesitated because it would mean I could be moved to a new section.

That night I began experiencing frequent cramping, and the bleeding became worse. Rachel finally took me off to the infirmary. When we say infirmary, at Le Vernet it was a small barrack much like the others with a few bunks, a dearth of anything resembling medical instruments, and no medicines of note. Two doctors, both inmates, ruled this poor imitation of an infirmary. One was a French physician arrested for black market dealings. He was the bad one, noted for his lack of concern, his lethargic approach to helping others, and his wheedling manner to enrich himself. The other was an older man, a northern European Jew, who had been a physician in Paris and had been arrested in Marseille in a roundup. He was the one that people hoped would come to their aid. Luckily, perhaps because of the late hour, he came in response to my situation.

"How long?" he asked, pulling on his unkempt beard.

"Three months."

"Any cramping?"

"Yes."

"How frequently?"

"This evening, it was happening every hour or maybe more frequently."

"Back pain?"

"Yes."

"It's not a good sign. Take off your underwear." I removed a pair of shorts for warmth and my filthy panties, now bloody.

He examined me. "Hmm. You are dilated and effaced." He listened to my belly with a stethoscope. "No heartbeat. The body is delivering the embryo. It's just a matter of time. Is this your first pregnancy?"

I nodded my head, tears rolling down my cheeks.

"It's fairly common. Can't be helped, and the conditions here are not optimal for pregnancy. It happens more than you would imagine. You can spend the night here, and there are extra blankets. Nothing much I can do. You're relatively healthy. Just watch for excessive bleeding. The cramps will continue, but it should be over soon. I'll check in tomorrow morning." He turned to Rachel. "Can you stay with her?"

"Of course."

"Good. Her body is in charge, just watch for excessive bleeding. You know the process?" She nodded. "Here's a basin. Keep everything. She'll be fine." He left.

"Why didn't you tell me, Gabrielle?"

"I told no one."

"I know. I had four kids and two miscarriages. I finally had to put my husband out."

"The doctor doesn't talk much, does he." I said.

"No, but he didn't seem worried."

That night was a hard one for me, the hardest ever. Hard because I knew what was happening. I was losing my baby. The cramps continued strongly and frequently, for hours. Finally in the false dawn, my body expelled the embryo. The pain was not too much, but the thought of losing my baby made me crazy. I thought I couldn't feel more miserable. I have never felt such a failure and such sadness. I am not a crier, but that night I couldn't help myself. I felt so alone. So helpless. So lost. Rachel tried to comfort me, but my spirits had reached a new low, one that certainly must be near the bottom. What could be worse than this? So much was wrong with the camp, my incarceration, my health, the world, and now added to that I had lost my baby, our baby. Paul knew nothing of the joy of carrying his child or of the appalling trauma of my loss.

The doctor examined me the next day and said I had had a complete miscarriage and should be on my feet that afternoon. Then, what only a camp occupant could find amusing, he said flippantly as he departed: "Rest, drink plenty of fluids, and eat well."

***

One day, Marta, the guard gave me a pencil and a piece of paper, and I sent a note through proper channels:

>My dearest Paul,
>
>I miss you desperately. I have lost so much here, I can't describe it. What I have learned is to treasure what I have. How I took you for granted. I'll never forgive myself. I feel shame at how I treated you. It is so wrong to value yourself over others without thought. Life here is unpleasant and uncertain, but I am surviving. A number of ██████████████████████████ a few days ago ██████████████. They never declare the ███████████. But people have come from camps all over, in France, Poland, and Germany, and ███████████████████████. They call certain ones "███████████████████." I have a friend, Rachel, who is older and is kind to me. We have a group who stick together. I never heard from Paco. We know ██████████████████ ████████████ ███████████████████████ and hope you can avoid it. I love you with all my soul, and I pray for you. Your loving wife forever,
>
>Gabrielle

27

March 1943

> *Yes, I love you*
> *And I dedicate this poem to you*
> *Yes I love you*
> *In joy and in sadness*
> *Sweet France*
> *Dear country of my childhood*
> *Cradle of tender lighthearted memories*
> *I have always cherished you in my heart.*
> « *Douce France,* » *C. Trenet*

Paul and Miguel walk along the frothy, coursing Ariège River in Le Vernet. This time they are joined by a local Resistance fighter by the name of Royo, a dark-faced young man, slight of build, chain-smoking, nervous, dressed in worker's clothes with a black béret. The morning exudes spring, and the song birds team in full force. During the past few weeks in Perpignan, the weather has turned variable, light snows and cold snaps interspersed with hints of warmth and growth: the cottony white blooms on the almond trees and yellow acacia, the cafés filling up in the mornings, and an increase in bicycles along the roads. Paul has become a frequent commuter on the train from Perpignan to Toulouse and the local to Le Vernet, and he and Miguel have become fast friends. The three men look like chess pieces: one tall and thin, one nervously slight, and one short and squat. They speak in a mixture of Catalan and Spanish.

"We've done this before," Royo says rapidly, his eyes moving, scanning the horizon. To Paul, he seems tense, a little crazy. "We're not ready to battle face-to-face with German ordinary troops, but we're able to cause problems. We've been in the business since forty-one, longer than most of the other Maquis, and we're talking with some of the coastal groups about combining forces or coordinating our activities. I know Paco Macias. He's a good man. We have talked."

"What about the Milice?" Paul asked.

"They're not so strong here. We're soldiers. They're informers and crooks. Our life depends on what we do, and we'll continue until Franco's hanging from a lamppost in El Retiro in Madrid. We work with the Maquis of Foix and Varilhes. We are talking with the Mouvements Unis de la Résistance (MUR). When unification proceeds and London decides to take us seriously, we'll have better weapons and capabilities. In the Garonne and Ariège, we make sure we are well-liked by the people; we protect them, and they can count on us. We have caused numerous interruptions to Vichy with the high-power lines and the trains. But we are only bees. We sting and depart. We annoy them, but we're growing rapidly with over eighty *guérilleros* and a few women. All the groups are growing. We're currently without sufficient or modern arms, but we're mostly Republicans with plenty of experience. We have stopped trains before."

"Trains with guards?" Miguel asks.

"No, but the trains coming from Le Vernet camp are not well-guarded. Everyone knows that. Mostly with local policemen, and not the best of those. Old men and boys. They have rail priority and move rapidly. That's their only defense."

"That's changing," Paul says. "They may have German soldiers on board."

"Well, with better weapons, we'll face the *Boches*. We're not afraid of them."

"Are you able to buy better arms?"

"Yes. We have contacts in Toulouse. The English are providing weapons selectively. The FFI are cautious to begin serious operations."

"You get the arms, and I will pay for them." Paul says, looking at Miguel. "The train has to stop or at worst to slow way down. I don't want a battle. Too many innocents. I want five minutes, and then we're out of there."

"Certainly, *Senyor*. I understand."

"We can't afford to have this go wrong. We have to trust you." Miguel adds.

"*No som Republicans, eh?*"

"*Si*," Miguel agreed, "but we get only one chance, and no slipups. *Entens?*"

"*Cierto*. We will be there for you."

They continue walking along the river discussing the operation, the location, and the timing. They plan another meeting the following week, and Royo leaves them.

Paul is concerned about Royo. He questions some of his braggadocio, and his confidence leads one to suspect that he is not credible, only a shadow, or a bee as he says, trying to aggrandize his group. "What do you think?"

"He's all we have in this region. If we can get him some arms, he seems to have the men. And if they are Republicans, then they will be fighters."

"What's happening at the camp? I got a note from Gabrielle a few days ago, but she was not able to say much."

"According to Marta, the guard in the women's barrack, they had a surprise transport a few weeks ago, where they sent the recent arrivals to the north, but the camp barracks continue to fill up. Several large roundups in the south took place last week. So another transit is in the planning and may come next month, or so they say. Gabrielle was sick for a few weeks, but is doing better now. The Germans have slowly enforced management of the camp, though remaining offsite, but the guards have been made aware that their lives are at stake if they get caught helping the internees or are sympathetic or even rest lethargic. Marta is still with us, but less willing. She's frightened. It's a new regime, and the rations have been reduced and everyone is now expected to work."

"I have some funds to get Gabrielle out, but I want to be very careful in using this money to its best advantage. It has to be used effectively at the right time and place. I'd be willing to help Royo, if we can trust him."

"Let's go slow for the moment and see what he has to say when we meet next week. No commitments or payments yet."

"I can't thank you enough, Miguel. I don't know what I would have done without you."

"Our only goal is to get Gabrielle out."

Paul smiles, which he hasn't done in many weeks.

***

Back in Perpignan, Paul meets with Léon, his forger when he worked at the Prefecture. Léon is still in business, prosperous and better dressed. He agrees to provide papers for Gabrielle and him, a married couple, including exit visas, temporary transit visas in Spain, and falsified arrangements for entry and departure from Portugal, including travel documents to England by steamer: the works.

"Don't worry, I'll make you a set of documents no one can break. Give me a week, and I give you a *'client fidèle'* discount." He laughed. "Just like *le Bon Marché.*"

"I guess things have been slowing down."

"Not really. There're always people wanting to get out of France. It's that time of the year, like marriage."

"How do you stay out of the STO?"

"That cost is supplementary."

***

This time it was easier to meet with Bouloc. We met at an outside table of the Palmarium. The sun was warm in a clear sky. He ordered a red wine, and I took a coffee. I wanted to talk to Bouloc about the reasonableness of the escape plan and the plan to support Royo and his group.

"Damn Vichy," Bouloc said, "can't find a good Pastis anymore. That's their largest mistake." He was wearing his well-used tweed jacket and black béret, just as at our last meeting. He looked fit.

"Any news on Paco?" I asked immediately.

"He was pretty beaten up during the interrogation. When they finally determined they could get no more out of him, they sent him to Gurs. That saved all of us. If they had been smart and knew his value, it would have been far worse for him, and they might have cracked him open like a *noisette*. He gave them nothing. Last I heard, he was going to be sent to Drancy in the north, which is another transit camp. He's strong though. He'll make it, if given half a chance. How's your wife?"

"She's okay. I've received a couple of letters, and we've set up communications, so I hear about her. She's fine at this point. I've been talking with the local Maquis about a plan to free her."

"Who's that?"

"His nom de guerre is Royo. Says he has many contacts in the Ariège and Garonne. They're mostly Spanish Republicans. They want to overthrow Franco and see the Resistance as a first step to achieving that goal. He talks a good game, but I'm not sure I trust him to carry out an operation."

"What are you thinking of doing."

"We have inside help, so I'm hoping to set up an escape from a train heading out of the camp. I don't want to stop the trains, because that could mean a firefight, with lots of casualties. I want a group I can count on to slow the train over a distance of about a kilometer, allowing time and the conditions for someone to escape fairly safely from the train, while at the same time not raising too much notice among the guards."

"I've heard this happening in the north, but never here. In the low countries, the trains move more slowly through busy rail networks leading into Germany. In the open country of the Garonne, it would be more difficult due to their speed and open track access. Plus, the Wehrmacht controls these transports. With the Allied advances in North Africa and the surrender of the Sixth Army at Stalingrad, our Occupant is scrambling. He's spread out thin. The English and American flyers are causing havoc in northern France and Germany. He's being attacked from all directions, including the east. I can't understand why these transports are so important, but they seem to be, and Vichy is collaborating. You have to wonder why. It doesn't serve them one bit."

"I just want to free Gabrielle."

"Good. I understand. Sorry. Let me do a little research on this Royo."

"He claimed to know Paco."

"Possible, not likely, maybe a Republican connection. Give me a week."

"He claims to have eighty men with close connections with other groups, but he lacks arms and is mostly making mischief with isolated sabotage: power transformers, rail interruptions, mainly inconveniences. He talked about MUR, but I just don't have complete confidence."

"If he talked with MUR, we have a fix on him. Leave that one to me."

***

I return to the apartment. It's a mess. I haven't cared to do anything like clean up or dust or sweep the floors. I exist one day at a time, one mental note to the next, my mind focused on Gabrielle. Without my job and in the absence of Paco, Georges, and Robert, I have no friends. I don't see anyone. When I'm hungry enough, I go out to a local brasserie for a quick meal. I smoke constantly, my one indulgence. I walk frequently to nowhere in particular. With the coming of warmer weather, I roam farther along the river, and I have taken the truck out a few times into the mountains to visit Grand-mère, but mostly it has remained in the parking area behind the apartment, as indolent as I am. I can't concentrate enough to read. I listen to news reports with little comprehension. I sleep. I dream.

What can possibly become of us? Assuming that the direction of the war continues, the Occupant will ultimately depart. What then? How can we ever recover? We are so torn apart in spirit and loyalty. Hatred rules. How can we forgive ourselves as a society? Certainly, we cannot continue as we are. The government is floundering, run by a senile old man and a power-driven fascist megalomaniac. The Milice, the latest attempt by Laval to corral the population into the arms of the Occupant, is the very incarnation of Vichy: spiteful, prejudicial, hateful, xenophobic, made up of uneducated and narrow-minded young men, taking out their feelings of inferiority on thoughtful and intelligent people. They blame everyone else for their problems, and Vichy gives them a route to act out their frustration.

When the doorbell rings, I'm in total despondency. Feeling hopeless, trusting no one, feeling weak and useless. The grating noise of the doorbell brings me back to reality with a crash. I can only think of jumping out the fourth-floor window. With great trepidation, I go to the door. No one has visited in months. I crack the door.

"Paul?" It's Henri Bardou, Robert's father.

"Monsieur Bardou."

"*Bonsoir*. May I come in?"

"*Bonsoir*. Of course. Of course. Come in."

He looks around the salon in amazement like the owner he is.

"Edith tells me you don't go out so much anymore. What's up?"

"First, they arrested Georges and Bernadette, my mentor in Perpignan. I've lost total touch with them. Then, early this year they arrested Gabrielle."

"Gabrielle? Really? What for?"

"The man she worked for was in the Resistance. She was there, so they took her along."

"Where is she."

"Camp du Vernet."

"What is that?"

"It's a concentration camp in the Ariège, a transit camp to the north."

"I see." He looked shocked. "Can I help?"

"I doubt it. She's not allowed visitors, and I've received only a few cards over the last three months. She's basically out of contact. I get short glimpses. She's okay. She's sick. She's better. That's about it."

"May I sit down?"

"I'm sorry. I'm not prepared for visitors. I'm afraid the apartment is a mess. I've been somewhat occupied, not with my schedule, but in my head."

"I'm really sorry. It's a terrible time. I've received exactly one note since the holidays from Robert. He apologized for not seeing me, but didn't say much more. He's totally committed to this man in Lyon, Joseph Mercier, or Max. Neither one exists. I've done a little research. And God knows what they do."

He seems stunned for the moment, and a little embarrassed, surveying the hardwood floor, covered in dust, and the mess throughout. "I came to see if you could help out temporarily, but I see that is the least of your concerns. We share this in common: you have lost contact with Gabrielle, and I with Robert. It's difficult to focus on anything else."

Paul nodded. "Right now, I'm trying to see if I can help Gabrielle. I never registered for the STO, but I, like many, was given more time when the records were destroyed. I won't be around much longer in Perpignan. I'm thinking of joining the thousands hiking over the Pyrenees. Only, I have to wait awhile. So I keep my head down."

"I don't blame you, at your age. Anything I can do to help, let me know."
He sat solidly, for a moment staring into space.

"I'd offer you something, but I haven't shopped in months."

"You've lost weight."

"I know. I eat at cheap restaurants, when I feel the need."

"You know, Paul. This is a time you need to focus. Nothing is hopeless.
You've had rough times before, and you survived…a better person."

"I'm trying, believe me. I have plans, but everything moves so slowly
and is so uncertain."

"I know you, Paul. Nothing is beyond you if you set your mind and body
to it. I look forward to your success."

He stood like a beaten man. "I better go."

"I've heard nothing from Robert or Nuria. I think for the time being
that's a good thing."

"I understand. Anything you need, just ask."

"Thanks. I would give anything to be able to come and work for you.
Believe me. I feel honored that you thought of me. One day I'll be better
prepared. I may be leaving soon, so the management of the building may
come to an end. Edith will let you know. Oh, by the way, I'll clean up here."

"I understand. Thanks."

"*Bonne nuit,* Monsieur," and he shows him out.

***

A few days later, a note arrives from Gabrielle, the third. Paul has written
her at least one note a week, but he is pretty sure by her lack of responses
that she has received none of them. Every day he looks for something from
her and is devastated when there is nothing in their postal box. And when
there is one of her notes, he takes it with him upstairs, smelling it, feeling it,
knowing that she touched it. Then after reading it, he feels even worse. It's
like the anticipation of torture that turns out worse than torture itself. He sits
on his unmade bed and reads:

My darling Paul,

I am okay. Life continues, sprinkled with moments of bitter snow. But the sun returns more frequently now. We are supposed to work nowadays, but there is little to do. Sweep out the barrack. Clean up the yard, which is soupy and never dries. Clear the latrine. Make work. Stay busy. ███████████████████████████████ The ██ ████████████████████████████████ I think of my parents, hoping they are doing well. I think of my father's bright, saturated colors. Here there is only mud, dirt, dust: grays and browns. I am finding it more and more difficult to remember our life together and ███████████████████████████████████████ ████████Perpignan. Les Nouvelles Galeries seems such an anomaly, so useless, without meaning. I have nothing. Only my thoughts of you and hope beyond reason. Writing is so difficult and hurtful, my Paul, my heart, my soul, you are so near, yet so far away. It rips me apart. I hold you closely in my heart, but oh that I could hold you in my arms. Love,

Your Gabrielle

He reads the note again and again. He feels her despair and feels her moving away from him, at least in her daily thoughts, to maintain her sanity. It's too hurtful, comparing the past and the present for her. He understands that, but her letters cannot satisfy the terrible visions in his mind of what she is going through and his inability to aid her. She is changing. He can see that.

So much has been lost. He wonders if he will ever find her again, and, if by some miracle they are reunited, what he will find.

***

A few days of turmoil later, I receive a call on the telephone: my second in a matter of months. I had been mind-traveling: trudging through the past, angry at the present, and fearing the future. Even the best moments only serve to point out the depth of the basest moments, serving only to depress me further.

"*Allo?*"

"One moment please," an operator says.

"Paul?"

"Yes"

"It's Miguel, Miguel Serrano. Are you there? Paul?"

"Yes, I'm here."

"Paul, our friend has come up with a pretty good idea."

"He has?"

"Yes. It's urgent we meet."

"I can't for a few days. I'm meeting with someone here."

"We don't have much time. We've heard from our contact. They are planning the next move in late March. We are guessing Sunday the twenty-eighth or Monday."

"I'll be there next week. Tuesday morning around noon. Okay?"

"Okay. *Fins aviat.*"

"A bientôt. "

I put down the phone and sit for a moment in the hallway. I can't continue like this. I have to do something. I have no life. I'll talk with Bouloc and then meet with Miguel and Royo, and then I'm at the end of my rope.

***

At the Grand Café de France, in the center, Paul sits in the cool sunshine, feeling the heat on his face, his coffee before him, waiting for Bouloc. People are feeling good with the warmer temperature and sunshine. There is some joy in watching others take pleasure in themselves, in living.

He watches a family: a couple with their two young daughters sitting at a table bordering the pedestrian walk. The two young girls in fresh Sunday dresses joke around, their parents in conversation, ignoring them. The attractive older girl of twelve or thirteen sits feeling quite pleased with herself, her legs crossed, resting them on an empty chair in front of her. She prattles on with her younger sibling in the warmth of the spring sun. Paul observes the older sister with curiosity. She exudes a budding confidence and a relaxed innocence, feeling sensuous without understanding it and yet still capable of playing a silly girl with her sister.

A guard troop of five German soldiers approaches from the shopping area. They are led by an immaculately dressed SS officer, in grey-green uniform with an officer's cap with a shiny black bill, a death head on the band. His butter polished high boots reflect the morning light, and he sports a short leather horse crop, striking his thigh as he walks, clearly feeling pleased with himself in his own way, just as the girl does. The juxtaposition intrigues Paul.

To his surprise, as the soldiers enter the plaza, the officer notes the young girls playing at the café. As he passes the table, he stops and reaches down and grabs the older girl's right ankle in his gloved hand and lifts it slightly and holds on forcefully. He smiles and says something in German, laughing and keeping his hold. The girl's face suddenly turns deathly frightened, knowing full well the stories of the Occupant's cruelty. She clutches her dress to keep her thighs from being exposed. The shocked parents are immobilized, not knowing what to do. The German officer continues to hold her leg and raises it slightly, caressing her calf mockingly with his crop. The girl, not struggling, is frozen in fear. Paul feels himself tense, about to rise from his chair, but then the officer says something to his troops and laughs loudly to their delight, and drops her leg. He says something to her in German in a warning tone, wagging his crop, and then in accented French:

"*Bonne journée monsieur, madame, mesdemoiselles,*" and salutes.

Paul isn't surprised to see the family rise immediately and depart as the guard troop marches off. All the people who observed the scene are horrified and sit silently for some time,. He shakes his head in disbelief and resentment and empathy for the poor girl.

Bouloc arrives a few minutes later.

"Royo has only one problem," Bouloc said to the point, after greeting Paul, lighting his pipe. "He's Spanish."

"So?" Paul asks.

"He's Spanish, man. Never forget that. He's always looking ahead. He may help you, but it's because he sees it as part of his strategy. He has a group of guérilleros. You can call them Maquis, but their primary goal is to do battle against Franco. These are Republicans, mostly Communists and Anarchists, outside their home fighting to return. They are well organized and disciplined, and their chief is competent. They work closely with the other Maquis from that region and are one of the spearhead groups."

"Sounds like he can do the job?"

"He can if he wants. That's between you and him. He works with French Maquis and includes some French among his fighters. Eighty may be an exaggeration, but he has some good men. Listen, Paul, I couldn't find anything bad about him. He has talked with MUR, and he sees the benefits of a unified Resistance movement. He'll be a big help in the future. But right now, he's doing what he can without exposing himself. It's a little like hiring a cobra. He can do the trick, but you always have to keep out of his way and make sure you control him and watch which direction he strikes."

"I kind of like him. Just too much bravado."

"Don't get me wrong. He's capable. He'll work for you, particularly if it furthers his goals. Just watch him."

"Thanks."

"Good luck."

***

As the train journeyed toward Toulouse, he thought of how he had managed others, always a committed team member, although always with doubts. He had spent too much time on his own, solely responsible for himself. He couldn't ignore his doubts and concerns attempting to rescue Gabrielle. He didn't know Royo, and, although he liked Miguel, he didn't know how far he could trust any of them. In this case, trust was essential. Everything had to go according to plan, or the operation would be a total disaster. There would be no second chance, ever.

With two weeks to the estimated convoy departure, Paul had pulled himself out of his useless despondency. Whenever in doubt, just as his Grand-mère had taught, he went to work. He cleaned the apartment. Warned Edith of his possible departure. Ate better. Perhaps it was the words of Monsieur Bardou or Gabrielle's latest note, but he made himself busy getting everything in order. Surprisingly, in addition to their papers, Léon had obtained two Spanish passports, based on Paul's middle name and his father's nationality. If they were counterfeit, it was impossible to tell, and he was an expert. Supplies had to be purchased and moved to the Ariège. He detailed plans, considering the many possible variables: the schedule of the train, the makeup of the train, the kinds of carriages, the composition of the guards, the other deportees, the location of the operation, the timing, and many other unknowns, including the Maquis and their ability and commitment.

Each unknown was a moving target, interlaced with all the others, depending on the others. It was a complicated equation. He went through as many scenarios as he could conceive. It was endlessly branching like a giant tree to each tiny meristem, but he had to consider everything. He recalled the childhood fantasy stories of Cockaigne, the land where everything is possible, where abbots suffer abuse by their monks, where skies rain cheeses, where girls are as free as the breezes.

The spring was becoming remarkably warm with little precipitation or snow in the mountains. He watched as the train approached Toulouse. The vineyards were budding early and the fruit trees were still blooming. Wild iris, yellow forsythia, white lilac, acacia, mimosa, and chestnut, all showy in bright colors along the way. He transferred trains and arrived at Le Vernet station at noon, where Miguel welcomed him.

"*Hola, amigo.*"

"*Hola,* how are you?"

"Good news. We're lucky."

"What's the good news?"

"Let's have some snacks first and then we talk."

They walked into town to the local café and took an outside table. The sun was warm, and winter was becoming a mean memory. They ordered the daily soup and a carafe of the regional wine from a pretty young waitress.

"The news is that this next convoy is one of the largest and the last one for several months. They are cleaning house, so to speak. So if they plan to send Gabrielle north, this will be the transit. But the really good news is that we were able to identify and contact the train engineer, and he is willing to help out for a price. We may not need Royo. No western gun fights like John Wayne. He will cooperate for a few hundred francs. Sure."

"What is he offering to do?"

"Slow down, and that's important."

"You're right about that. It's been one of my main concerns. Royo can be a distraction, but I'll use him only if necessary."

"The best would be to escape from the train without the knowledge of the guards. Plus, we will know the makeup of the train and the exact schedule."

"I'm on board, so to speak."

"I know you are. We'll need transportation."

"You know my occupation," Paul said feeling better. "I'm a truck driver. I have access to a Renault AGR. Two thousand five hundred kilograms. We can carry twenty people easily. And it's covered. Similar trucks are being used as prisoner wagons in many towns.

They finished their meal and walked to the river, where they were to meet Royo. He hadn't arrived yet, so they sat smoking on a low stone wall, watching the river.

"You have children?" Paul asked.

"One boy and two girls. My boy is about your age and is considering joining the Free French Forces. He knows the hills and has passed many people into Spain. The girls are still at home, adolescents."

"And your wife?"

"We married young, never regretted it. She's all there is for me. That's one reason I wanted to help you from the start. Give you a chance. You know?"

Paul nodded, looking at this man, feeling grateful. "Well, it's no fun without her. That was an easy lesson. I know how important it is to get her back."

"We will. Here comes Royo."

He was limping, which Paul hadn't noticed before. They welcomed him. How are you?" Paul asked, noting his leg.

"Oh, that's the war. No matter. You okay?"

"Yes. You still interested?"

"*Cierto*. We help you."

"Good. I've heard some good things about you. I want to avoid a fight. Hopefully, you will watch and nothing more, but if something goes wrong, I want you to create a diversion to the guards. A small explosion maybe, something to take them away from what is happening on the opposite side of the train. The train will slow without you doing anything."

"I found some automatic rifles," Royo said. "Thompson SMGs. Two thousand francs each."

"That's a lot."

"Five will give us the ability to contain the guards, even German soldiers. These trains usually have no more than fifteen guards, and they're spread out front, middle, and back."

"Okay," Paul said. "We hope you won't have to earn it."

"We will. I'm telling you."

"We have to establish a place and project the time," Miguel said. "We will know in advance when the train plans to leave the camp: date and time and itinerary. You can count on French trains, always on schedule."

"Miguel will let you know the timing," Paul said. "The date is variable. You'll have to be ready toward the end of the month. Okay?"

"Sure, boss."

Paul wasn't sure whether Royo was joking or being sarcastic. "We are counting on you, Royo. Is that clear? This is serious. No joking around. It should be an easy operation for you. Let's keep it that way. Okay?"

"*Cierto*. No problem." The two men looked at each other soberly, appraising each other.

"It should give you the resources to be a power here in the Ariège. *Entens*?"

"I understand, *Senyor*."

"Royo, I have to be able to trust you. MUR is aware of this operation, and it must succeed."

They discussed in broad terms what they were attempting to do. This had happened only a few times in northern France. Convoys of internees were common, but few had experienced escapes, and none had been stopped with mass escapes. By the time Royo departed, he had become much more serious, and Paul hoped that Bouloc's intelligence was correct. How strongly he was committed was still not clear. He departed with ten thousand francs in his pocket and a firm handshake.

"Assuming all goes well," Miguel said, "what are your plans afterwards."

"I meant to discuss that. We have exit visas, and we have papers for Spain, but I want to go over the mountain rather than test our papers. We need to cross the border, and we'll need a safe-house for a few days, possibly weeks. We'll go by way of Bagneres-de-Luchon, but we'll need a passeur to avoid the patrols. Once in Spain, we should have no problem."

"Okay. Maybe my son, Armando, will take you. He knows the mountains and the best routes, and we have several safe-houses in St. Girons. He currently lives there with my sister. I'll talk to him. You'll need to be here several days before the transport. You can stay with us. You're bringing the truck?"

"Yes."

"We'll need to get tools into the camp before."

"You'll have them."

"Yes, Marta will require some incentive."

"How much do you think?"

"A few hundred francs."

Paul nodded his head and handed him two, one-hundred-franc notes.

"Thanks, Miguel."

"Believe me, we'll do this."

They shook hands, and Paul walked to the train, feeling better, but in the back of his head he wondered what the chances were. Everything had to be perfect. Each step faultless. One mistake threatened the entire structure. So much depended on the actions of the Occupant, his deportation orders, his participation, either remotely or directly in the transit, the camp officials, the local police, the SNCF, and, of course, the train engineer.

28

28 March 1943

No, nothing at all, I regret nothing
Neither the good that others have done
Nor the bad; it's all the same to me
No, nothing at all, I regret nothing
It's all paid, swept away, forgotten
I don't give a damn for the past
With my memories I light the fire
My sorrows, my pleasures
I have no need of them
All my loves swept away with their complications
Swept away forever, I begin again at zero.
    « *Non, je ne regrette rien,* » *Charles Dumont, lyrics*
    Michel Vaucaire

"Get your arses out of bed," the head yells with sadistic pleasure. "Up and at'em. Drop your cocks and grab your socks," she says laughing, quoting some B-movie. "Out. Out. Rise and shine, my jollies." Another movie.

It's still night, still dark. God knows what time it is. I'm awakened from another terrible dream of running and an endless fall from heights, cold, yet covered in sweat. I never remember the dreams in the morning, but when I'm rudely awakened, the dreams are implanted like watching a pyrotechnic display, and then closing your eyes I see it all. I'm lost in the mountains, snow spotting the higher elevations, lost in the wind and rain, with the clouds swirling above me. I cannot find my way home. Cold, my heart pumping erratically, tense, breathing rapidly, I know where I am, but I can't find my way home.

Since my miscarriage, I have suffered similar nightmares. Nightmares of escape and helplessness. I have recovered to an extent, but only an extent. I think I placed all my thoughts of that terrible failure into a sealed compartment for my own survival, to open at some time in the future, if God willed it. This morning I know exactly what is happening.

"Roll call," the head yells again and again. "Bring all your personal items. Quick now. Everyone."

The two long lines of bunks come to life: grumbling, swearing, women running down the aisle to the latrine, others putting on extra clothing, trying to maximize what they take with them. Others stand in stupor. The sick remain in their bunks. We have all heard second-hand stories, but most know what early morning roll call means.

"Let's go. Everyone out. That means everyone. No matter if you're sick." She walks up and down the aisle pulling blankets off women who are trying to avoid the reality of what's occurring.

Slowly the barrack empties into the drizzly morning fog. Recent spring showers have made the yard once again almost impassable, each footstep sinks into the sludgy mud, and the ruined shoe, or what passes as a shoe, rises with caked mire. The latrine is hazardous, as any misstep can result in a filthy disaster. I'm one of the first to leave. I have nothing to carry: my blanket, my eating implements, a few extra clothes in a small suitcase I salvaged from the last group to leave our barrack. I'm wearing my overcoat, which hides the small tools rolled into my blanket.

A few days before, Marta, the guard who has spoken to me in the past and given me word on Paul, found me alone in the yard and walked me back to the barrack. Alone, except for a few sick women, she surreptitiously handed me some tools from her adequate waist. They were small and did not take up much space. I hid them in my blanket. She proceeded to whisper the use of each one.

"You and your group will be leaving in a few days," she began without introduction. I gasped. "There's an operation to free you, and anyone else who wants to get out. You will have one chance, and if it doesn't work, God protect you."

"Wait, how do you know my name will be called?" I asked breathlessly.

"Everyone's going."

"Oh…"

"Now listen, when you enter the railcar head to the rear on the east side. Any car, but east side rear. You understand? There are four wooden shutters covering the openings on the platform side of the carriage. They will be shut and fastened in place. This is critical. Last opening on the east side. Remember that, if nothing else. The shutters open from the outside by an armature for raising, lowering, and locking the shutter in place. There is a rod exactly centered on the shutter. The rods rest in place on a support, half way from the bottom of the floor of the carriage. Is that clear? You'll see it.

"First, you must cut a hole in the side of the carriage on the sixth slat up. Not in the center, where the metal armature is, about six centimeters off center on either side. Cut the hole just wide enough to get your arm outside to release the shutter by forcing the rod off its support. The siding is rotten and should not present a problem to open a space. Use this lever to force the rod off the support. The shutter will fall exposing the entire opening. Careful to avoid the falling shutter. This is a keyhole saw. Get someone to help you. It can easily cut through the rotten wood siding. You have two saws, just in case. You might have to lift the rod a bit to help release it.

"While someone is cutting the hole, you want to be cutting the metal bar across the opening. There are three bars on the inside of the car. You cut close to one side of the center bar so you can bend it entirely out of the way. This is a small hacksaw. It should easily cut through the metal due to the age of the carriages and years of rust. You can bend it back to allow a person to slide through to the outside. You have two hack saws and a wrench to bend the bar out of the way. Okay?"

I concentrated, but I was not at my best, and Marta went quickly, and I was never very mechanical, but I thought I understood.

"That's it. Now, with the middle bar open, getting out is easy. But wait for the train to slow or stop. This will be about an hour after you depart. One hour. Understand? You have one hour to get the shutter open and the bar bent back. It'll be well after Auterive, near Labarthe-sur-Leze just after a rail bridge crossing the Leze River, in a shady forested area. The train will slow. You'll feel and hear the bridge. If you are not out by the time the train crosses the larger Garonne bridge, you will know that you have failed.

"Now, when you feel it slowing, someone must help you out the window feet first. Don't jump. Hang on the lower bar and drop. You'll be a little over a meter above the ground. Try to land in the direction the train is moving." She was watching me the whole time, concentrating on imparting this information as quickly as possible, but making sure I was taking it in.

"Thank you, Marta. I'll never forget you."

"You understand?" she asked firmly, ignoring me.

"Yes."

"You've got a good man. That should be an incentive. Mine is null." Other people were entering the barrack, so she left. I hid the few tools away and revisualized her instructions.

That was four days ago. Now on a Sunday morning before dawn, we are running around like the cooped chickens we are. I visit the horrid latrine, and then join a growing group of women in front of our barrack. We wait for a while in the cold with our blankets thrown over our shoulders. Why they allow us this luxury, I'm not sure.

Finally, a group of guards and the *Chef du Camp* walk into the enclosure. The chief looks us over like he was seeing us for the first time and perhaps the last. We never see him at any other time.

"Ladies, today we are sending you to a labor camp in the north. You'll find it much improved over this facility. With better food and accommodations. You will be able to work and help the war effort. I will read your names, and you will advance to the gate and wait."

Some of us know the process, and our reactions are muted. I have made my peace with this evil determinant of my fate. The new arrivals less so.

"Yael Goldfranck, Aymee-Lee Hirsch, Delia Oppenheimer, Bastienne Halphen. Simone Seidenbach, Devorah Kiel Liebermann, Claire Maar, Rivka Tichenor, Judith Anselm, Adina Murkowski..."

As he calls out our names, I hear isolated gasps and groans, but not the emotional reactions of my first roll call. I wait as if before Saint Peter's gates, the image so removed from the reality that I giggle to myself, my breath piercing my chest, uncontrollable. I know and yet I know nothing.

"Liseann Weiser, Claudette Wertheim, Ruth Bachstein, Nicole Barach, Sarah Rastenhausen, Frieda Marcelle Dachs, Charlotte Jessel, Denise Hire-Dreyfus, Esther Gabriel Solano, Eliana Raabe, Marie-Gabrielle Solomon, Tamar Frank, Moriah Judenberg, Peronne Gouston Stiller, Leah Reynard, Moriah Ernst-Silberman, Susanne Gustavo, Gabrielle Daniel, Rachel Caan, Maya Aronsfeld..." He continues on and on.

Rachel touches my elbow. Then it dawns to me, the familiar sound ringing in my ears. I look at Rachel, who has not been called yet, but knows that her name is coming up. I move off alone over to the waiting area before the barbed wire gate, and I no longer listen to the names being called. The grating noise continues so long I cannot grasp its meaning. It is our entire barracks, over one hundred. I think of Homer's roll call of the ships, where he calls out the names of the Greek fighters, most of them going to their deaths. Does God hear our names? Does he note our accomplishments? Our villages, our towns, our cities? Our faithful conscientiousness? Our good works, as the priests always mention first off. Our loves? Our failures and mistakes? Our tears? Our regrets?

At the end, a multitude of the barrack internees are huddled before the gates. We hold our blankets close in the cold morning with rosy-fingered dawn breaking as the gate opens. We begin moving en masse toward the station, a march of three hundred meters or so. We are Convoy No. 11 from le Vernet. When we come to the platform, we are unable to progress farther, since we are no longer alone. Other barracks are being loaded onto the same waiting train. As we gradually approach the platform, it's chaos. As people in the front of the throng come onto the platform, they are forced to wait as others are pushed into the carriages by many more guards than usual, all with truncheons, until each carriage is filled. Then the next carriage begins filling, as people behind push forward. Some of the people are old, some infirm, some sick, and for the first time I see mothers with their children being loaded. The guards treat, or mistreat, everyone the same.

Marta, the guard, appears from nowhere to our group, since we have reassembled.

"Come," she addresses me.

I follow her, as do Rachel and other women from our group. She leads us through and around other groups. We follow like good sheep.

The carriages are old, designed for cattle or industrial freight. I examine the cars and see exactly what Marta described: the shutters covering the openings and the apparatus for raising and lowering the shutter and keeping it in place. I see the supporting rod in a vertical position without any padlocks.

Marta practically pushes me into a near-empty car, No. 413 chalked on the door in large numerals, and the others follow. I hold onto Rachel, as we move into the carriage, pulling her quickly to the back of our car on the platform side, the east side, just as Marta said. There are other women from our barracks mounting into the car behind us. And then others enter: men and boys and even some children, huddling in fright, alone and unsupervised. I am glad to be among some friends. Inside, I note the openings now shuttered. Our car fills rapidly, until people refuse to cede further place to others. It must have over a hundred people, with room enough for only a few people to sit on the floor at a time. Otherwise, everyone stands, waiting nervously for departure. Then the door is slammed shut, and it's near pitch black. I hadn't counted on that. Thin glimmers of light come from the roof vent or penetrate through slits in the old wooden siding.

The train sits on the rail spur for some time as people continue to fill other carriages, and then when we hear no more commotion on the platform, we continue to wait. An older man in the center of the internees yells for us to be quiet, and most everyone quiets down.

"Bonjour, everyone," a man yells. He is obscured from our view at the front of the car. "I have been selected as *Wagonführer* of this carriage and will report to the *Obersturmführer*," he yells. "That's better. We are all going to the same destination. We are all being deported. We need to cooperate and make of this the best we can. There is a single container for piss and shit. Please be careful. Only a few of us can sit at one time. Please reserve this for the elderly and infirm. I've also been informed that if anyone disobeys me, behaves out of control, or acts crazy, all our lives will be in jeopardy. Let's make the most out of something I believe that all of us detest. Thank you."

I wonder who this man is. I wonder how far this man will take his assumed responsibility, and if he truly believes our lives depend on acting correctly on the way to our execution? Does anyone with half a mind expect some German official at the end of the line to question each *Wagonführer*, as he calls himself, while the cars are emptied? I saw no one counting the deportees as they entered the cars. Where are these carefully notated lists of all persons in each car? The only list is of the names called from a score of barracks, hundreds of names. We were just randomly pushed into cars as we came, and no one paid much attention, except Marta, thank God.

But my mind is consumed with information few people have: information on the eventual destination, the welcome in store, the value of our lives, and, thanks to Nuria and Robert, a clear vision of the process. Further, I have a goal that exists before the terminal stop. I am not focused on the final destination, only an hour ahead.

The train begins with a jerk, upsetting many people, throwing them against their neighbors with much grumbling. We are lucky to be at the end of the car as the train jerks forward. People are standing mostly eye to eye. Many look slightly deranged. Several sick people are lying on the floor, but in general the carriage is so crowded that there is no possible communication between people in one part of the car and elsewhere. The air is immediately stifling, with the stench of filthy people, over-crowded and fearful, and the rancid smell of waste begins to permeate the car. There is no water and certainly no food. Most everyone is quiet in anonymity, dwelling deep within their own psyche. Moans and groans. Nauseating stench of offal and sickness and filth.

A small broken board in the wall at the back of the car allows a bit of light to fall near us. During the slow start, people approached our group with paper notes they had prepared, asking us to push them out of the train once we leave le Vernet. They call them white snow. Commonly, white snow is released from these transport trains with notes to family and friends and addresses, hoping without hope, that someone will find them and forward them.

I start working immediately, knowing we have an hour to complete our tasks.

"Rachel," I say, "can you cut the hole in the carriage wall while I cut the bar." We had discussed the tools and the plans beforehand, and she agreed that we had to attempt our escape. She nods.

I take the keyhole saw from my sac, which had remained on my shoulder the entire time, and give it to her, showing her exactly where to cut the hole in the wall.

"Not exactly centered, slightly off, large enough to allow an arm through." She is far better than I at this type of work.

There are three bars fairly widely spaced at the shuttered window. I pull the small hacksaw from the sac and begin sawing the right side of the middle bar. With the middle bar out of the way, a small person could slip through. The bar is slightly above my head and near the closed shutter, making it difficult to cut, but the height gives me leverage to saw. The metal is old and rusty, but the hacksaw makes slow progress. People around us note what we are doing, but in their stupor say nothing. Rachel's having better luck. The rotten wood of the siding collapses and disintegrates as she cuts through quickly. She works on enlarging the hole. We both are rapt in our work, when we hear some voices behind us.

"*Hé*, what are you doing?" A man's voice. I can't see his face, so I don't answer and continue working. Our group of friends from our barrack provides a shield. Rachel has enlarged her hole easily. I estimate about ten minutes. She pushes the wooden pieces out, and a hole appears, and the morning light falls onto our legs and the wooden flooring.

"Just reach through," I say. "Jimmy the support with this lever to release the shutter. Watch out for your arm when it falls."

I stop sawing to watch her. Part of her forearm extends through the wall, and I can see her moving, feeling the mechanism, struggling to force the lever with her shoulder. Suddenly the entire exterior shutter descends gradually due to the rust, finally banging loudly at the bottom of its track. Light floods the car like a spotlight, shocking everyone around us, and cool air blows into the compartment. She looks at me victoriously.

"Eh, what's that," the same voice says, more irritated. "Where's the *Wagonführer*," he yells loudly this time. There is some commotion, but I ignore it, my saw now halfway through the bar, making slow progress on the ancient metal. I don't want to get sidetracked.

"Stop that."

I turn to see a small, balding man standing directly behind me. Some functionary. Officious. Doing his job. He has forced himself between the people surrounding us.

"Who are you?" I ask, guessing at his intent.

"I'm the *Wagonführer*. You didn't hear what I said earlier?"

"I did, but who are you, and what is a *Wagonführer?*"

"You are endangering everyone in this car."

Another man, old, orthodox by his appearance, pushes through. "If you flee, you will have all our deaths on your conscience...forever."

I stare at both of them. "What is wrong with you?" I practically scream. "Didn't you learn anything from your time in the camp? Did you talk to no one?" I hand my saw to Rachel and indicate that she should continue. I shield her with my body. Suddenly, I'm angry.

"Listen, you're idiots. Listen to yourselves."

"Have you given thought to the people in this car?" the old man continues, ignoring me. "The sick and the old? The Germans will kill us all."

"Do you have any idea of where we're going?" I demand, crazed beyond any time in my life. "Do you? Do you?'

My fervor unseats him. "To a work camp," the *Wagonführer* repeats mindlessly. "That's what I was told."

"You're absolutely blind and deaf. The Germans care nothing of what we do. They do not know we exist and have no plans for us to work. Why send sick people to work? And children? And mothers? They want us gone. Do you think God is watching over us? Where is he? Use your head."

They say nothing in reply.

"We're going to a death camp," I continue angrily. "Look around you. We're all Jews on our way to a Nazi extermination camp. Talk to some of our internees from the north. They know. Whether you or I remain in this car or escape has no meaning. We will all die."

They don't reply. The guards were at the front and rear of the train in separate carriages. The people in the car remain out of the argument, have no opinion, are apathetic, or are too far gone to care. Some few come to our aid.

"Leave them be," someone yells.

The *Wagonführer* makes no further effort to stop us, but watches us indignantly.

During this confrontation, Rachel has managed to saw through the bar. She is much stronger and faster than I am. I hand her the wrench, and she begins attempting to bend the bar out of the way. It doesn't budge. She strains, but cannot move it.

"It's too strong."

"Cut the other side," I order, at the end of my patience. "Quickly." We are about a half hour into our trip.

A large man appears, hairy and bearded, seemingly in better health, a new arrival perhaps. He takes the wrench from Rachel, and we back up to give him a little more room. He tightens the wrench at the tip of the cut and begins forcing the bar back. This time it slowly gives way. Once he pulls it away to some extent, he changes the leverage of the wrench to the other side and begins pushing it farther backward. This is more effective, and he manages to bend it entirely out of the way against the back wall, and a half-meter opening appears with the blue sky outside between the two remaining bars, top and bottom.

"You might be able to get out, but I never could," he says stoically with passive acceptance. He hands the wrench back. "And you're right, this is a death train. Our only hope is escape."

"Okay," I reply. "I promise if I can get out alive, I'll open the door of this carriage. It depends on the train speed. Then everyone here can choose to leave or remain.

The *Wagonführer* and the old Jew continue to stand there, unconvinced. A strapping teenage boy pushes his way through the crowded car.

"I want to try," he says eagerly.

"The train is going too fast," Rachel warns him. "You'll kill yourself."

"You just said we will all be killed anyway. Let me go."

"Wait," I said. "The train will be slowing down in a few minutes. You can go then. It's in a forested area, and you should be able to survive the fall. At this speed you might seriously hurt yourself or be killed. What good does that do?

"I don't care." He begins climbing into the opening. The bearded man helps him up. The entire car is focused on the open space and the adolescent.

"No," I tell him, "Feet first on your belly."

The boy turns in the man's arms and pokes his feet out and wiggles his body, until his stomach rests on the bottom bar.

"Grab the lower bar and thrust yourself away from the train," I say.

He changes his hands to the lower bar and pushes up. He smiles at me and then slides outside until all we can are his two fists clinging to the bar. And then the fingers open and disappear. He's gone. No sound. The car is silent. Only the clacking of the rails and wind blowing through the opening. Everyone around the opening is silently amazed, but not willing to try themselves with the speeding train.

We wait awhile, everyone relieved to have the fresh air flowing through the car. No one speaks, but every eye is glued on the opening, looking at the blue sky and a few cumulus clouds in the distance as if heaven existed and was within their reach.

Most of the internees have been in the camp at least several months, and some many more than that. I'm a recent arrival, but long enough to understand. They have been arrested, tortured, interned in atrocious conditions, deprived of food, clean water, and hygiene. They come with a polyglot of languages and cultures. They suffer a multitude of ills: malnutrition, open sores, broken bones, dysentery, diabetes, mental disorders, nerve problems, heart disease, cancers, disorders of age, all without treatment or medicine. Their will power is eradicated, their humanity progressively denied, their faith extinguished. Beaten, nameless, they have been transformed into ignoble slaves. We come from a world of negation, the untouchables, the Untermenschen. I can't blame them for anything, and I understand them: I'm one of them.

The brakes come on suddenly, squealing, and we are thrown forward against the others. People scream and groan. Their complaints continue until the train finally slows. Our speed declines until we are moving at a crawl. I give Rachel a big kiss on each cheek.

"A bientôt."

"Merci," she says. "Thanks for giving us hope."

I indicate to the large man to heft me as he had the boy. He picks me up with ease and puts my feet through the opening. I feel foolish in this position, my ragged tunic thrown back, my legs and shorts exposed. At that moment, the train suddenly squeals to a complete stop. I hear an explosion in the distance, but the man continues to help me. Hesitant, I grab the upper bar as my body is hefted through the opening. Then I am supported by the bottom bar on my stomach with my legs hanging outside. I hear some distant sporadic gun shots and then a more concerted response with rapid fire. Then nothing. Total silence.

I'm not about to let that keep me in the railcar. As the boy did, I manage to wiggle myself onto the lower bar to a point where I grasp it. I look back into the carriage. Everyone's eyes are on me. I take a deep, welcome breath of the fresh and clean air with the smell of herbs and grass and the invigorating greenness of the surrounding trees. A feeling of independence builds in my chest, no matter the outcome. With my legs hanging against the carriage wall in the still air, I push my chest up, feeling a gentle draft across my body. I thank the large man, whose eyes have not left me for a moment, and I glance warmly at Rachel.

I push against the bar, and for a moment I hang on the lower bar just as I had as a small girl on the high bar in the middle school gymnasium, feeling grown up and proud of my body. I am completely outside the train. Remembering Marta's words, I turn my body in the direction of travel. I glimpse the carriages ahead on a straightaway, steam rising in a cloud from the locomotive in the distance among high trees on both sides. I swing my legs away from the train and release my grip, free-falling toward the gravel and grass below, having no fear of the outcome, just feeling the wonderful, humid freshness of freedom.

29

28 March 1943

> *Symphony of a day that sings forever in my heavy heart*
> *Symphony, symphony of an evening in spring*
> *It's you I hear evermore*
> *The harmony of your scent remains*
> *And I remember the days that are no more*
> *Symphony, symphony.*
> « *Symphonie,* » *Fred Adison, Alstone, Tabat,*
> *Bernstein /French lyrics Marlène Dietrich*

I arrive at Miguel Serrano's farm in le Vernet early Saturday evening. The weather vane has swung back toward winter, with a spring storm the night before and scattered showers on the way from Toulouse. I'm driving my truck with plenty of extra charcoal from the depot and park it behind the small house out of sight in front of the barn. Miguel comes out to welcome me with a dog barking behind him.

"*Hola, amigo.*"

"Bonjour, Miguel. All's well?"

"Yes. Come in. Come in."

He leads me into the house. This is my second visit to his home; our many rendezvous have been mostly in cafés or walking the river. I have been dreading this day and yet couldn't survive without its advent. I am prepared to do all to regain Gabrielle. Of all the dangerous risks I have taken over the last two years, this is the most treacherous. The stakes are enormous, the chances slim, and potentially innumerable uncertainties. So much is out of our control. I cannot hide my fear of what we're doing, which could end lives and send us into the very arms from which we are intending to save Gabrielle. It's better not to think of the downside. After careful planning, we focus on executing and ignore all else, allowing the winds their direction.

A friend once theorized on the secret of the Germans' success. German soldiers, he said, accept orders without scrutiny, examining nothing too closely for fear of awakening questions or feelings of uncertainty. This trait is general, he went on, and is imbibed with their mother's milk. The acceptance of facts without questioning influences every act, every relation, every thought, from the words of their leaders to the mores of their society. In contrast, our civilization is erratic and messy, created by people who examine everything deeply, question authority, and fight for what they believe right. There are always arguments, anger, and tears, but ultimately the results are worth every spent emotion.

Miguel's home is warm and comfortable, crammed with oversized furniture, throw rugs, doilies, paintings on the walls, crosses, images of Jesus, and general brick-a-brac covering every surface. Two teenagers are playing a board game on the floor and ignore our entry. Miguel's wife comes forward to welcome me. In her forties, she's attractive and vivacious, with her hair tied unsuccessfully into a bun, not at all as he described her.

"This is Paul. My wife Carmen." Miguel introduces me in Spanish.

"I've heard so much about you. Welcome."

"Thank you."

"Are you hungry?"

"I could eat something."

"*Albondigas de pollo,* fresh.*"

"Sounds delicious. As a bachelor, I haven't been eating very well lately."

"I'm so sorry about your wife," Carmen says.

I nod.

"Those two hunks are my daughters." They turn their heads in our direction. Probably fourteen and sixteen. "Up," he orders. The two attractive adolescents rise reluctantly, but welcome me with firm handshakes, too old for bisous.

"Something to drink?" Miguel asks. "A sweet wine?"

"Sounds great."

After an excellent dinner of fresh chicken meatballs in soup, we sit at the table and talk. The two daughters are in lycee, both speak perfect French, disdaining Spanish and Catalan, which they also speak fluently. It's wonderful to be in a family situation, both joking and serious. The two girls turn attentive when I tell them about meeting Charles Trenet and Georges Ulmer. They know many of the popular tunes we sang, and I'm judged acceptable.

After a few hours, the daughters retire to their room, and Carmen leaves us alone in the warm family room. Miguel pours a red wine, and we discuss the operation for several hours.

"They are leaving tomorrow in the early morning," Miguel says of the convoy. "The location to slow the train is in a forested glade outside of Labarthe-sur-Leze, about an hour by train from the camp. Just after a small train trestle across the Leze River. It's sheltered, away from the village, with easy access for your truck."

"I've grown to love the reluctant monster. It's been very useful."

"Plenty of space to carry Royo's men in the back and supplies. We'll leave about four in the morning to pick up Royo. I'm told they've had three recent convoys without a hitch, and the camp authorities have grown comfortable. Shouldn't be heavily guarded.

"Royo and I visited the site, and we talked to the engineer of the local train to Toulouse, and he has agreed to slow down at the selected location. Money well spent. Most of the employees of the SNCF are not enthusiastic in supporting the German convoys. Royo has prepared some signage as well. This is not his first operation with the rail system, and he's quite knowledgeable of the conventions of signaling, including the electric signals."

"I thought we had decided to stop the train."

"It's a delicate balance and will depend. The train will slow. That's guaranteed. But our intent is to stop it. We will be prepared for any contingency."

"Without a firefight." I said.

"Again, we all agree. Royo doesn't want a fight. Even if he could keep the guards pinned down, which he believes he can, it would have follow-on consequences, with possible retaliation and a massive police response against the local Maquis. Stopping the train sends a message to the Occupant that you cannot continue to ship people across France with impunity, at least not without some resistance. We decided to wait until we can assess the guard contingent and their assertiveness and the extent of cooperation of the train engineer."

"The train may not even slow," I say pessimistically, feeling tired and frankly uncertain about our loose plans and lack of control.

"That's possible."

We continue to discuss the potential deviations and outcomes, but in general we have a course of action from start to finish, requiring plenty of latitude for reacting to the unknown.

With only a few hours before departure, Miguel retires to his bedroom, and I settle under a quilt on the large sofa.

***

We rise early the next morning, Sunday, before sunrise. I go out to the truck to add charcoal and light the combustion chamber. After coffee and bread, we drive to a neighboring village to pick up Royo. Carmen waves as we leave, attempting to conceal her concern.

Royo and five experienced Maquis are waiting when we arrive at the rear of an isolated farmhouse, all in work clothes and bérets, Royo in his wool newsboy hat. They pile quickly into the back with their equipment and arms hidden. Royo and Miguel ride with me in the front cab. Before getting into the truck, Royo hands us two police revolvers. I have never even held a gun. It's cold to the touch and heavy. He explains the safety catch.

"These are MAB-D's. Just a measure of insurance, if things get out of control. They are off-safety, so be careful. If you get into trouble, you have some protection. You have seven rounds. Put them inside your pants and belt on your left side, if you're right handed."

When I refuse, he is insistent. I look at Miguel, who seems more accustomed to firearms, and he places his in his belt without comment. I follow suit. Suddenly, the operation is real, the danger manifest. I'm not alone in being nervous. Everyone is nervous and quiet.

"How are the Thompson machine guns?" I ask. I assume he had done as he said and purchased these guns that rank with anything the Germans issue.

"Great. We've been practicing. The cartridges are not that common here and expensive, so we were careful. Plenty of ammunition for the time being. Now we're well equipped, not for just making a nuisance of ourselves. This should help when we cleanse the region of the Boches and their supporters.

"We got the Thompson M1A1 with thirty-shot magazines. Directly from London. Someone high up in our region okayed this, thinking it important enough to allow us the guns. These are new versions of the standard, more dependable at close range. We are better equipped than any of the police guards, carrying old five-round, bolt-action MAS carbines. German infantry normally carry Karabiner rifles, comparable to the MAS carbine. MG 42s are unlikely, though comparable to the Thompsons. The Wehrmacht guards are at the bottom of the food chain. The French will likely be less aggressive than the Germans. But we don't know what to expect."

"We just want to stop the train with the minimum of exposure." I say, repeating myself.

"Yes, boss," Royo replies in his enigmatic fashion.

We arrive at the site as the sun rises in a clear blue sky with a distant bank of high cumulus clouds. The field mist slowly departs, and the day awakens clear of rain. Royo directs me to a narrow farm road, and we park the truck under the train trestle next to a stream.

No one is about, and we walk along the sheltered tracks, carrying our bags of supplies and arms. At the signal post on the trestle, Royo cuts the electric system wires and uncoils a yellow diamond placard, used in emergencies when electric signals fail. The yellow diamond warns the engineer to slow to below thirty kilometers per hour, with a possible stop ahead. About two hundred meters farther along, they place a blinking red lantern on the left-hand side of the tracks, a warning to the engineer of a stop ahead. Four hundred meters farther down, on a straightway through a forested area with high trees on both sides, they put up a red carré placard on the signal post. In normal operations, the carré warns the driver to stop and not pass. The red carré sign is easily visible from the blinking red lantern.

"The engineer is not expecting the danger signage," Royo says, "and may believe it's real. At least it reminds him of his agreement to slow down. These convoys are not supposed to slow or stop and have priority through all blocks. This is a long BAPR (*bloc automatique à permissivité restreinte*), about fifteen kilometers, normally without restraints. We'll see."

448

"We'll split up. Four of us on the west side behind the carré stop sign. You and Miguel and two of our men will be hidden a hundred meters back at the center of the train on the opposite side. If someone jumps from the train, you should be able to see them. If it stops, wait to see the reaction of the guards. There are three cars with guards: one at the front, one at the center, and the final car. Never more than fifteen guards in passenger carriages with windows. You'll see them, and a passenger car provides little protection for them. We have a small smoke bomb, which we will set off as the train approaches the red carré. That should confuse things and divert the attention of the guards to our side. You can approach the train once their attention is diverted. But it's not clear which car your wife is in, or if others will attempt an escape. Our success depends on how interested the guards are in exposing themselves and how aggressively they want to keep any prisoners from escaping."

"And if the train doesn't stop?" I ask nervously.

"Not much we can do. It will slow. And at least initially the attention of the guards will be focused on us to the west."

"What if the guards chose to make a fight and leave their carriages?" Miguel asks.

"Then we welcome them. A big surprise. Okay? Should make a statement that this shit of deporting people can't continue."

By this time, the sun is shining, and the sky is clearer. We leave Royo and his men and walk back to our location, hidden behind trees and bushes quite close to the tracks, but well concealed. And we wait.

So much is in doubt, so much left up to the unfolding of events. I feel the revolver in my pants; the whole thing is goddamn dangerous. I light a cigarette and offer one to Miguel. I don't think I have ever been so nervous. We sit in silence. The two Maquis spread out from us: one midway, the other at what should be the last car. A slight breeze blows. Through the trees, we have a straight view back up the tracks and can see where the trestle ends and the back of the first yellow placard on the signal post. We wait.

It's difficult to believe we have come this far. Can we actually free Gabrielle? Yet we are close. As close as we will ever be. To be close to her, only to fail, would be the worst. I can't conceive what I would do. Leave the country? Disappear? Join the Maquis? My life would be over. This has to work; it cannot fail.

After more than two hours waiting, with the sun high in the sky, light streaking through the trees in places, the first sign materializes: the unmistakable chugging of a steam locomotive approaching from afar. My heart skips a beat. We wait, not breathing. The next sign is steam above the tree line. A train is nearing. Only one train is on this line, and it approaches slowly. Before we see the locomotive, there is a loud screeching of brakes. The engine appears and crosses the trestle. We can't tell if the brakes are still slowing the train, but it is not approaching rapidly. We wait. It seems forever before the engine is opposite our position. We can see the engineer. Then the first carriage passes, a passenger car with a few heads looking out in surprise. The next cars are freight cars, completely closed. They look like old cattle cars, long out of service, with their painted sides looking decrepit, layers of paint peeling, marked by graffiti, broken siding in spots, and chalked directions and numbers.

The train is definitely slowing. It's not too long, maybe fifteen carriages. Now we see the middle passenger car, with men standing at the windows looking out. The train is coming to a halt, the brakes squealing. We see the end of the train on the trestle and the engine approaching the carré sign. We wait. It comes to a squealing stop. Suddenly, a loud explosion and smoke at the front of the train on the opposite side.

I watch a Maquis sprint toward the end of the train to keep the final car under his control. The other Maquis lies on the ground, his rifle trained on the middle guard car. For a moment, everything is silent and motionless. Then I note a carriage two cars ahead of the final passenger car. One of its shutters is open. It's the only one open in the entire convoy. Standing up within the trees, I move in that direction. I hear the sound of single shots at the front: a few shots, and then a quick reply with many louder shots in quick succession: machine guns resounding in the trees. Then there is silence. Suddenly, the heads in the passenger cars disappear. Neither of the two guard cars near us is showing any sign of life. They must be hiding on the floor of the cars.

I jog down toward the car with the open shutter, hoping that the plan is happening as we conceived. I remain within the tree line. When I see two legs hanging from the opening and then the lower trunk of what appears to be a woman, with bare legs and shorts and back. She pushes against the lower part of the window, and I begin running alongside the train, watching her slowly lower herself out. For a moment, she hangs in the air, as though looking at the engine, and then she drops. It's about a meter and a half drop. I'm there just as she lands on her feet at first, but then falls backwards. I'm able to break her fall, so she actually lands on her feet. She turns toward me. Somehow, after all our planning and discussions, I can't believe it's happening. Of all the miracles, it's Gabrielle, looking thin, but beautiful beyond all belief. She's there, looking at me in equal amazement, not really focusing on what's happening. I lift her into my arms and hold her, but she struggles free.

"Wait. Wait."

She rushes to the door of the train and attempts to raise the large lever on the side of the sliding doors. She lifts and pushes with all her might but cannot move the lever. I run to her side. I see what she's doing and grab the large latch and am able to raise it above the hook keeping it in place. I push the door open, and suddenly we are standing below a group of people looking out into the forest and at us in amazement, eyes blinking, dressed in rags. Almost immediately, they begin sitting on the edge and pushing off or turning around and dropping their legs first as Gabrielle had done. Gabrielle helps them, but as more get out, they begin helping the others. Soon there are fifty people milling around the open door. They are hugging Gabrielle, and she is hugging them. I note another carriage down the way with people jumping out, a similar scene. The other freight carriages remain closed.

I watch as Gabrielle hugs an older man, looking lost, obviously Jewish.

"I'm so happy," she says.

The old man replies seriously, "I may be an old Jew, but I'm never too old to learn. Thank you, my daughter."

Miguel has come up to us and is watching intensely both ends of the train. No guards appear. I look around and see both of the Maquis at the end and middle cars. They are covering the car with their guns in position. There have been no further shooting or explosions.

"We have to get out of here," Miguel says. I pull Gabrielle away.

"We can't just leave them," she says. At the same time, the train starts moving with a jolt. People from the car are still jumping into the arms of others. I can see some irresolute people in the back of the car, confused and uncertain, but not making any attempt to escape. The people on the ground are exhorting the others to jump as the train begins moving. The train slowly accelerates. Only two freight carriages have been opened, and the people are standing away from the rails not knowing what to do.

I take Gabrielle aside. "We can take a few people, but not many. The others have to move off on their own."

"Okay Paul. I will…it's impossible…it's a miracle…oh my God." Looking closer, I see how terrible she looks: waif thin, pallid, and dirty, hair unkempt and filthy, arms thin, and dressed in rags like the others, and smiling oddly.

"What did they do to you?"

She says nothing.

"Come on." I pull her back into the trees. The train is now moving more rapidly. I see the last passenger car move by, still with no one appearing in the windows. Royo was correct about the French guards and that the train contained no German troops.

In less than a few minutes, the train is gone. Everything is deathly quiet, except the voices of the freed deportees. I can see Royo and his three companions running with big smiles on their faces.

"Once the guards got the idea," he yells, "they disappeared under their seats. *Salauds*. We did it. First time ever a convoy has been stopped in France. *Fichons le camp*."

"We've got to go, Gabrielle." She doesn't reply, but I take her hand and lead her away.

"Rachel." She breaks free and runs into the arms of an older woman. All the people look equally terrible: drawn, thin, scraggly, in prison gowns or rags.

"We've got to go," Miguel repeats, as Royo comes up to us.

"Gabrielle, bring her and the old man," I say. She turns and pulls the old man along with her friend to our sides. "Let's go. We can't help these people. They may find help in the community. I just don't know." People begin to move away in all directions, some alone and others in small groups. Maybe they can find help.

We walk rapidly back to the trestle, descending the tracks to the farm road below. Gabrielle and her friend are helping each other down the hillside. The Maquis wait by the truck, packing their weapons. Everyone gets into the truck. It takes a while to get the engine started, but we have not seen a single person from the town or in the open fields. I struggle getting the truck started. Finally, the temperature of gas combustion comes up, and I'm able to start the engine. In the cab Gabrielle is sitting next to me, and Miguel is to her right. She grabs my hand and makes it difficult for me to shift, but she won't let go. I'm able to back up on the farm road and then join the highway back in the direction of Le Vernet. Very few cars are on the road, and we return to Le Vernet without incident and no indication of police activity or anything else that might signify news of a train stoppage and escape of deportees.

At Le Vernet, on the far side of town, I let Miguel and the Maquis out of the truck. The old Jew joins them, somewhat abashed, having accepted Miguel's offer of a safe-house and change of clothes and some nourishment. Gabrielle hugs him, and he shyly hugs her back.

Miguel gives Gabrielle a strong hug and then comes to me.

"I owe you more than you will ever know," I say, not knowing how to express my gratitude, feeling guilty at my vacillating faith in him, tears filling my eyes.

"You have already repaid me, Paul. I will see you soon in the new world. Good luck. Tell my sister I love her. Now, get out of here. The farther away the better. The Ariège is going to be a rough place for a while, and I'm sure the Occupant will seek retribution. But we took a chip out of his armor." Miguel and the old man depart as rapidly as possible along the river toward his home.

The Maquis give us big hugs, and then Royo and his men quickly leave. Everyone is excited, pleased with the operation and intending to lie low for the next few weeks.

I mount the cab. Gabrielle and the older woman are waiting. The truck bed is empty. We move off on the highway south toward the mountains.

"Paul, this is Rachel," Gabrielle says once we are on the move. "She saved my life. Without her I would have succumbed to the evil of that place." I nod in her direction. She appears to be in decent shape, although both of them could not be mistaken for anything except escaped prisoners.

"We need to get you some clothes and fixed up."

"I have a cousin in Foix," Rachel says. "Can you drop me?"

"Of course."

"We can change clothes there, and you can spend the night."

"We have an appointment at a safe-house. Foix is on the way. I want to get out of the region."

Gabrielle continues to hold onto my hand and refuses to let go. We're on the road now, traveling south toward the Pyrenees. I cast a glance at her. A different apparition, and yet it's her. Her eyes, her hand, her strength. I feel her warmth next to me.

High clouds in the distance, but the sun is strong, and the temperature is warmer than the past few days. I can't believe it all worked out and we are on our way. I wonder about the other escapees. Where will they go without transportation and dressed as they are? Villagers may help them out, once they understand. I can't help thinking that their chances of escaping are not good, but anything is better than that train to the north. I wonder about us, and the truck. If we were stopped for any reason, the women would be a dead giveaway. The truck is also easily recognizable. I'll have to part with it at some point. We probably have some hours before the authorities will begin searching in earnest for the escaped deportees, but they will. Probably once the train reaches Toulouse, which is about now. Some will be immediately recaptured and raise the entire issue. I look at Gabrielle again and squeeze her hand. We're not home yet: every car, every truck, every village, every person along the road I feel in my gut. But we are together and will not be parted again.

30

April 1943

It was a love story
Like a beautiful holiday
Full of sunshine and dancing
When spring courted me
But when love stories are too beautiful
They cannot last forever
It was a love story
Of which nothing hereafter will remain
In order to have a love story
Someone must always be hurt.
　　« C'était une histoire d'amour, » Jean Jal, lyrics
　　Henri Contet

The stop at Foix lasted no more than a few minutes. No introductions. Gabrielle's prison rags were exchanged for ill-fitting garments. Her face washed and her filthy, uncut, scruffy, scraggly hair brushed. Without reloading the combustion chamber, hoping to have enough fuel to make it to St. Girons, they left after a few bites to eat, tears, and deathly embraces. No policeman would be deceived for an instant from Gabrielle's appearance and stupor that she is not a fugitive and he is not a facilitator. They had to make it to the safe-house or fail entirely.

The distance from Foix to St. Girons is no more than forty kilometers, but it felt like an eternity, with Gabrielle slumped, exhausted, sick next to him.

They finally arrived at a two-storey farmhouse with a large grange connected on one side. It was situated in a suburb of St. Girons on the chemin de Pujole on a hillside within walking distance to town. Madame Lépinay, a robust woman, quite pretty with beautifully coiffed blond hair, in her mid-fifties, welcomed them in the waning afternoon sun, opening a large iron gate, indicating that Paul should drive into the courtyard, waving him into the open barn. The ignition had no fuel remaining. He parked inside the large structure next to a commercial tractor behind the large sliding door that Madame closed, Paul felt much more comfortable. This would eliminate wandering eyes or questions from the neighbors.

Realizing immediately the situation, Madame helped the near-comatose Gabrielle down from the truck. Paul quickly came to her aid.

"Miguel has spoken of you and put me on notice," she said. "We are very proud to have you with us. Both of you. Please come in, my dears." Seeing Gabrielle more closely, she grabbed her around the waist and kept her from falling, hugging her tightly. "We will need to care for you, to eat, and to change out of these horrible clothes. My goodness girl, you are so tiny, so frail. My clothes won't do, not at all, but we'll find something. Come in. Come in."

Together with Paul, she guided Gabrielle into the house both supporting her tightly the entire way. The tears poured from Gabrielle's eyes. The plain stone and mortar exterior turned into a spacious and elegant dwelling, with the exposed stone walls, open beam ceilings, and antique furnishings A large, leather davenport dominated the salon on an enormous Persian carpet and chairs surrounded a carved coffee table in the center with a carefully polished wood top. Several large oil paintings hung from the walls. One was an enormous landscape painted by Auguste Daniel. The room was sparsely furnished, but elegantly. No brick-a-brac in sight.

"Sit down for a moment," Madame Lépinay said, indicating the sofa. Her focus was on Gabrielle, who could barely keep her eyes open. She knew exactly what Gabrielle had been through and rapidly placed three small snifter glasses on the table, pouring a dark amber cognac, almost filling two of the glasses and a dribble in the third. "Drink," she ordered warmly.

Paul tasted the drink, which flooded his mouth with an intense flavor of figs and cherries. Gabrielle drank deeply of hers.

"I'm sure you two are dead-tired. You've been through a lot. Let me show you to your room. You are welcome to stay here as long as you need. You must feel at home. Of course Miguel told you I am his sister, and his son, Armando, lives with me. And you are members of our family. He made that clear." She could see just how depleted the two were. "Please, just let me know if there is anything you need or anything I can do for you."

"You are very kind to take us in," was all Paul could say.

"You have quite a following, Paul. And Gabrielle, I have the largest painting your father ever did, or at least at the time: le Roussillon. He was my husband's favorite contemporary artist, and we visited him on several occasions. My husband's in Germany now, one of the many officers captured during the German offensive. It's been almost three years, and every evening of every day they expect some of the soldiers to return, but the Germans know the value of a good hostage, and our government, *bah*, enough said." Then stopped herself, realizing how beat they were.

During the three-hour ride, Gabrielle had come to realize the enormity of her escape. She was physically and emotionally consumed, as well as ill and suffering from malnutrition. What she had hoped would be pure joy quickly transformed into a terrible feeling of guilt and melancholy. Nothing remained to regain her footing.

They walked up a curving staircase, Paul supporting her, into a hallway running the length of the house. Their room was at one end. Madame opened the door, and they entered a gorgeous room with the afternoon sunlight streaking the carpets and wood flooring. One window opened onto the rear garden and fallow fields, with colossal, snow-covered mountains in the far distance. The opposite window had a view of the street below and the forest and hillside beyond. A large double bed occupied the back wall of the room, with a breakfast table and chairs in the center. Paul was fully supporting her at this point: her body totally enervated.

"Your bath is the first door on your right, opposite the WC. My room is at the other end of the hallway. Armando is not here, but will return in a few days. He's next to the stairwell. Please rest, and I'll call you for dinner." She left, abruptly closing the door.

Alone at last. Gabrielle managed to rush to the WC, and Paul waited, taking off his jacket and sweater. He tested the soft bed. After the few hours of sleep the week before, the constant worry of the operation, and then the tension of the drive, he was totally exhausted, not like Gabrielle, but enough to feel at the end of his resources. He took off his boots and lay back on the bed. The room was warm from the radiant sunlight. With the truck stowed away, he felt relieved of any fear of being immediately discovered by the police.

Gabrielle came into the room and closed the door, saying nothing.

"Are you okay?" Paul asked.

"No," shaking her head. "I can't believe it. Such a nightmare. I dreamed of this. It's all different." She began crying again.

"We'll talk about it later. Come and lie down." He pulled the cover up and folded it to the end of the bed, and threw back a heavy duvet. She approached on the opposite side, kicking off some pumps that Rachel had given her and dropping a heavy coat onto the floor.

"I'm so filthy. God." She had on a wool sweater and a full length skirt, both old and unsuited. She sat down on the bed, as though she meant to disrobe, but instead fell backwards. She lifted her legs onto the bed, pulling herself into a fetal position with her back to him and her arms hugging herself, and passed out immediately, breathing heavily. Paul covered her with the duvet.

He watched her as he would a wounded animal, having difficulty believing her return, but disconcerted by her lack of strength and mental confusion, aware that the doe was on the verge of running away once again and disappearing into the woods. He recognized the terrible effort of the coming struggle as her rescue continued, and he wondered about its depth and duration.

Paul lay down on top of the duvet reliving the operation and chaotic escape, listening to her irregular breathing, large gasps followed by great exhalations, and he finally fell asleep in his turn.

***

Four hours later, Madame Lépinay gently knocked on the door. Paul woke from a deep sleep, rubbing his eyes, feeling disoriented, and opened the door to her. Gabrielle never budged.

"I'm sorry to bother you," she whispered in the hall backlight, "but I thought you might need something to tide you over." She entered the room and placed a giant silver platter on the table. "Don't bother returning anything tonight. Good night." She closed the door. In the moonlight, Paul had no idea of the actual time; from somewhere he counted ten chimes.

Gabrielle had not stirred. Paul sat at the table and viewed the unbelievable platter. Food he had not seen in years: cut sausage and ham, two real baguettes, three fresh cheeses, glorious pâté, a plate of homemade cookies, and two pitchers, one of wine and the other of water. Miracle of miracles: a small ramekin filled to the top with butter. He poured some wine and began eating disjointedly, anxious about Gabrielle and still distracted. In the confusion of their flight, he had failed to return the MAB revolver to Royo. He took it out and placed it in a bedside table, making sure the safety was on. He would hide it in the truck tomorrow. He ate more than he intended, unable to resist the prewar flavors, undressed, and got into bed under the sheets. Gabrielle never stirred.

Some time during the night, Gabrielle awoke. She ran to the toilet and finally returned. She didn't speak. She returned to the bed and lay down sobbing.

"You should have left me," she said barely audibly.

"What?"

"I don't deserve you."

He shook his head, not believing this continuation of a nightmare.

"I'm such a failure," she said, beginning to cry again. "I'm rotten, a piece of empty flesh." She turned once again away from him and cried silently into her pillow.

"There's food on the table," Paul said.

"I don't want any," she said angrily. "I'm an empty vessel. I have no need of food. It would only make me sicker."

"I love you, Gabrielle. I will do anything for you."

"That's what I mean."

"What?"

"Worthless." She lay still for a moment, her body shaking. He moved closer to her and put his arms around her. She was under the duvet, but not under the sheets, and she still had on that awful skirt and sweater. He waited, as she seemed to be attempting to express some thought.

"I lost it."

"You lost what?"

"Your baby."

"My baby?" he said almost to himself, surprised, but he believed her.

"I lost our baby."

"You never told me you were pregnant."

"I was. But not now. They treated us like sewage."

"You need something to eat."

"No," she shouted angrily. "I don't."

Paul rose from his side of the bed and went around. He lifted the duvet from her. He stripped off her sweater and unclasped an ill-fitting bra. She didn't resist, helping him like a little girl. He unbuttoned her skirt and pulled it off. She wore Rachel's panties, way too large for her. He viewed her body, all bones, her stomach flaccid, emaciated, her small breasts flat against her chest, her ribs prominent, her arms and legs unnaturally thin. He wondered about lice and fleas, but decided that would have to wait. Then he gently lifted her. She weighed almost nothing. He pulled the sheets from underneath, re-covering her with the warmed sheets, tucking her in, and pulling the duvet around her neck. He moved the pillow more securely under her head. He went around the bed and got in, enveloping her as best he could. There he remained, never releasing her, listening to her breathing, at times even and soft and at other times rough and intermittent, as though suffering some dreadful nightmare. He lightly held her, always aware of her, but never releasing her for the rest of the night, until the dawn light tiptoed into the room.

He went to the bath and washed himself. He brushed his teeth with a toothbrush in the holder, no dentifrice. He looked at himself in the mirror. He hadn't shaved in days and had no way to do it now. His eyes looked gaunt and deep-seated. He realized that this bad dream would not end as long as they were running. They were both fugitives and could easily be arrested and find themselves in another camp and another train to the north. They had no home. Their only chance was to leave the country and find a safe haven from this cloudy tempest, a refuge, a sanctuary: somewhere to reassemble the losses and begin again.

When he returned, Gabrielle was sitting immodestly at the table in her ill-fitting panties, having consumed much of the remaining meal and water. She looked at him shyly. "I was hungry," and she smiled. An ironic smile, a cheerless smile of momentary satisfaction. He realized once again that her return would not be easy, and he wondered if he could help. All he could do was love her patiently and aid her to focus on her recovery. Between the two of them, they might be able to find a way forward, not as in the past perhaps, but a new way.

"You feeling better?"

"Understand, Paul, I'm not the same person you married. I've aged. I'm an old witch. I have no country. I'm not Christian. I'm not Jewish. I am loosed into this world without care or thought. An impersonal world that doesn't give a hoot for anything or anyone. I'm alone. I came to that understanding early on. Other people can only harm you. At best, they can temporarily befriend you. They will depart in a storm. You can't count on anything or anyone." She took a sip of wine. "Oh, my god," and she ran off to the WC.

She returned and went to the bed and lay down exhausted and seemed to fall asleep again. At least, she wanted no further conversation. Paul dressed and took the dinner platter downstairs to the kitchen, where he found Madame Lépinay.

"Bonjour, Madame."

"Bonjour, Paul. How goes it? I hope you slept well."

"I did. I'm afraid it will be some time before Gabrielle finds peace. She's under attack."

"It takes time. My husband's cousin returned from the camp at Rivesaltes, and it took almost a year before you could talk to him. And he's still suffering. It's a scar that remains, and the goal must be to learn to live with it. There's coffee and croissants and butter. It pays to live in a rural community. How long was she in the camp?"

"Almost six months."

"Miguel has worked for years with the people at Camp du Vernet, trying to get them out or help the ones that remain, fighting for decent conditions. He knows. He spent almost a year there in thirty-nine. I tell him he needs to move away. His son is similar to his dad, but the two girls are fed up. I worry for them, but he refuses to listen."

"He certainly helped us."

Paul could tell that sister and brother had taken different routes after the Spanish Civil War. She had moved on. She spoke French. Married a French man. While Miguel continued to fight the battle, just as so many other Spanish Republicans did in France, hoping to return to Spain one day.

"Do you think I can take a walk?"

"Of course."

"I mean is it safe?"

"The people here mostly work together. There are so many refugees today. Every city, town, or village in the region has its refugees and temporary citizens from the coast. St. Girons probably has more than most due to its proximity to the border. The people here are comfortable with the strangers appearing in the last few years. They don't ask questions. You'll be fine. You can walk into town. No problem."

"Thanks for your help."

"Stop saying that. You have risked helping many others, now it is our turn. I'll get some clothes for your wife. Now, you go on. Both of you need some mothering. I'll check in on her."

***

I went upstairs for my heavy coat. Gabrielle remained asleep. The day was crisp and fresh, the sky clear and the sun strong. I looked at the mountains covered in snow in the distance and realized it was far too early to attempt a crossing. I checked the truck and hid the gun in the cab. Then I walked down a road in the direction of town. No cars. It felt good to be outside and moving without fear. Walking always reanimated me. I wondered about Gabrielle. What had she gone through? How much had it wounded her? All the pain and losing a baby. How soon would she recover her equilibrium? How far could she return? I have heard tales of released service men, who never returned to their former selves. They had become aliens in their own villages, some committing suicide, others lost to themselves.

I too have changed. My makeshift family has been decimated. Robert and Nuria have departed Perpignan. Georges and Bernadette have been arrested and sent north. God only knows where they are. Auguste and Julie disappeared into les Fenouillèdes. And then Paco Macias and Gabrielle were taken away and sent to separate camps. I've floated through the last months, listlessly, consumed with Gabrielle's ordeal. My only ambition was to save her, and although I achieved this, I've lost much at the same time. I've lost my direction, my ambition, all my friends, and my ability to move through troubles. I've always prided myself on surviving, having done it my entire life, but now I seem lost.

For years, I carefully protected myself by ignoring or avoiding misfortune, call it what you will. I managed to keep myself moving forward. One of the better beans in the school according to my mathematics teacher, Monsieur Boucher. Climbing obstacles. Getting accepted at the Prefecture. Singing with the greats. Helping others. Hard work, a trait Grand-mère worshiped.

But now all that seems foolish and has not worked. All the furnishings of my house have disappeared. All that remains are the walls and foundation. This winter everyone was angry. The war should have been over. Not another harsh summer of deadly fighting with the government doing nothing, except offering its citizens and economy up to work for Germany. When will they realize who the real enemy is? People have discovered that staying on their rations means starving. They are tired of being consumed by hunger, while a few are fat and happy. This winter, shoe manufacturers suddenly discovered stored leather inventories, which they had hoarded since the war began, and were now making new leather shoes for local consumption, at expensive prices.

In Perpignan, two cars ran into each other. The drivers jumped out and accused each other. The bystanders in the street joined the fray. Everyone was arguing, yelling, cursing, when a German officer entered the dispute, hoping to end it. At first the French ignored him and continued fighting and yelling. Suddenly, they looked around and realized their foolishness. Everyone departed. The two men got into their cars and drove off. The people who had watched the spectacle disappeared. The German was left alone on the street.

The war, which so many predicted would end soon, has continued unabated, if not with increased intensity. And our government is useless, worse. My marriage, which has been my one refuge, has dissolved, and now Gabrielle, previously my strength, is fighting to recover her losses. For once in my life, I do not know what to do or where to go, like a spinning top slowing until it wobbles into a disorderly spiral and finally falls spent.

Is there some purpose or is it just gravity, as Gabrielle has said? Could I recreate something out of nothing, as one reads about protagonists doing in novels, moving in directions determined by choices and effort, not by chance, and not determined by others. A determinant life, a sensible, rational progression, not a hodgepodge of random events leading nowhere.

I returned to the safe-house feeling weak. A lone billiard ball ricocheting from one cushion to the other without achieving anything, just moving heedlessly and aimlessly.

Yes, I saved my wife, but the joy I expected may take years of hard work to appreciate. I promised her with my being, and that is our contract.

***

Armando arrived a few weeks later. Gabrielle had regained some weight and her mood swings had declined. She was still distant, not always available, small mental walkabouts, but slowly rediscovering her former self as she gained confidence in her surroundings and liberty. We ate dinners in the dining room, took short walks, became familiar with the farm, and even became friendly with neighbors, remaining ever vigilant of strangers and the police. We helped out as much as possible, although Madame was resistant. Gabrielle and Béatrice, for she insisted we call her by her first name, became fast friends, going shopping in town, always talking together, comfortable and loving with each other. I tried to help as much as possible, not to be a burden to Béatrice. She was the sort of person I would have loved to have had as a mother, accepting, knowledgeable, demonstrably loving, and caring. I seem always in search of parents.

At first blush, Armando was nothing like his dad: tall, my height, nervous, high-strung, with stringy long blond locks. He talked at a fast clip in perfect French, sometimes slurring his words and liaising to a point where I couldn't understand him. I liked him immediately. He was honest and straightforward, confident, someone you could trust. He inherited that from his dad.

"You're famous, man," he said.

"Why's that?"

"You know, I've known many local *passeurs*, but you're a legend."

"That's not good."

"Not by name. How many?"

"How many?" Although he comes across much younger, he's about my age. He looks at me as if I were some old veteran.

"Yea. How many did you pass?"

"No idea. Do you know how many you've helped?"

"Not exactly, a few dozen or so, but we move in groups. This mountain range is rough. The English send their airmen elsewhere. Takes someone who is desperate, really, really desperate, who will attempt anything to escape. No morning stroll. And we're out of business for six or nine months of the year because of the mountain conditions. My dad says you want to cross. You could do it, but your wife..." He shook his head.

"When will the mountain passes open?'

"The lower ones are open now, under twenty-two hundred meters. But that's not high enough to get into Spain. By next month, we can have a go. Depends on the warming days. We've lost a few recently. The weather can't be trusted once you're on the mountains."

"We crossed at lower altitudes, when I was doing it, and those passages are mostly closed now by the police."

"These mountains are higher, steeper, and more treacherous, even in good weather. You've got to be prepared. We can do some hiking first. Get a feeling for the climb. Build up some muscles. You know. My aunt said there's no rush. This is a nice place. Being raised in Le Vernet. Not so hot. You know what I mean. Glad to be out."

"What are your plans?"

"Probably school. Don't know. My aunt wants me to stay. They've got twenty hectares here. You know her husband's been in Germany the entire war. She gets a card now and then. He had been mayor of St. Girons. Called up. A colonel, you know. Tough guy, but fair. It's hard to know how he's doing."

Gabrielle and Madame entered the room.

"Well, you look comfortable," Béatrice said, sitting opposite them. "Man talk?" Gabrielle remained standing.

"Just comparing notes, Auntie."

"I'm going upstairs," Gabrielle said. *"Bonne nuit."*

"Bonne nuit."

"I'll be up in a few minutes," I said looking at her, assessing her state of mind. She was still too thin. She was less confident, less cheerful. What did I expect? She had taken hits in many different ways, mostly invisible. Her health was just one of them.

"Did you two get a chance to talk?" Béatrice asked.

"We did," I replied. "Armando thinks we need some training before attempting the crossing. At the same time, we must wait until the snow melts at the higher points."

"You know you're free to stay here as long as necessary," Madame said. "I enjoy having you, and it's no work. You help out immensely. It goes without saying that Gabrielle is not ready. She needs to rebuild her strength. She's come a long way, but she needs more time."

"She had a miscarriage," I say, wanting her to know.

"She told me. Leave her to me. She has had some terrible blows. We've known many men who took years to recover. Miguel struggled for years with some of them: alcohol, drugs, bouts of anger, rage, and crimes. I don't know how he does it. Working and fighting with the camp administration and the town council. Now with the Germans in command, there are no discussions. They see the camp as a temporary stop; they are focused on sending people north. It's changed. Let me help Gabrielle."

"Any help would be gladly accepted."

"Don't misunderstand. You're great with her. I'm impressed with your ability to handle her and with your patience."

"We're going to prepare," Armando said. "You need to get her walking outside of the house."

"Don't worry, Armando. She'll be fine in a few weeks."

"I'm going up. Thanks, Armando and Madame. Good night."

"Bonne nuit."

I enter the room. The lights are off, and she seems to be sleeping, or trying to. I go off to the bathroom and WC and return. Undressing, I get carefully into the bed, not to disturb her, and wait for the heavy sheets to warm up. The sunshine warms the earth, but the nights are still freezing cold. At times, there are light rains or snow flurries.

"Paul?"

"Yes."

"I worry about you."

"About me? Why. You need to take care of yourself. I'm fine."

"I know, I'm trying."

"I know you are."

"I worry that I'm a drag on you like an anchor."

"You are no anchor, my dear." She is turned toward her side of the bed. I place my hand on her narrow waist. "I just want to get us to a place where we can no longer be afraid."

She puts her hand on mine. "I wonder how my parents are doing."

"I'm sure they're fine. Your dad would have it no other way. It was a surprise they left so precipitously. He never mentioned anything to me."

"Me either. Did you know he was in the Resistance?"

"Some. I learned later that he had been instrumental in establishing MUR in our region. Paco never said anything, but he knew more than we did. I wonder how much Julie knew?"

"She never said anything to me."

"Anyway, they're fine. I'm sure of it." I pulled her gently, and she turned toward me."

"I'm sorry I'm so gloomy all the time."

"You're not gloomy. You've gone through a terrible experience. You're coming back."

"I'll never be the same, Paul. I try, but it's difficult."

"I know it is." I pulled her into my arms. She was warm and snuggled into my embrace. I held her, listening to her breathing. We remained that way for a long while.

"You can make love to me," she said. "You know that."

"I do. But I want to make love with you."

I continued to hold her.

"I never imagined I would ever be in your arms again. I thought I was dead, like everyone else. I never expected to see you again. And the worst was I had to prepare myself to lose all the people I loved. I had to leave. I had to disconnect myself emotionally. It was just too hard loving you."

We were quiet.

"I was sent away. You know why? Because I was Jewish. Jewish. A year ago I would have never believed it. It was the farthest thing from my mind. It had nothing to do with working for Paco. Somehow, they knew my parents and grandparents. The officer didn't care about anything else, and he barely interrogated me, just sent me away. Never said a word, and there I was in a barrack for Jewish women, only a few Christians. Strange, but, you know, I think I'm Jewish. Do you mind having a Jewish wife?"

"Not in the least. I want you as my wife. I love your parents, but the rest, *je m'en fou*. I could care less."

She put her hands under my t-shirt and began rubbing my chest. I massaged her, up and down her frail back, her shoulders and neck, along her spine, feeling the wonderful reverse curve of her waist and hips and her buttocks. For a long time, we just touched each other, as though we had never felt our bodies before. I treated her like the doe she was, glad just to be with her, never wanting her to run away, never wanting her to feel that she must perform or accept me, wanting her to desire me as she did before.

As in a dream, it happened without trying or thinking. We made love slowly, more concerned for the other than we were for ourselves. We wanted to be wanted, and we wanted to feel each other's desire, and we wanted to express our love. We wanted to love and to be loved, all in a delicious combination of emotions of missing, of returning, of retrieving, and of somehow coming back together as one, consumed by our love for each other. Stronger together than alone, rooted against the winds, invincible together, two hearts beating as one.

31

May 1943

Before the barracks at the end of day
The old lantern suddenly lit and gleamed
Here we awaited the evening full of hope
The two of us, Lily Marlène
The two of us, Lily Marlène
And in the somber night our bodies entwined
Forming a single shadow when I kissed you
We exchanged our simple vows cheek to cheek
The two of us, Lily Marlène
The two of us, Lily Marlène...
This tender story of our twenties
Sings to me in my memory despite the days, the years
It's as if I hear your steps and hold you in my arms
Lily...Lily Marlène, Lily...Lily Marlène.
  « Lily Marlène, » Norbert Schultze, French lyrics
  Henri Lemarchand, as sung by Suzy Solidor

I woke with Paul lying next to me. What overweening indulgence and good fortune. I never thought it would happen again. I thought it had all been stolen. All hope had been taken from me. The repetitive and demeaning daily demands of living in the camp left me mindless and empty. The detainees soon learned the true intent of their incarceration: a mechanical process of dehumanization leading unquestionably and intractably to death. The daily schedule, our lack of clothing, limited nourishment, irrational rules and punishments, acceptance of death as a common occurrence, loss of privacy and all modesty, bitter cold and sleep deprivation, roll calls, and fights between the other internees: all mechanically combined for destruction. A construct of a debauched human without conscience or charity. Had it not been for Rachel and our small coterie of friends, I would surely not have survived.

I'm convinced that convoy No. 11 was headed to Germany for extermination of its passengers. This fact was attested to by the many deportees caught up for a second or third time in the Nazi web. They freely warned anyone who would listen. The others, if they'd listened at all, should have known. Once we were stuffed into cattle carriages, they should have recognized that we were never returning. Even that old Jewish man realized that his inability to accept the reality of the train had been wrong. Hope is the most powerful of human hormones, even in miniscule doses.

If Paul had not intervened, I would have been lost.

I realize now that the infernal machinations of the camp had almost achieved their end. Dante's warning at the gates of the Inferno, the city of pain, could not be more appropriate: *lasciate ogni speranza, voi ch'entrate*. I had given up all hope, including my baby, the quintessence of hope. That awful doctor had offhandedly remarked the morning after that the miscarried embryo had been male. How dare he? How dare I not react to his lack of humanity, quietly accepting what I could not control. Except, he too was a victim of the camp, neither better nor worse. Who am I to judge?

Once the body's appetite is minimally satiated, the mind turns immediately to other areas of concern: the desire for home, the urgent need for love and companionship, and the yearning for meaning. After several weeks of freedom, I'm beginning to feel that I may be able to rejoin the living, able once again to accept hope.

I lean over and see his eyes are open. I kiss his sweet lips, an early morning buss, with such satisfaction and freedom. You cannot imagine my momentary happiness? He smiles a sleepy smile, and I touch his taut body, stretching against my own, and I feel his warmth, and I love his acceptance, his sleepiness, his patience. I love being warm in a clean bed with him. A Catalan proverb: if this is war, then may peace never come.

***

The return of Armando is like a fresh sirocco, making me aware that there is one more step to conquer to recover freedom and hope, and that is this mighty mountain that makes its presence felt above us, snow-capped, ever changing with wisps of fog circling and a mysterious clouded aura, ever changing. I rise before Paul, wash up, which is still a privilege, dress in long pants and a man's shirt; my small wardrobe from Béatrice is comfortable and utilitarian and slowly expanding with nice, used clothing. I head down to the kitchen, where I hear the sounds of breakfast.

"Bonjour, Béatrice."

"Bonjour, Gabrielle. Feeling better this morning? Your color is great." She smiles, knowingly. In the kitchen, she always wears her full-length white apron, which is freshly washed daily, hung out in the sun, when possible, and pressed. She must have many. She smells good when I lean in to give her a morning bisou.

"Shalimar by Guerlain."

"Right. You know your perfumes."

"I do, after years in the makeup boutique of Les Nouvelles Galeries."

"I see. We'll have to confer. Bread's in the oven. Fruit compote on the table. Warm milk and tea on the stove. Help yourself."

I join her at the table. She eats almost nothing, I have learned, and her cute figure becomes her.

"Feeling like shopping this morning?" she asks brightly.

"Absolutely. Paul gave me some money to buy clothes."

"You're nearly my size of several decades ago. The same height. Let's first explore the attic carefully. See if we can find some things. Then we go. Since the war, I've been very conservative. Buying little and making everything go a little longer. With Albert gone, my life has changed."

She's very stylish, like the ladies in Perpignan, knows herself, always smart. We never see her dressed down, even when she's puttering in the garden. She has a gardener, but she loves to collect vegetables for dinner, even in the spring, without a great selection. My mother never cared much about clothes or makeup or fresh vegetables for that matter.

"Armando said he and Paul are headed out this morning to the mountains."

"I'd prefer staying with you. I'm not exactly ready for hiking. Not yet."

"You will be."

"This morning is the first day I possibly believe you."

"Good."

***

Paul and Armando head out to one of the tamer trails, walking through the center of the village, past the cathedral St. Lizier, crossing the Salat

River on the old bridge, following the river to the south. Through the center of town, Armando greets people right and left, as though he is a celebrity, the nephew of the ex-mayor. A police car sits beside the road, and Paul passes with anxiety. He has seen some police activity and some German patrols, but he has never heard any news report of a stopped train and escape of deportees.

Their destination is Soueix-Rogalle, about fifteen kilometers out. They are both dressed warmly with heavy coats, hats, and boots. It's a gentle incline up a farm road to about five hundred meters, well below the snow line at two thousand meters.

"Spain is a four-day hike," Armando says. "Arduous. Even the military find it demanding. I worry about Gabrielle being able to keep up."

"She's coming along. At full health, she would put us both to shame. In the Albères, we're much closer to the border and at a much lower elevation. It's one night: go and come."

"You have to be crazy to do this one, or without any choice. One thing going for it is that the police and German patrols are less vigilant and stick to the roads. The going is rough for them too. It's not a common route, and we avoid the villages and roads, traveling most often at night at full moon. Today, we would find it impossible to cross some of the snowed-in cols. That will change as the snow melts. It's been a warm spring. I would guess we can do it in June, if the weather holds. We'll be ahead of the border guards, police, and German troops, waiting for the summer season, but maybe not the Milice. They're a dedicated group, and they know the paths, but they're primarily rural types, not too bright."

"You do this frequently in season?"

"No. Maybe four times last summer. But we move with larger groups."

"No problems?"

"None yet."

It takes them four hours to reach Rogalle. They greet people along the way, who are not surprised to see strangers hiking. No police patrols or border guards are sighted. They are both in good shape, although Armando keeps to a quicker pace.

"Do you always move so fast?" Paul asks, not prepared.

"Sorry. I have a natural pace. I rarely get to move this fast. Far too fast for most people. When I'm with older people, I slow down. This is the route we'll take on the first day."

At the village, they pay for lunch at the house of one of Armando's friends. Bread, soup, and fresh cheese.

"How did you get into the business?" Armando asks.

"Sort of fell into it. Growing up I knew all the paths in the region. When immigrants began trying to get out, that was the beginning. As time went on, the easier trails became too dangerous. Passeurs were caught and taken away. A few that we know about were executed on the mountain, which was enough to discourage others. But by then, British airmen became more common. And the government paid for them to cross. We moved west and became smarter. That's when I met Paco and began helping him. I believe you know him."

"I don't really, but he visited my dad a few times. They had something going."

"Now Paco has been arrested, and we've heard no word from him."

"My dad never talks about it. Never tells me anything. Probably for the best. Didn't you worry about the risks?"

"It was a slow process. At first I just wanted to help. I had worked at the Prefecture at first just helping people, eventually getting into forged documents. The passeur was the next step, leading me deeper into the Resistance. I knew the trails, and it was on an informal basis. Working with Paco was a whole new thing, organized and deeply involved with the Resistance networks. I never knew exactly how deep until Paco was arrested." I felt free to talk to Armando, a sign that we were not returning any time soon to France once in Spain.

"Well, you were very courageous."

"Scared most of the time. I never got used to it."

"You ready?"

"Okay, let's do it."

They return to St. Girons before nightfall, and Paul is exhausted. Eight hours is a long hike, even with only a small change in elevation. He has trouble imagining four days and elevations of two thousand plus meters.

473

Ascents of more than a thousand meters in a day, and equally long descents. He wonders if Gabrielle can do it.

They arrive at the house to a nice supper.

"We went into town and shopped," Gabrielle says. "Nothing serious. How about the hike?"

"It's not going to be easy," Armando says, "and the snow is still at an elevation that would make it dangerous. We have to wait for the weather to turn. You need to think of a hiking outfit and boots, warm and resistant to all kinds of adverse weather, and probably crampons, and a backpack, maybe hiking poles. We've got some equipment here. My aunt used to hike."

"What are crampons?"

"Metal plates for your boots to keep you from slipping on ice and snow."

"I don't know if I can do it," Gabrielle admits, visualizing ice and snow.

"We'll help," Paul adds. "But we don't have much choice. The authorities are most likely withholding any news of the train stoppage and escape. We didn't see any police activity on our hike, but believe me, they will not forget."

"Early night for you guys." Béatrice announces brightly. "You both look exhausted. Don't worry about the dishes."

Ignoring her, both Gabrielle and Paul jump up to clear the table and wash the dishes. They soon depart for their room.

***

I remembered an outing with my father a few years before the war. Auguste had been involved in an art exhibition at the Prieuré de Serrabone, a beautiful priory church on the slopes of Mount Canigou. After the opening of the exhibition, we were returning toward Perpignan. As on all his searches for painting sites, this day led us through back roads and through tiny mountain villages. As we drove, Auguste noted a small parish church dedicated to St. Saturnin just outside the village of Boule d'Amont in deep forest, not too far from the exhibition. He stopped, parked the car, and began investigating the site walking around it as he sketched different views in his notebook. Papa never painted on site, instead he did multiple sketches in a diary, noting paint colors, highlights, and his thoughts for a future painting.

At St. Saturnin, he made several sketches, and then entered the church after a local spotted our interest and opened the church to us.

The church was typical of small village churches in the region: Romanesque with a single apse and altar without great elaboration, a few paintings on the walls, and simple capital sculptures. According to the small entry portal, construction dated from the twelfth century. The church still functioned, with a priest occasionally coming from a neighboring village for services. Auguste sat down before the altar on a bench in the first row. I stayed in the rear, watching as he silently prayed. He sat for a long time. One of the paintings lured his interest. It was an eighteenth century portrait of *La Sanch*, a traditional Perpignan procession on Good Friday. This local ceremony dated back hundreds of years.

I've seen the procession many times in Perpignan. It always attracts a large crowd, both locals and tourists. Under the current government, it is discontinued. The ceremony is a strange amalgam of the Passion of Christ and a march of condemned men to their execution. At the head of the procession is the *Regidor*, dressed in red satin with a red conical hood hiding his head and shoulders. He rings a hand bell to warn people of the approach of the procession. Only his eyes are visible through two small holes. Following him are black-robed penitents, their heads entirely covered with black-peaked hoods, similar to the *Regidor's*, some with tambour drums. These are the condemned being taken to their execution. Traditionally, their identities were hidden to avoid any violent reactions from the spectators. Behind them follow church members, some carrying heavy objects portraying the Passion.

At times the church has attempted to ban the tradition, but it always comes back due to its popularity, and finally the church accepted it, and priests and lay people now march together. The focus of *La Sanch* is on the scary penitents in black.

As a child, it always frightened me. I felt an unease in my stomach at the sights and sounds. Now as an adult and after my horrible experiences at Camp du Vernet, I better understand its attraction and emotive impact. *La Sanch* commemorates a single truth. We are all condemned, whether pious or guilty, whether saint or sinner, we must suffer our own Passion, just as

Jesus did. We all must acknowledge this reality. Some choose to ignore it. Some drink their way through it. Some pray through it. However, we cannot understand, help, or love others without acknowledging our shared journey.

I watched Papa deep in reverie. He stayed there far longer than his habit, and when we departed he was silent for a long while. We walked slowly back into the village, crossing through the shadows of the tall trees with glimpses of blue sky, in search of a café or restaurant.

Finally, he spoke, "We have to remember where we come from and where we are going."

I regarded him, whom I loved and admired more than anyone on earth. I was used to his periods of intense introspection, his silences, just as I was used to his rare times of elation.

"When we are born into the family of man, we must always remember our legacy. Although I'm unique, my journey is not. We all share this same journey, and it must serve to unite us."

We ate a nice lunch in a friendly restaurant in an ancient stone building. There was a mixture of locals and visitors. The waitress focused on me, asking about my schooling and desires. A village dog came in and sat at our feet while we ate, perhaps scenting Gribouille. It was a magical moment.

"Did you find a subject for a painting?" I asked finally.

"Yes. I think I did. Not a painting of the church or the village, but a painting of *La Sanch*. Its vital meaning."

Why did I think of this visit? Perhaps my recent incarceration face to face with people who failed to comprehend this idea. Perhaps the war itself. It could also have been my knowledge of my father's Jewish heritage and his empathy with what was happening to Jews throughout Europe, but also people in general.

I never recognized a specific painting of Papa's epiphany of *La Sanch*, but I better understand his unconditional feelings of love and understanding of his fellow man. I'm not sure I can ever rid myself of my own feelings of anger, injustice, and desire for retribution against the people who sent me away, but at least I can take pity on them for their failure to appreciate their shared journey.

32

June 1943

> *The farmer saw it flowering in his fields*
> *The old curé loved it in the clear sky*
> *Flower of hope, flower of happiness*
> *All those who fought for our liberty*
> *Saw it shining at daybreak before their eyes*
> *The three colored flower of France*
> *It flowered everywhere, the flower of return*
> *The return of summer days*
> *For four long years its colors were guarded in our hearts*
> *Blue, white, red*
> *It was truly the flower of our country.*
> « *Fleur de Paris,* » *H. Bourtayre, lyrics M. Vandair*

Vichy replaced May Day with the *Fête du travail et de la concorde sociale* (celebration of labor day and social harmony). Its mean-spirited significance to the coming of spring was not lost on anyone. Bouquets of lily-of-the-valley and dog-rose flowers appeared joyously. Spring announced itself warmer than normal, with fruit trees blossoming early in the plains and the wild flowers running wild in the hills surrounding St. Girons: white asphodel, poppies, yellow Pyrenean lily, purple Turk's cap, and blue iris. The light, warm rains in May melted the snows in the mountains and quickened the streams, with a temperate flourish spreading across the south in mid-May.

Armando wanted to avoid crossing to Spain during the high summer season. He knew of two large groups preparing to head out in mid-June at the full moon and wanted to avoid them. Also the annual movement of sheep and goats into the mountains began about this same time, with herders and their dogs leading large herds for high-altitude summer grazing pastures, and he hoped to avoid them as well.

Gabrielle and Paul had lived with Béatrice for more than two months since the escape. Based on numerous hikes with Armando, Paul felt in his best shape ever. Cared for by Madame Lépinay with her unusual access to products and foodstuffs from her garden and the surrounding farms,

Gabrielle had filled out and no longer experienced periods of doubt and despair. She too felt ready, perhaps to an unrealistic degree, knowing that they had to depart soon. To wait invited disaster, increasing the risk each day of being discovered by the police and of arrest in the high season on the mountain.

Armando never took the arduous hike for granted. On the mountain, weather can change instantly from sunshine to nasty rain squalls and dangerous snow blizzards. Vicious winds can come up without warning. A minimum of four days of hiking, sleeping in primitive conditions, and the high-altitude exertion make for a perilous venture, with eight to ten hours hiking each day or more, depending on the weather and conditions of the route. This ignores the danger of arrest by border guards, German troops, and the local Milice.

"We can't pretend to be anything but what we are," Armando said one evening after dinner. "We are not peasants working our fields or herders with their goats. We will be seen as illegal emigrants, fleeing without authorization. We will be arrested if we are observed by the authorities or worse. We can't pretend to be on an evening stroll, because we will have to carry sufficient supplies and equipment. Traffic along this difficult route is for one reason only: to arrive in Spain. It's not what you are used to, Paul, on the eastern end of the Pyrenees.

"This route is the longest of them all. It's used by the local passeurs because it's what they know best. The passage alone is difficult, exhausting, and dangerous, even ignoring the patrols. Its one advantage is that military and police maintain limited surveillance due to their own discomfort at the difficult terrain and the hostile weather conditions. They cannot post guards in the high mountains, so they depend on interrupting escapees early at the lower elevations. We are ahead of the season, but you can never count on any fixed routine. This will be the Occupant's first summer guarding the border, and we don't know how aggressive he will be. The scenery of the high Pyrenees, you know, is as beautiful as anything in this world, but you will be too concerned with each step, struggling for breath, and too exhausted to appreciate the view. And there is no turning back once we begin."

"We could get a start in the truck," Paul suggested.

"That might save us a day, but the risk of being stopped would be very high. There are police and guard stations at Seix, and they patrol the road from there to St. Girons. Whereas they are lazy on the many arduous paths into Spain, they are active on the easily accessible roads. Are your papers in order?"

"Yes. We have exit visas from France. We have other papers as well for transit, exit, and entrance to Portugal, but we also have Spanish passports for both of us, which I hope will do the trick. My father is Spanish."

On Saturday June 5, we listened to Prime Minister Laval's address concerning the *Chantiers de Jeunesse*, a compulsory civil service of young men formed after the armistice to take the place of military service. It became a tool of the administration. The radio broadcast was initiated by Vichy's rising fear of the growing strength of the Maquis in the central and southern regions.

> Two hundred thousand French men will be needed in Germany…to put an end to injustice and arbitrariness, I call the entire class of 1942 to their duty…this is in response to those who have shirked and failed to report…I want to repeat, we will not allow freeloaders (*défaillants*) to win, and stringent actions will be taken, even against their families…no one will avoid or postpone a duty required of all…

That made it clear the time had come to escape, regardless of the danger. To remain in France was like a hog wallowing in the mud hoping to be overlooked by the farmer at slaughter time.

The last evening before their departure on Monday June 17, Gabrielle and Paul went into the kitchen to thank Madame Lépinay. The kitchen was spotless, and Béatrice seemed to be expecting them.

"Teaming up, eh?"

"We just wanted to thank you for everything," Paul said formally.

Gabrielle threw her arms around the older woman and gave her a bear hug. "You have made all the difference. I would have been lost without you, and we owe you everything. You saved my life." Tears began rolling down Gabrielle's cheeks.

"Now, now. Enough," Béatrice said, tearing up. "You'll be fine. I have a little present for you. Since we wear the same size shoe, I want you to have my leather hiking boots and two pairs of heavy socks. The boots are well worn and should be very comfortable. You'll need them."

"You've given us so much," Gabrielle said, blotting the tears with her sleeve.

"I haven't done much for the cause. A few people passing through, but not like my brother and Armando and you. I just pray it will all end soon. I may even have a husband one day. God bless you two. You have so much to give and look forward to." She hugged Gabrielle again.

Paul stood awkwardly watching the two women. Soon enough, Béatrice was hugging him strongly with bisous. "We'll return to visit," he said "when it's over."

"Please do," she replied, "and bring a few babies. Now you two get to bed. This will be your last comfortable evening for some time. Is everything arranged?"

"Yes," Paul nodded.

"I'll see you off tomorrow morning. Day one is the easiest. I've done it…once, and that was enough. Now to bed."

***

On a cool and misty morning long before sunrise, they crossed over the bridge on the Salat River at the southern extreme of the town. No inhabitants were seen as they walked past several rural houses in the darkness. Dogs barked and roosters crowed, but the three hikers walked on in silence. No cars or trucks. Armando led the way with his indomitable stride, Gabrielle attempted to keep up.

The plan was to arrive at Aunac, a small village about twenty kilometers distant on a gentle ascent from St. Girons to an elevation of seven hundred and fifty meters, well below the snow line, which was currently above twenty-two hundred meters. The entire approach to the Pyrenees had been declared a forbidden zone by the Germans. Their destination was a safe-house outside of Aunac. They avoided all roads, since this zone was the most dangerous in terms of border guards and police.

The water below the iron bridge sloshed and struggled over the winter deposits of branches and other debris caught in the rocks and piers. They stood for a moment watching the water passing rapidly as though their recent lives had been caught up in this troubled flooding waterscape, reflecting the starry sky and the gibbous moon.

Before leaving, Paul had visited his truck. In the clandestine area of the tool box, he took out the revolver that Royo had given him. It was wrapped in a greasy waste cloth. He checked the seven rounds and secreted it in his rucksack. He reviewed his beloved Renault. Together, they had lived through a lifetime of overcoming fear and doing what he felt was right. He left the keys on the front seat, along with a note to Miguel thanking him for his help in freeing Gabrielle and offering the truck for Royo's use, as Miguel saw fit. He had no idea when they would return to France or even if they would. That last night, he had tried to give some money to Béatrice, just for her expenses, but she would not hear of it. He promised himself to return to see her one day for the warmth of her welcome, once free of the future hanging above his head like a sword.

In the predawn morning, Béatrice, in her elegant and revealing white nightgown, had awaited them with a large breakfast: a cheese omelette of real eggs and lardons and fresh coffee and baguettes. How she secured her near-prewar menus was never revealed. She had packed an abundant amount of food for the trip: dry fruit, chocolates, nuts, dry sausages, cured ham, crackers, cookies, lemons, and fresh carrots and celery.

"That's too much to carry," Armando complained.

"I'll carry the bulk of it," Paul intervened, knowing he could never repay her kindnesses.

"Do as I say," was Béatrice's terse, though pleasant reply. "And remember eat small bits frequently, don't procrastinate or ignore your body. This is a Herculean trip."

"Yes, Mother," Paul replied lightheartedly, but so full of meaning to him.

Gabrielle came into the kitchen dressed entirely in men's clothing, from her heavy wool toque, ear muffs, and scarf to her leather boots. She had on an insulated coat and leather gloves.

"You certainly look prepared. How do the boots feel?" Béatrice asked.

"As though I've been wearing them my entire life, thank you." She gave Béatrice a bisou and kissed Paul. "Mon Dieu, such a breakfast," but she sat down and ate with gusto.

Last to appear was Armando, looking ready for the hike in his heavy gear. "We have to move to get out of town long before general reveille."

"Eat and then you can go," Béatrice ordered. "I'm in no mood for banter. I'm losing my favorite people in the world, and I want you all to return soon. Is that clear?"

"Yes," Armando replied, sitting down. "I'll be back in a fortnight."

"*Bon.* Just make sure."

"We'll miss you," Gabrielle said, tearing up. "You've been so welcoming, and what would I have done without you? I hope you'll be able to meet my parents, and I'll see to it that you add another painting to your collection. You will always be dear to me. Thank you for everything."

The real tears came as they departed. Often in stressful moments, people are at their finest. Béatrice could not have done more to welcome them, care for them, bring them both back to health, understanding their situations without explanation, and finally to facilitate their departure. They would never forget Madame Lépinay of St. Girons, wife of the ex-mayor, and she would never forget them.

They soon found themselves on a three-quarter moonlit woodland path under a clear sky, the town receding. The trail was easy, well-traveled, and dry. The path took them into a humid wood, smelling of herbs and grasses, the air redolent of moist freshness and the acrid smell of the box and beech trees. Armando slowed to Gabrielle's gait, which was fine for a relatively easy day's journey. As they gained altitude, they glimpsed from afar the muted lights of the small rural villages of Eycheil and Lacourt along the main road, always within the sound of the barking village dogs. They met no one on the path, as they walked quietly and easily, stopping occasionally to drink from their canteens or take a quick snack. They passed scattered unoccupied huts, failing barns, and deserted makeshift hunters' lodges. Their ascent continued past a soaring *falaise*, or high cliff, pockmarked in the near light with caves and waffle-shaped outcroppings, begging to be searched. They walked on.

They entered an area covered in brambles, overgrown, and difficult to walk through, with huge boulders strewn about as if some giant had torn them from the mountains and scattered them in rage. Once back on a reasonable path, they gently descended past small villages, still sleeping. After crossing a stone bridge, the river valley lead up to the somewhat larger village, Alos. Avoiding the village, they began a steeper climb.

Before the dawn could splash the mountain ranges with crimson hues, they arrived at the Col d'Artigue, the highest point of the day's trek and began a mild descent on a wide trail past several ruined stone barns and then a steeper descent leading to a rest stop.

"Here we can see our final destination," Armando said, waking them from their reverie, concentrating on the path and the near obstacles. The magnificent view suddenly registered. The dark sky overflowed with millions of stars, extending into the heavens, and the trail of Hera's Milky Way circled the dome like a medieval crown of baby's breath flowers. To the west, the black silhouette of a high peak could be seen partially blocking the pyrotechnical sky.

"You can see the highest peak, Mont Valier. On the north side is a v-shaped cleft called the Col de Craberous at about twenty-three hundred meters." He let them contemplate the dark image in the dawning sky. "We will pass that col in two days' time."

Gabrielle and Paul viewed the distant scene with more self-interest, both arriving at the same conclusion. This would be impossible. The distant and foreboding cascades of dark mountains and then, the highest of them all, Mont Valier.

"That's a challenge," Paul finally said in understatement.

"*A poc a poc, eh?*" Armando smiled, using the Catalan, chewing on a sausage.

"Yes," Gabrielle reminded herself, feeling abruptly full of misgivings after a gentle hike, "little by little." She liked that and shook her head in wonder and took a deep breath. Her mind was full of doubts: doubts of her return to full health. One thing she knew, this challenge meant much more than the challenge of a difficult hike for her; it meant returning to the world of the living.

After a short break, they began descending to the Col d'Escots. As they walked, the sky turned crimson, the lights reflected on the snowy peaks. Then a slight descent, crossing the road from Seix, a larger village, careful not to be observed since this served as the center of the border control. They proceeded on a gentle climb of four kilometers to the darkly wooded hamlet of Aunac with widely scattered homes and barns.

Avoiding the village, they found the safe-house before noon at a small farm that Armando knew well. Gabrielle was exhausted, but Paul and Armando were feeling good. They all rested in a barn, only slightly warmer than the exterior temperature, but their heavy clothing and the hay made for a comfortable afternoon and evening.

"You did well today," Armando complimented Gabrielle. "Tomorrow will be a little harder, and then, well, we'll take it day by day."

"How do you feel?" Paul asked Gabrielle.

"Fine. Béatrice gave me some extra socks and salve."

"We should all remove our boots and socks to allow them to dry out and our feet to recover. We've made it past the most populated area with the highest probability of being stopped. Now, we just have to depend on our bodies to get us through. From this point on, it's unlikely we'll meet any patrols."

"Did you expect to meet any?" Paul asked.

"No. Not really. I've never had any trouble, and it's early, but with the Occupant here since November, things are tightening up. The Germans are asleep, or possibly not here yet, and the Gendarmes don't know the region well, particularly the mountains. We'll be okay."

"I only had one close call," Paul remembered. "I took this man over the hill hidden in the truck. After an unexpected stop by the border guard on the roadway, I could see that he was up to no good. So I left him in the forest. I know he was trying to trap me. The border guards never showed much interest in me. Mostly, I knew them and supplied them with charcoal. When the Germans arrived, everything changed, but that was near the end of my career. Now I'm the 'package,' and, frankly, I'm glad to be ignorant of the risks."

"This may be the most demanding crossing, but the least risky."

"That's good to know," Gabrielle said. "Let's get some rest." She was exhausted, but at the same time knew she was moving in a direction that spelled freedom. "Otherwise you'll have to carry me. *Bon repos*."

They all rested well after eight hours hiking, knowing that the most difficult lay ahead.

***

Early the next day, again long before sunrise, they begin day two of their march. After snacking, they leave the chilly barn and return to the trail, wishing for sunlight. During their first day, they had glimpsed only a few locals, who ignored the small party. They feel comfortable that they are alone on this track.

"Today," Armando announces, "only ten kilometers or so, a short day. We'll climb to about fifteen hundred meters, well below the snowline, a steady climb. Enough to get our pulses beating. Our goal will be the Cabane de Subéra, a mountain refuge used by shepherds during the summer months. We'll rest at the Fontaine de la Gore, a small waterfall near our final altitude. It's a couple of hours. Then a steeper climb near the Col de Soularil toward our final destination."

"You know," Paul says, "in our Pyrenees, we pass normally in the evening or night. Not in daylight."

"You'll understand why that's not possible the next two days. Just too dangerous. Today, we're leaving all villages and signs of habitation behind and will travel in the daylight after a few hours." Armando takes his lead position, moving forward.

Paul looks about as he assumes the pace. He can make out the majesty of the mountains in the dawn, but also their expanse in all directions, always with the highest peaks ahead. Too much time in this trek is wasted on worrying about the next step, the next corner, the next climb, and not enough on experiencing the natural expanses: a banquet for the eyes. Under any other circumstances, this would be a magnificent hike with views of the river plain behind and of the mountains ahead.

Gabrielle is silent, making her way studiously, uncomplaining, a darkly moving shade against the sky and mountains.

"What are you thinking about?" he asks her. They lag a bit behind with Paul following.

"I don't know. Did you expect all this? All that's happened?"

"How could I?" he laughs ironically.

"It's like we have become the exiles we used to talk about. Exiles from our own country. I know it happens, but I never thought it would happen to us."

"On my truck," Paul replies, "the rearview mirror is tiny in comparison to the windshield and side windows. The view forward is far larger and all-encompassing and welcoming."

"I know. I guess I love that about you. But the rearview mirrors are useful, no?"

"Yes, but not to be studied too intensely."

"I'll try to look forward."

After a half hour they begin a steeper ascent, walking through a dense beech forest, with a jungle of undergrowth, brambles, and low bushes slowing their pace. They reach the tiny waterfall and rest alongside the path in an open area outside the dense wood of beech trees, breathing heavily, watching the light begin to caress the mountains. The path forward remains in obscurity.

"How are you doing?" Armando asks Gabrielle. She's lying back in the grass looking up into the sky.

"Okay."

"Just okay?"

"I'm fine," she finally replies testily.

They munch on nuts and dried fruit.

"Let's go," Armando announces.

They struggle up and continue climbing in the growing light, moving slowly, through alternating beech stands with undergrowth obscuring the path and open areas. The path begins to level out after an hour, and the walking is easier. After two more hours, and several rest stops, they cross another path leading to the Col de Soularil, but they keep walking to the southwest. Full sunlight is now finding its way among the dense trees, with the sun burning off the mist and making the trail easier to navigate.

"About two kilometers to go," Armando says.

They're beginning to flag, but they continue walking, happy to be on a level track with increased visibility and good weather, not too cold in the sunlight. It's harder going in the thick woods, avoiding the growth of brambles making the path more difficult, particularly in the low light.

"Wait a minute," Paul says quickly, holding his hand in the air. "Wait."

Ahead, Armando stops and turns.

"Someone behind us."

"What? How do you know?"

"I heard some talking. Let's get off the path and make sure."

"Up ahead." Armando points to a ravine at a sharp turn in the path with brush and trees.

At the next jog in the path in a clear area, they turn off into a copse of beech trees slightly above the track. From their secluded site, they can glimpse the road directly below. The path is now in full sun. They wait expectantly in the cool shade. They drink and a take a bit of sausage and vegetables. They wait. After a few minutes, they see two locals and a dog walking along, relaxed and unhurried. They watch them pass below on the track.

"Hunters," Armando says.

"Not so sure," Paul replies. "Look how they're dressed. Too neat and not outfitted for the cold. They're wearing bérets, for God's sake. Hunting? That dog's a herder, not a hunting dog. They have a rifle. That doesn't bother you?"

"It does. I just don't know what to make of it. They don't look dangerous."

"I think we should huddle here for a while," Paul says. "See if they return or are searching for something...like us, for instance."

They settle down, eat a little more, rest, but the men do not return. After an hour, Armando becomes restless.

"Let's move," he suggests."You might be right. They're herders returning to their flock. It's early in the season, but there's plenty of forage."

"They're not herders. Not dressed for it. And they're too old. Let's follow them carefully."

They descend to the track and begin walking. All of a sudden, the splendor of the mountains turns into an agonizing march, watching constantly the next step, listening, anticipating the next turn in the path. The sun is falling on their backs and warming. They sweat in their heavy clothing. After an hour without seeing or hearing the two men, they are within a couple of kilometers of the refuge of Subéra.

Hunkering down off the path, they rest and have a bite to eat. At this height, they have a wide view to the east and the receding high Pyrenees, thousands of meters above them.

"What do you think?" Armando asks.

"I think they were following us. They must have seen us in the village where we spent the night. They've lost us for the moment, but they know there is only one track and which direction we're headed."

"We can wait here a while." Armando says, somewhat frustrated. "They're not going to Spain. That's for sure. They have to return."

Silently, Gabrielle watches Armando, who may be twenty, a smart young man but definitely not prepared for adversity. A product of his father, an idealist with the right ideas, not ready for a fight, or even to allow it into his head.

"They're not Milice clearly," Paul says. "Just a couple of village rustics. Possibly operating at the orders of someone in the village. No one is expecting anyone on the trail at this time of year. It's too early, so they send out a couple of locals to patrol."

They wait, and Gabrielle rests. She listens to the continuing discussion, but somehow is removed, skeptical of the explanations. Too much of stark reality in her recent past, but at the same time she remembers the camp and the guards and the administrators. She says nothing. The sun is warm, and only a gentle wind reminds them of the capricious nature of these mountains.

Finally, after a half an hour or so Armando says, "Let's move. Let me lead by about a minute, then you follow. The path is clear, and the refuge is close. We don't know what to expect. They may be waiting." He takes off.

The path zigs and zags, so they are unable to see far ahead. There is no relaxing their anticipation though, with each turn in the track possibly leading them to a confrontation with the two men. Paul walks behind Gabrielle, who at this point is moving more slowly, although they remain on level ground, still not talking. He watches her anxiously, noting the effort she is making. He loves the fact that she is such a fighter, so determined to play her role, even though she is far from recovered. Ahead he catches a quick glimpse of Armando counting his steps, aware that he may be leading them into a trap. Paul is gratified to see him taking the lead, giving them some flexibility should there be a problem. The only sounds are the wind in the occasional tree and the shuffling of their boots, step by step, as they steadily, monotonously march.

After fifteen minutes or so, they come to a turn and see across a wide crevasse a barbed wire barrier of concertina wire blocking the road. Armando warns them back. They lose sight of him as he rounds the bend, but they suddenly hear barking.

The hike abruptly transforms from a physical effort into a far more sinister endeavor with perilous uncertainty.

"Let's back up," Paul says. Gabrielle follows him to a rock cache just above the trail. "Wait here. I'll check on Armando."

Gabrielle watches him as he reaches into his rucksack and pulls out a revolver that she had not noticed before. Her heart begins beating rapidly and her breath comes in spurts as she realizes the extent of the danger.

"I got this from the Maquis who helped liberate you. I never needed it, and forgot it was in the pack until we left St. Girons." He hands it to her.

Startled, she pushes it away. "What would I do with that?"

"Just to protect yourself and warn us if anyone comes...in either direction. I don't take those men too seriously, but you never know."

She looks at the revolver and then Paul. "That's the first thing you've said...and Armando too...that I agree with. Evil does not come with a mask announcing itself. But Paul, I know nothing about guns. Papa detested them.

Felt they only hurt people. Never had one in the house. I don't think I could use it."

"I know, but this can help all of us." Paul takes it off safety and hands it to her again. "Just use it as a signal. You can pull the trigger, can't you."

Gabrielle stops herself. "Of course I can. I just don't know how that would help."

"Just trust me. The gun can be fired by the trigger, or if it is too difficult, by pulling back the hammer. These men are not out for a stroll, but they are untrained…not Milice."

"Okay." She nods, distrusting the value of the gun, but hesitantly accepts the heavy, cold weapon and lays it on her lap like a sharp knife to be avoided.

"If someone comes along the trail in either direction, just fire a warning shot in the air. That's all. Okay?"

"Okay," she says reluctantly.

***

Paul carefully descends the ten meters to the trail. She hears his receding footsteps and the continuing occasional barks of the dog on the other side of the curve in the trail. She can't make out the sound of any voices.

Barely fifty meters from where he leaves Gabrielle, Paul comes around a turn and sees Armando sitting on the ground with the two men standing over him, threatening him with the rifle. They see Paul, and the dog begins barking loudly again, the sound echoing off the hillside. An older man, perhaps in his sixties, with the rifle turns and directs it toward Paul and waves him to approach. Strangely, Paul has no fear of them, assessing who they are, only the familiar pain of fear in his stomach.

"*¿El que està passant aquí,*" he asks casually in Catalan, approaching the two men. They're short and overweight. Too many cigarettes, too much wine, and not enough hard work. The man holding the rifle, which turns out to be an old small-gauge, single-barrel bird gun, looks nervous.

"What are you doing here?" the younger man counters.

"What do you think? We're crossing the mountains into Spain. You have a problem with that, *Senyor?*"

"You're a foreigner?"

"No *Senyor*. Catalan, French-born. What are you doing here?"

"We're Milice guards."

"You don't look it," Paul says affably, brazenly standing a few meters from the man, "There's no need for the rifle. We're not enemies. *Bon*, we're all on the same side, no?" He pauses never looking away from the man's dark set eyes, nervously twitching. "If you continue this, you will regret it."

"Eh? You don't know who we are."

"I don't need to. I asked you to lower that musket," Paul repeats strongly.

The older man makes an unconscious movement backward, apprehensively, but keeps his rifle pointed at Paul.

"Let me be clear," Paul says, feeling master of this confrontation. "Either you lower that or you will be killed. No second warning." He glances at Armando, who stares at him in shocked disbelief at what he's hearing.

The man, taken aback, is clearly nervous, glancing over Paul's shoulder. He knows there's a third person.

"I don't want to hurt you," Paul says, but the man's doubt is apparent. "Last chance. Put the rifle down."

Paul approaches the man, who mechanically lowers the barrel.

"*Eh, que fots, Joan?*" the younger man demands loudly, jumping in front of them to grab the rifle from his companion's hands. The dog begins barking again. He raises the rifle, cocks the single hammer. "I will kill you. Get down with your friend."

For the first time, Paul is surprised, as he was the time his package in the mountains surprised him by demanding to be released from the tool compartment. He sees the hatred in this man's eyes, less nervous, more intense. He looks at Armando and then chooses to sit next to him, not surrendering.

***

Gabrielle waits nervously. The afternoon is rapidly departing, and she pulls her jacket above her neck and throws a scarf around her neck. A cold breeze begins to chill, as the sun departs behind the high mountains. She waits. Her mind wanders to the Camp du Vernet, and she remembers her vulnerability and impotence. She promised herself that if she ever gained her freedom all would change. She would not allow herself to be made helpless, dependent, powerless. Even with the birth of her child. Tears come to her eyes, even now, after so much, but also an anger at herself, allowing herself to be vulnerable. Even at the Nouvelle Galeries. Even at school.

Without planning, she shrugs off her backpack and stands. Climbing down to the trail, she carries the revolver in her right hand carefully avoiding the trigger. On the trail she listens for sounds from the men, but hears nothing. Keeping close to the hill-side of the trail, she makes her way toward where she spied the concertina wire crossing the track.

It's dusky. She now sees the barbed wire on one side of the trail and slows, realizing the turn will reveal them soon enough. As she rounds the curve, she ducks and hugs the rock face. She hears the men. She waits behind an outcropping.

"What are you doing here?" she hears Paul ask.

"We're keeping fugitives from escaping."

"Do we look like fugitives?"

"No, *Senyor*," the other says.

"Miliciens?" Paul asks. "You getting paid?"

"We live near the trail…"

"Shut up," another voice says. "Where's that woman?"

"She'll be here," Paul says.

Gabrielle lowers herself onto the ground and begins to snake her way along the rocky wall. As she advances the scene becomes clearer. She sees Paul and Armando sitting on the side of the trail being interrogated by the two men, their profiles to her. She crawls closer, a low ledge somewhat hiding her. She places the revolver in front of her with a clear view of the two men, about ten meters distant.

"You'll never take us back," Paul says.

For a moment there is silence. The two locals considering their situation and how much to believe.

Gabrielle aims the gun at the younger man with the rifle. Should she try to kill him? Her finger rests on the trigger and her other hand grasps the side of the revolver resting on the ground. She aims with her arms outstretched.

She has a clear view of the men. A feeling of anger wells up in her mind. Should she kill him? She has seen so much death. Every day. Every morning. She was given no quarter. They attempted to kill her. She is convinced. She will fight for her freedom. Never to return. She loves Paul and will do anything for him, just as he did for her. Slowly her finger tightens on the trigger, aiming at the man with the rifle. The trigger will not move. She tries as hard as she can, but she cannot pull the trigger. She remembers and with both thumbs, pulls the hammer back into position. Again, she takes aim at the younger man, touches the trigger and to her surprise the gun explodes, the force and sound of the explosion stunning her, kicking the barrel back.

The men are totally startled as the shot rings through the crevasse. The two locals duck and turn toward the sound. Paul, the first to understand, jumps to his feet and grabs the rifle. The younger man is unhurt, but immobile. Paul angrily throws the rifle far into the brush down the hillside. At that, the dog attacks him, but Paul catches him with a kick under his jaw that sends him head over heals. Both of the locals remain stunned. The dog scampers off, whimpering in pain. Armando stands to confront the locals.

Gabrielle stands with the gun in her hand and approaches.

Paul quickly comes to her, carefully taking the gun from her, and hugs her as he never has before. Her eyes are full of tears.

"I wanted to kill them."

"I know. But you did enough."

"I wanted to kill them," she repeats and begins crying.

"That's okay. At the very least they would have sent us to internment camps. You saved us."

"Did you know?" she asks seriously, still in his arms.

"Let's just say I was hoping it would not come to this. I'm so proud of you." He turns to the locals, still shocked, and in Catalan says. "Now, take down the barbed wire,"

The two locals look at him in disbelief, but slowly climb the hillside to release the wire being held in place by a stump.

"I'm so proud of you," Paul repeats with his arms still wrapped around her.

"You saved us," Armando says hugging them both. "You saved us, Gabrielle. I'll never forget."

The locals finally disconnect the wire, allowing it to collapse on itself, with the contraction sending the entire roll spinning off the road over the side of the hill.

"The Milice won't like this," the younger local swears when they return to the trail.

"Listen," Paul says. "We could kill you right now with impunity, but I'm not going to. After this filthy war ends, I'm coming back. My Maquis friends don't take kindly to the Milice. So I'm depending on you to be less helpful in the future. Understood?"

"Yea." the older begrudges. The younger man is silent. Paul walks directly into his face. "You don't believe me?"

"We're just farmers."

"Then act like it. Make up some story for your health and stay out of it."

"Okay, agreed. But what about my rifle."

"You can return tomorrow and collect it. Now, go home."

The two men amble off, dismayed and downcast, back along the trail, followed by their woeful dog. Not talking; they do not turn around.

Gabrielle looks at Paul and then back at Armando. "I was worried," she says honestly.

"So were we," Paul replies, both laughing with relief.

***

They continue their trek, soon arriving at the stone refuge of Subéra, built against a large rock cliff, soaring above the small building. It's after noon; their destination achieved on day two. They settle down in the refuge, collect debris from the surrounding hills, and build a fire outside to warm up.

In the afternoon, they hear the noisy chorus of tingling bells, baaing, mehing, and bleating of sheep and barking of dogs. They watch as a large herd of sheep enters the clearing with two dogs keeping them together. Two herders follow. The sheep are herded into a pasture near the refuge with plenty of grass, since they appear to be the first herd of the season. Paul loads the fire with more kindling from the woods and welcomes the herders.

"*Hola.*"

They shake hands with the young herders, both shyly friendly, one a talkative dark-skinned Catalan, the other, a Spaniard, who never says a word. They settle down near the fire once the sheep are grazing and the dogs on duty.

"Headed for Spain?" The Catalan asks.

"Yes," Armando says.

"Shouldn't be too bad. Less snow this winter. That's why we're out early: plenty of grass and herbs." He's bright-eyed, hirsute with a heavy beard, already looking like he's been in the mountains all summer.

"Did you meet some men on their way out?" Paul asks.

"Yes. They're from Aunac. We know them. See them on the trail sometimes." He stopped himself.

"They tried to detain us," Paul said.

"Yea. The Milice think they own the road. They rob people, and this winter they killed a man at the refuge on the down slope from Col de Soularil. With a larger group, they wouldn't have stopped you. They act like hedgehogs: they look cute, but they're cannibals and dangerous. This summer will be interesting."

"Yeah?"

"You're past the worst. The police never come this far, but we don't know about the Boches. Would you like some fresh cheese?"

"Sure, we have some fruit and sausages."

The evening is enjoyable, talking with the herders around a warm fire. They know the mountain trail and offer advice on the trail and conditions. During the night, the refuge provides protection from the wind and cold. They all bundle up and share the space with the herders. They decide to leave at sunrise tomorrow, feeling out of the reach of any patrols or guards, seeking a good night's rest. Besides, Armando explains, the next day will be tougher going, and they need the light to navigate safely. Paul finds Gabrielle's hand and holds it until they fall asleep.

***

The night at the Subéra refuge passes unbearably slowly, as we waited for dawn, sleeping fitfully, sharing a single blanket, while the herders sleep soundly. They finally give up on sleep, and after snacking they begin immediately walking uphill in the near-dawn light, for several kilometers, before the longest, steepest climb of the journey: about three kilometers of torturous ascent. Day three will take all day, thirteen kilometers, and possibly longer.

They walk through another beech forest, crossing a slope of scree, where small, loose pebbles constantly fall from the hillsides and make each step difficult and dangerous. The sky is full of birds of prey. They see buzzards, vultures, kites, and an eagle soaring at higher altitudes. Wild azaleas grow under the trees and are blooming in reds and pinks. All along the way are signs of *sanglier*, the wild boars that forage nocturnally, digging up the soft soil searching for bulbs, roots, mushrooms after a downpour, as well as small animals, worms, and insects. Grasshoppers proliferate along the way, jumping across the road, hitting them, and frightening Gabrielle. A stable chorus of birdcalls and insects and wind accompanies them, as the sun slowly rises.

The steep ascent slows them. They are forced to rest often to catch their breath, their hearts thumping in their chests. Armando demonstrates the rest step. With each step forward, you rest your weight on the forward leg, and then bring your other leg forward and rest on it. Each step is a rest in itself. But nothing works to make the climb easier. They encounter spotty snow on the track, solid drifts in the heights above them, but now also on the hillsides and in ditches and ravines. The temperature drops as they climb higher.

For the first time, Gabrielle is winded. They have to stop frequently for her to regain her breath, but she never complains.

"I'm sorry I'm such a drag," she says.

"You're not a drag," Paul says, taking her in his arms. He too is breathing hard. "We just have to take it slowly. No rush."

"Keep in mind," Armando says, "we're halfway there, halfway to Spain.

"Only halfway," Paul groans. "God, I've been walking forever."

After three hours of progress, half of the time spent resting, particularly as they approach the saddle of Col de Craberous. The sky has clouded over, and the sun peeks through only occasionally. It's colder then ever, and they find themselves marching through a coating of snow remaining along the track, slowing them down further. By the time they reach Craberous, they are walking in several centimeters of sloppy snow, wet and muddy, and the path has become crusty and watery in spots. Snow melts cross the road. The constant wind blows light snowfall in their faces. The sun has disappeared. They rest in a sheltered area out of the swirling wind and snow, but it's cold, and moving is preferable. They begin to eat the chocolates and sweets. Thank God for Béatrice; she is still helping them along.

The entire morning, they have been walking around the margin of the snow-covered Pic de Lampau at twenty-five hundred meters. After a long rest and snacks, they consider the conditions.

"I think we should put on the crampons, just to be safe," Armando suggests. "It's not too deep, but the snow can hide ice, and we will be crossing some deep gullies covered in snow drifts, which mask what is happening beneath. Also, we have ice picks if the ice on the northern slopes becomes more difficult and slippery."

"I'm getting scared I can't make it," Gabrielle admits for the first time.

"Gabrielle," Armando says, "I shouldn't have mentioned our location. Just keep placing one foot before the other. You'll make it. Don't worry about how much more we have left. Okay?"

"I'm not sure."

"We've just completed the most difficult ascent. You can do it, and we will help."

Paul takes Gabrielle's hand and holds tight. He understands her feelings, since he feels the same. It seems impossible. The conditions seem to be getting worse, combining to make every step hazardous. "I feel exactly as you do. We're in this together. Don't worry. It's just like walking on Canigou."

She glances at him, but doesn't smile. "Yes, Canigou during the worst storm of the season."

He knows how hard this is for her. They are not all starting from the same point: she has been climbing her own mountain each day before this trek all by herself.

They fix their crampons and begin a dizzying descent. The weak, obscured sun is high in the sky, and they face their ultimate destination to the south, Mont Valier, the highest landmark, straddling the border of France and Spain. To the east is a panorama of peaks, ridges, and steep ravines, all bathed in snow, and valleys smothered in smooth planes of clouds. It's become a white world. All greenery has disappeared. The stony, rocky terrain is covered in starkly white snow.

The steep descent is only about a kilometer, but it's worse than the climb. Their knees begin to ache. They step carefully to avoid falling or sliding down the steep slope the path crosses. The route is covered in snow, hiding more scree, with rivulets crossing the path, and iced puddles.

"Be careful not to stamp your legs as you descend, and watch your feet," Armando warns. "Try to land each step gently, otherwise by tomorrow you'll really feel the pain. Your knees will be worthless."

After the descent, the route levels off, and they make their way across the down-slope with a sheer drop-off to their right. They can see several large ice lakes far below covered in a smooth snow blanket. After two hours, they begin another climb. This one to the Col de Pécouch at about twenty-five hundred meters. They are once again climbing steeply in a light snow covering. The pain of descent is forgotten. Step by step, they climb up the steep incline, crossing frozen areas and gullies, breathing hard. They rest frequently, advancing slowly. Time has slowed to a crawl. The continuing light snow has soaked them, and their extremities are wet and freezing. Suddenly, a new hazard. The perilous terrain is frightening. Narrow ledges on the edges of dizzying drop-offs. Wide snow gullies require ice picks to avoid slipping. Also, they are visually impaired, with ice forming on their eyelashes and the constant snowfall. They are silent, their facial muscles frozen, even with scarves entirely covering their faces. The snow gusts continue.

They pass a large frozen lake covered in deep snow, but they are too focused on each step to acknowledge the scenery. The sun has left them entirely, and it's freezing. As they continue, they stop frequently to recover their breath and give their legs a rest. They are focused on themselves, on the track, and on the dangerous slopes. Everything at this altitude is covered under a solid white blanket. Their muscles are aching at each movement. The diffuse daylight slowly fades. Fortunately, the snow on the track is not deep. The ice-covered puddles have mostly melted during the hours of sunlight. The track remains visible, but it's wet and muddy, soaking their shoes and lower trouser legs. The wind continues to swirl, full of ice particles, reducing visibility and covering every centimeter of their bodies. They have become a part of this white world. They all focus silently on taking one step after another, carefully placing their feet, counting their progress on the fingers in their minds. The terrain passes interminably, meter by meter.

In the late afternoon, they reach the Col de Pécouch, the highest altitude of their journey and huddle together for a rest stop without any shelter. The light, icy snow continues, with the wind driving it against them. They are literally freezing, drenched through all the layers of their clothing. The trek has been a steep saddleback: a long, difficult ascent to a peak, then down to lower elevation, then up again, finally leading to another steep descent.

Thoughts of giving up, quitting, getting out of the weather enter their heads. Their passage has turned real, distressing, painful, making them wretched. They cannot talk. To quit would be deadly. Gabrielle is completely covered; only her eyes show through the wrapped scarf. Melting snow drips from her, like a snowman. They are all miserable snowmen lost in a horizontal blizzard. They have to keep moving, eking out slow progress, one step by one step.

"Only a few kilometers remain, downhill," Armando calls out, barely able to speak with frozen lips and cheeks and the constant wind. "Stone refuge at snow level."

No response. Armando glances at his partners, but they are too tired, their heads down to ward off the snow and water, and too cold to respond. They are concentrating on placing their crampons for best advantage, fearing a slip into deeper snow or into a deep gully. They stare into the earth, forcing themselves to eat some nuts and dried fruit. Ironically, they drink water thirstily. They are too tired, too wet, too cold to stop for long. Managing to struggle on, they begin the detestable descent once again. Each step takes them to a lower elevation, which is a gift, barely appreciated but accepted.

They finally arrive at the refuge of Estagnous in the dark, almost totally obscured. It's been an entire day of walking, twelve hours or more. Armando is marvelous at finding the refuge. They could be wandering around in search of it for hours in the freezing and wet snow and lack of visibility. A step farther and they would have frozen. The sky is covered. An eddy of fog surrounds them, no moon or stars, and no reflected light: total darkness. The snow is spotty and wet, but the lower elevation feels a bit better. They are cold, soaking stuffed dolls, too tired to move. Their minds are empty of all thought save warmth.

The refuge is tiny, nothing but four stone walls and a wood beam roof. It was recently rebuilt as a refuge for travelers on this hazardous section of the trail. There are no amenities, neither fireplace nor wood. At least there is a low shack with a wooden door that shelters them from the wind. They crawl in and flop down on the hardpan floor, cover themselves as best they can with the single blanket. They snuggle together, snacking under cover, waiting for the blood to begin recirculating through their bodies. They have to choose between remaining wet or freezing. The wet clothes have taken on some heat from their bodies and the blanket. They cower in their wet outer garments, praying for relief.

"Why do you do it?" Gabrielle asks Armando, shivering without respite. She is lying in Paul's arms, their bodies providing a modicum of heat.

"I don't, normally, at this time of year. Mountains are unforgiving." He too is worn out. "Take your shoes off so they can at least partially dry out."

"When your father suggested his son as a passeur," Paul says, shivering, "I never imagined the trek would be this difficult, entailing this much pain. As a kid, we used to play in the Albère Mountains, but they are foothills in comparison to this and warm." He sits up and begins beating his left calf. "My leg is cramping. I'm totally wiped out. I can't feel my extremities. And Gabrielle. I'm so proud of you." She doesn't reply, her head hidden beneath the blanket still wrapped in the wet scarf and cap. "This is torture. I don't ever want to see another mountain in my life. I'm finished. It sounds nice, mountaineering, intriguing, exciting, crossing the Pyrenees. All lies. All lies."

"Shut up, Paul," Gabrielle grumbles from beneath the blanket. "You're making it worse." They begin laughing hysterically.

"What are we doing here? We could be in France. I could be in the STO, working in some beautiful earthly paradise in Germany. You could be in Buchenwald or Auschwitz, enjoying yourself. And Armando could be fighting it out with the Milice. We should have thought harder about this little hike across the Pyrenees."

"You're right, Paul," Armando says. "It could be worse. I learned a lot today. Thanks."

They realize their bodies are beginning to warm up, and food tastes good, and the next night might possibly be better than the last, and tomorrow might be better than today. The only undeniable disaster in life is failure of hope, the fuel motivating the soul.

***

We woke late in the darkness of the Estagnous refuge, our last night on the mountain, beginning day four. We felt better, having been able to sleep uncomfortably for hours, totally exhausted. The small enclosed room had been a true refuge, and without it, we would have frozen. A wet night in the cold, freezing air would have killed us, and I knew that I had little remaining in my frozen body. I also knew I was going to make this trek. My love for Paul fortified me, while he continued to amaze me. My love of my parents and my country kept me going as well, and I knew I had to make it. Although I never imagined so much agony.

I struggled into my less wet socks from the day before and pulled on my frozen shoes and tightened them with the frozen leather shoestrings. My scarf was still damp, but I had no substitute, and the wool cap was not much better. When I exited the refuge, I could barely see. My eyes were shocked by the intense luminosity. Slowly, they adjusted to the brightly lit scene that only God could have imagined. The fog had lifted, and the snow and wind had died down overnight. The morning light was partially blocked by Mont

Valier to the east, reflected by the mountains that surrounded us. The sky was clear blue. Spotty snow surrounded the refuge and covered the rocky terrain, yet small areas of green announced the appearance of spring in this world of white. Before us lay range after range of mountains, stretching out far into the horizon to the south. Directly below lay a thick carpet of clouds covering the valleys and canyons between monstrous peaks poking through. I looked down on all this like a Medieval angel observing earth from heaven. It seemed as if you could walk on the white carpet from one precipice to the next.

I was still thoroughly damp. My headgear had dried to an extent, but my coat and pants remained damp. My jacket as well was wet, but it had managed to keep my heavy wool shirt and long johns relatively dry. I felt better, seeing that there might be some sun today. I had no idea of what was next on our painful journey.

Paul joined me. He looked like I felt, but was cheerful, no dryer than I was. For a moment we stood together, his arms around me, looking out into this stationary sea of monstrous fixed white clouds blanketing the rocks below. We were all that existed on this peak, alone, away from all, forgotten. No sound disturbed us, no birds above and no motion of any kind. A gentle breeze rose from below.

"Feeling better?"

"I am. I think I can make it. I had my doubts yesterday. Now I think it may be possible."

"We all had our doubts. I'm in awe of you, Gabrielle."

Such delicious words at an altitude unfit for man. I hugged him and held on.

Armando was last to rise and joined us.

"Pretty amazing," he said, squinting.

"Yes." I could only say yes. "Yes, it truly is."

"This may partially answer your question, Gabrielle, on why I do this."

"After last night, I doubt that this extraordinary seascape has anything to do with it."

"Now, Gabrielle…"

Armando looked at her half-amused.

We filled our canteens in a swift rivulet and set off after snacking. We still had plenty of provisions, but all our packs felt lighter and our hearts fuller.

"We'll move more rapidly today. We've only one steep ascent remaining. We should be in the village of Isil before sundown. That's in Spain."

From Estagnous, we descended alongside a shallow stream. We crossed it to a high rock cliff too steep to retain snow and a narrow path with plenty of small scree. The path bordered a large oblong frozen lake. After a while, we began an arduous climb toward the final pass at twenty-five hundred meters, the Col de Claouère. This climb turned out to be the worst ascent of all. I always try to be the optimist. I inherited that from my mother. I thought yesterday was impossible, but this day was worse. It was the most painful and difficult climb of the journey. It was not the highest. That was the Col de Pécouch. I can't describe the agony of each step. My joints burned. The cold and dampness continued. The punishment of our minds might have been the worst, knowing that to die might be preferable to continuing this torture. Our legs were rotten. The snow became deeper as we climbed, making every step agonizing, forcing us to return to crampons and for the first time, a tether rope holding us together for safety. Our shoes had not dried out, and our socks and shoes and pants rapidly filled with cold water. We had to cross a narrow rock chimney near the top with a frightening drop on the left side. I tried not to look. I took each painful step, ignoring the potentially deadly drop, my ice pick in my right hand.

We crossed a large valley: a glacier, Armando said, but it looked pretty much like the rest of the snow-covered mountains, and our minds focused once again on each step, ensuring our crampons held onto the hard-packed snow and ice. Time slowed to a near stop once again. The nightmare regenerated. Armando was enthusiastic about the clear skies and sun, though tepid. It could have been far worse, he said. I didn't believe him. We had no protection for our eyes from the intensity of the light. I shielded my eyes as well as I could without endangering my climbing. The path was filled with loose rocks buried under the snow, once again making each step a trial. A mistake could result in a fall, a twisted ankle, or a deathly slide down an alleyway or a wide gutter. We moved slowly, resting often, rest-stepping the higher grades. I have never experienced such a test of every facet of my body and mind. I hate even to think about it.

We reached the Col de Claouère at midday after an interminable, difficult, dangerous ascent, more resting than hiking. Every bone, every muscle in my body ached. My breath came in spurts, my heart beating rapidly, sounding in my ears as though through a loudspeaker. We camped on the Spanish side of the col, snacking and looking out into the expanse. It was cold, and snow covered everything. The wind was stronger and colder, but from this knife-blade col everything before our eyes was Spain.

We struggled down a precipitous descent, our last painful rocky descent, removing our crampons and rope. We crossed stretches of scree, occasionally setting off small avalanches of loose pebbles. We traversed gullies of hard-packed snow, once again requiring crampons. We remained on the edge of the universe. Slipping meant sure death, but for the first time, each step became firmer, drier, and warmer.

Armando had to rouse us physically, tugging us to our feet, urging us forward. We are near the end. Our minds could not believe him. We came to a large unfrozen lake and continued the descent, perhaps three hours of careful walking in all. At midday, we came to the intersection where two rivers joined, becoming the Noguera Pallaresa. The track followed the swiftly flowing river into the valley d'Aneu, cascading down the hillside beside us. Ahead of us, we could see the dry plains of the valley without snow. Soon, the track took on a gentler descent, and the river flattened out. We began seeing signs of life: domestic animals, fields, even farmers. Colors surrounded us: green grass, tiny ivory wildflowers, leafing trees, frothy water, azure sky. Unthreatening bubble clouds drifted lazily among the mountains. We had entered a new world, a magnificent panoply bursting with vibrant hues, welcoming and embracing us.

We left the track and began walking on country roads with rut marks from wagons and animal detritus. Suddenly, we felt a second wind. The temperature was warmer, and the snow had disappeared. We saw cows comfortably grazing. Each step seemed to buttress us, giving us back some of our wasted strength, slowly drying us out.

We stopped for a rest, and I hugged Paul.

"We've made it, haven't we."

"Yes. I think we have."

"We're in Spain. They speak Spanish here."

"Right. What's your point?"

"We're free."

"You're right, at least for the moment."

"Always the optimist."

We both hugged Armando, who shyly allowed us.

"Still some walking left," he cautioned, "but the worst is long behind us. History. Only a memory. You made it."

"Do I look as bad as you?" I asked Paul.

"Far worse."

"Thanks."

The increased temperature and gentler slope permitted us to quicken our pace. We felt tired but glad to be away from the snow-filled gullies and cols and jagged cliffs. Our clothes and shoes began to dry out. We came to a hamlet, Alós d'Isil, a small mountain village with more animals than people. We were greeted by a Roman bridge and an ancient church. They comforted us in their civility. The locals barely glanced at us. They were used to people descending the mountainside, most commonly in terrible shape as we were, haggard and exhausted. Theirs was the first of the villages along the river valley, and we found a café serving hot coffee, which was one of the best and most fortifying coffees I have ever tasted. The heat alone filled my belly and warmed my mind.

We began walking downhill along the river in the village, when a policeman spotted us and signaled us to halt. We waited as he crossed the road. He was a local policeman, obese, walking with difficulty, but clearly pleased with himself. Paul eyed him with annoyance mixed with fatigued forbearance. All I could imagine was that we had come so far to be arrested and sent to a Spanish jail, reputedly somewhat better than the French internment camps, but that was yet to be seen.

The policeman finally bustled up to us, looking searchingly at our filthy attire and miserable shape.

"Your papers, *por favor, señores y señorita.*"

"*Estem català, senyor,*" Paul said, playing the Catalan card.

"Your papers, please."

Paul rummaged though his disordered and near-empty rucksack, looking for the Spanish passports, hoping beyond hope, they would pass muster, and I watched nervously as he fought through the papers at the bottom to produce the passports without exposing any of the other documents or gun. In the meantime, Armando had produced his own Spanish passport, this one presumably not forged, which the policeman perused.

"Here you are, sir," Paul offered his and mine, but the policeman busily ignored him.

Finally, the policeman took the two other passports Paul offered and began flipping through all three, going back and forth between them, looking up at us from the photo identifications, and then returning to the documents.

"You are married?" he asked Paul.

"Yes, sir."

"And why are you coming from France?"

"We cannot live in France," Paul said, "too difficult, and my father is here to help us." A lie, I well knew, but nonetheless, his Spanish father finally came to his aid.

"And you?" the policeman asked Armando.

"I'm here to meet my fiancée."

"Ah, and where is she?"

"Isil."

"I see."

He seemed unable to believe that we three young people, obviously having crossed over from France, the first of the season, were not foreigners. He was sure he had spotted some illegal aliens and could take credit for another arrest. He continued to futz with the passports, and then handed them back indignantly. I'm sure he felt something was not right, but couldn't put his finger on it.

"*Benvinguda a Espanya,*" he finally said begrudgingly, welcoming us to Spain with a sour look, telling us to get lost, which we did happily.

"Thank you, *senyor. Adéu.*"

We moved along as rapidly as we could without arousing any further suspicion and began walking to our final destination, Isil, three kilometers farther down the valley, three dry kilometers, three easy kilometers. The policeman watched us walk away.

"Fiancée?" Paul asked.

"Yes," Armando said firmly.

"Your father know?"

"Not really. No."

We left it at that, happy to have passed muster, allowed entry without complications, and now we knew the real reason he endured this difficult crossing of the Pyrenees: anything for love. Feeling joyful and totally physically wrung out at the same time. We began laughing and walking more rapidly in the warm afternoon sunlight. Perhaps Paul's Catalan playing card had worked, and his Spanish father as well, allowing us the benefit of doubt.

We arrived in the late afternoon at La Promesa, a small inn near the church in the public square of Isil. Few people were in evidence. An attractive young woman welcomed us to the inn. She knew Armando, and they embraced warmly. The fiancée no doubt. She smiled at us and invited us into the restaurant, which had three tables and a small but warm fire in the hearth. She knew exactly who we were and where we had come from and how we had gotten here. She welcomed us with fresh coffee and warm bread and butter, though the temperature of the inn was a tremendous soporific, and I could barely keep my eyes open.

"I need to lie down," I said honestly. "Can you show us our room?" I asked the young woman. She took us immediately up a narrow circular staircase to the rooms. All rooms were vacant, and we chose one with a double bed.

"Can we have a late dinner this evening?" Paul asked.

"Of course. This is Spain. I'll call you at nine, if that's okay."

"That's fine. Armando?' He seemed more interested in the young woman than anything else.

"Of course. Of course. Get some rest. We'll talk."

507

"The WC is at the end of the hall," the woman indicated with her hand. I left immediately for the toilet. This was the first real toilet in four days.

When I returned to the room, Paul was passed out on the bed in all his clothes. I untied his shoes, pulled off his damp socks, and left them on the steam heater, barely warm, but enough. I pulled off his jacket and hung it with my own, pulling my boots and socks off and placing them next to his. I pushed him bodily over to one side of the bed, which did not disturb his deep sleep. I pulled off all my damp clothes and climbed under the covers. It smelled fresh and clean. I have never felt such fatigue in all my life. It's funny how short our memories are when pain is concerned: we remember happy moments, but the painful ones flee without return. My mind flashed on the barrack at Le Vernet, but the bed was soft and warming, and I fell asleep immediately.

When I heard a knocking on the door, it seemed only an instant later, but actually it was four hours later, and the sunlight was gone, and the room was dark.

"Thank you. We're coming," I called, once I returned to reality.

For a long moment I lay in bed, amazed at our voyage, at our escape, at our feat. I had done it. Who would have thought? I was never very good at sports as a girl, always the worst in my class. I was known for my awkward throwing arm and maladroit kicking style. The boys always chose me last for any competition. Nuria was always the first girl chosen. Today, I felt proud of myself. My body still ached, but I had accomplished something that I would have never believed possible. I did it on my own. No one had to push or coerce me. I never complained or asked for help.

Paul sat up groggily. "What are you doing?"

"Call to dinner."

"Dinner?" He looked at me crazily. "I don't need dinner. I need you." He grabbed at me, but I avoided his grasp. I guess he also was returning from our ordeal as well.

"I'm hungry. We can celebrate later."

He looked at me sheepishly, boyishly. The boy I love.

"We did it," he said smiling. "We're in Spain. Even our passports worked, we'll soon be on our way to Barcelona."

"Yes, we did it, now dinner. I'm starving for something hot."

I jumped up, my body aching, especially my legs, and cleaned myself with a washcloth in the sink. There was no bath in sight. I had brought a change in clothes, thanks to Béatrice's foresight, a wool dress, a blouse, and a light sweater. My hiking outfit was a mess, filthy, and useless until washed. Paul too changed his shirt and trousers and combed his hair, and the miracle was that our rucksacks had kept the spare clothes somewhat dry. His beard made him look a little wild, a little untrustworthy, but I liked it, liked the feeling when he kissed me. Our boots had dried to a degree, but we had nothing else. I did change back to my drier socks, and I combed out my hair, which looked like a drunken hornet's nest, and put on some lipstick, rubbing a little onto my cheeks. I was, at least, presentable.

Armando and the young woman were seated at the table when we entered the front room, and they looked perfectly comfortable together. He must have had a change of clothes in the inn, and he was shaved. She was olive-skinned and pretty, Catalan. We greeted them and received bisous in return.

"Now, I understand why you make this trip," Paul said with a grin on his face.

Armando stood formally. "This is my fiancée, Sofia. Her parents own this inn, but she runs it."

I gave her a big hug. "Without Armando, we'd be frozen snowmen in the mountains somewhere. His father was instrumental in obtaining my freedom." The word rang in my mind: freedom. It was true, and such an important word, and here we were. I'm free, and Paul is out of harm's way as well. No more dangerous assignments. That was something. The tears came to my eyes, and Paul held me in his arms for a moment and kissed me. I think we were all near the breaking point, drained, and on the precipices of our emotions.

"Please sit down," Sofia said swiftly. "Let me bring your supper." She moved rapidly off to the kitchen, allowing us to reassemble our minds and wherewithal.

"I can't believe we made it," I repeated. "I can't believe I kept up with you two. I don't see how you do it, Armando."

"Listen, Gabrielle, this was the most difficult hike I have ever made to cross the Pyrenees. And we were very lucky the weather was with us most of the way. It could have been far worse, murderous. We left too early in the season. Few people could have made this, and you are not accustomed to hiking. I'm so impressed by your courage and determination."

The tears reappeared in my eyes. I'm so foolish.

"Now, Gabrielle," Paul said, "let's enjoy our freedom and try to get hold of our emotions."

"I'm sorry." He's always the realist, so boring, so correct.

"No need to be sorry. We are all at the same point. Let's just focus on the here and now."

The here and now? How can I? Such a man's way of thinking. I have just suffered for months, living with constant fear, trying to make the best of awful situations: the camp, the carriage car, the escape from the train, the ordeal in the mountains. It's just too much. I'm not the same person as before, and, by the way, Paul is not the same man. We are a new couple: stronger for sure, but initiating a new life together, an uncertain life. I think of our lost baby. I think of my friends. I have not heard from Nuria since the holidays, which now seem to be an old novel long forgotten, barely remembered, but fondly. Catie. God bless her, who knows what she's up to? My parents. Georges and Bernadette. Robert. All entering new existences, while my country struggles, forgetting much of our foundation, requiring a wrestling match of such magnitude as to equal the revolution in order to remember and to recover and, most importantly, to forgive ourselves.

"Gabrielle." Paul interrupted my reverie.

"I'm sorry."

"Quit being sorry. Eat."

He treats me like a little girl. I attempt to eat, but cannot. Although I'm too tired to be hungry, the warmth of the fire and the delicious food force me to fight to eat. I can scarcely taste the wild black mushroom omelette with sausage, real butter, and crisp, warmed bread. I sample the red wine in my glass. I can eat no more.

"I must excuse myself," I said. I rose from the table and left quickly, ignoring what anyone thought.

"I'll be there in a moment," Paul said softly, understanding.

***

I ran up the stairs, undressed, and got back under the covers. I lay in the bed alone at peace. The darkness of the room enveloped me and caressed me.

The present dissolved from my vision. I only saw the silver screen of my mind. I remembered as a child being interrogated by my parents. This was the result of a few mistakes I made growing up, nothing serious: surreptitiously taking a bite out of an apple at a market stall in Ceret, yelling at a playmate in our primary schoolyard, shoplifting a beautiful blue ribbon at the tabac in our neighborhood. My father would only express his disappointment, and that was the worst punishment of all. It took days to recover. He didn't withdraw his love and kindness, just forced me to question myself on what was important. Living up to my parents' expectations became ingrained. It pointed me toward self-control and independence. They would be amazed by my performance on this trek.

I have experienced all the disunity and enmity of hate in my country. All the clouds lowered on my wonderful and beautiful home will one day be buried in the deep bosom of the sea. Victory wreaths will crown our brows. The beast, risen once again revealing the ancient underbelly of our country, will retreat to his wintry lair. The Nazis, Zola's "scourge of our time," will return to hibernation. Some day we will learn, God willing, to temper the beast – for the beast is us. We will vanquish the Cyclops of bigotry and hatred and war.

I realize now the immense danger I ran by working for Paco. I minimized it, and it was important that I did. One cannot live knowing that each day may be the last. Paco did the same. And poor Paul ran the real risks and somehow survived on a daily basis. I am so proud of him, but we did it because we had to. There was no choice. Staying out of the fray would have been cowardly and weak. I couldn't have continued as I was. I had to accept the risks in my fashion. The camp taught me one thing: in adversity you have to struggle to survive. I saw too many give up, unable to live with themselves, and sink into oblivion.

Michael Barnes Selvin

Each day that I wake, I will endeavor to thank God and move forward. I love everyone as I love myself, and I will treat everyone as I would have myself treated. I am Gabrielle, and I understand them all, since I'm one of them, and I forgive them all.

I will have my lover, my delicious lover. Together, we will have my baby boy. My lover will sing beautiful lullabies, and we'll dance a sardane. We'll laugh and raise fine young people and work hard to raise them right and worry about them forever. They'll inherit all that we have accomplished and all that we have attempted in good spirit, and they will make this earth something amazing to behold.

I refuse to stop. I'll never be frustrated again or slowed, by myself or others. I've proved capable. I worked in the Resistance. I walked over that enigmatic Pyrenean, snow-capped mountain. I refuse to waste the precious time allotted to me. I refuse to give over my life to others.

I'm proud of my Jewish progenitors, their blood flowing wondrously through my body like an obstinate river seeking the hospitable sea. I'm whole. My parts are all consonant and suit me. I want nothing more.

I thank you, Paul, my love, you befriended me in the cold and swirling snow and darkest uncertainty and swore to release me and did it. Love is providing a high platform for free flight and a welcoming nest to come home to. How much I love you. You told me I obliterated the sun's radiance, and somehow I believed you. I am an everyday girl, yet you made me feel mysterious. You sing songs to me and display your love like a peacock's train, always with respect. The sounds of our laughter rolled off our lips like the call of a dove to dying ears.

And you made me feel beautiful, the wondrous gift of a stingy God, and extravagantly desirable. No other in the world could satisfy your desire. Like a naked Artemis, I clutched the moon and rolled it into the universe, and you made me discard any fears or regrets of revealing myself. I trusted your love. Like the wild girl of the waterfall. I could be capricious and reckless and tender, and, what's more, love you with all abandon. I danced like Salome, floating among my transparent veils, without modesty, all transfixed on my arrogant display. Edith Piaf sings: "No, nothing at all, I regret nothing, because my life, my joys, today begin with you."

512

Time is the most precious of all commodities, more precious than the three diamonds you gave me this evening at the inn of La Promesa. I feel like a flower made glorious by the knowledge of its impermanence. I feel like a bird swooping down to a welcome return to its balmy nest. Time makes everything worthwhile. Instead of making us servants to its dreadful march, it turns us into handmaidens dancing around a tree of liberty. Never deny the importance of dance and song. I know nothing of my fate, but I follow the dictates of my heart, which speak loudly to me, burning all illusions in its wake. The heart is the most perceptive organ and the most easily damaged: the abode of the soul.

I'm the girl that obliterates light like a dark presence of love and acceptance, like a giant void to be cherished, like a chasm of concentrated promise of life made eternal through its incandescence in a never-ending arc through the universe. I know only that I have been loved and that's enough. Enough for a lifetime. Enough for an eternity. Love is the phosphorescent streak of a meteor across the night sky, whose luminous trajectory abides and continues on boundlessly, infinitely.

33

Barcelona, August 1945
> *It's here where my story ends*
> *Will you have trouble believing me*
> *If I tell you that they loved each other every day*
> *That they grew old with their tender love*
> *That they founded an admirable family*
> *And that they had adorable children*
> *That they died gently, unknown, yes*
> *In leaving as they had come.*
> « *La romance de Paris,* » *Charles Trenet*

In a small cabaret in Barcelona, Bar Rei dels Conills, on the Via Laietana, a quartet of three young jazz musicians and a singer entertained a mixture of tourists and locals. The bar had occupied this old cellar since the turn of the century, primarily serving alcohol, but after the Civil War, in order to survive, it became a restaurant and cabaret on weekend nights. Nostalgia of better times was on order, after seven years of two wars: the future was painted uncertainly in irresolute and unsaturated colors. The young players reminded the audience of happier and more innocent times: dancing freely in tight-waisted, nylon stockings, and plastic zips with short, tight skirts, cloche hats, and loosely strung pearls.

On 25 August 1944, Paris was liberated by General Leclerc's Ninth Armored Company, led by veteran volunteers from the Spanish Civil War. The next day, the Second French Armored Division followed, accompanied by Allied troops. Germany surrendered nine months later on 7 May 1945. On 14 August, the US ended the war in the Pacific with the surrender of Japan, after the terrible destruction of Hiroshima and Nagasaki. The world breathed a sigh of relief before beginning reconstruction. War is like a wildfire: easy to start, impossible to control, and extinguished only after everyone has suffered hell. Never again: the pathetic avowal of the inexperienced and guileless romantics. God's voice can be heard by the innocents and ignored by the powerful.

The musicians consisted of a quick-witted pianist, a wild drummer, a seemingly disinterested bassist, and an earnest young singer, lately making a name for himself in the city. They played a pre-war French Swing style. Due to the war recovery, new recordings have been halted, and radio play has reverted to the pre-war tunes. Music has returned to the streets.

Spain is the last remaining Fascist holdout in Europe, and Barcelona, a stronghold of the Republicans during the Civil War, is uncomfortably under occupation by Spanish troops and local Fascists. Franco is attempting to unify Spain by suppressing the disparate echoes in his country; he wages a battle against the local expressions of language and culture. In Barcelona, the sole language permitted in public is Castilian. Catalan is banned from schools. Few if any books are published in Catalan. Catalan culture, such as the sardane, traditional celebrations, and holidays, are outlawed. Symbols of Catalan nationalism, statues, art, flags, are removed from public view. Even the names of streets are changed to Castilian. The new symbols have become the fascist salute, the *Cara al Sol* anthem, and the Spanish flag.

At a break later in the evening, Paul came down from the stage to join Gabrielle at her table with Nuria and Paco Macias. Drying his face with a towel, he gave bisous to them all. Gabrielle and Nuria had arranged this reunion after many letters and failed plans. Paco had returned to teaching at the University of Perpignan and had been allowed a temporary Spanish visa to attend a conference in Barcelona. It seemed an ideal time.

Paul seated himself and looked at his old friends and his wife. They all gave us so much, took on danger as a normal occurrence, and put their lives at risk. It seems astounding that they were all survivors. They had lived on the edge of danger and uncertainty for so long. The fact that they saved themselves is irrelevant. So many others attempted to and failed. It's not exactly a happy reunion. They were happy enough to see each other, somewhat at a loss perhaps, somewhat distanced by time and events. Too much had changed in their individual lives.

"You look good," Nuria said to Paul, after his bise. She was wearing a man's shirt and loose trousers, with a grey silk scarf around her neck, her auburn hair cut short. She arrived this afternoon and had not yet seen him. "And you can still carry a tune."

Paul simply smiled, didn't reply.

"He always looks good and sounds good," Gabrielle added. "He's charmed. He's in architecture school and loving it. And teaching must agree with you," she said, turning to Paco.

He looked older, wearing a tweed jacket and dark tie, but more distinguished with long unkempt white hair. He returned to working on his three-volume study of Lope de Vega, *The Path to the Future*. Gabrielle and Paul haven't seen Paco since the winter of 1943, and of all of them, he seemed to be the most scarred by his wartime experience, the most abridged.

"How's school going?" Nuria asked Paul.

"Well," he said, smiling at Gabrielle. "It's a practical art."

"Aren't you planning on returning?" Nuria asked again. "We have an architecture school in Perpignan."

"I know, only Gabrielle is doing so well at Puig, the local producer of perfumes, that we decided to stay on for a while."

"Not surprising." Paco said quietly. "I always knew you were talented. Vice-president of a major company."

"I started at the right time, in the right place. I joined shortly after we arrived and was hired as a secretary in the department responsible for Agua Lavanda Puig. It became one of the flagship products of the company. I never realized that I was learning anything at Les Nouvelles Galeries, but I soon made myself useful in marketing. I knew the public better than anyone in the company and how to sell cosmetics."

"She's being modest," Paul added. "She helped promote the growth of the top-selling product, made locally with the highest margin, and it's just beginning. '*Que se enriquece con salvia y tomillo.*'" He quoted the slogan printed on every package of Agua Lavanda Puig: enriched with sage and thyme, both local ingredients.

"We're preparing to go international once the government eases up on restrictions to selling overseas."

"And you," Paul turned to Nuria. "What are you doing?"

"I'm back with la Cimade, helping immigrants and the postwar recovery, but I really want to go into politics. I'm running next year as a deputy in the Socialist MRP alliance for the Constituent Assembly to write a new constitution."

"Gabrielle stared at her constant companion. "Was it difficult after Robert's death?"

Nuria blanched, looking at her friend."Yes, impossible."

"How did it happen?" Paco asked carefully, knowing only the sketchiest of details and not wanting to upset her. After the war ended, people got into the habit of not talking about it, especially their roles. De Gaulle minimized everyone's role, foul or fair, including the Allies, the Resistance, and the *attentistes*, and somehow returned the country to a unified whole after a period of perturbation.

"He was arrested in June 1943 after his boss, Jean Moulin, was arrested by the Gestapo at a meeting outside of Lyon. All of the participants were taken and interrogated by Klaus Barbie. Jean Moulin died of the beatings he received. Robert was one of many taken to the Fresnes prison. He never returned. There was never any explanation, but that was common. Information was carefully controlled and parsed out, and only one among the assistants survived…" She stopped talking, obviously still entangled in her emotions.

"I'm so sorry," Paco said, changing the conversation. "Your parents made it through."

"Yes," Gabrielle said. "They returned to their home in Perpignan after liberation, and Papa is back in the government as curator of a city museum. My grandparents weren't as lucky. They were sent to Germany. That was the last word we ever heard. Today, that isn't surprising by what we know. An entire generation was murdered."

"We never heard what became of Georges and Bernadette either," Paul added soberly. He had written to Franco at the Prefecture after liberation, but had never heard back. He had no idea if Franco Plana was still there.

The list went on of people they had known and their outcomes. Paco remained silent.

"We know one thing for sure," Nuria said. "Our friend Isabelle Lefèvre and her lover Joseph Tena where both hanged on the streets by the Resistance. First to go. I always believed she was behind the problems you and your family had, Gabrielle, but you were not the only ones she harmed."

"I heard that Mireille Printemps had her head shaved," Paul said. "And Marie Dubas died naturally in Switzerland."

"Who are they?" Paco asks.

"Oh, just some people caught up in it. You faced some hard times too, Paco." He looked older and was distant and reserved.

"I did, though I was far luckier than Gabrielle. I was sent to Gurs, a camp outside of Pau, much like Camp du Vernet, originally set up to house the Spanish Republicans, but after the armistice Gurs became another transit camp for Jews, like le Vernet, and like Drancy, but also for dissidents. I remained there until the Germans left in August 1944. I lost fifty kilos, but gained most of it back. You saved my life, Gabrielle. Remember?"

She shook her head, having no idea.

"At your suggestion, we discarded a bunch of files at the last moment. Without those files, they had little to convict me of espionage or resistance activities. They never sent me to the special section for deportation, where many of the convicted Resistance members were sent, which allowed me to survive. But it was not easy...as you know." His stentorian voice and madcap manner were no longer in evidence: his self-described "two personalities" morphed together into a more sober and sadder one.

Paul noted the musicians gathering for their final set of the night.

"Excuse me, I have to go."

The quartet opened the second set with a slow rendition of Trenet's "La Mer," which had become a local standard and popular worldwide. The truly great works are prescient with time. He continued with a survey of Trenet until late into the night and completed with several requests and a great reception by the remaining audience.

They walked back to Gabrielle and Paul's apartment off the Passeig de Gràcia on Carrer de Valencia, a walkup to the fifth floor with three rooms, but with a sunny exposure south above the buildings across the street. They left a quiet and restrained Paco at his hotel with bisous and promises to keep in touch. Perhaps he was more damaged by his interrogation than they had believed.

In the apartment, Paul opened a bottle of wine, and, dropping their shoes, they settled on the couch and easy chair. The furnishings were all well used.

They had collected them at flea markets over the last two years. The evening was warm and humid; the days had been hot, but the evenings always turned comfortable. It was late, and everyone was tired.

"Have you talked with Robert's father," Paul asked Nuria.

"No. I can't. I only met him once, and Robert never talked about him. So I haven't contacted him. Someday maybe."

"He knows?"

"I'm not sure."

"You should, just to let him know. He used to visit us every so often to ask about Robert. It's funny about parents: so much hope at birth, and then your child grows up and leaves. Some return as adults, but most just move on with their lives. I haven't dared to ask about my grandmother. She's close to ninety."

"You need to return," Nuria said.

"I don't know," Gabrielle replied sleepily. "I miss my parents, but I'm not that eager to return. We may when Paul graduates from university. Maybe Puig will open an office in Paris. Catie married shortly after liberation, you know, but I haven't heard from her."

"It's a new world and not in any good sense," Nuria said.

"It's as though our lives were diverted by a waterway," Gabrielle replied, "and the shores and beaches of our childhood memories were destroyed. The war marked us, marked our generation, and we have different bodies and damaged hearts, less idealistic, less trusting, less esteem for others. It robbed us of our youth and our innocence. Five years of hatred and disrespect like a cancer."

"You're right," Nuria said. "That's why I want to be involved in structuring our society. Before the war, there was so much anger and division. No wonder we failed wretchedly to live up to our ideals and split into camps like cockerels, spitting and fighting. It seems the only way to come together is to have a common purpose. An agreed goal…easy to say."

"I'm going to bed," Paul announced.

"I'll join you soon," Gabrielle replied.

He kissed both and traipsed off to the bedroom.

***

I undress and put my clothes in a corner, leaving my shorts, which I always sleep in, and enter the bed on my side, sheets only. Gabrielle's side remains vacant. The window is wide open with the shutters cracked. The city noises have abated, but the balmy heat perseveres. Nuria seems lost, engaged in a political career, but lost personally. And Paco is a ghost of his former self. I'm so proud of Gabrielle, and I surely could not survive without her. Three more years of school remain. A long time. We have talked of returning, but are hesitant. Her parents are the primary reason to return, but we look at our country differently today; just as we are marked, so is our country.

I don't think much about the danger of what I did during the war. Why would I think of that now, since I thought little of it then. I knew I might be arrested or even killed. It happened to many. I did what I could, and I never thought too much about the risks. Of course, my days were filled with fear and dread. I wasn't a hero. I did what I could because I believed it was right. We all did. Somehow I survived. Now it is the past, and I don't think about it. I rarely talk about it. Maybe seeing old friends. But not a day goes by that it does not cross my mind. Not a minute. Not a second. It's engraved in my soul, for better or worse.

The future. What is ahead? It's like we are on a conveyor belt moving forward, attempting to find our stability, our dynamic equilibrium, to give us comfort as time moves on relentlessly, regardless of all, malleable in its impact, but tenacious in its pursuit. What is important? Finding your equilibrium, knowing that nothing lasts. Preparing to encounter the next change, until, for you, all change ends.

The one repudiation of a conveyor belt of time is the love for another. I now realize that my life had no value before I met Gabrielle. She made me realize the importance of others and of love for others. I never saved her. She saved me, and not by escaping over the mountains, but by making me see the importance of love. I now understand my mother better. She was consumed by her love for my father, who never reciprocated. Against all my grand-mère's wishes and small town gossip, she attempted to fashion her love for a man into a living and breathing entity. My mother risked all for his love, even the love of her children; all for an impossible love, for he never cared. I cannot understand my father. Had he love for anyone? When he wrote to me on my twelfth birthday to inform me that he was paying my tuition at Trinité, he also enclosed an offer of fatherly advice. What right did he have to do this? Advice so absurd and vague as to be meaningless: "*Ne prends pas des vessies pour des lanternes.*" What was that? I have thought about this for years. It's always with me, in its absurdity. I'm not even sure he understood the old French idiom, and that was all he offered: "Don't get gypped" or "Don't take a wooden nickel." What did that mean to him?

I have not written to him since coming to Spain. We have not communicated since well before the war. He doesn't know if I'm dead or alive. He probably doesn't think much about it. I don't even know what he does for a living. Did he find love with his second family? I wonder. I hope he did, but somehow I doubt it.

Few people find, or build, a relationship with all curtains raised, no lies, no façades, no excuses. Some fall in love with the feeling of falling in love, but cannot ever move beyond that, and tend to repeat it unhappily. Grand-mère fell in love with the church, and for her that was enough: the thoughts of a father long dead and the Catholic church. What is it about Gabrielle? She obliterated all light, and I could see nothing else, but that was not enough to sustain us, just an entry. A momentary eclipse. Yet, she made me see permanence in impermanence. She brought me the fruits of love from her garden that I had never tasted before. She made me promises with her actions and words that I had never experienced before. She gave me strength, the will to be myself, to do what was possible, to discard anxiety and self-doubt and to find comfort in our combined eternal motion. She gave me herself. She had been bathed in love growing up, and she showed me what that meant. I had not existed before her. She suppressed all caution in herself, for nothing can dampen a song of love like caution and restraint. The great singers stand before you revealing their innermost feelings. Without that it is just an act. Feigned emotions are neither transmitted nor received. What she made me recognize was that the moment counts: the time between what just happened and what will happen next. An instant. But then, love cannot be measured by time or space. There are no degrees of love, no substance, no physicality.

It's like the lifting of clouds after a powerful rainstorm, the pattern of light suddenly illuminating the fretful ocean:

> *Que reste-t-il de nos amours? Et dans un nuage le cher visage de mon passé, un souvenir que me poursuit, sans cesse."**

Love is a song admitting weakness, offering an opening, making an exchange, a disclosure, a giving and a receiving. The song is a saving grace. It does not begin and end, but advances and recedes like the channeled rhythmic sounds of the eternally blown waves: a wink of God's eye, a mourning dove's gift, a fragrant smile, the hope contained in a promise, and a mutual assent, a future imagined…

* "What remains of our loves? In a cloud, the cherished silhouette of my past, a memory that pursues me, forever." Charles Trenet, 1942

Acknowledgements

Fernand Jude: who started it all: talking about the region, war, music, and internment camps, and all his experiences over the war years, providing primary documentation and letters, always open and welcoming

Angèle Jude: spending hours conveying her knowledge of her husband and what he went through

Johnny Barnes Selvin: for her encouragement, support, editing, and love

Marc and Luisette Aroles: talking for hours on WW2 stories of the region

Jacqueline Vivès and Paul Nadal: our pathfinders to the region and our French family

Alain and Josette Marco: neighbors for 25 years with loving information and advice on their native country

Mike Staples: editor and proof reader par excellence

Scott Goodall: (*The Freedom Trail*), whom we sadly missed in St. Girons

Tanja von Fransecky: ("Escape and Attempted Escape of Jewish Deportees from Deportation Trains in France, Belgium and the Netherlands")

Jean Barrès: stories of les Nouvelles Galeries

Yves and Marie-Christine Péan: neighbors and friends

Jean-Marie and Marie-Brigitte Baille: local information and contacts

Bernard and Marina Tournet

Germaine (Zoë) Oudouin

Michèle Bayar

Insightful readers: Francis Furey, Anthony Holdsworth, Wendy Ruebman, Dan and Françoise Hunter, Susan Charlot, Denis Slavich, Martin Limbird

Photo Credits:

Frontispiece image of Mont Valier: permission of Pierre Goujet (PierreG_09, via Flickr)

Portrait of Gaby: permission of family of Martin Vivès, master painter

Images of Paul and Gabrielle: permission of Marc and Luisette Aroles

Image of Camp du Vernet: Département d'Occitanie: Centre de documentation du Patrimoine Régie des Recettes, Service Connaissance du Patrimoine, Direction de la Culture

All other images property of the author